ONE WOMAN, ANCHORED TO HER OWN TIME AND PLACE . . . INTENSELY HERSELF, YET UNIVERSAL

"In bewitching, often hilarious language, Gibbon tells the tale of Chris Guthrie over the course of the years 1911 to 1933. Chris Guthrie endures. And Gibbon deserves to endure with her, in *A Scots Quair.*"
—*The Chicago Sun-Times*

"Its emotional range from tender poignancy to brutality, its diversity of characters and its lyrical sense of the Scottish highlands . . . an undoubted masterwork memorably beautiful"
—*The Wall Street Journal*

"Authentic, powerful, beautiful . . . Gibbon sees deep into the heart of his heroine as she lives her harsh life, bears up under the blows of changing times and changing fortunes. It all comes to an end far too soon."
—*Publishers Weekly*

"*The* great Scottish novel"
—Alistair Cooke, introducing *Sunset Song* on public television

Lewis Grassic Gibbon

A SCOTS QUAIR

A TRILOGY OF NOVELS

Sunset Song
Cloud Howe
Grey Granite

**WITH A FOREWORD
BY IVOR BROWN**

PUBLISHED BY POCKET BOOKS NEW YORK

POCKET BOOKS, a Simon & Schuster division of
GULF & WESTERN CORPORATION
1230 Avenue of the Americas, New York, N.Y. 10020

Library of Congress Catalog Card Number: 77-4988

ISBN: 0-671-82166-0

First Pocket Books printing February, 1979

10 9 8 7 6 5 4 3 2 1

Trademarks registered in the United States and other countries.

Printed in the U.S.A.

CONTENTS

FOREWORD

By IVOR BROWN

Books about modern Scotland now commonly, and justly, include the name of Lewis Grassic Gibbon as one of the great interpreters of Scottish scene and character. His early death, at the age of thirty-four, and his rather peculiar pseudonym, which was used for only part of his work, have made him an elusive figure. Now that his notable trilogy of the hard life lived between the Grampians and the North Sea and in the granite towns and cities thereabout is being printed in one volume, some information about his origins and his work is due to the reader. I am proud to have been asked to give it.

My interest in—which became a devotion to—this writer was due to various causes. My forefathers all sprang from the lands in Aberdeenshire, north of Don, where James Leslie Mitchell (the real name of Lewis Grassic Gibbon) was born. In London, thirty years after his birth, I became, all too late, his friend. I shared some of his opinions, disputed others, and found in him a spirit in tune with my own racial and local sympathies and my acquired philosophies. His utterance was of north-east Scotland in idiom and phrase. He was the voice of Scotland's past, almost of all antiquity in his great sense of pre-history and his addiction to primitive (the very opposite of barbaric and savage) men and things. He was a voice of humanity in his anger and compassion; his wrath flamed against oppression (he died in 1935, knowing full well what Fascism would do to the world). His pity for all poor and hunger-bitten men came out of his experience. He had lived with folk who lived hard, riving their food from an often grudging earth in an air that nips the blood.

Even more than any other of his qualities did I admire his superb mastery of words and rhythms, his spate of images, his prose of the earth which continually dissolved into air to become the poetry of sky and cloud. Has anybody ever written better about the mist of Scotland and the 'far-off mountains turnéd into clouds,' the steam of the land in summer, the sharp savours of the root-fields after rain, the aroma of fir-trees on the hillside, and the glitter of dew as it melts into the morning's canopy of jewelled Grampian air? Neil Gunn has said that you can hear the earth itself speaking in Gibbon's prose. I would add that the sky is in it too, a sky where the peesies (lapwings) ribbon and cry, a sky where the whaups (curlews) are eternally keening over the stones of the archaic men.

James Leslie Mitchell was born in February, 1901, at the farm of Hill of Seggat, near Auchterless, in Central Aberdeenshire. His mother, whose maiden name was Lily Gibbon, came from Kildrummy. When he was only eight young Mitchell changed his county, his father moving to a farm at Drumlithie in the Mearns (otherwise known as Kincardineshire), the county whence Robert Burns's father had migrated to Ayrshire. It is a land of hills and the sea, containing the whole essence of Scotland in small compass, the large hills sweeping to the sky, the farmlands sweeping to the cliffs. Here are the towns of granite, the harbours of the herring-fleet, the cloth-mills, and the crofts.

At the local school he was, I fancy, very lucky in his dominie, Alexander Gray, who saw and knew how to shape the immense promise in the boy. In his leisure the pupil was far readier to escape with a book than to help the work on the farm. At fifteen he went to Mackie Academy, Stonehaven, where he was a gifted pupil, writing essays far above the ordinary level. But he left after a year and found work as a reporter on the *Aberdeen Journal;* later he moved to the *Scottish Farmer* in Glasgow. At the age of twenty he fell ill and came back for a short while to help in the fields in the Mearns.

I was greatly struck later on by his width of reading and his knowledge of languages. How he found time for it all, I never knew. His boyhood must have been cruelly strenuous in self-chosen bookishness, strenuous at the cost of his physique. It happens often so with the eager Scottish scholar. Leslie Mitchell was one of several Aberdonians whom I have known, greatly gifted in various ways, who spent themselves in studenthood and died in early manhood. At the age of sixteen, young Mitchell had even picked up enough Russian to try to interview M. Krassin in the latter's native language. Mitchell has related that Krassin was being deported from England by way of Aberdeen and that he met the cub-reporter's gallant Russian with English, explaining that in any case, he was not allowed to make a statement in any language. Meanwhile the young reporter dreamed of an Aberdeen Soviet and walked the grey city by the moon, thinking of Scotland's old pains and planning remedies to come. His mind ranged always, with a passionate eagerness, from the bright beginnings of mankind to its escape from present anguish.

After the illness followed eight years as a clerk in the Army and later in the R.A.F. That this brilliant boy should have wasted his time in military form-filling may seem strange, but he had no money and wanted to travel. It is on record that he did not mix well and was odd man out in the barrack-room, and one can well believe it. But the experience did get him out to the Middle East, where he could survey the greater relics of antiquity and muse upon the origins of society and of the martyrdom of man. It was there, he told me, that he met an archæologist who later took him to Central America, where he studied the remains of the Maya civilisation, thus gaining the material for a book written later. He attributed some of his subsequent ill-health to that excursion: he told me once that his digestion had never recovered from the diet of maize on which he lived for some time amid the Maya ruins, following some years of a Service diet.

By 1928 he was free of Army forms. In 1935 he was dead. In seven years he wrote sixteen books; his fertility was tremendous, his energy hectic, his planning of a career absurd. (And still the myth endures that Aberdonians always know how to look after themselves.)

If he had gone back to his early craft of journalism he could have earned a steady moderate income and written a few books in his leisure, until he was able to live decently on books alone. But he slogged away at books and stories, dividing the day into three portions and expecting to write some 1,500 words in each. He tried to sell his short pieces to the wrong magazines till H. G. Wells noticed him and put him on the right lines. His books were, as a rule, written too quickly, but his quality was always there in one form or another. The Near East was a fruitful and a frequent background. The writer's life, though short and busy, was a blessed change from his old routine, and he was happily married, with children, a daughter and son, arriving later.

The trilogy here presented was his salute to Scotland. A 'quair' is the same word as a 'quire,' and means a set of papers or a volume. Mitchell himself marked that return by a change of name to Lewis Grassic Gibbon. The first book, *Sunset Song,* was published in 1932 and rapidly won the attention it deserved. Next year the tale of Chris Guthrie was carried further in *Cloud Howe,* which I find no less haunting. *Grey Granite* followed in 1934. This last gives the impression of being hasty and the end is unworthy of the whole. The great pattern appears to crumble in the author's hands, and the talent, which had been so finely maturing, suddenly seems younger and cruder. The book has some tiresome coarseness. Yet, being by a master, it has rarely beautiful things in it. When I said to Eric Linklater that it had disappointed me, he retorted that, whatever its faults, it had passages worthy of the great Scots ballads. And what greater praise could there be?

So here is the trilogy, the story of a small farm among the peesie-haunted 'parks' of the Mearns, a story linked with the early age of Scotland, a story returning continually to the standing stones of the ancient colonists who came, metal-hunting and exploring, from the Mediterranean to these far hills.

Two points of explanation must be made. Leslie Mitchell's philosophy of life was a belief in original innocence. The early, unpropertied men, who are usually regarded as warring savages, he believed to have been care-free and peaceable. (All the evidence about the real primitives, simple food-gathering folk, is on his side.) Then came, with the discovery of agriculture in Egypt and the misuse of the civilisation which settled farming created, the flow of follies and corruptions, the worship of tyrannous gods and tyrannous kings, the cults of property and power, war, and all the miseries of modern man. To him the savage and the barbarian were the primitive in decay and his creed was a passionate assertion of the initial, the pre-savage, the primitive goodness which man must somehow recover.

This is no place to expound his whole doctrine of the archaic civilisation, its diffusion, and its decay. It can be read in many of his books, in his contributions to *Scottish Scene* (a volume shared with Hugh MacDiarmid), in his record of the early explorers, *Nine Against the Unknown*, and in the earlier 'Leslie Mitchell' novels. I mention it here because the reader of this trilogy may be puzzled by the constant return to the standing-stones above Blawearie, the standing-stones which in his view linked Scottish earth to all enduring and universal things, symbol of the early men who were happy until they missed the way.

A second point needing explanation is the idiom and the rhythm of these books. Leslie Mitchell was born a peasant and his mind was divided about the peasant and his lot. At one moment he would hate the drudgery of the land; at another he was conscious of a powerful pride that the land was so closely and intimately his. 'My mother,' he wrote, 'used to hap me in a plaid in harvest time and leave me in the lea of a stook while she harvested.' These divisions of opinion, love of the earthy savours and the tang of the wind, resentment of the servitude under the 'on-ding' of the rain, hatred of the sweat and the shivering and the poverty, are constantly occurring in *Sunset Song* and *Cloud Howe*. There the Scottish peasants appear in all their roughness and coarseness as well as in their humours and their honour, just as the land itself appears in all its grudging and grinding dominion over labouring flesh as well as in the shimmering beauty of the Mearns upon a summer's day and in the foison of earth well dunged and well cropped by Scottish skill and endurance.

To utter this voice of the land and the landsman Mitchell chose a mannered, lilting style. When I first met this, it struck me as an affectation. But suddenly I realised what he was attempting and indeed achieving, which was 'to mould the English language into the rhythms and cadences of Scots spoken speech.' He used dialogue scantily, but in a sense he used it all the time. For his descriptions of men and places were the voice of one talking, say, the voice of Scotland itself. The vocabulary was a little antique, a trifle old-fashioned when it was first made. (So, they say, was that of Robert Burns.) That boy meets girl so often as 'childe meets quean' may irritate some. I am not here to defend all the means employed to achieve a certain result. That result was to make Scottish earth vocal, and I would claim that in the lilting, anapaestic prose of Lewis Grassic Gibbon you can indeed feel the swing of the horses at the plough, the rhythm of the wind upon the woods, the surge of the tumbling land where the mountains run down to the sea, and 'the speak' of the men who toiled and loved and quarrelled, the men of the little farms upon whose passing there is so noble a valediction at the close of *Sunset Song*.

The author has said that working in this convention helped him to turn out *Sunset Song* in six weeks. It kept his typewriter flowing. That was his surface talk. I believe that the rhythm did, in fact, come from deep fountains of his own feeling for the land and for its people. In any case, once the reader has settled down to the swing of it, he is likely to find the melody most apt to the subject and sweet to the senses.

In the autumn of 1934 Leslie Mitchell complained to me of increasing pains which he took to be due to a duodenal ulcer. Early in 1935 he underwent an operation for this affliction from which he did not rally, I shared the melancholy task of paying a tribute at his cremation at Golder's Green. His ashes were later buried at Arbuthnott in the Mearns.

He was just thirty-four. He had never, I think, been able to spend time on any book. His life had been various, uneven, hustled. He was just touching success which would have given him leisure to stretch himself instead of rushing to his typewriter. He had begun a book which might have been a Scottish classic. At his wish what he had written was destroyed. But, at any rate, he had left this trilogy and in it were his head and his heart and the cunning of as quick a hand as ever put a landscape in a sentence. I do

not think that the creator of Chris Guthrie, the colourist of
the red-clay Guthrie fields and of the misty beauty of the
Howe, and the recorder of 'the speak' of the Mearns in
town and tavern, will easily be forgotten. Nor should he be.

IVOR BROWN.

SUNSET SONG

A NOVEL

CONTENTS

PRELUDE

THE SONG

EPILUDE

A NOTE THE READER
IS ADVISED TO READ

THOSE who read and run—or who find all antique history a weariness—or have little relish for meeting the characters, one by one, in detailed biography, before the story begins—*are advised to skip the Prelude and begin the Song at page 27*. If they feel the urge, they may later delve in the Prelude as a handy reference to the off-stage history of this soul and that.

Similarly, should the context refuse to give up the meaning of a Scots word used, the reader may turn to the Glossary. But the author hopes that that will be seldom: the author, indeed, has quite failed in his purpose if the Glossary proves a pressing need.

For the author (whose humility may be taken for granted) can be best regarded as a sagaman arrived in the house of the English with the salvage of his own ruined house of words; and the tongue of his hosts, so it seems to him, may be yet enriched with this salvage of words that are only half-alien.

L. G. G.

PRELUDE

THE UNFURROWED FIELD

KINRADDIE lands had been won by a Norman childe, Cospatric de Gondeshil, in the days of William the Lyon, when gryphons and such-like beasts still roamed the Scots countryside and folk would waken in their beds to hear the children screaming, with a great wolf-beast, come through the hide window, tearing at their throats. In the Den of Kinraddie one such beast had its lair and by day it lay about the woods and the stench of it was awful to smell all over the countryside, and at gloaming a shepherd would see it, with its great wings half-folded across the great belly of it and its head, like the head of a meikle cock, but with the ears of a lion, poked over a fir tree, watching. And it ate up sheep and men and women and was a fair terror, and the King had his heralds cry a reward to whatever knight would ride and end the mischieving of the beast.

So the Norman childe, Cospatric, that was young and landless and fell brave and well-armoured, mounted his horse in Edinburgh Town and came North, out of the foreign south parts, up through the Forest of Fife and into the pastures of Forfar and past Aberlemno's Meikle Stane that was raised when the Picts beat the Danes; and by it he stopped and looked at the figures, bright then and hardly faded even now, of the horses and the charging and the rout of those coarse foreign folk. And maybe he said a bit

5

prayer by that Stone and then he rode into the Mearns, and
the story tells no more of his riding but that at last come
he did to Kinraddie, a tormented place, and they told him
where the gryphon slept, down there in the Den of Kinraddie.

But in the daytime it hid in the woods and only at night,
by a path through the hornbeams, might he come at it,
squatting in bones, in its lair. And Cospatric waited for the
night to come and rode to the edge of Kinraddie Den and
commended his soul to God and came off his horse and
took his boar-spear in his hand, and went down into the
Den and killed the gryphon. And he sent the news to
William the Lyon, sitting drinking the wine and fondling
his bonny lemans in Edinburgh Town, and William made
him the Knight of Kinraddie, and gave to him all the wide
parish as his demesne and grant to build him a castle there,
and wear the sign of a gryphon's head for a crest and keep
down all beasts and coarse and wayward folk, him and the
issue of his body for ever after.

So Cospatric got him the Pict folk to build a strong castle
there in the lithe of the hills, with the Grampians bleak
and dark behind it, and he had the Den drained and he
married a Pict lady and got on her bairns and he lived
there till he died. And his son took the name Kinraddie, and
looked out one day from the castle wall and saw the Earl
Marischal come marching up from the south to join the
Highlandmen in the battle that was fought at Mondynes,
where now the meal-mill stands; and he took out his men
and fought there, but on which side they do not say, but
maybe it was the winning one, they were aye gey and
canny folk, the Kinraddies.

And the great-grandson of Cospatric, he joined the English against the cateran Wallace, and when Wallace next
came marching up from the southlands Kinraddie and other
noble folk of that time they got them into Dunnottar Castle
that stands out in the sea beyond Kinneff, well-builded and
strong, and the sea splashes about it in the high tides and
there the din of the gulls is a yammer night and day. Much
of meal and meat and gear they took with them, and they
laid themselves up there right strongly, they and their
carles, and wasted all the Mearns that the Cateran who
dared rebel against the fine English king might find no
provision for his army of coarse and landless men. But
Wallace came through the Howe right swiftly and he heard

of Dunnottar and laid siege to it and it was a right strong
place and he had but small patience with strong places.
So, in the dead of one night, when the thunder of the sea
drowned the noise of his feint, he climbed the Dunnottar
rocks and was over the wall, he and the vagabond Scots,
and they took Dunnottar and put to the slaughter the noble
folk gathered there, and all the English, and spoiled them
of their meat and gear, and marched away.

Kinraddie Castle that year, they tell, had but a young
bride new home and she had no issue of her body, and
the months went by and she rode to the Abbey of Aber-
brothock where the good Abbot, John, was her cousin, and
told him of her trouble and how the line of Kinraddie was
like to die. So he lay with her that was September, and
next year a boy was born to the young bride, and after that
the Kinraddies paid no heed to wars and bickerings but
sat them fast in their Castle lithe in the hills, with their
gear and bonny leman queans and villeins libbed for service.

And when the First Reformation came and others came
after it and some folk cried *Whiggam!* and some cried
Rome! and some cried *The King!* the Kinraddies sat them
quiet and decent and peaceable in their castle, and heeded
never a fig the arguings of folk, for wars were unchancy
things. But then Dutch William came, fair plain a fixture
that none would move, and the Kinraddies were all for
the Covenant then, they had aye had God's Covenant at
heart, they said. So they builded a new kirk down where
the chapel had stood, and builded a manse by it, there in
the middle of the yews where the cateran Wallace had hid
when the English put him to rout at last. And one Kinraddie, John Kinraddie, went south and became a great man
in the London court, and was crony of the creatures John-
son and James Boswell and once the two of them, John
Kinraddie and James Boswell, came up to the Mearns on
an idle ploy and sat drinking wine and making coarse talk
far into the small hours night after night till the old laird
wearied of them and then they would steal away and as
James Boswell set in his diary, *Did get to the loft where the*
maids were, and one Πεγγι Δυνδας ωας φατ εν τhε βυττοχς
ανδ ι διδ λιε ωιτh her.

But in the early days of the nineteenth century it was
an ill time for the Scots gentry, for the poison of the
French Revolution came over the seas and crofters and

common folk like that stood up and cried *Away to hell!*
when the Auld Kirk preached submission from its pulpits.
Up as far as Kinraddie came the poison and the young
laird of that time, and he was Kenneth, he called himself
a Jacobin and joined the Jacobin Club of Aberdeen and
there at Aberdeen was nearly killed in the rioting, for
liberty and equality and fraternity, he called it. And they
carried him back to Kinraddie a cripple, but he would still
have it that all men were free and equal and he set to
selling the estate and sending the money to France, for he
had a real good heart. And the crofters marched on Kinraddie Castle in a body and bashed in the windows of it,
they thought equality should begin at home.

More than half the estate had gone in this driblet and
that while the cripple sat and read his coarse French books;
but nobody guessed that till he died and then his widow,
poor woman, found herself own no more than the land that
lay between the coarse hills, the Grampians, and the farms
that stood out by the Bridge End above the Denburn,
straddling the outward road. Maybe there were some twenty
to thirty holdings in all, the crofters dour folk of the old
Pict stock, they had no history, common folk, and ill-reared
their biggins clustered and chaved amid the long, sloping
fields. The leases were one-year, two-year, you worked
from the blink of the day you were breeked to the flicker
of the night they shrouded you, and the dirt of gentry sat
and ate up your rents but you were as good as they were.

So that was Kenneth's leaving to his lady body, she wept
right sore over the pass that things had come to, but they
kittled up before her own jaw was tied in a clout and they
put her down in Kinraddie vault to lie by the side of her
man. Three of her bairns were drowned at sea, fishing off
the Bevie braes they had been, but the fourth, the boy
Cospatric, him that died the same day as the Old Queen,
he was douce and saving and sensible, and set putting the
estate to rights. He threw out half the little tenants, they
flitted off to Canada and Dundee and parts like those, the
others he couldn't move but slowly.

But on the cleared land he had bigger steadings built and
he let them at bigger rents and longer leases, he said the
day of the fine big farm had come. And he had woods of
fir and larch and pine planted to shield the long, bleak
slopes, and might well have retrieved the Kinraddie fortunes but that he married a Morton quean with black blood

in her, she smitted him and drove him to drink and death, that was the best way out. For his son was clean daft, they locked him up at last in an asylum, and that was the end of Kinraddie family, the Meikle House that stood where the Picts had builded Cospatric's castle crumbled to bits like a cheese, all but two-three rooms the trustees held as their offices, the estate was mortgaged to the hilt by then.

So by the winter of nineteen eleven there were no more than nine bit places left the Kinraddie estate, the Mains the biggest of them, it had been the Castle home farm in the long past times. An Irish creature, Erbert Ellison was the name, ran the place for the trustees, he said, but if you might believe all the stories you heard he ran a hantle more silver into his own pouch than he ran into theirs. Well might you expect it, for once he'd been no more than a Dublin waiter, they said. That had been in the time before Lord Kinraddie, the daft one, had gone clean skite. He had been in Dublin, Lord Kinraddie, on some drunken ploy, and Ellison had brought his whisky for him and some said he had halved his bed with him. But folk would say anything.

So the daftie took Ellison back with him to Kinraddie and made him his servant, and sometimes, when he was real drunk and the fairlies came sniffering out of the whisky bottles at him, he would throw a bottle at Ellison and shout *Get out, you bloody dish-clout!* so loud it was heard across at the Manse and fair affronted the minister's wife. And old Greig, him that had been the last minister there, he would glower across at Kinraddie House like John Knox at Holyrood, and say that God's hour would come. And sure as death it did, off to the asylum they hurled the daftie, he went with a nurse's mutch on his head and he put his head out of the back of the waggon and said *Cockadoodledoo!* to some school bairns the waggon passed on the road and they all ran home and were fell frightened.

But Ellison had made himself well acquainted with farming and selling stock and most with buying horses, so the trustees they made him manager of the Mains, and he moved into the Mains farmhouse and looked him round for a wife. Some would have nothing to do with him, a poor creature of an Irishman who couldn't speak right and didn't belong to the Kirk, but Ella White she was not so particular and was fell long in the tooth herself. So when

Ellison came to her at the harvest ball in Auchinblae and
cried *Can I see you home to-night, me dear?* she said *Och,
Ay.* And on the road home they lay among the stooks and
maybe Ellison did this and that to make sure of getting
her, he was fair desperate for any woman by then.

They were married next New Year's Day, and Ellison
had begun to think himself a gey man in Kinraddie, and
maybe one of the gentry. But the bothy billies, the ploughmen and the orra men of the Mains, they'd never a care
for gentry except to mock at them and on the eve of Ellison's wedding they took him as he was going into his house
and took off his breeks and tarred his dowp and the soles
of his feet and stuck feathers on them and then they threw
him into the water-trough, as was the custom. And he
called them *Bloody Scotch savages,* and was in an awful
rage and at the term-time he had them sacked, the whole
jingbang of them, so sore affronted he had been.

But after that he got on well enough, him and his mistress, Ella White, and they had a daughter, a scrawny bit
quean they thought over good to go to the Auchinblae
School, so off she went to Stonehaven Academy and was
taught to be right brave and swing about in the gymnasium
there with wee black breeks on under her skirt. Ellison
himself began to get well-stomached, and he had a red face,
big and sappy, and eyes like a cat, green eyes, and his
mouser hung down each side of a fair bit mouth that was
chokeful up of false teeth, awful expensive and bonny, lined
with bits of gold. And he aye wore leggings and riding
breeks, for he was fair gentry by then; and when he would
meet a crony at a mart he would cry *Sure, bot it's you, thin,
ould chep!* and the billy would redden up, real ashamed, but
wouldn't dare say anything, for he wasn't a man you'd
offend. In politics he said he was a Conservative but everybody in Kinraddie knew that meant he was a Tory and the
bairns of Strachan, him that farmed the Peesie's Knapp,
they would scraich out

> *Inky poo, your nose is blue,*
> *You're awful like the Turra Coo*

whenever they saw Ellison go by. For he'd sent a subscription to the creature up Turriff way whose cow had been
sold to pay his Insurance, and folk said it was no more than

a show off, the Cow creature and Ellison both; and they laughed at him behind his back.

So that was the Mains, below the Meikle House, and Ellison farmed it in his Irish way and right opposite, hidden away among their yews, were kirk and manse, the kirk an old, draughty place and in the wintertime, right in the middle of the Lord's Prayer, maybe, you'd hear an outbreak of hoasts fit to lift off the roof, and Miss Sarah Sinclair, her that came from Netherhill and played the organ, she'd sneeze into her hymnbook and miss his bit notes and the minister, him that was the old one, he'd glower down at her more like John Knox than ever.

Next door the kirk was an olden tower, built in the time of the Roman Catholics, the coarse creatures, and it was fell old and wasn't used any more except by the cushat-doves and they flew in and out the narrow slips in the upper storey and nested there all the year round and the place was fair white with their dung. In the lower half of the tower was an effigy-thing of Cospatric de Gondeshil, him that killed the gryphon, lying on his back with his arms crossed and a daft-like simper on his face; and the spear he killed the gryphon with was locked in a kist there, or so some said, but others said it was no more than an old bit heuch from the times of Bonny Prince Charlie. So that was the tower, but it wasn't fairly a part of the kirk, the real kirk was split in two bits, the main hall and the wee hall, and some called them the byre and the turnip-shed, and the pulpit stood midway

Once the wee hall had been for the folk from the Meikle House and their guests and suchlike gentry but nearly anybody that had the face went ben and sat there now, and the elders sat with the collection bags, and young Murray, him that blew the organ for Sarah Sinclair. It had fine glass windows, awful old, the wee hall with three bit creatures of queans, not very decent-like in a kirk, as window-pictures. One of the queans was Faith, and faith she looked a daft-like keek for she was lifting up her hands and her eyes like a heifer choked on a turnip and the bit blanket round her shoulders was falling off her but she didn't seem to heed, and there was a swither of scrolls and fiddley-faddles all about her.

And the second quean was Hope and she was near as unco as Faith, but had right bonny hair, red hair, though maybe you'd call it auburn, and in the winter-time the light in the morning service would come splashing through the yews in the kirkyard and into the wee hall through the red hair of Hope. And the third quean was Charity, with a lot of naked bairns at her feet and she looked a fine and decent-like woman, for all that she was tied about with such daft-like clouts.

But the windows of the main hall, though they were coloured, they had never a picture in them and there were no pictures in there at all, who wanted them? Only coarse creatures like Catholics wanted a kirk to look like a grocer's calendar. So it was decent and bare-like, with its carved old seats, some were cushioned and some were not, if you weren't padded by nature and had the silver to spend you might put in cushions to suit your fancy. Right up in the lithe of the pulpit, at angles-like to the rest of the kirk, were the three seats where the choir sat and led the hymn-singing; and some called it the calfies' stall.

The back door, that behind the pulpit, led out across the kirkyard to the Manse and its biggings, set up in the time of the Old Queen, and fair bonny to look at, but awful damp said all the ministers' wives. But ministers' wives were aye folk to complain and don't know when they're well off, them and the silver they get for their bit creatures of men preaching once or twice a Sunday and so proud they hardly know you when they meet you on the road. The minister's study was high up in the house, it looked out over all Kin-raddie, at night he'd see from there the lights of the farm-houses like a sprinkling of bright sands below his window and the flagstaff light high among the stars on the roof of the Meikle House. But that nineteen eleven December the Manse was empty and had been empty for many a month, the old minister was dead and the new one not yet voted on; and the ministers from Drumlithie and Arbuth-nott and Laurencekirk they came time about in the Sunday forenoons and took the service there at Kinraddie; and God knows for all they had to say they might well have bidden at home.

But if you went out of the kirk by the main door and took the road east a bit, and that was the road that served kirk and Manse and Mains, you were on to the turnpike then. It ran north and south but opposite to the road you'd just come down was another, that went through Kinraddie by the Bridge End farm. So there was a cross-roads there

and if you held to the left along the turnpike you came to
Peesie's Knapp, one of the olden places, no more than a
croft of thirty-forty acres with some rough ground for pasture, but God knows there was little pasture on it, it was
just a fair schlorich of whins and broom and dirt, full up
of rabbits and hares it was, they came out at night and ate
up your crops and sent a body fair mad. But it wasn't bad
land the most of the Knapp, there was the sweat of two
thousand years in it, and the meikle park behind the
biggings was black loam, not the red clay that sub-soiled
half Kinraddie.

Now Peesie's Knapp's biggings were not more than twenty years old, but gey ill-favoured for all that, for though the
house faced on the road—and that was fair handy if it
didn't scunner you that you couldn't so much as change
your sark without some ill-fashioned brute gowking in at
you—right between the byre and the stable and the barn
on one side and the house on the other was the cattle-court
and right in the middle of that the midden, high and yellow
with dung and straw and sharn, and Mistress Strachan could
never forgive Peesie's Knapp because of that awful smell
it had.

But Chae Strachan, him that farmed the place, he just
said *Hoots, what's a bit guff?* and would start to tell of the
terrible smells he'd smelt when he was abroad. For he'd
been a fell wandering billy, Chae, in the days before he
came back to Scotland and was fee'd his last fee at Netherhill. He'd been in Alaska, looking for gold there, but damn
the bit of gold he'd seen, so he'd farmed in California till
he was so scunnered of fruit he'd never look an orange or
a pear in the face again, not even in a tin. And then he'd
gone on to South Africa and had had great times there,
growing real chieflike with the head one of a tribe of
blacks, but an awful decent man for all that. Him and Chae
had fought against Boers and British both, and beaten them,
or so Chae said, but folk that didn't like Chae said all the
fighting he'd ever done had been with his mouth and that
as for beaten, he'd be sore made to beat the skin off a bowl
of sour milk.

For he wasn't well liked by them that set themselves up
for gentry, Chae, being a socialist creature and believing
we should all have the same amount of silver and that there
shouldn't be rich and poor and that one man was as good
as another. And the silver bit of that was clean daft, of

course, for if you'd all the same money one day what
would it be the next?—Rich and Poor again! But Chae said
the four ministers of Kinraddie and Auchinblae and
Laurencekirk and Drumlithie were all paid much the same
money last year and what had they this year?—Much the
same money still! *You'll have to get out of bed slippy in the
morning before you find a socialist tripping and if you
gave me any of your lip I'll clout you in the lug, my mannie.*

So Chae was fell good in argy-bargying and he wasn't the
quarrelsome kind except when roused, so he was well-liked,
though folk laughed at him. But God knows, who is it they
don't laugh at? He was a pretty man, well upstanding, with
great shoulders on him and his hair was fair and fine and
he had a broad brow and a gey bit coulter of a nose, and
he twisted his mouser ends up with wax like that creature
the German Kaiser, and he could stop a running stirk by
the horns, so strong he was in the wrist-bones. And he was
one of the handiest billies in Kinraddie, he would libb a calf
or break in a horse or kill a pig, all in a jiffy, or tile your
dairy or cut the barns' hair or dig a well, and all the time
he'd be telling you that socialism was coming or if it
wasn't then an awful crash would come and we'd all go
back to savagery, *Dam't ay, man!*

But folk said he'd more need to start socializing Mistress
Strachan, her that had been Kirsty Sinclair of Netherhill,
before he began on anybody else. She had a fell tongue,
they said, that would clip clouts and yammer a tink from
a door, and if Chae wasn't fair sick now and then for his
hut and a fine black quean in South Africa damn the hut
or the quean had he ever had. He'd feed'd at Netherhill
when he came back from foreign parts, had Chae, and there
had been but two daughters there, Kirsty and Sarah, her
that played the kirk organ. Both were wearing on a bit,
sore in the need of a man, and Kirsty with a fair letdown
as it was, for it had seemed that a doctor billy from Aberdeen was out to take up with her. So he had done and left
her in a gey way and her mother, old Mistress Sinclair,
near went out of her mind with the shame of it when
Kirsty began to cry and tell her the news.

Now that was about the term-time and home to Netherhill from the feeing market who should old Sinclair of
Netherhill bring but Chae Strachan, with his blood warmed
up from living in those foreign parts and an eye for less
than a wink of invitation? But even so he was gey slow to

get on with the courting and just hung around Kirsty like a futret round a trap with a bit meat in it, not sure if the meat was worth the risk; and the time was getting on and faith! Something drastic would have to be done.

So one night after they had all had supper in the kitchen and old Sinclair had gone pleitering out to the byres, old Mistress Sinclair had up and nodded to Kirsty and said *Ah well, I'll away to my bed. You'll not be long in making for yours, Kirsty?* And Kirsty said *No*, and gave her mother a sly bit look, and off the old mistress went up to her room and then Kirsty began fleering and flirting with Chae and he was a man warm enough and they were alone together and maybe in a minute he'd have had her couched down right well there in the kitchen but she whispered it wasn't safe. So he off with his boots and she with hers and up the stairs they crept together into Kirsty's room and were having their bit pleasure together when *ouf!* went the door and in burst old Mistress Sinclair with the candle held up in one hand and the other held up in horror. *No, no*, she'd said, *this won't do at all, Chakie, my man, you'll have to marry her*. And there had been no escape for Chae, poor man, with Kirsty and her mother both glowering at him.

So married they were and old Sinclair had saved up some silver and he rented Peesie's Knapp for Chae and Kirsty, and stocked the place for them, and down they sat there, and Kirsty's bairn, a bit quean, was born before seven months were past, well-grown and finished-like it seemed, the creature, in spite of its mother swearing it had come fair premature.

They'd had two more bairns since then, both laddies, and both the living spit of Chae, these were the bairns that would sing about the Turra Coo whenever they met the brave gig of Ellison bowling along the Kinraddie Road, and faith, they made you laugh.

Right opposite Peesie's Knapp, across the turnpike, the land climbed red and clay and a rough stone road went wandering up to the biggings of Blawearie. *Out of the World and into Blawearie* they said in Kinraddie, and faith! it was coarse land and lonely up there on the brae, fifty-sixty acres of it, forbye the moor that went on with the brae high above Blawearie, up to a great flat hill-top where lay a bit loch that nested snipe by the hundred; and some said there was no bottom to it, the loch, and Long Rob of the

Mill said that made it like the depths of a parson's depravity.

That was an ill thing to say about any minister, though Rob said it was an ill thing to say about any loch, but there the spleiter of water was, a woesome dark stretch fringed rank with rushes and knifegrass; and the screeching of the snipe fair deafened you if you stood there of an evening. And few enough did that for nearby the bit loch was a circle of stones from olden times, some were upright and some were flat and some leaned this way and that, and right in the middle three big ones clambered up out of the earth and stood askew with flat sonsy faces, they seemed to listen and wait. They were Druid stones and folk told that the Druids had been coarse devils of men in the times long syne, they'd climb up there and sing their foul heathen songs around the stones; and if they met a bit Christian missionary they'd gut him as soon as look at him. And Long Rob of the Mill would say what Scotland wanted was a return of the Druids, but that was just a speak of his, for they must have been awful ignorant folk, not canny.

Blawearie hadn't had a tenant for nearly a year, but now there was one on the way, they said, a creature John Guthrie from up in the North. The biggings of it stood fine and compact one side of the close, the midden was back of them, and across the close was the house, a fell brave house for a little place, it had three storeys and a good kitchen and a fair stretch of garden between it and Blawearie road. There were beech trees there, three of them, one was close over against the house, and the garden hedges grew as bonny with honeysuckle of a summer as ever you saw; and if you could have lived on the smell of honeysuckle you might have farmed the bit place with profit.

Well, Peesie's Knapp and Blawearie were the steadings that lay Stonehaven way. But if you turned east that winter along the Auchinblae road first on your right was Cuddiestoun, a small bit holding the size of Peesie's Knapp and old as it, a croft from the far-off times. It lay a quarter-mile or so from the main road and its own road was fair clamjamfried with glaur from late in the harvest till the coming of Spring. Some said maybe that accounted for Munro's neck, he could never get the glaur washed out of it. But others said he never tried. He was on a thirteen years' lease there,

Munro, a creature from down south, Dundee way, and he was a good six feet in height but awful coarse among the legs, like a lamb with water on the brain, and he had meikle feet that aye seemed in his way. He was maybe forty years or so in age, and bald already, and his skin was red and creased in cheeks and chin and God! you never saw an uglier brute, poor stock.

For there were worse folk than Munro, though maybe they were all in the jail, and though he could blow and bombast till he fair scunnered you. He farmed his bit land in a then and now way, and it was land good enough, the most of it, with the same black streak of loam that went through the Peesie parks, but ill-drained, the old stone drains were still down and devil the move would the factor at Meikle House make to have them replaced, or mend the roof of the byre that leaked like a sieve on the head of Mistress Munro when she milked the kye on a stormy night.

But if anybody, chieflike, were to say, *God, that's an awful byre you have, mistress,* she would flare up in a minute *It's one and good enough for the like of us.* And if that body, not knowing better, poor billy, were to agree that the place was well enough for poor folk, she'd up again *Who's poor? Let me tell you we've never needed anybody come to our help, though we don't boast and blow about it all over the countryside, like some I could mention.* So the body would think there was no pleasing of the creature, and she was right well laughed at in all Kinraddie, though not to her face. And that was a thin one and she had black hair and snapping black eyes like a futret, and a voice that fair set your hackles on edge when she girned. But she was the best midwife for miles around, right often in the middle of the night some poor distracted billy would come chapping at her window *Mistress Munro, Mistress Munro, will you get up and come to the wife?* And out she'd get, and into her clothes before you could whistle, and out into the cold of Kinraddie night and go whipping through it like a futret, and soon be snapping her orders round the kitchen of the house she'd been summoned to, telling the woman in childbed she might easily be worse, and being right brisk and sharp and clever.

And the funny thing about the creature was that she believed none spoke ill of her, for if she heard a bit hint of such, dropped sly-like, she'd redden up like a stalk of rhubarb in a dung patch and look as though she might start to cry, and the body would feel real sorry for her till next minute she'd be screeching at Andy or Tony, and fleering them out of the little wits they had, poor devils.

Now, Andy and Tony were two dafties that Mistress Munro had had boarded out on her from an Asylum in Dundee, they weren't supposed to be dangerous. Andy was a meikle slummock of a creature, and his mouth was aye open, and he dribbled like a teething foal, and his nose wabbled all over his face and when he tried to speak it was just a fair jumble of foolishness. He was the daftest one, but fell sly, he'd sometimes run away to the hills and stand there with his finger at his nose, making faces at Mistress Munro, and she'd scraich at him and he'd yammer back at her and then over the moor he'd get to the bothy at Upperhill where the ploughmen would give him cigarettes and then torment him till he fair raged; and once tried to kill one with an axe he caught up from a hackstock. And at night he'd creep back to Cuddiestoun, outside he'd make a noise like a dog that had been kicked, and he'd snuffle round the door till the few remaining hairs on the bald pow of Munro would fair rise on end. But Mistress Munro would up and be at the door and in she'd yank Andy by the lug, and some said she'd take down his breeks and skelp him, but maybe that was a lie. She wasn't feared at him and he wasn't feared at her, so they were a gey well-matched pair.

And that was the stir at Cuddiestoun, all except Tony, for the Munros had never a bairn of their own. And Tony, though he wasn't the daftest, he was the queer one, too, right enough. He was small-bulked and had a little red beard and sad eyes, and he walked with his head down and you would feel right sorry for him for sometimes some whimsy would come on the creature right in the middle of the turnpike it might be or half-way down a rig of swedes, and there he would stand staring like a gowk for minutes on end till somebody would shake him back to his senses. He had fine soft hands, for he was no working body; folk said he had once been a scholar and written books and learned and learned till his brain fair softened and right off his head he'd gone and into the poorhouse asylum.

Now Mistress Munro she'd send Tony errands to the wee shop out beyond the Bridge End, and tell him what she wanted, plain and simple-like, and maybe giving him a bit clout in the lug now and then, as you would a bairn or a daftie. And he'd listen to her and make out he minded the messages and off to the shop he'd go, and come back without a single mistake. But one day, after she'd told him the things she wanted, Mistress Munro saw the wee creature writing on a bit of paper with a pencil he'd picked up somewhere. And she took the paper from him and looked at it and turned it this way and that, but feint the thing could she made of it. So she gave him a bit clout in the lug and asked him what the writing was. But he just shook his head, real gowked-like and reached out his hand for the bit of paper, but Mistress Munro would have none of that and when it was time for the Strachan bairns to pass the end of the Cuddiestoun road on their way to school down there she was waiting and gave the paper to the eldest the quean Marget, and told her to show it to the Dominie and ask him what it might mean.

And at night she was waiting for the Strachan bairns to come back and they had an envelope for her from the Dominie; and she opened it and found a note saying the writing was shorthand and that this was what it read when put in the ordinary way of writing: *Two pounds of sugar The People's Journal half an ounce of mustard a tin of rat poison a pound of candles and I don't suppose I can swindle her out of tuppence change for the sake of a smoke, she's certainly the meanest bitch unhung this side of Tweed.* So maybe Tony wasn't so daft, but he got no supper that night; and she never asked to see his notes again.

Now, following the Kinraddie road still east, you passed by Netherhill on your left, five places had held its parks in the crofter days before Lord Kenneth. But now it was a fair bit farm on its own, old Sinclair and his wife, a body that was wearing none so well—soured up the creature was that her eldest daughter Sarah still bided all unwed—lived in the farm-house, and in the bothy was foreman and second man and third man and orra lad. The Denburn lay back of the Netherhill, drifting low and slow and placid in its hollow, feint the fish had ever been seen in it and folk said that was just as well, things were fishy enough at Netherhill without the Denburn adding to them.

Through the rank schlorich of moor that lay between the place and Peesie's Knapp were the tracks of an old-time road, some said it was old as Calgacus, him that

chased the Romans all to hell at the battle of Mons
Graupius, others said it was a Druid work, laid by them
that set the stone above Blawearie loch. And God! there
must have been an unco few idle masons among the creatures, they'd tried their hands at another stone circle in
the Netherhill moor, right midway the old-time road. But
there were no more than two-three stones above the ground
in this later day, Netherhill's ploughmen swore the rest must
have been torn up and broadcast over the arable land, the
parks were as tough and stony as the heart of the old wife
herself.

But it was no bad place for turnips and oats, the Netherhill, sometimes the hay was fair to middling but the most
of the ground was red clay and over coarse and wet for
barley, if it hadn't been for the droves of pigs old Mistress
Sinclair fed and sold in Laurencekirk maybe her man would
never have sat where he did. She came of Gourdon stock,
the old wife, and everybody knows what they are, the
Gourdon fishers, they'd wring silver out of a corpse's wame
and call stinking haddocks perfume fishes and sell them at
a shilling a pair. She'd been a fishing quean before she took
up with old Sinclair, and when they settled down in Netherhill on borrowed money it was she that would drive to
Gourdon twice a week in the little pony lorry and come
back with it stinking out the countryside for miles around
with its load of rotten fish to manure the land. And right
well it manured it and they'd fine crops the first six years
or so and then the land was fair bled white and they'd to
stop the fish-manure. But by then the pig-breeding was
fine and paying, their debts were gone, they were coining
silver of their own.

He was a harmless stock, old Sinclair, and had began to
doiter and Mistress Sinclair would push him into his chair
at night and take off his boots and put slippers on him
there in front of the kitchen fire and say to him *You've tired
yourself out again, my lad.* And he'd put his hand below her
chin and say *Och, I'm fine, don't vex yourself. . . . Ay your
lad still, am I, lass?* And they'd look at each other, daft-
like, two wrinkled old fools, and their daughter Sarah that
was so genteel would be real affronted if there were visitors
about. But Sinclair and his old wife would just shake their
heads at her and in their bed at night, hiddling their old
bones close for warmth, give a bit sigh that no brave billy
had ever show inclination to take Sarah to *his* bed. She'd

hoped and peeked and preened long years, and once there
had seemed some hope with Long Rob of the Mill, but
Rob wasn't the marrying sort. God! If Cuddiestoun's dafties
were real dafties what would you say of a man with plenty
of silver that bided all by his lone and made his own bed
and did his own baking when he might have had a wife to
make him douce and brave?

But Rob of the Mill had never a thought of what Kinraddie said of him. Further along the Kinraddie road it
stood, the Mill, on the corner of the side-road that led up to
Upperhill, and for ten years now had Rob bided there alone,
managing the Mill and reading the books of a coarse creature Ingersoll that made watches and didn't believe in God.
He'd aye two-three fine pigs about the Mill had Rob, and
fine might well they be for what did he feed them on but
bits of corn and barley he'd nicked out of the sacks folk
brought him to the Mill to grind? Nor could a body deny
but that Long Rob's boar was one of the best in the
Mearns; and they'd bring their sows from as far afield as
Laurencekirk to have them set by that boar of his, a
meikle, pretty brute of a beast.

Forbye the Mill and his swine and hens Rob had a
Clydesdale and a sholtie beast he ploughed his twenty acres
with, and a cow or so that never calved, for he'd never
time to send them to the bull though well might he have
taken the time instead of sweating and chaving like a daft
one to tear up the coarse moorland behind the Mill and
turn it into a park. He'd started that three years before
and wasn't half through with it yet, it was filled with great
holes and ponds and choked with meikle broom-roots thick
as the arm of a man, you never saw a dafter ploy. They'd
hear Rob out in that coarse ground hard at work when they
went to bed, the rest of Kinraddie, whistling away to himself as though it were nine o'clock in the forenoon and the
sun shining bravely. He'd whistle *Ladies of Spain* and
There was a young maiden and *The lass that made the bed
for me,* but devil the lass he'd ever taken to his bed, and
maybe that was as well for the lass; she'd have seen feint
the much of him in it beside her.

For after a night of it like that he'd be out again at the
keek of day, and sometimes he'd have the Clydesdale or
the sholtie out there with him and they'd be fine friends,
the three of them, till the beasts would move off when he

didn't want them or wouldn't move when he did; and then he'd fair go mad with them and call them all the coarsest names he could lay tongue to till you'd think he'd be heard over half the Mearns; and he'd leather the horses till folk spoke of sending for the Cruelty, though he'd a way with the beasts too, and would be friends with them again in a minute, and when he'd been away at the smithy in Drum-lithie or the joiner's in Arbuthnott they'd come running from the other end of the parks at sight of him and he'd get off his bicycle and feed them with lumps of sugar he bought and carried about with him.

He thought himself a gey man with horses, did Rob, and God! he'd tell you stories about horses till you'd fair be grey in the head, but he never wearied of them himself, the long, rangy childe. Long he was, with small bones may-be, but gey broad for all that, with a small head on him and a thin nose and eyes smoky blue as an iron coulter on a winter morning, aye glinting, and a long mouser the colour of ripe corn it was, hanging down the sides of his mouth so that the old minister had told him he looked like a Viking and he'd said *Ah well, minister, as long as I don't look like a parson I'll wrestle through the world right content,* and the minister said he was a fool and godless, and his laughter like the thorns crackling under a pot. And Rob said he'd rather be a thorn than a sucker any day, for he didn't believe in ministers or kirks, he'd learned that from the books of Ingersoll though God knows if the creature's logic was as poor as his watches he was but a sorry prop to lean on. But Rob said he was fine, and if Christ came down to Kinraddie he'd be welcome enough to a bit meal or milk at the Mill, but damn the thing he'd get at the Manse. So that was Long Rob and the stir at the Mill, some said he wasn't all there but others said Ay, that he was, and a bit over.

Now Upperhill rose above the Mill, with its larch woods crowning it, and folk told that a hundred years before five of the crofter places had crowded there till Lord Kenneth threw their biggins down and drove them from the parish and built the fine farm of Upperhill. And twenty years later a son of one of the crofters had come back and rented the place, Gordon was the name of him, they called him Upprums for short and he didn't like that, being near to gentry with his meikle farm and forgetting his father the crofter that had cried like a bairn all the way from Kinraddie that night the Lord Kenneth drove them out. He was a small bit man with a white face on him, and he'd long, thin hair and a nose that wasn't straight but peeked away to one side of his face and no moustache and wee feet and hands; and he liked to wear leggings and breeks and carry a bit stick and look as proud as a cock on a midden.

Mistress Gordon was a Stonehaven woman, her father had been a bit post-office creature there, but God! to hear her speak you'd think he'd invented the post office himself and taken out a patent for it. She was a meikle sow of a woman, but aye well-dressed, and with eyes like the eyes of a fish, fair cod-like they were, and she tried to speak English and to make her two bit daughters, Nellie and Maggie Jean, them that went to Stonehaven Academy, speak English as well. And God! they made a right muck of it, and if you met the bit things on the road and said *Well, Nellie, and how are your mother's hens laying?* the quean would more than likely answer you *Not very meikle the day* and look so proud it was all you could do to stop yourself catching the futret across your knee and giving her a bit skelp.

Though she'd only a dove's flitting of a family herself you'd think to hear Mistress Gordon speak that she'd been clecking bairns a litter a month since the day she married. It was *Now, how I brought up Nellie*—or *And the specialist in Aberdeen, said about Maggie Jean*—till folk were so scunnered they'd never mention a bairn within a mile of Upperhill. But Rob of the Mill, the coarse brute, he fair mocked her to her face and he'd tell a story *Now, when I took my boar to the specialist in Edinburgh, he up and said 'Mister Rob, this is a gey unusual boar, awful delicate, but SO intelligent, and you should send him to the Academy and some day he'll be a real credit to you.'* And Mistress Gordon when she heard that story she turned as red as a fire and forgot her English and said Rob was an orra tink brute.

Forbye the two queans there was the son, John Gordon, as coarse a devil as you'd meet, he'd already had two-three queans in trouble and him but barely eighteen years old. But with one of them he'd met a sore stammy-gaster, her brother was a gardener down Glenbervie way and when he heard of it he came over to Upperhill and caught young Gordon out by the cattle-court. *You'll be Jock?* he said, and young Gordon said *Keep your damned hands to your-self,* and the billy said *Ay, but first I'll wipe them on a dirty clout,* and with that he up with a handful of sharn and splattered it all over young Gordon and then rolled him in the greip till he was a sight to sicken a sow from its supper.

The bothy men heard the ongoing and came tearing out but soon as they saw it was only young Gordon that was being mischieved they did no more than laugh and stand around and cry one to the other that here was a real fine barrow-load of dung lying loose in the greip. So the Drum-lithie billy, minding his sister and her shame, wasn't sharp to finish with his tormenting, young Gordon looked like a half-dead cat and smelt like a whole-dead one for a week after, a sore affront to Upperhill's mistress. She went tearing round to the bothy and made at the foreman, a dour young devil of a Highlandman, Ewan Tavendale, *Why didn't you help my Johnnie?* and Ewan said *I was fee'd as the fore-man here, not as the nursemaid,* he was an impudent brute, calm as you please, but an awful good worker, folk said he could smell the weather and had fair the land in his bones.

Now the eighth of the Kinraddie places you could call hardly a place at all, for that was Pooty's, midway along the Kinraddie road between the Mill and Bridge End. It was no more than a butt and a ben, with a rickle of sheds behind it where old Pooty kept his cow and bit donkey that was nearly as old as himself and faith! twice as good-look-ing; and folk said the cuddy had bided so long with Pooty that whenever it opened its mouth to give a bit bray it started to stutter. For old Pooty was maybe the worst stutterer ever heard in the Mearns and the worst of that worst was that he didn't know it and he'd clean compel any minister creature organising a concert miles around to give him a platform part. Then up he'd get on the platform, the doitered old fool, and recite *Weeeee, ssss-leek-ed, cccccccowering TIMROUS BEASTIE* or such-like poem and it was fair agony to hear him.

He'd lived at Pooty's a good fifty years they said, his father the crofter of the Knapp before that time, hardly a soul knew his name, maybe he'd forgotten it himself. He was the oldest inhabitant of Kinraddie and fell proud of it, though what there was to be proud of in biding all that while in a damp, sour house that a goat would hardly have stopped to ease itself in God knows. He was a shoe-maker, the creature, and called himself the Sutor, an old-fashioned name that folk laughed at. He'd grey hair aye falling about his lugs and maybe he washed on New Year's Days and birthdays, but not oftener, and if anybody had ever seen him in anything but the grey shirt with the read neckband he'd kept the fact a dead secret all to himself.

Alec Mutch was farmer of Bridge End that stood beyond the Denburn head, he'd come there up from Stonehaven way, folk said he was head over heels in debt, and damn it you couldn't wonder with a slummock of a wife like that to weigh him down. A grand worker was Alec and Bridge End not the worst of Kinraddie, though wet in the bottom up where its parks joined on to Upperhill. Two pairs of horses it was stabled for but Alec kept no more than three bit beasts, he'd say he was waiting for his family to grow up before he completed the second pair. And fast enough the family came, if she couldn't do much else, Mistress Mutch, fell seldom a year went by but she was brought to bed with a bairn, Mutch fair grew used to dragging himself out in the middle of the night and tearing off to Bervie for the doctor. And the doctor, old Meldrum he was, he'd wink at Alec and cry *Man, Man, have you been at it again?* and Alec would say *Damn it, you've hardly to look at a woman these days but she's in the family way.*

So some said that he must glower at his mistress a fell lot, and that was hard enough to believe, she was no great beauty, with a cock eye and a lazy look and nothing worried her, not a mortal thing, not though her five bairns were all yammering blue murder at the same minute and the smoke coming down the chimney and spoiling the dinner and the cattle broken into the yard and eating up her clean washing. She'd say *Ah well, it'll make no difference a hundred years after I'm dead,* and light up a bit cigarette, like a tink, for aye she carried a packet of the things about with her, she was the speak of half the Mearns, her and her smoking.

Two of the five bairns were boys, the oldest eleven, and the whole five of them had the Mutch face, broad and boney and tapering to a chinney point, like the face of an owlet or a fox, and meikle lugs on them like the handles on a cream-jar. Alec himself had such lugs that they said he flapped them against the flies in the summer-time, and once he was coming home on his bicycle from Laurence-kirk, and he was real drunk and at the steep brae above the Denburn bridge he mistook the flow of the water for the broad road and in between coping and bank he went and head over heels into the clay bed twenty feet below; and often he'd tell that if he hadn't landed on a lug he might well have been brained, but Long Rob of the Mill would laugh and say *Brained? Good God, Mutch, you were never in danger of that!*

So that was Kinraddie that bleak winter of nineteen eleven and the new minister, him they chose early next year, he was to say it was the Scots countryside itself, fathered between a kailyard and a bonny brier bush in the lee of a house with green shutters. And what he meant by that you could guess at yourself if you'd a mind for puzzles and dirt, there wasn't a house with green shutters in the whole of Kinraddie.

The Song

I

PLOUGHING

BELOW and around where Chris Guthrie lay the June
moors whispered and rustled and shook their cloaks, yellow
with broom and powdered faintly with purple, that was the
heather but not the full passion of its colour yet. And in the
east against the cobalt blue of the sky lay the shimmer of
the North Sea, that was by Bervie, and maybe the wind
would veer there in an hour or so and you'd feel
the change in the life and strum of the thing, bringing a
streaming coolness out of the sea.

But for days now the wind had been in the south, it
shook and played in the moors and went dandering up the
sleeping Grampians, the rushes pecked and quivered about
the loch when its hand was upon them, but it brought more
heat than cold, and all the parks were fair parched, sucked
dry, the red clay soil of Blawearie gaping open for the
rain that seemed never-coming. Up here the hills were
brave with the beauty and the heat of it, but the hayfield
was all a crackling dryness and in the potato park beyond
the biggings the shaws drooped red and rusty already. Folk
said there hadn't been such a drought since eighty-three
and Long Rob of the Mill said you couldn't blame *this* one
on Gladstone, anyway, and everybody laughed except
father. God knows why.

Some said the North, up Aberdeen way, had had rain

enough, with Dee in spate and bairns hooking stranded
salmon down in the shallows, and that must be fine enough,
but not a flick of the greeve weather had come over the
hills, the roads you walked down to Kinraddie smithy or up
to the Denburn were fair blistering in the heat, thick with
dust so that the motor-cars went shooming through them
like kettles under steam.

And serve them right, they'd little care for anybody, the
dirt that rode in motors, folk said; and one of them had
nearly run over wee Wat Strachan a fortnight before and
had skirled to a stop right bang in front of Peesie's Knapp,
Wat had yowled like a cat with a jobe under its tail and
Chae had gone striding out and taken the motorist man
by the shoulder. And *What the hell do you think you're
up to?* Chae had asked. And the motorist, he was a fair
toff with leggings and a hat cocked over his eyes, he'd said
Keep your damn children off the road in future. And
Chae had said *Keep a civil tongue in your head* and had
clouted the motorist man one in the ear and down he had
flumped in the stour and Mistress Strachan, her that was old
Netherhill's daughter, she'd gone tearing out skirling
Mighty, you brute, you've killed the man! and Chae had
just laughed and said *Damn the fears!* and off he'd gone.

But Mistress Strachan had helped the toff up to his
feet and shook him and brushed him and apologised for
Chae, real civil-like. And all the thanks she got was that
Chae was summonsed for assault at Stonehaven and fined
a pound, and came out of the courthouse saying there was
no justice under capitalism, a revolution would soon
sweep away its corrupted lackeys. And maybe it would, but
faith! there was as little sign of a revolution, said Long Rob
of the Mill, as there was of rain.

Maybe that was the reason for half the short tempers
over the Howe. You could go never a road but farmer billies were leaning over the gates, glowering at the weather,
and road-menders, poor stocks, chapping away at their hill-
ocks with the sweat fair dripping off them, and the only
folk that seemed to have a fine time were the shepherds up
in the hills. But they swore themselves dry when folk cried
that to them, the hill springs about a shepherd's herd would
dry up or seep away all in an hour and the sheep go straying and baying and driving the man fair senseless till he'd
led them weary miles to the nearest burn. So everybody
was fair snappy, staring up at the sky, and the ministers

all over the Howe were offering up prayers for rain in between the bit about the Army and the Prince of Wales' rheumatics. But feint the good it did for rain; and Long Rob of the Mill said he'd heard both Army and rheumatics were much the same as before.

Maybe father would have done better to keep a civil tongue in his head and stayed on in Echt, there was plenty of rain there, a fine land for rain, Aberdeen, you'd see it by day and night come drenching and wheeling over the Barmekin and the Hill of Fare in the fine northern land. And mother would sigh, looking out from Blawearie's windows, *There's no land like Aberdeen or folk so fine as them that bide by Don.*

She'd bidden by Don all her life, mother, she'd been born in Kildrummie, her father a ploughman there he'd got no more than thirteen shillings a week and he'd had thirteen of a family, to work things out in due ratio, maybe. But mother said they all got on fine, she was never happier in her life than those days when she tramped barefooted the roads to the little school that nestled under the couthy hills. And at nine she left the school and they packed a basket for her and she bade her mother ta-ta and set out to her first fee, no shoes on her feet even then, she hadn't worn shoes till she was twelve years old. It hadn't been a real fee that first one, she'd done little more than scare the crows from the fields of an old bit farmer and sleep in a garret, but fine she'd liked it, she'd never forget the singing of the winds in those fields when she was young or the daft crying of the lambs she herded or the feel of the earth below her toes. *Oh, Chris, my lass, there are better things than your books or studies or loving or bedding, there's the countryside your own, you its, in the days when you're neither bairn nor woman.*

So mother had worked and ran the parks those days, she was blithe and sweet, you knew, you saw her against the sun as though you peered far down a tunnel of the years. She stayed long on her second fee, seven or eight years she was there till the day she met John Guthrie at a ploughing-match at Pittodrie. And often once she'd tell of that to Chris and Will, it was nothing grand of a match, the horses were poor and the ploughing worse and a coarse, cold wind was soughing across the rigs and half Jean Murdoch made up her mind to go home.

Then it was that it came the turn of a brave young childe
with a red head and the swackest legs you ever saw, his
horses were laced in ribbons, bonny and trig, and as soon
as he began the drill you saw he'd carry off the prize. And
carry it off he did, young John Guthrie, and not that alone.
For as he rode from the park on one horse he patted the
back of the other and cried to Jean Murdoch with a glint
from his dour, sharp eye *Jump up if you like.* And she
cried back *I like fine!* and caught the horse by its mane and
swung herself there till Guthrie's hand caught her and set
her steady on the back of the beast. So out from the ploughing-match at Pittodrie the two of them rode together, Jean
sitting upon the hair of her, gold it was and as long, and
laughing up into the dour, keen face that was Guthrie's.

So that was beginning of their lives together, she was
sweet and kind to him, but he mightn't touch her, his face
would go black with rage at her because of that sweetness
that tempted his soul to hell. Yet in two-three years they'd
chaved and saved enough for gear and furnishings, and
were married at last, and syne Will was born, and syne
Chris herself was born, and the Guthries rented a farm in
Echt, Cairndhu it was, and sat themselves down there for
many a year.

Winters or springs, summers or harvests, bristling or sun-
ning the sides of Barmekin, and life ploughed its rigs and
drove its teams and the dourness hardened, hard and cold,
in the heart of Jean Guthrie's man. But still the glint of her
hair could rouse him, Chris would hear him cry in agony at
night as he went with her, mother's face grew queer and
questioning, her eyes far back on those Springs she might
never see again, dear and blithe they had been, she could
kiss and hold them still a moment alone with Chris or Will.
Dod came, then Alec came, and mother's fine face grew
harder then. One night they heard her cry to John Guthrie
Four of a family's fine; there'll be no more. And father
thundered at her, that way he had *Fine? We'll have what
God in His mercy may send to us, woman. See you to that.*

He wouldn't do anything against God's will, would father,
and sure as anything God followed up Alec with the twins,
born seven years later. Mother went about with a queer look
on her face before they came, she lost that sweet blitheness
that was hers, and once, maybe she was ill-like, she said to
father when he spoke of arranging a doctor and things,
Don't worry about that. No doubt your friend Jehovah will

see to it all. Father seemed to freeze up, then, his face grew black; he said never a word, and Chris had wondered at that, seeing how mad he'd been when Will used the word, thoughtless-like, only a week before.

For Will had heard the word in the kirk of Echt where the elders sit with shaven chins and the offering bags between their knees, waiting the sermon to end and to march with slow, sleeked steps up through the pews, hearing the penny of penury clink shy-like against the threepenny of affluence. And Will one Sunday, sitting close to sleep, heard fall from the minister's lips the word *Jehovah,* and treasured it for the bonniness and the beauty of it, waiting till he might find a thing or a man or beast that would fit this word, well-shaped and hantled and grand.

Now that was in summer, the time of fleas and glegs and golochs in the fields, when stirks would start up from a drowsy cud-chewing to a wild and feckless racing, the glegs biting through hair and hide to the skin below the tail-rump. Echt was alive that year with the thunder of herds, the crackle of breaking gates, the splash of stirks in tarns, and last with the groans of Nell, the old horse of Guthrie's, caught in a daft swither of the Highland steers and her belly ripped like a rotten swede with the stroke of a great, curved horn.

Father saw the happening from high in a park where the hay was cut and they set the swathes in coles, and he swore out *Damn't to hell!* and started to run, fleetly as was his way, down to the groaning shambles that was Nell. And as he ran he picked up a scythe-blade, and as he neared to Nell he unhooked the blade and cried *Poor quean!* and Nell groaned, groaning blood and sweating, and turned away her neck, and father thrust the scythe at her neck, sawing till she died.

So that was the end of Nell, father waited till the hay was coled and then tramped into Aberdeen and bought a new horse, Bess, riding her home at evening to the raptured starings of Will. And Will took the horse and watered her and led her into the stall where Nell had slept and gave to her hay and a handful of corn, and set to grooming her, shoulder to heel, and her fine plump belly and the tail of her, long and curled. And Bess stood eating her corn and Chris leant against the doorjamb, her Latin Grammar held in her hand. So, working with fine, strong strokes, and

happy, Will groomed till he finished the tail, and then as he
lifted the brush to hit Bess on the flank that she might
move to the other side of the stall and he complete his
grooming there flashed in his mind the fine word he had
treasured. *Come over, Jehovah!* he cried, smiting her
roundly, and John Guthrie heard the word out across the
yard and came fleetly from the kitchen, wiping oatcake
from his beard, and fleetly across the yard into the stable
he came——

But he should not have stricken Will as he did, he fell
below the feet of the horse and Bess turned her head, dripping corn, and looked down at Will, with his face bloody,
and then swished her tail and stood still. And then John
Guthrie dragged his son aside and paid no more heed to
him, but picked up brush and curry-comb and cried *Whoa,
lass!* and went on with the grooming. Chris had cried and
hidden her face but now she looked again. Will was sitting
up slowly, the blood on his face, and John Guthrie speaking
to him, not looking at him, grooming Bess.

*And mind, my mannie, if I ever hear you again take your
Maker's name in vain, if I ever hear you use that word
again, I'll libb you. Mind that. Libb you like a lamb.*

So Will hated father, he was sixteen years of age and
near a man, but father could still make him cry like a
bairn. He would whisper his hate to Chris as they lay in
their beds at night in the loft room high in the house and
the harvest moon came sailing over the Barmekin and the
peewits wheeped above the lands of Echt. And Chris would
cover her ears and then listen, turning this cheek to the
pillow and that, she hated also and she didn't hate, father,
the land, the life of the land—oh, if only she knew!

For she'd met with books, she went into them to a magic
land far from Echt, out and away and south. And at school
they wrote she was the clever one and John Guthrie said
she might have the education she needed if she stuck to her
lessons. In time she might come out as a teacher then, and
do him credit, that was fine of father the Guthrie whispered
in her, but the Murdoch laughed with a blithe, sweet face.
But more and more she turned from that laughter, resolute,
loving to hear of the things in the histories and geographies,
seldom thinking them funny, strange names and words like
Too-long and Too-loose that convulsed the classes. And at
arithmetic also she was more than good, doing great sums
in her head so that always she was first in the class, they

made her the dux and they gave her prizes, four prizes in
four years she had.

And one book she'd thought fair daft, *Alice in Wonderland* it was, and there was no sense in it. And the second,
it was *What Katy did at School,* and she loved Katy and
envied her and wished like Katy she lived at a school, not
tramping back in the spleiter of a winter night to help muck
the byre, with the smell of the sharn rising feuch! in her
face. And the third book was *Rienzi, the Last of the Roman
Tribunes,* and some bits were good and some fair wearying.
He had a right bonny wife, Rienzi had, and he was sleeping
with her, her white arms round his neck, when the Romans
came to kill him at last. And the fourth book, new given
her before the twins came to Cairndhu, was *The Humours
of Scottish Life* and God! if that stite was fun she must have
been born dull.

And these had been all her books that weren't lesson-
books, they were all the books in Cairndhu but for the
Bibles grandmother had left to them, one to Chris and one
to Will, and in Chris's one were set the words *To my daw-
tie Chris: Trust in God and do the right.* For grandmother,
she'd been father's mother, not mother's mother, had been
fell religious and every Sunday, rain or shine, had tramped
to the kirk at Echt, sitting below some four-five ministers
there in all. And one minister she'd never forgiven, for he'd
said not GAWD, as a decent man would, but GOHD, and
it had been a mercy when he caught a bit cold, laid up he
was, and quickly passed away; and maybe it had been a
judgment on him.

So that was Chris and her reading and schooling, two
Chrisses there were that fought for her heart and tormented her. You hated the land and the coarse speak of
the folk and learning was brave and fine one day and the
next you'd waken with the peewits crying across the hills,
deep and deep, crying in the heart of you and the smell of
the earth in your face, almost you'd cry for that, the beauty
of it and the sweetness of the Scottish land and skies. You
saw their faces in firelight, father's and mother's and the
neighbours', before the lamps lit up, tired and kind, faces
dear and close to you, you wanted the words they'd known
and used, forgotten in the far-off youngness of their lives,
Scots words to tell to your heart, how they wrung it and
held it, the toil of their days and unendingly their fight. And
the next minute that passed from you, you were English,

back to the English words so sharp and clean and true—
for a while, for a while, till they slid so smooth from your
throat you knew they could never say anything that was
worth the saying at all.

But she sat for her bursary, won it, and began the con-
jugating Latin verbs, the easy ones only at first, *Amo, amas,
I love a lass* and then you laughed out loud when the Dominie said that and he cried *Whist, whist* but was real
pleased and smiled at you and you felt fine and tingly and
above all the rest of the queans who weren't learning Latin
or anything else, they were kitchen-maids in the bone. And
then there was French, fair difficult, the u was the worst;
and an inspector creature came to Echt and Chris near
dropped through the schoolroom floor in shame when he
made her stand out in front of them all and say *o-oo, o-oo,
o-oo-butin.* And he said *Put your mouth as though you were
going to weesel, but don't do it, and say 'o-oo, o-oo, o-oo.'*
And she said it, she felt like a hen with a stone in its
thrapple, after the inspector creature, an Englishman he was
with an awful belly on him and he couldn't say whistle, only
weesel.

And he went away down to the gig that was waiting to
drive him to the station he went, and he left his brave
leather bag behind, and the Dominie saw it and cried *Whist,
Chrissie, run after the Inspector man with his bag.* So she
did and caught him up at the foot of the playground, he
growked at her and said *Haw?* and then gave a bit laugh
and said *Haw?* again and then *Thenks.* And Chris went
back to the Dominie's room, the Dominie was waiting for
her and he asked if the Inspector had given her anything,
and Chris said *No,* and the Dominie looked sore disappointed.

But everybody knew that the English were awful mean
and couldn't speak right and were cowards who captured
Wallace and killed him by treachery. But they'd been beaten
right well at Bannockburn, then, Edward the Second hadn't
drawn rein till he was in Dunbar, and ever after that the
English were beaten in all the wars, except Flodden and
they won at Flodden by treachery again, just as it told in
The Flowers of the Forest. Always she wanted to cry when
she heard that played and a lot of folk singing it at a parish
concert in Echt, for the sadness of it and the lads that came
back never again to their lasses among the stooks and the
lasses that never married but sat and stared down south to

the English border where their lads lay happed in blood
and earth, with their bloodied kilts and broken helmets.
And she wrote an essay on that, telling all how it happened,
the Dominie said it was fine and that sometimes she should
try to write poetry: like Mrs. Hemans.

But then, just after writing the essay, the twins were born
and mother had as awful a time as she'd always had. She
was sobbing and ill when she went to bed, Chris boiled
water in kettles for hours and hours and then towels came
down, towels clairted with stuff she didn't dare look at,
she washed them quick and hung them to dry. The doctor
came in with the evening, he stayed the whole night, and
Dod and Alec shivered and cried in their room till father
went up and skelped them right sore, they'd something to
cry for then but they didn't dare. And father came down
the stairs again, fleet as ever, though he hadn't been in bed
for forty hours, and he closed the kitchen door and sat with
his head between his hands and groaned and said he was a
miserable sinner, God forgive him the lusts of the flesh,
something about the bonny hair of her also he said and then
more about lust, but he hadn't intended Chris to hear for
he looked up and saw her looking at him and he raged
at her, telling her to spread a table with breakfast for the
doctor—*through in the parlour there, and boil him an egg.*

And then mother began to scream, the doctor called
down the stairs *Man, it's a fair tough case, I doubt I'll need
your help,* and at that father turned grey as a sheet and
covered his face again and cried *I dare not, I dare not!*
Then the doctor childe called him again *Guthrie man, do
you hear me?* and father jumped up in a rage and cried
Damn't to hell, I'm not deaf! and ran up the stairs, fleet as
ever, and then the door in the room closed fast and Chris
could hear no more.

Not that she wanted to hear, she felt real ill herself,
cooking the egg and laying a meal in the parlour with a
white cloth spread above the green plush cloth and all the
furniture dark and shadowed and listening. Then Will came
down the stair, he couldn't sleep because of mother,
they sat together and Will said the old man was a fair beast
and mother shouldn't be having a baby, she was far too old
for that. And Chris stared at him with horrified imaginings
in her mind, she hadn't known better then, the English bit
of her went sick, she whispered *What has father to do with*

it? And Will stared back at her, shamed-faced, *Don't you know? What's a bull to do with a calf, you fool?*

But then they heard an awful scream that made them leap to their feet, it was as though mother were being torn and torn in the teeth of beasts and couldn't thole it longer; and then a little screech like a young pig made followed that scream and they tried not to hear more of the sounds above them. Chris boiled the egg over and over till it was as hard as iron. And then mother screamed again, Oh God! your heart stopped to hear it, and that was when the second twin came.

Then quietness followed, they heard the doctor coming down the stairs, the morning was close, it hung scared beyond the stilled parks and listened and waited. But the doctor cried *Hot water, jugs of it, pour me a basin of water, Chris, and put plenty of soap near by it.* She cried *Ay, doctor,* to that but she cried in a whisper, he didn't hear and was fell angry. *D'you hear me?* And Will said to him, calling up the stair, *Ay, doctor, only she's feared,* and the doctor said *She'll have a damned sight more to fear when she's having a bairn of her own. Pour out the water, quick!* So they poured it and went through to the parlour while the doctor passed them with his hands held away from them, and the smell of his hands was a horror that haunted Chris for a day and a night.

That was the coming of the twins at Cairndhu, there'd been barely room for them all before that time, now they'd have to live like tinks. But it was a fell good farm, John Guthrie loath to part with it though his lease was near its end, and when mother came down from her bed in a fortnight's time with the shine of the gold still in the sweet hair of her and her eyes clear eyes again, he raged and swore when she spoke to him. *More rooms? What more room do we want than we have? Do you think we're gentry?* he cried, and went on again to tell that when he was a bairn in Pittodrie his mother had nine bairns all at home, nought but a butt and ben they had and their father nought but a plough-childe. But fine they'd managed, God-fearing and decent all he'd made them, and if one of Jean Murdoch's bairns were half as good the shame need never redden the face of her. And mother looked at him with the little smile on her lips, *Well, well, we're to bide on here,*

then? and father shot out his beard at her and cried *Ay,
that we are, content yourself.*

But the very next day he was driving back from the mart,
old Bob in the cart, when round a corner below the Barmekin came a motor-car spitting and barking like a tink dog
in distemper. Old Bob had made a jump and near landed
the cart in the ditch and then stood like a rock, so feared
he wouldn't move a step, the cart jammed fast across the
road. And as father tried to haul the thrawn beast to the
side a creature of a woman with her face all clamjamfried
with paint and powder and dirt, she thrust her bit head
out from the window of the car and cried *You're causing
an obstruction, my man.* And John Guthrie roused like a
lion: *I'm not your man, thank God, for if I was I'd have
your face scraped with a clart and then a scavenger wash
it well.* The woman nearly burst with rage at that, she fell
back in the car and said *You've not heard the last of this.
Take note of his name-plate, James, d'you hear?* And the
shover looked out, fair shamed he looked, and keeked at
the name-plate underneath Bob's shelvin, and quavered
Yes, madam, and they turned about and drove off. That
was the way to deal with dirt like the gentry, but when
father applied for his lease again he was told he couldn't
have it.

So he took a look at the *People's Journal* and got into
his fine best suit, Chris shook the moth-balls from it and
found him his collar and the broad white front to cover
his working sark; and John Guthrie tramped into Aberdeen
and took a train to Banchory to look at a small place there.
But the rent was awful high and he saw that nearly all the
district was land of the large-like farm, he'd be squeezed
to death and he'd stand no chance. It was fine land though,
that nearly shook him, fine it looked and your hands they
itched to be at it; but the agent called him *Guthrie,* and he
fired up at the agent: *Who the hell are you Guthrie-ing?
Mister Guthrie to you.* And the agent looked at him and
turned right white about the gills and then gave a bit laugh
and said *Ah well, Mr. Guthrie, I'm afraid you wouldn't
suit us.* And John Guthrie said *It's your place that doesn't
suit me, let me tell you, you wee dowp-licking clerk.* Poor
he might be but the creature wasn't yet clecked that might
put on its airs with him, John Guthrie.

So back he came and began his searchings again. And

the third day out he came back from far in the south. He'd
taken a place, Blawearie, in Kinraddie of the Mearns.

Wild weather it was that January and the night on the
Slug road smoring with sleet when John Guthrie crossed
his family and gear from Aberdeen into the Mearns. Twice
the great carts set with their shelvins that rustled still stray
binder-twine from September's harvest-home laired in
drifts before the ascent of the Slug faced the reluctant
horses. Darkness came down like a wet, wet blanket, weariness below it and the crying of the twins to vex John
Guthrie. Mother called him from her nook in the leading
cart, there where she sat with now one twin at the breast
and now another, and her skin bare and cold and white and
a strand of her rust-gold hair draped down from the darkness about her face into the light of the swinging lantern:
*We'd better loosen up at Portlethen and not try the Slug
this night.*

But father swore at that *Damn't to hell, do you think
I'm made of silver to put up the night at Portlethen?* and
mother sighed and held off the wee twin, Robert, and the
milk dripped creamily from the soft, sweet lips of him: *No,
we're not made of silver, but maybe we'll lair again and
all die of the night.*

Maybe he feared that himself, John Guthrie, his rage
was his worriment with the night, but he'd no time to answer her for a great bellowing arose in the road by the
winding scurry of peat-moss that lined the dying light of the
moon. The cattle had bunched there, tails to the wind,
refusing the Slug and the sting of the sleet, little Dod was
wailing and crying at the beasts, Polled Angus and Short-
horns and half-bred Highland stirks who had fattened and
feted and loved their life in the haughs of Echt, south there
across the uncouthy hills was a world cold and unchancy.

But John Guthrie dropped the tarpaulin edge that shielded
his wife and the twins and the furnishings of the best room
and gear good and plentiful enough; and swiftly he ran
past the head of the horse till he came to where the cattle
bunched. And he swung Dod into the ditch with one swipe
of his hand and cried *Have you got no sense, you brat?*
and uncoiled from his hand the length of hide that served
him as a whip. Its crackle snarled down through the sting
of the sleet, the hair rose in long serrations across the backs
of the cattle, and one in a minute, a little Highland steer it

was, mooed and ran forward and fell to a trot, and the rest
followed after, slipping and sprawling with their cloven
hooves, the reek of their dung sharp and bitter in the sleet
smore of the night. Ahead Alec saw them coming and
turned himself about again, and fell to a trot, leading up
the Slug to Mearns and the south.

So, creaking and creaking, and the shelvins skirling
under the weight of their loads, they passed that danger
point, the carts plodded into motion again, the first with its
hooded light and house gear and mother suckling the twins.
In the next, Clyde's cart, the seed was loaded, potato and
corn and barley, and bags of tools and implements, and
graips and forks fast tied with esparto twine and two fine
ploughs and a driller, and dairy things and a turnip machine
with teeth that cut as a guillotine cuts. Head down to the
wind and her reins loose and her bonny coat all mottled
with sleet went Clyde, the load a nothing to her, fine and
clean and sonsy she marched, following John Guthrie's
cart with no other thing or soul to guide but that ever and
now, in this half-mile and that she heard his voice cry
cheerily *Fine, Clyde, fine. Come on then, lass.*

Chris and Will with the last cart, sixteen Will and fifteen
Chris, the road wound up and up, straight and unwavering,
and sometimes they hiddled in the lithe and the sleet sang
past to left and right, white and glowing in the darkness.
And sometimes they clambered down from the shelvins
above the laboured drag of old Bob and ran beside him,
one either side, and stamped for warmth in their feet, and
saw the whin bushes climb black the white hills beside them
and far and away the blink of lights across the moors where
folk lay happed and warm. But then the upwards road
would swerve, right or left, into this steep ledge or that,
and the wind would be at them again and they'd gasp,
climbing back to the shelvins, Will with freezing feet and
hands and the batter of the sleet like needles in his face,
Chris in worse case, colder and colder at every turn, her
body numb and unhappy, knees and thighs and stomach
and breast, her breasts ached and ached so that nearly she
wept. But of that she told nothing, she fell to a drowse
through the cold, and a strange dream came to her as they
plodded up through the ancient hills.

For out of the night ahead of them came running a man,
father didn't see him or heed to him, though old Bob in
the dream that was Chris's snorted and shied. And as he

came he wrung his hands, he was mad and singing, a
foreign creature, black-bearded, half-naked he was; and he
cried in the Greek *The ships of Pytheas! The ships of Pytheas!* and went by into the smore of the sleet-storm on the
Grampian hills, Chris never saw him again, queer dreaming that was. For her eyes were wide open, she rubbed them
with never a need of that, if she hadn't been dreaming she
must have been daft. They'd cleared the Slug, below was
Stonehaven and the Mearns, and far beyond that, miles
through the Howe, the twinkling point of light that shone
from the flagstaff of Kinraddie.

So that was their coming to Blawearie, fell wearied all of
them were the little of the night that was left them, and
slept late into the next morning, coming cold and drizzly
up from the sea by Bervie. All the darkness they heard that
sea, a shoom-shoom that moaned by the cliffs of lone Kinneff. Not that John Guthrie listened to such dirt of sounds,
but Chris and Will did, in the room where they'd made their
shake-down beds. In the strangeness and cold and the sighing of that far-off water Chris could find no sleep till Will
whispered *Let's sleep together.* So then they did, oxtering
one the other till they were real warm. But at the first keek
of day Will slipped back to the blankets of his own bed,
he was feared what father would say if he found them
lying like that. Chris thought of that angrily, puzzled and
angry, the English Chris as sleep came on her again. Was
it likely a brother and a sister would do anything if they
slept together? And besides, she didn't know how.

But Will back in his bed had hardly a minute to get warm
or a wink of sleep when John Guthrie was up and about the
place, rousing them all, and the twins were wakened and
crying for the breast, and Dod and Alec trying to light the
fire. Father swore up and down the strange Blawearie
stairs, chapping from door to door, weren't they sick with
shame lying stinking in bed and half the day gone? Then
out he went, the house quietened down as he banged the
door, and he cried back that he was off up the brae to look
at the loch in Blawearie moor—*Get out and get on with
the breakfast and get your work done ere I come back else
I'll warm your lugs for you.*

And faith, it was queer that the notion took father to
climb the brae at that hour. For as he went up through the
broom he heard a shot, did John Guthrie, cracking the

morning so dark and iron-like, and he stood astounded, was not Blawearie his and he the tenant of it? And rage took him and he ceased to dander. Up through the hill among the dead broom he sped like a hare and burst in sight of the loch, grass-fringed and chill then under the winter morning, with a sailing of wild geese above it, going out east to the sea. All but one winged east in burnished strokes under the steel-grey sky, but that one loped and swooped and stroked the air with burnished pinions, and John Guthrie saw the feathers drift down from it, it gave a wild cry like a bairn smored at night below the blankets, and down it plonked on the mere of the loch, not ten yards from where the man with the gun was standing.

So John Guthrie he went cannily across the grass to this billy in the brave leggings and with the red face on him, and who was he standing so sure-like on Guthrie's land? He gave a bit jump, hearing Guthrie come, and then he swithered a laugh inside the foolish face of him, but John Guthrie didn't laugh. Instead, he whispered, quiet-like, *Ay, man, you're been shooting,* and the creature said *Ay, just that.* And John Guthrie said *Ay, you'll be a bit poacher, then?* and the billy said *No, I'll not be that. I'm Maitland, the foreman at Mains,* and John Guthrie whispered *You may be the archangel Gabriel, but you're not to shoot on MY land, d'you hear?*

The Standing Stones reared up above the two, marled and white-edged with snow they were, and a wind came blowing fit to freeze the chilblains on a brass monkey as they stood and glowered one at the other. Then Maitland muttered *Ellison at Mains will see about this,* and made off for all the world as if he feared the crack of a kick in the dowp of him. And right fairly there, midmost his brave breeks John Guthrie might well have kicked but that he restrained himself, cannily, for the goose was still lying by the side of the loch, jerking and slobbering blood through its beak; and it looked at him with terror in its slate-grey eyes and he waited, canny still, till Maitland was out of sight, syne he wrung the neck of the bird and took it down to Blawearie. And he told them all of the meeting with Maitland, and if ever they heard a shot on the land they were to run to him at once and tell him, he'd deal with any damn poacher—Jew, Gentile, or the Prince of Wales himself.

So that was how father made first acquaintance with the

Standing Stones, and he didn't like them, for one evening
in Spring after a day's ploughing and tired a bit maybe,
he went up on a dander through the brae to the loch and
found Chris lying there, just as now she lay in the summer
heat. Tired though he was he came to her side right fleet
enough, his shoulders straight and his frightening eyes on
her, she had no time to close the story-book she read and
he snatched it up and looked at it and cried *Dirt! You've
more need to be down in the house helping your mother
wash out the hippens.* And he glanced with a louring eye
at the Standing Stones and then Chris had thought a foolish
thing, that he kind of shivered, as though he were feared,
him that was feared at nothing dead or alive, gentry or
common. But maybe the shiver came from his fleetness
caught in the bite of the cold Spring air, he stood looking
at the Stones a minute and said they were coarse, foul
things, the folk that raised them were burning in hell, skin-
clad savages with never a skin to guard them now. And
Chris had better get down to her work, had she heard any
shooting that evening?

But Chris said *No,* and neither she had, nor any other
evening till John Guthrie himself got a gun, a second-hand
thing he picked up in Stonehaven, a muzzle-loader it was,
and as he went by the Mill on the way to Blawearie Long
Rob came out and saw it and cried *Ay, man, I didn't mind
you were a veteran of the '45.* And father cried *Losh, Rob,
were you cheating folk at your Mill even then?* for sometimes he could take a bit joke, except with his family. So
home he brought the old gun and loaded it up with pellets
and stuffed in wadding with a ram-rod; and by night he
would go cannily out in the gloaming, and shoot here a
rabbit and there a hare, no other soul must handle the gun
but himself. Nor did any try till that day he went off to the
mart at Laurencekirk and then Will took down the gun and
laughed at the thing and loaded it and went out and shot
at a mark, a herring box on the top of a post, till he was
fell near perfect. But he wished he hadn't, for father came
home and counted his pellets that evening and went fair
mad with rage till mother grew sick of the subject and
cried *Hold your whist, you and your gun, what harm was
in Will that he used it?*

Father had been sitting at the neuk of the fire when he
heard that, but he got to his feet like a cat then, looking at
Will so that the blood flowed cold in Chris's veins. Then he

said, in the quiet-like voice that was his when he was going to leather them, *Come out to the barn with me, Will*. Mother laughed that strange, blithe laugh that had come out of the Springs of Kildrummie with her, kind and queer in a breath it was, looking pityingly at Will. But Chris burned with shame because of him, he was over-old for that, she cried out *Father, you can't!*

As well have cried to the tides at Kinneff to keep away from the land, father was fair roused by then, he whispered *Be quiet, quean, else I'll take you as well*. And up to the barn he went with Will and took down his breeks, nearly seventeen though he was, and leathererd him till the weals stood blue across his haunches; and that night Will could hardly sleep for the pain of it, sobbing into his pillow, till Chris slipped into his bed and took him into her arms and held him and cuddled him and put out her hand below his shirt on to his body and made gentle her fingers to pass and repass across the torn flesh of his body, soothing him, and he stopped from crying after a while and fell asleep, holding to her, strange it seemed then for she knew him bigger and older than she was, and somehow skin and hair and body stranger than once they had been, as though they were no longer children.

She minded then the stories of Marget Strachan, and felt herself in the darkness blush for shame and then think of them still more and lie awake, seeing out of the window as it wore on to midnight a lowe in mauve and gold that crept and slipt and wavered upon the sky, and that was the lowe of the night-time whin-burning up on the Grampians; and next morning she was almost too sleepy to stiter into her clothes and set out across the fields to the station and the College train for Duncairn.

For to the College she'd been sent and found it strange enough after the high classes in Echt, a little ugly place it was below Duncairn Station, ugly as sin and nearly as proud, said the Chris that was Murdoch, Chris of the land. Inside the main building of it was carved the head of a beast like a calf with colic, but they swore the creature was a wolf on a shield, whatever the brute might be doing there.

Every week or so the drawing master, old Mr. Kinloch, marched out this class or that to the playground in front of the wolf-beast; and down they'd all get on the chair they'd brought and try and draw the beast. Right fond of the gentry was Kinloch, if you wore a fine frock and your hair was well brushed and your father well to the fore he'd sit beside you and stroke your arm and speak in a slow sing-song that made everybody laugh behind his back. *Noooooooooooo, that's not quate raight,* he would flute, *More like the head of one of Chrissie's faaaaaaaather's pigs than a heraaaaaaaaaaldic animal, I'm afraaaaaaaaaaaaaaaaaid.*

So he loved the gentry, did Mr. Kinloch, and God knows he was no exception among the masters there. For the most of them were sons and daughters of poor bit crofters and fishers themselves, up with the gentry they felt safe and unfrightened, far from that woesome pit of brose and bree and sheetless beds in which they had been reared. So right condescending they were with Chris, daughter of a farmer of no account, not that she cared, she was douce and sensible she told herself. And hadn't father said that in the sight of God an honest man was as good as any school-teacher and generally a damned sight better?

But it vexed you a bit all the same that a creature like the Fordyce girl should be cuddled by Mr. Kinloch when she'd a face like a broken brose-cap and a voice like a nail on a slate. And but little cuddling her drawing warranted, her father's silver had more to do with it, not that Chris herself could draw like an artist, Latin and French and Greek and history were the things in which she shone. And the English master set their class an essay on *Deaths of the Great* and her essay was so good that he was forced to read it aloud to all the class, and the Fordyce quean had snickered and sniffed, so mad she was with jealousy.

Mr. Murgetson was the English master there, not that he was English himself, he came from Argyll and spoke with a funny whine, the Highland whine, and the boys swore he had hair growing up between his toes like a Highland cow, and when they'd see him coming down a corridor they'd push their heads round a corner and cry *Moo!* like a lot of cattle. He'd fly in an awful rage at that, and once when they'd done it he came into the class where Chris was waiting her lesson and he stood and swore, right out and horrible, and gripped a black ruler in his hands and glared round as if he meant to murder a body. And maybe he would if the French teacher, her that was bonny and brave, hadn't come simpering into the room, and then he lowered the ruler and grunted and curled up his lip and

said *Eh? Canaille?* and the French teacher she simpered
some more and said *May swee*.

So that was the college place at Duncairn, two Chrisses
went there each morning, and one was right douce and
studious and the other sat back and laughed a canny laugh
at the antics of the teachers and minded Blawearie brae
and the champ of horses and the smell of dung and her
father's brown, grained hands till she was sick to be home
again. But she made friends with young Marget Strachan,
Chae Strachan's daughter, she was slim and sweet and fair,
fine to know, though she spoke about things that seemed
awful at first and then weren't awful at all and you wanted
to hear more and Marget would laugh and say it was Chae
that had told her. Always as Chae she spoke of him and
that was an unco-like thing to do of your father, but maybe
it was because he was socialist and thought that Rich and
Poor should be Equal. And what was the sense of believing
that and then sending his daughter to educate herself and
herself become one of the Rich?

But Marget cried that wasn't what Chae intended, she
was to learn and be ready for the Revolution that was some
day coming. And if come it never did she wasn't to seek out
riches anyway, she was off to be trained as a doctor, Chae
said that life came out of women through tunnels of pain
and if God had planned women for anything else but the
bearing of children it was surely the saving of them.

And Marget's eyes, that were blue and so deep they
minded you of a well you peeped into, they'd grow deeper
and darker and her sweet face grow so solemn Chris felt
solemn herself. But that would be only a minute, the next
and Marget was laughing and fleering, trying to shock her,
telling of men and women, what fools they were below
their clothes; and how children came and how you should
have them; and the things that Chae had seen in the huts
of the blacks in Africa. And she told of a place where the
bodies of men lay salted and white in great stone vats till
the doctors needed to cut them up, the bodies of paupers
they were—*so take care you don't die as a pauper, Chris,
for I'd hate some day if I rang a bell and they brought me
up out of the vat your naked body, old and shrivelled and
frosted with salt, and I looked in your dead, queer face,
standing there with the scalpel held in my hand, and cried
'But this is Chris Guthrie!'*

That was awful, Chris felt sick and sick and stopped

midway the shining path that led through the fields to
Peesie's Knapp that evening in March. Clean and keen and
wild and clear, the evening ploughed land's smell up in
your nose and your mouth when you opened it, for Netherhill's teams had been out in that park all day, queer and
lovely and dear the smell Chris noted.

And something else she saw, looking at Marget, sick at
the thought of her dead body brought to Marget. And that
thing was a vein that beat in Marget's throat, a little blue
gathering where the blood beat past in slow, quiet strokes,
it would never do that when one was dead and still under
grass, down in the earth that smelt so fine and you'd never
smell; or cased in the icy darkness of a vat, seeing never
again the lowe of burning whins or hearing the North Sea
thunder beyond the hills, the thunder of it breaking through
a morning mist, the right things that might not last and so
soon went by. And they only were real and true, beyond
them was nought you might ever attain but a weary dream
and that last dark silence—Oh, only a fool loved being
alive!

But Marget threw her arms around her when she said
that, and kissed her with red, kind lips, so red they were
that they looked like haws, and said there were lovely
things in the world, lovely that didn't endure, and the
lovelier for that. *Wait till you find yourself in the arms of
your lad, in the harvest time it'll be with the stooks round
about you, and he'll stop from joking—they do, you know,
and that's just when their blood-pressure alters—and he'll
take you like this—wait, there's not a body to see us!—
and hold you like this, with his hands held so, and kiss you
like this!*

It was over in a moment, quick and shameful, fine for
all that, tingling and strange and shameful by turns. Long
after she parted with Marget that evening she turned and
stared down at Peesie's Knapp and blushed again; and suddenly she was seeing them all at Blawearie as though they
were strangers naked out of the sea, she felt ill every time
she looked at father and mother. But that passed in a day
or so, for nothing endures.

Not a thing, though you're over-young to go thinking of
that, you've your lessons and studies, the English Chris, and
living and eating and sleeping that other Chris that stretches
your toes for you in the dark of the night and whispers a
drowsy *I'm you.* But you might not stay from the thinking

when all in a day, Marget, grown part of your life, came waving to you as you neared the Knapp with the news she was off to Aberdeen to live with an auntie there—*it's a better place for a scholar, Chae says, and I'll be trained all the sooner.*

And three days later Chae Strachan and Chris drove down to the station with her, and saw her off at the platform, and she waved at them, bonny and young, Chae looked as numb as Chris felt. He gave her a lift from the station, did Chae, and on the road he spoke but once, to himself it seemed, not Chris: *Ay, Marget lass, you'll do fine, if you keep the lads at bay from kissing the bonny breast of you.*

So that was your Marget gone, there seemed not a soul in Kinraddie that could take her place, the servant queans of an age with Chris were no more than gowks and gomerils a-screech round the barn of the Mains at night with the ploughmen snickering behind them. And John Guthrie had as little use for them as Marget herself. *Friends? Stick to your lessons and let's see you make a name for yourself, you've no time for friends.*

Mother looked up at that, friendly-like, not feared of him at all, she was never feared. *Take care her head doesn't soften with lessons and dirt, learning in books it was sent the wee red daftie of Cuddiestoun clean skite, they say.* And father poked out his beard at her. *Say? Would you rather see her skite with book-learning or skite with*—and then he stopped and began to rage at Dod and Alec that were making a noise in the kitchen corner. But Chris, a-pore above her books in the glow of the paraffin lamp, heeding to Cæsar's coming in Gaul and the stour the creature raised there, knew right well what father had thought to speak of—*lust* was the word he'd wanted, perhaps. And she turned a page with the weary Cæsar man and thought of the wild career the daftie Andy had led one day in the roads and woods of Kinraddie.

Marget had barely gone when the thing came off, it was fair the speak of the place that happening early in April. The sowing time was at hand, John Guthrie put down two parks with grass and corn, swinging hand from hand as he walked and sowed and Will carried the corn across to him from the sacks that lined the rigs. Chris herself would help of an early morning when the dew had lifted quick,

it was blithe and lightsome in the caller air with the whistle
of the blackbirds in Blawearie's trees and the glint of the
sea across the Howe and the wind blowing up the braes
with a fresh, wild smell that caught you and made you
gasp. So silent the world with the sun just peeking above
the horizon those hours that you'd hear, clear and bright
as though he paced the next field, the ringing steps of
Chae Strachan—far down, a shadow and a sunlit dot, sowing his parks behind the steadings of Peesie's Knapp.

There were larks coming over that morning, Chris
minded, whistling and trilling dark and unseen against the
blaze of the sun, now one lark now another, till the sweetness of the trilling dizzied you and you stumbled with
heavy pails corn-laden, and father swore at you over the
red beard of him *Damn't to hell, are you fair a fool, you
quean?*

That morning it was that the daftie Andy stole out of
Cuddiestoun and started his scandalous rampage through
Kinraddie. Long Rob of the Mill was to say he'd once had
a horse that would do that kind of thing in the early Spring,
leap dykes and ditches and every mortal thing it would if
it heard a douce little mare go by. Gelding though it was,
the horse would do that, and what more was Andy, poor
devil, than a gelding? Not that Mistress Ellison had thought
him that—faith no!

It was said she ran so fast after her meeting with the
daftie she found herself down two stone in weight. The
coarse creature chased her nearly in sight of the Mains and
then scrabbled away into the rough ground, beyond the
turnpike.

She'd been out fell early for her, Mistress Ellison, and
was just holding along the road a bit walk to Fordoun
when out of some bushes Andy jumped, his ramshackle
face all swithering and his eyes all hot and wet. She thought
at first he was hurted and then she saw he was trying to
laugh, he tore at her frock and cried *You come!* She nearly
fainted, but didn't, her umbrella was in her hand, she broke
it over the daftie's head and then turned and ran, he went
louping after her along the road, like a great monkey he
leapt, crying terrible things to her. When sight of the Mains
put an end to that chase he must have hung back in the
hills for an hour or so and seen Mistress Munro, the futret,
go sleeking down the paths to the Mains and Peesie's Knapp
and Blawearie, asking sharp as you like, as though she

blamed every soul but herself, *Have you seen that creature Andy?*

While she was up Blawearie way he must have made his road back across the hills, high up above the Cuddiestoun, till Upperhill came in sight. For later one of the plough-men thought he'd seen the creature, shambling up against the skyline, picking a great bunch of sourocks and eating them. Then he got into the Upperhill wood and waited there, and it was through the wood at nine o'clock that Maggie Jean Gordon would hold her way to the station—close and thick larch wood with a path through it, where the light fell hardly at all and the cones crunched and rotted underfoot and sometimes a green barrier of whin crept up a wood ditch and looked out at you, and in the winter days the deer came down from the Grampians and sheltered there.

But in the April weather there were no deer to fright Maggie Jean, even the daftie didn't frighten her. He'd been waiting high in the wood before he took her, but maybe before that he ran alongside the path she was taking, keep-ing hidden from view of the lass, for she heard a little crackle rise now and then, she was to remember, and won-dered that the squirrels were out so early. Gordon she was, none the better for that it might be, but a blithe little thing, thin body and bonny brown hair, straight to walk and straight to look, and you liked the laugh of her.

So through the wood and right into the hands of the daftie she went and when he lifted her in his hands she was frightened not even then, not even when he bore her far back into the wood, the broom-branches whipped their faces and the wet of the dew sprayed on them, coming into a little space, broom-surrounded, where the sun reached down a long finger into the dimness.

She stood up and shook herself when he set her down, and told him she couldn't play any longer, she must really hurry else she'd miss her train. But he paid no heed, crouching on one knee he turned his head this way and that, jerking round and about, listening and listening, so that Maggie Jean listened as well and heard the ploughmen cry to their horses and her mother at that moment calling the hens to feed—*Tickie-ae! Tickie-ae!*—*Well, I must go*, she told him and caught her bag in her hand and hadn't moved a step when he had her in his hands again; and after a minute or so, though she wasn't frightened even then, she didn't

like him, and please she'd have to go. And she looked up
at him, pushing him away, his mad, awful head, he began
to purr like a great, wild cat, awful it must have been to
see him and hear him.

And God alone knows the next thing he'd have done but
that then, for it was never such a morning before for that
bright clearness, far away down and across the fields a man
began to sing, distant but very clear, with a blithe lilt in
the voice of him. And he broke off and whistled the song
and then he sang it again:

> Bonny wee thing,
>   Cannie wee thing,
> Lovely wee thing,
>   Wert thou mine
> I wad wear thee
>   In my bosom
> Lest my jewel
>   I should tine!

And at that, crouching and listening, the daftie took his
hands from Maggie Jean and began to sing the song himself; and he took her in his arms again, but gentle, folding
her as though she were a cat, and he set her on her feet
and tugged straight the bit frock she wore; and stood up
beside her and took her hand and guided her back to the
path through the larch wood. And she went on and left
him and once she looked back and saw him glowering after
her; and because she saw he was weeping she ran back to
him, kind thing, and patted his hand and said Don't cry!
and she saw his face like that of a tormented beast and
went on again, down to the station. And only when she
came home that night did she tell the story of her meeting
with Cuddiestoun's Andy.

But as the day wore on and Long Rob, working in that
orra field above the Mill, still sang and sweated and swore
at his horses, the singing must have drawn the Andy creature down from the larch wood, by hedges creeping and
slipping from the sight of the Upperhill men in the parks.
And once Rob raised his head and thought he saw a moving shadow in a ditch that bounded the orra ground. But
he thought it a dog and just heaved a stone or so in case
it was some beast in heat or on chicken-killing. The shadow
yelped and snarled at that, but was gone from the ditch

when Rob picked up another stone; so he went on with his work; and the daftie, tearing along the Kinraddie road out towards the Bridge End, with the blood red trickling down his woesome face, was all unseen by him.

But right at the corner, close where the road jerked round by Pooty's place, he nearly ran full tilt into Chris herself, coming up from Auchinblae she was with the messages her mother had sent her on, her basket over her arm and her mind far off with the Latin verbs in *-are*. He slavered at her, running towards her, and she screamed, though she wasn't over-frightened; and then she threw the basket clean at his head and made for Pooty's. Pooty himself was sitting just inside the door when she reached it, the louping beast was close behind, she heard the pant of his breath and was to wonder often enough in later times over that coolness that came on her then. For she ran fleet as a bird inside the door and banged it right in the daftie's face and dropped the bar and watched the planks bulge and crack as outside the body of the madman was flung against them again and again.

Pooty mouthed and stuttered at her in the dimness, but he grew real brave when she made him understand, he sharpened two of his sutor's knives and prowled trembling from window to window—the daftie left them untouched. Then Chris took a keek from one window and saw him again: he was raking about in the basket she'd thrown at his head, he made the parcels dirl on the road till he found a great bar of soap, and then he began to eat that, feuch! laughing and yammering all to himself, and running back to throw himself against the door of Pooty's again, the foam burst yellow through the beard of him as he still ate and ate at the soap.

But he soon grew thirsty and went down to the burn, Pooty and Chris stood watching him, and then it was that Cuddiestoun himself came ben the road. He sighted Andy and cried out to him, and Andy leapt the burn and was off, and behind him went Munro clatter-clang, and out of sight they vanished down the road to Bridge End. Chris unbarred the door in spite of Pooty's stutterings and went and repacked the bit basket, and everything was there except the soap; and that was down poor Andy's throat.

Feint the thing else he'd to eat that day, he was near the end of his tether; for though he ran like a hare and Cuddiestoun behind him was more than coarse in the legs, yet luck would have it that Mutch of Bridge End was just guiding his team across the road to start harrowing his yavil park when the two runners came in sight, real daft-like both of them, Andy running near double, soap and madness a-foam on his face, Cuddiestoun bellowing behind.

So Mutch slowed down his team and called out to Andy, *Ay, man, you mustn't run near as fast as that,* and when Andy was opposite threw out a foot and tripped him up, and down in the stour went Andy, and Cuddiestoun was on top of him in a minute, bashing in the face of him, but Alec Mutch just stood and looked on, maybe working his meikle ears a bit, it was no concern of his. The daftie's hands went up to his face as the bashings came and then Cuddiestoun gripped him in a tender private part, he screamed and went slack, like a sack in Cuddistoun's hands.

And that was the end of Andy's ploy, for back to the Cuddiestoun he was driven and they said Mistress Munro took down his breeks and leathered him sore; but you never know the lies they tell, for others said it was Cuddiestoun himself she leathered, him having let the daftie out of the house that morning to scandalize her name with his coarse on-goings. But he'd no chance more of them, poor stock, next day the asylum officials came out and took him away in a gig, his hands fast tied behind his back; and that was the last they ever saw of Andy in Kinraddie.

Father raged when he heard the story from Chris, queer raging it was, he took her out to the barn and heard the story and his eyes slipped up and down her dress as she spoke, she felt sickened and queer. *He shamed you then?* he whispered; and Chris shook her head and at that father seemed to go limp and his eyes grew dull. *Ah well, it's the kind of thing that would happen in a godless parish like this. It can hardly happen again with the Reverend Gibbon in charge.*

Three minister creatures came down to Kinraddie to try for its empty pulpit. The first preached early in March, a pernickety thing as ever you saw, not over five feet in height, or he didn't look more. He wore a brave gown with a purple hood on it, like a Catholic creature, and jerked and pranced round the pulpit like a snipe with the staggers, working himself up right sore about *Latter-Day Doubt in the Kirk of Scotland.* But Kinraddie had never a doubt of *him,* and Chris coming out of the kirk with Will and father heard Chae Strachan say he'd rather sit under a clucking hen than *that* for a minister. The second to try was an old bit man from Banff, shaking and old, and some said he'd be best, he'd have quietened down at his age, not aye on the look for a bigger kirk and a bigger stipend. For if there's a body on earth that would skin a tink for his sark and preach for a pension in purgatory it's an Auld Kirk minister.

But the poor old brute from Banff seemed fair sucked dry. He'd spent years in the writing of books and things, the spunk of him had trickled out into his pen, forbye that he read his sermon; and that fair settled his hash to begin with.

So hardly a soul paid heed to his reading, except Chris and her father, she thought it fine; for he told of the long dead beasts of the Scottish land in the times when jungle flowered its forests across the Howe and a red sun rose on the steaming earth that the feet of man had still to tread; and he pictured the dark, slow tribes that came drifting across the low lands of the northern seas, the great bear watched them come, and they hunted and fished and loved and died, God's children in the morn of time; and he brought the first voyagers sailing the sounding coasts, they brought the heathen idols of the great Stone Rings, the Golden Age was over and past and lust and cruelty trod the world; and he told of the rising of Christ, a pin-point of the cosmic light far off in Palestine, the light that crept and wavered and did not die, the light that would yet shine as the sun on all the world, nor least the dark howes and hills of Scotland.

So what could you make of that, except that he thought Kinraddie a right coarse place since the jungles had all dried up? And his prayers were as short as you please, he'd hardly a thing to say of the King or the Royal Family at all, had the Reverend Colquohoun. So that fair put him out with Ellison and Mutch, they were awful King's men both of them, ready to die for the King any day of the week and twice on Sundays, said Long Rob of the Mill. And his preaching had no pleasure at all for Chae Strachan either, he wanted a preacher to praise up socialism and tell how Rich and Poor should be Equal. So the few that listened thought feint the much of the old book-writer from Banff, he stood never a chance, pleasing Chris and her father only, Chris didn't count, John Guthrie did, but his vote was only

one and a hantle few votes the Banff man got when it came
to the counting.

Stuart Gibbon was the third to make try for Kinraddie
manse, and that Sunday when Chris sat down in the kirk
and looked up at him in the pulpit she knew as well as she
knew her own hand that he was to please all of them,
though hardly more than a student he was, with black hair
on him and a fine red face and shoulders strong and well-
bulked, for he was a pretty man. And first his voice took
them, it was brave and big like the voice of a bull, and
fine and rounded, and he said the Lord's Prayer in a way
that pleased gentry and simple. For though he begged to be
forgiven his sins as he forgave those that sinned against
him—instead, as was more genteel, crying to be forgiven
his trespasses as he forgave those that trespassed against
him—still he did it with a fine solemnity that made everybody that heard right douce and grave-like; and one or two
joined in near the end of the prayer, and that's a thing gey
seldom done in an Auld Kirk kirk.

Next came his sermon, it was out of the *Song of Solomon*
and well and rare he preached on it, showing that the Song
had more meaning than one. It was Christ's description of
the beauty and fine comeliness of the Auld Kirk of Scotland, and as such right reverently must it be read; and it
was a picture of womanly beauty that moulded itself in the
lithe and grace of the Kirk, and as such a perpetual manual
for the women of Scotland that so they might attain to
straight and fine lives in this world and salvation in the
next. And in a minute or so all Kinraddie kirk was listening to him as though he were promising to pay their taxes
at the end of Martinmas.

For it was fair tickling to hear about things like that read
out from a pulpit, a woman's breasts and thighs and all the
rest of the things, in that voice like the mooing of a holy
bull; and to know it was decent Scripture with a higher
meaning as well. So everybody went home to his Sunday
dinner well pleased with the new minister lad, no more than
a student though he was; and on the Monday Long Rob of
the Mill was fair deaved with tales of the sermon and put
two and two together and said *Well, preaching like that's a
fine way of having your bit pleasure by proxy, right in the
stalls of a kirk, I prefer to take mine more private-like*. But
that was Rob all over, folk said, a fair caution him and his
Ingersoll that could neither make watches nor sense. And

feint the voter it put off from tramping in to vote for Kinraddie's last candidate.

So in he went with a thumping majority, the Reverend
Gibbon, by mid-May he was at the Manse, him and his
wife, an English creature he'd married in Edinburgh. She
was young as himself and bonny enough in a thin kind of
way, with a voice as funny as Ellison's, near, but different,
and big, dark eyes on her, and so sore in love were they
that their servant quean said they kissed every time he
went out a bit walk, the minister. And one time, coming
back from a jaunt and finding her waiting him, the minister picked up his wife in his arms and ran up the stairs
with her, both cuddling one the other and kissing, and
laughing in each other's faces with shining eyes; and into
their bedroom they went and closed the door and didn't
come down for hours, though it was bare the middle of the
afternoon. Maybe that was true and maybe it wasn't for
the servant quean was one that old Mistress Sinclair had
fee'd for the Manse in Gourdon, and before a Gourdon
quean speaks the truth the Bervie burn will run backwards
through the Howe.

Now every minister since Time was clecked in Kinraddie
had made a round of the parish when he was inducted.
Some did it quick, some did it slow, the Reverend Gibbon
was among the quick. He came up to Blawearie just after
the dinner hour on a Saturday and met in with John Guthrie
sharpening a hoe in the close, weeds yammered out of
Blawearie soil like bairns from a school at closing time, it
was coarse, coarse land, wet, raw, and red clay, father's
temper grew worse the more he saw of it. So when the
minister came on him and cried out right heartily *Well,
you'll be my neighbour Guthrie, man?* father cocked his
red beard at the minister and glinted at him like an icicle
and said *Ay, MISTER Gibbon, I'll be that.* So the minister
held out his hand and changed his tune right quick and
said quiet-like *You've a fine-kept farm here, Mr. Guthrie,
trig and trim, though I hear you've sat down a bare six
months.* And he smiled, a big sappy smile.

So after that they were chief enough, sitting one the
other on a handle on the sharn-barrow right in the middle
of the close, the minister none feared for his brave, black
clothes; and father told him the coarse land it was in Kinraddie, and the minister said he well believed him, it was

only a man from the North could handle it so well. In a
minute or so they were chief as brothers, father brought
him over into the house, Chris stood in the kitchen and
father said *And this quean's my daughter, Chris.* The minister smiled at her with his glinting eyes and said *I hear
you're right clever, Chrissie, and go up to the Duncairn
College. How do you like it?* And Chris blushed and said
Fine, sir, and he asked her what she was to be, and she
told him a teacher, and he said there was no profession
more honourable.

Then mother came ben from putting the twins to sleep
and was quiet and friendly, just as she always was with
loon or laird, crowned with gold with her lovely hair. And
she made the minister some tea, and he praised it and said
the best tea in his life he'd drunk in Kinraddie, it was
the milk. And father asked whose milk they got at the
Manse and the minister said *The Mains,* and father shot
out his beard and said *Well may it be good, it's the best
land in the parish they've a hold of, the dirt,* and the minister said *And now I'll have to be dandering down to the
Manse. Come over and see us some evening, Chrissie, maybe the wife and I'll be able to lend you some books to help
in your studies.* And off he went, swack enough, but no
more fleet than father himself who swung alongside him
down to where the turnip-park broke off from the road.

Chris made for the Manse next Monday night, she
thought maybe that would be the best time, but she said
nothing to father, only told mother and mother smiled
and said *Surely,* far-off she seemed and dreaming to herself
as so often in the last month or so. So Chris put on the
best frock that she used for Sundays, and her tall lacing
boots, and prigged out her hair in front of the glass in the
parlour, and went up across the hill by Blawearie loch, with
the night coming over the Grampians and the snipe crying
in their hundreds beyond the loch's grey waters—still and
grey, as though they couldn't forget last summer nor hope
for another coming.

The Standing Stones pointed long shadow-shapes into
the east, maybe just as they'd done of an evening two thousand years before when the wild men climbed the brae and
sang their songs in the lithe of those shadows while the
gloaming waited there above the same quiet hills. And a
queer, uncanny feeling came on Chris then, she looked
back half-feared at the Stones and the whiteness of the

loch, and then went hurrying through the park paths till she came out above kirkyard and Manse. Beyond the road the Meikle House rose up in its smother of trees, you saw the broken walls of it, the flagstaff light was shining already, it would soon be dark.

She unsnecked the door of the kirkyard wall, passing through to the Manse, the old stones rose up around her silently, not old when you thought of the Standing Stones of Blawearie brae but old enough for all that. Some went back to the old, unkindly times of the Covenanters, one had a skull and crossed bones and an hour-glass on it and was mossed half over so that but hardly you could read the daft-like script with its esses like effs, and it made you shudder. The yews came all about that place of the oldest stone and Chris going past put out her hand against it and the low bough of a yew whispered and gave a low laugh behind her, and touched her hand with a cold, hairy touch so that a daft-like cry started up on her lips, she wished she'd gone round by the plain, straight-forward road, instead of this near-cut she'd thought so handy.

So she whistled to herself, hurrying, and just outside the kirkyard stood the new minister himself, leaning over the gate looking in among the stones, he saw her before she saw him and his voice fair startled her. *Well, Chrissie, you're very gay,* he said, and she felt ashamed to have him know she whistled in a kirkyard; and he stared at her strange and queer and seemed to forget her a minute; and he gave an unco half-laugh and muttered to himself, but she heard him, *One's enough for one day.* Then he seemed to wake up, he mooed out at her *And now you'll be needing a book, no doubt. Well, the Manse is fair in a mess this evening, spring-cleaning or something like that, but if you just wait here a minute I'll run in and pick you something light and cheerful.*

Off he set, she was left alone among the black trees that bent over the greyness of the kirkyard. Unendingly the unseen grasses whispered and rustled above the stones' dim, recumbent shapes, and she thought of the dead below those stones, farmers and ploughmen and their wives, and little bairns and new-born babes, their bodies turned to skeletons now so that if you dug in the earth you'd find only their bones, except the new-buried, and maybe there in the darkness worms and awful things crawled and festered in flesh grown rotten and black, and it was a terrifying place.

But at last came the minister, not hurrying at all but just drifting towards her, he held out a book and said *Well, here it is, and I hope you'll like it.* She took the book and looked at it in the dying light, its name was *Religio Medici*, and she mastered her shyness and asked *Did you, sir?* and the minister stared at her and said, his voice just even as ever, *Oh, like hell!* and turned about and left her to go back through the terror of the yews. But they didn't terrify at all, climbing home and thinking of that word he used, swearing it has been and nothing else, should she tell of it to father?

No, that wouldn't do, a minister was only a man, and he'd loaned her a book, kind of him though he looked so queer. And besides, father didn't know of this errand of hers down to the Manse, maybe he'd think she was trying to hold in with gentry and would swear himself. Not that he swore often, father, she told herself as she hurried across the brae, and, hurrying, climbed out of the dimness into the last of the May daylight with the sunset a glow and a glimmer that danced about her feet, waiting for her; not often, except when things went clean over him, as that day in the sowing of the park below Blawearie when first the cart-shaft had broken and then the hammer had broken and then he'd watched the rain come on, and he'd gone nearly mad, raging at Will and Chris that he'd leather them till they hadn't enough skin to sit a threepenny bit on; and at last, fair skite, he'd shaken his fist at the sky and cried *Ay, laugh, you Mucker!*

Chris took a bit peep or so in *Religio Medici* and nearly yawned her head off with the reading of it, it was better fun on a spare, slow day to help mother wash the blankets. In the sun of the red, still weather Jean Guthrie had every bed in Blawearie cleared and the blankets piled in tubs half-filled with lukewarm water and soap, and Chris took off her boots and her stockings and rolled her knickers far up her white legs and stepped in the grey, lathered folds of blankets and tramped them up and down. It felt fine with the water gurgling blue and iridescent up through your toes and getting thicker and thicker; then into the next tub while mother emptied the first, lovely work, she felt she could trample blankets for ever, only it grew hot and hot, a red forenoon while they did the washing. So next time mother was indoors she took off her skirt and then her petticoat and mother coming out with another blanket cried *God, you've stripped!* and gave Chris a slap in the knickers friendly-like, and said *You'd make a fine lad, Chris quean*, and smiled the blithe way she had and went on with the washing.

But John Guthrie came home from the fields then, him and Will, and as soon as she saw her father's face she went all shrivelled up and he cried *Get out of that at once, you shameful limmer, and get on your clothes!* And out she got, white and ashamed, shamed more for father than herself, and Will turned red and led off the horses, awkward-like, but John Guthrie went striding across the close to the kitchen and mother and began to rage at her. *What would folk say of the quean if they saw her sit there, near naked? We'd be the speak and laughing-stock of the place.* And mother looked at him, sweet and cold, *Ah, well, it wouldn't be the first time you've seen a naked lass yourself; and if your neighbours haven't they must have fathered their own bairns with their breeks on.*

Father had been in a fair stamash at that, he left mother and went out with his face dead-white, not red, and he didn't say another word, he didn't speak to mother all that evening nor all the next day. Chris went to her bed that night and thought of the happening, lying close-up and alone, it had been as though she saw a caged beast peep from her father's eyes as he saw her stand in the tub. Like a fire that burned across the close, it went on and on as though she still stood there and he glowered at her. She hid her face below the blankets but she couldn't forget, next morning she was able to bear thinking of it no longer, the house had quietened with the folk gone out, she went to mother and asked her straight, she'd never asked anything of the kind before.

And then an awful thing happened, mother's face went grey and old as she stopped from her work at the kitchen table, she went whiter and whiter second on second, Chris near went out of her mind at the sight. *Oh, mother, I didn't mean to vex*, she cried and flung her arms round mother and held her tight, seeing her face then, so white and ill-looking it had grown in the last month. And mother smiled at her at last, putting her hands on her shoulders. *Not you, Chris quean, just life. I cannot tell you a thing or advise you a thing, my quean. You'll have to face men for yourself when the time comes, there's none can stand and help*

you. And then she said something queerer, kissing Chris,
Mind that for me sometime if I cannot thole it longer—
and stopped and laughed and was blithe again. *We're daft,
the two of us, run out and bring me a pail of water.* And
Chris went out with the pail, out and up to the pump in
the hot red weather, and then something came on her, she
crept back soft-footed and there mother stood as she'd left
her, white and lonely and sad, Chris didn't dare go into
her, just stood and looked.

Something was happening to mother, things were happening to all of them, nothing ever stayed the same except
maybe this weather and if it went on much longer the
Reverend Colquohoun's bit jungles would soon be sprouting
back across the parks of the Howe. The weary pleiter of
the land and its life while you waited for rain or thaw!
Glad she'd be when she'd finished her exams and was into
Aberdeen University, getting her B.A. and then a school of
her own, the English Chris, father and his glowering and
girning forgotten, she'd have a brave house of her own
and wear what she liked and have never a man vexed with
sight of her, she'd take care of that.

Or maybe she wouldn't, queer that she never knew herself for long, grown up though she was, a woman now,
near. Father said that the salt of the earth were the folk
that drove a straight drill and never looked back, but she
was no more than ploughed land still, the furrows went
criss and cross, you wanted this and you wanted that, books
and the fineness of them no more than an empty gabble
sometimes, and then the sharn and the snapping that sickened you and drove you back to books——

She turned over on the grass with a jerk when she came
to that troubled thinking. The sunset was painting the loch,
but hot as ever it was, breaking up for one of those nights
when you couldn't bear a blanket above you and even the
dark was a foul, black blanket. It had died off, the wind,
while she lay and thought, feint the loss was that, but there
was sign of nothing in the place of it, the broom stood up
in the late afternoon, not moving, great faces massed and
yellow like the faces of an army of yellow men, looking
down across Kinraddie, watching for the rain. Mother below would be needing her help, Dod and Alec back from
the school already, father and Will soon in from the fields.

There somebody was crying her already!

She stood up and shook out her frock and went through

the grass to the tail of the brae, and looked down and saw
Dod and Alec far below waving up at her. They were crying her name excitedly, it sounded like the lowing of calves
that had lost their mother, she went slow to tease them till
she saw their faces.

It was then, as she flew down the hill with her own face
white, that the sky crackled behind her, a long flash zig-
zagged across the Grampian peaks, and far across the
parks by the hills she heard the hiss of rain. The drought
had broken at last.

II

DRILLING

LYING down when her climb up the cambered brae was done, panting deep from the rate she'd come at—skirt flying and iron-resolute she'd turn back for nothing that cried or called in all Blawearie—no, not even that whistle of father's!—Chris felt the coarse grass crackle up beneath her into a fine quiet couch. Neck and shoulders and hips and knees she relaxed, her long brown arms quivered by her side as the muscles slacked away, the day drowsed down an aureal light through the long brown lashes that drooped on her cheeks. As the gnomons of a giant dial the shadows of the Standing Stones crept into the east, snipe called and called——

Just as the last time she'd climbed to the loch: and when had that been? She opened her eyes and thought, and tired from that and closed down her eyes again and gave a queer laugh. The June of last year it had been, the day when mother had poisoned herself and the twins.

So long as that and so near as that, you'd thought of the hours and days as a dark, cold pit you'd never escape. But you'd escaped, the black damp went out of the sunshine and the world went on, the white faces and whispering ceased from the pit, you'd never be the same again, but the world went on and you went with it. It was not mother

62

only that died with the twins, something died in your
heart and went down with her to lie in Kinraddie kirkyard
—the child in your heart died then, the bairn that believed
the hills were made for its play, every road set fair with its
warning posts, hands ready to snatch you back from the
brink of danger when the play grew over-rough. That died,
and the Chris of the books and the dreams died with it, or
you folded them up in their paper of tissue and laid them
away by the dark, quiet corpse that was your childhood.

So Mistress Munro of the Cuddiestoun told her that awful night she came over the rain-soaked parks of Blawearie
and laid out the body of mother, the bodies of the twins
that had died so quiet in their crib. She nipped round the
rooms right quick and pert and uncaring, the black-eyed
futret, snapping this order and that, it was her that terrified
Dod and Alec from their crying, drove father and Will out
tending the beasts. And quick and cool and cold-handed
she worked, peeking over at Chris with her rat-like face.
*You'll be leaving the College now, I'll warrant, education's
dirt and you're better clear of it. You'll find little time for
dreaming and dirt when you're keeping the house at
Blawearie.*

And Chris in her pit, dazed and dull-eyed, said nothing,
she minded later; and some other than herself went searching and seeking out cloths and clothes. Then Mistress
Munro washed down the body that was mother's and put it
in a night-gown, her best, the one with blue ribbons on it
that she hadn't worn for many a year; and fair she made
her and sweet to look at, the tears came at last when you
saw her so, hot tears wrung from your eyes like drops of
blood. But they ended quick, you would die if you wept
like that for long, in place of tears a long wail clamoured
endless, unanswered inside your head, *Oh, mother, mother,
why did you do it?*

And not until days later did Chris hear why, for they
tried to keep it from her and the boys, but it all came out
at the inquest, mother had poisoned herself, her and the
twins, because she was pregnant again and afraid with a
fear dreadful and calm and clear-eyed. So she had killed
herself while of unsound mind, had mother, kind-eyed and
sweet, remembering those Springs of Kildrummie last of
all things remembered, it may be, and the rooks that cried

across the upland parks of Don far down beyond the tunnels of the years.

A month later Dod and Alec went back to school and as they left to go home that night first one scholar cried after them and others took it up *Daftie, daftie! Whose mother was a daftie?* They ran for Blawearie and came stumbling into the house weeping and weeping, father went fair mad at the sight of them and skelped them both, but skelping or not they wouldn't go back to the school next day.

And then Will spoke up, he cared not a fig for father now. All in a night it seemed the knowledge had come on him father wouldn't dare strike him again, he bought an old bicycle and would ride off in an evening as he pleased, his face cold and hard when he caught the glint of father's eye. Of a morning John Guthrie grumbled and girned at him, crying *Where do you wander each night like a tink?* But Will would say never a word, except once when John Guthrie made at him and then he swung round and whispered *Take care.* And at that father stopped and drew back, Chris watched them with angry eyes, angry and frightened in a breath as now when Will spoke up for his brothers.

Why should they go back? I wouldn't. Oh, and you needn't glower at me. You take damn good care you never go near a mart or a market yourself nowadays—I've to do all your dirty work for you!

Father louped to his feet at that, Will was on his as well, they stood with fists clenched in the kitchen and Dod and Alec stopped from their greeting and stared and stared. But Chris thrust the table in between the two, she made out she wanted it there for baking; and they dropped their fists and John Guthrie swore, but soft; and Will reddened up and looked foolish.

But father that night, he said never a word to the rest of them in Blawearie, he was over-proud for that, wrote off to his sister Janet in Auchterless and asked that she take Dod and Alec in her care and give them an Aberdeen schooling. In a week she was down from the North, Auntie Janet and her man. Uncle Tam he was, big and well-bulked and brave, and his watch-chain had rows and rows of wee medals on it he'd gotten for playing quoits. And they were fell kind, the two of them, Alec and Dod were daft with delight when they heard of the Auchterless plan. But

Auntie and Uncle had never a bairn of their own and soon made plain if the boys went with them it would be for aye, they wanted to adopt the pair of them.

Father sneered and thrust out his beard at that *So you'd like to steal the flesh of my body from me?* and Auntie Janet nodded, right eye to eye, *Aye, John, just that, we've never a wean of our own, though God knows it's not for want of the trying;* and father said *Ill blood breeds ill:* and Auntie said *Ay, it'll be long ere I have to kill myself because my man beds me like a breeding sow;* and father said *You dirty bitch.*

Chris stuck the dirl of the tow till her head near burst and then ran out of the kitchen, through the close into the cornyard, where Will was prowling about. He'd heard the noise and he laughed at them, but his eyes were angry as his arm went round her. *Never heed the dirty old devils, one's bad as the other, father, auntie, or that midden that's covered with its wee tin medals. Come off to the park with me and we'll bring home the kye.*

Deep in clover the cows as they came on them, Chris and Will; and they went in no hurry at all, unanxious to be back in Blawearie. And Will seemed angry and gentle and kind all at once. *Don't let them worry you, Chris, don't let father make a damned slave of you, as he'd like to do. We've our own lives to lead.* And she said *What else can I do but bide at home now?*

He said he didn't know, but he'd be libbed and poleaxed and gutted if *he* did for long, soon as he'd saved the silver he was off to Canada, a man was soon his own master there. Chris listened to that with eyes wide opened, she caught at the hope of it and forgot to smack at the kye that loitered and boxed and galumphed in their cloverful-foolishness up the brae. *Oh, Will, and you could send for me as your housekeeper!* He turned a dull red and smacked at the kye and Chris sighed and the hope went out, he'd no need to answer *Ay, maybe, but maybe it would hardly suit you.*

So then she knew for sure he'd a lass somewhere in Drumlithie, it was with her he planned to share a bed and a steading in the couthy lands of Canada.

And when they got back to Blawearie they found the row ended, father'd given in to his sister Janet, ill the grace though he did it with. In three days time but three of them were sitting to meat at the kitchen table, Chris listened for

days for voices of folk that were dead or gone, both far
enough from Blawearie. But even that lost strangeness in
time, the harvest drew on, she went out to the park to help
with it, lush and heavy enough it had sprung and yellowed
with the suns and rains of the last two months.

He'd no binder, father, wouldn't hear of the things, but
he'd brought an old reaper from Echt and with that they
cut the corn; though Will swore he'd be the fool of Kinraddie seen driving a thing like that. Father laughed at him
over his beard, like a spitting cat, *If Kinraddie's laughing
can make you a bigger fool than nature made you it'll be
a miracle, and don't fret the sark from your dowp, my mannie, I'LL do the driving*. And though Will muttered at that
he gave in all the same, for every harvest there came something queer and terrible on father, you couldn't handle the
thing with a name, it was as if he grew stronger and crueller
then, ripe and strong with the strength of the corn, he'd
be fleeter than ever and his face filled out, and they'd hear
him come up from the parks, astride the broad back of
Bess, singing hymns, these were the only things that he
ever sang, singing with a queer, keen shrillness that brought
the sweat in the palms of your hands.

Now in the park below Blawearie, steading and house,
the best crop, and that was the ley, was the first they cut,
a great swither of a crop with straw you could hardly break
and twist into bands for sheaves. Sore work Chris found it
to keep her stretch of each bout cleared for the reaper's
coming, the weather cool and grey though it was. But a
sun was behind the greyness and sometimes when you
raised your head from the sheaves you'd see a beam of
light on the travel far over the parks of Upperhill or lazing
across the moor or dancing a-top the Cuddiestoun stooks,
a beam from the hot, grey haze of that sky that watched
and waited above the sweat of the harvesting Howe.

First ere the cutting in the ley began there'd been roads
to clear all round the corn, wide bouts that father scythed
himself, he swore that the scythe would yet come back to
its own when the binders and reapers rotted in rust and
folk bred the old breed again. But its time was past or was
yet to come, the scythe's, out the reaper was driven and
yoked, Chris followed down at the tail of it. The best of
weather for harvest, folk said, it was ill to cut in a swither
of heat; and so still was the air by morn and noon it re-
minded you of the days in Spring, you'd hear the skirl of

the blades ring down the Howe for mile on mile, the singing of Long Rob of the Mill, the Cuddiestoun creatures swearing at Tony as he stood and gowked at the stooks. Then Blawearie's reaper clanged in through the gates with Bess and Clyde at the pole, and the blades flashed and brightened like the teeth of a beast and snarled in a famished freedom. And then John Guthrie cried *Get up!* and swung the horses down the bout, and the hungry snarl changed to a deep, clogged growling as the corn was driven on the teeth by the swinging reaper flails; and down the bout, steady and fine, sped the reaper, clean-cutting from top to bottom, with never a straggling straw as on other farms, John Guthrie saw to that.

But feint the time had you for glowering at rip or reaper, soon as the horses were off and the flail drove the first sheaf from the tail-board Chris had pounced on that sheaf and gathered and bound it and flung it aside before you could say *Glenbervie!* and had run to the next and twisted its band, and gathered and bound and bound and gathered with her hands like a mist below her eyes, so quick they were. Midway the bout Will met with her, working up from the foot, and flicking the sweat from his face. And just as they straightened and stretched and looked up to the head of the park the clong, clong of the empty reaper would change to the snarling engaging whirr as father guided the horses to the cutting again. Still the sun smouldered behind its mists and out by Kinneff the fog-horn moaned all hours, you felt like moaning like that yourself long ere the day was out and your back near cracked and broke with the strain of the bending.

But in three days time the ley was cut, the yavil glowed yellow across the dykes and they moved to that without stop. And then suddenly the mists cleared up and the fog-horn stopped from its droning, it came on real blistering weather of heat, but hardly you'd bear to touch on the wood of the reaper shaft when you loosed the horses, so hot it grew. Kinraddie gasped and then bent to its chaving again, this heat wouldn't last, the rain was due, God help the crops that waited cutting then.

The second day of the yavil cutting a tink climbed up the Blawearie road from the turnpike and cried to John Guthrie for work, and father said *Maybe, maybe. Let's see the work that you've in you first,* and the tink said *Ay, fine that.* And he off with his coat and took the middle of the bout, and was up it in a jiffy, gathering and binding to the manner born, you might say, and giving Chris a bit smile when he met with her. So, coming down the next bout father cried to the tink that he'd take him on for a day or so, if the weather held; and Chris could get up to the house and see to the supper—*no idling, quean, mind that.* He was a black-like, gypsy childe, the tink, father wouldn't have him into the kitchen for meat, the creature might be all lice; and he wouldn't have him sleep in the house.

So Chris made him a shake-down out in the barn, he said he was real content with that. But when she carried him his supper over to the barn the first night she felt shamed for him suddenly, and told him she'd have had him eat in the house if it hadn't been father. And he said *Don't let that fash you, lass, I'm as little anxious for his company as he is for mine. Forbye, he's only a Kinraddie clown!* Chris felt her face flame at that, it just showed you there was no good doing kindness to tinks, but she made out she hadn't heard and turned back to go over the close.

Then it was the tink put out his arm, round her legs before she could move, almost he pulled her down on the hay beside him. *You've never lain with a man yet, lass, I can see, and that's a sore waste of hot blood like yours. So mind I'm here if you want me.* He loosed her then, laughing low, she couldn't do anything but stare and stare at him, sick and not angry, something turned in her stomach and her knees felt weak. The tink put out his hand and patted her leg again, *Mind, if you want me I'll be here,* and Chris shook her head, she felt too sick to speak, and slipped out of the barn and crossed the close and washed and washed at her hands and face with hot water till father lowered his paper and asked *Have you gone clean daft?*

But up in her room that night, the room that was hers and hers only now, Will slept where his brothers had slept, she saw a great moon come over the Grampians as she undressed for bed. She opened the window then, she liked to sleep with it open, and it was as though the night had been waiting for that, a waft of the autumn wind blew in, it was warm and cool and it blew in her face with a smell like the smell of late clover and the smell of dung and the smell of the stubble fields all commingled.

She leant there breathing it, watching the moon with the hills below it but higher than Blawearie, Kinraddie slept like a place in a picture-book, drifting long shadows that danced a petronella across the night-stilled parks. And without beginning or reason a strange ache came in her, in her breasts, so that they tingled, and in her throat, and below her heart, and she heard her heart beating, and for a minute the sound of the blood beating through her own head. And she thought of the tink lying there in the barn and how easy it would be to steal down the stairs and across the close, dense black in its shadows, to the barn.

But it was only for a second she thought of that, daftly, then laughed at herself, cool and trim and trig, and closed the window, shutting out the smells of the night, and slowly took off her clothes, looking at herself in the long glass that had once stood in mother's room. She was growing up limber and sweet, not bonny, perhaps, her cheek-bones were over high and her nose over short for that, but her eyes clear and deep and brown, brown, deep and clear as the Denburn flow, and her hair was red and was brown by turns, spun fine as a spider's web, wild, wonderful hair.

So she saw herself and her teeth clean-cut and even, a white gleam in that grave brown stillness of face John Guthrie's blood had bequeathed to her. And below face and neck now her clothes were off was the glimmer of shoulders and breast and there her skin was like satin, it tickled her touching herself. Below the tilt of her left breast was a dimple, she saw it and bent to look at it and the moonlight ran down her back, so queer the moonlight she felt the running of that beam along her back. And she straightened as the moonlight grew and looked at the rest of herself, and thought herself sweet and cool and fit for that lover who would some day come and kiss her and hold her, so.

And Chris saw the brown glimmer of her face grow sweet and scared as she thought of that—how they'd lie together, in a room with moonlight, and she'd be kind to him, kind and kind, giving him all and everything, and he'd sleep with his head here on her breast or they'd lie far into the mornings whispering one to the other, they'd have so much to tell!

And maybe that third and last Chris would find at last for the whimsies that filled her eyes, and tell of rain on the roof at night, the terror and the splendour of it across the long slate roofs; and the years that faded and fell, dissolved as a breath, before those third clear eyes; and mother's face, lying dead; and the Standing Stones up

there night after night and day after day by the loch of
Blawearie, how around them there gathered things that
wept and laughed and lived again in the hours before the
dawn, till far below the cocks began to crow in Kinraddie
and day had come again. And all that he'd believe, more
than so often she believed herself, not laugh at, holding and
kissing her, so. And faith! no more than a corpse he'd hold
if she didn't get into her bed-gown and into her bed, you
may dream of a lad till you're frozen as a stone, but he'll
want you warmer than that.

So that was the harvest madness that came on Chris, mild
enough it had been, she fell fast asleep in the middle of it.
But it scored her mind as a long drill scores the crumbling
sods of a brown, still May, it left neither pleasure nor pain,
but she'd know that track all the days of her life, and its
dark, long sweep across the long waiting field. Binder and
reaper clattered and wheeped through the brittle weather
that held the Howe, soon the weather might break and the
stooking was far behind in Blawearie. But Will would have
nothing to do with night-time work, he laughed in John
Guthrie's face at the mention of it and jumped on his bicycle and rode for Drumlithie evening on evening. Father
would wander out by the biggins and stare at the parks and
then come glinting into the house and glower at Chris, *Get
off to your bed when you've milked the kye;* and she made
little protest at that, she was tired enough at the end of a
day to nearly sleep in the straw of the byre.

But one night she didn't dare sleep, for up in the room
he'd shared with mother she heard John Guthrie get out
of bed and go slow padding about in his stocking soles,
like a great cat padding there, a beast that sniffed and
planned and smelled at the night. And once he came soft
down the cowering creak of the stairs and stopped by her
door, and she held her breath, near sick with fright, though
what was there to be feared of? And she heard his breath
come quick and gasping, and the scuffle of his hand on the
sneck of the door; and then that stopped, he must have
gone up or down, the house was quiet, but she didn't dare
sleep again till Will came clattering home in the still, small
hours.

For the harvest madness was out in Kinraddie if Chris
had been quick to master hers. And though a lad and a
quean might think their ongoings known to none but them-

selves, they'd soon be sore mistaken, you might hide with your lass on the top of Ben Nevis and have your bit pleasure there, but ten to one when you got up to go home there'd be Mistress Munro or some claik of her kidney, near sniggering herself daft with delight at your shame.

First it was Sarah Sinclair and the foreman at Upperhill, Ewan Tavendale he was, that the speak rose round: they'd been seen coming out of the larch wood above the Upperhill, that wood where the daftie had trapped Maggie Jean, and what had they been doing there on their lone? It was Alec Mutch of Bridge End that met them, him taking a dander over the moor to the smithy with a broken binder-blade for mending. The two hardly saw him at first, Miss Sinclair's face was an unco sight, raddled with blushing it was like the leg of a tuberculous rabbit when you skinned the beast, Ewan slouched along at her side, hang-dog he looked as though it was his mother he'd bedded with, said Alec, and maybe that's how it had felt. Alec cried a *Good night!* to the pair, they near jumped out of their skins, and went on with the story to the smithy beyond the moor. And from there you may well be sure it went through Kinraddie fast enough, the smith could tell lies faster than he could shoe horses; and he was fell champion at that.

Truth or no, Chae Strachan got hold of the story and went over to Upperhill to see Ewan Tavendale and ask in a friendly way what he meant to do about Sarah, his sister-in-law, the daft old trollop. And maybe he'd have settled things canty and fine but that he came on Ewan at the wrong bit minute, he was sitting outside the bothy door with the rest of the bothy billies; and when Chae came up there rose a bit snigger, that fair roused Chae, he stopped bang in front of them and asked what the hell they were laughing at? And Sam Gourlay said *Little, damned little*, looking Chae from head to foot; and Ewan said he felt more in the way of weeping than laughing at such a sight, and he spoke in a slow, impudent way that fair roused Chae's dander to the boiling point.

So, being a fell impatient man, and skilly with his hands, he took Sam Gourlay a clout in the lug that couped him down in the stour and then before you could wink he and Ewan were at it, ding-dong, like a pair of tinks, all round the Upperhill close; and Upprums came running in his leggings, the creature, fair scandalized, but he got a shove in the guts that couped him right down in the greip where

once his son Jock had been so mischieved; and that was
the end of *his* interfering. In a minute or so it was plain
that Ewan, fight though he might, was like to have the
worst of the sett, he was no match for that madman Chae.
So the rest of the bothy lads up and went for Chae; and
when he got back to Peesie's Knapp he'd hardly a stitch
on his back. But Ewan, the coarse, dour brute, had a cut
in the face that stopped *his* mouth for a while, and a black
eye big enough to sole the boots on Cuddiestoun's meikle
feet, folk said.

And faith! if it shouldn't be Cuddiestoun himself that
began the next story, running into the middle of it himself,
you might say, going up to the Manse to get a bit signature
on some paper or other for his lawyer man. But Mr. Gibbon they told him wasn't at home, Mistress Gibbon herself
came out to tell him that, kind and fine as she was, but he
didn't like her, the English dirt.

So, fair disgruntled he turned from the door, maybe the
poor brute's big sweating feet were fell sore already with a
hot day's stooking. But just down at the end of the Manse's
garden, where the yews bent thick above the lush grass their
boughs that had sheltered the lost childe Wallace in the
days before the coarse English ran him to earth and took
him to London and there hanged and libbed him and
hewed his body in four to hang on the gates of Scotland—
there, in that grass in the half-dark was a rustling and
squealing as though a drove of young pigs was rootling
there. And Cuddiestoun stopped and picked up a handful
of gravel from the minister's walk and flung it into the
grass and cried *Away with you!* for maybe it was dogs in
heat that were chaving there, big collies are none so chancy
to meet when the creatures are set for mating. But instead
of a collie up out of the grass rose the Gourdon quean,
her that old Mistress Sinclair had fee'd for the Manse; and
Munro saw her face then with a glazed look on it, like the
face of a pig below the knife of its killer; and she brushed
the hair from her face, daft-like, and went trailing past
Munro, without a word from her, as though she walked
half-asleep.

But past him, going into the Manse, she began to whistle,
and laughed a loud scraich of a laugh—as though she'd
tried desperately for something, and won, and beaten all
the world in the winning of it. So it seemed to Cuddiestoun, and faith! you couldn't put that down to imag-

ination, for he'd never had any, the ugly stock; so fair
queer it must well have been, he stood and stared after her,
dumbfoundered-like, and was just turning at last, to tramp
down to the road, when he found Mr. Gibbon himself at
his elbow.

It had grown fell dark by then but not so dark that Cuddiestoun couldn't see the Minister was without a hat and
was breathing in great deep paichs as though he'd come
from the running of a race. And he barked out, *Well,
speak up, man, what do you want?* Munro was sore took
aback at hearing a fine childe like the minister snap at him
that way. So he just said *Well, well, Mr. Gibbon, you've
surely been running a bit race?* and then he wished he
hadn't, for the minister went by him without another word,
and then flung over his shoulder *If you want me, come to-
morrow.*

And into the Manse he went and banged the door with a
clash that fair made Cuddiestoun loup in his meikle boots.
So there was nothing for him but to taik away home to
Mistress Munro, and faith! you might well believe the
story lost nothing in the telling she gave it, and soon every
soul in Kinraddie had a different version, Long Rob's was
cried to John Guthrie as he went by the Mill. He never
spread scandal about folk, Long Rob—only horses, was
the joke they told of him—but maybe he classed ministers
lower than them.

It seemed like enough to John Guthrie, the story, though
he'd no coarse notions like Rob and his Ingersoll, the
world was rolling fast to a hell of riches and the old slave
days come back again, ministers went with it and whored
with the rest. For the bitterness had grown and eaten away
into the heart of him in his year at Blawearie. So coarse
the land proved in the turn of the seasons he'd fair been
staggered, the crops had fared none so bad this once, but
he saw in a normal year the corn would come hardly at
all on the long, stiff slopes of the dour red clay.

Now also it grew plain to him here as never in Echt that
the day of the crofter was fell near finished, put by, the
day of folk like himself and Chae and Cuddiestoun, Pooty
and Long Rob of the Mill, the last of the farming folk that
wrung their living from the land with their own bare
hands. Sign of the times he saw Jean Guthrie's killing of
herself to shame him and make of his name a by-word in
the mouths of his neighbours, sign of a time when women

would take their own lives or flaunt their harlotries as they
pleased, with the country-folk climbing on silver, the few,
back in the pit, the many; and a darkness down on the land
he loved better than his soul or God.

And next it was Will himself that started the claiks of
Kinraddie, him and his doings in Drumlithie. But Chris
met the story ere it reached Kinraddie, she met it in Drumlithie itself, in the yard of the gardener Galt. The tink had
been gone from Blawearie that day she set out with her
basket, no sign of the rain showed even then, the heat held
still as the white, dull heat from a furnace door. Down in
the turnpike, the motor-cars went whipping by as she set
her feet for Mondynes there where the battle was fought
in the days long syne. Below the bridge went the wash of
the burn west to the Bervie Water, bairns cried and
splashed in the bridge's lithe, they went naked there when
they dared, she saw them glance white and startled in the
shelter of the stones.

Soon the heat grew such that she took off her hat and
swung that in her hand and so climbed the road, and there
to the left rose Drumlithie at last, some called it Skite to
torment the folk and they'd get fell angry at that in Skite.
No more than a rickle of houses it was, white with sunshine below its steeple that made of Skite the laugh of the
Howe, for feint the kirk was near it. Folk said for a joke
that every time it came on to rain the Drumlithie folk ran
out and took in their steeple, that proud they were of the
thing, it came from the weaver days of the village when
damn the clock was there in the place and its tolling told
the hour.

So that was Skite, it rose out of its dusts and its ancient
smells, the berries hung ripe in the yard of the gardener
Galt and he looked at Chris in a queer kind of way when he
heard her name. Syne he began a sly hinting and joking as
he weighed her berries, a great sumph of a man the creature was, fair running with creash in that hot weather, you
near melted yourself as you looked at him. *And how's Will?*
he asked. *We haven't seen much of him here of late—faith,
the roses are fair fading from Mollie Douglas's cheeks.* And
Chris said *Oh?* right stiff-like, and then *And I'll have two
pounds of your blackberries too.* So he packed her that,
hinting and gleying like a jokesome fat pig, she could have
taken him a clout in the face, but didn't, it would only

stir up more scandal, there seemed enough and to spare of
that. Whatever could Will have been doing; and what had
he done to his quean that he'd left her?

Right glad she was to be out from the stink of Skite with
the road of Mondynes in front of her. Then she heard
the bell of a bicycle far down the road behind and drew
to one side, but the thing didn't pass, it slowed down and
somebody called out, timid-like, *Are you Will Guthrie's
sister?* Chris turned and saw her then, knew her at once
Will's quean, young and white-faced and fair, and heard
her own voice, near troubled as the eyes that looked at her
as she answered *Yes; and you'll be Mollie Douglas?*

The face of the girl blushed slow at that, slow and sweet,
and she looked away back at the steeple of Skite as though
she feared the thing spied on them; and then suddenly,
near crying, she was asking Chris to tell Will he must ride
over and see her again, come again that night, she couldn't
bear it longer—she didn't care were she shameless or not,
she couldn't! And then she seemed to read the question in
Chris's eyes, the blood drained off from her face in a minute and then came back, it seemed to Chris she must be
blushing all over under her clothes, right down to the soles
of her feet as she herself sometimes blushed. But she cried
Oh, you think THAT, like all of them, but it isn't true!
Staring at her surprised and shamed Chris found she just
couldn't speak up and deny that THAT was indeed what
she thought, what else was a body to think?

Then she found Mollie Douglas's face bent close to hers,
sweet and troubled and shamed as her own. And Mollie
tried to look at her and then looked away, blushing as
though she'd sink into the ground, such a fool of herself
she was making. *It's not that at all, only I love him so sore
I can't live if I don't see Will!*

So there they were in the middle of the road, so shamed
to look one at the other they'd nothing to say; and then a
gig came spanking along from the station, at sight of it
Mollie jumped on her bicycle again, and wheeled it about,
and looked over her shoulder with a smile you couldn't forget, and stammered and cried *Ta-ta!*

But Chris couldn't forget that look in her eyes, she
went home with that in her mind and at supper that night
couldn't take her own eyes from Will. She saw him then
for the first time in years, almost a man, with his fair hair
waving across his head and spreading to his cheeks in a

rust-red down, like the down on a new-hatched chick; and his eyes blue and dark as a quean's, and kind when they looked at her, sulky when they turned on father. Not that they turned there often, there was never a word between Will and father unless they were clean compelled to it; like dumb folk working and eating together that needed no speech for hate.

Father ate his supper and climbed down the hill with his gun, Will loitered from door to window, whistling and idle, till he saw right across the Howe, up on Drumtochty hills, something that rose and coiled ash-grey and then darker against the autumn sky, a great shape like a snake there in the quiet of the evening air, with its tail a glimmer that wasn't the sunset, burning up red in the lithe of the hills. *Whin-burning,* he called to Chris, *they're burning the whins up Drumtochty way, come on up the moor and have a try at ours. They're damned sore in the need of it.——But I've my jelly to make, you gowk!——Oh, to hell with your jelly, we'll soon be jelly and bones in a grave ourselves, come on!*

So she went, they gathered great piles of old papers for twisting in torches, and made up the brae to the moor. They sat down on the grass and breathed a while, Kinraddie below them all cut and close-stooked, waiting the coming of the night, the lowe of the Bervie lights as the glow of another whin-burning there by the sea. They spread out to left and right below the moor-gate, Chris held to the left and ran through the whins, stopping to kick holes down close to the ground wherever a meikle bush rose up. Then far round the knowe Will cried he was starting, she saw him a long way off with the sky behind him and called back *All right!* and knelt by the biggest bush she'd struck; and kindled her torch and set its light to the crackling dryness of the grass.

It whoomed in an instant, the whin, she set her torch into it and ran to the next and fired that; and so in and out, backwards and forwards worked round the brae, you'd to speed quick as your legs could carry you to fire the frontward bushes when those behind raged out with their flames and smoke at your hair. In the dry, quiet evening the fire crackled up and spread and roared through the bushes and caught on the grass and crept and smoked on quick, searching trains to bushes unlit, and fired them, half you thought those questing tongues alive and malignant as they lapped through the grass. By the time Chris met with Will at the moor-gate there spread before them a park like an upland sea on fire, sweeping the hill, now the sun had quite gone and the great red roaring beast of a thing hunted and postured unchallenged, all Kinraddie was lit with its glare.

Will was black as a nigger, his eyebrows scorched, he pulled Chris down to rest on the grass. *By God, I hope the fire doesn't catch on the fence up there, else old Guthrie will be casting me out of Blawearie for bringing his grey hairs in sorrow to the grave!*

He said that sneering-like, mocking at father's Aberdeenshire voice, and Chris stirred half-angry, and sighed, and then asked *What would you do if he did put you out?* and Will said *Go.——Would you get a fee?——Damn the fears of that.*

But he didn't sound over-confident, Chris knew right well that he'd find it none so easy if it came to the push, with the harvest over now in the Howe. And then, for she'd clean forgot her in the excitement of the fires, she minded the quean Mollie Douglas—it was as though she saw her white face by Will's in the firelit dark. *I met Mollie Douglas in Drumlithie to-day, she asked me to ask you to go down and see her.*

He sat stock-still, he mightn't have heard, she pushed at his elbow *Will!* and at that he shook off her hand, *Oh, I hear. What's the good? I can't have a quean like other folk —I haven't even a fee.——Maybe she doesn't want your fee, just you. Will, they're saying things about her and you in Drumlithie—Galt and coarse tinks like that.——Saying things? What things?——What they aye say—that she's with a baby to you and you're biding away from her now. ——Galt said that?——Hinted at it, but he'll do more than hint when he's not speaking to a sister of yours.*

She'd never heard him swear as he did then, jumping to his feet with his fists tight-clenched. *That about Mollie— they said that, the orra swine! I'll mash that bloody Galt's head till his own mother won't know it!* But Chris told him that wouldn't help much, folk would just snigger and say there was something, sure, in the story of Mollie's condition. *Then what am I to do?* Will asked, raging still, and Chris blushed and said *Wait. Do you love her, Will?* But she might have known well enough how he'd take that question, maybe he blushed himself in the lithe of the dark,

he threw down the paper torches he'd saved and muttered
I'm away to Drumlithie, and was running down the hill before she could stop him.

Maybe, as he told Chris later, he went with no other
intention than seeing his Mollie herself. But as luck would
have it, who should he near run down with his bicycle outside the Drumlithie Hotel but Galt himself, the great
creash, gey drunk, and Alec Mutch in his company.

And Alec cried, *Fine night, Will,* but Galt cried *Don't
take her out to-night, Will lad, the grass is overwet for lying
on.* Will stopped and jumped off and left his bicycle lying in the road and went up to Galt—*Speaking to me?*
And the fat creash, panting like a sow in litter and sweating
all down the great face of him, hiccoughed drunken-like
Who else?——Well take that then, Will said and let drive
at the great belly of Galt; but Mutch caught his arm and
cried *Young Guthrie, you've fair gone daft, the man's old
enough to be your father.* Will said if he'd a father like
that he'd kill him and then go and drown himself, and
tried to break away from Mutch and get at the Galt creash
again. But Galt was right unkeen for that, in a minute he'd
turned, for all his fat, and made off like a hare up the
Drumlithie lanes, real swack with his girth and all, and was
out of sight in a second.

Well, sure you may be there were claiks enough in Skite
for Mutch to get all the story and drive home with it to the
Bridge End. In a day or so it was all about the place, Will
was the laughing-stock of Kinraddie. Father heard it first
from the postman, who waved him down to the road to tell
him, and soon's he heard it John Guthrie went back to Will
stooking in the yavil field and said *What's this I hear about
you and some orra tink bitch in Drumlithie?*

Now Will had been in a fair fine temper all that day from
seeing his Mollie again: and she'd made him swear he'd
not fly in a rage or go making a fool of himself if he heard
their coarse hinting at her. So he just went on with the
stooking and said *What the devil are you blithering about?*
Father shot out his beard and cried *Answer my question,
Will!* and Will said *Put a question with sense in it, then.
How am I to know what you've been hearing? I'm not a
thought-reader,* and father said *Damn't to hell, you coarse
brute, am I to stand your lip as well as your whoring every
night? Is't true there's a tink called Mollie Douglas that's
with a bairn by you?* and Will said *If you call Mollie*

Douglas a tink again, I'll knock the damned teeth down the throat of you, father though you be.

And they stopped their stooking, glaring at each other, and father made to strike at Will but Will caught his arm and cried *Mind!* So father lowered his arm, white as a ghost he'd turned, and went on with the stooking. Will stared at him, white himself, and then went on with the stooking as well. And that might well have been the end of it so far as Blawearie went, but that evening they heard a clatter outside in the close and there was the minister's bicycle and Mr. Gibbon himself new off it; and into the kitchen he came and said *Good evening, Chris, good evening, Mr. Guthrie. Can I have a word with Will?*

So Chris was sent to bring Will from the byre where he bedded the kye, he came back with her grey in the gills, there sat the minister and father, solemn as two owls in the loft of a barn, it was plain they'd been taking the matter through hand together. Father said *Chris, go to your room,* and there was nothing else for her but go; and what happened after that she was never sure, for Will wouldn't tell her, but she heard the sound of the three of them, all speaking at once and Will getting in a rage: and then suddenly the kitchen-door banged and there was Will striding across the close to the barn where he stored his bicycle. Mr. Gibbon's voice cried after him, angry-like, with a boom, *Just a minute, Will, where are you going?* and Will looked back and said *You're so anxious I should lie with my lass and get her with a bairn that I'm off to try and oblige you.* And he wheeled his bicycle out by the honeysuckle hedge and pedalled away down the road and didn't come back to Blawearie till one o'clock in the morning.

Chris hadn't been able to sleep, she lay listening for him, and when she heard him come up the stairs she cried his name in a whisper *Will!* He stopped uncertain outside her door and then lifted the sneck and came in soft-footed and sat on the side of her bed. Chris raised herself on an elbow and peered at him, there was little light in the room and no moon that night though the sky was white with stars, and Will no more than a shadow hunched on her bedside there, with a whitish blotch for a face. And Chris whispered *Will, I heard what you said when you went away. But you didn't do it?* and Will gave a low laugh, he wasn't in a rage, *It wouldn't be for want of prigging by half the holy*

*muckers in Kinraddie if I had. But you needn't be feared
for that, I'd as soon cut my own throat as do hurt to—HER.*

So the minister's interfering brought no harm, faith! he'd
more need to roust round his own bit byre with a clart if
Cuddiestoun's story of the Gourdon quean were true. And
soon enough after that a worse scandal went on the rounds
about him, folk shook their heads and made out they were
fell affronted: all but Long Rob of the Mill, and he swore
B'God, it was the best he'd heard since Nebuchadnezzar
went out to grass!

And the way of it was that in early November a bit
daughter was born to the Manse, and the Reverend Gibbon
was proud as punch, he preached a grand sermon that
Sunday, *For unto us a child is born;* and it was so affecting
that old Mistress Sinclair of the Netherhill broke down
and cried in her hanky about it; but Long Rob of the Mill,
when he heard that, said: *She shouldn't take whisky sweeties
to the kirk with her.* Everybody else was fell impressed,
folk who'd been a bit off the Manse for months agreed
he'd maybe his faults, the Gibbon childe, but who hadn't
these days? and feint the many could wag a pow like that
in a Mearns pulpit. But damn't! if the next day he didn't
go off and spoil the whole thing, the Monday it was, he was
just setting out for the train to Aberdeen, Mr. Gibbon, when
the nurse cried out to him he might bring a small chamber-
pot for the girlie, none in the Manse was suitable. He gave
a bit blush, the big, curly bull, and said *Very well, nurse,*
in a bull-like voice, and off to the station he went, it was
Fordoun, and left his bicycle there and caught his train.

About what happened after that some told one thing and
some another and some told both together. But it seems
that fair early in the day in Aberdeen the Reverend Gibbon
fell in with some friends of his; and they'd have it that a
dram there must be to celebrate the occasion. So off the
whole lot of them went to a public house and had their
dram and syne another on top of that to keep the first one
down, syne two-three more to keep the wind out, it was
blowy weather on the edge of winter. Some said that midway the carouse Mr. Gibbon had got up to make a bit
prayer: and one of the barmaids had laughed at him and
he chased her out of the bar up to her room and finished
his prayer with her there. But you couldn't believe every
lie you heard.

Sometime late in the afternoon he minded his train, the
minister, and hired a cab and bought the bit chamber, and
caught the train by the skin of the teeth. No sooner was he
down in his carriage than, fell exhausted, he went fast
asleep and blithely snored his way south through many a
mile, right dead to the world he was.

Most of the story till then was maybe but guessing, ill-
natured guessing at that, but the porter at the Bridge of
Dunn, a good twenty miles south from Fordoun, swore to
the rest. He was just banging the doors of the old 7.30
when out of a carriage window came a head, like a bull's
head out of the straw, he'd fair a turn, had the porter,
when he saw the flat hat that topped it. *Is this Fordoun?* the
meikle head mooed, and the porter said *No, man, it's a
damned long way from being that.*

So he opened the door for Kinraddie's minister, and
Mr. Gibbon came stumbling out and rubbed his eyes, and
the porter pointed to a platform where he'd find a slow
train back to Fordoun. This platform lay over a little bridge
and the minister set out to cross; and the first few steps he
managed fell well, but near the top he began to sway and
missed his footing and flung out his hands. The next thing
that the porter saw was the chamber-pot, burst from its
paper, rolling down the steps of the bridge with the minister's hat in competition and the minister thundering behind.

And then, when the porter had picked him up and was
dusting him, the Reverend Gibbon broke down and sobbed
on the porter's shoulder what a bloody place was Kinraddie!
And how'd the porter like to live 'tween a brier bush and
a rotten kailyard in the lee of a house with green shutters?
And the minister sobbed some more about the shutters,
and he said you couldn't lie down a minute with a quean
in Kinraddie but that some half-witted clod-hopping crofter
began to throw stones at you, they'd feint the respect for
God or kirk or minister down in Kinraddie. And the
porter said it was awful the way the world went, he'd
thought of resigning from the railway himself and taking
to preaching, but now he wouldn't.

Syne he helped the minister over to an up-going train
and went home to his wife and told her the tale: and she
told it to her sister from Auchenblae: and *she* told it to her
man who told it to Mutch; and so the whole thing came out.
And next time he rode down by the Peesie's Knapp, the
minister, a head shot out of a hedge behind him, it was wee

Wat Strachan, and cried loud as you like *Any chambers
to-day?*

Not that they'd much to shout for that winter themselves,
the Strachans; folk said it was easy to see why Chae was
so strong on Rich and Poor being Equal: he was sore in
need of the sharing out to start ere he went clean broke
himself. Maybe old Sinclair or the wife were tight with the
silver that year, but early as December Chae had to sell his
corn, he brought the first threshing of the season down in
Kinraddie. John Guthrie and Will were off at the keek of
dawn when they saw the smoke rise from the engines, Chris
followed an hour later to help Chae's wife with the dinner
and things. And faith! broke he might be but he wasn't
mean, Chae, when the folk came trampling in to eat there
was broth and beef and chicken and oat-cakes, champion
cakes they made at the Knapp; and loaf and jelly and
dumpling with sugar and milk; and if any soul were that
gutsy he wanted more he could hold to the turnip-field,
said Chae.

The first three men to come in Chris hardly saw, so busied
she was pouring their broth for them. Syne, setting the
plates, she saw Alec Mutch, his great lugs like red clouts
hung out to dry: and he cried *Ay, Chris!* and began to sup
as though he hadn't seen food for a fortnight. Beside him
was Munro of the Cuddiestoun, he was eating like a collie
ta'en off its chain, Chae's thresh was a spree to the pair
of them. Then more trampling and scraping came from the
door, folk came drifting in two-three at a time, Chris over-
busied to notice their faces, but some watched her and give
a bit smile and Cuddiestoun cried to father, *Losh, man,
she's fair an expert getting, the daughter. The kitchen's
more her style than the College.*

Some folk at the tables laughed out at that, the ill-nature
grinned from the faces of them, and suddenly Chris hated
the lot, the English Chris came back in her skin a minute,
she saw them the yokels and clowns everlasting, dull-brained
and crude. Alec Mutch took up the card from Cuddiestoun
then and began on education and the speak ran round the
tables. Most said it was a coarse thing, learning, just teaching your children a lot of damned nonsense that put them
above themselves, they'd turn round and give you their lip
as soon as look at you.

But Chae was sitting down himself by then and he

wouldn't have that. *Damn't man, you're clean wrong to think that. Education's the thing the working man wants to put him up level with the Rich.* And Long Rob of the Mill said *I'd have thought a bit balance in the bank would do that.* But for once he seemed right in agreement with Chae—*the more education the more of sense and the less of kirks and ministers.* Cuddiestoun and Mutch were fair shocked at that, Cuddiestoun cried out *Well, well, we'll hear nothing coarse of religion,* as though he didn't want to hear anything more about it and was giving out orders. But Long Rob wasn't a bit took aback, the long rangy childe, he just cocked an eye at Cuddiestoun and cried *Well, well, Munro, we'll turn to the mentally afflicted in general, not just in particular. How's that foreman of yours getting on, Tony? Is he still keeping up with his shorthand?* There was a snicker at that, you may well be sure, and Cuddiestoun closed up quick enough, here and there folk had another bit laugh and said Long Rob was an ill hand to counter. And Chris thought of her clowns and yokels, and was shamed as she thought—Chae and Long Rob they were, the poorest folk in Kinraddie!

At a quarter past six the mill loosed off again from its bumble-bee hum, the threshers came trooping down to the tables again. More dumpling there was, cut up for tea, and bread and butter and scones and baps from the grocer, and rhubarb and blackberry jam, and syrup for them that preferred it, some folk liked to live on dirt out of tins. Most of the mill folk sat down in a right fine tune, well they might, and loosed out their waistcoats. Will was near last to come in from the close, a long, dark young childe came in at his heels, Chris hadn't set eyes on him before, nor he on her by the way he glowered. The two of them stood about, lost-like and gowked, looking for seats in the crowded kitchen till Mistress Strachan cried over to Chris *Will you lay them places ben in the room?*

So she did and took them their supper there, Will looked up and cried *Hello, Chris, how have you gotten on?* and Chris said *Fine, how've you?* Will laughed *Well, God, my back would feel a damned sight easier if I'd spent the day in my bed. Eh, Tavendale?* And then he minded his manners. *This is Ewan Tavendale from Upprums, Chris.*

So that was who; Chris felt queer as he raised his head and held out his hand, and she felt the blood come in her face and saw it come dark in his. He looked over young for the coarse, dour brute folk said he was, like a wild cat, strong and quick, she half-liked his face and half-hated it, it could surely never have been him that did THAT in the larch wood of Upperhill? But then if you could read every childe's nature in the way he wiped his nose, said Long Rob of the Mill, it would be a fine and easy world to go through.

So she paid him no more heed and was out of the Knapp a minute later and ran nearly all the way up to Blawearie to see to the milking there. The wind was still up but the frost was crackling below her feet as she ran, the brae rose cold and uncanny with Blawearie's biggings uncertain shadows high up in the cold mirk there. She felt tingling and blithe from her run, she said to herself if she'd only the time she'd go out every winter night and run up over hills with frost and the night star coming in the sky.

But that night as Blawearie went to its bed Will opened his bedroom door and cried *Father! Chris! See that light down there in the Knapp!*

Chris was over at her window then in a minute, barefooted she ran and peered by the shadow of the great beech tree. And there was a light right plain enough, more than a light, a lowe that crackled to yellow and red and rose in the wind that had come with the night. Peesie's Knapp would be all in a blaze in a minute, Chris knew; and then father came tearing down the stairs, crying to Will to get on his clothes and follow him, Chris was to bide at home, mind that. They heard him open the front door and go out and go running right fleetly down the night of Blawearie hill, Chris cried to Will *Wait for me, I'm coming as well,* and he cried back *All right, but for God's sake hurry!*

She couldn't find her stockings then, she was trembling and daft; and when found they were, her corsets were missing, slipped down the back of the kist they had, Will came knocking at the door *Come on!*——*Light a match and come in,* she called and in he came, knotting his muffler, and lighted a match and looked at her in her knickers and vest, reaching out for the new-seen corsets. *Leave the damn things where they are, you're fine, you should never have been born a quean.* She was into her skirt by then, and said *I wish I hadn't,* and pulled on her boots and half-laced them, and ran down the stairs after Will and put on her coat at the foot.

In a minute they were out in the dimness then, under

the starlight, it was rimed with frost, and running like mad down to the lowe that now rose like a beacon against the whole of Kinraddie. *I hope they've wakened!* Will panted, for every soul knew the Strachans went straight to bed at the chap of eight. Running, they could see by then it was the barn itself that had taken alight, the straw sow seemed burned to a cinder already, and the barn had caught and maybe the house. And all over Kinraddie lights were springing up, as they ran Chris lifted her eyes and saw Cuddiestoun's blink and shine bright down through the dark.

And faith, quick though they were, it was father that saved Chae Strachan's folk. He was first down at the blazing Knapp, John Guthrie; and he ran round the biggings and saw the flames lapping and lowing at the kitchen end of the house, not a soul about or trying to stop them though the noise was fair awful, the crackling and burning, and the winter air bright with flying sticks and straw. He banged at the door and cried *Damn't to hell do you want to be roasted?* and when he got no answer he smashed in the window, they heard him then and the bairns scraiched, there was never such a lot for sleep, folk said, Chae'd have slept himself out of this world and into hell in his own firewood if John Guthrie hadn't roused him then. But out he came stumbling at last, he'd only his breeks on; and he took a keek at John Guthrie and another at the fire and cried out *Kirsty, we're all to hell!* and off he tore to the byre.

But half-way across the close as he ran the barn swithered and roared and fell, right in front of him, and he'd to run back, there was no way then of getting at the byre. By then Long Rob of the Mill came in about, he'd run over the fields, louping dykes like a hare, and his lungs were panting like bellows, he was clean winded. He it was that helped Mrs. Strachan with the bairns and such clothes as they could drag out to the road while Chae and John Guthrie tried to get at the byre from another angle: but that was no good, the place was already roaring alight.

For a while there was only the snarling of the fire eating into the wooden couplings, the rattle of falling slates through the old charred beams, and then, the first sound that Will and Chris heard as they came panting down the road, a scream that was awful, a scream that made them think one of the Strachans was trapped down there. And at that sound Chae covered his ears and cried *Oh God, that's*

old Clytie, Clytie was his little horse, his sholtie, and she
screamed and screamed, terrible and terrible, Chris ran
back to the house trying not to hear and to help poor Kirsty
Strachan, snivelling and weeping, and the bairns laughing
and dancing about as though they were at a picnic, and
Long Rob of the Mill smoking his pipe as cool as you
please, there was surely enough smell and smoke without
that? But pipe and all he dived in and out of the house and
saved chairs and dishes and baskets of eggs; and Mistress
Strachan cried *Oh, my sampler!* and in Rob tore and rived
that off a blazing wall, a meikle worsted thing in a cracked
glass case that Mistress Strachan had made as a bairn at
school.

And then came the clip-clop of a gig, it was Ellison down
from the Mains, him and two of his men, and God! he
might be little more than a windy Irish brute but he'd sense
for all that, the gig was crammed with ropes and pails, Ellison strung out the folk and took charge, the pails went
swinging from hand to hand over the close from the well
to the childe that stood nearest the fire, and he pelted the
fire with water. But feint the much good that did for a
while and then there was an awful sound from the byre,
the lowing of the cattle with the flames among them, and
Long Rob of the Mill cried out *I can't stand it!* and took a
pick-axe and ran round the back of the close; and there he
found the sow was nothing but a black heap then, hardly
burning at all, and he cried back the news and himself
louped through the smoke and came at the back wall of
the byre and started to smash it in fast as he could.

Chae followed and John Guthrie, and the three of them
worked like madmen there, Ellison's men splashed water
down on the roof above them till suddenly the wall gave
way before them and Chae's oldest cow stuck out its head
and said *Moo!* right in Chae's face. The three scrambled
through into the byre then, that was fell dangerous, the
rafters were crumbling and falling all about the stalls, and
it was half-dark there in spite of the flames. But they
loosed another cow and two stirks before the fire drove
them out, the others they had to leave, their lowing was
fair demented and the smell of their burning sickening in
your throat, it was nearly a quarter of an hour later before
the roof fell in and killed the cattle. Long Rob of the Mill
sat down by the side of the road and was suddenly as sick

as could be, and he said *By God, I never want to smell roasting beef again.*

So that was the burning of the Peesie's Knapp, there was a great throng of folk in about by then, the Netherhill folk and the Upperhill, and Cuddiestoun, and Alec Mutch with his great lugs lit up by the fire, some had come on bicycles and some had run across half Kinraddie and two had brought their gigs. But there was little to do now but stand and glower at the fire and its mischief. Ellison drove off to the Mains with Mistress Strachan and the bairns, there for the night they were bedded. The cattle he'd saved from the byre Chae drove to Netherhill, folk began to put on their jackets again, it was little use waiting for anything else, they'd away home to their beds.

Chris could see nothing of either father or Will, she turned to make for Blawearie then. Outside the radiance of the burning Knapp it was hard and cold, starless but clear, as though the steel of the ground glowed faintly of itself; beyond rose the darkness as a black wall, still and opaque. On the verge of its embrasure it was that she nearly ran into two men tramping back along the road, she hardly saw them till she was on them. She cried *Oh, I'm sorry,* and one of them laughed and said something to the other, next instant before she knew what was happening that other had her in his arms, rough and strong, and had kissed her, he had a face with a soft, grained skin, it was the first time a man had ever kissed her like that, dark and frightening and terrible in the winter road.

The other stood by, Chris, paralysed, heard him breathing and knew he was laughing, and a far crackle rose from the last of the lowe in the burning biggings. Then she came to herself and kicked the man that held her, young he was with his soft, grained face, kicked him hard with her knee and then brought her nails down across his face. As he swore *You bitch!* and let go of her she kicked him again, with her foot this time, and he swore again, but the other said *Hist! Here's somebody coming,* and the two of them began to run, the cowardly tinks, it was father and Will on the road behind them.

And when Chris told Will of what happened, next morning it was that she told him when father wasn't by, he looked at her queerly, half-laughing, half-solemn, and made out he thought nothing of the happening, all ploughmen were like that, aye ready for fun. But it hadn't seemed fun

to her, dead earnest rather; and lying that night in her bed
between the cold sheets, curled up so she might rub her
white toes to some warmth and ease, it was in her memory
like being chased and bitten by a beast, but worse and with
something else in it, as though half she'd liked the beast and
the biting and the smell of that sleeve around her neck and
that soft, unshaven face against her own. Sweet breath he
had had anyway, she thought, and laughed to herself, that
was some consolation, the tink. And then she fell asleep
and dreamed of him, an awful dream that made her blush
even while she knew she was dreaming, she was glad when
the morning came and was sane and cool and herself again.

But that dream came to her often while the winter wore
on through Kinraddie, a winter that brought hardly any
snow till New Year's Eve and then brought plenty darkening the sky with its white cascading. It was funny that
darkening the blind fall and wheep of the snow should
bring, like the loosening of a feather pillow above the hills,
night came as early as three in the afternoon. They redd
up the beasts early that evening, father and Will, feeding
them well with turnips and straw and hot treacle poured
on the straw; and then they came in to their supper and had
it and sat close round the fire while Chris made a fine
dumpling for New Year's Day. None of them spoke for
long, listening to that whoom and blatter on the window-
panes, and the clap-clap-clap of some loose slate far up on
the roof, till father whispered and looked at them, his
whisper hurt worse than a shout, *God, I wonder why Jean
left us?*
Chris cried then, making no sound, she looked at Will
and saw him with his face red and shamed, all three of them
thinking of mother, her that was by them so kind and
friendly and quick that last New Year, so cold and quiet
and forgotten now with the little dead twins in the kirkyard
of Kinraddie, piling black with the driving of the snow it
would be under the rustle and swing and creak of the yews.
And Will stared at father, his face was blind with pity, once
he made to speak, but couldn't, always they'd hated one the
other so much and they'd feel shamed if they spoke in
friendship now.
So father took up his paper again and at ten o'clock
Chris went out to milk the kye and Will went with her over
the close, carrying the lantern, the flame of it leapt and

starred and quivered and hesitated in the drive of the snow. In the light of it, like a rain of arrows they saw the coming of the storm that night swept down from the Grampian heuchs, thick and strong it was in Blawearie, but high in the real hills a smoring, straight wall must be sweeping the dark, blinding down against the lone huts of the shepherds and the faces of lost tinks tramping through it looking for lights the snow'd smothered long before. Chris was shaking, but not with cold, and inside the byre she leant on a stall and Will said *God, you look awful, what is't?* And she shook herself and said *Nothing. Why haven't you gone to see Mollie to-night?*

He said he was going next day, wasn't that enough, he'd be a corpse long ere he reached Drumlithie to-night—*listen to the wind, it'll blow the damn place down on our lugs in a minute!* And the byre shook, between the lulls it seemed to set its breath to rise and take from the hill-side into the air, there was such straining and creaking. Not that the calves or the stirks paid heed, they slept and snored in their stalls with never a care, there were worse things in the world than being a beast.

Back in the house it seemed to Chris she'd but hardly sieved the milk when the great clock ben in the parlour sent peal after peal out dirling through the place. Will looked at Chris and the two at father, and John Guthrie was just raising up his head from his paper, but if he'd been to wish them a happy New Year or not they were never to know, for right at that minute there came a brisk chap at the door and somebody lifted the sneck and stamped the snow from his feet and banged the door behind him.

And there he was, Long Rob of the Mill, muffled in a great grey cravat and with leggings up to the knees, covered and frosted from head to foot in the snow, he cried *Happy New Year to you all! Am I the first?* And John Guthrie was up on his feet, *Ay, man, you're fairly that, out of that coat of yours!* They stripped off the coat between them, faith! Rob's mouser was nearly frozen, but he said it was fine and laughed, and waited the glass of toddy father brought him and cried *Your health!* And just as it went down his throat there came a new knock, damn't if it wasn't Chae Strachan, he'd had more than a drink already and he cried *Happy New Year, I'm the first foot in am I not?* And he made to kiss Chris, she wouldn't have

minded, laughing, but he slithered and couped on the
floor. Long Rob peered down at him and cried out, shocked-
like, *Good God, Chae, you can't sleep there!*

So he was hoisted into a chair and was better in a
minute when he'd had another drink; and he began to tell
what a hell of a life it was he'd to live in Netherhill now,
the old mistress grew worse with the years, she'd near girn
the jaws from her face if the Strachan bairns so much as
gave a bit howl or had a bit fight—fell unreasoning that,
no bairns there were but fought like tinks. And Long Rob
said Ay, that was true, as it said in the hymn 'twas dog's
delight to bark and bite, and faith! the average human
could out-dog any cur that ever was upped.

Now, horses were different, you'd hardly ever meet a
horse that was naturally a quarreller, a coarse horse was
a beast they'd broken in badly. He'd once had a horse—a
three-four years come Martinmas that would have been, or
no! man, it was only two—that he bought up in Auchinblae
at the fall of the year, a big roan, coarse as hell, they said,
and he'd nearly kicked the guts out of an old man there.
Well, Rob had borrowed a bridle and tried to ride home
the beast to the Mill, and twice in the first mile the horse
threw him off with a snort and stood still, just laughing, as
Rob picked himself up from the stour. But Rob just said to
himself, *All right, my mannie, we'll see who'll laugh last;*
and when he'd got that horse home he tied him up in his
stall and gave him such a hammering, by God he nearly
kicked down the stable.

Every night for a week he was walloped like that, and
damn't man! in the shortest while he'd quietened down and
turned into a real good worker, near human he was, that
horse, he'd turn at the end of a rig as it drew to eleven
o'clock and begin to nicker and neigh, he knew the time
fine. Ay, canty beast that, he'd turned, and sold at a profit
in a year or so, it just showed you what a handless man did
with a horse, for Rob had heard that the beast's new owner
had let the horse clean go over him. A sound bit leathering
and a pinch of kindness was the only way to cure a coarse
horse.

Chae hiccuped and said *Damn't ay, man, maybe you're
right. It's a pity old Sinclair never thought of treating his
fish-wife like that, she'd deave a door-nail with her whines
and plaints, the thrawn old Tory bitch.* And Long Rob said
there were worse folk than Tories and Chae said if there

were they kept themselves damn close hidden, if he'd his way he'd have all Tories nailed up in barrels full of spikes and rolled down the side of the Grampians; and Long Rob said there would be a gey boom in the barrel trade then, the most of Kinraddie would be inside the barrels; and Chae said *And a damned good riddance of rubbish, too.*

They were both heated up with the toddy then, and raising their voices, but father just said, cool-like, that he was a Liberal himself, and what did they think of this bye-election coming off in the February? Chae said it would make no difference who got in, one tink robber was bad as another, Tory as Liberal; damn't if he understood why Blawearie should be taken in by those Liberals. Long Rob said *Why don't you stand as the Socialist man yourself, Chae?* and winked at Chris, but Chae took it real serious and said maybe he'd do that yet once Peesie's Knapp was builded again. And Long Rob said *Why wait for that? You're allowing your opinions to eat their heads off in idleness, like a horse in a stall in winter. Losh, man, but they're queer beasts, horses. There's my sholtie, Kate——* But Chae said *Och, away to hell with your horses, Rob. Damn't, if you want a canty kind of beast there's nothing like a camel,* and maybe he'd have just begun to tell them about the camel if he hadn't fallen off his chair then, nearly into the fire he went, and John Guthrie smiled at him over his beard, as though he'd really rather cut his throat than smile. And then Will and Long Rob helped Chae to his feet, Long Rob gave a laugh and said it was time they went dandering back to their beds, he'd see Chae far as the Netherhill.

The storm had cleared a bit by then, it was bright starlight Chris saw looking after the figures of the two from her bedroom window—not very steady, either of them, with shrouded Kinraddie lying below and a smudge there, faint and dark, far down in the night, that was the burned-out steading of Peesie's Knapp.

And there the smudge glimmered through many a week, they didn't start on Peesie's new steading till well in the February. But faith! there was clatter enough of tongues round the place right from the night of the fire onwards. All kinds of folk came down and poked in the ash with their walking-sticks, the police and the Cruelty came from Stonehaven; and the factor came, he was seldom seen unless there was money in question; and insurance creatures buzzed down from Aberdeen like a swarm of fleas, their humming and hawing and gabbling were the speak of all Kinraddie.

Soon all kinds of stories flew up and down the Howe, some said the fire had been lighted by Chae himself, a Drumlithie billy riding by the Knapp late that night of the fire had seen Chae with a box of spunks in his hand, coming from the lighting of the straw sow, sure; for soon as he saw the billy on the bicycle back Chae had jumped to the lithe again. Others said the fire had been set by the folk of Netherhill, their only chance of recovering the silver they'd loaned to Chae. But that was just a plain lie, like the others, Chris thought, Chae'd have never cried for his burning sholtie like that if he'd meant it to burn for insurance.

But stories or no, they couldn't shake Chae, he was paid his claims up to the hilt, folk said he'd made two-three hundred pounds on the business, he'd be less keen now for Equality. But faith! if he'd won queer silver queerly, he'd lost feint the queer notion in the winning of it.

Just as the building of the new bit Knapp began so did the bye-election, the old member had died in London of drink, poor brute, folk said when they cut his corpse open it fair gushed out with whisky. Ah well, he was dead then, him and his whisky, and though he'd maybe been a good enough childe to represent the shire, feint the thing had the shire ever seen of him except at election times. Now there came a young Tory gent in the field, called Rose he was, an Englishman with a funny bit squeak of a voice, like a bairn that's wet its breeks. But the Liberal was an oldish creature from Glasgow, fell rich he was, folk said, with as many ships to his name as others had fields. And real Radical he was, with everybody's money but his own, and he said he'd support the Insurance and to Hell with the House of Lords, *Vote for the Scottish Thistle and not for the English Rose.*

But the Tory said the House of Lords had aye been defenders of the Common People, only he didn't say aye, his English was a real drawback; and it was at the meeting where he said that, that Chae Strachan up and asked if it wasn't true that his own uncle was a lord? And the Tory said *Yes,* and Chae said that maybe *that* lord would be glad to see him in Parliament but there was a greater Lord who heard when the Tories took the name of poor folk in vain. The God of old Scotland there was, aye fighting on the side of the people since the days of old John Knox, and He would yet bring to an end the day of wealth and waster throughout the world, liberty and equality and fraternity were coming though all the damned lordies in the House of Lords should pawn their bit coronets and throw their whores back in the streets and raise private armies to fight the common folk with their savings.

But then the stewards made at Chae, he hadn't near finished, and an awful stamash broke out in the hall; for though most of the folk had been laughing at Chae they weren't to see him mishandled by an English tink and the coarse fisher brutes he'd hired from Gourdon; to keep folk from asking him questions. So when the first steward laid hands on Chae, John Guthrie, who was sitting near, cried *Ay, man, who'll you be?* And the fisher swore *You keep quiet as well*, and father rose and took him a belt in the face, and the fisher's nose bled like the Don in spate, and somebody put out a leg and tripped him up and that was the end of his stewarding. And when the other steward made to come to his help Long Rob of the Mill said *Away home to your stinking fish!* and took him by the lug and ran him out of the hall and kicked him into the grass outside.

Then everybody was speaking at once, Mr. Gibbon was the Tory lad's chairman and he called out *Can't you give us fair play, Charles Strachan?* But Chae's blood was up, strong for the Kirk though he was in a way he clean forgot who he spoke to—*Come outside a minute, my mannie, and I'll fair-play you!* The minister wasn't such a fool as that, though, he said that the meeting was closed, fair useless it was to go on; and he said that Chae was a demagogue and Chae said that he was a liar, folk cried out *Wheest, wheest!* at that and begun to go home. The Tory childe got hantle few votes in the end, Chae boasted it was his help put in the old Liberal stock; and God knows if he thought that fine he was easily pleased, they never saw the creature again in Kinraddie.

But that was the last time father struck a man, striking in cold anger and cold blood as was the way of him. Folk said he was an unchancy childe to set in a rage; but his next rage mischieved himself, not others. For a while up into the

New Year, April and the turnip-time, things at Blawearie went fair and smooth, Will saying no more than his say at plate or park, never countering father, hardly he looked at him even; and father maybe thought to rule the roost as he'd done before when Will was no more than a boy that cowered when he heard that sharp voice raised, frightened and beaten and lying through nights with his sore wealed body in the arms of Chris. But Chris, knowing none of his plannings, guessed right well something new it was kept Will quiet, so quiet day on day, yet if you looked at him sudden you'd more likely than not seeing him smiling to himself, lovely the face that he smiled with, brown and clean, and his eyes were kind and clear and the hair grew down on his head in a bonny mop, Will took after mother with that flame of rusty gold that was hers.

Ah well, he kept to his whistling and his secret smiling, and every night after loosening and suppering was done, off down the road on his old bit bicycle he'd go, you'd hear through the evening stillness nothing but the sound of the old machine whirring down Blawearie road, and the weet-weet of the peewits flying twilit over Kinraddie, wheeling and circling there in the dark, daft creatures that made their nests in this rig and that and would come back next day and find them robbed or smothered away. So for hundreds of years they'd done, the peewits, said Long Rob of the Mill, and hadn't learned the sense of the thing even yet; and if you were to take that as a sample of the Divine Intelligence that had allotted a fitting amount of brain to each creature's needs then all you could suppose was that the Divine had more than a spite against the peesie.

Chris heard him say that one day she looked in at the Mill to ask when a sack of bruised corn, left there by Will, would be ready. But there on the bench outside the Mill, in the shade from the hot Spring weather, sat Rob and Chae and Mutch of Bridge End, all guzzling beer from long bottles they were, Rob more bent on bruising their arguments than on bruising Blawearie's corn.

Peewits were flying round the Mill fell thick, peewits and crows that nested in the pines above the Mill, and the birds it was had begun the argument. Chris waited for a while, pleased enough with the shade and rest, hearkening to Long Rob make a fool of God. But Alec Mutch wagged his meikle lugs, *No, man, you're fair wrong there. And man, Rob, you'll burn in hell for that, you know.* Chae was half on his side and half wasn't, he said *Damn the fears, that's nothing but an old wife's gabble for fearing the bairns. But Something there IS up there, Rob man, there's no denying that. If I thought there wasn't I'd out and cut my throat this minute.* Then the three of them sighted Chris and Rob got up, the long, rangy childe with the glinting eyes, and cried *Is't about the bruised corn, Chris? Tell Will I'll do it to-night.*

But Will had unyoked and made off to Drumlithie, his usual gait, when Chris got home, and father was up on the moor with his gun, you heard the bang of the shots come now and then. Chris had a great baking to do that night, both father and Will would eat oat-cakes and scones for a wager, bought bread from the vans soon scunnered them sore. Warm work it was when you'd heaped a great fire and the girdle glowed below, you'd nearly to strip in fine weather if you weren't to sweat yourself sick. Chris got out of most things but a vest and a petticoat, she was all alone and could do as she pleased, it was fine and free and she baked a will.

She was lifting the last cake, browned and good and twice cross cut, when she knew that somebody watched her from the door of the kitchen, and she looked, it was Ewan Tavendale, him she hadn't seen since the day of the thresh at Peesie's Knapp. He was standing against the jamb, long and dark with his glowering eyes, but he reddened when she looked, not half as much as she did herself, she could feel the red warm blushing come through her skin from tip to toe; *such a look he's taking,* she thought, *it's a pity I'm wearing a thing and he can't study the blush to its end.*

But he just said *Hello, is Will about?* and Chris said *No, in Drumlithie I think,* and they stood and glowered like a couple of gowks, Chris saw his eyes queer and soft and shy, the neck of his shirt had fallen apart, below it the skin was white as new milk, frothed white it looked, and a drop of sweat stood there where the brown of his tanning and the white of his real skin met. And then Chris suddenly knew *something* and blushed again, sharp and silly, she couldn't stop, she'd minded the night of the fire at Peesie's Knapp and the man that had kissed her on the homeward road, Ewan Tavendale it had been, no other, shameless and coarse.

He was blushing himself again by then, they looked at each other in a white, queer daze, Chris wondered in a kind of a panic if he knew what she knew at last, half-praying she was he wouldn't speak of it when he began to move off from the door, still red, stepping softly, like father, like a limber, soft-stepping cat. *Well, I was hoping I'd see him in case he should leave us suddenlike.*

She stared at him all awake, that kissing on the winter road forgotten. *Leave? Who said Will was leaving?——— Oh, I heard he was trying for a job in Aberdeen, maybe it's a lie. Tell him I called in about. Ta-ta.*

She called *Ta-ta, Ewan,* after him as he crossed the close, he half-turned round and smiled at her, quick and dark like a cat again, *Ta-ta, Chris.* And she stood looking after him a long while, not thinking, smiling, till the smell of a burning cake roused her to run, just like the English creature Alfred.

And next morning she said to Will after breakfast, casual-like, but her heart in her throat, *Ewan Tavendale was down to see you last night, he thought you'd be leaving Blawearie soon.* And Will took it cool and quiet, *Did he? God, they'd haver the breeks from a Highlandman's haunches, the gossipers of Kinraddie. Tavendale down to see me? More likely he was down to take a bit keek at you, Chris lass. So look after yourself, for he's Highland and coarse.*

In July it came to the hay-time, and John Guthrie looked at Will and said he was going to have down the hay with a scythe this year, not spoil the bit stuff with a mower. Fair plain to Chris he expected Will to fly in a rage at that and say he wasn't to chave and sweat in the forking of rig after rig when a mower would clear Blawearie's park in a day or two at the most. But Will just said *All right* and went on with his porridge, and went out to the field in the tail of father, a fork on his shoulder and whistling happy as a lark, so that father turned round and snapped *Hold your damned wheeber, you'll need your breath for the bout.* Even at that Will laughed, as a man at a girning bairn, right off they were worse friends than even the year before. But all that time, Will was making his plans and on the morning of the August's last Saturday, Chris aye remembered that morning with its red sun and the singing of the North Sea over the Howe, that morning he said to father *I'm off to Aberdeen to-day.*

Father said never a word, he went on with his porridge and finished it, he mightn't have heard Will speak, he

lighted his pipe and stepped out of the house, fleet as ever
he went, and began coling the hayfield in front of the
house; Will could see him then and be shamed of himself
and his idle jaunting. But Will wasn't ashamed, he looked
after father with a sneer, *The old fool thinks he can frighten
me still,* and said something else Chris didn't catch, syne
looked at her suddenly, his eyes bright and his lips moving,
Chris—Lord, I wish you were coming as well!

She stared at that amazed, pleased as well. *What, up to
Aberdeen? I'd like it fine but I can't. Hurry and dress else
you'll miss your train.*

So he went and dressed, fell slow-like he seemed at the
business, she thought, the morning and a jaunt in front of
him. She went to the foot of the stairs and cried up to
ask if he were having a sleep before he set out? And instead of answering her back with a jest and a fleer he
laughed a shaky laugh and called out All right, he'd soon
be down. And when he came she saw him in his Sunday
suit, with his new boots shining, he'd on a new hat that
suited him fine. *Well, will I do?* he asked and Chris said
You look fair brave, and he said *Havers!* and picked up
his waterproof, *Well, ta-ta, Chris;* and suddenly turned
round to her and she saw his face red and strange and he
kissed her, they hadn't kissed since they were children lying
in a bed together on a frosty night.

She wiped her mouth, feeling shamed and pleased, and
pushed him away, he tried to speak, and couldn't, and said
Oh, to hell! and turned and ran out of the door, she saw
him go down the Blawearie road fast as he could walk,
looking up at the hills he was with the sun on them and the
slow fog rising off the Howe, jerking his head this way and
that, fast though he walked, but he didn't once look in
father's direction nor father at him. Syne she heard him
whistling bonny and clear, *Up in the Morning,* it was, they'd
used that for a signal in the days when they went the
school-road together, and down on the turnpike edge he
looked round and stood still, and waved his hand, he knew
she was watching. Then a queer kind of pain came into her
throat, her eyes smarted and she told herself she was daft,
Will was only off for the day, he'd be back at night.

But Will didn't come back that night, he didn't come back
the next day, he came back never again to John Guthrie's

Kinraddie. For up in Aberdeen he was wed to his Mollie
Douglas, he'd altered his birth certificate for that; and the
earth might have opened and swallowed them up after that,
it seemed not a soul in Aberdeen had seen them go. So
when father went into Aberdeen on the track of the two
there wasn't a trace to be found, he went to the police and
raged at them, but they only laughed—had he lain with
the quean himself, maybe, that so mad he was with this
son of his?

So father came home, fair bursting with rage, but that
didn't help. And ten days went by before they heard of the
couple again, it came in a letter Will sent to Chris at
Blawearie; and it told that through Mollie's mother, old
Mistress Douglas, Will had got him a job in the Argentine,
cattleman there on a big Polled Angus ranch, and he and
Mollie were sailing from Southampton the day he wrote;
and oh! he wished Chris could have seen them married;
and remember them kindly, they would write again, and
Mrs. Douglas at Drumlithie would aye be a friend to her.

So that was Will's going, it was fair the speak of the
parish a while, folk laughed at father behind his back and
said maybe that would bring down his pride a bit; and they
asked Chae Strachan, that well-travelled childe, where was
this Argentine, was it a fine place, would you say? And
Chae said *Och,* fine, he'd never been actually there, you
might say, but a gey fine place it was, no doubt, a lot of
silver was there; and *Damn't man, young Guthrie's no fool
to spread his bit wings, I was just the same myself.* But most
said it was fair shameful of Will to go off and leave his
father like that, black burning shame he might think of
himself; it just showed you what the world was coming to,
you brought bairns into the world and reared them up and
expected some comfort from them in your old age and
what did you get? Nothing but a lot of damned impudence,
it was all this education and dirt. You might well depend
on it, that coarse young Guthrie brute would never thrive,
there'd be a judgment on him, you'd see, him and his coarse
tink quean.

Judgment or not on Will, it was hardly a week before
his own rage struck down John Guthrie. He'd been setting
up ricks in the cornyard when Chris heard a frightened
squawk break out from the hens. She thought maybe some
strange dog was among them and caught up a spurtle and
ran out to the close and there saw father lying still in his

blood, black blood it looked on his face where he'd fallen and mischieved himself against a stone.

She cried out to him in fright and then cooled herself down, and ran for water from the spring and dipped her hanky in it and bathed his face. He opened his eyes then, dazed-like he seemed, and he said *All right, Jean lass,* and tried to rise, and couldn't. And rage came on him again, he put out his hand and gave Chris a push that near threw her down, he tried and tried to rise up, it was sickening to see. He chaved on the ground as though something tied him there, all one of his sides and legs, and the blood veins stood out blue on his face; and he cursed and said *Get into the house, you white-faced bitch!* he wouldn't have her looking at him. So she watched from behind the door, near sick she felt, it was as though a great frog were squattering there in the stour, and the hens gathered and squawked about him.

And at last he stood up and staggered to a stone, and Chris didn't look more, going on with her work as well as she could with hands that quivered and quivered. But when he came in for supper he looked much as ever, and grumbled at this and that, and ate his egg as though it would do him ill, syne got his gun and went off to the hill as fleet as ever.

He was long up there, Chris went to the window and watched for him, seeing the August late night close in, Cuddiestoun's sheep were baaing high up in the Cuddiestoun moor and a sprig of the honeysuckle that made the Blawearie hedges so bonny through the summer tapped and touched against the window-pane, it was like a slow hand tapping there; and the evening was quiet in the blow of the night-wind, and no sign of father till Chris grew alarmed and nearly went out to look for him. But then she heard his step in the porch, in he came and put down his gun and saw her stand there and cried out *Damn't to hell, is that all you've to do, stand about like a lady?* So you could hardly believe there was much wrong with him then, except ill-nature, he'd plenty of that, you'd no foreseeing that next morning he'd try to get out of bed and lie paralysed.

She wouldn't in a hurry forget the sight of him then, nor the run she had down Blawearie brae till the new Knapp came in sight, brave with its biggings and house. But there at last was Chae Strachan, he was busied letting a strainer into the ground, smoking, the blue smoke of his pipe rose into the air, blue, like a pencil-stroke, a cock was crowing across the Denburn and he didn't hear her cry for a while. But then he did and was quick enough, he ran up to meet her, *What's wrong, Chris lass?* and she told him and he turned and ran down—*Go back to your father and I'll get to the doctor myself and send the wife up to Blawearie.*

And up she came, the fat, fusionless creature, all she could do was to stand and gowk at father, *Mighty me, Mr. Guthrie, this is a sore, sore sight, whatever will you do now, eh?* And father mouthed and mowed at her from the bed as though the first thing he'd be keen on doing was braining her, paralysis or not he'd still plenty of rage. For when the doctor came up at last from Bervie and bustled into the room, peering and poking with the sharp, quick face of him, and his bald head shining, and snapped in his curt-like way, *What's this? what's wrong with you now, Blawearie?* father managed to speak out then right enough—*That's for you to find out, what the hell do you think you're paid for?*

So the doctor grinned behind his hand, *One of you women must help me strip him.* And he looked from Kirsty to Chris and said *You, Chris lass,* and that she did while Mrs. Strachan went down to the kitchen to make him tea and trail around like a clucking hen, God! what might be happening in Peesie's Knapp without her? Chris lost her temper at last, she lost it seldom enough, this time it went with a bang—*I don't know either what's happening in Peesie's Knapp but if you're in such tune about it you'd better go home and find out.* Mrs. Strachan reddened up at that, bubbling like a hubbley-jock, that wasn't the way for a quean to speak to a woman that might well be her mother, she might think shame to curse and swear with her father lying at death's door there. And Chris said she hadn't sworn, but she was over-weary to argie about it, and knew right well that whatever she said now Mistress Strachan would spread a fine story about her.

And sure as death so she did, it was soon all over the Howe that that coarse quean at Blawearie had started to swear at Mistress Strachan while her father was lying near dead in the room above their heads. Only Chae himself didn't believe it, and when he came up to Blawearie next day he whispered to Chris, *Is't true you gave Kirsty a bit*

of a damning yesterday? and when she said she hadn't he
said it was a pity, it was time that somebody did.

So there father lay and had lain ever since, all those five
weeks he'd lain there half-paralysed, with a whistle beside
his bed when he wanted attention, and God! that was often
enough. Creeping to her bed half-dead at night Chris would
find herself thinking a thing that wouldn't bear a rethinking
out here in the sun, with the hum of the heather-bees,
heather-smell in her face, Lord! could she only lie here a
day how she'd sleep and sleep. Fold over her soul and her
heart and put them away with their hours of vexing and
caring, the ploughing was done, she was set to her drilling,
and faith! it was weary work!

She started and sighed and took her hands down from
her face and listened again. Far down in Blawearie there
rose the blast of an angry-blown whistle.

III

SEED-TIME

SHE'D thought, running, stumbling up through the moor, with that livid flush on her cheek, up through the green of the April day with the bushes misted with cobwebs, *I'll never go back, I'll never go back, I'll drown myself in the loch!* Then she stopped, her heart it seemed near to bursting and terribly below it moved something, heavy and slow it had been when she ran out from Blawearie but now it seemed to move and uncoil. Slow, dreadfully, it moved and changed, like a snake she had once seen up on this hill, and the sweat broke out on her forehead. Had anything happened with it? Oh God, there couldn't be anything! If only she hadn't run so, had kept herself quiet, not struck as she'd done, deaved and angry and mad she had been!

Sobbing, she fell to a slow walk then, her hand at her side, and through the gate into the moorland went with slow steps, the livid flush burning still on her cheek, she felt it was branded there. Tears had come in her eyes at last, but she wouldn't have them, shook them off, wouldn't think; and a pheasant flew up beneath her feet, *whirroo!* as she came to the mere of the loch. She bent over there through the rushes, raising her hands to her hair that had come all undone, and parted it from her face and looked down at her face in the water. It rippled a moment, it was brown with detritus, at first she could see nothing of herself but a tremulous amorphousness in the shadow of the rushes; and then the water cleared, she saw the flush below her cheek-bone, her own face, strange to her this last month and stranger now.

Below in Kinraddie the carts were rattling up every farm-road, driving out dung to the turnip-planting, somewhere there was a driller on the go, maybe it was Upperhill's, the clank was a deafening thing. Nine o'clock in the morning and here up on the hill she was, she didn't know where to go or where to turn.

There were the Standing Stones, so seldom she'd seen them this last nine months. Cobwebbed and waiting they stood, she went and leant her cheek against the meikle one, the monster that stood and seemed to peer over the water and blue distances that went up to the Grampians. She leant against it, the bruised cheek she leaned and it was strange and comforting—stranger still when you thought that this old stone circle, more and more as the years went on at Kindaddie, was the only place where ever she could come and stand back a little from the clamour of the days. It seemed to her now that she'd had feint the minute at all to stand and think since that last September day she'd spent up here, caught and clamped and turning she'd been in the wheel and grind of the days since father died.

But at the time a thing fine and shining it had been, she hadn't cared if folk deemed her heartless and godless—fine she thought it, a prayer prayed and answered, him dead at last with his glooming and glaring, his whistlings and whisperings. *Chris, do this,* and *Chris, do that* it went on from morn till night till but hardly she could drag herself to the foot of the stairs to heed him.

But a worse thing came as that slow September dragged to its end, a thing she would never tell to a soul, festering away in a closet of her mind the memory lay, it would die sometime, everything died, love and hate; fainter and fainter it had grown this year till but half she believed it a fancy, those evening fancies when father lay with the red in his face and his eye on her, whispering and whispering at her, the harvest in his blood, whispering her to come to him, they'd done it in Old Testament times, whispering *You're my flesh and blood, I can do with you what I will, come to me, Chris, do you hear?*

And she would hear him and stare at him, whispering

also, *I won't*, they never spoke but in whispers those
evenings. And then she'd slip down from his room, frightened and frightened, quivering below-stairs while her
fancies raced, starting at every creak that went through
the harvest stillness of Blawearie house, seeing father somehow struggling from his bed, like a great frog struggling,
squattering across the floor, thump, thump on the stairs,
coming down on her while she slept, that madness and
tenderness there in his eyes.

She took to locking her door because of that wild fear.
The morning of the day she woke to find him dead she
leaned out from her bedroom window and heard Long Rob
of the Mill, far ayont the parks of Peesie's Knapp, out even
so early, hard at work with his chaving and singing, singing
Ladies of Spain with a throat as young and clear as a boy's.
She had slept but little that night, because of the fear upon
her and the tiredness, but that singing was sweet to hear,
sweet and heart-breaking, as though the world outside Blawearie were singing to her, telling her this thing in the
dark, still house could never go on, no more than a chance
and an accident it was in the wind-loved world of men.

She got into her clothes then, clearer-headed, and slipped
down to the kitchen and put on the kettle and milked the
kye and then made breakfast. Below the windows the parks
stood cut and stooked and trim, Ellison and Chae and Long
Rob had done that, good neighbours John Guthrie had, had
he never aught else. There came no movement from father's
room, he was sleeping long, and setting the tray with porridge and milk she hoped he'd have nothing to say, just
glower and eat, she'd slip away then.

So she went up the stair and into his room without
knocking, he hated knocking and all such gentry-like notions, she put down the tray and saw he was dead. For a
moment she looked and then turned to the curtains and
drew them, and took the tray in her hand again, no sense
in leaving it there, and went down and ate a good breakfast,
slowly and enjoyingly she ate and felt quiet and happy,
even though she fell fast asleep in her chair and awoke to
find it gone nine. She lay and looked at her outspread arms
a while, dimpled and brown, soft-skinned with the play of
muscles below them. Sleep? She could sleep as she chose
now, often and long.

Then she tidied the kitchen and found a spare sheet and
went out to the hedge above the road and spread the sheet

there, the sign she'd arranged with Chae should she need
him. In an hour or so, out in his parks he saw it and
came hurrying up to Blawearie, crying to her halfway up
Chris, lass, what's wrong? Then only she realized she hadn't
yet spoken that day to a soul, wondered if her voice would
shake and break, it didn't, was ringing and clear as a bell
crying down to Chae, *My father's dead.*

It was fair a speak in Kinraddie, her coolness, she knew
that well but she didn't care, she was free at last. And
when Mistress Munro, her that came to wash down the
corpse, poked out her futret face and said, *A body would
hardly think to look at you that your father was new dead*,
Chris looked at the dark, coarse creature and saw her so
clearly as she'd never done before, she'd never had time to
look at a soul through her own eyes before, Chris-come-
here and Chris-go-there. Not a pringle of anger she felt,
just smiled and said *Wouldn't you, now, Mistress Munro?*
and watched her at work and watched her go, not caring
a fig what she thought and did. Then she roused herself
for a while, free yet she could hardly be for a day or so,
and got ready the big room for Auntie Janet and her man
to sleep in, medals and all, when they came down to the
funeral.

Down the next day they came, the two of them, Auntie
as cheery as ever, Uncle as fat, he'd another bit medal
stuck on his chain; and when they saw she wasn't sniftering
or weeping they put off the long decent faces they'd set for
her sight, and told her the news, Dod and Alec did fine and
had sent their love. And Auntie said they must sell up the
things at Blawearie and Chris come and bide with them in
the North, some brave bit farmer would soon marry her
there.

And Chris said neither yea nor nay, but smiled at them,
biding her time, waiting till she found if a will had been left
by father. Chae Strachan and old Sinclair of Netherhill saw
to the funeral, old Sinclair moving so slow up the road,
you'd half think he'd stop and take root, clean agony it was
to watch him, and his face so pitted and old, father had
been young by the like of him. And Mr. Gibbon came over
to see her, he'd been drinking a fell lot of late, folk said,
maybe that accounted for the fact that as he crossed the
twilit brae he was singing out loud to himself, Auntie heard
the singing and ran up and out and hid in the lithe of a
stack to try and make out what he sang. But he left off

then and left her fair vexed, she said later she could have
sworn it was a song they sang in the bothies about the bedding of a lad and a lass.

But Chris didn't care, keeping that secret resolve she'd
made warm and clean and unsoiled in her heart, taking it
out only alone to look at it, that old-time dream of hers.
She'd never looked at herself so often or so long as now she
did, the secret shining deep in her eyes, she saw her face
thinner and finer than of yore, no yokel face it seemed.
So she cared nothing for Mr. Gibbon and his singing, the
great curly brute and his breath that smelt so bad, he went
up with her to father's room where father lay in his coffin,
in a fine white shirt and a tie, his beard combed out and
decent and jutting up, you'd say in a minute he'd raise those
dead eyelids and whisper at you.

Down on his knees the minister went, the great curly
bull, and began to pray, Chris hesitated a minute and looked
at the floor, and then, canny-like, when he wasn't seeing her,
dusted a patch and herself knelt down. But she didn't heed
a word he was saying, honeysuckle smell was drifting in
on the air from the night, up on the hills the dog of some
ploughman out poaching was barking and barking itself to
a fair hysteria following the white blink of some rabbit's
tail, in the closing dark she could see across the brae's
shoulder the red light of Kinraddie House shine like a quiet
star. So the curly bull prayed and boomed beside her, it
was what he was paid for, she neither listened nor cared.

And that brought the funeral, it was raining early in the
dawn when they woke, a fine drizzle that seeped and seeped
from the sky, so soft and fine you'd think it snow without
whiteness; there was no sun at all at first but it came up at
last, a red ball, and hung there so till ten o'clock brought
up the first of the funeral folk, and that was Chae, and
his father-in-law, syne Ellison and Maitland in a gig they
loosed in the corn-yard, setting the sholtie to graze. And
Ellison cried out, but low and decent, *I'll leave him here,
me dear, sure he'll be all right, won't he?* and Chris smiled
and said *Fine, Mr. E'llison,* and he goggled his eyes, Irish
as ever, you could never change Erbert Ellison, not even
for the worse, folk said.

Next there came a whole drove of folk, the factor, the
minister, Cuddiestoun with his ill-marled face like a potato-
park dug in coarse weather, but a fine white front, new-
starched, to cover his working sark, and cuffs that fair

chafed his meikle red hands, right decent, and he'd on fine
yellow boots on his meikle feet. Rob of the Mill and Alec
Mutch came next, you could hear their tongues from the
foot of Blawearie brae, folk were affronted and went out
and cried *Wheest-wheest!* down to them, and Rob called
back *What is't?* and faith! it would have been better if they'd
been left alone, what with the wheesting and whispering
that rose.

But they were real good, Rob bringing a bottle of
whisky, Glenlivet it was, and Alec a half-bottle, they
whisked them over to Uncle Tam when nobody looked; or
anyway not a body but looked the other way and spoke,
canny-like, of the weather. The kitchen was fair crowded,
so was the room, like a threshing-day, folk sat and each had
a dram, Mr. Gibbon said *Spirits? Yes, thank you, I'll have
a drop,* there'd have been barely enough to go round but
for Rob and Alec. Then they heard another gig come up the
hill, it was Gordon's from Upperhill, him and his foreman.
Uncle Tam winked at the whisky. *You'll have a dram,
Upperhill, you and your man?* but Mr. Gordon said, sniffy-
like, *I hardly think it shows respect and Ewan's tee-tee as
well.*

Long Rob of the Mill sat next the door, he winked at
Chris and then at Ewan Tavendale, Ewan turned fair red
and said nothing. So he hadn't a dram, he'd have liked
one fine, Chris guessed, and felt mean and pleased and shy,
and then gave herself a shake inside, what did it matter to
her? Then the minister looked at his watch and the undertaker came in about, and then last of all, they hadn't expected the poor old stock, there was Pooty on the doorstep,
he'd on a clean collar and shirt and an old hat, green but
well-brushed; and when Uncle whispered if he'd have a
dram he said *Och, ay, it's the custom, isn't it?* and had
two.

The undertaker had gone up by then, Uncle with him,
folk followed them one by one and came down, syne Auntie
beckoned Chris to the neuk of the stair and said *Would you
like to see him before he's screwed down?*

Uncle Tam and Long Rob of the Mill were there and as
Chris went in Long Rob said *Well, well, good-bye, Blawearie man,* and shook father's hand, his eyes looked queer
when he turned away, he said *He was a fine neighbour* and
went out and closed the door. Chris stood and looked at
her father, seeing him so plain as never in life she'd seen

him, he'd been over-restless for that and quick enough he'd have raged at you had you glowered at his face like this.

Still enough now, never-moving there in the coffin, he seemed to have changed already since he died, the face sunk in, it wasn't John Guthrie and yet it was. Uncle whispered behind her, him and the undertaker, and then Auntie was beside her. *They're to screw it down now, kiss your father, Chris.* But she shook her head, she couldn't do that, the room was still as they looked at her, for a moment she felt almost sick again as in those evening hours when *that* in the coffin had lain and whispered that she should lie with it. Then she just said *Good-bye, father,* and turned from him and went down to her own room and put on her coat and hat, it wasn't decent for a quean to go to a funeral, folk said, but in Blawearie's case there was no son or brother to see him into the kirkyard.

Chae and Long Rob and Ellison and Gordon carried the coffin down to the stair-foot, and settled it on their shoulders there, and went slow with it out through the front door then; and the rain held off a little, wind blowing in their faces, though, as they held down the hill. Behind walked the Reverend Gibbon, bare-headed, all the folk were bare-headed but Chris, Long Rob and Chae stepping easily and cannily, Ellison as well, but Gordon quivering at his coffin corner, he'd have done better with a dram to steady him up. But Chris walked free and uncaring, soon as the burial was over she'd be free as never in her life she'd been, she lifted her face to the blow of the wet September wind and the world that was free to her.

Then it was that she saw Ewan Tavendale walked beside her, he glanced down just then and straight and fair up into his eyes she looked, she nearly stumbled in the slow walk because of that looking. They came to the turnpike then, there Ewan took Gordon's corner and Alec Mutch Ellison's, and these two fell back beside the minister, but Chae and Long Rob shook their heads when others offered to change with them, they'd manage fine.

The rain still held off, presently the wind soughing down the Howe died away and a little peek of sun came through, not down the Denburn it came but high up in the hill peaks, the lost, coarse ground where never a soul lived or passed but some shepherd or gillie, you could see them far off, lone and lonesome there on a still, clear day. Maybe so the dead walked in a still clear, deserted land, the coarse lands of death where only the chance wanderer showed his face, Chris thought, and the dead lapwings wheeled and cried against another sun. Then she ceased from that, startled out a moment from the calm that had come to her with her father's dying—daft to dream these things now when she planned so much. Step, step, steadily and cannily went Long Rob and Chae, Chae getting bald and sandy in the crown, but Rob still with the corn hair clustered thick and the great moustaches swinging from his cheeks as they turned up the road that led to the kirkyard.

Then the sun went again, it was eleven o'clock perhaps, and Chris raised her eyes and saw through the trees the blinded windows of the Mains, the curtains were all drawn, decent-like, in respect for the funeral; and she felt a queer, sick thrill just below her left breast, not ill or sick, but just like a starting of the blood there, as though she'd leant on that place too long, and it had grown numb. It was dark under the yews, they dripped on the coffin and Long Rob, then there came a pattering as they passed by slow beneath, and Chris saw the long, oval leaves suddenly begin to quiver, it was as though a hand shook them, and through the leaves was the sky, it had blackened over and the rain was coming driving in a sheet down the brae from the Grampian haughs. It came and whipped the wet skirts about her legs, she saw Long Rob and Chae and Ewan stagger and then stand leaning against the drift, and then go on, not a soul put on his hat, there'd be bad colds by night and ill-tunes over this funeral yet.

That wasn't decent to think, but what did it matter to her? She wished she were back in Blawearie, and hoped the minister would not be over long-winded when he said his say. There was the grave-digger, a man from the Mains, a big scrawny childe who lived ill with his wife, folk said, he had his coat collar up and came out below the eaves of the kirk and motioned them along a path. And ben it they went, then Chris saw the grave, red clay and bright it was, not as she'd expected his grave somehow to be, they weren't burying him in mother's grave. For that land was over-crowded, folk said that every time the grave-digger stuck his bit spade in the ground some bone or another from the dead of olden time would come spattering out, fair scun-nering you. But this was an old enough bit as well, right opposite rose the stone with the cross-bones, maybe all the dead bodies had long mouldered away into red clay here, clay themselves, and folk were glad they left the earth free for new-comers.

Uncle had come to her elbow then and he stood with her, the others stood back, it was strange and silent but for the soft patter of the rain on the yews and the Reverend Gibbon shielding his Bible away from the wet drive of it, beginning to read. And Chris listened, her head bent against the rain's whisper, to the words that promised Resurrection and Life through Jesus Christ our Lord, who had died long syne in Palestine and had risen on the third day and would take from that thing that had been John Guthrie quick, and was now John Guthrie dead, the quickness and give it habitation again.

And Chris thought of her dream looking up at the coarse lands of the hills and thinking of the lands of death, was that where Christ would meet with father? Unco and strange to think, standing here in the rain and listening to that voice, that father himself was there in that dark box heaped with the little flowers that folk had sent, father whom they were to leave here happed in red clay, alone in darkness and earth when the night came down. Surely he'd be back waiting her up in Blawearie, she'd hear his sharp, vexed voice and see him come fleetly out of the house, that red beard of his cocked as ever at the world he'd fought so dourly and well——

Somebody chaved at her hand then, it was the grave-digger, he was gentle and strangely kind, and she looked down and couldn't see, for now she was crying, she hadn't thought she would ever cry for father, but she hadn't known, she hadn't known this thing that was happening to him! She found herself praying then, blind with tears in the rain, lowering the cord with the hand of the grave-digger over hers, the coffin dirling below the spears of the rain. *Father, father, I didn't know! Oh father, I didn't KNOW!*

She hadn't known, she'd been dazed and daft with her planning, her days could never be aught without father; and she minded then, wildly, in a long, broken flash of re-membrance, all the fine things of him that the years had hidden from their sight, the fleetness of him and his justice, and the fight unwearying he'd fought with the land and its masters to have them all clad and fed and respectable. he'd never rested working and chaving for them, only God had beaten him in the end.

And she minded the long roads he'd tramped to the kirk with her when she was young, how he'd smiled at her and called her his lass in days before the world's fight and the fight of his own flesh grew over-bitter, and poisoned his love to hate. *Oh father, I didn't know!* she prayed again, and then that was over, she was in the drive of the rain, hard and tearless, the grave-digger was pointing to the ground and she picked up a handful of soft, wet earth, and heard the Reverend Gibbon's voice drone out *Dust to dust, ashes to ashes,* and leant over the grave and dropped the wet earth; and then the grave-digger was throwing in the turf, the coffin rang as though it were hollow, she stared at it till Uncle had her by the elbow, speaking to her, and so was the Reverend Gibbon but she couldn't hear them at first: and folk were to say she must have been real fond of her father after all, the best of a coarse bit family in the end.

And then she was walking back through the kirkyard and the folk at the gate were stopping to shake her hand, Long Rob and Chae to say they'd aye help her, and Ellison, kind and solemn and Irish, and old Sinclair dripping in the rain, he should never have been out in a day like this. The last was Ewan Tavendale, he said *Ta-ta, Chris,* his hand was wet meeting hers as her own hand was, but he put up his left hand as well as his right and held both of hers a minute; and he didn't look ashamed and shy any more, but as though he was so sorry he'd help her in any way, not only the ways he could.

That was the last of them she saw and the end of father's funeral. Back in Blawearie Auntie Janet made her strip from her clothes and get into bed, *God be here, it's you that'll be next in your grave!* she cried. And Chris slept throughout the remainder of that day, undreaming, she didn't wake till late in the night, Blawearie listening and hearkening about her. And then she was afraid, awfully afraid, sitting up in bed and hearkening to that Something that walked the house with sharp, quick footsteps, running so fleetly up the stairs, impatient and unresting, a shadow with footfalls that were shadows; and into the night and far towards the dawn it roamed the house of Blawearie till the cocks were crowing and Uncle and Auntie moving, and

Chris didn't feel afraid at all by then, only lay and wept softly for the father she'd never helped and forgot to love.

And the next forenoon the lawyer man came down from Stonehaven, it was Peter Semple, folk called him Simple Simon but swore that he was a swick. Father had trusted him, though, and faith! you'd be fell straight in your gait ere John Guthrie trusted you. Not that he'd listened to advice, father, he'd directed a will be made and the things to be set in that will; and when Mr. Semple had said he was being fell sore on some of his family father had told him to mind his own business, and that was a clerk's.

So Mr. Semple drew up the will, it had been just after Will went off to the Argentine, and father had signed it; and now the Blawearie folk sat down in the parlour, with whisky and biscuits for Mr. Semple, to hear it read. It was short and plain as you please, Chris watched the face of her uncle as the lawyer read and saw it go white in the gills, he'd expected something far different from that. And the will told that John Guthrie left all his possessions, in silver and belongings, to his daughter Christine, to be hers without let or condition, Mr. Semple her guardian in such law matters as needed one, but Chris to control the goods and gear as she pleased. And folk were to say, soon as Kinraddie heard of the will, and faith! they seemed to have heard it all before it was well out of the envelope, that it was an unco will, old Guthrie had been fair spiteful to his sons, maybe Will would dispute his sister's tocher.

The money was over three hundred pounds in the bank, it was hard to believe that father could have saved all that. But he had; and Chris sat and stared at the lawyer, hearing him explain and explain this, that, and the next, in the way of lawyers: they presume you're a fool and double their fees. Three hundred pounds! And now she could do as she'd planned, she'd go up to the College again and pass her exams and go on to Aberdeen and get her degrees, come out as a teacher and finish with the filthy soss of a farm. She'd sell up the gear of Blawearie, the lease was dead, it had died with father, oh! she was free and free to do as she liked and dream as she liked at last!

And it was pity now that she'd all she wanted she felt no longer that fine thrill that had been with her while she made her secret plans. It was as though she'd lost it down in Kinraddie kirkyard; and she sat and stared so still and white at the lawyer man that he closed up his case with a snap. *So think it well over, Christine,* he said and she roused and said *Oh, I'll do that;* and off he went, Uncle Tam drew a long, deep breath, as though fair near choked he'd been *Not a word of his two poor, motherless boys!*

It seemed he'd expected Alec and Dod would be left their share, maybe that was why he'd been so eager to adopt them the year before. But Auntie cried *For shame, Tam, how are they motherless now that I've got them? And you'll come up and live with us when you've sold Bla-wearie's furnishings, Chris?* And her voice was kind but her eyes were keen, Chris looked at her with her own eyes hard, *Ay, maybe,* and got up and slipped from the room, *I'll go down and bring home the kye.*

And out she went, though it wasn't near kye-time yet, and wandered away over the fields; it was a cold and lour-ing day, the sound of the sea came plain to her, as though heard in a shell, Kinraddie wilted under the greyness. In the ley field old Bod stood with his tail to the wind, his hair ruffled up by the wind, his head bent away from the smore of it. He heard her pass and gave a bit neigh, but he didn't try to follow her, poor brute, he'd soon be over old for work. The wet fields squelched below her feet, oozing up their smell of red clay from under the sodden grasses, and up in the hills she saw the trail of the mist, great sailing shapes of it, going south on the wind into Forfar, past Laurencekirk they would sail, down the wide Howe with its sheltered glens and its late, drenched harvests, past Brechin smoking against its hill, with its ancient tower that the Pictish folk had reared, out of the Mearns, sailing and passing, sailing and passing, she minded Greek words of forgotten lessons, Greek to come *Nothing endures.*

And then a queer thought came to her there in the drooked fields, that nothing endured at all, nothing but the land she passed across, tossed and turned and perpetually changed below the hands of the crofter folk since the oldest of them had set the Standing Stones by the loch of Bla-wearie and climbed there on their holy days and saw their terraced crops ride brave in the wind and sun. Sea and sky and the folk who wrote and fought and were learnéd, teaching and saying and praying, they lasted but as a breath, a mist of fog in the hills, but the land was forever, it moved and changed below you, but was forever, you were close to it and it to you, not at a bleak remove it held you and hurted you. And she had thought to leave it all!

She walked weeping then, stricken and frightened because of that knowledge that had come on her, she could never leave it, this life of toiling days and the needs of beasts and the smoke of wood fires and the air that stung your throat so acrid, Autumn and Spring, she was bound and held as though they had prisoned her here. And her fine bit plannings!—they'd been just the dreamings of a child over toys it lacked, toys that would never content it when it heard the smore of a storm or the cry of sheep on the moors or smelt the pringling smell of a new-ploughed park under the drive of a coulter. She could no more teach a school than fly, night and day she'd want to be back, for all the fine clothes and gear she might get and hold, the books and the light and learning.

The kye were in sight then, they stood in the lithe of the freestone dyke that ebbed and flowed over the shoulder of the long ley field, and they hugged to it close from the drive of the wind, not heeding her as she came among them, the smell of their bodies foul in her face—foul and known and enduring as the land itself. Oh, she hated and loved in a breath! Even her love might hardly endure, but beside it the hate was no more than the whimpering and fear of a child that cowered from the wind in the lithe of its mother's skirts.

And again that night she hardly slept, thinking and thinking till her head ached, the house quiet enough now, without fairlies treading the stairs, she felt cool and calm, if only she could sleep. But by morning she knew she couldn't go on with Uncle and Auntie beside her, they smothered her over with their years and their canny supposings. Quick after breakfast she dressed and came down and Auntie cried out, real sharp-like, *Mighty be here, Chris, where are you going?* as though she owned Blawearie stick and stone, hoof and hide. And Chris looked at her coolly, *I'm away to Stonehaven to see Mr. Semple, can I bring you anything?*

Uncle Tam rose up from the table then, goggling, with his medals clinking, *Away to Stonehive? What are you jaunting there for? I'll transact any business you have.* Their faces reddened up with rage, she saw plain as daylight how near it lay, dependence on them, she felt herself go white as she looked at them. *I'll transact my own busi-*

ness fine, she said hardly, and called *Ta-ta* from the door
and heard no answer and held down the Blawearie road
and ran over the parks to the station, and caught the early
scholar's train that went to Stonehaven Academy.

It was crowded fell close, there were three-four scholars
in the carriage she got in to, she didn't know any, they
were learning French verbs. And she'd wanted to go back
to things as silly!

They were past Drumlithie and the Carmont then, you
could smell the woods of Dunnottar and look out at them
from the window, girdling Stonehaven down to its bay,
shining and white, the sun was out on the woods and the
train like a weasel slipped through the wet smell of them.
And there was Stonehaven itself, the home of the poverty
toffs, folk said, where you might live in sin as much as
you pleased but were damned to hell if you hadn't a white
sark. She'd heard Chae Strachan say that, but it wasn't
all true, there were fell poor folk in Stonehaven as well as
the come-ups; and douce folk that were neither poor nor
proud and had never a say when Stonehaven boomed of its
braveness. And that it did fair often, the Mearns' capital,
awful proud of its sarks but not of its slums and it thought
itself real genteel, and a fine seafront it had that the English came to in summer—daft, as usual, folk said, hadn't
they a sea in England?

Because it was early in the day and the lawyer's office
still shut Chris loitered on the road in the tail of the hasting
scholars, the little things they were, all legs and long boots,
funny how they tried to speak English one to the other,
looking sideways as they cried the words to see if folk
thought them gentry. Had Marget and she been daft as
that?

But the sun was out now on the long Stonehaven streets
and Chris went past the Academy down to the market, still
at that hour with just a stray cat or so on the sniff around,
genteel and toff-like, Stonehaven cats. Down through a
lane she caught a glimmer of the North Sea then or maybe
it was the sunlight against the sky, but the smell of the sea
came up. And she still had plenty of time.

So she went down to the shore, the tide was out, thundering among the rocks, not a soul on the beach but herself,
gulls flying and crying, the sun strong and warm. She sat
on a seat in the glow of it and shut her eyes and was happy.
Below her feet the ground drummed and trembled with

reverberations from that far-off siege of the rocks that the sea was making out there by the point of the bay, it was strange to feel it and be of it, maybe folk there were who felt for the sea as last night she had felt in the rain-drenched fields of Kinraddie. But to her it seemed restless, awaiting and abiding nowhither, not fine like the glens that nestled and listened high up the coarse country, or the parks sun-heavy with clover that waited your feet at evening.

She fell asleep then, she slept there two hours in the sun and woke feeling fresher than she'd done since father's funeral. So hungry also she felt she couldn't wait the ending of the business she'd come on but went into a tea-house up in the square, two women kept it, old bodies they were that moved backward and forward the room, slow and rheumatic. One looked like the cats she'd seen in the square that morning, sleeked and stroked, the other was thin as a lathe, their tea-room looked scrubbed and clean and their tea had a taste to match. They were sharp and stroked and genteel, Chris thought for the first time then in her life how awful it would be to grow old like them, old maids without men, without ever having lain with a man, or had him kiss you and hold you, and be with you, and have children of his, or the arm of a man when you needed it, kind and steadfast and strong. If she'd lived her plan to train as a teacher she'd have grown like them.

She might grow so still! she thought, and daft-like suddenly felt quite feared, she paid for her tea in a hurry and went out to the square again, thinking of herself as an old maid, it wouldn't bear thinking about. So she hurried to the office of Simple Simon and a little clerk asked her business, perky-like, and she looked at him coolly and said her business was Mr. Semple's. And then she minded the old maids, was she herself one by nature? And in a cold fear she smiled at the clerk, desperately, with her lips and eyes, it was fine, the boy smiled also and blushed and thawed, and said *Sit down, this is fine and comfortable;* and pulled out a padded chair for her; and down she sat, light-hearted again. Then the clerk came back and led her through a passage to Semple's room, he looked busy enough, with a telephone beside him and heaps of papers, and rows of little black boxes round the shelves. Then he rose and shook hands, *Well, well, it's Miss Guthrie come up; you've been thinking of the will, no doubt?*

She told him, Yes, just that; and she was going to live on

at Blawearie a while, not roup the gear out at once, could he see to that with the factor?

He stared at her with his mouth fallen open, *But you can't live there alone!*

She told him she'd no such intention, couldn't he get her some woman come live with her, some old bit body who'd be glad of a home?

He said *Oh, God, there are plenty of them!* and began to chew at his mouser.

She told him it mightn't be for more than a month or so, till she'd made up her mind, just.

He said absent-like, *Just? Hell, a woman's mind just!* and then pulled himself up right sudden as she looked at him hardly and cool. Then he argued a bit, but Chris hardly listened, father's will had said she could do what she liked.

And presently, seeing she cared not a fig for him, Semple gave in and said he'd settle up with the factor, and he knew an old widow body, Melon, he'd send down to Blawearie the morn.

So Chris said *Thank you, good-bye,* and went out from the office, cool as she'd come, the sun was a fell blaze then and the streets chock-a-block with sheep, great droves of them, driven in to the weekly mart. Collies were running hither and yon, silent and cocked of ear, clean and quick as you'd wish, paying heed to none but shepherd and sheep. Drovers and beasts, they took a good look at Chris both, as she stood in her black clothes watching them; and just as she wondered what she'd do next, walk down to the sea and sit on a bench till it neared to dinnertime in the hotels, or go up to the station and take the 11.0, a gig going by slowed down of a sudden, a man jumped down and cried back to the driver.

The man that had jumped was the foreman at Upperhill, Ewan Tavendale, the driver old Gordon himself, he looked in a rage about something. And he cried *Mind the time then!* and gave Chris a sore glower and drove spanking away.

And then Ewan had crossed the pavement and was standing in front of her, he lifted his cap and said, shy-like, *Hello!* Chris said *Hello,* and they looked at each other, he was blushing, she minded the last time, she didn't like him half as she'd done at the funeral. He said *Are you in for the day?* and she mocked him, not knowing why she did that, it wasn't decent and father new dead, *Och ay, just that.*

He blushed some more, she felt cool and queerly giddy in
a breath, looking at the fool of a lad, folk were glowering
at them both they were later to learn, not Gordon only but
Ellison: and back the two of them went to Kinraddie and
told every soul it was a sore shame there wasn't somebody
about to heed to the Guthrie girl from the hands of that
coarse tink brute, Ewan Tavendale.

But they hadn't known that and mightn't have cared,
suddenly Chris felt herself hungry again, happy as well,
not caring about Ewan himself but not wanting either he
should leave her and go on to the mart. She said *I'm going
up to the Inn for dinner,* and he looked at her, still shy, but
with a kind of smoulder in the shyness, his eyes like the
smoulder of a burning whin—*Maybe we can eat together?*
And she said, as he turned by her side, *Oh, maybe. But
what will Mr. Gordon do?* And Ewan said he could dance
a jig on the head of the mart with sheer rage, for all he
cared.

So in they went to old Mother White's, not that they
saw the old body herself; and there was a fine room to eat
in, with white cloths set, and a canary that sang above them,
the windows fast closed to the dust and dirt. And they'd
broth, it was good, and the oat-cakes better; and then boiled
beef and potatoes and turnip; and then rice pudding with
prunes; and then some tea, Ewan found his tongue as they
drank the tea and said to-day was his holiday, for he'd
worked all the last Sunday on a job libbing lambs. And
Chris said, it was out of her mouth before she thought,
So you're in no hurry to be back? and Ewan leaned across
the table, the smoulder near kindled to a fire, *Not unless
you should be? What train are you taking up to Kinraddie?*

And then how it all came about, their planning to spend
the day together and their walk to Dunnottar, Chris never
knew, maybe neither did Ewan. But half an hour later,
Stonehaven a blinding white glimmer behind, Dunnottar
in front, they were climbing down the path that led to the
island. The air was blind with the splash of the incoming
tide above you the rock rose sheer as the path wound down-
wards sheer; and high up, crowning the rock were the
ruins of the castle walls, splashed with sunlight and the
droppings of sea-birds. Gulls there were everywhere, Chris
was deafened in the clamour of the brutes, but quiet enough
in the castle it proved, not a soul seemed visiting there but
themselves.

They paid their shillings and the old man came with them from room to room, a scunner to Ewan, Chris guessed, for his eyes kept wandering, wearied, to her from this ruin and that. In walls little slits rose up, through these it was that in olden times the garrisons had shot their arrows at besiegers; and down below, in the dungeons, were the mouldering clefts where a prisoner's hands were nailed while they put him to torment. There the Covenanting folk had screamed and died while the gentry dined and danced in their lithe, warm halls, Chris stared at the places, sick and angry and sad for those folk she could never help now, that hatred of rulers and gentry a flame in her heart, John Guthrie's hate. Her folk and his they had been, those whose names stand graved in tragedy:

HERE : LYES : IOHN : STOT : IAMES : ATCHI
SON : IAMES : RUSSELL : & WILLIAM : BRO
UN : AND : ONE : WHOSE : NAME : WEE :
HAVE : NOT : GOTTEN : AND : TWO :
WOMEN : WHOSE : NAMES : ALSO : WEE :
KNOW : NOT : AND : TWO : WHO : PERISHED :
COMEING : DOUNE : THE : ROCK : ONE :
WHOSE : NAME : WAS : IAMES : WATSON
THE : OTHER : NOT : KNOWN : WHO : ALL :
DIED : PRISONERS : IN : DUNNOTTAR :
CASTLE : ANNO :   1685 : FOR : THEIR :
ADHERENCE : TO : THE : WORD : OF : GOD :
AND : SCOTLANDS : COVENANTED : WORK :
OF : REFORMATION :
                              REV : II CH : 12 VERSE

But Ewan whispered, *Oh, let's get out of this,* though it was he himself that had planned they come to Dunnottar. So out in the sun, at the shelving entrance, they stood awhile in the cry of the gulls; and then Ewan said *Come down to the sea: I know a nook.*

And they climbed down and then up again, along the cliff-edge, it made you dizzy to look over and down at the incoming wash of froth, and sometimes, far under their feet, there rose a loud *boom!* like a gun going off. Ewan said that the rocks were sometimes hollow and the water ran far below the fields, so that ploughmen ploughed above the sea and in stormy weather they'd sometimes see their furrows quiver from that storm that raged under their feet.

So they came to a crumbling path, it seemed to fall sheer away, a seagull sailed up to meet them, and Ewan with his feet already out of sight turned back and asked, *You'll not be dizzy?* And Chris shook her head and followed him, it seemed to her between sea and sky, down and down, and then Ewan was gripping her ankle, she swung almost loose for a moment, looking down in his face, it was white and strained, then her foot and hand caught again, Ewan called that it wasn't much further; and they got to the bottom and sat and looked at each other on a ledge of sand.

The sun poured in there, the tide whispered and splashed and threw out its hands at them on the sand, but it didn't come further up. And Chris saw that the place was closed in, you couldn't see a thing of the coast but the rocks over-hanging, and only a segment of the sea itself a mile or so out a boat had tacked, it flashed its wings like a wheeling gull; and Ewan was sitting beside her, peeling an orange.

They ate it together and Chris took off her hat, she felt hot and uncouth in her sad black clothes. And suddenly, for no reason, she thought of a time, years before, when she'd been trampling blankets for mother a fine summer day in May, and had taken off her skirts and her mother had come out and laughed at her, *You'd make a fine lad!* It was as though she heard mother speak, she looked up and around, daftly, dazed-like a moment, but there was not a soul near but Ewan Tavendale lying on an elbow, looking at the sea, the sun in his face, young and smooth with its smouldering eyes. And she found she didn't mislike him any longer, she felt queer and strange to him, not feared, but as though he was to say something in a moment that she knew she couldn't answer. And then he said it, blushing, but his smouldering eyes didn't waver, *Chris, do you like me a bit?*

Can't thole you at all, that's why we're out lazing in this place together.

But a nervousness came on her, not that she feared him, she'd known all along she was safe with Ewan as Mollie with Will in those long-gone days of the court at Drum-lithie. Only, it was as though her blood ran so clear and with such a fine, sweet song in her veins she must hold her breath and hark to it; and for the first time she knew the strange thing her hand was, held there dripping sand, it seemed as though all her body sat a little apart from herself, and she looked at it, wondering. So it was that she

knew she liked him, loved him as they said in the soppy
English books, you were shamed and a fool to say that in
Scotland. Ewan Tavendale—that it should be him! And then
she minded something, it didn't matter at all, but she wanted
to know for all that. *Ewan, was it true that story they told
about you and old Sarah Sinclair?*

It was as though she had belted him in the face. He
went white then, funnily white leaving brown the red tan
in the little creases of his face that the coarse field weather
had made; and he sat up, angrily, and glowered at her, the
great black cat, so sleeked and quick to anger. And the
feeling she'd had for him, that dizziness that made earth
and sea and her heart so light, quite went from her. She
said *Oh, I don't want to know*, and began to hum to herself; and then Ewan reached out his hand and gripped her
arm, it hurt, he said *Damn well listen now that you've
asked me.* And it was awful, awful and terrible, she didn't
want to listen to him, covering her face with her hands, he
went on and on and then stopped at last—*Now you're
frightened, frightened that a woman should feel like that,
maybe some day you'll feel it yourself.*

She jumped to her feet then, angry as him, forgetting to
feel ashamed. *Maybe I will, but when I do I'll get a better
man than you to serve me!* And before he could answer
that she had caught up her hat and was up the cliff path
so quick she didn't know how she did it, her fingers and
feet were nimble and sure, she heard Ewan cry below her
and paid no need. He was barely half-way up when she
reached the top and looked down, and then the rage quite
went from her, she leaned over the edge instead, holding
down her hand, and he caught it and smiled, and they stood
and panted and smiled one at the other, fools again as
they'd been in the market-square of Stonehaven.

But suddenly Ewan whipped out his watch, *God, it must
be getting fell late,* and as he said it the sunshine went.
Chris raised her head and saw why, they'd been sitting
down there in the last of it, the gloaming was down on the
countryside and the noise of the gulls rising up through
the mirk. Ewan caught her hand and they ran by the cliff-
edge of the gloaming-stilled parks, there were great dap-
pled kye that stopped their grazing to look; and up in front,
dark and uncanny, they saw Dunnottar rise on its rock.
And then they reached the main road and slowed down,
but she still left her hand in Ewan's.

And in Stonehaven they caught by the skin of the teeth the six o'clock train, the mart was long over and folk gone home. In the carriage were only themselves all the way to Kinraddie, Ewan sat on the opposite seat, she liked him sit there, liked him not wanting to hold her hand, she'd have hated him touch her now. And they didn't say a word till they neared Kinraddie, and then he said *Chrissie! Tired?* and she said *Losh, no, and my name's Chris, Ewan.* Then she saw him blush again in the flicker of the gaslight; and a strange, sweet surge of pity came on her, she leant over and patted his knee, he was only a boy in spite of his Sarah Sinclair.

But she thought of Sarah all the same that night, lying listening in bed to the coming of the rain again, a wet winter it promised the Howe. So women were like that when they didn't have the men they wanted?—many of them maybe like that, hiding it away even from themselves till a summer of heat drove on here and there to such acts as affronted Kinraddie. But she didn't feel affronted, it was maybe because she was over young, had read over many of the books, had been the English Chris as well as this one that lay thinking of Ewan; and the old ways of sinning and winning, having your own pleasure and standing affronted at other folk having theirs, seemed often daft to her. Sarah Sinclair might well have obliged her and met with some other lad than Ewan that August night; but then she wasn't to know Chris Guthrie would ever lie and think of him in her bed, hearing the batter of the rain against her window and the swish of the great Blawearie trees.

It was then, in a lull of the swishing, she heard the great crack of thunder that opened the worst storm that had struck the Howe in years. It was far up, she thought, and yet so close Blawearie's stones seemed falling about her ears, she half-scrambled erect. Outside the night flashed, flashed and flashed, she saw Kinraddie lighted up and fearful, then it was dark again, but not quiet. In the sky outside a great beast moved and purred and scrabbled, and then suddenly it opened its mouth again and again there was the roar and the flash of its claws, tearing at the earth, it seemed neither house nor hall could escape. The rain had died away, it was listening—quiet in the next lull, and then Chris heard her Auntie crying to her *Are you all right, Chrissie?* and cried back she was fine. Funny Uncle Tam had cried never a word, maybe he was still in the sulks,

he'd plumped head-first in when he'd heard of the old
woman that Semple was sending to help keep house in Blawearie. They were off to Auchterless the morn, and oh!
she'd be glad to see them go, she'd enough to do and to
think without fighting relations.

The thunder clamoured again, and then she suddenly sat
shivering, remembering something—Clyde and old Bob
and Bess, all three of them were out in the ley field there,
they weren't taken in till late in the year. Round the ley
field was barbed wire, almost new, that father had put up
in the Spring, folk said it was awful for drawing the lightning, maybe it had drawn it already.

She was out of bed in the next flash, it was a ground
flash, it hung and it seemed to wait, sizzling, outside the
window as she pulled on stockings and vest and knickers
and ran to the door and cried up *Uncle Tam, Uncle Tam,
we must take in the horses!* He didn't hear, she waited, the
house shook and dirled in another great flash, then Auntie
was crying something, Chris stood as if she couldn't believe
her own ears. Uncle Tam was feared at the lightning, he
wouldn't go out, she herself had best go back to her bed
and wait for the morning.

She didn't wait to hear more than that, but ran to the
kitchen and groped about for the box of matches and lighted
the little lamp, it with the glass bowl, and then found the
littlest lantern and lighted that, though her fingers shook
and she almost dropped the funnel. Then she found old
shoes and a raincoat, it had been father's and came near
to her ankles, and she caught up the lamp and opened the
kitchen door and closed it quick behind her just as the
sky banged again and a flare of sheet lightning came flowing down the hill-side, frothing like the incoming tide at
Dunnottar. It dried up, leaving her blinded, her eyes ached
and she almost dropped the lantern again.

In the byre the kye were lowing fit to raise the roof,
even the stirks were up and stamping about in their stalls.
But they were safe enough unless the biggings were struck,
it was the horses she'd to think of.

Right athwart her vision the haystacks shone up like
great pointed pyramids a blinding moment, vanished, darkness complete and heavy flowed back on her again, the
lantern-light seeking to pierce it like the bore of a drill.
Still the rain held off as she stumbled and cried down the
sodden fields. Then she saw that the barbed wire was alive,

the lightning ran and glowed along it, a living thing, a
tremulous, vibrant serpent that spat and glowed and hid its
head and quivered again to sight. If the horses stood anywhere near to that they were finished, she cried to them
again and stopped and listened, it was deathly still in the
night between the bursts of the thunder, so still that she
heard the grass she had pressed underfoot crawl and quiver
erect again a step behind her. Then, as the thunder moved
away—it seemed to break and roar down the rightward hill,
above the Manse and Kinraddie Mains,—something tripped
her, she fell and the lantern-flame flared up and seemed almost to vanish; but she righted it, almost sick though she
was because of the wet, warm thing that her body and
face lay upon.

It was old Bob, he lay dead, his tongue hanging out, his
legs doubled under him queerly, poor brute, and she shook
at his halter a minute before she realized it was useless and
there were still Bess and Clyde to see to. And then she
heard the thunder and clop of their hooves coming across
the grass to her, they loomed suddenly into the light of the
lamp, nearly running her down, they stood beside her and
whinnied, frightened and quivering so that her hand on
Bess's neck dirled as on the floor of a threshing-machine.

Then the lightning smote down again, quite near, though
the thunder had seemed to move off, it played a great zig-
zag over the field where she stood with the horses, and
they pressed so near her she was almost crushed between
them; and the lantern was pressed from her hand at last,
it fell and went out with a crash and a crinkle of breaking
glass. She caught Bess's bridle with one hand, Clyde's with
another, and the lightning went and they began to move forward in the darkness, she thought she was in the right direction but she couldn't be sure. The next flash showed a
field she didn't know, close at hand, with a high staked
dyke, and then she knew she had gone utterly wrong, it was
the dyke on the turnpike.

The thunder growled satisfiedly and Clyde whinnied
and whinnied, she saw then the reason for that, right ahead
was the waving of a lantern, it must be Uncle come out to
look for her at last, she cried *I'm here!* and a voice cried
Where? She cried again and the lantern came in her direction, it was two men climbing the dyke. The horses started
and whinnied and dragged her forward and then she found
herself with Chae Strachan and Ewan, they had seen to

their own horses on Upperhill and the Knapp, and had met
and had minded hers on Blawearie; and up they had come
to look for them. In the moment as they recognized one
the other the lightning flared, a last sizzling glow, and then
the rain came again, they heard it coming far up in the
moors, it whistled and moaned and then was a great driving swish. Chae thrust his lantern upon Ewan, *Damn't man,
take that and the lass and run for the house! I'll see to the
horses!*

Ewan caught Chris under the arm, he swung the lantern
in his other hand, they ran for a gate that led to the turnpike, the horses galloped behind them, Chae dragging at
their halters and cursing them; and the rain overtook them
as they gained the road, it was a battering wet hand that
beat at them, Chris was soaked to the skin in a moment.

But in another they'd gained the new biggings of Peesie's
Knapp, there shone a light in the kitchen, Ewan opened
the door and pushed Chris in, *Bide here and I'll off and
help Chae!* He disappeared into the blackness, the door
closed behind him, Chris went forward into the kitchen and
the glow of the fire. She felt daft and deaf in the sudden
silence and out of the rain, in the stillness of the new
kitchen with its meikle clock wagging against the wall, and
its calendars and pictures all spaced about, it looked calm
and fine. Then she realised how wetted she was and took
off the raincoat, it rained a puddle on the kitchen floor,
she was dressed below only in knickers and vest, she'd not
remembered that!

There came a rattle and clatter outside in the close as
the men ran to the house, Chris slipped on the coat again
and was tugging at the buttons as the two came stamping in.
Chae cried, *Damn't, Chris, get out of that coat, you must
fair be soaked. Here, I'll stir up the fire, the old wife's in
bed, she'd sleep through a hundred storms.*

He bent over the fire then, poking it up, Chris found
Ewan beside her, his hair black with the rain, the great
cat, to help her off with her coat. She whispered, *I can't,
Ewan, I've nothing on below!* and he blushed as red as a
girl himself, and dropped his hands, and looked like a foolish boy so that she lost her own shyness at once, and told
the same thing to Chae when he turned him round. He
laughed at her with his twinkling eyes, *What, nothing at
all?*——*Well, not very much, Chae*——*Then come ben
and I'll get you a coat of the wife's, you can slip into that.*

The rain was pelting on the roof as she followed him through to Mistress Strachan's new parlour, it sounded loud enough to wake the dead let alone her that had been Kirsty Sinclair. Chae opened the wardrobe and brought out a fine coat, Mistress Strachan's best for the Sunday, lined and fine and smelling of moth-balls; and then a pair of her slippers. *Get out of your things, Chris lass, and bring them to dry. I'll have something warm for you and Ewan to drink.*

Left alone with the candle she wished she'd asked for a towel; Chae was kind but a man had no sense. But she managed without, though stripping from vest and knickers and stockings felt like parting wetly from her own skin, almost, so soaked she had been. Then she put on the coat and slippers and gathered up the wet under-things and went through with them to the kitchen; and there was Chae one side of the fire with a bottle of whisky at his elbow, making toddy, and Ewan at the other, with his coat off, warming his hands and looking at the door for her to come ben. They didn't look at her over-close, either of them, Chae pulled in one chair for her to sit on and another for her things to dry on, and when she'd spread them out he stopped in his toddy-making and said *Damn't, Chris, was that ALL you'd on?* And she nodded and he said *You'll have your death of cold, sit closer—*

And that was fine, sitting next to Ewan, close to the blaze of the meikle larch logs that Chae had put on, they were swack with resin, Syne Chae had the toddy made and he handed a glass to Ewan first, as was right with a man, and another to Chris, with three spoonfuls of sugar in it, Mistress Strachan might have had something to say about that if she'd seen such wastry. But she was fast asleep up in Chae's bed, and knew nothing of it all till the morning, she made up for it then, folk said she accused both Chae and Ewan of cuddling and sossing with the Guthrie quean all the hours of the night.

So that was the ongoing there was that night of lightning, nor was it the only one in Kinraddie, for the lightning, and maybe it was the big flash Chris had seen as she gained the brae leading down to the horses, drove a great hole through the Manse spare bedroom, and let in the rain and fair ruined the place. Folk said that when the Reverend Gibbon heard the bolt strike the house, he'd been awake and listening, he dived like a rabbit below the blankets and cried *Oh, God, keep it away from me!* Which wasn't the kind of conduct you'd have expected from a minister, but there was a fair flock of folk the lightning scared that night in one place or another, Jock Gordon at Upperhill ran to his mother's bedroom and wept all over the counterpane there like a bairn.

And Alec Mutch of Bridge End went out about midnight to look for his sheep, but he was half-drunk when he went and got drunker every minute as he chaved about, not seeing a thing. And at last he came to a big stook out in the corn-parks and crawled into that, it was a stook that stood near the turnpike, and feint the thing else was seen of him till late the next morning when the postman was going by and the sun was shining fine, and out Alec's face and meikle lugs were stuck from the stook and gave the postman such a turn in the wame he was nearly sick on the spot.

But of all that Chris knew nothing, she'd plenty to think of with her own bit ploys. For after the rain cleared and her under-things dried she went through to the parlour and got in them again, and into the raincoat of father's, and Chae lighted a lantern, fair yawning with sleep was Chae, and Ewan was to guide home to Blawearie both Chris and the horses. So out to the night again, the rain had cleared and freshened it, there was a wind from off the sea blowing in the stars, and clouds like the drifting of great women's veils, fisher-wives' veils, across the sad faces of the coarse high hills.

Then the horses champed in the courtyard, Ewan had their halter-ropes in his hand, Chris was beside him swinging the lantern, they cried *Ta-ta!* to Chae and Chae nearly uncovered the back of his gums, so sleepy he was, poor stock; and he started to cry something to Chris about coming up the morn and seeing to old Bob whom the lightning had killed, they'd be able to sell him to the knacker in Brechin. But a yawn put an end to whatever he'd to say, it hardly mattered, it was morn already, you could see far down by Bervie a band of greyness stroke the horizon, as though an idle finger stroked it there on a windowpane.

Tramp, tramp, with a nicker now and then and long snortings through their nostrils, the horses, glad to be roaded up to Blawearie, Ewan big by the side of Chris, she hadn't realised before how big he was. He said nothing at all, except shy-like, once *Are you warm enough?* and she laughed and said *Fine,* she'd never again be shy with Ewan Tavendale. And it seemed to her even then it would be

long before she forgot this walk through the night that was
hardly night at all, an hour poised on the edge of the morning like a penny on its rim, the flutter of the wind in their
faces and the wet country sleeping about them, it smelt like
Spring, not a morning in fore-winter.

Then she was yawning, stopping from that, it was still
a bit way to the house, she wondered if Uncle or Auntie
had known she went out to the horses in the lightning. But
she needn't have worried, not a thing they'd guessed and
didn't till the morning came. Blawearie was black as the
inside of a lum-hat when they climbed to it, the kye quietened down, it hardly seemed home at all she had come to,
a strange place this, with Ewan beside her. She opened the
stable door for him, he led in the horses and made a shake-
down, and came out and closed and barred up the door,
she held him the lantern to see to that. And then he turned
round, they were standing there in the close, his arms went
round her, below her arms, and she said *Oh, don't!* and
turned away her face; and he did nothing and she turned
up her face to him again, peeping to see what he did.

Dark still it was but she saw his teeth, laughing at her,
and then she put down the lantern and somehow resistance
went from her, she hadn't wanted to resist, he was holding
her close to him, kissing her, her cheeks and the tip of her
nose because he couldn't see well in the darkness. And
then he waited a moment and his lips came to hers and
they were trembling as her own were, she wanted to cry and
she wanted to laugh in a breath, and have him hold her
for ever, so, in the close, and his trembling lips that came
into hers, sweet and terrible those lips in hers.

There was a great power of honeysuckle that year, the
smell of it drenched all the close in wet, still weather, it
perfumed the night and that kiss, she wouldn't ever forget
them both though they lived unkissed again till she died.
And then she knew they were near to other things, both of
them, Ewan's breath was quicker than it should, he'd
stopped from kissing her that kiss in the lips, his lips were
urgent on her neck; and she let him, standing so still, it was
warm and sweet, she was his, he hers, for all things and
everything, she never wanted better than that.

And then, in that ultimate moment, close at hand Chris
heard the Blue Wyandotte, already so cocky that he was,
stir on his ree, he gave a bit squawk before he stirred
and peeked for the day he would crow so lustily. Somehow

that stirring brought Chris to her senses, she wasn't afraid, only this could wait for another night's coming, it was sweet and she wanted it to live and last, not snatch it and fumble it blindly and stupidly. And she caught Ewan's hand and kissed him, he stopped with that kiss of hers on his cheek, his cheek with the soft brown skin; and she whispered *Wait, Ewan!*

He let her go at once, shamed of himself, he had little need to be that, she saw him troubled and uncertain in the dim light and put her arms about him and kissed him again and whispered *Come down and see me to-morrow evening,* and he said *Chris, when'll you marry me?* and she quivered strangely and sweetly as he said that, his hands holding her again, but gently. And then something happened, and the happening was a yawn, she yawned as though her head would fall off, she couldn't stop yawning; and a laugh came in the middle of it and that only made it worse. And Ewan let go of her again, maybe he was nearly in a rage at first, and then he yawned himself, they stood like two daft geese, yawning, and then they were laughing together, holding hands, not laughing too loud in case they'd be heard. And five minutes after that Ewan was far on his way to the steading of Upperhill and Chris lying in her bed, she'd hardly touched it when she thought of Ewan, she wanted to think of him long and long, only next minute she was fast asleep.

It didn't seem that minute had passed when she heard Uncle Tam come chapping at her door, fair testy, *Come away, come away, now; there's a fire to light and your Auntie wants her tea.* She sat up in bed, still sleepy and dazed, *All right, Uncle Tam,* and yawned and didn't move for a minute, remembering the things of the night and day she'd forgotten in sleep. And then she threw off the blankets and got out from the bed, and stretched till each muscle was taut and quivering, she felt light and free and fine, not at all Chris Guthrie with the grave brown face and heavy hair, light and free as a feather; and without a stitch on she did a little dance at her window in the splash of early sun that came there—what a speak for Kinraddie were she seen! And she was singing to herself as she dressed and went slipping downstairs, Uncle was kneeling at the kitchen fire, like a cow with colic, and fair sour in the face. *You're in fine tune this morning,* he glowered and she said *Ay,*

Uncle, I'm that, give the sticks to me, and had them out
of his hand and the fire snapping into them all in a minute.

Uncle went out to the close then, to look over the fields
for the horses, and came back at a run, his little quoit
medals swinging and clashing from his meikle belly, *Mighty,
Chris, there's no sign of a horse!* She didn't turn round, just
said *You could hardly have looked in the stable*, and heard
him stop and breathe a great breath, and then go out again.
And not a word more he said at the breakfast, he went up
to their room to pack; but Auntie asked how the horses
came to be in and was told Chris had done it herself, with
Chae Strachan and Ewan to help. She seemed fair shamed
to hear that, Auntie Janet, but angry as well, she whisked
round the house like a wasp, *Ah well, it's plain you've no
use for your relatives here, I only pray you don't come to
disaster*. And Chris said *That's awfully fine of you, Auntie*,
and that made her madder than ever, but Chris didn't care,
she didn't care though all the world, all Kinraddie and the
Howe, went mad and choked itself with its bootlaces over
the things that had been between her and Ewan.

If it wasn't in a rage it was fair in a stir of scandal by
postman time, Kinraddie. Not a thing but it knew of her
day in Stonehaven with that coarse tink brute, Ewan Tavendale, they'd been seen to go wandering out to Dunnottar
together, they'd hidden away down in a hole by the sea—
what did they that for if they'd nothing to hide?

The postie told this to Auntie while Chris meated the
chickens, Auntie fair grew worked up and forgot to rage,
near crying she was as she told the story to Chris. How
funny were folk! Chris thought, standing and fronting that
trembling face. You knew them, saw through them, tied
them up in little packets stowed away in your mind,
labelled COARSE or TINKS or FINE; and they came
tumbling from the packets at the very first shake, mixed
and up-jumbled, she'd never known a soul bide neat and
sure in his packet yet. For here was Auntie near crying because she thought her niece had been raped by Ewan
Tavendale overnight, ashamed for her, sorry for her, fair
set to carry her off to Aberdeen and cover her shame. But
Chris said *There's nothing to cry about yet, Auntie Janet,
Ewan and I haven't lain together. We'll wait till we're married*, and laughed at her Auntie's face, it was funny and
pitiful both at once. And Auntie said *He's to marry you
then?* and Chris said she hoped so, but you never knew, and

Auntie fell in a fearsome stew again, it wasn't fair to torment her like that, but that was the mood of Chris that
morning.

Then Chae Strachan came up from the Knapp and looked
at old Bob lying dead in his park. He shook his head over
him, he doubted if the knacker would pay more than a
pound—the closest muckers in Scotland, knackers, and *that*
was fair saying a lot. Syne he promised to drive Auntie and
her man to the station, and went back to the Knapp for his
gig and was up and waiting before you could blink. And
Chris helped her relatives up in the gig, and sent them her
love to her brothers, and off the gig spanked, they looked
over their shoulders and saw her stand laughing, she didn't
care a button, coarse quean that she was.

And fair a relief was the riddance, the place to herself
again; and then as she watched the gig whip round the
corner into the turnpike it came on her that it wasn't *again*,
it was just the first time! Blawearie was hers, there wasn't
a soul in the place but herself, nobody had a right to come
near it but if she allowed. The honeysuckle was blinding
sweet in the sun, wet still and as she stood beside it and
buried her face in it, laughed into it, blushed in it, remembering herself of the night before. And Ewan would be up
to see her soon, to see her . . . and she wouldn't think of
more! she had hundreds of things to do.

By noon she had dinner set for the old wife sent from
Stonehaven. And then she heard Chae's gig come driving
up to Blawearie and there was Chae and an old bit body,
fair tottery she seemed as she got from the gig, with a
black mutch on and a string bag gripped in her hand. But
when she reached the ground she was none so tottery, she
said that the heights aye feared her legs; and she looked
Chris all over as though to make sure of her, living or dead,
and asked *Where'll I put my box, Mem?* And Chris blushed
for shame that any old soul should *Mem* at her, *Maybe
Chae will carry it up for us?* And Chae said *Och, fine that,*
and hoisted the old tin thing on his shoulder, and went
swaggering into the house, and Mrs. Melon followed after
and Chris turned to Chae's gig.

By the time Chae came down she had nearly unyoked it,
Chae cried *Damn't Chris, what's on?* and she told him
Dinner, you're to stay for that. So he was fell pleased,
though he hummed and hawed a minute about rousting
back to the Knapp. But she smiled at him, that way she

had done to the boy in Semple's office, and Chae stared at
her and wound up his waxed mouser and twinkled his eyes
and gave her shoulder a slap *Lord, Chris, they'll right soon
be after you, the lads, with your eyes like that!* And he
gave a bit sigh as though, other times, other ways, he'd
have headed the band himself.

So into the kitchen he came and sat himself down with
old Mistress Melon, and Chris dished up the rabbit stew
and they had a great dinner, Mistress Melon was a funny
old wife as soon as she saw you put on no airs. She'd a
great red face as though she'd just unbended from a day's
hard baking, and pale blue eyes like a summer sky, and
faded hair that had once been brown, and Chris soon saw
she was maybe the biggest gossip that had ever come into
Kinraddie, and faith! that meant the challenging of many
a champion.

But her stories of Stonehaven had a lilt and a laugh, and
the best was the one of the Provost that had lost his stud
in his tumbler when speaking to a teetotal gathering. And
Chae said that was a fine one, *Damn't, mistress, when I was
in Africa* . . . and he told them a story of a man he knew,
a black he'd been, real brave, and he found a diamond, on
his own ground too, but as soon as the British heard of it
they sent to arrest him for't. And what had that black
childe done? Swallowed the damned thing and nothing of
him could the British make, and they couldn't arrest him,
and the black got his diamond back in a day or so in the
course of nature, they were awful constipated folk, the
blacks.

All the time he was telling the story Chae had been tearing into his rabbit and oat-cake; and soon's he'd finished
one plate he took a look over the pot and cried *God, that
was right fine, Chris quean. Is there more on the go?* Chris
liked that, it was fine to have somebody that was hungry
and liked his meat and didn't make out he was gentry or
polite, there was less politeness about Chae than about a
potato fork.

Mistress Melon was eating right heartily too, and syne
Chae told them another story, about a lion that he and the
black head childe had hunted, they'd been awful chief together. . . . And Mistress Melon asked *What, you and the
lions?* and winked at Chris, but Chae wasn't a bit put out,
he just said *Damn't no, mistress, me and the head man,*
and went on with the story again, it was plain Mistress

Melon thought he was a bit of a liar till suddenly, casual-like, Chae opened the front of his sark and finished up, *And that was the bit momento the damned beast left on me.* Syne they saw the marks on his chest, the marks of great raking claws they were they had torn fair deep and sure, and Chae's dark body-hair didn't grow in them. So Mistress Melon was fair stammy-gastered at that; and said so to Chris when Chae was gone.

Soon as that was Chris set to arranging with the Melon wife how the two of them would partition the work, Mistress Melon could do the cooking and cleaning, Chris preferred the outside, she'd milk and see to the kine; and they'd get on bravely, no doubt. Mistress Melon was a fell good worker in spite of her awful tongue, she'd cleared up the dinner things and washed them and put them away ere Chris was well out of the house. Then down on her knees she went and was scrubbing the kitchen floor. Chris was glad enough to see her at that, she hated scrubbing herself. If only she'd been born a boy she'd never had such hatings vexing her, she'd have ploughed up parks and seen to their draining, lived and lived, gone up to the hills a shepherd and never had to scunner herself with the making of beds or the scouring of pots. But neither would she ever have had Ewan hold her as last night he had.

And then she blushed and went on in silence with the cleaning of the byre, thinking of his coming and what she would say to him and the thing it was they'd arrange. Before she knew it the new plan came shaping up bravely in her mind, neat and trim and trig, and when she looked out and saw the gloaming near and went over the close and down through the parks for the kye, she had everything fixed, it didn't matter a fig what folk might say.

So when Ewan came in by at last she waited him ben in the parlour, with a great fire kindled there and the two big leather chairs drawn close. It was Mistress Melon that brought him through, her meikle red face fair shaking with ill-fashionce, agog to know what was toward. But Chris just said *Thank you, Mistress Melon.* and ticed Ewan over to his chair, and took his cap from him and made him sit down and fair closed the door in the old wife's face.

It was bright and warm in the room, she turned round and saw her lad sit so; and then she raised her head and saw herself in the long, old mirror of the parlour wall, and thought how she'd changed, it crept on you and you hardly noticed, in ways you were still as young as the quean with the plaits that had run by Marget to catch the scholar's train. But she saw herself then in her long green skirt, long under the knee, and her hair wound in its great fair plaits about her head, and her high cheek-bones that caught the light and her mouth that was well enough, her figure was better still; and she knew for one wild passing moment herself both frightened and sorry she should be a woman, she'd never dream things again, she'd live them, the days of dreaming were by; and maybe they had been the best; and there was Ewan waiting for her, the great quiet cat, reddening and turning his head up with its smouldering eyes.

She went to him then and put her hand on his shoulder and before she knew it they were close together and so stayed long after they had finished with kissing, just quiet, in the firelight, his arms about her, her head on his shoulder, watching the fire. And when at last they began to speak she put her hands over his lips, whispering to him to whisper in case Mistress Melon should be listening out by. Maybe she wasn't but in the shortest while they heard her go stamping about in the kitchen, singing a hymn fell loud, and that was a bit suspicious.

But they ceased from heeding her soon enough, they'd a hundred things to plan and discuss, there in the fire-glow, they lit no lamp, Chris listened with her head down-bent as he told her he couldn't marry he'd no more than a hundred pounds saved up, they'd have to wait. And she told him *she* had three hundred pounds, no credit to her, it was her father's saving, but if she and Ewan married fair soon he could take over Blawearie's lease, they could stay where they were, *and that would be fine, no need for you any day then to go back through the parks to Upperhill.* He kissed her again at that, hurting her lips, but she didn't heed, it was fine to be hurt like that; but she wouldn't kiss back till he'd put him his Highland pride in his pouch and muttered *All right.*

They'd planned to be married in December and as they'd planned so the thing worked out without any hitch at all. In November Ewan found and fee'd a substitute foreman for Upperhill, a quite-like childe James Leslie; and though old Gordon was none so pleased he couldn't well afford to fall out with so near a neighbour as the new Blawearie. Chris went into Stonehaven again with Ewan and saw the man Semple, he was fair suspicious, at first, but she argued him soon from that, and he got the lease changed to Ewan's name, and well-feathered his own nest in the changing, no doubt.

By then the news was no news, Kinraddie knew all, and when they came from the station that night they met in with Ellison down from the Mains, he'd been waiting them there to go by and he wouldn't have it but that they go up to the house and drink their own healths in a dram. Mistress Ellison was gentry and nice, more gentry than nice, poor thing, she was still no more than a servant quean and fleered and arched to make Chris and Ewan blush, she managed with Ewan. But Chris kept cool as ice, and nearly as friendly, she didn't see that a joke was less dirty if a neighbour spoke it. She and Ewan fair quarrelled over that when they left the Mains, it was their first quarrel and she wouldn't let him touch her, she said *If you like foul stories, I don't,* and he said, prigging at her, *Oh, don't be a fool, Chris quean,* and she said *There's no need for you marry a fool, then,* and the Highland temper quite went with him then, he flared up like a whin with a match at it, *Don't be feared, I've no such intention!* and off he went, up over the hill through the evening parks.

Chris walked on prim and cold and quick, it was near to sunset, she turned her head, she couldn't but help it, to see if he wasn't looking back, he wasn't; and that was too much, she stopped and cried *Ewan!* and he wheeled like a shot and came running to her, she was crying in earnest by then, she cried up against his coat while he held her and panted and swore at himself, *Oh, Chris, I didn't mean to hurt you!* And she sniffed *You didn't, it was myself;* and they made it all up again. She walked home subdued-like that night, it wouldn't be always plain sailing, they'd awful tempers, both of them. Then she saw the light of Blawearie shine steadfast across the parks and her heart kindled to a queer, quiet warmth at that.

They'd arranged to be married on New Year's Eve, most folk would be free to come that day. For three evenings they sat in Blawearie parlour and wrote their invitations to folk they knew and some they didn't, nearly every soul in Kinraddie was asked, they couldn't well miss out one of them. And to Auntie and Uncle and Dod and Alec they wrote, and to Ewan's friend, McIvor, a Highlandman out of Ross. He hadn't any near relatives, Ewan, and faith! they were feint the loss.

Chris knew that some would be sore affronted she should marry so close to her father's death, and with all the stir they intended, too. But Ewan said *Damn it, you're only married once as a general rule, and it won't hurt the old man in Kinraddie kirkyard.* So when Uncle wrote down from Auchterless that he'd think black, burning shame to attend such a marriage, Ewan said he could blacken and burn till he was more like a cinder heap than a man, for all they need care.

Chris was sorry they wouldn't let her brothers come, but it couldn't be helped, she wasn't to weep for that. So they planned out a wedding they'd mind on when they grew old, ordering food enough to feed the French, as the saying went. Mistress Melon near burst her meikle face with amaze as the packages came pouring in; and she spread the story of Chris's extravagance out through the Howe, she'd soon see the end of old Guthrie's silver. Folk shook their heads when they heard of that, it was plain that the quean wouldn't store the kiln long.

When Ewan went over to see to the banns the Reverend Gibbon tried to read him a lecture about such a display so close to John Guthrie's death. But he gave it up quick enough when Ewan began to spit like a cat and say the service he wanted was a wedding, not a sermon. Syne it grew plain they couldn't meet so often, Ewan would have to bide at the Upperhill all the day before the marriage. Chris kissed him good-bye that evening and told him to look after himself, and herself looked after him, troubled, knowing the kind of coarse things they might try him with in the bothy. And try they did, but Ewan couped one of them into the midden and threw young Gordon into the horse-trough when that brute was trying the same on Ewan himself; so they let him be, dour devils to handle, those High-landmen.

And down in Blawearie next day, what with cooking and chaving and tending to beasts, and wrestling with the worry of the barn, it wasn't half spruced for the dance, Chris might well have gone off her head if Chae and Long Rob of the Mill hadn't come dandering up the road in the afternoon, shy-like, bringing their presents. And Rob's was fine, two great biscuit barrels in oak and silver: and Chae's was from him and Kirsty, sheets and pillows, kind of Mis-

tress Strachan, that, when you minded how the two of you'd
fallen out over father ill.

And when they heard of the barn they cast off their
coats, *Leave it to us, Chris, just tell's what you want;* and
they set to with ladders and tow and fancy frills and
worked till near it was dark, redding up the place, it looked
fine as a fairy-palace in a picture-book when they finished.
Chae said *And who's your musician?* Chris nearly dropped
through the floor with shock, she and Ewan had fair forgot
about music. But Chae said it didn't matter, he'd bring his
melodeon and Long Rob his fiddle; and faith! if that didn't
content the folk they were looking for a church parade of
the Gordons, not a wedding.

Syne they bade good night to Chris, and they laughed at
her, kind-like, and said *This time the morn you'll be a married woman, Chris, not a quean. Sleep sound to-night!* And
she laughed back and said *Oh, fine that;* but she blushed
when Long Rob began to glint his grey eyes at her, he'd
have to think of getting married himself, he said, fine it
must be to sleep with a slim bit the like of herself those
coldrife winter nights. And Chae said *Away, Rob, feint the
much sleep you'd give her!*

And then they cried their good nights again and went off,
leaving Chris with such lonesome feeling as she'd seldom
had, all had been done that could be done, she wanted to
sleep but couldn't sleep; and she wandered from room to
room till Mistress Melon was fair upset and cried *For God's
sake gang to your bed, lass, I'll tend to the rest; if you don't
lie down you'll look more like a bull for the butcher's than
a bride the morn.* And Chris laughed, she heard her laugh
funny and faint-like, and said she supposed so, and went off
to her room, but not to bed. She sat by the window, it was
a night that was rimed with a frost of stars, rime in the
sky and rime on the earth, the Milky Way shone clear and
hard and the black trees of Blawearie waved their leafless
boughs up against the window, sparkling white with the
hoar; and far across the countryside for hours she watched
the winking of the paraffin-lights in the farmhouses, till
they sank and went out, and she was left in a world that
might well have been dead but that she lived.

Strange and eerie it was, sitting there, she couldn't move
from the frozen flow of thoughts that came to her then,
daft things she'd no need to think on her marriage eve . . .
that this marriage of hers was nothing, that it would pass

on and forward into days that had long forgotten it, her
life and Ewan's, and they pass also, and the face of the
land change and change again in the coming of the seasons
and centuries till the last lights sank away from it and the
sea came flooding up the Howe, all her love and tears for
Ewan not even a ripple on that flood of water far in the
times to be. And then she found herself cold as an icicle
and got to her feet and at last began to get from her
clothes—strange to think that to-morrow and all the tomorrows Ewan would share her room and her bed with
her.

She thought that cool and unwarmed, still in the grip of
the strange white dreaming that had been hers, looking
down at herself naked as though she looked at some other
than herself, a statue like that of the folk of olden time
that they set in the picture galleries. And she saw the light
white on the satin of her smooth skin then, and the long,
smooth lines that lay from waist to thigh, thigh to knee,
and was glad her legs were long from the knee to the ankle,
that made legs seem stumbling and stumpy, shortness there.
And still impersonally she bent to see if that dimple still
hid there under her left breast, it did, it was deep as ever.
Then she straightened and took down her hair and brushed
it, standing so, silly to stand without her night-gown, but
that was the mood she was in, somehow it seemed that
never again would she be herself, have this body that was
hers and her own, those fine lines that curved from thigh
to knee hers, that dimple she'd loved when a child—oh,
years before!

And then a clock began to strike, it struck two, and suddenly she was in a panic to be bedded and snug and herself
again; and was in between the sheets in an instant, cuddling herself to some warmth and counting how many hours
it would be till morning. And oh! it was still so long!

It came in snow that morning; she looked out from her
window and saw it sheeting across the countryside, all
silent; but still the daft peewits wheeped and wheeled
against the hills, looking for the nests they'd lost in the
harvest and couldn't forget. In the race and whip of the
great broad flakes the leafless trees stood shivering; but
down below Mistress Melon was already at work. Chris
heard the clatter of the breakfast things, it was time she
herself was into her clothes, there were hundreds of things
to do.

Then she took out of the chest of drawers her under-things, there was no need to wait to change them, and looked at them, the silken vest, awful price it had been, and knickers and petticoat, vest, knickers and petticoat all of a shade, blue, with white ribbon; and they looked lovely and they smelt fine, she buried her face in them, so lovely they were and the queer feeling they brought her. And she changed her mind, she couldn't wear anything now she'd be wearing when she was married, she put on her old things and her old skirt and went down the stairs; and there was Mistress Melon smiling at her, *How do you feel on your marriage-morn, Chris?*

And Chris said *Fine,* and Mistress Melon said that was a good job, too, she'd known creatures of queans come down fair hysterical, others that just shook with fright, still others that spoke so undecent you knew fine a man's bed was no unco place for *them.* She hoped Chris would be awful happy, no fear of that, and soon have a two-three bairns keep her out of longer. And Chris said *You never know,* and she ate her porridge and Mistress Melon hers, and they cleared the table and scrubbed the kitchen and then Chris went out and tended the beasts, the very horses seemed to guess there was unco thing on the go, Bess noz-zled up against her shoulder; and there in the barn when she peeked in it, right in the middle of the floor, were two great rats, sitting up on their tails, sniffing at each other's mouths, maybe kissing, and that was so funny, she tried not to laugh, but gave a choked gurgle and flirt! the rats were out of sight and into their holes.

In the cornyard the hens came tearing about her, mad with hunger, she gave them meat hot from the pot and then a bushel of corn, they liked that fine. But first the little bit Wyandotte got up on the cartshaft and gave a great crow that might have been heard in the Upperhill; and he cocked a bright eye on her, first one eye and then the other, and Chris laughed again.

She didn't feel hurried after that, then the postman came, fell dry, they gave him a dram and he licked his lips and said *Here's to you, Chris!* as blithe to drink to her health as to blacken her character. He'd brought him two parcels, one was a lovely bedspread from Mistress Gibbon of the Manse, nice of the quiet-voiced English thing, and the other from the Gordons of Upperhill, a canteen of cutlery, full enough of knives and forks and things to keep you cleaning them a week on end and not be finished, said Mistress Melon.

Then up the road came the wife of the grave-digger, Garthmore, him that had buried father. Sore made as always she was, poor thing, they'd asked her to come and lend them a hand more out of pity than anything else; and when the three sat down to dinner she said *Eh, me! it's fine to be young and be married, and maybe he'll treat you all right, but mine, my first man, him that's now dead, God! he was a fair bull of a man and not only the first night, either. He was aye at it, near deaved me to death he would if he hadn't fallen over the edge of a quarry on the road from the feeing-market some nine-ten years come Martinmas.* But Mistress Melon said, *Havers, are you trying to frighten the lass? She'll be fine, her lad's both blithe and kind;* and Chris loved her for that, she'd never seemed to see and know Mistress Melon before, thinking her just a hard-working, hard-gossiping old body, now she saw the kindliness of her shine out, her gossiping no more than the dreams she aye dreamt and must tell to others. And then Mistress Melon cried *Away and get into your dress now, Chris, before the folk come up.*

It had left off snowing, Chris, dressing, saw from her window, a sunless day; and a great patching of clouds was upon the sky, the light below bright and sharp, flung by the snow itself; and the smoke rose straight in the air. Far over the braes by Upperhill where Ewan would be getting set in his clothes—unless he'd done that long before in the morning—the sheep were baaing in their winter buchts. Then Chris took off her clothes, and stood white again, and put on the wedding things, mother'd have like to see them, mother lying dead and forgotten in Kinraddie kirkyard with the twins beside her. She found herself weep then, slowly, hardly, lost and desolate a moment without mother on her marriage-day. And then she shook her head, *Oh, don't be a fool, do you want to look a fright before Ewan and the folk?*

She peered at her face in the glass, then, fine! her eyes were bright, the crying had helped them. Pretty in a way, not only good-looking, she saw herself, dour cheek-bones softened for the hour in their chilled bronze setting. And she combed out her hair, it came far past her middle, thick and soft and sweet-smelling and rusty and tarnished gold. Then last was her dress, blue also, but darker than

her underclothes because so short was the time since
father had died, she threaded the neck with a narrow black
ribbon but round her own neck put nothing, her skin was
the guerdon there.

So, ready, she turned herself round a minute, and held
back the skirt from her ankles and liked them, they were
neat and round, she had comely bones, her feet looked
long and lithe in the black silk stockings and shoes. She
found herself a hanky, last, and sprinkled some scent in
that, only a little; and hid it away in her breast and went
down the stairs just as she heard the first gig drive up.

That was the Strachans from Peesie's Knapp, Mistress
Strachan fell long in the face at first. But Chae soon kindled her up with a dram, he whispered to Chris that he'd
look after the drink; and Mistress Melon said it was aye
best to have a man body at that end of the stir. And before they could say much more there come a fair stream
of traffic up from the turnpike, all Kinraddie seemed on
the move to Blawearie: except the old folk from Netherhill, and they sent their kind wishes and two clucking hens
for Chris's nests.

The hens broke the ice, you might say, for they got
themselves loose from the gig of the Netherhill folk and
started a wild flutter and chirawk everywhere, anywhere
out of Blawearie. Long Rob of the Mill was coming up
the road at that minute, in his Sunday best, and he met
the first hen and heard the cry-out that followed her, and
he cried himself, *Shoo, you bitch!* The hen dodged into
the ditch, but Rob was after her, grabbing her, she
squawked fair piercing as he carried her up to the house,
his fine Sunday coat was lathered with snow; and he said
that such-like work would have been nothing to Chae,
who had chased the bit ostriches out in the Transvaal, but
he'd had no training himself. Syne he took up the dram
that Chae had poured him and cried *Here's to the bonniest
maid Kinraddie will mind for many a year!*

That was kind of him, Chris had been cool and quiet
enough until then, but she blushed at that, seeing Rob stand
like a viking out of the picture books with the iron-grey
glint in his eyes. Mistress Munro, though, was right sore
jealous as usual, she poked her nose in the air and said,
and not over-low, *The great fool might wait for the tea
before he starts his speechifying;* she was maybe mad that

nobody had ever said *she* was bonny; or if anybody ever had, he was an uncommon liar.

Then the Bridge End folk came up, then Ellison and his wife and their daughter, and then the Gordons, and then the minister, riding on his bicycle, it looked as though he'd had a fall or two and he wasn't in the best of temper, he wouldn't have a dram, *No, thank you, Chae,* he said, real stiff-like. And when Rob gave him a sly bit look, *You've been communing with Mother Earth, I see, Mr. Gibbon,* he just turned his back and made out he didn't hear, and folk looked fair uncomfortable, all except Long Rob himself and Chae, they winked one at the other, and then at Chris.

She thought the Minister a fusionless fool, and went to the door to see who else was coming; and there, would you believe it, was poor old Pooty toiling up through the drifts with a great parcel under his oxter, his old face was white with snow and he shivered and hoasted as he came in, peeking out below his old, worn brows for Chris. *Where's the bit llllass!* he cried, and then saw her and put the parcel in her hands, and she opened it then, as the custom was, and in it lay a fine pair of shoes he had made for her, shoes of glistening leather with gay green soles, and a pair of slippers, soft-lined with wool, there wouldn't be a grander pair in Kinraddie. And she said *Oh, thank you,* and she knew that wasn't enough, he stood peering up at her like an old hen peers, she didn't know why she did it but she put her arms round him and kissed him, folk laughed at that, all but the two of them, Pooty blinked and stuttered till Long Rob reached out a hand and pulled him into a chair and cried *Wet your whistle with this, Pooty man, you've hardly a minute ere the wedding begins.*

And he was right, for up the road came walking the last two, Ewan and his best man, the Highlander McIvor, near six feet six, red-headed, red-faced, a red Highlandman that bowed so low to Chris that she felt a fool; and presented his present, and it was a ram's horn shod with silver, real bonny and unco, like all Highland things. But Ewan took never a look at Chris, they made out they didn't see one the other, and Mistress Melon whispered to her to go tidy her hair, and when she came down again all the place was quiet, there was hardly a murmur. She stopped at the foot of the stairs with the heart beating so against her skin it was like to burst from her breast; and there was Chae

Strachan waiting her, he held out his arm and patted her hand, when she laid it on his arm, and he whispered *Ready then, Chris?*

Then he opened the parlour door, the place was crowded, there were all the folk sitting in chairs, solemn as a kirk congregation, and over by the window stood the Reverend Gibbon, very stern and more like a curly bull than ever; and in front of him waited Ewan and his best man, Mc-Ivor. Chris had for bridesmaids the little Ellison girl and Maggie Jean Gordon, they joined with her, she couldn't see clear for a minute then, or maybe too clear, she didn't seem to be seeing with her own eyes at all. And then Chae had loosed her hand from his arm and she and Ewan stood side by side, he was wearing a new suit, tweed it was, and smelt lovely, his dark face was solemn and frightened and white, he stood close to her, she knew him more frightened than she was herself. Something of her own fear went from her then, she stood listening to the Reverend Gibbon and the words he was reading, words that she'd never heard before, this was the first marriage she'd ever been at.

And then she heard Chae whisper behind her and listened more carefully still, and heard Ewan say *I will,* in a desperate kind of voice, and then said it herself, her voice was as happy and clear as well you'd have wished, she smiled up at Ewan, the white went from his face and the red came in spate. The Red Highlander behind slipped something forward, she saw it was the ring, and then Ewan fitted it over her finger, his fingers were hot and unsteady, and Mr. Gibbon closed his eyes and said, *Let us pray.*

And Chris held on to Ewan's hand and bent her head and listened to him, the minister; and he asked God to bless their union, to give them courage and strength for the difficulties that the years might bring to them, to make fruitful their marriage and their love as pure and enduring in its fulfilment as in its conception. They were lovely words, words like the marching of a bronze-leafed beech on the lips of a summer sky. So Chris thought, her head down-bent and her hand in Ewan's, then she lost the thread that the words were strung on, because of that hand of Ewan's that still held hers; and she curbed her little finger into his palm, it was hard and rough there and she tickled the skin secretly, and his hand quivered and she took the littlest keek at his face. There was that smile of his, fliting like a startled cat; and then his hand closed firm and warm

and sure on hers, and hers lay quiet in his, and the minister had finished and was shaking their hands.

He hesitated a minute and then bent to kiss Chris; close
to hers she saw his face older far than when he came to
Kinraddie, there were pouches under his eyes, and a weary
look in his eyes, and his kiss she didn't like. Ewan's was a
peck, but Chae's was fine, it was hearty and kind though
he reeked of the awful tobacco he smoked, and then Long
Rob's, it was clean and sweet and dry, like a whiff from the
Mill itself; and then it seemed every soul in Kinraddie was
kissing her, except only Tony, the daftie, he'd been left at
home. Everybody was speaking and laughing and slapping
Ewan on the back and coming to kiss her, those that knew
her well and some that didn't. And last it was Mistress
Melon, her eyes were over bright but careful still, she nearly smothered Chris and then whispered *Up to your room
and tidy yourself, they've messed your hair.*

She escaped them then, the folk trooped out to the kitch-
en where the fire was roaring, Chae passed round the
drams again, there was port for the women if they wanted
it and raspberry drinks for the children. Soon's the parlour
was clear Mistress Melon and Mistress Garthmore had the
chairs whisked aside, the tables put forward and the cloths
spread; and there came a loud tinkling as they spread the
supper, barely past three though it was. But Chris knew it
fell likely that few had eaten much at their dinners in Kinraddie that day, there wouldn't have been much sense with
a marriage in prospect: and as soon as they'd something
solid in their bellies to foundation the drink, as a man
might say, the better it would be.

In her room that wouldn't be her room for long Chris
brushed her hair and settled her dress and looked at her
flushed, fair face, it was nearly the same, hard to believe
though you thought it. And then something felt queer
about her, the ring on her hand it was, she stood and
stared at the thing till a soft whispering drew her eyes to
the window, the snow had come on again, a scurry and a
blinding drive from down the hills; and below in the house
they were crying *The bride, where is she?*

So down she went, folk had trooped back in the parlour
by then and were sitting them round the tables, the minister at the head of one, Long Rob at the head of another,
in the centre one the wedding cake stood tall on its stand
with the Highland dirk beside it that Ewan had gotten

from McIvor to do the cutting. The wind had risen storming without as Chris stood to cut, there in her blue frock with the long, loose sleeves, there came a great whoom in the chimney and some looked out at the window and said that the drifts would be a fell feet deep by the morn. And then the cake was cut and Chris sat down, Ewan beside her, and found she wasn't hungry at all, about the only soul in the place that wasn't, everybody else was taking a fair hearty meal.

The minister had thawed away by then, he was laughing real friendly-like in his bull-like boom of a voice, telling of other weddings he'd made in his time, they'd all been gey funny and queer-like weddings, things that you laughed at, not fine like this. And Chris listened and glowed with pride that everything at hers was just and right; and then again as so often that qualm of doubt came down on her, separating her away from these kindly folk of the farms—kind, and aye ready to believe the worst of others they heard, unbelieving that others could think the same of themselves. So maybe the minister no more than buttered her, she looked at him with the dark, cool doubt in her face, next instant forgot him in a glow of remembrance that blinded all else: she was married to Ewan.

Beside her: he whispered *Oh, eat something, Chris, you'll fair go famished*, and she tried some ham and a bit of the dumpling, sugared and fine, that Mistress Melon had made. And everybody praised it, as well they might, and cried for more helpings, and more cups of tea, and there were scones and pancakes and soda-cakes and cakes made with honey that everybody ate; and little Wat Strachan stopped eating of a sudden and cried *Mother, I'm not right in the belly!* everybody laughed at that but Kirsty, she jumped to her feet and hurried him out, and came back with him with his face real frightened. But faith! It didn't put a stop to the bairn, he started in again as hungry as ever, and Chae cried out *Well, well, let him be, maybe it tasted as fine coming up as it did going down!*

Some laughed at that, others reddened and looked real affronted, Chris herself didn't care. Cuddiestoun and his wife sat opposite her, it was like watching a meikle collie and a futret at meat, him gulping down everything that came his way and a lot that didn't, he would rax for that; and his ugly face, poor stock, fair shone and glimmered with the exercise. But Mistress Munro snapped down at her

plate with sharp, quick teeth, her head never still a minute,
just like a futret with a dog nearby. They were saying
hardly anything, so busied they were, but Ellison next to
them had plenty to say, he'd taken a dram over much already and was crying things across the table to Chris, Mistress Tavendale he called her at every turn; and he said
that she and Mistress Ellison must get better acquaint.
Maybe he'd regret that the morn, if he minded his promise:
and that wasn't likely.

Next to him was Kirsty and the boys and next to that the
minister's table with Alec Mutch and his folk and young
Gordon; a real minister's man was Alec, awful chief-like
the two of them were, but Mistress Mutch sat lazy as ever,
now and then she cast a bit look at Chris out of the lazy,
gley eyes of her, maybe there was a funniness in the look
that hadn't to do with the squint.

Up at Rob's table an argument rose, Chris hoped that it
wasn't religion, she saw Mr. Gordon's wee face pecked up
to counter Rob. But Rob was just saying what a shame it
was that folk should be shamed nowadays to speak Scotch
—or they called it Scots if they did, the split-tongued sourocks! Every damned little narrow dowped rat that you met
put on the English if he thought he'd impress you—as
though Scotch wasn't good enough now, it had words in it
that the thin bit scraichs of the English could never come
at. And Rob said *You can tell me, man, what's the English
for sotter, or greip, or smore, or pleiter, gloaming or
glanching or well-henspeckled? And if you said gloaming
was sunset you'd fair be a liar; and you're hardly that, Mr.
Gordon.*

But Gordon was real decent and reasonable, *You can't
help it, Rob. If folk are to get on in the world nowadays,
away from the ploughshafts and out of the pleiter, they
must use the English, orra though it be.* And Chae cried
out that was right enough, and God! who could you blame?
And a fair bit breeze got up about it all, every soul in the
parlour seemed speaking at once; and as aye when they
spoke of the thing they agreed that the land was a coarse,
coarse life, you'd do better at almost anything else, folk
that could send their lads to learn a trade were right wise,
no doubt of that, there was nothing on the land but work,
work, work, and chave, chave, chave, from the blink of
day till the fall of night, no thanks from the soss and sotter,
and hardly a living to be made.

Syne Cuddiestoun said that he'd heard of a childe up Laurencekirk way, a banker's son from the town he was, and he'd come to do farming in a scientific way. So he'd said at first, had the childe, but God! by now you could hardly get into the place for the clutter of machines that lay in the yard; and *he* wouldn't store the kiln long. But Chae wouldn't have that, he swore *Damn't, no, the machine's the best friend of man, or it would be so in a socialist state. It's coming and the chaving'll end, you'll see, the machine'll do all the dirty work.* And Long Rob called out that he'd like right well to see the damned machine that would muck you a pigsty even though they all turned socialist to-morrow. And they all took a bit laugh at that, Chris and Ewan were fair forgotten for a while, they looked at each other and smiled, Ewan reached down and squeezed her hand and Chris wished every soul but themselves a hundred miles from Blawearie.

But then Chae cried *Fill up your glasses, folk, the best man has a toast.* And the red Highlander, McIvor, got up to his feet and bowed his red head to Chris, and began to speak; he spoke fine, though funny with that Highland twist, he said he'd never seen a sweeter quean than the bride or known a better friend than the groom; and he wished them long and lovely days, a marriage in the winter had the best of it. For was not the Spring to come and the seed-time springing of their love, and the bonny days of the summer, flowering it, and autumn with the harvest of their days? And when they passed to that other winter together they would know that was not the end of it, it was but a sleep that in another life would burgeon fresh from another earth. He could never believe but that two so young and fair as his friend and his friend's wife, once made one flesh would be one in the spirit as well; and have their days built of happiness and their nights of the music of the stars.

And he lifted his glass and cried *The bride!* looking at Chris with his queer bright eyes, the daft Highland poet, they were all like that, the red Highlanders. And everybody cried *Good luck to her!* and they all drank up and Chris felt herself blush from head to foot under all the blue things she wore.

And then Long Rob of the Mill was making a speech, different from McIvor's as well it might be. He said he'd never married himself because he'd over-much respect for

those kittle folk, women; but if he'd been ten years younger
he was damned if his respect would have kept him from
having a try for Chris Guthrie, and beating that Highland
childe, Ewan, at his own fell game. That was just Ewan's
luck, he thought, not his judgment, and Chris was clean
thrown away on her husband, as she'd have been on any
husband at all: but himself. Ah well, no doubt she'd train
him up well, and he advised Ewan now, from the little
that he knew of marriage, never to counter his wife; not
that he thought she wasn't well able to look after herself,
but just that Ewan mightn't find himself worsted though
he thought himself winner.

Marriage, he took it, was like yoking together two two-
year-olds, they were kittle and brisk on the first bit rig—
unless they'd fallen out as soon as they were yoked and
near kicked themselves and their harness to bits—but the
second rig was the testing time, it was then you knew when
one was pulling and one held back, the one that hard
sheer sweirty—and that was a word for Mr. Gordon to
put into English—in its bones, and the one with a stout
bit heart and a good guts. Well, he wouldn't say more
about horses, though faith! it was a fascinating topic, he'd
just come back to marriage and say they all wished the
best to Chris, so sweet and trig, and to Ewan, the Highland
cateran, and long might they live and grow healthy,
wealthy, and well content.

Then they all drank up again, and God knows who
mightn't have made the next speech if Chae then hadn't
stood up and cried *The night's near on us. Who's game for
a daylight dance at Chris's wedding?*

So out they all went to the kitchen, it was cold enough
there from the heat of the room, but nothing to the cold
rife air of the barn when the first of them had crossed the
close and stood in the door. But Mistress Melon had kindled a brazier with coal, it crackled fine, well away from
the straw, Rob tuned up his fiddle, Chae squeaked on his
melodeon, it began to feel brisk and warm even while you
stood and near shivered your sark off. Chris was there with
the men, of course, and the children and Mistress Gordon
and Mistress Mutch and Mistress Strachan were there, Mistress Munro had stayed behind to help clear the tables,
she said, and some whispered it was more than likely she'd
clear most of the clearings down her own throat, by God
she couldn't have eaten a mouthful since Candlemas.

But then Chae cried *Strip the Willow*, and they all lined up, and the melodeon played bonnily in Chae's hands, and Long Rob's fiddle-bow was darting and glimmering, and in two minutes in the whirl and go of *Strip the Willow*, there wasn't a cold soul in Blawearie barn, or a cold sole either. Then here, soon's they'd finished, was Mistress Melon with a great jar of hot toddy to drink, she set it on a bench between Chae and Long Rob. And whoever wanted to drink had just to go there, few were bashful in the going, too; and another dance started, it was a schottische, and Chris found herself in the arms of the minister, he could dance like a daft young lad. And as he swung her round and around he opened his mouth and cried *Hooch!* and so did the red Highlander, McIvor, *Hooch!* careering by with fat Kirsty Strachan, real scared-like she looked, clipped round the waist.

Then Chae and Long Rob hardly gave them a breather, they were at it dance on dance; and every time they stopped for a panting second Chae would dip in the jar and give Rob a wink and cry *Here's to you, man!* and Rob would dip, solemn-like as well, and say *Same to you!* and off the fiddle and melodeon would go again, faster than ever. Ewan danced the schottische with prim Mistress Gordon, but for waltzing he found a quean from the Mains, a red-faced, daft-like limmer, she screamed with excitement and everybody laughed, Chris laughed as well. Some were watching to see if she did, she knew, and she heard a whisper she'd have all her work cut out looking after him, coarse among the queans he was, Ewan Tavendale. But she didn't care, she knew it a lie, Ewan was hers and hers only; but she wished he would dance with her for a change.

And here at the *Petronella* he was, he anyway hadn't been drinking, in the noise of the dance as they swayed up and down the barn he whispered *Well, Chris?* and she whispered back *Fine*, and he said *You're the bonniest thing even seen in Kinraddie, Long Rob was right*. And she said she liked him to think so, and he called her back in the darkness away from the dancers, and kissed her quickly and slowly, she didn't hurry either, it was blithe and glad to stand there kissing, each strained to hear when they'd be discovered.

And then they were, Chae crying *Where's the bride and the groom? Damn't it, they're lost!* and out they'd to come. Chae cried was there anyone else could play the melodeon?

and young Jock Gordon cried back to him *Ay, fine that*, and came stitering across the floor and sat himself down by the toddy jar, and played loud and clear and fine.

Then Chae caught Chris, he said to Ewan *Away, you greedy brute, wait a while till she's yours forever and aye*, and he danced right neatly, you didn't expect it from Chae, with his grey eyes laughing down at you. And as he danced he said suddenly, grave like, *Never doubt your Ewan, Chris, or never let him know that you do. That's the hell of a married life. Praise him up and tell him he's fine, that there's not a soul in the Howe can stand beside him, and he'll want to cuddle you till the day he dies; and he'll blush at the sight of you fifty years on as much as he does the day.* She said *I'll try*, and *Thank you, Chae*, and he said *Och, it must be the whisky speaking,* and surrendered her up to Ellison, and took the melodeon from Gordon again, but staggered and leant back against the sack that hung as a draught-shield behind the musician's place. Down came the sack and there among the hay was the minister and the maid from the Mains that had scraiched so loud, she'd her arms round him and the big curly bull was kissing the quean like a dog lapping up its porridge.

Chris's heart near stopped, but Chae snatched up the sack, hooked it back on its hook again, nobody saw the sight except himself and Chris and maybe Long Rob. But you couldn't be sure about Rob, he looked as solemn as five owls all in one, and was playing as though, said Chae, he was paid by piece-work and not by time.

Between eight and nine Mistress Melon came out to the barn and cried them to supper, the storm had left off, all but a flake that sailed down now and then like a sailing gull in the beam from the barn door. On the ground the snow crinkled under their feet, frost had set in, the folk stood and breathed in the open air, and laughed, and cried one to the other, *Man, I'll have aching joints the morn!* The women ran first to the house, to tidy their hair, Ewan saw everybody in, except Munro of the Cuddiestoun, he was nowhere to be seen.

And then Ewan heard a funny bit breathing as he passed by the stable; and he stopped and opened the door and struck a match, and there was Munro, all in his Sunday-best, lying in the stall beside Clyde the horse, and his arms were round the beast's neck, and faith! the beast looked real disgusted. Ewan shook him and cried *Munro, you can't sleep*

here, but Munro just blinked the eyes in his face, daft-like,
and grumbled *Why not?* Syne Alec Mutch turned back from
the house to see what all the stir was about, and both he
and Ewan had another go at the prostrate Munro, but
damn the move would he make, Alec cried *To hell with
him, leave him there with the mare, she's maybe a damned
sight kinder a bedmate then ever was that futret of a wife
of his.*

So they closed the door of the stable and went into their
supper, everybody ate near as well as at tea-time, fair
starved they were with the dancing and drink. Chris had
thought she herself was tired till she ate some supper, and
then she felt as fresh ever, and backed up Long Rob, who
looked twice as sober as any of the men and had drunk
about twice as much as any three of them, when he cried
Who's for a dance again? Mistress Melon had the toddy-jar
filled fresh full and they carried that out, everybody came
to the barn this time except Mistress Munro, *No, no, I'll
clear the table.*

And young Elsie Ellison, wondering for why the creature
should stay behind, stayed herself and took a bit keek round
the corner of the door: and there was Mistress Munro,
with a paper bag in her hand, stuffing it with scones and
biscuits and cake, and twisting her head this side and that,
like the head of a futret. So Elsie, fair scared, ran off to
the barn and caught at her father's tails and cried *The
Cuddiestoun wife's away home with the pieces,* and Ellison,
he was whisked up to high tune by then, cried *Let her run
to hell and be damned to her.*

Syne he started a tale about how once she insulted him,
the dirty Scotch bitch. But Long Rob and Chae were
striking up a dance again and Chris heard no more of the
Ellison story, dancing a waltz with young Jock Gordon, it
was like flying, Jock's face was white with excitement. The
fourth dance Alec Mutch, the fool, began to stiter the floor,
backwards and forwards, he was a real nuisance till he
passed Long Rob and then Rob cried *Hoots, Alec, man,
your feet are all wrong!* and thrust out a foot among Alec's
and couped him down and Chae shoved him aside to the
straw with a foot and a hand, and played on with the other
foot and hand, or maybe with a foot and his teeth, a skilly
man, Chae.

Mistress Mutch said nothing, just standing and laughing
and smoking at her cigarette. There were more men than

women in the barn, though, even when the men made do
with a little quean, and soon Chris found herself dancing
with Mistress Mutch, the great, easy-going slummock, she
spoke slow and easy as though she'd just wakened up from
her sleep. Chris couldn't tell what way she looked with that
gleying eye, but what she spoke was *Take things easy in
married life, Chris, but not over-easy, that's been MY ruin.
Though God knows it'll make not a difference in a hundred
years' time and we're dead. Don't let Ewan saddle you with
a birn full of bairns, Chris, it kills you and eats your heart
away, forbye the unease and the dirt of it. Don't let him,
Chris, they're all the same, men; and you won't well steer
clear of the first or the second. But you belong to yourself,
mind that.*

Chris went hot and cold and then wanted to ask something
of Mistress Mutch and looked at her and found she couldn't,
she'd just have to find the thing out for herself. Long Rob
came down to dance with her next, he'd left the fiddle to old
Gordon, and he asked what that meikle slummock had been
saying to her? And Chris said *Oh, just stite,* and Rob said
*Mind, don't let any of those damned women fear you,
Chris; it's been the curse of the human race, listening to
advice.* And Chris said *But I'm listening to yours, Rob, now,
amn't I?* He nodded to her, solemn, and said, *Oh, you've
your head screwed on and you'll manage fine. But mind, if
there's ever a thing you want with a friend, not to speak it
abroad all over Kinraddie, I'll aye be there at the Mill to
help you.* Chris thought that a daft-like speak for Rob,
kind maybe he meant it, but she'd have Ewan, who else
could she want?

And then the fun slackened off, the barn was warm, folk
sat or lay on the benches or straw, Chris looked round and
saw nothing of the minister then, maybe he'd gone. She
whispered to Chae about that, but he said *Damn the fears,
he's out to be sick, can't you hear him like a cat with a
fish-bone in its throat?* And hear him they could, but Chris
had been right after all, he didn't come back. Maybe he
was shamed and maybe he just lost his way, for next noon
there were folk who swore they'd seen the marks of great
feet that walked round and round in a circle, circle after
circle, all across the parks from Blawearie to the Manse;
and if these weren't the minister's feet they must have
been the devil's, you could choose whichever you liked.

No sooner was the dancing done than there were cries

Rob, what about a song now, man? And Rob said *Och, ay, I'll manage that fine,* and he off with his coat and loosened his collar and sang them *Ladies of Spain;* and then he turned round to where Chris stood beside her Ewan and sang *The Lass that Made the Bed to Me:*

> Her hair was like the link o' gowd,
> Her teeth were like the ivorie,
> Her cheeks like lilies dipt in wine,
> The lass that made the bed to me.

> Her bosom was the driven snaw,
> Two drifted heaps sae fair to see,
> Her limbs, the polished marble stane,
> The lass that made the bed to me.

> I kissed her owre and owre again,
> And aye she wist na what to say,
> I laid her between me and the wa',
> The lassie thought na long till day.

Folk stared and nodded at Chris while Rob was singing and Ewan looked at first as though he'd like to brain him; and then he blushed; but Chris just listened and didn't care, she thought the song fine and the lass lovely, she hoped she herself would seem as lovely this night—or as much of it as their dancing would leave. So she clapped Rob and syne it was Ellison's turn, he stood up with his meikle belly a-wag and sang them a song they didn't know:

> Roses and lilies her cheeks disclose,
> But her red lips are sweeter than those,
> Kiss her, caress her,
> With blisses her kisses,
> Dissolve us in pleasure and soft repose.

and then another, an English one and awful sad, about a young childe called Villikins and a quean called Dinah, and it finished:

> For a cup of cold pizen lay there on the ground
>   .   .   .   .   .   .
> With a tooril-i-ooril-i-oorily-i-ay.

Chae cried that was hardly the kind of thing that they wanted, woeful as that; and they'd better give Chris a rest about her roses and lips and limbs, she had them all in safe-keeping and would know how to use them; and what about a seasonable song? And he sang so that all joined in seasonable enough, for the snow had come on again in spite of the frost:

> Up in the morning's no for me,
> Up in the morning early,
> When a' the hills are covered wi' snaw
> I'm sure it's winter fairly!

Then Mistress Mutch sang, that was hardly expected, and folk tittered a bit; but she had as good a voice as most and better than some, she sang *The Bonnie House o' Airlie,* and then the *Auld Robin Gray* that eye brought Chris near to weeping, and did now, and not her alone, with Rob's fiddle whispering it out, the sadness and the soreness of it, though it was long, long syne:

> When the sheep are in the fauld, and the kye at hame
> And a' the warld to its rest has gane,
> The waes o' my heart fa' in showers frae my e'e
> While my gudeman lies sound by me.

and all the tale of young Jamie who went to sea and was thought to be drownded in an awful storm; and his lass married Auld Robin Gray and syne Jamie came back but couldn't win his lass away from the auld man, though near brokenhearted she was:

> I gang like a ghaist, and I carena to spin,
> I daurna think on Jamie, for that wad be a sin,
> But I'll do my best a gude wife aye to be,
> For auld Robin Gray he is kind unto me.

Old Pooty was sleeping in a corner; he woke up then, fell keen to recite his TIMROUS BEASTIE; but they pulled him down and cried on the bride herself for a song. And all she could think of was that south country woman crying in the night by the side of her good man, the world asleep and grey without; and she whispered the song to Rob and he tuned his fiddle and she sang, facing them, young and earnest, and she saw Ewan looking at her solemn and proud, *The Flowers of the Forest:*

I've heard the lilting at our ewe-milking,
    Lasses a-lilting before the dawn o' day;
But now they are moaning in ilka green loaning,
    The Flowers o' the Forest are a' wede away.

Dule and wae for the order, sent oor lads
    tae the Border!
    The English for ance, by guile wan the day,
The Flowers o' the Forest, that foucht aye the foremost,
    The prime o' our land are cauld in the clay.

Chae jumped up when she finished, he said *Damn't folk, we'll all have the whimsies if we listen to any more woesome songs! Have none of you a cheerful one?* And the folk in the barn laughed at him and shook their heads, it came on Chris how strange was the sadness of Scotland's singing, made for the sadness of the land and sky in dark autumn evenings, the crying of men and women of the land who had seen their lives and loves sink away in the years, things wept for beside the sheep-buchts, remembered at night and in twilight. The gladness and kindness had passed, lived and forgotten, it was Scotland of the mist and rain and the crying sea that made the songs—And Chae cried *Let's have another dance, then, it's nearly a quarter to twelve, we must all be off soon as midnight chaps.*

And they all minded what midnight would bring, and Chae and Rob had the melodeon and fiddle in hand again, and struck up an eightsome, and everybody grabbed him a partner, it didn't matter who was who, McIvor had Chris and danced with her as though he would like to squeeze her to death, he danced light as thistle-down, the great red Highlander; and no sooner was one dance finished than Rob and Chae swept forward into another, they played like mad and the lights whipped and jumped as the couples spun round and round; and the music went out across the snowing night; and then Chae pulled out his great silver watch, and laid it beside him, playing on.

And suddenly it was the New Year, the dancing stopped and folk all shook hands, coming to shake Chris's and Ewan's; and Long Rob struck up the sugary surge of *Auld Lang Syne* and they all joined hands and stood in a circle to sing it, and Chris though of Will far over the seas in Argentine, under the hot night there. Then the singing finished, they all found themselves tired, somebody began to take down the barn lights, there was half an hour's scramble of folk getting themselves into coats and getting their shivering sholts from out the empty stalls in the byre. Then Chris and Ewan were handshook again, Chris's arm began to ache, and then the last woof-woof of wheels on snow thick-carpeted came up the Blawearie road to them, it was fell uncanny that silence in the place after all the noise and fun of the long, lit hours. And there was Mistress Melon in the kitchen-door, yawning fit to swallow a horse, she whispered to Chris *I'm taking your room now, don't forget,* and cried them *Good night, and a sound sleep, both!* and was up the stairs and left them alone.

He hardly seemed tired even then, though, Ewan, prowling locking the doors like a great quiet cat till Chris called to him softly *Oh, sit by me!* So he came to the chair she sat in and picked her out of it, so strong he was, and himself sat down, still holding her. They watched the fire a long time and then Chris's head dropped down, she didn't know she had been asleep till she woke to find Ewan shaking her, *Chris, Chris, you're fair done, come on to bed.* The fire was dying then and the paraffin had run low in the lamp, the flame swithered and went out with a plop! as Ewan blew on it; and then they were in the dark, going up the stairs together, past the room that had been Chris's and where Mistress Melon slept for a night ere she went back to Stonehaven.

And to Chris going up that stair holding the hand of her man there came a memory of one with awful eyes and jutting beard, lying in that room they came to, lying there and whispering and cursing her. But she put the memory away, it had never happened, sad and daft to remember that, she was tired. Then, with her hand on the door, Ewan kissed her there in the dark, sweet and wild his kiss, she had not thought he could kiss her like that, not as though he wanted her as a man might do in that hour and place, but as though he minded the song he had heard her sing. She put up her face to the kiss, forgetting tiredness, suddenly she was wakeful as never she had been, the sleep went out of her head and body and the chill with it, Ewan's hand came over hers and opened the door.

A fire burned bright in the fireplace, they had thought the

place would be black and cold, but Mistress Melon had seen to that. And there was the bridal bed, pulled out from the wall, all in white it was, with sheet and blanket turned back, the window curtains were drawn, and in the moment they stood breathing from their climb of the stairs Chris heard the sound of the snow that stroked the window, with quiet, soft fingers, as though writing there.

Then she forgot it, standing by the fire getting out of her blue things, one by one. She found it sweet to do that, so slowly, and to have Ewan kiss her at last when there was no bar to his kisses, lying with him then, with the light put out and the radiance of the fire on the walls and ceiling. And she turned towards him at last, whispering and tender for him, *We're daft, we'll catch cold without anything on!* and then she saw his face beside her, solemn and strange, yet not strange at all. And he put his left hand below her neck, and he took her close to him, and they were one flesh, one and together; and far into the morning she woke, and was not cold at all, him holding her so, and then she heard again the hand of winter write on the window, and listened a moment, happy, happy, and fell fast asleep till morning brought Mistress Melon and two great cups of tea to waken Ewan and herself.

So that was her marriage, not like wakening from a dream was marrying, but like going into one, rather, she wasn't sure, not for days, what things they had dreamt and what actually done—she and this farmer of Blawearie who would stir of a morning at the jangle of the clock and creep from bed, the great cat, and be down the stairs to light the fire and put on the kettle. She'd never be far behind him, though, she loved even the bitterness of those frozen mornings, and a bitter winter it was, every crack and joint of the old house played a spray of cold wind across the rooms. He'd be gone to the byre and stable as she came down and sought out the porridge meal and put it to boil, Blawearie's own meal, fine rounded stuff that Ewan so liked. She'd leave it to hotter there on the fire and then bring the pails from the dairy and open the kitchen door on the close and gasp in the bite of the wind, seeing a grey world on the edge of morning, the bare stubble of the ley riding quick on the close, peering between the shapes of the stacks, the lights of the lanterns shining in byre and stable and barn as Ewan feeded and mucked and tended horses and kye.

And the byre would hang heavy with the breaths of the kye, they'd have finished their turnips as she came in, and Ewan would come swinging after her with a great armful of straw to spread them in front, he'd tickle her neck as she sat to milk and she'd cry *Your hand's freezing!* and he'd say *Away, woman, you're still asleep. Up in the morning's the thing!* and go whistling out to the stable, Clyde and Bess stamping there, getting fell cornfilled and frolicsome, they more than wanted exercise. She would carry the milk back herself most mornings and make the breakfast, but sometimes Ewan would come with her, so young and daft they were, folk would have laughed to see them at that, both making breakfast and sitting them close to eat it.

Then Ewan would light his pipe when he'd done and sit and smoke while she finished more slowly; and then he'd say that he'd meat the hens, and she'd tell him not to haver, she'd do that herself, and he'd argue, maybe sulk, till she kissed him back to his senses again. Then he'd laugh and get up and get down John Guthrie's gun, and be out and up in the moors till eleven, sometimes he'd bring a great bag and Chris would sell the spare rabbits to the grocer that came on Tuesdays.

There was little to be done, such weather on Blawearie. Ewan tidied the barn they'd danced in, it seemed years ago since that night, and got ready plough and sock and coulter for the time when the weather would break. And then he found the bruised corn running low in the great kist there, that was his first out-going from the place since his marriage, Chris watched him go, sitting in the front of the box-cart, Clyde in the shafts, the cart loaded down with corn for the Mill, and Ewan turning to wave to her from the foot of Blawearie brae. And all that afternoon he was away she fretted from room to room, oh! she was a fool, there was nothing could happen to him! And when at last he came back she ran out to him, fair scared he was at the way she looked, and thought her ill, and when she cried she had missed him so he went white and then blushed, just a boy still, and forgot to unyoke Clyde left in the cold, he was kissing Chris instead. And faith! for the bairns of farmers both they might well have had more sense.

But, and it crept into her mind that night and came often in the morning and days that followed, somehow that going of Ewan's to the Mill had ended the foolishness that shut them in fast from Kinraddie and all the world, they two alone, with all the gladness that was theirs alone and her kisses the most that Ewan'd ever seek and his kisses ending days and nights, and almost life itself for her. Kinraddie came in again, something of her own cool reliance came back, the winter wore on to its close, and mid-February brought the sun, weather that might well have come out of a May.

Looking out from her window as every morning still she did, Chris saw the steam of the lands below the house, it was as though the earth had swung round the fields of Kinraddie into the maw of the sun, a great furnace, and left them there to dry. The hills marched their great banners of steam into the face of each sunrise and through the whisper and wakening and shrouding of the morning came presently the moan of the foghorn at Todhead, a dreadful bellow, like a sore-sick calf, it went on and on, long after the mist had cleared, it rose and faded into the sun-dazzle overhead as great clouds of gulls came wheeling in from the sea. They knew what was toward on Kinraddie's land, Chris heard the call of them as she went about the day's work, and looked out on the ley field then, there was Ewan with the horses, ploughing his first rig, bent over the shafts, one foot in the drill, one the rig side, the plough-share, sharp and crude and new, cleaving the red-black clay. The earth wound back like a ribbon and curved and lay; and the cloud of gulls cawed and screamed and pecked on the rig and followed at Ewan's heels again.

All over Kinraddie there were horse-pairs out, though none so early as Ewan's, it seemed, folk had stayed undecided about the weather, they'd other things to do, they'd say, than just wait about to show off like that young Blawearie. But, when the day rose and at nine Chris set her a jug of tea in a basket, and set by it scones well buttered and jammed, and carried out the basket to Ewan *wishing* up the face of the rig, Chae Strachan, far away and below, was a-bend above his plough-shafts at the tail of his team, Upperhill had two pairs in the great park that loitered up to the larch-wood, and there was Cuddiestoun's pair, you guessed it him and his horses, though they never came full in sight, their heads and backs just skimmed the verge of the wood and hill.

Spring had come and was singing and rilling all over

the fields, you listened and heard, it was like listening to
the land new wake, to the burst and flow of a dozen burns
in this ditch and that; and when you turned out the cattle
for their first spring dander, in case they went off the legs,
they near went off the face of the earth instead, daft and
delighted, they ran and scampered and slid, Chris was
feared that the kye would break their legs. She tried driving
them down to the old hayfield, but the steers broke loose
and held down the road, and Ewan saw them and left his
plough and chased them across the parks, swearing blue
murder at them as he ran; and faith! if it hadn't been for
the postman meeting them and turning them at the end of
the road they might well have been running still.

Chris had known then mazes of things to do in that
bright coming of the weather, the house was all wrong, it
was foul and feckless, Ewan unyoking at midday would
come in and make hardly his way through the kitchen,
heaped high with the gear of some room, Chris saw her
long hands grow sore and red with the scrubbing she did
on the sour old walls. Ewan said she was daft, the place
was fine, what more did she want? And she said *Less dirt;*
and that maybe he liked dirt, she didn't; and he laughed
Well, maybe I do, I like you right well! and put his arm
round her shoulders and they stood and kissed in the mid
of the heaped and littered kitchen—awful to be like that,
said Chris, they could hardly be sane.

In March the weather broke, the rain came down in
plashing pelts, you could hardly see a hand's-length in front
of your face if you ran through the close. Ewan sat in the
barn, winnowing corn or tying ropes, or just smoking and
swearing out at the rain. Chae Strachan came up for a talk
on the second day, all in oilskins he came; and he sat in the
barn with Ewan and said he'd seen it rain like this in
Alaska, and the mountains move when the snows were melt-
ing. And Ewan said he didn't care a damn though Alaska
moved under the sea the morn, when would it clear on
Blawearie? Munro came next, then Mutch of Bridge End,
they'd nothing on their hands but watch the rain and shake
their heads and swear they were all fair ruined.

But at last it went, the unending rain of a fortnight went,
and that morning they woke and found it fine, Ewan took
him a look at the land from the bedroom window and
prompt lay back in the bed again. *Damn Blawearie and all*

that's on't, let's have a holiday the day, Chris quean. She
said *I can't, I'm cleaning the garret,* and Ewan got angered,
she'd never seen him angry like that before, Highland and
foreign then, spitting like a cat. *Are you to spend all your
days cleaning damned rooms? You'll be old and wizened
and a second Mistress Munro before you're well twenty.
Off on a holiday we're going to-day.*

And, secretly glad, she lay back, lying with her hands
under her head, lazy, and looking at him, thinking how
different he was from that lad she'd tramped to Dunnottar
with, so close she knew him now, the way he thought and
the things he liked and his kindness and slowness to take
offence, and the bitter offence, how it rankled in him, once
it was there! Like and not like what she'd thought and
wanted in those days before they had married. Spite of their
closest moments together, Ewan could still blush at a look
or a touch of hers; she touched him then to make sure,
and he did! He said *Hold off! you're a shameless limmer,
for sure, and not nineteen yet. Come on, let's get out and
get off.*

So they raced through the morning's work and by nine
were down at the Peesie's Knapp, and borrowed Chae's
gig and heard Chae promise to milk and take in Blawearie's
kye. Then out they drove and swung left through Kinraddie, into the Laurencekirk road, the sun shining and the
peewits calling, there were snipe in a loch they passed, the
North Sea was gloom-away by Bervie as the sholtie trotted
south. You could see then as the land rose higher the low
parks that sloped to the woods and steeple of Drumlithie,
beyond that the hills of Barras, the Reisk in its hollow
among its larch-woods. West of that rose Arbuthnott, a
fair jumble of bent and brae, Fordoun came marching up
the horizon in front of them then, and they were soon
going through it. Ewan said if he bided in Fordoun he'd
lay his neck on the railway line and invite the Flying Scots-
man to run over it, so tired he'd be of biding in a place
that looked like a barn painted by a man with nothing but
thumbs and a squint in both eyes.

But Chris liked the little place, she'd never seen it before
and the farms that lay about it, big and rich, with fine black
loam for soil, different from the clay of bleak Blawearie.
Ewan said *To hell with them and their fine land too, they're
not farmers, them, only lazy muckers that sit and make
silver out of their cotters;* and he said he'd rather bide in a

town and wear a damned apron than work in this countryside. And then they were near Laurencekirk, the best of
weather the day held still, Laurencekirk looked brave in the
forenoon stir, with its cattle mart and its printing office
where they printed weekly the *Kincardineshire Observer*,
folk called it *The Squeaker* for short. It had aye had a hate
for Stonehaven, Laurencekirk, and some said that it should
be the county capital, but others said God help the capital
that was entrusted to it; and would speak a bit verse that
Thomas the Rhymour had made, how ere Rome—

> became a great imperial city,
> Twas peopled first, as we are told,
> By pirates, robbers, thieves, banditti;
> Quoth Tammas: 'Then the day may come
> When Laurencekirk shall equal Rome.'

And when Laurencekirk folk heard that they would
laugh, not nearly cry as they did in Drumlithie when you
mocked at their steeple, or smile sick and genteel as they
did in Stonehaven when you spoke of the poverty toffs.
Ewan said it was a fine town, he liked Laurencekirk, and
they'd stop and have dinner there.

So they did, it was fine to eat food that another had
cooked. Then they looked at the day and saw how it wore
and planned to drive over to Edzell Castle—*There's nothing
to see there but a ruckle of stones,* said Ewan, *but you'll
like them fine, no doubt.*

So they did as they'd planned, the afternoon flew, it
was golden and green. Under Drumtochty Hill they passed,
Ewan told that in summer it came deeper with the purple
of heather than any other hill in Scotland; but it hung dark
and asleep like a great cloud scraping the earth as they
trotted past. There was never a soul at the castle but
themselves, they climbed and clambered about in the ruins,
stone on stone they were crumbling away, there were little
dark chambers in the angle walls that had sheltered the
bowmen long syne. Ewan said they must fair have been
fusionless folk, the bowmen, to live in places like that; and
Chris laughed and looked at him, queer and sorry, and
glimpsed the remoteness that her books had made.

She was glad to be out in the sun again, though, clouds
were racing it up from the North and Ewan said they'd not
need to loiter long. In the garden of the castle they wan-

dered from wall to wall, looking at the pictures crumbling there, balls and roses and rings and callipers, and wild heraldic beasts without number, Ewan said he was glad that they'd all been killed. But Chris didn't laugh at him, she knew right well that such beasts had never been, but she felt fey that day, even out here she grew chill where the long grasses stood in the sun, the dead garden about them with its dead stone beasts of an ill-stomached fancy.

Folk rich and brave, and blithe and young as themselves, had once walked and talked and taken their pleasure here, and their play was done and they were gone, they had no name or remembered place, even in the lands of death they were maybe forgotten, for maybe the dead died once again, and again went on. And, daft-like, she tried to tell Ewan that whimsy, and he stared at her, pushing his cap from his brow, and looked puzzled and said *Ay*, half-heartedly; he didn't know what she blithered about. She laughed then and turned away from him, angry at herself and her daftness; but once she'd thought there wouldn't be a thing they wouldn't understand together.

And the rain that had held away all the day came down at last and caught them on their way back home, overtaking them near to Laurencekirk, in a blinding surge that they watched come hissing across the fields, the sholtie bent its head to the storm and trotted on cannily, it grew dark all of a moment and Ewan found there was never a lamp on Chae's bit gig. He swore at Chae and then drove in silence, and the wind began to rise as they came on the long, bare road past Fordoun, near lifting the sholt from its feet; and out in the darkness they heard the foghorn moaning by Tod-head lighthouse. They were a pair of drookéd rats when they turned the gig into the close at Peesie's Knapp, and Chae cried to them to come in and dry, but they wouldn't, they ran all the way to Blawearie and the wet trees were creaking in the wind as they reached to their door.

Now that was the last wet day of the Spring and to Chris the weeks began to slip by like posts you glimpse from the fleeing window of a railway train in a day of summer—light and shade and marled wood, light and shade and the whoom of the train, life itself seemed to fly like that up through the Spring, Ewan had the corn land all ploughed and sown himself almost early as was the Mains; only in the yavil did Chris go out and carry the corn for him.

And that she liked fine, not a chave and a weariness as
it was with father, Ewan brisk and cheerful with the
smoulder gone from his eyes, they had settled to a clear,
slow shining, it seemed to Chris, now he had his own home
and wife. Then in the days of the harrowing Chris drove
the harrows while he carted manure to the turnip-land, she
was glad that she hadn't that work, glad to tramp behind
the horses instead, with kilted skirts, a switch in her hand
and the reins there and the horses plod-plodding steadily,
they knew her fine, and she spoiled them with bits of loaf
and jam so that Ewan, coming to drive them himself, cried
vexedly, *Hold up your head from my pockets, Clyde! What
the hell are you sniff-sniff-sniffing for?*

Then he went down to Stonehaven and bought a new
sower and sowed the turnips; and the night he finished
and unloosed and came back to the biggings for his supper,
he couldn't find Chris though he called and called. She
heard him calling and didn't answer, herself lying out in
the garden under the beeches, brave and green and rustling
their new Spring leaves, whispering without cease over her
head that was buried in the grass while she lay and thought.
A little insect ran over her hand and she hated it, but it
mightn't disturb her for this time at the least, nothing might
do that, she lay so certain and still because of this thing
that had come to her.

She felt neither gladness nor pain, only dazed, as though
running in the fields with Ewan she had struck against a
great stone, body and legs and arms, and lay stunned and
bruised, the running and the fine crying in the sweet air
still on about her, Ewan running fee and careless still not
knowing or heeding the thing she had met. The days of love
and holidaying and the foolishness of kisses—they might be
for him yet but never the same for her, dreams were fulfilled and their days put by, the hills climbed still to sunset
but her heart might climb with them never again and long
for to-morrow, the night still her own. No night would she
ever be her own again, in her body the seed of that pleasure
she had sown with Ewan burgeoning and growing, dark,
in the warmth below her heart. And Chris Guthrie crept
out from the place below the beech trees where Chris
Tavendale lay and went wandering off into the waiting
quiet of the afternoon, Chris Tavendale heard her go, and
she came back to Blawearie never again.

But she did not tell Ewan, not that night nor the week

that followed, nor the weeks after that, watching her own body with a secret care and fluttering eyes for the marks and stigmata of this thing that had come to her. And she saw her breast nipples change and harden and grow soft again, the breasts that Ewan had kissed and thought the wonder of God, a maid's breasts a maid's no longer, changing in slow rhythm of purpose with the sway and measure of each note in the rhythm, her belly rounding to plumpness below the navel, she looked in the glass and saw also her eyes changed, deeper and most strange, with red lights and veinings set in them.

And in the silences of the night, when the whit-owl had quieted out by the barn, once something moved there under her heart, moved and stirred drowsily, a sleeper from dreams; and she gasped and cried and then lay still, not wakening Ewan, for this was her rig and furrow, she had brought him the unsown field and the tending and reaping was hers, even as with herself when she lay in her own mother's body. And she thought of that, queer it seemed then how unclearly she had thought of that aforetime, shamed, indecent and coarse for a quean to think of such things—that her mother had once carried her as seed and fruit and dark movingness of flesh hid away within her.

And she wakened more fully at that, lying thinking while Ewan slept at her side, turned away from him, thinking of mother, not as her mother at all, just as Jean Murdoch, another woman who had faced this terror-daze in the night. They went sleepless in the long, dark hours for the fruitage of love that the sower slept all unaware, they were the plants that stood dark and quiet in the night, unmoving, immobile, the bee hummed home and away, drowsy with treasure, and another to-morrow for the hunting his.

So was the way of things, there was the wall and the prison that you couldn't break down, there was nothing to be done—nothing, though your heart stirred from its daze and suddenly the frozenness melted from you and still you might not sleep. . . . But now it was because of that babble of words that went round and around in your mind, soundless and scared of your lips, a babble of hours in the hills and loitering by lochs and the splendour of books and sleeping secure—babble of a world that still marched and cried beyond the prison walls, fair and unutterable its loveliness still outside the doors of Blawearie house, mocked by its ghost, a crying in the night for things that were lost and foregone and ended.

It quietened away then, morning came tapping at the window, she turned and slept, sleeping exhausted, rising with white face and slow steps so that she was long in the kitchen. And Ewan came hasting in, hurried that morning, the first of the turnips were pushing their thin, sweet blades of grass above the drills, he wanted to be out to them. *Damn't, Chris, are you still asleep?* he cried, half-laughing, half-angry, and Chris said nothing, going back to the dairy, Ewan stared and then moved uneasily and followed her with hesitant feet, *What's wrong? What's up?*

Turning to look at him, suddenly Chris knew that she hated him, standing there with the health in his face, clear of eyes—every day they grew clearer here in the parks he loved and thought of noon, morning and night; that, and the tending to beasts and the grooming of horses, herself to warm him at night and set him his meat by day. *What are you glowering for?* he asked, and she spoke then at last, calmly and thinly, *For God's sake don't deave me. Must you aye be an old wife and come trailing after me wherever I go?*

He flinched like a horse with the lash on its back, his eyes kindled their smoky glow, but he swung round and away from her. *You're out of bed the wrong side this morning,* and out he went. She was sorry then, wanted to cry to him, dropped the pails to run after him, when he spoilt it all, crying from the middle of the close: *And I'd like my breakfast before the night comes down.*

It was as though she were dry whin and his speech a fire to it, she ran out and overtook him there in the close, catching his shoulder and whirling him round, so surprised he was that he almost fell. *Speak to me like that?* she cried, *Do you think I'm your servant? You're mine, mind that, living off my meat and my milk, you Highland pauper! . . .* More than that she said, so she knew, no memory of the words abided with her, it was a blur of rage out of which she came with Ewan holding her shoulders and shaking her: *You damned bitch, you'd say that to me? To me? . . .* he was glaring like a beast, then he seemed to crumple, his hands fell from her. *Och, you're ill, you should be in your bed!*

He left her in the close then, striding to the barn, she stood like a fool with the tears of rage and remorse blinding her eyes. And as she went back to the kitchen and came out with the pails Ewan went striding away over the fields, his hoe on his shoulder, it was barely yet light, he was going to the parks without his breakfast. Milking the kye she hurried, her anger dying away, hurrying to be finished and have the breakfast ready, for he'd sure to be back again soon.

So she planned; but Ewan didn't come back. The porridge hottered to a thick, tough mess, beyond the raised blind the day broke thick and evilly red, hot like a pouring steam across the hills; the tea grew cold. Herself half-desperate with hunger she waited, couldn't sit, wandering from fire to door and door to table; and then she caught sight on the dresser of the whistle that had lain by father while he lay in paralysis in bed, and snatched it down, and all in a moment had run over the close to the lithe of the corn ricks.

Shading her eyes she saw Ewan then, down in the turnip-park, swinging steady and quick in lunge and recovery, Kinraddie's best hoer. Then she whistled to him loud and clear down through the morning, half Kinraddie must have heard the blast, but he took no notice. Then she went desperate in a way, she stopped from whistling and screamed to him, *Ewan, Ewan!* and at her first scream he looked up and dropped his hoe—he'd heard her whistling all right, the thrawn swine! She screamed again, he was running by then over the parks to the close; him not ten yards away she screamed a third time, hurting her throat, but she did it calmly, anger boiled in her, yet in a way she was cool enough.

And Ewan cried *God, Chris, have you gone clean daft? What are you screaming for, what do you want?* He towered up above her, angry, amazed, it was then that she knew for sure, she gathered up all the force in her voice and body for the reply that sprang to her lips and the thing that followed it. *That!* she said, and struck him across the face with her arm's full force, her fingers cried agony and then went numb, on Ewan's face a great red mark sprang up, the clap of the blow went echoing around the Blawearie biggings.

So she saw and heard, only a moment, next minute he was at her himself like a cat, her head rang and dirled as he struck her twice, she tried to keep her footing and failed and fell back, against the rick-side, clutching at the thing, staring feared at Ewan, the madness on his face, his fists coming up again. *Get up, get up!* he cried, *Damn you, get up!* and she knew he would strike her again, and rising shielded her face with her arm, trying to cram back the sobs in her throat, too late for that. Dizzy, she saw him in front of her swaying and moving, she couldn't see him but she cried *No, no!* and turned then and ran stumbling up through the close, up the hill to the moor. Twice he called as she ran, the second time so that nearly she stopped, *Chris, Chris, come back!* in a voice that was breaking as her own had been. But she couldn't stop running, a hare that the snare had whipped. *Never again, never again, the loch, the loch!* she sobbed as she ran and panted, the Standing Stones wheeling up from the whins to peer with quiet faces then in her face.

A quarter of an hour, half an hour, how long had she lain and dozed? Still morning in the air, she was soaked with dew. She turned and half-rose, heard the whistling of the broom and sank down again.

It was Ewan by the moor-gate, searching, he'd stopped to stare at the loch, thinking the thing she had thought, not seeing her yet. She sighed. She felt tired as though she had worked a great day in the sweat of the land, but Ewan would see to her, Ewan would take heed.

So she raised her voice and called to him and he came.

IV

HARVEST

It seemed to her that but hardly could she have left the place since that May-day more than six years ago when Ewan had come seeking her through the red, evil weather. She closed her eyes and put out a hand against the greatest of the Standing Stones, the coarse texture of the stone leapt cold to her hand, for a shivering wind blew down the hills. She started at thought of another thing then, opening her eyes to look round; but there he was, still and safe as he stood and looked at her. She cried *Stay by me, Ewan!* and he came running to her side; and she caught his hand and closed her eyes again, praying in a wild compassion of pity for that Ewan whose hand lay far from hers.

Six years: Spring rains and seeding, harvests and winters and springs again since that day that Ewan had come seeking her here with his white, chill face that kindled to warmth and well-being when she called him at last. She'd cried in his arms then, tired and tired, as he carried her down the hill; and the rage was quite gone from him, he bore her into the house and up to their bed, and patted her hand, and said *Bide you quiet!* and went off down the hill at a run.

So she learned he had run, and to Peesie's Knapp, but she didn't know then, she sank and sank away into sleep, and awakened long after with Ewan and still another man come in the room, it was Meldrum from Bervie, the doctor.

He peeled off his gloves from his long white hands, and peered at her like a hen with his gley, sharp eye. *What's this you've been doing, Chris Guthrie?*

He didn't wait a reply but caught up her hand and wrist and listened, still like a hen, head on one side while Ewan stared at him greyly. Then he said *Well, well, that's fine, let's see a bit more of you, young Mistress Tavendale.*

While he listened with the funny things at his ears and the end of it on her chest, she closed her eyes, ill no longer though drowsy still, and peeked sideways at Ewan, smiling at him. And then the doctor moved his stethoscope further down, it tickled her bared skin there and she knew he knew, and he straightened up *And you tell me you didn't know what the thing was, Chris Tavendale?*

She said *Oh, yes,* and he said *But not Ewan?* and she shook her head and they both laughed at Ewan standing there staring from one to the other, black hair unbrushed, she had gone near to killing him that morning. And then Dr. Meldrum shook him by the arm, *You're going to be a father, Blawearie man, what think you of that? Away and make me a cup of tea while Chris and I go into more intimate details—you needn't bide, she's safe enough with an old man, bonny though she be.*

All that he said as canny as ordering a jug of milk, Ewan gasped, and made to speak, and couldn't but his face was blithe as he turned and ran down the stairs. They heard him singing below and old Meldrum cocked his head to the side and listened, *Damned easy for him to sing, eh, Chris? But you'll sing yourself when this bairn of yours comes into the world. Let's see if everything's right.*

It was. He put his hand on her shoulder when he finished and gave her a shake. *A body as fine and natural and comely as a cow or a rose, Chris Guthrie. You'll have no trouble and you needn't fret. But look after yourself, eat vegetables, and be still as kind to Ewan as the wear of the months will let you be. Good for him and good for you.* She nodded to that, understanding, and he gave her another shake and went down to Ewan, and drank the tea that Ewan had made, if tea it was, which you doubted later when you smelt the cups.

Ewan knowing, Meldrum knowing, it was as though a bank had gone down behind which she had dreamt a torrent and a storm would burst and blind and whelm her. But there was nothing there but the corn growing and the peewits calling, summer coming, marching up each morning with unbraided hair, the dew rising in whorling mists from the urgent corn that carpeted Ewan's trim fields. Nothing to fear and much to do, most of all to tell Ewan not to fret, she wasn't a doll, she'd be safe as a cow though she hoped to God she didn't quite look like one. And Ewan said *You look fine, bonnier than ever,* saying it solemnly, meaning it, and she was glad, peeking at herself in the long mirror when she was alone, seeing gradually that smooth rounding of belly and hips below her frock—lucky she had never that ugliness that some poor folk have to bear, awful for them.

She took pleasure in being herself, in being as before, not making a difference, cooking and baking and running to the parks with the early morning piece for Ewan, he'd cry *Don't run!* and she'd cry *Don't blether!* and reach beside him, and sink down beside him midway the long potato rows he was hoeing, growing low and broad and well-branched, the shaws, it was set a fine year for potatoes. And as he sat and ate she'd gather his coat below her head for a pillow, and lean back with her arms outspread in the sun, and make of that few minutes her resting-time, listening to Ewan on the crops and the weather that was so good folk didn't believe it could last, there must soon be a break of the fine interplay of the last two months.

That was late in June he said that, and all the dour Howe watched the sky darkly, certain some trick was on *up there.* For the rain that was needed came in the night, just enough, not more, as though cannily sprinkled, and the day would be fine with sun, you couldn't want better; but it wasn't in the nature of things it would last. And Chris said, dreamily, *Maybe things are changing for the better all round,* and Ewan said *Damn the fears!* his gaze far off and dark and intent, the crops and the earth in his bones and blood, and she'd look in his face and find content, not jealous or curious or caring though she herself found in his eyes a place with the crops and land. And she'd close her eyes in the sun-dazzle then, in the smell, green, pungent, strong and fine, of the coming potato shaws, and sometimes she'd doze and waken sun-weary, Ewan working a little bit off, not clattering his hoe lest she wake.

She made up her mind she'd have the baby born in the room that had once been her own. So she rubbed it and scrubbed it till it shone again and brought out the bed mattress and hung it to air, in the garden, between the

beeches, all in leaf they were, so thick. You could hardly
see the sky looking up in that malachite, whispering dome;
and by as she looked came Long Rob of the Mill to settle
his bills with Ewan, he saw Chris then and came to lean on
the hedge, hatless, and long as ever, with the great moustaches and the iron blue eyes.

And he picked a sprig of the honeysuckle and bit it
between his teeth. *This'll be for the son, eh, Chris? And
when are you having him born?* She said *Late September
or early October, I think,* and Rob shook his head, it wasn't
the best time for bairns, though feint the fear for hers.
And he laughed as he leaned there, minding something,
and he told Chris of the thing, his own mother it was, the
wife of a crofter down in the Reisk. She'd had her twelve
children in sixteen years, nine of them died, Rob was the
oldest and only a lad and he'd seen the youngest of his
brothers born. *Seen? I helped, think of that, Chris quean!*
And think she did and she shivered, and Rob said *That was
daft, the telling of that. But things are fair right with you,
then, Chris?*

So maybe, going home, he told of Blawearie's news;
soon Kinraddie knew more than did Chris herself. Folk
began to trail in about in the quiet of an evening, out of ill-
fashionce, and nothing much more, they'd gley sidewise at
Chris as they'd argue with Ewan, syne home they would go
and tell it was true, *Ay, there'll soon be a family Blawearie
way, Chris must have fair have taken at the first bit sett.*
But others knew better, Mutch and Munro, and the speak
went round that the taking was well ere the marriage, Ewan
had married the quean when she threatened him with law.
Kinraddie mouthed that over, it was toothsome and tasty,
and the speak came creeping up to Blawearie, Chris never
knew how she heard it. But she did, Ewan did, and he
swore to go out and kick the backsides of Mutch and Munro till they'd dream of sitting as a pleasure and a passion.
And off he'd have set in the rage of the moment but Chris
caught him and held him, that would only be daft, folk
would think it the truer, the scandal; and if it made them
the happier to think as they did, let them think!

And then it seemed to Chris that her world up Blawearie
brae began to draw in, in and about her and the life she
carried, that moved now often and often, turning slow
under her heart in the early days, but jerking with sudden-

ness, a moment at a stretch now, sometimes, so that
she would sit and gasp with closed eyes. In, nearer and
nearer round herself and the house the days seemed to
creep, Will in Argentine was somebody she'd met in a
dream of the night, Aberdeenshire far away, nothing living
or moving but shadows in sunlight or night outside the
circle of the hills and woods she saw from Blawearie's
biggings. Then fancies came on her and passed, but were
daft and straining and strange while they lasted, she couldn't
break herself of the things, they'd to wear and fade at their
own bit gait.

One night it was that she couldn't touch kye, Ewan had
to do the milking himself, sore puzzled and handless he was
but she couldn't help that, though next morning she laughed
at herself, what was there to fear in the milking of kye?
Then came the day when they drove Chae Strachan's sheep
to the buchts and the libbing of the lambs went on till it
nearly drove her mad, the thin young baaing that rose an
unending plaint, the folk with their pipes and knives and
the blood that ran in the sunlight. All in a picture it rose
to her on the sound of that baaing, and she hid in the
dairy at last, the only place that shut out the sound.

But another fad, and the one that lasted the longest,
was fear that all sounds would go, fear of the night when it
might be so nearly still, Ewan sleeping with his head in his
arm as he sometimes did, soundless, till she'd think him dead
and shake him to a sleepy wakefulness; and he'd ask *What's
wrong? Have I been stealing the blankets from you?* and
she'd say *Yes*, ashamed to let him know of that fear of hers.

So she found the days blithe enough then, the scraich and
scratch of hens in the close, the sound of the mower that
Ewan drove up and down the rigs of the hay, the mooing
of the calves wild-plagued with flies, Clyde's neighing to a
passing stallion. Only night was the time to be feared, if
she woke and there was that stillness; but even the quietest
night if she listened hard she'd hear the wisp-wisp of the
beech leaves near to the window, quietening her, comforting her, she never knew why, as though the sap that swelled
in branch and twig were one with the blood that swelled
the new life below her navel, that coming day in the
months to be a thing she'd share with that whisperer out in
the darkness.

And oh, but the time was long! She could almost have
wished that she and Ewan had bedded unblessed as Mutch

said they had, the baby would have been here by now and not still to come, still waiting harvest and stooking and the gathering of stooks. But it lay with her, warm and shielded, and saw with her the growth and ripening of that autumn's corn, yellow and great, and the harvest moons that came so soon in that year, red moons a-slant and a-tilt on the rim of the earth they saw as they went to bed, you felt it another land and another world that hung there in the quietness of the sky.

One night, the mid-days of August as they sat at meat, the door burst open and in strode Chae Strachan, a paper in his hand, and was fell excited, Chris listened and didn't, a war was on, Britain was to war with Germany. But Chris didn't care and Ewan didn't either, he was thinking of his close that the weather might ruin; so Chae took himself off with his paper again, and after that, though she minded it sometimes, Chris paid no heed to the war, there were aye daft devils fighting about something or other, as Ewan had said; and God! they could fight till they were black and blue for all that he cared if only the ley field would come on a bit faster, it was near fit for cutting but the straw so short it fair broke your heart.

And out he'd go in the evening light, down to the ley park and poke about there, rig to rig, as though coaxing the straw to grow and grow in the night for his delight in the morning. A bairn with a toy, Chris thought, laughing as she watched him then; and then came that movement in her body as she watched Ewan still—a mother with his child he was, the corn his as this seed of his hers, burgeoning and ripening, growing to harvest.

The corn was first. Up and down the rigs on his brave new binder, Clyde and Bess each aside the pole, rode Ewan; and the corn bent and was smitten on the flyboard, and gathered up on the forking teeth and wound and bound and ejected. Up and down went the whirling arms, and fine harvest weather came then in Kinraddie, though it rained in Dee, folk said, and down in Forfar the year was wet. Park by park Ewan rode it down, Chris still could carry him a piece as he worked, but she walked slow now, careful and slow, and he'd jump from the binder and come running and meet her, and down he would sit her in the lithe of a stook while he stood and ate, his gaze as ever on the fields and sky, there was still the harvest to finish.

But finished it was, September's end, and there came a

blatter of rain next day, Chris saw the coming of the rain
and the bright summer went as the stook stood laden and
tall in the fields. And Chris found herself sick, a great pain
came and gripped at her breast, at her thighs, she cried
Ewan! and nearly fell and he ran to her. They stared in
each other's faces, hearing the rain, and then again the
pain drove through and through Chris like a heated sword,
and she set her teeth and shook Ewan free, she knew the
things she'd to do. *It'll maybe be a long time yet, but get
Chae to drive for the doctor and nurse. He'll bring the nurse
back from Bervie, Chae.*

Ewan stood and stared and his face was working, she
smiled at him then though the pain of the sword was as
nothing now, iron hooks were tearing in her body instead,
rusty and dragging and blunt. She held up her face to be
kissed and kept her teeth fast and said *Hurry, though I'm
fine!* and syne watched him run down the road to the
Knapp. Then, white, in a daze of pain, she began to walk
backwards and forwards on the kitchen floor, as she knew
she must do to bring on the birth quick, everything else was
ready and waiting in the room upstairs. And after a while
the pain waned and went, but she knew it would soon be
back.

So she filled her a hot-water bottle and almost ran up
the stairs to put it in the bed, almost running lest the pain
come midway and catch her unaware. But it held off still,
she smoothed out the sheets, brought out the rubber one
she'd had bought, and tied that down, firm and strong, and
set the great basin on the rug by the window and wondered
what else there might be. Then she saw her face in the
glass, it was flushed and bright and her eyes all hot; and
suddenly she thought how strange it would be if she died,
like the many women who died in childbed, she felt well
and strong, they had felt the same, strange to think that
her face might be dead and still in another day, that face
that she looked at now, it couldn't be hers, it was still the
face of a quean.

From the window she saw Ewan running back and as she
reached to the foot of the stairs to meet him the pain came
on her again, she had to sit down. But that was daft, it
would make it last longer, she struggled to her feet and
walked in the kitchen again, Ewan was in the doorway, a
white blur of a face and nothing else unless she looked at
him hard and hard. He kept saying *Chris, go and lie down!*

and she opened her mouth and gasped and meant to tell him she was fine; and instead found herself swearing and swearing, terrible words she hadn't known she knew, they were wrung from her lips as she went stumbling to and fro, better than screaming, women screamed, but she wouldn't.

And then came relief again, the kitchen straightened and she sat down, Ewan emerged from his blur and made her tea. Something kept worrying her—what was he to have for his dinner? She couldn't remember the thing she'd intended, and gave it up, her tormentors were nearby again. *Boil yourself an egg, Ewan!* she gasped, and he didn't understand, he thought it something she wanted—*Boil what?* And at that a frenzy of irritation came on her, *Oh, boil your head if you like!* and she dragged herself to her feet, the clock on the mantelshelf was expanding and contracting, its dial blurred and brightened as she stood. And then she was sure, she cried *Ewan, help me up to the room,* for she knew that her time had come.

What happened then she didn't know, there came a clear patch and she found herself nude, all but a stocking, it wouldn't come off, she sat on the bedside and tried, Ewan tried, it was so funny she giggled in spite of the pain. And then she saw Ewan's face, it had grown to the face of an old man, now, she must lie and get him out of the room. She cried *Mind the fire, Ewan, there's no wood there, run and hack some,* and when he was out of the room she could heed to herself and her agony at last; and she bit the sheets, she rolled herself tight in a ball, the pain seemed to go for a moment, maybe she had smothered the baby, she didn't care, she couldn't abide it, not through hours and hours and days and days, for weeks it had gone on now, she had seen the room darken and lighten and night come, tormented by Ewan and father her body, and Will was dead, they had tortured him first.

She cried *Will!* then opened her eyes from an hour-long sleep. In the room was the doctor and the nurse from Bervie, he came over to her side, old Meldrum, *Well Chris lass, how do you feel? Fine to send for us in such a stour, and here we coming tearing up to find you sleeping like a lamb! This is Mrs. Ogilvie, you've heard of her.*

Chris tried to speak, and managed, her body was a furnace, but she managed to speak, she didn't get it clear and she tried again. And Mrs. Ogilvie patted her and said *Don't bother with that. Do you feel you're getting on fine?* Dr.

Meldrum came back then, *Well, let's see;* and Chris poised
herself on the rim of a glistening cup of pain while they
looked at and felt at and straightened something alien and
white, it was her own body she remembered. Meldrum
said *Fine, fine, it shouldn't be long, I'll wait below,* and
went out and closed the door, he hated confinements. Mrs.
Ogilvie sat down and next minute jumped to her feet again,
*Don't do that, Mrs. Tavendale, don't grip yourself up!
Slacken and its easy, wish it to come, there's a brave girl!*

Chris tried: it was torment: the beast moved away from
her breasts, scrabbled and tore and returned again, it wasn't
a beast, red-hot pincers were riving her apart. Riven and
riven she bit at her lips, the blood on her tongue, she
couldn't bite more, she heard herself scream then, twice.
And then there were feet on the stairs, the room rose and
fell, hands on her everywhere, holding her, tormenting her,
she cried out again, ringingly, deep, a cry that ebbed to a
sigh, the cry and the sigh with which young Ewan Tavendale came into the world in the farm-house of Blawearie.

So quick as all that, she was lucky, folk said, bringing a
birth in a forenoon, just; it was twelve when Ewan was born.
Some folk, Mrs. Ogilvie told, had to thresh from dawn to
dusk and through another night to another day, and Chris
lay and nodded and said *Yes, I know,* and fell fast asleep,
she didn't dream at all. And, waking, she found herself
washed and dried, a new nightgown put on her and Mrs.
Ogilvie knitting by the side of the bed, nothing else, oh!
she couldn't have dreamt and not known it. She whispered,
scared, *My baby?* and Mrs. Ogilvie whispered *Beside you,
don't crush him,* and Chris turned round her head and saw
then beside her a face as small as though carved from an
apple, near, perfect and small, with a fluff of black hair and
a blue tinge on long eyelids, and a mouth that was Ewan's
and a nose her own and she nearly cried out *Oh, my baby!*

So she lay and wondered, near cried again, and put out
her hand, it felt strong and quick, only heavy, and her
fingers passed up and along, under its swathings, a body as
small and warm as a cat's, with a heart that beat steady
and assured. And the baby opened his eyes and fluttered
them at her and yawned and she saw a tongue like a little
red fish in the little red mouth; and the blue-shaded eyelids
went down again and young Ewan Tavendale slept.

Sweet to lie beside him in the hours that went by, sleeping herself now and then and wakening to watch him, not ugly as she'd thought he'd be, lovely and perfect. And then he moved and whimpered, unrestful, and was picked from the bed in Mrs. Ogilvie's hands, and fluttered his eyelids at her, Chris saw, and opened his mouth and weeked like a kitten. And Mrs. Ogilvie said *He's hungry now,* Chris found him in her arms at last, and hugged him, just once, and held him to her breast.

The blind little mouth came kissing and lapping, he wailed his disappointment, his little hands clawing at her. Then his lips found her nipple, it hurt and it didn't, it was as though he were draining the life from her body, there was nothing better than to die that way, he was hers close and closer than his father had been, closer than again could any child be. And she wondered above him and kissed his black hair, damp still from the travail of birth; and looked at the eyes that stared so unwinkingly as the hungry lips clung to her breast. So at last he was finished, then Ewan came up, he'd come while she slept before and he bent and kissed her and she cried *Mind the baby!* and he said *By God, am I like to forget?* And he wiped his forehead, poor Ewan!

In a week Mrs. Ogilvie was gone and Chris felt so well she was up and about, it was daft to lie wearied and feckless when she felt so fine. So down to the kitchen and the shining of the October sun she came, she and her baby, into the whisper and murmur of that war that had so excited Chae Strachan.

For it was on, not a haver only, every soul that came up to look at young Ewan began to speak of it sooner or later. Chae came and looked at young Ewan and tickled his toes and said *Ay, man!* And he told them they'd brought out a fine bit bairn between them, every man might yet have to fight for bairn and wife ere this war was over; and he said that the Germans had broken loose, fair devils, and were raping women and braining bairns all over Belgium, it was hell let loose. And Ewan said *Who'll win, then?* and Chae said if the Germans did there'd be an end of both peace and progress forever, there wouldn't be safety in the world again till the Prussians—and they were a kind of German, with meikle spiked helmets, awful brutes, and the very worst—were beaten back to the hell they came from. But Ewan just yawned and said *Oh, to hell with them and their hell both, Chae! Are you going to the mart the morn?*

For he didn't care, Ewan; but the mart was as bad, nobody spoke of anything but war, Munro of the Cuddiestoun was there, and Mutch, they'd a fair drink in their bellies, both, and swore they'd 'list the morn were they younger, by God. That was just the drink speaking, no doubt, but the very next day the Upperhill foreman, James Leslie he was that had taken Ewan's place, went into Aberdeen and joined in the Gordons, he was the first man to go from Kinraddie and was killed fell early. But folk thought him fair daft, showing off and looking for a holiday, just, there was no use coming to such stir as that when the war would so soon be over. For the papers all said that it would, right fierce they were, *Man, some of those editors are right rough creatures, God pity the Germans if they'd their hands on them!* And folk shook their heads, and agreed that the newspaper billies were ill to run counter.

But the Germans didn't care—maybe they didn't read the papers, said Long Rob of the Mill; they just went on with their raping of women and their gutting of bairns, till Chae Strachan came up to Blawearie one night with a paper in his hand and a blaze on his face, and he cried that he for one was off to enlist, old Sinclair could heed to the Knapp and to Kirsty. And Ewan cried after him, *You're havering, man, you don't mean it!* but Chae cried back *Damn't ay, that I do!* And sure as death he did and went off, by Saturday a letter came to Peesie's Knapp that told he had joined the North Highlanders and been sent to Perth.

So there was such speak and stir as Kinraddie hadn't known for long, sugar was awful up in price and Chris got as much as she could from the grocer and stored it away in the barn. Then Ewan heard funny things about the sermon that the Reverend Gibbon had preached the Sunday before, and though he couldn't bear with a kirk he broke his habit and put on his best suit and went down to the service next Sabbath.

There was a fell crowd there, more than Ewan had heard of the last week's sermon, and the place was all on edge to hear what the Reverend Gibbon would say. He looked bigger and more like a bull than ever, Ewan thought, as he mounted the pulpit, there was nothing unusual as he gave out the hymn and the prayer. But then he took a text, Ewan couldn't mind which, about Babylon's corruptions, they'd been right coarse there. And he said that God was sending the Germans for a curse and a plague on the world because of its sins, it had grown wicked and lustful, God's anger was loosed as in the days of Attila. How long it would rage, to what deeps of pain their punishments would go, only God and His anger might know. But from the chastisement by blood and fire the nations might rise anew, Scotland not the least in its ancient health and humility, to tread again the path to grace.

And just as he got there, up rose old Sinclair of the Netherhill, all the kirk watched him, and he put on his hat and he turned his back and went step-stepping slow down the aisle, he wouldn't listen to this brute defending the German tinks and some friend that he called Attila. Hardly had he risen when Mutch rose too, syne Cuddiestoun, and they too clapped on their hats; and Ellison half made to rise but his wife pulled him down, he looked daft as a half-throttled turkey then, Ella White wasn't to have him make himself a fool for any damned war they waged. But the minister turned red and then white and he stuttered when he saw folk leaving; and his sermon quietened down, he finished off early and rattled off the blessing as though it was a cursing. Outside in the kirkyard some young folk gathered to clout him in the lug as he came from the kirk, but the elders were there and they edged them away, and Mr. Gibbon threaded the throngs like a futret with kittle, and made for the Manse, and padlocked the gate.

But Ewan didn't care one way or the other, as he told to Chris. The minister might be right or be wrong with his Babylons and whores and might slobber Attila every night of the week, Blawearie had its crop all in and that was what mattered. And Chris said *Yes, what a blither about a war, isn't it, Ewan?* and tickled young Ewan as he lay on her lap. And he laughed and kicked and his father sat down and looked at him, solemn, and said it was fair wonderful, *Did you see him look up at me then, Chris quean?*

So they were douce and safe and blithe in Blawearie though Kinraddie was unco with Chae Strachan gone. Kirsty came up on a visit and cried when she sat in the kitchen beside the crib, Chris made her tea but she wouldn't take comfort. She said she knew well enough Chae'd never come back, he was in such a rage with the Germans he'd just run forward in his bit of the front and kill and kill till he'd fair lost himself. Chris said *And they're maybe not such bad folk as the papers make out,* and at that Kirsty Strachan jumped up *So, you're another damned pro-German as well, are you? There's over-many of your kind in Kinraddie.* Chris stared clean amazed, but out Kirsty Strachan went running, still crying, and that was the last they saw of her in many a week, maybe she was ashamed of her outburst.

Whether or not *she* was, there could be never a doubt about the Reverend Gibbon. For the next Sabbath day, when another great crowd came down to the kirk to hear him preach, they got all the patriotism they could wish, the minister said that the Kaiser was the Antichrist, and that until this foul evil had been swept from the earth there could be neither peace nor progress again. And he gave out a hymn then, *Onward, Christian Soldiers* it was, and his own great bull's voice led the singing, he had fair become a patriot and it seemed likely he thought the Germans real bad. But Long Rob of the Mill, when he heard the story, said it was a sight more likely that he thought the chance of losing his kirk and collections a damned sight worse than any German that was ever yet clecked.

For, and it grew a fair scandal all through the Howe, you could hardly believe it, it was funny enough, Long Rob of the Mill didn't hold with the war. He said it was a lot of damned nonsense, those that wanted to fight, the M.P.s and bankers and editors and muckers, should all be locked up in a pleiter of a park and made to gut each other with graips: there'd be no great loss to the world and a fine bit sight it would make for decent folk to look on at. But for folk with sense to take part in the soss and yammer about King and country was just plain hysteria; and as for Belgium invaded, it got what it needed, what about the Congo and your Belgians there? Not that the Germans weren't as bad, they were all tarred with the same black brush.

But, though folk weren't patriots as daft as Chae Strachan, that didn't look when he was being laughed at, they knew right well that Long Rob couldn't lie like that, the long, rangy childe, without being pro-German, as the papers called it. For all the papers were full of pro-Germans then, British folk that thought that the German rascals were right; and in England folk went and smashed in their windows, such a rage they were in with the pro-Germans for being so coarse. There was little danger that they'd smash Rob's windows, there were few that cared to tackle the childe except Chae Strachan that was training in Perth.

So the whole stour might well have blown over, Rob was
a well-liked billy and you needn't heed his blithers, if the
Reverend Gibbon hadn't taken to the business and preached
a sermon about tinks and traitors and a lot he preached
about a jade called Jael, fell uncanny she'd been, right holy,
though, and she'd killed a childe Sisera that she couldn't
thole, because he was coarse to the Jews. And the Reverend
Gibbon boomed out she was fine, a patriot and a light unto
Israel she'd been, and we in like manner must act the same,
right here in our midst were traitors that sided with the
Antichrist, shame on Kinraddie that it should be so!

Folk listened to the sermon and fair got excited, and
after dinner that Sabbath a horde of billies, some came from
Kinraddie though most did not, but Upperhill's new foreman was there, and an awful patriot childe just like Gordon
himself, they went down to the Mill, and there was Long
Rob sitting out by his door, smoking at his pipe and reading in a book, coarse stite about God and God knows what.
And the Upperhill foreman cried out *Here's the Kaiser's
crony, let's duck the mucker!* and the lot made a run at
Rob and got him gripped in their hands, Rob thought it
some joke and he laughed at them, setting by his bit book.
But they soon let him know they were serious enough, they
were clean worked up about the sermon and Long Rob
the Antichrist's friend, and they started to haul Rob over
to the mill-course then, where the water was sparkling and
raging from a good bit spate in the hills.

Syne at last Rob knew they meant what they said, folk
told that he gave a great cry that wasn't a curse and wasn't
a shout, it was both together; and as they dragged him he
lifted his foot, real coarse-like, and he kicked the foreman
at the Upperhill right in the tender parts then, and the foreman at the Upperhill he screamed like a fell stuck pig; and
God! folk laughed right well when they heard about that.
Well, the next thing that happened was that Rob got a hand
free then, and he took a childe near him, a meikle man from
the Mains, a clout in the ear that stretched him flat; and
then Rob was free and he ran, all the rest at his heels, for
the house. But he could run right well, could Rob and fair
outdistanced the pack, and he leapt inside and he barred
the door.

So they threw some stones and rammed at the door with
their shoulders, half-shamed by then at the stour they were
raising, and maybe they knew they'd feel fools by Monday;

and they might have gone home in another minute if it
hadn't been that the meikle Mains man, him that Rob had
couped on the ground with a clout in the ear, crawled up
to his feet and picked up a great stone; and crack! through
the kitchen window it went with a bang and a splinter inside!

Next minute the door flung open, they turned and looked
and there was Long Rob, a gun in his hand and his face
fair grey with rage. Some cried *Take care, man, now, put
down that gun!* but they edged away back for all that. And
Rob cried out *Smash in my window you would, then,
would you, you scum?* and he swung the gun at the nearest
billy and let drive at him. The pellets sang past the billy's
head and he'd had enough of the war, he turned and ran
like a rabbit; and the others scattered and ran as well, and
Long Rob ran after them, and his gun went bang! again
and again, you could hear it all over Kinraddie.

Folk ran to their doors, they thought the Germans had
landed and were looting the Mearns; Chris, who had run
across the Blawearie cornyard, shaded her eyes and looked
over the country and at last she saw them, the running
figures, like beetles in the distance, they fanned out and
ran from the Mill as focus. And behind ran another that
stopped now and then, and a puff of smoke went up at each
stopping, and there came the bang of the gun. Mist was
coming down and it blinded the battlefield, and through it
the attacking army ran in an awful rout, Chris saw them
vanish into its coming and Long Rob, still shooting, go
scudding in chase.

So that was the result of the Reverend Gibbon's sermon,
Kinraddie fair seethed with the news next day, all about
the attack on the Mill and how Rob had chased the childes
that came up against him, some could hardly sit down for
a week after that, so full were their backsides with pellets.
And some said that Long Rob was a coarse tink brute, if
he was willing to fight like that at the Mill it was him that
should go out to France and fight; but others, though they
weren't so many, Chris and Ewan were among them, liked
Long Rob and sided with him, and said it was a damn poor
show for Scotland if her patriots aye ran as they had at
the Mill. That had been the Sunday, but on Wednesday was
another happening, and God knows what mightn't have
come of *it* but for the interfering of the daftie Tony, him
that bided at Cuddiestoun.

He'd been stitering along the Denburn road, had Tony,
when he rounded a bend and there, on the road outside the
Mill, was the Reverend Gibbon, his bicycle was lying in the
stour and Long Rob had him gripped by the collar, and if
he wasn't in danger of a bash in the face appearances were
sore deceptive. For Long Rob had seen the minister come
riding in the distance and knew his black coat and stopped
the Mill and ran down to the road to ask what the hell the
Reverend had meant by saying he was friends with the Antichrist. And the Reverend Gibbon turned red with rage and
cried *Stand out of my way there, Rob*, and Rob cried *Stand
still you first, my man, for we've a bit bone to pick!* and as
the minister tried to ride him down Rob caught the handles
and twisted them sore, and off the minister came, like a
sack of corn, right flump in Rob's hands.

And Rob gave him a bit shake and asked *Who's pro-
German?* and the minister swore himself blue and made at
Rob, and Rob shook him like a futret a rabbit, and syne
stood back and looked close at his face, and made up his
mind that he'd smash in the minister's bit nose right then,
he'd seen that kind of thing done before and it fair sossed
up a pretty man, you just struck and struck till the bone
gave way.

So Rob was just starting to mash up the minister childe
when round the bend with a funny bit screech came the
daftie Tony, he scraiched like a hen with a seed in its throat
and ran and caught at Rob's arm. *He's only a half-witted
cleric, Rob, you'll dirty your hands on him*, he cried, and
both Rob and minister, sore astounded, stopped from their
fighting and stared at the creature, the impudence of him
with his wee red beard, and him only a daftie, like. But he
nodded to the minister *Get while the going's good and your
hide's still intact*, he said, and if you'd believe it the minister
louped on his bicycle without a word, and off he rode; and
Long Rob turned and asked the daftie where he'd hidden
his sense all the time they'd known him, but Tony stood
still like a stock of rags, a daft-like look on his face. And
when Rob spoke to him again he just smiled like a gowk,
and went shuffling away through the stour.

Some said that if all things were true that wouldn't be
a lie, but Rob swore to it, he wasn't boasting what he'd done
to the minister, he said, he was just so astonished at Tony
he'd to tell them the story to make Tony's part plain. Cuddiestoun swore 'twas a lie from beginning to end, the thing

you'd expect from a damned pro-German, like; but he didn't
say that to Long Rob, he was over coarse in the feet, Munro,
to run as fleet as the other billies had when Rob got in
action. But he stopped his trade with Long Rob and he
carted his corn for crushing and bruising over to the mill
at Mondynes, syne Mutch of Bridge End did the same. Ah
well, they might do that if they liked, folk as a rule were
hardly so daft as leave the best miller for miles around just
because of his saying that all the Germans could hardly be
tinks. Maybe, you know, there was something in what the
man said, coarse devils though most of the Germans were.

But Chris didn't care, sitting there at Blawearie with
young Ewan at her breast, her man beside her, Blawearie
theirs and the grain a fine price, forbye that the stirks sold
well in the marts. Maybe there was war and bloodshed and
that was awful, but far off also, you'd hear it like the North
Sea cry in a morning, a crying and a thunder that became
unending as the weeks went by, part of life's plan, fringing
the horizon of your days with its pelt and uproar. So the
new year came in and Chris watched young Ewan change
and grow there at her breast, he was quick of temper like
his father, good like his mother, she told Ewan; and Ewan
laughed *God, maybe you're right! You could hardly be
wrong in a thing after bringing a bairn like that in the
world.* And she laughed at him *But you helped a little!* and
he blushed as red as he always did, they seemed daft as
ever in their love as the days wore on.

It was still as strange and as kind to lie with him, live
with him, watch the sweat on his forehead when he came
from tramping a day in the parks at the heels of his horses;
still miracle to hear beside her his soundless breathing in
the dark of the night when their pleasure was past and he
slept so soon. But she didn't herself, those nights as the
Winter wore to March, into Spring: she'd lie and listen to
that hushed breathing of his one side of her, the boy's
quicker breath in his cradle out by—content, content, what
more could she have or want than the two of them, body
and blood and breath? And morning would bring her out
of her bed to tend young Ewan and make the breakfast and
clean out the byre and the stable singing: she worked never
knowing she tired and Long Rob of the Mill came on her
one morning as she cleaned the manure from the stable and

he cried *The Spring of life, eh, Chris quean. Sing it and
cherish it 'twill never come again!*

Different from the old Rob he looked, she thought, but
thought that carelessly, hurried to be in to young Ewan.
But she stopped and watched him swing down the rigs to
Ewan by the side of his horses, Ewan with his horses halted
on the side of the brae and the breath of them rising up
like a steam. And she heard Ewan call *Ay, man, Rob,* and
Rob call *Ay, man, Ewan,* and they called the truth, they
seemed fine men both against the horizon of Spring, their
feet deep laired in the wet clay ground, brown and great,
with their feet on the earth and the sky that waited behind.
And Chris looked at them over-long, they glimmered to her
eyes as though they had ceased to be there, mirages of men
dreamt by a land grown desolate against its changing sky.
And the Chris that had ruled those other two selves of herself, content, unquestioning these many months now, shook
her head and called herself daft.

That year's harvest fell sharp away, but the price of corn
made up for it, other prices might rise but farming folk
did well. So it went in the winter and into the next year too,
Ewan took in a drove of Irish steers to eat up the lush green
grass of nineteen-sixteen. They grew fat and round in the
shortest while, Chris proud to see them, so many beasts had
Blawearie. You'd hardly believe 'twas here father had
chaved and fought for a living the way he did; but that was
before the War.

For it still went on, rumbling its rumours like the thunder
of summer beyond the hills. But nobody knew now when
it would finish, not even Chae Strachan come home, a soldier all the way from the front, as they called it; in the
orra-looking khaki he came, with two stripes sewn on his
arm, he said they had made him a corporal. He came up to
Blawearie the night he got home and scraped his feet on the
scraper outside and came dandering into the kitchen as aye
he had done, not knocking but crying through the door,
Ay, folk, are you in?

So there was Chae, Chris gave a loud gasp to see him,
Chae himself, so altered you'd hardly believe it, Chae himself, thin, his fine eyes queered and strained somehow. Even
his laugh seemed different, hearty as it was, and he cried
God, Chris, I'm not a ghost yet! and syne Chris and Ewan
were shaking his hands and sitting him down and pouring
him a dram and another after that. And young Ewan came

running to see and cried *soldier!* and Chae caught him and swung him up from the floor and cried *Chris's bairn—God, it can't be, I mind the day he was born, just yesterday it was!*

Young Ewan took little to strangers, most, not frightened but keep-your-distance he was, but he made no try to keep distant from Chae, he sat on his knee as Chris spread them supper and Chae spoke up about things in the War, it wasn't so bad if it wasn't the lice. He said they were awful, but Chris needn't be feared, he'd been made to stand out in the close by Kirsty and strip off everything he had on, and fling the clothes in a tub and syne get into another himself. So he was fell clean, and God! he found it a change not trying to reach up his shoulders to get at some devil fair sucking and sucking the life from his skin.

And he gave a great laugh when he told them that, his old laugh queerly crippled it was. And Ewan asked what he thought of the Germans, were they truly coarse? And Chae said he was damned if he knew, he'd hardly seen one alive, though a body or so you saw now and then, gey green and *feuch! there's a supper on the table!* Well, out there you hardly did fighting at all, you just lay about in those damned bit trenches and had a keek at the soil they were made of. And man, it was funny land, clay and a kind of black marl, but the French were no good as farmers at all, they just pleitered and pottered in little bit parks that you'd hardly use as a hanky to wipe your neb. Chae didn't like the French at all, he said they were damned poor folk you'd to fight for, them, meaner than dirt and not half so sweet.

And Ewan listened and said *So you don't think that I should join up, Chae?* and Chris stared at him, Chae stared at him, young Ewan stared, and they all three stared till Chae snorted *There are fools enough in the fighting as it is.* Chris felt something holding her throat, she'd to cough and cough, trying to speak, and couldn't, and Ewan looked at her shamed-like and blushed and said *Och, I was asking, only.*

Chae went round all Kinraddie on his leave that time and found changes enough to open his eyes, maybe he was fell wearied with the front, folk thought, there was nothing on there but their pleitering and fighting. And the first change he saw the first morning, did Chae, lying down on his bed for the pleasure of it and Kirsty at the making of his breakfast. And Chae sat up in his bed to reach for his pipe when he looked from the window and he gave a great roar; and he louped from his bed in his sark so that Kirsty came running and crying *What is't? Is't a wound?*

But she found Chae standing by the window then, cursing himself black in the face he was, and he asked how long had *this* been going? So Mistress Strachan looked out the way he looked and she saw it was only the long bit wood that ran by the Peesie's Knapp that vexed him, it was nearly down the whole stretch of it, now. It made a gey difference to the look-out faith! but fine for Kinraddie the woodmen had been, they'd lodged at the Knapp and paid high for their board. But Chae cried out *To hell with their board, the bastards, they're ruining my land, do you hear!* And he pulled on his trousers and boots and would fair have run over the park and been at them; but Kirsty caught at his sark and held him back and cried *Have you fair gone mad with the killing of Germans?*

And he asked her hadn't she got eyes in her head, the fool, not telling him before that the wood was cut? It would lay the whole Knapp open to the north-east now, and was fair the end of a living here. And Mistress Strachan answered up that she wasn't a fool, and they'd be no worse than the other folk, would they? all the woods in Kinraddie were due to come down. Chae shouted *What, others?* and went out to look; and when he came back he didn't shout at all, he said he'd often minded of them out there in France, the woods, so bonny they were, and thick and grave, fine shelter and lithe for the cattle. No more than that would he say, it seemed then to Kirsty that he quietened down, and was quiet and queer all his leave, it was daft to let a bit wood go vex him like that.

But the last night of his leave he climbed to Blawearie and he said there was nothing but the woods and their fate that could draw his eyes. For over by the Mains he'd come on the woodmen, teams and teams of them hard at work on the long bit forest that ran up the high brae, sparing nothing they were but the yews of the Manse. And up above Upperhill they had cut down the larch, and the wood was down that lay back of old Pooty's.

Folk had told him the trustees had sold it well, they got awful high prices, the trustees did, it was wanted for aeroplanes and such-like things. And over at the office he had found the factor and the creature had peeked at Chae through his horn-rimmed glasses and said that the Govern-

ment would replant all the trees when the War was won.
And Chae had said that would console him a bloody lot,
sure, if he'd the chance of living two hundred years and
seeing the woods grow up as some shelter for beast and
man: but he doubted he'd not last so long. Then the factor
said they must all do their bit at a sacrifice, and Chae
asked *And what sacrifices have you made, tell me, you
scrawny wee mucker?*

That wasn't fair to the factor, maybe, who was a decent
childe and not fit to fight, but Chae was so mad he hardly
knew what he said, and didn't much care. So when he fell
in with old Ellison things were no better. For Ellison'd
grown fair big in the mind and the pouch, folk said he was
making silver like a dung-heap sourocks; and he'd bought
him a car and another piano; and he said *Ow, it's you,
Charles lad! Are you home for long?* and he said *And I'll
bet you want back to the front line, eh?* And Chae said that
he'd be wrong in the betting, faith ay! *Did you ever hear
tell of a body of a woman that wanted a new bairn put
back in her womb?* And Ellison gowked and said *No.* And
Chae said *And neither have I, you gowk-eyed gomeril,* and
left him at that; and it was hardly a kindly remark, you
would say.

But it seemed the same wherever he went in Kinraddie,
except at the Mill and his father-in-law's; every soul made
money and didn't care a damn though the War outlasted
their lives; they didn't care though the land was shaved of
its timber till the whole bit place would soon be a waste
with the wind a-blow over heath and heather where once
the corn came green. At Cuddiestoun he came on the
Munro pair, they were rearing up hundreds of chickens that
year and they sold them at great bit prices to the Aberdeen
hospitals. So busy they were with their incubators they'd
but hardly time to take notice of him, Mistress Munro
snapped and tweeted at him, still like a futret, and the
creature wrinkled its long thin neb: *Ah well, we'll have to
get on with our work. Fine being you and a soldier, Chae,
with your holidays and all. But poor folk aye have to work.*
Munro himself looked shamed at that and coloured all over
his ugly face, poor stock, but he'd hardly time to give Chae
a dram, so anxious he was with a new brood of hens.

So Chae left him fell quick, the place got on his stomach
and syne as he held through the parks he came bang on
Tony, standing right mid-way the turnip-field. And his eyes

were fixed on the ground and God! he might well have stood
there for days by the look of him. Chae cried out to him,
Ay, then, Tony man not expecting any reply, but Tony
looked up and aside, *Ah, Chae, so the mills of God still
grind?*

And Chae went on, and he thought of that, a real daft-
like speak he thought it at first, but further up the brae as
he held by Upprums, he scratched his head, was the thing
so daft? He stopped and looked back, and there, far below,
was the Tony childe, standing, glued to the ground. And
Chae shivered in a way, and went on.

So Chae wandered his round of Kinraddie, a strange place
and desolate with its crash of trees and its missing faces.
And not that alone, for the folk seemed different, into their
bones the War had eaten, they were money-mad or mad
with grief for somebody killed or somebody wounded—like
Mistress Gordon of the Upperhill, all her pride gone now
because of the Jock she had loved and aye called John.
But it was Jock she called him when Chae sat with her in
the parlour then, and she told him the news of her blinded
son in the hospital in England.

He wouldn't ever see again, it wasn't just a nervous trouble or anything like that, he'd drawn back the bandages
when she went to see him and shown her the great red holes
in his head; and syne he'd laughed at her, demented like,
and cried: *What think you of your son now, old wife?—
the son you wanted to make a name for you with his bravery
in Kinraddie? Be proud, be proud, I'll be home right soon
to crawl round the park and I'll show these holes to every
bitch in the Mearns that's looking for a hero.* He'd fair
screamed the words at his mother and a nurse had come
running and soothed him down, she said he didn't know
what he said, but Mistress Gordon had never a doubt about
that. And she told Chae about it and wept uncovered, her
braveness and her Englishness all fair gone; and when
Gordon came into the room he looked different too, shrivelled up he was, he'd taken to drink, folk said.

So Chae went out across the parks to the Bridge End
then and half-wished that he'd missed the Upperhill. But
across the nethermost park below the larch wood he ran
into young Maggie Jean, her that Andy the daftie had near
mischieved, grown a gey lass, and he hardly knew her. But
she knew him fine and smiled at him, blithe and open. *It's
Chae Strachan! You look fine as a soldier, Chae! And please*

can I have a button? So he cut off a button from his tunic for her and they smiled at each other, and he went out across the fields with a lighter heart then, she was sweet as a sprig of Blawearie 'suckle.

Bridge End he found with Alec away, he'd gone selling sheep in Stonehaven. But Mistress Mutch was there and she sat and smoked at a cigarette and told him that Alec was still a fell patriot, he'd enrolled in the volunteers of Glenbervie and every other night went down to Drumlithie for drill, a sight for sore eyes, the gowks, prancing about like dogs with diarrhœa, that's what they minded her of.

And she asked Chae when the War was to end, and Chae said *God only knows* and she asked *And you still believe in Him?* And Chae was real shocked, a man might have doubts and his disbelief, you expected a woman to be different, they needed more support in the world. But now that he thought of God for himself he just couldn't say, there was more of His enemy over in France, that minded him now he must give the Reverend Gibbon a look up at the Manse. But Mistress Mutch said *Haven't you heard, then? Mr. Gibbon's gone, he's a Colonel-chaplain in Edinburgh now, or something like that; and he wears a right brave uniform with a black hanky across the neck of it. His father's come down to take his place, an old bit stock that drinks German blood by the gill with his porridge, by the way he preaches.*

At Pooty's Chae knocked and knocked and got feint the answer. And folk were to tell him that wasn't surprising, old Pooty had taken to locking himself in nowadays, he got queerer and queerer, he said every night he heard men tramping the roads in the dark, chill hours, and they crept off the roads and slithered and slipped by the hedges and fields, and he knew who they were, they were Germans, the German dead from out of the earth that had come to work ill on Scotland. And even in the daytime if you but looked quick, right sharp and sudden between the bending of a bough or the bar of a gate, you'd see a white German face, distorted still in the last red pain, haunting the Scottish fields. And that was queer fancying well you might say.

But Chae knew nothing of the business, he near knocked in the door of the little house ere he gave it up and went ben the road to Long Rob's. And Rob saw him coming and turned off the Mill and ran to meet him, and they sat and argued the rest of the day, Rob brought out his bottle and they had a bit dram; and then Rob made them their supper

and they'd another long dram, and they argued far to the
wee, small hours. And Chae swore that he still believed the
War would bring a good thing to the world, it would end
the armies and fighting forever, the day of socialism at last
would dawn, the common folk had seen what their guns
could do and right soon they'd use them when once they
came back.

And Rob said *Havers, havers. The common folk when
they aren't sheep are swine, Chae man; you're an exception,
being a goat.*

Well, it was fine enough that long arguing with Rob, but
out in the dark by the side of Chae as they walked along
the road together Rob cried *Oh man, I'd go back with you
the morn if only*—and the words fair seemed to stick in his
throat. And Chae asked *If only, what, man?* and Rob said
*If only I wanted to be easy—easy and a liar. But I've never
gone that gait yet and I'm damned if I'll begin for any bit
war!*

And what he meant by that Chae didn't know, he left him
then and held over the moor land towards the Knapp under
the rising moon. And it was there that a strange thing happened to him, maybe he'd drunk over much of Long Rob's
whisky, though his head was steady enough as a rule for
thrice the amount he'd drunk.

Ah well, the thing was this, that as he went over an open
space of the vanished Standing Stones he saw right in front
of him a halted cart; and a man had got out of the cart and
knelt by the axle and looked at it. And Chae thought it
some carter billy from the Netherhill taking the near cut
through the moor, and steered out to go by and cried *Good
night, then.* But there wasn't an answer, so he looked again,
and no cart was there, the shingly stones shone white and
deserted under the light of the moon, the peewits were crying away in the distance. And Chae's hackles fair stood up
on end, for it came on him that it was no cart of the countryside he had seen, it was a thing of light wood or basket-
work, battered and bent, low behind, with a pole and two
ponies yoked to it; and the childe that knelt by the axle had
been in strange gear, hardly clad at all, and something had
flashed on his head, like a helmet maybe.

And Chae stood and swore, his blood running cold, and
near jumping from his skin when a pheasant started under
his feet with a screech and a whirr and shot away into the
dimness. And maybe it was one of the men of old time that

he saw there, a Calgacus' man from the Graupius battle
when they fought the Romans up from the south; or maybe
it had only been the power of Long Rob's Glenlivet.

So that was Chae's round of the countryside, in a blink
his leave was gone and Chae had gone with it, folk said he
was still the same old Chae, he blithered still about Rich
and Poor, you'd have thought the Army would have taught
him better. But Chris stuck up for him, Chae was fine, not
that she herself cared for the Rich and Poor, she was neither
one nor the other herself. That year the crops came so
thick Ewan said they must hire some help, and that they
did, an oldist stock from Bervie he was, gey handless at
first, John Brigson his name. But he soon got into the set
of Blawearie, sleeping in the room that had once been
Chris's, and making rare friends with young Ewan, it was
lucky they had him. And the harvest came fine and Chris
thought it near time that another baby should come to
Blawearie. They'd been careful as blithe in the thing so far,
but now it was different. Ewan'd love to have another.

And one night went on and then another and she whispered to herself *In the Spring I'll tell him;* and the New Year
went by; and then news came up to Blawearie in a wave of
gossip from all over the Howe. For the Parliament had
passed the Conscription Act that meant you'd to go out and
fight whatever you said, they'd shoot you down if you
didn't. And sure as death Ewan soon had his papers sent
to him, he'd to go up to Aberdeen and be there examined,
he'd been excused before as a farmer childe. Long Rob got
his papers on the very same day and he laughed and said
Fine, I'll like a bit jaunt.

And into Aberdeen they all went, a fair crowd of them
then, all in one carriage; and the ploughmen all swore that
they didn't care a button were they taken or not; and Ewan
knew right well that they wouldn't take him, they didn't
take folk that farmed their own land; and Long Rob said
nothing, just sat and smoked. So they came to Aberdeen
and went to the place and sat in a long, bare room. And
a soldier stood near the door of the room and cried out
their names one after the other; and Long Rob sat still and
smoked his pipe. So they finished at last with the ploughmen childes, the whole jing-bang were passed as soldiers.
And they called Long Rob, but he just sat still and smoked
his pipe, he wouldn't stir out of his jacket, even. So there

was a great bit stir at that, they danced around him and
swore at him, but he blew his smoke up in their faces, calm
like a man unvexed by midges met on a summer day.

They gave up the try, they did nothing to him then, he
came back to the Howe and sat down at the Mill. But next
he was called to appear at Stonehaven, the Exemption
Board sat there for the cases; and Rob rode down on his
bicycle, smoking his pipe. So they called out his name and
in he went and the Chairman, a wee grocer man that
worked night and day to send other folk out to fight the
Germans, he asked Long Rob how he liked the idea that
folk called him a coward? And Long Rob said *Fine, man,
fine. I'd rather any day be a coward than a corpse*. And
they told him he couldn't have exemption and Long Rob
lit up his pipe and said that was sad.

Home to the Mill he came again, and that night folk saw
him on the round of his parks, standing and smoking and
looking at his land and sky, the long rangy childe. Ewan
went by fell late that evening and saw him and cried *Ay,
Rob!* but the miller said never a word, Ewan went home
to Blawearie vexed about that. But Chris said it was just
that Long Rob was thinking of the morn, he'd been ordered
to report to the Aberdeen barracks.

And the next day passed and all Kinraddie watched from
its steadings the ingoings and outgoings of Rob at the Mill;
and damn the move all the day long did he make to set out
as they'd ordered him. The next day came, the policeman
came with it, he rode up to the Mill on his bicycle and bided
at the Mill a good two hours and syne rode out again. And
folk told later that he'd spent all that time arguing and
prigging at Rob to set out. But Rob said *If you want me,
carry me!* and faith! the policeman couldn't very well do
that, angered though he was, it would look fair daft wheeling Rob along the roads on his bicycle tail.

So the policeman went off to Stonehaven and out from
it late in the evening there drove a gig, the policeman again,
and two home-time soldiers, it needed all three to take Rob
of the Mill away to the war. He wouldn't move even then,
though he made no struggle, he just sat still and smoked
at his pipe, and they'd to carry him out and put him in the
gig. And off they drove, that was how Long Rob went off
to the War, and what happened to him next there rose this
rumour and that, some said he was in jail, some said he'd

given in, some said he'd escaped and was hiding in the hills: but nobody knew for sure.

And to Chris it seemed then, Chae gone, Rob gone, that their best friends were out of Kinraddie now, friends close and fine, but they had themselves, Ewan and her and young Ewan. And she held close to them both, working for them, tending them, seeing young Ewan grow straight and strong, with that slim white body of his, like his father's just; and it made a strange, sweet dizziness go singing in her heart as she bathed him, he stood so strong and white, she would mind that agony that had been hers at the birth of this body, it had been worth it and more. And now she wanted another bairn, Spring was coming, fast and fast, the land smelt of it, the caller sea winds came fresh with the tang that only in Spring they brought, it was nineteen-seventeen. And Chris said in her heart that in April their baby would be conceived.

So she planned and went singing those days about the kitchen of Blawearie toun, busy with this plot, she planned fresh linen and fresh clothes for herself, she grew young and wayward as before she married, and she looked at Ewan with secret eyes. And old John Brigson would cry *Faith, mistress, you're light of heart!*

But Ewan said nothing, strange enough that. She knew then that something troubled him, maybe he was ill and would say nothing about it, sitting so silent at meat and after, it grew worse as the days went on. And when he looked at her no longer was the old look there, but a blank, dark one, and he'd turn his face from her slowly. She was vexed and then frightened and out in the close one morning, over the stillness of the hen's chirawk, she heard his voice raised in cursing at Brigson, it was shameful for him to do that and not like Ewan at all to do it. Then he came back from the steading with quick stepping feet, as he passed through the kitchen Chris cried *What's wrong?* He muttered back *Nothing,* and went up the stairs, and he took no notice of young Ewan that ran after him, bairn-like, to show him some picture in a book he had.

Chris heard him rummage in their room, and then he came down, he was fully dressed, his dark face heavy and stranger than ever, Chris stared at him *Where are you going?* and he snapped *To Aberdeen, if you'd like to know,* and off he went. He had never spoken to her like that—he

was EWAN, hers! . . . She stood at the window, dazed,
looking after him, so strange she must then have looked
that little Ewan ran to her, *Mother, mother!* and she picked
him up and soothed him and the two of them stood and
watched Ewan Tavendale out of sight on the bright spring
road.

It seemed to Chris he had hated her that minute when he
looked at her in the kitchen, she went through the day with
a twist of sickness about her heart. Told Brigson, shamed
for her man, she said that Ewan had been worried with his
business and that, he'd been out of his temper that morning
and had gone to Aberdeen for the day. And John Brigson
said cheerily *Never heed, mistress. He'll be right as rain when
he's back the night,* and he helped her wash up the supper
things, and they had a fine long talk. Syne off he went to
tend to the beasts, and Chris grew anxious, looking at the
clock, till she minded that there was a later train still, the
ten o'clock train. So she bedded young Ewan and milked
the kye, and came back to the kitchen, and waited. John
Brigson had gone to his bed, Blawearie was quiet, she went
out and walked down to the road to meet Ewan in the fresh-
fallen dew of the night—so young the year and so sweet,
she'd make it this night, the night with Ewan that she'd
planned!

By Peesie's Knapp a snipe was sounding, she stood and
listened to the bird, and saw in the starlight the skeleton
timbers of the great wood that once fronted the north wind
there. A hare scuttled over the road, the ditches were running and trilling, hidden, filled with the waters of Spring,
she smelt the turned grass of the ploughlands and shivered
in the blow of the wind, Ewan was long on the road. At
the turnpike bend she stopped and listened for the sound
of his feet, and minded a thing out of childhood then, if
you put your ear to the ground you'd hear far off steps
long ere you'd hear them when standing and upright. And
she laughed to herself, remembering that, and knelt on the
ground, agile and fleet, as the Guthries were, and put close
her ear to the road, it was cold and crumbly with little
stones. She heard a flock of little sounds going home to their
buchts, far and near, each sound went home, but never the
sound of a footstep.

And then, Stonehaven way, a great car came flashing
down through the night, its headlights leaping from brae to
brae, Chris stood back and aside and she saw it go by, there

were soldiers in it, one bent on the wheel, she saw the floating ends of his Glengarry bonnet, the car whirled past and was gone in the night. She stared after it, dazed and dreaming, and shivered again. Ewan must have held over the hills and was already at Blawearie, it was daft to be here, he'd be anxious about her and go out seeking *her!*

So she ran back to Blawearie and she got there panting. But her heart was light, she'd play a trick on Ewan, creep in on him quiet as quiet, come up behind him sudden in the kitchen and make him jump. And she padded softly across the close to the kitchen door and looked in, and the lamp stood lit on the table, and the place was quiet in its glow. She went up the stairs to their room, there was no sign of Ewan, young Ewan lay sleeping with his face in the pillow, she righted him away from that and went down to the kitchen again. She sat in a chair there, waiting, and her heart froze and froze with the fears that came up in it, she saw Ewan run over by a car in the streets, and why hadn't they sent her a telegram?

But maybe she was wrong, maybe he missed the last train and taken one out to Stonehaven instead and was tramping from there in the darkness now. She piled new logs on the fire and sat and waited, and the night went on, she fell fast asleep and waking found the lamp gone out, in the sky between bar and blind was a sharp, dead whiteness like the hand of a corpse. And as she stretched herself, chilled and queer, up in John Brigson's room the alarum clock went. It was half-past five, the night had gone, and still Ewan had not come back.

Nor came he back that day, nor many a day beyond that. For the postman at noon brought Chris a letter, it was from Ewan and she sat in the kitchen and read it, and didn't understand, and her lip hurt, and she put up the back of her hand to wipe it and looked at the hand and saw blood on it. Young Ewan came playing about her, he took the letter out of her hand and ran off with it, screaming with laughter in his young, shrill voice, she sat and did not look after him and he came back and laughed in her face, surprised that she did not play. And she took him in her arms and asked for the letter again, and again she tried to read it. And what Ewan wrote was he'd grown sick of it all, folk laughing and sneering at him for a coward, Mutch and Munro aye girding at him. He was off to the War, he had joined the North Highlanders that day, he would let her

know where they sent him, she wasn't to worry; and *I am
yours truly Ewan.*

When John Brigson came in at dinner-time he found
Chris looking white as a ghost, but she wasn't dazed any
longer, it just couldn't be helped, Ewan was gone but maybe the war would be over before he had finished with his
training. And John Brigson said *Of course it will, I see the
Germans are retreating on all the fronts, they're fair scared
white, they say, when our men take to the bayonet.* Little
Ewan wanted to know what a bayonet was and why the
Germans were scared of them, and John Brigson told him
and Chris was sick, she'd to run out to be sick, for if you've
ever gutted a rabbit or a hen you can guess what is inside
a man, and she'd seen a bayonet going into Ewan there.
And John Brigson was awful sorry, he said he hadn't
thought, and she wasn't to worry, Ewan would be fine.

Oh, but that Spring was long! Out in the parks in the
day-time she'd go to help John Brigson and ease her weariness, she took little Ewan with her then and a plaid to wrap
him in for sleep, under the lithe of a hedge or a whin,
when he grew over-tired. And the fields were a comfort,
the crumble of the fine earth under your feet, swinging a
graip as you walked, breaking dung, the larks above, the
horses plodding by with snorting breath, old Brigson a-bend
above the shafts. He made fair poor drills, they were
better than none, and he aye was pleasant and canty, a fine
old stock, he did lots of the things that Ewan had done and
asked no more pay for the doing of them. That was as well,
he wouldn't have got it, the weather was bitter, corn spoiled
in the planting.

Early in the year, about May that was, the rain came
down and it seemed it never would end, there was nothing
to be done out of doors, the rain came down from the
north-east across Kinraddie and Chris wasn't the only one
that noted its difference from others years. In Peesie's
Knapp there was Mistress Strachan vexing herself in trying
to make out the change; and then she minded what Chae
had said would happen when the woods came down, once
the place had been sheltered and lithe, it poised now upon
the brae in whatever storm might come. The woodmen had
all finished by then, they'd left a country that looked as
though it had been shelled by a German army. Looking
out on those storms that May Chris could hardly believe

that this was the place she and Will had watched from the window that first morning they came to Blawearie.

And then the very next day as she made the butter, young Ewan was up the stairs with his blocks and books, John Brigson had gone to Mondynes with a load of corn, Chris heard a step in the close, somebody running in a hurry from the rain. Then the door burst open and a soldier came in, panting, in the queerest uniform, a hat with gold lacing and red breeches and leggings, Chris stared at the hat and then at the face. And the soldier cried *Oh, Chris, I believe you don't know me!* and she cried then, *Will!* and her arms went round him, they cuddled one the other like children, Chris crying, Will near to crying himself, patting her shoulder and saying *Oh, Chris!*

Then she pushed him away and looked at him and they cuddled each other again and Will danced her all round the kitchen, and little Ewan up the stairs heard the stir and came tearing down and when he saw a strange man holding his mother in his arms he made at Will and whacked his legs and cried, *Away, man!* Will cried *Good God, what's this you've got, Chris?* and swung Ewan high and stared in his face and shook his head *You're a fine lad, ay, but you're over much of your father in you ever to be as bonny as your mother!*

That wasn't true but fine to hear, Chris could hardly get any work done or a meal made ready, so many the things they'd to take through hand, Will sat and smoked and every now and then they'd look one at the other and Will would give a great laugh *Oh Chris, mind this . . . mind that . . . !* and his laughter had tears in it, they were daft, the pair of them. And when old John Brigson came home, they heard the noise of the wheels in the close and Will went out to lend him a hand, the old stock jumped off the cart and made for a fork that was lying to hand, he thought Will a German in that strange bit uniform. But he laughed right heartily when Will said who he was, and the two of them came in for dinner and Will sat at the table's head, in Ewan's place. And as he ate he told them how he came in the uniform, and all the chances and wanderings that were his and Mollie's when they went from Scotland.

And faith! he'd had more than enough of both, for in Argentine, as he'd told Chris already by letter. he'd left his first work after a while he and Mollie had both learned up the Spanish, and he took a job with a Frenchman there, an

awful fine stock. He liked Will well and Will liked him,
and he gave Will half of his house to bide in, it was a great
ranch out in the parks of that meikle country. So there they
had lived and were happy and blithe till the Frenchman had
to go to the War. Will had thought of going himself more
than once but the Frenchman had told him he'd be a fair
fool, he might well be glad there wasn't British conscription; besides, some body or other had to look to the ranch.

But in less than two years the Frenchman came back,
sore wounded he'd been, and soon as he came Will told him
it was *his* turn now, he'd see some of this War for himself.
And the Frenchman told him he was fair a fool, but he'd
get him a job with the French. So he did after cables and
cables to Paris, and Will said good-bye to Mollie and the
Frenchman and the Frenchman's wife, and sailed from
Buenos Ayres to Cherbourg; and in Paris they knew all
about him, he found himself listed as a sergeant-major in
the French Foreign Legion, an interpreter he was, for he
knew three languages fine. Then they'd given him a fortnight's leave and here he was.

And when he was alone with Chris that evening and she
told him about Ewan down training in Lanark, he said
Ewan was either soft or daft or both. *Why did you marry
the dour devil, Chris? Did he make you or were you going
to have a bairn?* And Chris didn't feel affronted, it was
Will that asked, he'd treat her just the same if she owned
up to a fatherless bairn once a year, or twice, if it came
to that. So she shook her head, *It was just because he was
to me as Mollie to you,* and Will nodded to that, *Ah, well,
we can't help when it gets that way. Mind when you wanted
to know . . . ?*

And they stood and laughed in the evening, remembering
that, and they walked arm in arm up and down the road
and Chris forgot all her worries remembering the days when
she and Will were bairns together, and the dourness and
the loveliness then, and Will asked *Do you mind when we
slept together—that last time we did it when the old man
had near killed me up in the barn?* And his face grew dark,
he still couldn't forgive, he said that folk who ill-treated
their children deserved to be shot, father had tormented and
spoiled him out of sheer cruelty when he was young. But
Chris said nothing to that, remembering the day of father's
funeral and how she had wept by his grave in Kinraddie
kirkyard.

But she knew she could never tell Will of that, he'd never understand, and they spoke of other things, Will of the Argentine and the life out there, and the smell of the sun and the warm weather and the fruit and flowers and flame of life below the Southern Cross. Chris said *But you'll come back, you and Mollie, to bide in Scotland again?* and Will laughed, he seemed still a mere lad in spite of his foreign French uniform, *Havers, who'd want to come back to this country? It's dead or it's dying—and a damned good job!*

And, daftly, Chris felt a sudden thrust of anger through her heart at that; and then she looked round Kinraddie in the evening light, seeing it so quiet and secure and still, thinking of the seeds that pushed up their shoots from a thousand earthy mouths. Daft of Will to say that: Scotland lived, she could never die, the land would outlast them all, their wars and their Argentines, and the winds come sailing over the Grampians still with their storms and rain and the dew that ripened the crops—long and long after all their little vexings in the evening light were dead and done. And her thoughts went back to the kirkyard, she asked Will would he like to come to the kirk next day, she hadn't been there herself for a year.

He looked surprised and then laughed *You're not getting religious, are you?* as though she had taken to drink. And Chris said *No*, and then thought about that, time to think for once in the pother of the days with Blawearie so quiet above them, young Ewan and old Brigson asleep. And she said *I don't believe they were ever religious, the Scots folk, Will—not really religious like Irish or French or all the rest in the history books. They've never BELIEVED. It's just been a place to collect and argue, the kirk, and criticise God.* And Will yawned, he said maybe, he didn't care one way or the other himself, Mollie in the Argentine had taken up with the Catholics, and faith! she was welcome if she got any fun.

So next day they set out for the kirk, the weather had cleared, blowing wet and sunny in a blink, there were teeth of rainbows out over Kinraddie, Chris said it was Will's uniform that messed up the sky. But she was proud of him for all that, how folk stared as the two of them went down the aisle! Chris was in her blue, with her new short skirt and long boots, and Will in *his* blue and red trousers and leggings, and his jacket with the gold lace on it and the high collar and the soft fine hat with the shiny peak. Old

Gibbon, him that preached for his son, near fell down the
stairs of the pulpit at sight of Will. But he recovered fell
soon and preached them one of the sermons that had made
such stir throughout the Howe a year or so back, he told
how the German beasts now boiled the corpses of their own
dead men and fed the leavings to pigs. And he ground his
teeth at the Germans, they were so coarse; and he said that
GUD would assuredly smite them.

But folk had grown sick of him and his ragings, there
was only a small attendance to hear him and when they
came out in the end Will said *It's good to be out of that
creature's stink!* Syne Ellison recognised Will and came
swaggering over, redder than ever and fatter than ever, and
he cried *If it ain't Will Guthrie! How are you?* and Will said
Fine. Most of the folk seemed pleased to see him, even
Mutch and Munro, excepting the Munro wife herself, she
snapped, *And what would you be, then Will? They've a
man at the picture palace in Stonehaven that wears breeks
just like that.* And Will said *Faith, Mistress Munro, you're
an authority on breeks. I hear you still wear them at the
Cuddiestoun.* Folk standing round gave a snicker at that,
real fine for the futret, she'd met her match.

And Will's leave went by like a shot, he was all over the
Howe in the first few days, up in Fordoun and down in
Drumlithie, and everywhere folk made much of him. But
after that he bided nearly all the time by Chris, he helped
her or Brigson in old clothes of Ewan's she'd raked out for
him. He went shooting with father's gun fell often, up in
the moor it was blithe to hear him and his singing, young
Ewan would go wandering up to meet him. And when it
came to the end and the last day, young Ewan in bed and
they sat by the fire and the June night came softly down
without, Chris didn't fear at all for Will, he was clean and
happy and quick, things went well with him. And next
morning only young Ewan cried at the parting, and off he
went, it seemed then at Blawearie that more than Will had
gone out of their lives, it was a happy voice that had sung
for itself a chamber in their hearts those weeks he had been
with them.

But the hills flowed up and down, day after day, in their
dark and sunshine, and even those weeks were covered and
laid past, and Chris saw the harvest near, so near, a good
harvest again in spite of the weather; and still the War

went on. Sometimes she'd a note or postcard from Ewan in
Lanark, sometimes she wouldn't hear for week on week
till she grew fair alarmed. But he just said it was that he
never could write, he didn't know how, they were awfully
busy and she wasn't to worry.

And then through Kinraddie a motor came driving one
day, it turned at the cross-roads and drove down by the
Denburn. It stopped at the Mill and folk ran to their doors
and wondered who it could be, the place was locked up
and deserted-like. And when the motor stopped a man got
out, and another came after, slow, and he took the arm of
the first one, and they went step-stepping at snail's pace up
to the Mill-house and folk could see no more. But soon the
story of it was known all over the place, it was Long Rob
himself come back, he had never given in, they had put
him in prison and ill-used him awful; but he wouldn't give
in whatever they did, he laughed in their faces, *Fine, man,
fine.* Last he went on the hunger-strike, that was when you
just starved to death to spite them, and grew weaker and
weaker. So they took him from prison to a doctor childe
and the doctor said it was useless to keep him, he'd never
be of use to his King and country.

So home at last he had come, folk told he was fairly a
wreck, he could hardly stand up and walk or make his own
meat, God knows how he ever got into his clothes. And
Mutch and Munro wouldn't go near him, neither would
Gordon, they said that it served him right, the coarse pro-
German. And when Chris heard that there came a stinging
pain in her eyes and she called old John Brigson to yoke
a cart and put corn in it, as though taking it to Rob for
bruising; and Chris got into the cart as well and took young
Ewan on her knee, and off they set from Blawearie. Outside
the Mill-house Chris cried on Brigson to stop, and found
the basket she'd laid on the bottom of the cart and ran
through the close to the kitchen door. It stood half-open,
the place was dark with hardly a glimmer from the fire, but
she saw someone sitting, she stopped and stared, an old man
it seemed with a white, drawn face, his hands fumbling at
the lighting of a pipe.

She called *Rob!* and he looked up and she saw his eyes,
they were filled with awful things, he cried *Chris! God is't
Chris Guthrie?* She was shaking his hand and his shoulder
then, minding things about him, not looking at him, minding the fine neighbour he'd been to her and Ewan in the

days they married. And she asked *What are you sitting here
for! You should be in your bed,* and Rob said *I'm damned
if I should, I've had over much of bed. I was waiting about
for the grocer childe, but he didn't stop, though he knows
I'm home. I suppose he's still an ill-will at pro-Germans,
like.*

Chris told him never to mind the grocer, and she spoke
to him roughly, in case she should weep at the sight of him;
and she told him to go out and see John Brigson. Then,
soon as he'd hirpled out with his stick she looked round the
place and started to clean it, and made a fine fire and a
meal with fresh eggs and butter, and oat-cakes and scones
and jam, she'd brought the lot from Blawearie. So when
Rob came in from his speak with Brigson, there it was
waiting for him on the table, he blinked and sat down and
said in a whisper, *You shouldn't have done this, Chris
quean.* But Chris said nothing, just sat him down at the
table and sat there herself and saw that he ate; and when
young Ewan came in with old Brigson she fed them as well;
and syne Brigson set off for the farm at Auchenblae where
Rob's horse and sholtie were housed.

When he'd gone Chris set to work on the place and
opened the windows to the air and cleaned out the rooms
and dragged off the dirty linen from the bed and made it
up in a bundle to take back with her. Syne she baked oat-
cakes for Rob and told him that each day he'd get him a
pail of milk from the Netherhill, till time came when he'd
kye of his own again, she'd arranged for that. And when
John Brigson came back in the evening with horse and
sholtie Long Rob was fast asleep in his chair, they didn't
rouse him but spread him his supper, and set him his breakfast as well, and left a lamp low-burning and clear beside
him, and a hot-water bottle in his bed. Syne they left him
and rode them back to Blawearie, all three were tired,
young Ewan asleep in the arms of Chris, dear to hold him
so with his dark head sleeping against her breast and old
Brigson's shoulder seen as a dark quiet bulking against the
night.

Next morning they looked out from Blawearie and saw
Rob's horse and sholtie at graze in a park of the Mill, and
Long Rob himself, a dot in the sunlight, making slow way
to the moor land he'd wrought at so long. And as they
looked they heard, thin and remote, the sound of a song

Kinraddie had missed for many a day. It was *Ladies of Spain*.

Soon maybe the War would end, Chris had dreamt as she listened to that singing, and they all be back in Kinraddie as once they had been, Chae and Long Rob and her dark lad, Ewan himself. So she'd dreamt that morning, she'd never grow out from long dreaming in autumn dawns like those. And fruition of dream came soon enough, it was a telegram boy that came riding his bicycle up to Blawearie. Chris read the telegram, it was Ewan that had sent it, *Home on leave to-night before going to France.* She stared at it and the lad that had brought it, and he asked, *Any reply?* and she said *Any what?* and he asked her again, and she said *No,* and ran into the kitchen and stared at the writing in the telegram. He was going to France.

It lingered at the back of her mind, dark, like a black cat creeping at the back of a hedge, she saw the fluff of its fur or the peek of its eyes, a wild and sinister thing in the sunlight; but you would not look often or see those eyes, how they glared at you. He was going out there, where the sky was a troubled nightmare and the earth shook night and day, into the lands of the coarse French folk, her Ewan, her lad with his dark, dear face and that quick, blithe blush. And suddenly she was filled with a weeping pity in her heart for him, a pity that brought no tears to her eyes, he must never see her shed tears all the time he was with her, he'd go out to the dark, far land with memories of her and Blawearie that were shining and brave and kind.

So all the forenoon she fled and bustled from room to room, brightening the place, she brought out fresh sheets and pillows for the bed she had found so lonely, she sent out young Ewan to gather roses and honeysuckle to set in a jar on the ledge above the bed. And she hung new curtains there and brought out Ewan's clothes and brushed them, he'd want to get out of his uniform, they were sick of the khaki the men that came back. Then she made a great baking against his coming, so much that she'd hardly time to make dinner for young Ewan and Brigson, but they didn't care, they were both excited as herself. She knew the train he would come by, the half-past five, and she swept and dusted the kitchen and set his tea, and punched a great cushion ready for his chair, and dressed herself in the blue he liked and young Ewan in his brave brown cords. John Brigson cried *This is hardly the place for me with your man come home, I'll away to Bervie then for the night.*

Off he set, Chris waved to the old, kind childe as he bicycled down Blawearie brae. And then she ran back, ben to the parlour to look at herself in the mirror again, in the long glass her figure seemed blithe and slim even still, she'd be fine to sleep with yet, she supposed—oh, Ewan! Her face hadn't changed, it was flushed and fair, the eyes may-be older, but shining and bright. And she finished with that looking and went over the close to stand by the side of young Ewan, looking down the hill for his father coming up. The sun flung the long shadows of Blawearie and the beeches far in the east, and across the Den, high in the fields of Upperhill, a lost sheep baaed in the whins.

She had hardly been able to believe it him lying awake after he slept, he slept with a snoring breath and fuddled mumblings, bulging out against her so that she had but little of the bed and less of the blankets. She closed her eyes and pressed her knuckles against her teeth that the pain might waken her, that she might know Ewan hadn't come home, was still the same Ewan she'd dreamt of in the silence of the night and her own lonely bed. But he moved, flinging out an arm that struck her across the face, she lay still below it, then it wabbled away. She took her knuckles from her mouth and lay quiet then, no need for her to hurt herself now.

Drunk he had come from the station and more than two hours late. Standing at last in the kitchen in his kilts he'd looked round and sneered *Hell, Chris, what a bloody place!* as she ran to him. And he'd flung his pack one way and his hat the other and kissed her as though she were a tink, his hands on her as quickly as that, hot and questing and wise as his hands had never been. She saw the hot smoulder fire in his eyes then, but no blush on his face, it was red with other things. But she smothered her horror and laughed, and kissed him and struggled from him, and cried *Ewan, who's this!*

Young Ewan held back, shy-like, staring, and just said *It's father.* At that the strange, swaying figure in the tartan kilts laughed, coarse-like, *Well, we'll hope so, eh Chris? Any supper left—unless you're too bloody stand-offish even to have that?*

She couldn't believe her own ears. *Stand-offish? Oh, Ewan!* and ran to him again, but he shook her away, *Och, all right, I'm wearied. For God's sake let a man sit down.* He staggered to the chair she'd made ready for him, a picture-book of young Ewan's lay there, he picked the thing up and flung it to the other side of the room, and slumped down into the chair. *Hell, what a blasted climb to a blasted place. Here, give us some tea.*

She sat beside him to serve him, she knew her face had gone white. But she poured the tea and spread the fine supper she'd been proud to make, it might hardly have been there for the notice he paid it, drinking cup after cup of the tea like a beast at a trough. She saw him clearer then, the coarse hair that sprang like short bristles all over his head, the neck with its red and angry circle about the collar of the khaki jacket, a great half-healed scar across the back of his hand glinted putrescent blue. Suddenly his eyes came on her, *Well, damn't, is that all you've to say to me now I've come home? I'd have done better to spend the night with a tart in the town.*

She didn't say anything, she couldn't, the tears were choking in her throat and smarting and biting at her eyelids, pressing to come, the tears that she'd sworn she'd never shed all the time he was home on leave. And she didn't dare look at him lest he should see, but he saw and pushed back his chair and got up in a rage, *Good God, what are you snivelling about now? You always were snivelling, I mind.* And out he went, young Ewan ran to her side and flung his arms round her, *Mother, don't cry, I don't like him, he's a tink, that soldier!* She'd pressed back the tears then, *Whist, Ewan, never say that again;* and got up and cleared off the supper things and went out to the close and cried gently *Ewan!*

He cried back *All right, all right!* still angrily; and at that some anger kindled within herself, she didn't wait for him to come back but turned and took young Ewan in her arms and climbed the stairs and put him to bed, he was vexed and troubled about her, kissing her as he lay there. *Sleep with me to-night, mother.* She laughed at him, she was sleeping with his father to-night, he must be good and sleep himself, quick and quick, there'd be such fun with father the morn. He said *I'll try,* and closed his eyes and she went down the stairs, it was dark there getting on for eight. She thought Ewan was still outside but as she made for the lamp something stirred in the chair, she thought it a cat, it was Ewan. He caught her and pulled her on to his knees and said *Be stand-offish now if you can, what the devil do you think I've come home for?*

It had been like struggling with someone deep in a nightmare, when the blankets are over your head and you can barely breathe, awful she should come to think that of Ewan. But it wasn't Ewan, her Ewan, someone coarse and strange and strong had come back in his body to torment her. He laughed as he fought her there in the chair and held her tight and began to tell stories—oh, he was drunk and didn't know what he said, terrible and sickening things, he'd had women when he pleased in Lanark, he said. And he whispered of them to her, his breath was hot on her face, she saw the gleam of his teeth, he told her how he'd lain with them and the things he'd done. Sickened and shamed she had felt and then worse than that, stopping from struggling, a shameful, searing desire come on her. And he knew, he knew at once, he said *Well, now that you know you can get!*

She had picked herself up from the floor and in a dream went out to milk the kye, leaving him there. When she came back he had gone from the kitchen, she was slow to finish sieving and skimming the milk and go up to the room she'd made ready that morning, singing she had made it ready. And up there he waited her, lying in the bed, he'd carried up a lamp from the kitchen, they who'd always gone to bed in the darkness and thought it fine to lie in each other's arms in the night-glimmer from the window. But now he grumbled *For God's sake hurry up!* and when she made to put out the light—*I'll do that, come on!* And she lay beside him and he took her.

She remembered that now, lying in the darkness the while he slept, why he had left the lamp alight; and at memory of that foulness something cold and vile turned and turned like a wheeling mirror inside her brain. For it had been other things than his beast-like mauling that had made her whisper in agony, *Oh Ewan, put out the light!* The horror of his eyes upon her she would never forget, they burned and danced on that mirror that wheeled and wheeled in her brain.

So that was Ewan's homecoming on leave and the days that went by were the same as that first night foreshadowed. He had gone away Ewan Tavendale, he came back a man so coarse and cruel that in place of love hate came singing in the heart of Chris—hate that never found speech, that but slowly found lodgement secure and unshaken. For often it seemed to her that a tortured, tormented thing looked out from Ewan's eyes while he told them his foulest tale, ill-used old Brigson and jeered at him, came drunken back to Blawearie night after night—that tortured thing that was the lost lad she had married. But the fancy wilted and vanished as the days went by. He stayed five days, had his breakfast in bed, and never got up till dinner-time; he never looked at the parks or stock or took notice of young Ewan; he dressed in his khaki and kilts alone, and to Chris's suggestion that he wear a suit—*What, me dress up like bloody conchy? I'll leave that to your friend, Rob Duncan.*

Every day he went swaggering down the road and was off to Drumlithie or Stonehaven or Fordoun, drinking there. Before he went he'd ask for money, Chris gave him all that he asked, not saying a word, but he'd fancy a reluctance and sneer at her. Wasn't he entitled to what was his own? Did she think him still the young fool he had been, content to slave and slave at Blawearie—*without as much as a dram to savour the soss, or a quean or so at night to waken your blood—nothing but a wife you hardly dared touch in case you put her in the family way, eh, Chris?*

He would say this at dinner-time, sneering and boasting, old Brigson would colour and look down at his plate and young Ewan stare and stare at his father till Ewan would say *God, what a damned glower! Eyes like your mother and a nature the same;* and he'd swear at the bairn, it was shameful to hear that. He'd made friends with Mutch, him that once he could hardly abide, and with him he went driving each night on their drunken sprees. As he went to bed John Brigson would look at Chris with trouble in his kind old eyes, but she didn't dare say a thing to him, he'd go stamping slow up above her head the while she sat down to await Ewan's return and have the hirpling note of the clock stamp each second in her heart, hating him home, wanting him home.

For after that first night he had ceased to touch her, she would lie beside him, quivering and waiting. And he'd lie quiet, she knew him awake and knew that he knew what she waited; and it was as though he were a cat that played with a mouse, he would laugh out after a while and then go to sleep, she herself to lie tortured in the hours thereafter. The last night she refused the torment, she got up near three o'clock and kindled a fire and made herself tea and watched the morning come down the hill passes—a fine summer morning, yellow and grey and lovely with its chirping of birds in the beeches. And suddenly then, as always these changes took her, she was calm and secure, putting Ewan from her heart, locking it up that he never could vex her again, she was finished with him, either loving or hating. And at that release she rose and went slow about her work, a great load had gone from her then, John Brigson coming down in the morning heard her sing and was cheery himself, cheery with relief, but she sang her release.

At nine o'clock Ewan cried down from his room *When the hell are you bringing some breakfast?* She took no notice of that, but she sent young Ewan out to play and then went on with her work. And at last she heard a clatter on the stairs, and there he stood at the kitchen entrance, glaring at her, *Have you gone clean deaf?* She answered him then, raising her head and looking at him, *If you're in need of a breakfast—get it.*

He said *You bitch!* and he made to strike her. But she caught up a knife from the table, she had it waiting there nearby, he swore and drew back. She nodded and smiled at that, calm, and put the knife down and went on with her work.

So he made his own tea, grumbling and swearing, a fine send-off this for a man that was going to France to do his bit. And Chris listened to the catch-phrase, contempt in her heart, she looked at him with curling lip, and he saw her look and swore at her, but was frightened for all that, always now she knew she had known him the frightened one. And a queer, cold curiosity came on to her then that so she should have slaved to tend him and love him and give him the best, body and mind and soul she had given, for a gift to the body of a drunken lout from the plough-stilts.

And now that body she saw with a cold repulsion him wash and shave and dress, she could hardly bear to look at him and went out and worked in the close, cleaning pots there in the shining weather, young Ewan played douce and content with his toys, it was hay-time all down the Howe and the hens came pecking around her. She heard Ewan stamp about in the kitchen, he wanted that she should look, go running and fetch him his things. And she smiled again, cold and secure and serene, and heard him come out and bang the door; and without raising her head she saw him then. He was all in his gear, the Glengarry on his head, his pack on his shoulder, his kilts a-swing, and he went past her jauntily, but she knew he expected her to stop him, to run after him and throw her arms about him: she saw in his eyes as he went by the fear that she'd pay no heed.

And none she paid, she did not speak, she did not unbend, young Ewan stopped from his playing and looked after his father incuriously, as at a strange alien that went from the place. At the gate of the close, as he banged it behind him, Ewan stopped to sort up his garters, red in the face, not looking at her still. And she paid him no heed.

He swung the pack on his shoulders then he went slow down the road to the turnpike bend, she saw that from the kitchen window, knew he believed she would cry to him at the last. And she smiled, cold and sure, that she knew him so, every action and thought, and why he stood there at last, not trying to look back. He fumbled for matches and lighted his pipe as she watched; and a cloud come over the sun and went on with Ewan, the two of them went down the turnpike then together, out of her sight in the shadow and flame of the bright sun weather, it was strange and impossibly strange. She stood long staring down at that point where he'd vanished, sharp under her breast, tearing her body, her heart was breaking, and she did not care! She was outside and away from its travail and agony, he had done all to her that he ever could now, he who had tramped down the road in that shadow that fled from the sun.

And then it was she found no salvation at all may endure for ever, or beyond the pitch that the heart may bear it, she was weeping and weeping, her arms flung over the kitchen table, weeping for that Ewan who had never come back, for the shamed, tormented boy with the swagger airs she had let go from Blawearie without a kiss or a parting word. *Ewan, Ewan!* her heart cried then, breaking and breaking, *Oh, Ewan, I didn't mean it!* Ewan—he was hers, hers still in spite of all he had done and said, he had lived more closely in her body than the heart that broke now, young Ewan was his, Oh God, she had never let him go like that! And in her desolation of weeping she began to pray, she had known it useless, but she prayed and prayed for him to come back, to kiss her and hold her in kindness just once before he went down that road. She ran wild-eyed and weeping to the close and there was John Brigson, he stared dumbfounded as she cried *Oh, don't let him go, run after him, John!*

And syne he said he didn't understand, if she meant her man, it was more than an hour since Ewan had gone down the road, he'd heard long syne the whistle of his train out across the hills.

It was a month before she heard from him, and then only a scrape and a score on a thing they called a field postcard written somewhere in France; and it said no more than that he was well. No more than a whisper out of the dark cave of days into which he had gone, it yet salved her mind from the searing agony that tormented the early weeks. They would never be the same again, but some day he would come back to her, their madness forgotten, back to her and young Ewan and Blawearie when the War was done, they'd forget and forget, busy themselves in new hours and seasons, there would never be fire and gladness between them again but still undying the labour of the fields in which she now buried her days.

For she sank herself in that, the way to forget, she was hardly indoors from dawn to dusk, in all the range of the harvest weather, running down the bouts behind the binder that John Brigson drove, little Ewan running and laughing beside her. He thought it a fun and a play she made, stooking and stooking so quickly then, her hands became as machines, tireless and quick and ceaseless through the long hours, she stooked so quickly that with an extra hour each evening, old Brigson helping her, she was close to the uncut rigs again. Corn and the shining hollow stalks of the straw, they wove a pattern about her life, her nights and days, she would creep to bed and dream of the endless rigs and her hands in the night would waken her, all pins and needles they would be. Once she went ben to the parlour to

look in the glass and saw then why pity came often in old
Brigson's eyes, she was thinner than ever she'd been, her
face was thin, it seemed to her some gloss had gone from
her hair, her eyes grown dull and patient and pupil-less;
like the eyes of a cow.

So, hurt and dazed, she turned to the land, close to it
and the smell of it, kind and kind it was, it didn't rise up and
torment your heart, you could keep at peace with the land
if you gave it your heart and hands, tended it and slaved
for it, it was wild and a tyrant, but it was not cruel. And
often, in the night-stooking with old John Brigson near, a
ghost of gladness would come to her then, working under
the coming of the moon before the evening dew came
pringling over Kinraddie, night-birds whistling over the
fields, so quiet, so quiet, stilling away the pain in her body,
the pain in her heart that this reaping and harvesting had
brought.

And then Long Rob of the Mill came up to Blawearie.
He came one morning as they started the yavil, he came
through the close and into the kitchen, long and as rangy
as ever he was, his face filled out and his eyes the same,
and he cried *How's Chris? Bonny as ever!* And he caught
young Ewan up on his shoulder and Ewan looked down at
him, dark and grave, and smiled, and thought him fine.

Rob had come over to help, he'd no cutting to do; and
when Chris said nay, he mustn't leave the Mill, he twinkled
his eyes and shook his head. And Chris knew he'd have little loss, folk changed and were changing again, not a soul
had driven his corn cart to the Mill since Long Rob came
back. He'd had nothing to do but pleiter about from park
to park and look out on the road for the custom that never
came; and if any came now it could damn well wait, he'd
come up to stook Blawearie.

So the two went down to the park, young Ewan went
with them, and they stooked it together, the best of the
crop, Rob cheery as ever it seemed to Chris. But sometimes his eyes would wander up to the hills, like a man
seeking a thing he had never desired, and into the iron-
blue eyes a shadow like a dark, quiet question would creep.
Maybe he minded the jail and its torments then, he spoke
never of that, and never a word of the War, nor Chris, all
the stooking of the yavil park. Strange she had hardly
known him before, Long Rob of the Mill, unco and atheist;
he'd been only the miller with the twinkling eyes, his sing-

ings by morn and his whistlings by night, his stories of
horses till your head fair reeled. Now it seemed she had
known him always, closely and queerly, she felt queer, as
though shy, when she sat by his side at the supper table
and he spoke to old Brigson that night. The pallor of the
jail came out in the lamp-light, under the brown that the
sun had brought, and she saw his hand by the side of her
hand, thin and strong, the miller's horse-taming hand.

He bedded young Ewan that night, for a play, and sung
him to sleep, Chris and old Brigson heard the singing as
they sat in the kitchen below, *Ladies of Spain* and *There
was a Young Farmer* and *A' the Blue Bonnets are Over
the Border.* Hardly anybody left in Kinraddie sang these
songs, it was full of other tunes from the bothy windows
now, *Tipperary* and squawling English things, like the
squeak of a rat that is bedded in syrup, the *Long, Long
Trail* and the like. It was queer and eerie, listening to Rob,
like listening to an echo from far in the years at the mouth
of a long lost glen.

And she never knew when and how in the days that followed, it came on her silently, secretly, out of the earth itself, maybe, the knowledge she was Rob's to do with as
he willed, she willed. She wanted more than the clap of his
hand on her shoulder as they finished the bout at evening
and up through the shadows took their slow way, by park-
side and dyke, to the close that hung drenched with honeysuckle smell. She wanted more than his iron-blue eye
turned on her, warm and clean and kind though she felt
her skin colour below that gaze, she wanted those things
that now all her life she came to know she had never
known—a man to love her, not such a boy as the Ewan
that had been or the poor demented beast he'd become.

And if old John Brigson guessed of those things that
whispered so shamelessly there in her heart he gave never
a sign, wise and canny and kind. And no sign that he knew
did Rob give either, swinging by her side in the harvest
that drew to its end. And in Chris as she bent and straightened and stooked the last day was a prayer to the earth
and fields, a praying that this harvest might never end, that
she and Long Rob would tramp it forever. But the binder
flashed its blades at the head of the last, long bout, and Long
Rob had his hand on her shoulder, *He's finished, Chris
quean, and it's clyak!*

That evening she went out with him to the gate of the

close, and he swung his coat on his shoulder, *Well, well, Chris lass, I've like this fine*. And then, not looking at her, he added *I'm away to Aberdeen to enlist the morn*.

For a moment she was stupefied and stared at him silently, but she had no place in his thoughts, he was staring across Kinraddie's stooked fields. And then he began to tell her, he'd resolved on this days before, he couldn't stay out of it longer, all the world had gone daft and well he might go with the rest, there was neither trade nor trust for him here, or rest ever again till this War was over, if it ever ended at all. *So I'm giving in at last, I suppose they'll say. And this is ta-ta, Chris; mind on me kindly some times*.

She held to his hand in the gloaming light and so he looked down at last, she was biting her lips to keep down the tears, but he saw them shine brimming then in her eyes. And his own changed, changed and were kind and then something else, he cried *Why, lass!* and his hand on her shoulder drew her close, she was close and against him, held tight so that she felt the slow beat of his heart, she wanted to rest there, safe and safe in these corded arms. And then she minded that to-morrow he'd be gone, it cried through the evening in every cry of the lapwings, *So near, so near!*

So this also ended as everything else, every thing she had ever loved and desired went out to the madness beyond the hills on that ill road that flung its evil white ribbon down the dusk. And it was her arms then that went round his neck, drawing down his head and kissing him, queer and awful to kiss a man so, kissing him till she heard his breath come quick, and he gripped her, pleading with her, *We're daft, Chris quean, we mustn't!* But she knew then she had won, she wound her arms about him, she whispered *The haystacks!* and he carried her there, the smell of the clover rose crushed and pungent and sweet from under her head; and lying so in the dark, held to him, kissing him, she sought with lips and limbs and blood to die with him then.

But that dark, hot cloud went by, she found herself still lying there, Rob was there, and she drew his head to her breast, lying so with him, seeing out below the rounded breasts of the haystacks the dusky red of the harvest night, this harvest gathered to herself at last, reaped and garnered and hers in her heart and body. So they were for hours, John Brigson never called out to them; and then she stood beside Rob at the head of the road again, drowsy and quiet and content. They made no promises, kissing for last, she knew already he was growing remote from her, his eyes already remote to that madness that beckoned beyond the hills. So it was that he went from her next, she heard him go step-stepping slow with that swinging stride of his down through the darkness, and she never saw him again, was never to see him again.

It had burned up as a fire in a whin-bush, that thing in her life, and it burned out again and was finished. She went about the Blawearie biggings next day singing under breath to herself, quiet and unvexed, tending to hens and kye, seeing to young Ewan's sleep in the day and the setting of old Brigson's supper ere he came at night. She felt shamed not at all, all the vexing fears had gone from her, she made no try to turn from the eyes in the glass that looked out at her, wakened and living again. She was glad she'd gone out with Long Rob, glad and content, they were one and the same now, Ewan and her.

So the telegram boy that came riding to Blawearie found her singing there in the close, mending young Ewan's clothes. She heard the click of the gate and he took the telegram out of his wallet and gave it to her and she stared at him and then at her hands. They were quivering like the leaves of the beech in the forecoming of rain, they quivered in a little mist below her eyes. Then she opened the envelope and read the words and she said there was no reply, the boy swung on his bicycle again and rode out, riding and leaning he clicked the gate behind him; and laughed back at her for the cleverness of that.

She stood up then, she put down her work on the hack-stock and read again in the telegram, and began to speak to herself till that frightened her and she stopped. But she forgot to be frightened, in a minute she was speaking again, the chirawking hens in the close stopped and came near and turned up bright eyes to her loud and toneless whispering, *What do I do—oh, what do I do?*

She was vexed and startled by that—what was it she did! Did she go out to France and up to the front line, maybe, into a room where they'd show her Ewan lying dead, quiet and dead, white and bloodless, sweat on his hair, killed in action? She went out to the front door and waved to the harvesters, Brigson, young Ewan, and a tink they'd hired, they saw her and stared till she waved again and then John Brigson abandoned the half-loaded cart and came waddling up the park, so slow he was, *Did you cry me, Chris?*

Sweat on his hair as sweat on Ewan's. She stared at that and held out the telegram, he wiped slow hands and took it and read it, while she clung to the door-post and whispered and whispered *What is it I do now, John? Have I to go out to France?* And at last he looked up, his face was grizzled and hot and old, he wiped the sweat from it slow. *God, mistress, this is sore news, but he's died like a man out there, your Ewan's died fine.*

But she wouldn't listen to that, wanting to know the thing she must do; and not till he told her that she did nothing, they could never take all the widows to France and Ewan must already be buried, did she stop from that twisting of her hands and ceaseless whisper. Then anger came, *Why didn't you tell me before? Oh, damn you, you liked tormenting me!* and she turned from him into the house and ran up the stairs to the bed, the bed that was hers and Ewan's, and lay on it, and put her hands over her ears trying not to hear a cry of agony in a lost French field, not to think that the body that had lain by hers, frank and free and kind and young, was torn and dead and unmoving flesh, blood twisted upon it, not Ewan at all, riven and terrible, still and dead when the harvest stood out in Blawearie's land and the snipe were calling up on the loch and the beech trees whispered and rustled. And *SHE KNEW THAT IT WAS A LIE!*

He wasn't dead, he could never have died or been killed for nothing at all, far away from her over the sea, what matter to him their War and their fighting, their King and their country? Kinraddie was his land, Blawearie his, he was never dead for those things of no concern, he'd the crops to put in and the loch to drain and her to come back to. It had nothing to do with Ewan this telegram. They were only tormenting her, cowards and liars and bloody men, the English generals and their like down there in London. But she wouldn't bear it, she'd have the law on them, cowards and liars as she knew them to be!

It was only then that she knew she was moaning, dreadful to hear; and they heard it outside, John Brigson heard it and nearly went daft, he caught up young Ewan and ran with him into the kitchen and then to the foot of the stairs; and told him to go up to his mother, she wanted him. And

young Ewan came, it was his hand tugging at her skirts
that brought her out of that moaning coma, and he wasn't
crying, fearsome the sounds though she made, his face
was white and resolute, *Mother, mother!* She picked him
up and then held him close, rocking in an agony of despair
because of that look on his face, that lost look and the
smouldering eyes he had. *Oh Ewan, your father's dead!* she
told him the lie that the world believed. And she wept at last,
blindly, freeingly, for a little, old Brigson was to say it was
the boy that had saved her from going mad.

But throughout Kinraddie the news went underbreath
that mad she'd gone, the death of her man had fair un-
hinged her. For still she swore it was a lie, that Ewan
wasn't dead, he could never have died for nothing. Kirsty
Strachan and Mistress Munro came up to see her, they
shook their heads and said he'd died fine, for his country
and his King he'd died, young Ewan would grow up to be
proud of his father. They said that sitting at tea, with long
faces on them, and then Chris laughed, they quivered away
from her at that laugh.

*Country and King? You're havering, havering! What
have they to do with my Ewan, what was the King to him,
what their damned country? Blawearie's his land, it's not his
wight that others fight wars!*

She went fair daft with rage then, seeing the pity in their
faces. And also it was then, and then only, staring through
an angry haze at them, that she knew at last she was living
a dream in a world gone mad. Ewan was dead, they knew
it and she knew it herself; and he'd died for nothing, for
nothing, hurt and murdered and crying for her, maybe,
killed for nothing: and those bitches sat and spoke of their
King and country. . . .

They ran out of the house and down the brae, and,
panting, she stood and screamed after them. It was fair
the speak of Kinraddie next day the way she'd behaved,
and nobody else came up to see her. But she'd finished
with screaming, she went quiet and cold. Mornings came
up, and she saw them come, she minded that morning she'd
sent him away, and she might not cry him back. Noons
with their sun and rain came over the Howe and she saw
the cruelty and pain of life as crimson rainbows that
spanned the horizons of the wheeling hours. Nights came
soft and grey and quiet across Kinraddie's fields, they

brought neither terror nor hope to her now. Behind the walls of a sanity cold and high, locked in from the lie of life, she would live, from the world that had murdered her man for nothing, for a madman's gibberish heard in the night behind the hills.

And then Chae Strachan came home at last on leave, he came home and came swift to Blawearie. She met him out by the kitchen door, a sergeant by then, grown thinner and taller, and he stopped and looked in her frozen face. Then, as her hand dropped down from his, he went past her with swinging kilts, into the kitchen, and sat him down and took off his bonnet. *Chris, I've come to tell you of Ewan.*

She stared at him, waking, a hope like a fluttering bird in her breast. *Ewan? Chae—Chae, he's not living?* And then, as he shook his head, the frozen wall came down on her heart again. *Ewan's dead, don't vex yourself hoping else. They can't hurt him more, even this can't hurt him, though I swore I'd tell you nothing about it. But I know right well you should know it, Chris. Ewan was shot as a coward and deserter out there in France.*

. . . .

Chae had lain in a camp near by and had heard of the thing by chance, he'd read Ewan's name in some list of papers that was posted up. And he'd gone the night before Ewan was shot, and they'd let him see Ewan, and he'd heard it all, the story he was telling her now—*better always to know what truth's in a thing, for lies come creeping home to roost on unco rees, Chris quean. You're young yet, you've hardly begun to live, and I swore to myself that I'd tell you it all, that you'd never be vexed with some twisted bit in the years to come. Ewan was shot as a deserter, it was fair enough, he'd deserted from the front line trenches.*

He had deserted in a blink of fine weather between the rains that splashed the glutted rat-runs of the front. He had done it quickly and easily, he told to Chae, he had just turned and walked back. And other soldiers that met him had thought him a messenger, or wounded, or maybe on leave, none had questioned him, he'd set out at ten o'clock in the morning and by afternoon, taking to the fields, was

ten miles or more from the front. Then the military policemen came on him and took him, he was marched back and
court-martialled and found to be guilty.

And Chae said to him, they sat together in the hut
where he waited the coming of the morning, *But why did
you do it, Ewan? You might well have known you'd never
get free.* And Ewan looked at him and shook his head, *It
was that wind that came with the sun. I minded Blawearie,
I seemed to waken up smelling that smell. And I couldn't
believe it was me that stood in the trench, it was just daft
to be there. So I turned and got out of it.*

In a flash it had come on him, he had wakened up, he
was daft and a fool to be there; and, like somebody minding things done in a coarse wild dream there had flashed
on him memory of Chris at Blawearie and his last days
there, mad and mad he had been, he had treated her as a
devil might, he had tried to hurt her and maul her, trying
in the nightmare to waken, to make her waken him up;
and now in the blink of sun he saw her face as last he'd
seen it while she quivered away from his taunts. He knew
he had lost her, she'd never be his again, he'd known it in
that moment he clambered back from the trenches; but he
knew that he'd be a coward if he didn't try though all
hope was past.

So out he had gone for that, remembering Chris, wanting to reach her, knowing as he tramped mile on mile that
he never would. But he'd made her that promise that he'd
never fail her, long syne he had made it that night when
he'd held her so bonny and sweet and a quean in his arms,
young and desirous and kind. So mile on mile on the laired
French roads: she was lost to him, but that didn't help,
he'd try to win to her side again, to see her again, to tell
her nothing he'd said was his saying, it was the foulness
dripping from the dream that devoured him. And young
Ewan came into his thoughts, he'd so much to tell her of
him, so much he'd to say and do if only he might win to
Blawearie. . . . .

Then the military policemen had taken him and he'd listened to them and others in the days that followed, listening and not listening at all, wearied and quiet. *Oh, wearied
and wakened at last, Chae, and I haven't cared, they can
take me out fine and shoot me to-morrow, I'll be glad for
the rest of it, Chris lost to me through my own coarse daftness. She didn't even come to give me a kiss at good-bye,*

Chae, we never said good-bye; but I mind the bonny head of her down-bent there in the close. She'll never know, my dear quean, and that's best—they tell lies about folk they shoot and she'll think I just died like the rest; you're not to tell her.

Then he'd been silent long, and Chae'd had nothing to say, he knew it was useless to make try for reprieve, he was only a sergeant and had no business even in the hut with the prisoner. And then Ewan said, sudden-like, it clean took Chae by surprise, *Mind the smell of dung in the parks on an April morning, Chae? And the peewits over the rigs? Bonny they're flying this night in Kinraddie, and Chris sleeping there, and all the Howe happed in mist.* Chae said that he mustn't mind about that, he was feared that the dawn was close, and Ewan should be thinking of other things now, had he seen a minister? And Ewan said that an old bit billy had come and blethered, an officer creature, but he'd paid no heed, it had nothing to do with him. Even as he spoke there rose a great clamour of guns far up in the front, it was four miles off, not more; and Chae thought of the hurried watches climbing to their posts and the blash and flare of the Verey lights, the machine-gun crackle from pits in the mud, things he himself mightn't hear for long: Ewan'd never hear it at all beyond this night.

And not feared at all he looked, Chae saw, he sat there in his kilt and shirt-sleeves, and he looked no more than a young lad still, his head between his hands, he didn't seem to be thinking at all of the morning so close. For he started to speak of Blawearie then and the parks that he would have drained, though he thought the land would go fair to hell without the woods to shelter it. And Chae said that he thought the same, there were sore changes waiting them when they went back; and then he minded that Ewan would never go back, and could near have bitten his tongue in half, but Ewan hadn't noticed, he'd been speaking of the horses he'd had, Clyde and old Bess, fine beasts, fine beasts—did Chae mind that night of lightning when they found Chris wandering the fields with those two horses? That was the night he had known she liked him well— *nothing more than that, so quick and fierce she was, Chae man, she guarded herself like a queen in a palace, there was nothing between her and me till the night we married. Mind that—and the singing there was, Chae? What was it that Chris sang then?*

And neither could remember that, it had vexed Ewan a while, and then he forgot it, sitting quiet in that hut on the edge of morning. Then at last he'd stood up and gone to the window and said *There's bare a quarter of an hour now, Chae, you'll need to be getting back.*

And they'd shaken hands, the sentry opened the door for Chae, and he tried to say all he could for comfort, the foreshadowing of the morning in Ewan's young eyes was strange and terrible, he couldn't take out his hand from that grip. And all that Ewan said was *Oh man, mind me when next you hear the peewits over Blawearie—look at my lass for me when you see her again, close and close, for that kiss that I'll never give her.* So he'd turned back into the hut, he wasn't feared or crying, he went quiet and calm; and Chae went down through the hut lines grouped about that place, a farm-place it had been, he'd got to the lorry that waited him, he was cursing and weeping then and the driver thought him daft, he hadn't known himself how he'd been. So they'd driven off, the wet morning had come crawling across the laired fields, and Chae had never seen Ewan again, they killed him that morning.

．　　　．　　　．　　　．　　　．　　　．　　　．

This was the story Chae told to Chris, sitting the two of them in the kitchen of Blawearie. Then he moved and got up and she did the same, and like one coming from a far, dark country, she saw his face now, he'd been all that time but a voice in the dark. And at last she found speech herself *Never vex for me or the telling me this, it was best, it was best!*

She crept up the stairs to their room when he'd gone, she opened the press where Ewan's clothes were, and kissed them and held them close, those clothes that had once been his near as ever he'd come to her now. And she whispered then in the stillness, with only the beech for a listener, *Oh, Ewan, Ewan, sleep quiet and sound now, lad, I understand! You did it for me, and I'm proud and proud, for me and Blawearie, my dear, my dear—sleep quiet and brave, for I've understood!*

The beech listened and whispered, whispered and listened, on and on. And a strange impulse and urge came on Chris Tavendale as she too listened. She ran down the stairs and found young Ewan and kissed him, *Let's go a jaunt up to the hill.*

Below them, Kinraddie; above, the hill; the loch shimmering and sleeping in the autumn sun; young Ewan at her feet; the peewits crying down the Howe.

She gave a long sigh and withdrew her hand from the face of the Standing Stone. The mist of memories fell away and the aching urge came back—for what, for what? Sun and sky and the loneliness of the hills, they had cried her up here—for what?

And then something made her raise her eyes, she stood awful and rigid, fronting him, coming up the path through the broom. Laired with glaur was his uniform, his face was white and the great hole sagged and opened, sagged and opened, red-glazed and black, at every upwards step he took. Up through the broom: she saw the grass wave with no press below his feet, her lad, the light in his eyes that aye she could bring.

The snipe stilled their calling, a cloud came over the sun. He was close to her now and she held out her hands to him, blind with tears and bright her eyes, the bright weather in their faces, her voice shaping a question that she heard him answer in the rustle of the loch-side rushes as closer his soundless feet carried him to her lips and hands.

Oh lassie, I've come home! he said, and went into the heart that was his forever.

Epilude

THE UNFURROWED FIELD

FOLK said that winter that the War had done feint the much good to Mutch of Bridge End. In spite of his blowing and boasting, his silver he might as well have flung into a midden as poured in his belly, though faith! there wasn't much difference in destination. He'd gone in for the Irish cattle, had Mutch, quick you bought them and quick you sold and reaped a fine profit with prices so brave. More especially you did that if you crammed the beasts up with hay and water the morning before they were driven to the mart, they'd fairly seem to bulge with beef. But sometimes old Aitken of Bervie, a sly old brute, would give a bit stirk a wallop in the wame and it would belch like a bellows, and Aitken would say, *Ay, Mutch, the wind still bloweth as it listeth, I see,* he was aye quoting his bits of poetry, Aitken.

But he'd made silver for all that, Mutch, and many an awful feed had his great red lugs overhung, there in the Bridge End while the War went on. For that was how it struck him and his family, they'd gorge from morn till night, the grocer would stop three times a week and out to him Alec and his mistress would come, the bairns racing at the heels of them, and they'd buy up ham and biscuits and cheese and sausage, and tins of this and tins of that, enough to feed the German army, folk told—it that was said to be so hungry it was eating up its own bit corpses, feuch!

Though faith! it was little more than eating their own corpses they did at Bridge End. And what little they left uneaten they turned to drink, by the end of the War he'd got him a car, had Alec, it was only a Ford but it clattered up and down the road to Drumlithie every day of the week, and back it would bump to the Bridge End place with beer in crates and whisky in bottles wagging drunken-like over the hinder end. But Alec would blow and boast as much as ever, he'd say the Bridge End was a fine bit place and could easily stand him a dram—*it's the knack of farming you want, that's all.*

Mutch had just got up and come out blear-eyed that day when the postman handed him the letter from Kinraddie House. So he had one read of it and then another, syne he cried to his wife *Nine hundred pounds—have YOU got nine hundred pounds, you?* And she answered him back, canty and cool, *No, I've seen neither silver nor sense since I married you. Why do you need nine hundred pounds?* So Alec showed her the letter, 'twas long and dreich and went on and on; but the gist of it was the Trustees were to sell up Kinraddie at last; and the farmers that wanted them could buy their own places; and if Mutch of Bridge End still wanted his the price was nine hundred pounds.

So that was how the Mutches left Kinraddie, they said never a word about buying the place, Alec sold off his stock fell quietly and they did a moonlight flit; some said they heard the Ford that night go rattling up by Laurencekirk, others swore that Mutch had gone north to Aberdeen and had got him a fine bit job in a public-house there. North or south, feint the thing more folk saw of him; and be-fore the New Year was out old Gordon of Upperhill had bought up the Bridge End forbye his own place, he said he would farm the fields with a tractor. But damn the tractor ever appeared, he put sheep on the place instead, and sometimes the shepherd would wander into the kitchen where that gley-eyed wife of Mutch had sat to smoke her bit cigarettes; and he said that the smell of the damned things lingered there still, they'd been as unco at changing their skirts, the Mutches, as ever old Pooty had been.

What with his Germans and ghosts and dirt, he'd fair been in a way, had old Pooty. Long ere the War had fin-ished he'd have nothing to do with the mending of boots,

he wouldn't let the grocer up to the door, but would scraich
at him to leave the messages out by the road. And at last
he clean went over the gate, as a man might say, he took
in his cuddy to live with him there in the kitchen, and the
farmer lads going by on their bicycles of a Saturday night
would hear the two of them speaking together, old Pooty
they'd hear, thinking himself back at some concert or other
in the olden days, reciting his TIMROUS BEASTIE, stut-
tering and stammering at the head of his voice. And then
he'd be heard to give the donkey a bit clout, and *Damn
you! Clap, you creature!* he'd cry; and it was a fair enter-
tainment.

But at last it grew overmuch to bear, that was just about
the month when the letters went out from the Trustee
childes, and folk said that fell awful sounds were heard
coming from the Pooty place, the creature was clean demented. Not a body would do a thing till at last old Gordon
did, he roaded off with his foreman, they went in old
Gordon's car, it was night, and the nearer they came to
Pooty's the more awful came the sounds. The cuddy was
braying and braying in an awful stamash, they tried to
look through the window, but there was a thick leather
blind there and feint the thing could they see. So the foreman tried the door and it wouldn't budge, but the braying
of the cuddy grew worse and worse; and the foreman was
a big bit childe and he took a great run at the door and
open it flew and the sight he saw would have scunnered a
sow from its supper, the coarse old creature was tormenting the donkey this way and that with a red-hot poker, he
scraiched the beast was a German, and they had to tie him
up.

So the foreman went back for his gun and to send a message to bring the police; and when the police came down
next day the donkey was shot, and some said old Pooty
should have been instead. But they took the old creature
away to the madhouse, fair a good riddance to Kinraddie it
was. For a while after that there was speak of the Upperhill's foreman biding at Pooty's, he wanted to marry and it
would be fine and close for his work. And the foreman
said the place was fine if you thought of breeding a family
of swine; but he was neither a boar himself nor was his
quean a bit sow.

So the place began to moulder away, soon the roof went
all agley and half fell in, it was fit for neither man nor

beast, the thistles and weeds were all over the close, right they'd have pleased old Pooty's cuddy if he'd lived to see them. It looked a dreich, cold place as you rode by at night, near as lonesome as the old Mill was, and not near so handy. For the Mill was a place you could take your quean to, you'd lean your bicycles up by the wall and take a peek through the kitchen window; syne off you'd go, your two selves, and sit inside the old Mill itself; and your quean would say *Don't!* and smooth her short skirts; and she'd tell you you *would* be lucky if you got two dances at the Fordoun ball, John Edwards was to take her there in his side-car, mind.

For Long Rob had never come back to the Mill. It had fair been a wonder him joining the soldiers and going off to the War the way he did—after swearing black was blue that he'd never fight, that the one was as bad as the other, Scotch or German. Some said it was just plain daft he had gone, with no need for him to enlist; but when Munro of the Cuddiestoun told that to Chris Tavendale up at Bla-wearie she said there had been more sweetness and sense in Rob's little finger than in all the Munro carcases clecked since the Flood. Ill to say that to a man of an age with your father, it showed you the kind of creature Chris Tavendale was, folk shook their heads, minding how she'd gone near mad when her man was killed; as if he'd been the only one! And there was her brother, Will was his name, that had come from the War in a queer bit uniform, French he had said that it was; but them that were fine acquainted with uniforms weren't so sure, the Uhlans had worn uniforms just like that.

They had been the German horse-billies away back at the War's beginning, you minded, and syne shook your head over that, and turned to thinking of Long Rob again, him that was killed in the April of the last year's fighting. He'd been one of the soldiers they'd rushed to France in such hurry when it seemed that the German childes were fair over us, and he'd never come back to Kinraddie again, just notice of his death came through and syne a bit in the paper about him. You could hardly believe your eyes when you read it, him such a fell pacifist, too, he'd been killed in a bit retreat, that they made, him and two-three more billies had stood up to the Germans right well and held them back while the Scots retreated; they'd held on long after the others had gone, and Rob had been given a

medal for that. Not that he got it, faith! he was dead, they
came on his corpse long after, the British, but just as a
mark of respect.

And you minded Long Rob right well, the long rangy
childe, with his twinkling eyes and his great bit mouser
and those stories of his that he'd deave you with, horses
and horses, damn't! he had horses on the brain. There'd
been his coarse speak about religion, too, fair a scandal
once in Howe, but for all that he'd been a fine stock, had
Rob, you minded him singing out there in the morning,
he'd sung——And you couldn't mind what the song had
been till maybe a bairn would up and tell you, they'd heard
it often on the way to school, and Ay, it was *Ladies of
Spain*. You heard feint the meikle of those old songs now,
they were daft and old-fashioned, there were fine new ones
in their places, right from America, folk said, and all about
the queer blue babies that were born there, they were clever
brutes, the Americans.

Well, that was the Mill, all its trade was gone, old
Gordon bought up its land for a two-three pounds, and
joined the lot on to Upperhill. Jock Gordon came blinded
back from the War, they said he'd been near demented at
first when he lost the use of his eyes. But old Gordon was
making silver like dirt, he coddled up Jock like a pig with
a tit, and he'd settled down fell content, as well the creature
might be, with all he could smoke or drink at his elbow,
and his mother near ready to lick his boots. Fell gentry
and all they were now, the Gordons, you couldn't get
within a mile of the Upperhill without you'd hear a blast of
the English, so fine and genteel; and the ploughmen grew
fair mad when they dropped in for a dram at Drumlithie
Hotel and some billy would up and ask, *Is't true they dish
you out white dickies at Upperhill now and you've all to
go to the Academy?*

He was one of the folk that broke up the ploughmen's
Union, old Gordon, right proud he was of it, too; and
faith, the man was but right, whoever heard tell of such
nonsense, a Union for ploughmen? But he didn't get off
scot-free, faith, no! For what should happen in the General Election but that the secretary of the Farm Servants'
Union put up as a candidate for the Mearns; and from far
and near over Scotland a drove of those socialist creatures
came riding to help him, dressed up in specs and baggy
breeks and stockings with meikle checks.

Now, one of them was a doctor childe and up to the Upperhill he came on a canvass, like, when old Gordon and the wife had driven off to lend help to the Coalition. The door was opened by Maggie Jean, she'd grown up bonny as a flower in spring, a fine quean, sweet and kind, with no English airs. And damn't if they didn't take up, the doctor and her, all in a minute, the doctor forgot about the bothy he'd come to canvass and Maggie Jean had him in to tea, and they spoke on politics for hours and hours, the servant quean told, she said it was nothing but politics; and there have been greater miracles.

Well, the next thing was that old Gordon found his men being harried to vote for the Labour man, harried by his own lass Maggie Jean, it sent him fair wild and the blind son too. But Maggie Jean didn't care a fig, the doctor childe had turned her head; and when the election was over and the Labour man beaten she told her father she wasn't going on to the college any longer, she was set on marrying her Labour doctor. Gordon said he'd soon put his foot on that, she wasn't of age and he'd stop the marriage. But Maggie Jean put her arms round his neck, *I know, but you wouldn't like people to point at you and say 'Have you heard of old Gordon's illegitimate grandchild?'* And at that they say old Gordon fair caved in, *Oh, my lass, my Maggie Jean, you haven't done that!* For answer Maggie Jean just stood and laughed, shaky-like, though, till ben came Mistress Gordon herself and heard the news, and started in on the lass. Syne Maggie Jean grew cool as ice, *Very well, then, mother, I hear there's a good bed in Stonehaven Workhouse where women can have their babies.*

So she won in the end, you may well be sure, the Gordons fair rushed the marriage, and every now and then the doctor and Maggie Jean would take a bit look at each other and laugh out loud, they weren't a bit ashamed or decent. And when the wedding was over Mistress Gordon said *It's glad I am that you're off from Kinraddie to Edinburgh, where the shame of your half-named bairn won't aye be cast in my face.* And Maggie Jean said *What bairn, mother? I'm not to have a baby yet, you know, unless George and I get over-enthusiastic to-night.* Fair dumb-foundered was Mistress Gordon, she gasped, *But you said that you were with a bairn!* and Maggie Jean just shook her head and laughed. *Oh, no, I just asked father if he'd like to grandfather one. And I don't suppose that he would.*

*I won't have time for babies for years yet, mother, I'm to
help ORGANIZING THE FARM SERVANTS!*

Ah well, folk said there was damned little chance of
Nellie, the other bit daughter, ever having anything legit-
imate or illegitimate, she was growing up as sour and
wizened as an old potato, for all her English she'd sleep cold
and unhandled, an old maid all her days. But faith! you're
sure of nothing in this world, or whoever would have
guessed that Sarah Sinclair, the daft old skate, would go
marrying? It all came through the War and the stir at the
Netherhill when old Sinclair bought up the Knapp and his
own bit place all at one whip. Soon's she heard of that Sarah
went to him and said *You did plenty for Kirsty and she'll
not be needing the Knapp any more, you can bravely settle
me there!*

Old Sinclair, he was nearly ninety and blind, he stared
at her like a stirk at a water-jump, and then cried for his
wife. And Sarah told them she meant what she said, Dave
Brown, the Gourdon childe, would marry her the morn if
they'd Peesie's Knapp to sit down in.

And she got her way, but she didn't get the land, old
Sinclair pastured his sheep on it, and Dave stayed on as a
Netherhill ploughman. So Sarah was married off at last
and taken to bed in the house that had been her sister's.
She soon had her man well in hand, had Sarah, folk said
she'd to take him to bed by the lug the first night, but there
are aye coarse brutes to say things like that. And damn it,
if before a twelve-month was up she didn't have a bairn, a
peely-wally girl, but a bairn for all that. It wasn't much,
but still it was something, and when old Sinclair heard the
news he got it all mixed, he was in bed by then and sinking
fast, he thought it was Kirsty's first bairn that they told
of, and all the time he kept whispering *Chae!* he wanted his
good-son, Chae, that had married Kirsty long syne.

But Chae had been gone long ere that, he was killed in
the first fighting of Armistice Day, an hour before the guns
grew quiet. You minded him well and the arguings he'd
have with Long Rob of the Mill; he'd have been keen for the
Labour candidate, for Rich and Poor were as far off being
Equal as ever they'd been, poor Chae. Ay, it struck you
strange that he'd gone, fine childe he had been though a
bit of a fool that you laughed at behind his back.

In his last bit leave folk said he'd been awful quiet, maybe he knew right well he would never come back, he

tramped the parks most of the time, muttering of the woods they'd cut and the land that would never get over it. And when he said good-bye to Kirsty it wasn't just the usual slap on the shoulder and *Well, I'm away!* He held her and kissed her, folk saw it at the station, and he said *Be good to the bairns, lass.* And Kirsty, the meikle sumph, had stood there crying as the train went out, you'd have thought she'd have had more sense with all the folk glowering at her. And that was the last of Chae, you'd say, except that in the November of nineteen-eighteen they sent home his pocket-book and hankies and things; and they'd been well washed, but blood lay still in the pouch of the pocket-book, cold and black, and when Kirsty saw it she screamed and fainted away.

Women had little guts, except one or two, said Munro of the Cuddiestoun, as though he himself had been killing a German for breakfast every day of the War. And maybe that's what he'd liked to think as he chased the hens and thrawed their necks for the hospital trade, or swore at the daftie, Tony, over this or that. Feint the much heed paid Tony, though, he'd just stand about the same as ever, staring at the ground and driving Mistress Munro fair out of her senses when she'd sent him to lower the heat in one incubator or raise it up in another. For it was more than likely the creature would do clean the opposite of what he'd been told, and syne stand and glower at the ground a whole afternoon till somebody came out to look for him and would find every damned egg hard-boiled or stone cold, as the case might be. Some said he wasn't so daft, he did it for spite, but you'd hardly believe that a daftie would have the sense for that.

But nobody could deny the Munros had got on, they'd clean stopped from farming every park except one to grow their potatoes in, all the rest were covered with runs and rees for the hens, they'd made a fair fortune with their poultry and all. You'd never hear such a scraich in your life as when night-time came and they closed up the Cuddiestoun rees, it was then that Mistress Munro would nip out a cockerel here and an old hen there and thraw the creature's neck as quick as you'd blink and syne sit up half the night in the plucking of the birds. They'd hardly ever a well-cooked meal in the house themselves, but if their stomachs had little in them their bank books knew no lack, maybe one more than consoled for the other. But

Ellison said that they made him sick, the only mean Scotch he'd ever met, and be damned if they didn't make up for all the free ones.

Though that was only the kind of speak you'd expect from an Irish creature, he still spoke like one, fell fat he'd grown, his belly wabbled down right near to his knees and his breeks were meikle in girth. When the Trustees sent out their notice to buy, folk wondered what he'd do, there'd be an end to Ellison now, they said. But sore mistaken they found themselves, he bought up the Mains, stock and all, he bought up the ruins of Kinraddie House, and he bought Blawearie when there were no bids, he got it for less than two hundred pounds. And where had he got all that money except that he stole it?

Fair Kinraddie's big man he thought himself, faith! folk laughed at him and called him the waiter-laird, Cospatric that killed the gryphon would have looked at him sore surprised. He spoke fell big about tractors for ploughing, but then the slump came down and his blowing with it, he bought up sheep for Blawearie instead. And that was the way things went in the end on the old bit place up there on the brae, sheep baaed and scrunched where once the parks flowed thick with corn, no corn would come at all, they said, since the woods went down. And the new minister when he preached his incoming sermon cried *They have made a desert and they call it peace;* and some had no liking of the creature for that, but God! there was truth in his speak.

For the Gibbons had gone clean out of Kinraddie, there'd be far more room and far less smell, folk said, Stuart Gibbon had never come back from the War to stand in the pulpit his father had held. Not that he'd been killed, no, no, you might well depend that the great, curled steer had more sense in him than that. But the gentry liked him in Edinburgh right well in his Chaplain's uniform, and syne he fell in with some American creatures that controlled a kirk in New York. And they asked him if he'd like to have that kirk, all the well-off Scots went to it; and he took the offer like a shot and was off to America before you could wink, him and that thin bit English wife of his and their young bit daughter. Well, well, he'd done well for himself, it was plain to see; no doubt the Americans would like him fine, they could stand near anything out in America, their stomachs were awful tough with all the coarse things that they ate out of tins.

As for the father, the old man that had had such an ill-will for the Germans, he'd grown over-frail to preach and had to retire; and faith! if the British armies had killed half the Germans with their guns that he did with his mouth it would have been a clean deserted Germany long ere the end of the War. But off he went at last and only two ministers made try for the pulpit, both of them young, the one just a bit student from Aberdeen, the other new out of the Army. There seemed little to choose between the pair, they'd no pulpit voices, either of them, but folk thought it only fair to give the soldier billy the chance.

And it was only after he headed the leet, Colquohoun was his name, that the story went round he was son to that old minister from Banff that made try for Kinraddie before the War and was fair out-preached by the Reverend Gibbon. You minded him, surely?—he'd preached about beasts and the Golden Age, that the dragons still lived but sometime they'd die and the Golden Age come back. Feuch ah! no sermon at all, you might say. Well, that was him and this was the son, thin and tall, with a clean-shaven face, and he lectured on this and he wrote on that and he made himself fair objectionable before he'd been there a month. For he chummed up with ploughmen, he drove his own coal, he never wore a collar that fastened at the back, and when folk called him the Reverend he pulled them up sharp—*reverent, I am, no more, my friend*. And he whistled when he went on a Sunday walk and he stormed at farmers for the pay they paid and he helped the ploughman's Union; and he'd preach just rank sedition about it, and speak as though Christ had meant Kinraddie, and folk would grow fair uncomfortable.

You couldn't well call him pro-German, like, for he'd been a plain soldier all through the War. Folk felt clean lost without a bit name to hit at him with, till Ellison said he was a Bolshevik, one of those awful creatures, coarse tinks, that had made such a spleiter in Russia. They'd shot their king-creature, the Tsar they called him, and they bedded all over the place, folk said, a man would go home and find his wife commandeered any bit night and Lenin and Trotsky lying with her. And Ellison said that the same would come in Kinraddie if Mr. Colquohoun had his way; maybe he was feared for his mistress, was Ellison, though God knows there'd be little danger of *her* being commandeered, even Lenin and Trotsky would fair be desperate before they would go to that length.

Well, that was your new minister, then; and next there came scandalous stories that he'd taken up with young Chris Tavendale. Nearly every evening of the week he'd ride up to Blawearie, and bide there all the hours of the night, or so folk said. And what could he want with a common bit quean like the Tavendale widow? Ministers took up with ladies if they meant no jookery-packery. But when Munro said that to old Brigson the creature fair flew into a rage; and he said that many a decent thing had gone out of Kinraddie with the War but that only one had come in, and that was the new minister.

Well, well, it might be so and it mightn't; but one night Dave Brown climbed up the hill from the Knapp, to see old Brigson about buying a horse, and he heard folk speaking inside the kitchen and he took a bit keek round the door. And there near the fire stood Chris herself, and the Reverend Colquohoun was before her, she was looking up into the minister's face and he'd both her hands in his. And *Oh, my dear, maybe the second Chris, maybe the third, but Ewan has the first for ever!* she was saying, whatever she meant by that; and syne as Dave Brown still looked the minister bent down and kissed her, the fool.

Folk said that fair proved the stories were true, but the very next Sunday the minister stood up in the pulpit, and calm as ever, read out the banns of Upperhill's foreman and his quean from Fordoun, and syne the banns of *Robert Colquohoun, bachelor of this parish, and Christine Tavendale, widow, also of this same parish.*

You could near have heard a pin drop then, so quiet it was in the kirk, folk sat fair stunned. And there'd never been such a claik in Kinraddie as when the service was over and the congregation got out—ay, Chris Tavendale had feathered her nest right well, the sleeked creature, who'd have thought it of her?

And that made the minister no more well-liked with Kinraddie's new gentry, you may well be sure. But worse than that came; he'd been handed the money, the minister, to raise a memorial for Kinraddie's bit men that the War had killed. Folk thought he'd have a fine stone angel, with a night-gown on, raised up at Kinraddie cross-roads. But he sent for a mason instead and had the old stone circle

by Blawearie loch raised up and cleaned and set all in
place, real heathen-like, and a paling put round it. And
after reading out his banns on that Sunday the minister
read out that next Saturday the Kinraddie Memorial would
be unveiled on Blawearie brae, and that he expected a fine
attendance, whatever the weather—*they'd to attend in ill
weather, the folk that fell.*

Fine weather for January that Saturday brought, sunny,
yet caller, you could see the clouds come sailing down from
the north and over the sun and off again. But there was
rain not far, the seagulls had come sooning inland; for
once the snipe were still. Nearly every soul in Kinraddie
seemed climbing Blawearie brae as the afternoon wore
on, a fair bit stir there was in the close, the place was
empty of horses and stock, Chris would be leaving there at
the term. Soon she'd be down at the Manse instead, and
a proud-like creature no doubt she'd be.

Well, up on the brae through the road in the broom
there drew a fell concourse of folk, Ellison was there, and
his mistress, and the Gordons and gentry generally, forbye
a reischle of ploughmen and queans, lying round on the
grass and sniggering. There was the old circle of the
Standing Stones, the middle one draped with a clout, you
wondered what could be under it and how much the mason
had charged. It was high, there, you saw as you sat in the
grass and looked round, you could see all Kinraddie and
near half the Howe shine under your feet in the sun, *Out
of the World and into Blawearie* as the old speak went.
And faith! the land looked unco and woe with its woods
all gone, even in the thin-sun-glimmer there came a cold
shiver up over the parks of the Knapp and Blawearie folk
said that the land had gone cold and wet right up to the
very Mains.

Snow was shining in the Grampians, far in the coarse
hills there, and it wouldn't be long ere the dark came. Syne
at last the minister was seen coming up, he'd on the bit
robes that he hardly ever wore, Chris Tavendale walked
by the side of him and behind was a third childe that nobody knew, a Highlander in kilts and with pipes on his
shoulder, great and red-headed, who could he be? And
then Ellison minded, he said the man had been friend to
young Ewan Tavendale, he'd been the best man at Ewan's
marriage, McIvor his name was.

The minister held open the gate for Chris and through
it she came, all clad in her black, young Ewan's hand held
fast in hers, he'd grown fair like his father, the bairn, dark-
like and solemn he was. Chris's face was white and solemn
as well except when she looked at the minister as he held
the gate open, it was hardly decent the look that she gave
him, they might keep their courting till the two were alone.
Folk cried *Ay, minister!* and he cried back cheerily and
went striding to the midst of the old stone circle, John
Brigson was standing there with his hands on the strings
that held the bit clout.

The minister said, *Let us pray,* and folk took off their
hats, it smote cold on your pow. The sun was fleering up
in the clouds, it was quiet on the hill, you saw young Chris
stand looking down on Kinraddie with her bairn's hand in
hers. And then the Lord's Prayer was finished, the minister
was speaking just ordinary, he said they had come to
honour the folk whom the War had taken, and that the
clearing of this ancient site was maybe the memory that best
they'd have liked. And he gave a nod to old Brigson and
the strings were pulled and off came the clout and there
on the Standing Stone the words shone out in their dark
grey lettering, plain and short:

> FOR : THE : MEMORY : OF : CHA
> RLES : STRACHAN : JAMES :
> LESLIE : ROBERT : DUNCAN :
> EWAN : TAVENDALE : WHO :
> WERE : OF : THIS : LAND : AND :
> FELL : IN : THE : GREAT : WAR .
> IN : FRANCE : REVELATION :
> II CH : 28 VERSE

And then, with the night waiting out by on Blawearie
brae, and the sun just verging the coarse hills, the minister
began to speak again, his short hair blowing in the wind
that had come, his voice not decent and a kirk-like bumble,
but ringing out over the loch:

FOR I WILL GIVE YOU THE MORNING STAR

*In the sunset of an age and an epoch we may write that
for epitaph of the men who were of it. They went quiet*

*and brave from the lands they loved, though seldom of
that love might they speak, it was not in them to tell in
words of the earth that moved and lived and abided, their
life and enduring love. And who knows at the last what
memories of it were with them, the springs and the winters
of this land and all the sounds and scents of it that had
once been theirs, deep, and a passion of their blood and
spirit, those four who died in France? With them we may
say there died a thing older than themselves, these were the
Last of the Peasants, the last of the Old Scots folk. A new
generation comes up that will know them not, except as
a memory in a song, they passed with the things that seemed
good to them with loves and desires that grow dim and
alien in the days to be. It was the old Scotland that perished
then, and we may believe that never again will the old
speech and the old songs, the old curses and the old bene-
dictions, rise but with alien effort to our lips.*

*The last of the peasants, those four that you knew, took
that with them to the darkness and the quietness of the
places where they sleep. And the land changes, their parks
and their steadings are a desolation where the sheep are
pastured, we are told that great machines come soon to
till the land, and the great herds come to feed on it, the
crofter has gone, the man with the house and the steading
of his own and the land closer to his heart than the flesh of
his body. Nothing, it has been said, is true but change,
nothing abides, and here in Kinraddie where we watch the
building of those little prides and those little fortunes on
the ruins of the little farms we must give heed that these
also do not abide, that a new spirit shall come to the land
with the greater herd and the great machines. For greed
of place and possession and great estate those four had
little head, the kindness of friends and the warmth of toil
and the peace of rest—they asked no more from God or
man, and no less would they endure.*

*So, lest we shame them, let us believe that the new
oppressions and foolish greeds are no more than mists that
pass. They died for a world that is past, these men, but
they did not die for this that we seem to inherit. Beyond
it and us there shines a greater hope and a newer world,
undreamt when these four died. But need we doubt which
side the battle they would range themselves did they live*

*to-day, need we doubt the answer they cry to us even now,
the four of them, from the places of the sunset?*

And then, as folk stood dumbfounded, this was just
sheer politics, plain what he meant, the Highland man
McIvor tuned up his pipes and began to step slow round
the stone circle by Blawearie Loch, slow and quiet, and
folk watched him, the dark was near, it lifted your hair
and was eerie and uncanny, the *Flowers of the Forest* as
he played it:

It rose and rose and wept and cried, that crying for the
men that fell in battle, and there was Kirsty Strachan weeping quietly and others with her, and the young ploughmen
they stood with glum, white faces, they'd no understanding
or caring, it was something that vexed and tore at them, it
belonged to times they had no knowing of.

He fair could play, the piper, he tore at your heart marching there with the tune leaping up the moor and echoing across the loch, folk said that Chris Tavendale alone shed never a tear, she stood quiet, holding her boy by the hand, looking down on Blawearie's fields till the playing was over. And syne folk saw that the dark had come and began to stream down the hill, leaving her there, some were uncertain and looked them back. But they saw the minister was standing behind her, waiting for her, they'd the last of the light with them up there, and maybe they didn't need it or heed it, you can do without the day if you've a lamp quiet-lighted and kind in your heart.

THE END

CLOUD HOWE

CONTENTS

NOTE

Colquohoun is pronounced *Ca-hoon,*
and
Segget as with one hard *g.*

PROEM

THE borough of Segget stands under the Mounth, on the southern side, in the Mearns Howe, Fordoun lies near and Drumlithie nearer, you can see the Laurencekirk lights of a night glimmer and glow as the mists come down. If you climb the foothills to the ruined Kaimes, that was builded when Segget was no more than a place where the folk of old time had raised up a camp with earthen walls and with freestone dykes, and had died and had left their camp to wither under the spread of the grass and the whins—if you climbed up the Kaimes of a winter morn and looked to the east and you held your breath, you would maybe hear the sough of the sea, sighing and listening up through the dawn, or see a shower of sparks as a train came skirling through the woods from Stonehaven, stopping seldom enough at Segget, the drivers would clear their throats and would spit, and the guards would grin: as though 'twere a joke.

But God alone knows what you'd want on the Kaimes, others had been there and had dug for treasure, nothing they'd found but some rusted swords, tint most like in the wars once waged in the days when the wife of the Sheriff of Mearns, Finella she was, laid trap for the King, King Kenneth the Third, as he came on a hunting jaunt through the land. For Kenneth had done her own son to death, and she swore that she'd even that score up yet; and he hunted slow through the forested Howe, it was winter, they tell, and in that far time the roads were winding puddles of glaur, the horses splashed to their long-tailed rumps. And the men of Finella heard of his coming, as that dreich clerk Wyntoun has told in his tale:

As through the Mernys on a day
  The kyng was rydand hys hey way
Off hys awyne curt al suddanly
  Agayne hym ras a cumpany
In to the towne of Fethyrkerne
  To fecht wyth hym thai ware sa yherne
And he agayne thame faucht sa fast,
  Bot he thare slayne was at the last.

So Kenneth was dead and there followed wars, Finella's carles builded the Kaimes, a long line of battlements under the hills, midway a tower that was older still, a broch from the days of the Pictish men; there they lay and long months withstood the folk that came to avenge the death of Kenneth; and the darkness comes down on their waiting and fighting and all the ill things that they suffered and did.

The Kaimes was left bare and ruined with walls, as Iohannes de Fordun tells in his time, a Fordoun childe him and had he had sense he'd have hidden the fact, not spread it abroad. Some kind of a cleric he was in those days, just after the Bruce drove out the English, maybe Fordoun then had less of a smell ere Iohannes tacked on the toun to his name. Well, the Kaimes lay there in Iohannes' time, he tells that the Scots folk halted there going north one night to the battle of Bara; and one man with the Scots, a Lombard he was, looked out that morn as the army roused and the bugles blew out under the hills, and he saw the mists that went sailing by below his feet the sun came quick down either slope of a brae to a place where a streamlet ran by a ruined camp. And it moved his heart, and he thought it an omen, in his own far land there were camps like that; and he swore that if he should survive the battle he'd come back to this place and claim grant of its land.

Hew Monte Alto was the Lombard's name and he fought right well at the Bara fight, and when it was over and the Bruce made King, he asked of the Bruce the lands that lay under the Kaimes in the windy Howe. These lands had been held by the Mathers folk, but they had made peace with

Edward the First and given him shelter and welcome the
night he halted in Mearns as he toured the north. So the
Bruce he took their lands from the Mathers and gave them
to Hew, that was well content, though vexed that he came
of no gentle blood. So he sent a carle to the Mathers lord
to ask if he had a daughter of age for wedding and bedding;
and he sent an old carle that he well could spare, in case
the Mathers should flay him alive.

For the Mathers were proud as though God had made
their flesh of another manure from men; but by then they
had come to a right sore pass in the mouldering old castle
by Fettercairn, where hung the helmet of good King Grig,
who first had 'stablished the Mathers there, and made of
the first of them Merniae Decurio, Captain-chief of the
Mearns lands. So the old lord left Hew's carle unskinned,
and sent back the message he had more than one daughter,
and the Lombard could come and choose which he liked.
And Hew rode there and he made his choice, and was
wedded and bedded to a Mathers quean.

But short was the time that he had for his pleasure, the
English again had come north to war. The Scots men
gathered under the Bruce at a narrow place where a black
burn ran, the pass of the Bannock burn it was. And Hew
was a well-skinned man in the wars, he rode his horse
lathered into the camp, and King Robert called him to
make the pits and set the spiked calthrops covered with
earth, traps for the charge of the English horse. So he did,
and the next day came, and the English, they charged right
brave and were whelmed in the pits. But Hew was slain
by an English arrow as he rode unhelmed to peer at his pits.

Before he rode south he had builded a castle within the
walls of the old-time Kaimes, and brought far off from his
Lombard land a pickle of weavers, folk of his blood. They
builded their houses down under the Kaimes in the green-
walled circle of the ancient camp, they tore down the walls
of that heathen place, and set their streets by the Segget
burn, and drove their looms, and were well-content, though
foreign and foolish and but ill-received by the dour, dark
Pictish folk of the Mearns. Yet that passed in time, as the
breeds grew mixed, and the toun called Segget was made
a borough for sake of the Hew that fell at the Burn.

So the Monte Altos came to be Mowat, and interbred
with the Mathers folk, and the next of whom any story is
told is he who befriended the Mathers who joined with

other three lairds against the Lord Melville. For he pressed
them right sore, the Sheriff of Mearns, and the four complained and complained to the King; and the King was
right vexed, and he pulled at his beard—*Sorrow gin the
Sheriff were sodden—sodden and supped in his brew!* He
said the words in a moment of rage, unthinking, and then
they passed from his mind; but the lairds remembered, and
took horse for the Howe.

There, as they'd planned, the four of them did, the
Sheriff went hunting with the four fierce lairds, Arbuthnott,
Pitarrow, Lauriston, Mathers; and they took him and bound
him and carried him up Garvock, between two stones a
great cauldron was hung; and they stripped him bare and
threw him within, in the water that was just beginning to
boil; and they watched while he slowly ceased to scraich,
he howled like a wolf in the warming water, then like a
bairn smored in plague, and his body bloated red as the
clay, till the flesh loosed off from his seething bones; and
the four lairds took their horn spoons from their belts and
supped the broth that the Sheriff made, and fulfilled the
words that the King had said.

They were hunted sore by the law and the kirk, the
Mathers fled to the Kaimes to hide, his kinsman Mowat
closed up the gates and defied the men of the King that
came. So they laid a siege to the castle of Kaimes; but the
burghers of Segget sent meat to the castle by a secret way
that led round the hills; and a pardon came for the Mathers
at last, the army withdrew and the Mathers came out, and
he swore if ever again in his life he supped of broth or
lodged between walls, so might any man do to himself as
he had done to the Sheriff Melville.

And for long the tale of Segget grows dim till there
came the years of the Killing Time, and the Burneses, James
and Peter they were—were taken to Edinburgh and put to
the question that they might forswear the Covenant and
God. And Peter was old, in the torment he weakened, and
by him his son James lay on the rack, and even when the
thummikins bit right sore and Peter opened his mouth to
forswear, his son was before him singing a psalm so loud
that he drowned the voice of Peter; and the old man died,
but James was more slow, they threw him into a cell at last,
his body broken in many places, the rats ate him there
while he still was alive; and maybe there were better folk
far in Segget, but few enough with smeddum like his.

His son was no more than a loon when he died, he'd
a little farm on the Mowat's land. But he moved to Glenbervie and there took a place, and his folk had the ups and
downs of all flesh till the father of Robert Burnes grew up,
and grew sick of the place, and went off to Ayr; and there
the poet Robert was born, him that lay with nearly as
many women as Solomon did, though not all at one time.

But some of the Burneses still bade in Segget. In the
first few years of King William's reign it was one of them,
Simon, that led the feud the folk of Segget had with the
Mowats. For they still owned most of Segget, the Mowats,
a thrawn old wife the lady was then, her sons all dead
in the wars with the French; and her wits were half gone,
it was seldom she washed, she was mean as dirt and she
smelt to match. And Simon Burnes and the Segget minister,
they prigged on the folk of Segget against her, the weaver
folk wouldn't pay their rent, they made no bow when they
met the old dame ride out in her carriage with her long
Mowat nose.

And at last one night folk far from Segget saw a sudden
light spring up in the hills; it waved and shook there all
through the dark, and from far and near as the dawn drew
nigh, there were parties of folk set out on the roads to see
what their fairely was in the hills. And the thing they saw
was the smoking Kaimes, a great bit fire had risen in the
night and burned the old castle down to its roots, of the
stones there stood hardly one on the other, the Segget folk
swore they'd all slept so sound the thing was over afore
they awoke. And that might be so, but for many a year,
before the Old Queen was took to her end and the weaving
entirely ceased to pay and folk went drifting away from
the Mearns, there were meikle great clocks in this house
and that, great coverlets on beds that lay neist the floor;
and the bell that rung the weavers awake had once been
a great handbell from the hall of the Mowats up on the
Kaimes high hill.

A Mowat cousin was the heritor of Kaimes, he looked
at the ruin and saw it was done, and left it there to the
wind and the rain; and builded a house lower down the
slope, Segget below, yew-trees about, and had bloodhounds
brought to roam the purviews, he took no chances of innocent sparks floating up in the night from Segget. But the
weavers were turning to other things now, smithying and
joinering and keeping wee shops for the folk of the farms

that lay round about. And the Mowats looked at the Segget burn, washing west to the Bervie flow, and were ill-content that it should go waste.

But it didn't for long, the jute trade boomed, the railway came, the two jute mills came, standing out from the station a bit, south of the toun, with the burn for power. The Segget folk wouldn't look at things, the Mowats had to go to Bervie for spinners, and a tink-like lot of creatures came and crowded the place, and danced and fought, raised hell's delight, and Segget looked on as a man would look on a swarm of lice; and folk of the olden breed moved out, and builded them houses up and down the East Wynd, and called it New Toun and spoke of the dirt that swarmed in Old Toun, round about the West Wynd.

The spinners' coming brought trade to the toun, but the rest of Segget still tried to make out that the spinners were only there by their leave, the ill-spoken tinks, with their mufflers and shawls; the women were as bad as the men, if not worse, with their jeering and fleering in Segget Square; and if they should meet with a farmer's bit wife as she drove into Segget to go to the shops, and looked neat and trig and maybe a bit proud, they'd scraich *Away home, you country cow!*

But the Mowats were making money like dirt. They built a new kirk when the old one fell, sonsy and broad, though it hadn't a steeple; and they lived and they died and they went to their place; and you'd hear the pound of the mills at work down through the years that brought the Great War; and that went by and still Segget endured, outlasting all in spite of the rhyme that some coarse-like tink of a spinner had made:

> Oh, Segget it's a dirty hole,
>   A kirk without a steeple,
> A midden-heap at ilka door,
>   And damned uncivil people.

I

CIRRUS

SEGGET was wakening as Chris Colquohoun came down the shingle path from the Manse. Here the yews stood thick, in a starlings' murmur, a drowsy cheep on the edge of the dawn; but down the dark, as you reached the door, you saw already lights twink here and there, in the houses of Segget, the spinners' wynds, a smell in the air of hippens and porridge. But she'd little heed for these, had Chris, she went quick as she looked at the eastern sky, the May air warm in her face as she turned, north, and went up the Meiklebogs road. So rutted it was and sossed with the carts that there was a saying in Segget toun: *There's a road to heaven and a road to hell, but damn the road to the Meiklebogs.*

But that didn't matter, she wasn't going there, in a while she turned by a path that wound, dark, a burn was hidden in the grass, over a stile to the hills beyond. And now, as she climbed swift up the slope, queer and sudden a memory took her—of the hills above the farm in Kinraddie, how sometimes she'd climb to the old Druid stones and stand and remember the world below, and the things that were done and the days put by, the fun and fear of the days put by. Was that why the Kaimes had so filled her sky the twenty-four hours she had been in Segget?

Now she was up on the lowermost ledge, it lay dark

about, the old castle of Kaimes, no more than a litter of
ruined walls, the earth piled high up over the stones that
once were halls and men-shielded rooms. There were yews
growing low in a corner outbye, they waved and moved
as they heard Chris come. But she wasn't feared, she was
country-bred, she wandered a little, disappointed, then
laughed, at herself, to herself, and the place grew still.
Maybe it thought, as did Robert Colquohoun, that her
laugh was a thing worth listening for.

She felt her face redden, faint, at that, and she thought
how over her face the slow blood would now be creeping,
she'd once or twice watched it, bronzed and high in the
cheek-bones her face, and a kindly smoulder of grey-gold
eyes, she minded how once she _had_ wished they were blue!
She put up her hand to her hair, it was wet, with the dew
she supposed from the dark Manse trees, it was coiled over
either ear in the way she had worn it now for over two
years.

She turned round then and looked down at Segget,
pricked in the paraffin lights of dawn. They were going out
one by one as the east grew wanly blind in the van of the
sun, behind, in the hills, a curlew shrilled—dreaming up
here while the world woke, Robert turning in his bed down
there in the Manse, and maybe out-reaching a hand to
touch her as he'd done that first morning two years ago, it
had felt as though he wakened her up from the dead . . .

So strange it had seemed a long minute she'd lain, half
feared, with his hand that touched her so. Then he'd
moved, quick breathing, deep in his sleep, and the hand
went away, she reached out in the dark and sought it again
and held to it, shy. It was winter that morning, they both
had slept late from their marriage night; and, as the winter
light seeped grey into the best bedroom of Kinraddie Manse,
Chris Colquohoun, who had once been married to Ewan,
and before that time was Chris Guthrie, just, had lain and
thought and straightened things out, like a bairn rubbing
its eyes from sleep. . . . This was new, she had finished
with that life that had been, all the love she had given to
her Ewan, dead, lost and forgotten far off in France: her
father out in the old kirkyard: that wild, strange happening
that had come to her the last Harvest but one there was of
the War, when she and another—but she'd not think of
that, part of the old, sad dream that was done. Had that

other remembered the happening at all, his last hour of all
in a Flanders trench?

And she thought that maybe he had not at all, you did
this and that and you went down in hell to bring the fruit
of your body to birth, it was nothing to the child that came
from your womb, you gave to men the love of your heart,
and they'd wring it dry to the last red drop, kind, dreadful
and dear, and deep in their souls, whatever the pretence
they played with you, they knew it a play and Life waiting
outbye.

So she lay and thought, and then wriggled a little—to
think these things on her marriage-morn, the hand she held
now never held so before! And she peered in his face in the
light that came, his hair lay fair on the pillow's fringe, fair
almost to whiteness, his skin ivory-white, she saw his brows
set dark in a dream, and the mouth came set in a straight
line below, she liked his mouth and his chin as well, and
his ears that were small and lay flat back, so, and the hand
that had tightened again in his sleep—oh! more than that,
you liked all of him well, with his kisses in the night that
had only just gone, his kisses, the twinkle-scowl in his eyes:
And now it's to bed, but I don't think to sleep. She had
laughed as well, feeling only half-shy. *An awful speak,
Robert, for Kinraddie's minister!* and he said *Don't ministers do things like that?* and she'd looked at him swift, and
looked quick away. *Maybe, we'll see;* and so they had seen.

She stretched then, softly, remembering that, warm under
the quilt her own body felt queer, strange and alive as
though newly blessed, and she smiled at that thought, in a
way it had been, one flesh she was made with a kirk minister! Funny to think she had married a minister, that this
was the Manse, that she was its mistress—oh! life was a
flurry like a hen-roost at night, the doors were banging, you
flew here and there, were your portion the ree or the
corner of a midden you could not foretell from one night
to the next.

She got from bed then and into her clothes, agile and
quick, and not looking back, if ministers ate as well as they
loved, Robert would be hungry enough when he woke.
Down in the kitchen she came on Else Queen, ganting as
wide as a stable-door, she stopped from that, the Manse's
new maid, a handsome quean, and she said *Hello!* Chris
felt the blood in the tips of her ears, she saw plain the
thing in the great lump's mind. *You call me Mrs. Colquo-*

*houn, you know, Else. And you get up smart in the morning
as well, else we'll need another maid at the Manse.*

Else went dirt-white and closed up her mouth. *Yes—
Mem, I'm sorry,* and Chris felt a fool, but she didn't show
it, and this kind of thing had just to be settled one way or
the other. *My name's not Mem, it's just Mrs. Colquohoun.
Get the water boiling and we'll make the breakfast. What
kind of a range is this that we've got?*

That was that, and she had no trouble at all with meikle
Else Queen in Kinraddie Manse, though the speak went out
and about the parish that Chris Tavendale, the new minister's new wife, had grown that proud that she made her
maid cry *Mem!* every time they met on the stairs, a fair
dog's life had that poor Else Queen, it just showed you the
kind of thing that happened when a creature got up a bit
step in the world. And who was she to put on her airs—
the daughter of a little bit farmer, just, and the wife of
another, killed in the War. Ay, them that were fond of
their men didn't marry as close as that on the death of the
first, the Manse and the minister's silver the things that the
new Mrs. Colquohoun had had in her mind.

Chris heard those stories in the weeks that went, if you
bade in Kinraddie and any ill tale were told about you—
and you fair had to be an angel in breeks if that weren't
done and even then, faith! they'd have said there were unco
things under your breeks—the very trees rose and sniggered
it to you, the kye lowed the news from every bit gate. But
she paid no heed, she was blithe and glad, happed in her
Robert and the nearness of him, young Ewan as well, a
third by the fire as they sat of a night and the storms came
malagarousing the trees down the length and breadth of the
shrilling Howe. Behind and far up you would hear the hills
quake, Robert would raise up his head and laugh, the
twinkle-scowl in his deep-set eyes—*The feet of the Lord on
the hills, Christine!*

Ewan would look up, staring and still, *Who's the Lord?*
and Robert would drop his great book and stare in the fire,
*That's a tough one, Ewan. But He's Something and sure,
our Father and Mother, our End and Beginning.*

Ewan's eyes would open wider at that. *My mother's here
and my father's dead.* Robert would laugh and upset his
chair, *A natural sceptic—come out of that chair, there's*

over many of your kind already squatting their hams in the thrones of the mighty!

So the two of them would crawl round the floor and would growl, play tigers and beasts of like gurring breeds, Ewan with his coolness and graveness forgot, Robert worse than a bairn, Chris sitting and watching, a book in her hand or darning and knitting, but not often those. Robert got angered when she sat and darned. *What, waste your life when you'll soon be dead? You're not going to slave for me, my girl!* And she'd say *But you won't like holes in your socks?* and he'd laugh *When they're holed we'll buy a new pair. Come out for a tramp, the storm's gone down.*

And out they would tramp, young Ewan in bed, the night black under their feet as cold pitch, about them the whistle and moan of the trees till they cleared the Manse and went up by the Mains, with the smell of the dung from its hot cattle-court, and the smell of the burning wood in its lums. You'd see and hear little about you by then, just the two of you swinging up the hill in the dark, till the blow of the wind would catch in your throats as you gained by the cambered edge of the brae.

Around them, dry, the whistle of the whins, strange shapes that rose and were lost in the dark, Robert would stop and would fuss at her collar, pretending he did it to keep out the old. But she'd grown to know him, the thing that he'd want, she'd put up her arms round close by his throat, and hug him, half-shy, she was still half-shy. He'd told her that once and Chris had been vexed, lying in his arms, for a sudden moment she had touched him with lips fierce and sudden with a flame that came up out of her heart, up out of the years when she still was unwed: and he'd gasped, and she'd laughed *Do you call that shy?* Then she'd been half-ashamed and yet glad as well, and fell fast asleep till the morning came, and they both woke up and looked at each other, and he said that she blushed and she hid her face and said that one or the other was a fool.

But best she minded of those night-time walks the first that took them up to the hills, a rousting night in December's close. They came at last on Blawearie's brae, and panting, looked down on the windy Mearns, the lights of Bervie a lowe in the east, the Laurencekirk gleams like a scattering of faggots, Segget's that shone as the blurring of stars, these were the lights of the jute mills there. So they stood a long while and looked down the brae, Kinraddie below them happed in its sleep; and Robert fell into a dreaming muse, as he often did, with his mind far off. Chris said nothing, content though she froze, after one peek at his stillness beside her. Queer with *him* here on Blawearie brae, that once was hers, if they walked down over that shoulder there they'd come to the loch and the Standing Stones to which she had fled for safety, compassion, so often and oft when she was a quean. . . .

She could smell the winter smell of the land and the sheep they pastured now on Blawearie, in the parks that once came rich with corn that Ewan had sown and they both had reaped, where the horses had pastured, their kye and their stock. And she minded the nights in the years of the War, nights such as this when she'd lain in her bed and thought of the times that would come yet again—Ewan come back and things as before, how they'd work for young Ewan and grow old together, and buy Blawearie and be happy forever.

And now she stood by a stranger's side, she slept in his bed, he loved her, she him, nearer to his mind than ever she had been to that of the body that lay mouldering in France, quiet and unmoving that had moved to her kisses, that had stirred and been glad in her arms, in her sight, that had known the stinging of rain in his face as he ploughed the steep rigs of Blawearie brae, and come striding from his work with that smile on his face, and his clumsy hands and his tongue that was shy of the things that his eyes could whisper so blithe. Dead, still and quiet, not even a body, powder and dust he with whom she had planned her life and her days in the times to be.

In a ten years' time what things might have been? She might stand on this hill, she might rot in a grave, it would matter nothing, the world would go on, young Ewan dead as his father was dead, or hither and borne, far from Kinraddie: oh, once she had seen in these parks, she remembered, the truth, and the only truth that there was, that only the sky and the seasons endured, slow in their change, the cry of the rain, the whistle of the whins on a winter night under the sailing edge of the moon——

And suddenly, daft-like, she found herself weep, quiet, she thought that she made no noise, but Robert knew, and his arm came round her.

It was Ewan? Oh, Chris, he won't grudge you me!

Ewan? It was Time himself she had seen, haunting their tracks with unstaying feet.

But the Spring was coming. You looked from the Manse at the hills as they moved and changed with each day, the glaur and the winter dark near gone, the green came quick and far on the peaks, the blink of the white snow-bonnets grew less, swallows were wheeling about the Manse trees, down in the fields of the Mains you could hear the click and spit of a tractor at work, far up by Upperhill parks rise the baa of the sheep they pastured now at Bridge End. It seemed to Chris when those first days came that she'd weary to death with a house and naught else, not to have fields that awaited her help, help in the seeding, the spreading of dung, the turning out of the kye at dawn, hens chirawking mad for their meat, the bustle and hurry of Blawearie's close. But now as she looked on the land so strange, with its tractors and sheep, she half-longed to be gone. It had finished with her, that life that had been, and this was her's now: books, and her Robert, young Ewan to teach, and set a smooth cloth on the Manse's table, hide in the little back room at the top and darn his socks when Robert didn't see.

He was out and about on the work of the parish, marrying this soul and burying that, christening the hopeful souls new-come to pass in their time to marriage and burial. He'd come back dead tired from a day of his work, Chris would hear him fling his stick in the hall and cry out *Else, will you run me a bath?* And because of those strange, dark moods she had met, Chris seldom met him now on the stairs, she'd wait till he changed and was Robert again, he'd come searching her out and tell her the news, and snatch the book from young Ewan's hand as Ewan squatted in the window-seat, reading. *A prig, a bookworm!* Robert would cry as he flung the book the other side of the room; and Ewan would smile in his slow, dark way, and then give a yell and they'd scuffle a while, while Chris went down and brought up the tea.

From that room you could see all Kinraddie by day and the lights of Kinraddie shine as night came, Robert would heave a great sigh as he sat and looked from Chris to Kinraddie below. *Wearied?* she'd ask, and he'd say, *Lord, yes,* and frown and then laugh: *Looks everywhere that would*

*sour the milk! But my job's to minister and minister I will
though Kinraddie's kirk grows toom as its head.* And would
think a while, *It's near that already.*

Faith! so it was, nothing unco in that, there was hardly
a kirk in the Mearns that wasn't, the War had finished your
fondness for kirks, you knew as much as any minister.
Why the hell should you waste your time in a kirk when
you were young, you were young only once, there was the
cinema down in Dundon, or a dance or so, or this racket
or that; and your quean to meet and hear her complain she's
not been ta'en to the Fordoun ball. You'd chirk to your
horses and give a bit smile as you saw the minister swoop
by on his bike, with his coat-tails flying and his wee, flat
hat; and at night in the bothy some billy or other would
mock the way that he spoke or moved. To hell with ministers and toffs of his kind, they were aye the friends of the
farmers, you knew.

All the farmers now of Kinraddie were big, but they had
as little liking as the bothy for the Reverend Colquohoun
and the things he said, Would a man go up to the kirk of
a Sabbath to sit down and hear himself insulted? You went
to kirk to hear a bit sermon about Paul and the things he
wrote the Corinthians, all of them folk that were safely
dead; but Kinraddie's minister would try to make out that
you yourself, that was born in Fordoun of honest folk,
were a kind of Corinthian, oppressing the needy, he meant
those lazy muckers the ploughmen. No, no, you were hardly so daft as take that, you would take the mistress a jaunt
instead, next Sunday like or maybe the next, up the Howe
to her cousin in Brechin that hadn't yet seen the new car
you had bought; or maybe you'd just lie happed in your
bed, and have breakfast, and read all about the divorces
the English had from their wives—damn't, man! they fair
had a time, those English tinks! You wouldn't bother your
head on the kirk, to hell with ministers of the kind of
Colquohoun, they were aye the friends of the ploughmen,
you knew.

And Chris would stand in the choir and sing, and sometimes look at the page in her hand and think of the days
when she at Blawearie had never thought of the kirk at all,
over-busied living the life that was *now* to bother at all on
the life to come. Others of the choir that had missed a

service would say to her with a shy-like smile, *I'm so sorry, Mrs. Colquohoun, I was late;* and Chris would say that they needn't fash, if she said it in Scots the woman would think, *Isn't that a common-like bitch at the Manse?* If she said it in English the speak would spread round the minister's wife was putting on airs.

Robert's stipend was just three hundred pounds, when he'd first told Chris she had thought it a lot, and felt deep in her a prick of resentment that he got so much, when the folk on the land that did all the work that really was work—they got not a third, with a family thrice bigger. But soon she was finding the money went nowhere, a maid to keep and themselves forbye, this and that charity that folk expected the minister should not only help but head. And they didn't in vain, he'd have given the sark from his back, would Robert, if Chris hadn't stopped him, and syne given his vest. When he heard of a cottar that was needy or ill he'd wheel out his old bike and swoop down the roads, he rode with old brakes and they sometimes gave way, and then he would brake with a foot on the wheel, his thoughts far off as he flew through the stour, if he hadn't a broken neck it was luck. That was his way and Chris liked him for it, though she herself would as soon have thought of biking that way as of falling off the old tower by the kirk, and lippening to chance she would land on her feet.

Well, so, and most likely sparked up with glaur, he'd come to the house where the ill man lay, and knock and cry *Well, are you in?* and go in. And sit him down by the bed of the man, and tell him a story to make him laugh, never mention God unless he was asked, and that was seldom enough, as you knew, a man just blushed if you mentioned God. So Robert would talk of the crops and fees, and *Where is your daughter fee'd to now?* and *The wife looks fine,* and *I'll need to be off.* And syne as he went he'd slip a pound note into the hand of the sick bit man; and he'd take it and redden up, dour, and say *Thank you;* and after Robert went they'd say, *What's a pound? Him that gets paid as much as he does.*

Chris knew that they said that kind of thing, Else told her the news as they worked in the kitchen; and she knew as well how the news went out from the Manse of every bit thing that was there—Ewan, her son, how he dressed, what he said; and the things they said and the things they sang and how much they ate and what they might drink; when they went to bed and when they got up; and how the minister would kiss his wife, without any shame, in the sight of the maid—Oh, Chris knew most and she guessed the rest, all Kinraddie knew better than she did herself how much she and Robert might cuddle in bed, and watched with a sneer for sign of a son. . . . And somehow, just once, you would hate them for that.

You knew these things, it was daft to get angry, you couldn't take a maid and expect her a saint, especially a lass from a cottar house, and Else was no worse than many another. So in time you grew used to knowing what you did—if you put your hair different or spoke sharp to Ewan or went up of an evening to change your frock—would soon be known to the whole of Kinraddie, with additional bits tacked on for a taste. And if you felt sick, once in a blue moon, faith! but the news went winged in the Howe, a bairn was coming, all knew the date, they would eye you keen as you stood in the choir, and see you'd fair filled out this last week; and they'd mouth the news on the edge of their teeth, and worry it to death as a dog with a bone.

But Chris cooked and cleaned with Else Queen to help, and grew to like her in spite of her claik, she'd tried no airs since that very first time, instead she was over-anxious to *Mem!* Chris couldn't be bothered in a while to stop her, knowing well as she did that in many a way she was a sore disappointment to Else.

In other bit places where a quean would fee, with the long-teethed gentry up and down the Howe or the poverty put-ons of windy Stonehive, the mistress would aye be glad of a news, hear this and that that was happening outbye, you'd got it direct from so and so's maid. But Mrs. Colquohoun would just listen and nod, maybe, polite enough in a way, but with hardly a yea or a nay for answer. And at first a lassie had thought the creature was acting up gentry, the minister's wife: but syne you saw that she just didn't care, not a button she cared about this place and that, and the things that were happening, the marryings and dyings, the kissings and cuddlings, the kickings and cursings, the lads that had gone and the farmers that broke; and what this cottar had said to his wife and what the wife had thrown at the cottar. And it fair was a shock, the thing wasn't natural, you made up your mind to give in your notice and go to a place where you wouldn't be lonesome.

So you'd have done if it hadn't been Ewan, the laddie that came from *her* first bit marriage, so quiet and so funny, but a fine little lad, he'd sometimes come down and sit in the kitchen and watch as you peeled the potatoes for dinner, and tell you things he had read in his books, and ask, *What's a virgin princess like—like you, Else?* And when you laughed and said *Oh, but bonnier a lot,* he would screw up his brows, *I don't mean that, is she like you under your clothes, I mean?*

You blushed at that, *I suppose she is,* and he looked at you calm as could be. *Well, that's very nice, I am sure*— so polite you wanted to give him a cuddle, and did, and he stood stock still and let you, not moving, syne turned and went out and suddenly went mad in the way that he would, whistling and thundering like a horse up the stairs, with a din and a racket to deafen a body, but fine for all that, you liked a place with a bairn at play; though not aye making a damned row, either.

So you stayed at the Manse as the summer wore on, and you liked it better, and sometimes you'd stop—when outbye or gone up home for a day—in the telling of this or that at the Manse, and be sorry you ever had started the tale. And your father would growl *Ay, and what then?* and you'd say, *Oh, nothing,* and look like a fool, and whoever was listening would be sore disappointed. But you'd minded sudden the face of the mistress, or young Ewan, polite, who thought you looked nice; and it didn't seem fair to tell stories of *them*.

And then, in the August, you were ill as could be, and they didn't send you off home to Segget, as most others would, to the care of your folk. Faith! you half thought as the mistress came in and dosed you with medicine and punched up your pillows and brought you your breakfast and dinner and tea, that she was well pleased to do all the work, you heard her singing washing the stairs, the minister himself went to help in the kitchen, you heard of that through the half-open door, then laugh as the mistress threw water at him and the scamper of feet as he chased her for that. When next dinner came the minister himself came in with the tray and his shirt-sleeves up, you blushed, and tried to cover your nightie, he cried, *All safe, Else, you needn't be shy. I'm old and I'm married, though you're pretty enough.*

And somehow you just didn't tell that outbye, folk

would have said that he slept with you next. So you lay
in your bed and had a fine rest but that they tormented you
to read books and brought great piles to put by your bed,
and themselves were so keen that you fair were fashed,
they would read you out bits, the mistress or minister, sometimes them both, and you never had had patience with
books in your life. You could never get in them or past the
long words, some thing there was that stood fast between,
though you knit up your brows and tried ever so hard.

And you'd drop the damn book when a minute was past
and listen instead to the birds in the trees, as the evening
drew in and they chirped in their sleep, and the low of the
kye in the parks of the Mains, and see through the swinging
of the casement window the light of the burning whins on
the hills, smell—you smelled with your body entire—the
tingle and move of the harvesting land. And then you'd be
wearied and lie half asleep, wondering what Charlie was
doing to-night, had he taken some other quean out to the
pictures, or was sitting about at some bothy fire? And
would he come to see you as he'd written he'd come?

He came that Sunday, and the mistress herself it was
brought him up, he stood with his cap in his hands and he
blushed, and you did the same, but the mistress didn't.
Now sit down and talk and I'll bring you both tea. And off
then she went, and you thought then, as often, she was
bonny in a way, in a dour, queer way, with her hair dark-
red and so coiled, and the eyes so clear, and the mouth like
a man's, but shaped to a better shape than a man's, you
stared at the door even after she'd gone, till Charlie whispered, *Do you think she'll come back?* And you said, *No,
you gowk,* and peeked at him quiet, and he looked round
about as slow as a sow and then cuddled you quick, and
that was fair fine, and you wanted a minute to cry in his
arms, because you were ill and weak and half-witted. You
told yourself that and pushed him away, and he smoothed
his hair and said, *You're right bonny,* and you said, *Don't
haver,* and he said, *Well, I don't.*

The mistress and Ewan brought up the tea, then left you
enough together alone for the two of you to have wedded
and bedded, as you thought in a peek of a thought that
came. And you looked at Charlie, he was sitting there
douce, telling of his place, and the hard work there was,
he'd as soon have thought ill as of dancing a jig. Like a
fool you felt only half-pleased to know that, of course

you didn't want anything to happen, but at least he should try to make out that *he* did, it was only nature a man should want that, especially if you looked as bonny as he said. So you were fell short with him in the end, and he took his leave and the mistress came up. And you suddenly felt a fool altogether, you were weeping and weeping, with her arm about you, safe you felt there and sleepy and tired. She said, *It's all right, Else, sleep, you'll be fine. You're tired now and you've talked so long with your lad.*

But you knew from her look she knew more than that, she knew the thing you yourself had thought; and you said to yourself when she left you that night, *If I ever hear any speak ill of the Colquohouns, I'll—I'll*—and afore you'd decided whether you'd blacken their eyes, or their character, or both, you fell fast asleep.

Sometimes a black, queer mood came on Robert, he would lock himself up long hours in his room, hate God and Chris and himself and all men, know his Faith a fantastic dream; and see the fleshless grin of the skull and the eyeless sockets at the back of life. He would pass by Chris on the stairs if they met, with remote, cold eyes and a twisted face, or ask in a voice that cut like a knife, *Can't you leave me alone, must you always follow?*

The first time it happened her heart had near stopped, she went on with her work in a daze of amaze. But Robert came from his mood and came seeking her, sorry and sad for the queer, black beast that rode his mind in those haunted hours. He said that the thing was a physical remembrance, only that just and Chris not to worry; and she found out that near the end of the War he'd been gassed by an awful gas that they made, and months had gone by ere he breathed well again, and the fumes of that drifting Fear were gone. And sometimes the shadows of that time came back, though his lungs were well enough now, he was sure, though 'twas in the months of his agony he'd known, conviction, terrible and keen as his pain, that there was a God Who lived and endured, the Tortured God in the soul of men, Who yet might upbuild the City of God through the hearts and hands of men of good faith.

But also Chris found it coming on Robert that here he could never do good or do ill, in a countryside that was dying or dead. One night he looked at Chris and said, *Lord!*

But for you, Christine, I was daft to come here. I'll try for a kirk in some other place, there's work enough to be done in the towns. And thought for a while, his fair head in his hands. *Would you like a town?*

Chris said, *Oh fine,* and smiled reassurance, but she bit at her lips and he saw, and he knew. *Well, then, not a town. I'll try to find something betwixt and between.*

So he did ere a month was out, news came from Segget its minister was dead, Robert brought the news home: *I'm to try for his kirk.* And Chris said, *Segget?* and Robert said *Yes,* and Chris quoted the bit of poetry there was, somebody they said in Segget had made it:

> Oh, Segget it's a dirty hole,
>   A kirk without a steeple,
> A midden-heap at ilka door
>   And damned uncivil people.

Robert laughed, *We'll make them both civil and clean.* Chris said, *But you haven't yet gotten the kirk,* and he said, *Just wait, for I very soon will.*

Three Sundays later they set out for Segget, Robert to preach there and Chris to listen, it was April, quiet and brown in the fields, drowsy under a blanket of mist that cleared as the sun rose, leaving the hills corona'd in feathery wispings of clouds, Chris asked their name, and Robert said, *Cirrus. They bring fine weather and they're standing still. There's little wind on the heights today.*

And Chris on her bicycle suddenly felt young, younger far than she'd felt for years, Robert beside her on his awful bike, it made a noise like a threshing machine, collies came barking from this close and that, but Robert ground on and paid them no heed, scowling, deep in his sermon, no doubt. But once he swung round. *Am I going too fast?* and Chris said, *Fast? It's liker a funeral,* and he came from the deeps of his thoughts and laughed. *Oh, Chris, never change and grow English-polite! Not even in Segget, when we settle in its Manse!*

Syne he said of a sudden, a minute or so later, they were past Mondynes and Segget in sight: *Do you mind how Christ was tempted of the devil? And so was I till you spoke just now, I'd made up my mind I'd butter them up, in the sermon I preached—just for the chance of getting*

out of Kinraddie, settled in Segget, and on with some work.
Well, I won't. . . . By God, I'll give them a sermon!

The old minister had died of drink, fair sozzled he was,
folk said, at the end; and his last words were, so the story
went, *And what might the feare's prices be today?* No
doubt that was just a bit lie that they told, but faith! he'd
been greedy enough for his screw, with his long grey face
and his bleary eyes and his way that he had of speaking
to a man, met out in the street or down by the Arms, as
though he were booming from the pulpit itself: *Why
didn't I see you in the kirk last Sabbath?* And a billy would
redden and give a bit laugh, and look this way and that,
were he one of New Toun. But more than likely, were he
one of the spinners, he'd answer: *Maybe because I wasn't
there!* in the awful twang that the creatures spoke; and go off
and leave old Greig sore vexed, he'd never got over the
fact that the spinners cared hardly a hoot for kirk session
or kirk.

Ah well, he was a dead and a two-three came to try for his
pulpit, more likely his stipend, two old men came, each
buttered up Segget, you'd have thought by the way the
creatures blethered the Archangel Michael could have
come to Segget, and bought a shop, and felt at home as he
sat at the back and sanded the sugar. Folk took that stite
with a dosing of salts, then the third man came and some
stories with him, 'twas the Reverend Colquohoun of Kinraddie, he'd been down there only a bare two years, and
half his congregation had gone, they'd go anywhere but
listen to him, he was aye interfering and preaching at folk
that had done him no harm, couldn't he leave them a-be?
Forbye that he'd married a quean of the parish, and if
there's a worse thing a minister can do than marry a woman that knows the kirk folk, it's only to suck sweeties
under the pulpit in the time he's supposed to be in silent
prayer.

Well, Mr. Colquohoun, he didn't suck sweets, but he did
near everything else, folk said, and most of Segget, though
it thronged to hear him, had no notion to vote for the
creature at all.

But when he was seen stride up to the pulpit, and he
leaned from the pulpit rails and he preached, the elders
were first of all ta'en with his way, and the old folk next
with the thing that he preached, not the mealy stuff that

you'd now hear often, but meaty and strong and preached with some fire—and man! he fairly could tell a bit tale!

For he took his text from a chapter in Judges, his sermon on Gath and the things that that Jew childe Samson did, how at last the giant was bound to a pillar but he woke from the stupor and looked round about, and cried that the Philistines free him his bonds; and they laughed and they feasted, paying him no heed, sunk in their swing-like glaurs of vice. Their gods were idols of brass and of gold, they lived on the sweat and the blood of men, crying one to the other, *Behold, we are great, we endure, and not earth itself is more sure. Pleasure is ours, and the taste of lust, wine in our mouths and power in our hands;* and the lash was heard on the bowed slave's back, they had mercy on neither their kith nor their kin.

And Samson woke and looked round again, he was shorn of his hair, bound naked there, in the lights of the torches, tormented and chained. And then sudden the Philistines felt the walls rock and they looked them about and saw the flames wave, low and sharp in a little wind; and again about them the great hall groaned, and Samson tore down the pillars of the roof, and the roof fell in and slew him and them. . . . And Samson was rising again in our sight, threatening destruction unless we should change, and free both him and the prisoners chained in the littered halls of our secret hearts.

And maybe it was because it was Spring, new-come, the sun a long, drowsy blink in the kirk, and folk heard the voice of the Reverend Colquohoun like the wind they'd hear up under the hills, fine and safe as they listened below, and who could be mean by Samson but them, ground down by the rents they'd to pay the Mowats? Maybe it was that and maybe it was because folk aye had prided themselves in Segget in taking no heed of what others said, that they licked up the sermon like calves at a cog; and a fair bit crowd watched Robert Colquohoun, him and his wife, she seemed decent and quiet, mount on their bikes and ride home to Kinraddie.

Robert said to Chris, *That's the end of my chance. But I'm glad I preached what I felt and thought.* But Chris had a clearer vision than his, *They liked the sermon and I think they liked you. They hadn't a notion what the sermon meant—themselves the Philistines and someone else Samson.*

Robert stared. *But I made it plain as plain.* Chris laughed, *To yourself; anyhow, we'll see.* And they rode to Kinraddie, and the days went by, Robert didn't believe he would head the leet. But he found out, for fun, all he could about Segget, from papers and Else and lists and old books, there was less than a thousand souls in Segget, and most of them lost, if you trusted Else.

Half of the Segget folk worked at the mills—the spinners, as the rest of Segget called them; the others kept shops or were joiners or smiths, folk who worked on the railway, the land, the roads, and the gardens of Segget House. Robert found an old map of the place and renewed it, playing as a boy with a toy town.

Chris leaned on his chair and looked over his shoulder, his fingers nimble in limning New Toun (where the folk had gone when the spinners came), Old Toun and its winding jumble of lanes that bunched and clustered around the West Wynd. South was the Arms, in the Segget Square, the East Wynd dotted with a joiner's, a school, a tailor's shop, a grocery, a sutor's—*and the Lord knows what,* Robert said as his pen swopped down the Wynd to the Segget Square. Then it wheeled about and went up The Close to the post-office-grocery-shop combined, dotted the Segget smiddy beyond, and syne lost itself in the Segget slums. . . . Chris saw on the northern outskirts of Segget two dots for the Manse and the steepleless kirk, and over to the west another one still, Segget House, where the Mowats lived, the old mill-owner, new-dead, said Else, and his son, young Stephen at an English college.

And Robert would whistle as he looked at his map— *What mightn't a minister do in Segget, with the help of young Mowat or the folk of the schools? And sutors are atheists, bound to have brains, and extremely religious, all atheists are. One could do great things with a village League. . . .*

Then he would laugh, *Just playing with bricks! Ewan, where are those toys you've outgrown?*

The news that he'd topped the leet at the poll was brought to Robert by an elder of Segget, it was Else who opened the door for the creature, she knew him well, but she didn't let on. It was wee Peter Peat, the tailor of Seg-

get, his shop stood mid-way the wind of Easy Wynd, with
his house behind it, he thought it a castle. And he spoke
right fierce, and he'd tell a man, before you were well in
the lithe of his door, that he made a fine neighbour to those
that were good, the best of friends to his friends, he was, but
God pity the man that fell out with him, he'd never forgive
an injury, never. And he was the biggest Tory in Segget, the
head of the Segget Conservative branch, and an awful patriot, keen for blood; but he'd loup in his shoes as he heard
his wife, Meg Peat that was slow and sonsy to look at,
come into the shop, she'd cry *Peter, I'm away. Mind the
fire and have tea set ready;* and he'd quaver, *Ay, Meg,*
like an ill-kicked cur. But soon's she was gone he'd look
fierce as ever, ready to kill you and eat you forbye, and
running his tape up and down your bit stomach as though
he were gutting you and enjoying it.

Well, here he was standing, fierce as a futret. *Is the
Reverend Mr. Colquhoun indoors?* And Else said, *I'll see;
what name shall I tell him?* And he said *Gang and tell him
Peter Peat's here.*

Else went and found the minister in his study, and the
minister said *Peat?* and looked at the mistress; and the mistress smiled in the quiet way she had, and shook her head,
and the minister shook his. *Still, kindling or peat, I suppose
I'd best see him!*

Else went down the stairs to where Peter stood. *Come
in, and wipe your feet on the mat.* He looked as though
he'd have liked to wipe them on *her,* but he came in, fierce
in his five feet two, the minister was waiting and rose when
he came. *I've come from Segget,* Else heard the thing say,
and the minister answer as she closed the door, *Oh, yes?
Well, won't you sit down, Mr. Peat?*

And then, half an hour or so after that, Chris heard the
closing of the Manse front door and syne the scamper of
feet on the stairs, she thought it was Ewan come in from
his play. But instead it was Robert, he burst into the room,
his face was flushed and he caught her arms, and plucked
her up from the chair she sat in, and danced her half
round the great-windowed room. She gasped, *What is't?*
and he said *What, that? Peter Peat, the tailor of Segget, of
course.* Then he dropped in the chair from which he had
plucked her, and sat there panting, still holding her hands.
Christine, you're now looking at Segget's minister. And

*he's promised that never as long as he lives he'll pray for
All-but the Prince of Wales!*

He told the story he'd gotten from Peter, and Chris
heard it later amended by Else, a warning that folk in a
pulpit speak plain. He was fell religious, wee Peter Peat,
an elder of the kirk and twice every Sunday he'd nip up
and down the pews with the bag; and look at you sharp to
see what you put in. And once he cried out to Dalziel of
Meiklebogs, that was stinking with silver but fair was right
canny. *No, no, I'll not have a button from you!* And
Meiklebogs reddened like a pig with rash, and dropped a
half-crown in the bag by mistake, he was so took aback
and affronted-like. That was back a good while, in the days
of old Nichols, the last minister but one, he was, as proud
and stuck-up as a hubbley-jock, English, and he never
learned to speak right; and his prayers at first had fair
maddened Peat. For when he came to the bit about Royalty, and he'd pray for the birn with might and with main,
he'd finish up *And all but the Prince of Wales!*

Now Peat he was Tory and fond of the Prince, he went
home to his wife in a fair bit stew, *What the hell ails him
at the Prince of Wales that he blesses all but him, I would
like to know?* And at last he tackled old Nichols on the
matter, and the creature gave a bit sniftering laugh, and
said to Scotch ears he supposed that *All-but* was how it
sounded when he said *Albert.* And he spoke this slow, in a
sneering bit way, as though he thought Scotch ears were
damn poor ears, mostly bad in the need of a clean—when
manners were being given out he hadn't even the manners
to stay and receive his, Peter Peat said.

Chris woke on the morning of the move to Segget with a
start of fear she had over-slept. It was May, and the light
came round about five, red and gold and a flow of silver
down the parks that she knew so well, she got from bed
at the very first blink. Robert yawned and sat up and remembered the day, and dived for his clothes, no bath this
morning she told him as each struggled into clothes. He
said, *Ah well, I'm not very foul,* and she thought that funny, and giggled and tangled her hair with her dress; and he
said, *Let me help,* and his help was a hinder, it was only an
excuse to take her and kiss her, this day of all!

She pushed him away at last and he went, whistling, two

steps at a time down the stair, Chris heard Else moving already in the kitchen and when she got down found breakfast near ready, and Else all excitement, and young Ewan up, his knickers pulled on the wrong way in his hurry. She'd to alter that and try answer his questions, and run to help Robert with the very last kist, full up to the brim with books and such-like; and he swore at the thing and Chris sat on the top, and Ewan came running and jumped there as well, and it closed with a bang, and they all of them cheered.

They sat down to breakfast, famished already. Suddenly Else came running in—*Mem, it's started to rain!* with her face as though it were raining ink, and thick ink forbye. So Chris had to quiet her, and see Ewan ate, and Robert forbye, excited as Else. Then they heard down the road the burr of a lorry, and Else came again: *It's Melvin from Segget.*

So it was, they'd hired him to do the Manse flitting, and had heard his character redd up by Else. He kept the only hotel in Segget, the Segget Arms that stood in the Square, the other inn down at the foot of West Wynd had been closed when the local option came. Will Melvin had been right well pleased over that, he said if this was their Prohibition, then he for one was all for the thing. He'd a face like a cat, broad at the eyes, and he'd spit like a cat whenever he spoke; he aye wore a dickey and a high, stiff collar and a leather waistcoat, and leggings and breeks, and he drove the two cars on hire in Segget, and carted folks' coals and attended the bar when Jim the potman, that folk called The Sourock, was down with the awful pains in his wame.

Will Melvin had married fell late in life, an Aberdeen woman, right thin and right north, she kept a quick eye on the bar and the till. And if she heard a billy give a bit curse, as a spinner or a cottar might do from outbye, knowing no better, they weren't Segget folk, she'd cry out sharp in the thin Aberdeen: *None of your Blasting and Blaspheming in here.* So folk called her the Blaster and Blasphemer for short, and if thoughts could have burned she'd have needed to go and take out a life insurance for fire.

Well, here was Will Melvin, he sat in the kitchen, but got to his feet when Chris came in. *Good morning, Mem,* and Chris said *Good morning,* and he asked, *Will I start*

then to load her up? meaning the lorry, Chris saw, not herself. And he said he had Muir, the gravedigger, to help,
and Chris called in Robert, and he came and scowled because he was thinking of some other thing. But he said,
*Hello, then, are we all ready? Would you like a dram be-
fore we begin?* Will Melvin said, genteel, *Just a drop,* and
would have sat and waited for the dram by himself but that
Chris asked, *Isn't there another with you?*

So John Muir was brought in from his seat in the lorry,
he was big and cheery and buirdly, John Muir, a roadman
of Segget, and the two had their dram, and John Muir as he
drank began to tell them of the awful time he'd once had
with a grave. He'd aye a horror of premature burial, a
fell few there were that were buried like that, when you
dug up the coffins of folk of old time and the boards fell
agley you would sometimes see, through the shrouds, the
bones all bulging and twisted, the creatures had struggled
down there in the earth, not dead at all, gasping for
breath....

Well, he'd been thinking of that one night as he went to
dig a new grave by the kirk, it was windy weather on the
winter's edge. He'd only finished digging the hole, and
turned about, and straightened his back, when the earth
gave way and his feet as well. Next minute his head went
over his heels and flat in a puddle of red earth he went,
right down at the bottom of the grave he had dug, his head
half-jammed in under his shoulder. He nearly fainted with
the awful shock, syne cried for help as loud as he could.
But he heard long nothing, it was winter time, the light was
waning up on the hills, he looked up and knew before long
he'd be dead. And he cried again and as luck would have it
the old minister heard his bit yowl, and came canny and
slow down through the graves, and looked in the hole where
John Muir was lying. And he said: *Who is't?* and John Muir
was sore vexed. *Oh, we've been introduced,* he cried back,
so stand on no ceremony—damn't, get a ladder!

Maybe that was why he still gleyed that way and went
with a kind of twist to his shoulder, Chris thought; but
Robert just laughed and looked at his watch. *Well, this is
a flitting, not yet a funeral.* John Muir set down his glass
and gleyed cheery. *Ah, well, it'll end in that, come time,*
you'd have thought he had something wrong with his stomach. But he gleyed at Chris cheery as a cock on a ree, and
fell to with a will, him and Will Melvin, and carried out

tables and presses and chairs, and kists and beds and boxes
of dishes, and piled them up till the lorry groaned. Will
Melvin near did the same at the sound and went spitting
around like a startled cat. Then they drove off, Robert
went with them to help, Else went as well in the back of
the lorry, clasping the best tea-set to herself, and giving
young Ewan a wave as she went.

The rain had cleared and Chris watched the lorry lurch
down by the Mains in the flare of the sun, they'd got a fine
day after all for the flitting. She liked John Muir, if not
Melvin much; but then it was daft to judge folk at first
sight. Young Ewan came running and asked for a piece,
they sat together in the half-tirred rooms, and ate some
biscuits and looked at each other, with the bizz of a fly
on the stripped window-panes. Ewan asked why they were
moving to Segget. Chris tried to tell him, and he listened,
polite, and then went out and drowsed in the grass till he
heard the lorry returning from Segget.

They loaded up the last of the stuff, John Muir climbed
gleying up in its midst, and Chris locked the door and left
the key for the folk of the Mains to come up and get, hid
in a little hole in the wall. Then she went to the lorry
where Melvin was waiting, young Ewan beside him, and
climbed in as well; and the lorry wound out through the
bending of yews where long, long ago the knight Wallace
had hidden as the English were looking for him in the
wars.

They saw not a soul as they passed the Mains, then they
swung out into the road that led south; and so as they went
Chris turned and looked back, at Kinraddie, that last time
there in the sun, the moors that smoothed to the upland
parks Chae Strachan had ploughed in the days gone by,
the Knapp with no woods to shelter it now, Upperhill set
high in a shimmer of heat, Cuddiestoun, Netherhill—last
of them all, high and still in the hill-clear weather, Blawearie up on its ancient brae, silent and left and ended for
you; and suddenly, daft, you couldn't see a thing.

But that went by, Chris glad to be gone; and the lorry
switched from the main road's ribbon up by the old
thatched toun of Culdyce, and she saw the Howe, spread
out like a map, there was Drumlithie down in its hollow,
a second Segget, but steepled enough. Mondynes that stood
by the Bervie Water, Fettercairn, where the soldiers of the

widow Finella had lain in wait to mischieve King Kenneth. All the parks were set with their hoeing squads, four, five, at a time they swung by the drills, here and there the hindmost man would stop, and straighten up slow, a hand at his back, to look at the lorry—who's could it be? And all the long line would straighten up, slow, and catch a glimpse of Chris, in her blue, and young Ewan in his, with his straight, black hair.

And there, as they swung by the Meiklebogs farm, the hills to the right, at last lay Segget, a cluster and crawl of houses white-washed, the jute-mills smoking by Segget Water, the kirk with no steeple that rose through the trees, the houses of the spinners down low on the left, though Chris didn't know that these were their houses. Then the lorry puffed up to the old kirk Manse, on the fringe of Segget, and Chris saw the lawn piled in a fair hysteria of furniture. She jumped down and stood a minute at gaze, in the shadows, the shadows the new yews flung, the grass seemed blue in the blaze of the heat.

Then as Melvin backed back the lorry and Ewan went running out over the lawn to the door, Robert came out and saw Chris and waved, and was pleased as though they'd been parted a year. He dropped the end of the press he'd picked up, near dropped it down on the toes of Muir (who gleyed as cheery as though 'twas a coffin) and cried to Chris, *Come and see the new study*. And nothing could content him but up she must go, leaving Melvin below to glower after the gowks.

Then two men came taiking up the Manse drive, Dalziel of the Meiklebogs and one of his men, Robert went down to see who they were. Dalziel said, *Ay, you'll be the minister?* and smiled, he was bad in the need of a shave, of middle height though he looked a lot less, so broad in the shoulders, hands like hams; and he smiled slow and shy with his red, creased face, and he said that he'd seen the lorries go by, and he knew right well the sore job it was to do a flitting without much help. And all the time he was smiling there, shy, he looked to Chris like a Highland bull, with his hair and his horns and maybe other things: there was something in his shyness that made her shiver. Beside him Robert seemed like a boy from school, thin and tall with his slim, thin face; and back of Robert was Else as she looked, not slim at all but big and well-made, her head flung back in that way she had and a look on her face as much as to say, *Good Lord, what's this that has come to us now?*

Then they all fell to carrying in the Manse gear, and Chris fled here and there in the house, a great toom place that shambled all ways, there were stairs that started and suddenly finished and steps that crumbled away into gloom, down to old cellars that never were used. And sometimes you'd think you would come to a room, and you didn't, you came slap-bang on another, the windows fast-closed and stiff with the heat. Chris told where and how to place all the things, and Meiklebogs and Else carried up the beds, and set them together, Chris heard Else give orders and Meiklebogs answer, canny and shy, *You'll be the new minister's bit maidie?* Else said, *There's damn the MAIDIE about me;* and Chris didn't hear more, but she guessed a bit.

John Muir came to her and asked where to put a press and a bed and some other things she'd brought from Blawearie the first flit she made. And she didn't know, in that crowding of rooms, till he said, *Would you maybe like the gear altogether?* and she said, *Just that, in a small-like room.* So he carried the bed up and back through the Manse, to a high-built room, it was three stairs up. The place was so lost that the cleaners had missed it, there were cobwebs looped from the walls like twine. But through the window, when you swung it out wide, you saw sudden hills rise up in your face, with below you the roll of long, grass-grown mounds. John Muir let down the bed with a bang, the great heavy bed that had once been her father's. Chris asked him what were the ruins up there, and he said, *You've heard of the Kaimes of Segget?*

Chris leaned from the window and looked to the west. *And what's that to the left, that hiddle of houses?—Where the spinners bide,* he told her, she stared, she had thought them abandoned byres or pig-sties. But Muir just gleyed and said they were fine—*good enough for the dirt that's in them. If you gave good houses to rubbish like them, they'd have them pig-rees in a damn short while. They're not Segget folk, the spinners, at all.*

Chris said *Oh!* and looked at him, quiet, then they went down to bring up the rest; and there was Meiklebogs met on the stair, smiling shy at that sumph of a maid. And John Muir thought, *You'd think he'd have quieted by now. A man that can't keep off the women by the time he's reach-*

ing to sixty or so should be libbed and tethered in a cattle-court.

Near twelve they'd the most of the furniture in, all but a long table brought from the north, from the Manse of Robert Colquohoun's old father, solid and oak and a hell of a weight. And then Else called that the dinner was ready, Chris said they all must stay and have dinner. Robert said *Let's eat it out on this table.*

So Else served them the dinner in the shade of the yews, and sat down herself when she'd finished with that, Meikle-bogs waiting to see where she sat, and sitting down next with a shy-like smile. Robert came out, getting into his coat, and stood at the end of the table a minute and bent his head, fair in the sunny weather, and said the grace, the grace of a bairn; and they bent and listened, all but young Ewan:

> God bless our food,
>   And make us good.
> And pardon all our sins,
>   For Jesus Christ's sake.

Then they all ate up, Muir, Melvin, and Meiklebogs, and the fee'd man that blushed and was shy, not just looked it. Chris liked him best, with that sudden compassion that always came on her as she looked at one of his kind—that conviction that he and his like were the REAL, they were the salt and savour of earth. She heard him, shy-like, say *Ay, I've a spoon,* as Else was asking, and knew by the way that he mouthed the *spoon* that he came from the North, as she did herself. And faith! so he did, like her 'twas from Echt, and he knew fine the place where once she had bidden. Cairndhu in the Barmekin's lithe. And he fair buckled up and he lost his shyness, *Ay, then, you're a Guthrie?* and she said that she was, and he said that they minded him long up in Echt, John Guthrie, her father, the trig way he farmed: and Chris felt herself colour up with sheer pleasure, her father could farm other folk off the earth!

Then she fell in a dream as she heard them talk, the rooks were cawing up in the yews, and you thought how they'd fringed your pattern of life—birds, and the waving leafage of trees: peewits over the lands of Echt when you were a bairn with your brother Will, and the spruce stood dark in the little woods that climbed up the slopes to the Barmekin bend; snipe sounding low on Blawearie loch as you turned in unease by the side of Ewan, and listened and heard the whisp of the beech out by the hedge in the quiet of the night; and here now rooks and the yews that stood to peer in the twisty rooms of the Manse. How often would you know them, hear them and see them, with what things in your heart in what hours of the dark and what hours of the day, in all the hours lying beyond this hour when the sun stood high and the yew-trees drowsed?

But she shook herself and came out of her dream, back to the table and the sun on the lawn, daft to go prowling those copses of night where the sad things done were stored with the moon. Here was the sun, and here was her son, Ewan, and Robert, the comrade of God, and those folk of Segget she had yet to know, and all the tomorrows that waited her here.

But that night she had slept in fits and in starts, waking early in that strange, quiet room, by the side of Robert, sleeping so sound. Then it was the notion had suddenly arisen, to come up to the Kaimes, as here she was now, watching the east grow pale in the dawn.

Pale and so pale: but now it was flushed, barred sudden with red and corona'd with red, as though they were there, the folk who had died, and the sun came washed from the sea of their blood, the million Christs who had died in France, as once she had heard Robert preach in a sermon. Then she shook her head and that whimsy passed, and she thought of Robert—his dream just a dream? Was there a new time coming to the earth, when nowhere a bairn would cry in the night, or a woman go bowed as her mother had done, or a man turn into a tormented beast, as her father, or into a bullet-torn corpse, as had Ewan? A time when those folk down there in Segget might be what Robert said all men might be, companions with God on a terrible adventure? Segget: John Muir, Will Melvin, Else Queen; the folk of the grisly rees of West Wynd——

Suddenly, far down and beyond the toun there came a screech as the morning grew, a screech like an hungered beast in pain. The hooters were blowing in the Segget Mills.

II

CUMULUS

CROSSING the steep of the brae in the dark, by the winding path from the Manse to the Kaimes, Chris bent her head to the seep of the rain, the wet November drizzle of Segget. Then she minded a wall of the Kaimes still stood, and ran quick up the path to stand in its lee. That gained, she stood and panted a while, six months since she'd been up here in the Kaimes—only six months, she could hardly believe it!

It felt like years—long and long years—since she'd worked as a farmer's wife in Kinraddie. Years since she'd felt the beat of the rain in her face as she moiled at work in the parks. How much had she gained, how much had she lost?—apart from her breath, she had almost lost that!

She felt the wall and then leant against it, wrapped in her ulster, looking at Segget, in its drowse of oil-lamps under the rain. Safe anyhow to go home this time. . . . And she smiled as she minded last time she had climbed to the Kaimes, and Segget had seen her go home—by the tale they told all Segget had seen her and stared astounded, a scan-dalled amaze——

But indeed, it was only Ag Moultrie that morning, as ill-luck would have it, who saw her go home. She had gone out early to the school to redd up, she went heavy with sleep and her great mouth a-agant, as you well might

believe, though he didn't tell that. Folk knew her fine, all
the Moultries forbye. Rob Moultrie had once been the
saddler of Segget, his shop lay down by the edge of the
Square. And as coarse an old brute as you'd meet, was Rob
Moultrie, though a seventy years old and nearing his grave.
'Twas only a saddler's shop in name now, the trade had
clean gone this many a year. There was still a britchen or
so in the shop, and a fine bit bridle Rob Moultrie had
made in the days long syne when he still would work. But
his trade had gone, and his sweirty had come, he was never
a popular man in the toun; he couldn't abide the sight of
the gentry, or the smell of the creatures either, he said,
and that was why he was Radical still.

And if he went on a dander somewhere, along the road
and he'd hear a car, toot-tooting behind him, would he get
off the road? Not him, he'd walk on bang in the middle,
dare any damn motorist try run him down. So sometimes
he'd come back to Segget from a walk, step-stepping cannily along the bit road, with a two-three motorists hard at
his heels, toot-tooting like mad, and the shovers red-faced.
Mrs. Moultrie would be looking from the window and see,
and cry as he came, *Losh, Rob, you'll be killed!* And he'd
stop and glower at her with his pocked old face, and his
eyes like the twinkling red eyes of a weasel, and sneer, the
old creature, shameful to hear. *Ay, that would be fine—
no doubt you'd get up to your old bit capers. Get out of
my way!* And he'd lift his stick, maybe more than do that,
syne hirple over to his armchair, and sit there and stare in
the heart of the fire or turn to the reading of his old bit
Bible.

For he'd never forgiven Jess Moultrie, the fact that
more than a forty years before, when he'd met her and
married her, she'd been with a bairn. She told how it was
before she would marry, and he'd glowered at her dour:
*More fool that I am. But I'm willing to take you and your
shame as well.* And he took her, and the bairn was born,
young Ag, no others came and maybe that was why he still
kept up the sneer at his wife. But she would say nothing she
was patient and bowed, little, with a face like a brown, still
pool; and she'd say not a word, getting on with her work,
making ready the supper for Ag when she came.

She cleaned out the school and the hall and such places,
did Ag, and in winter made the school broth, as nasty a
schlorich as ever you'd taste. She looked like a horse ta'en

out of a plough, and her voice was a neigh like a horse's as well, and she'd try to stand up for her mother with old Rob. *Don't speak that way to my mother!* she would cry, and he'd look at her dour, *Ay, ay, no doubt she's precious in your sight. You had only one mother, though three or four fathers;* and Ag more than likely would start to greet then, she wasn't a match for the thrawn old brute, though a good enough one for most other folk. And faith! she'd a tongue for news that was awful. Ake Ogilvie called her the Segget Dispatch, she knew everything that happened in Segget, and a lot that didn't, but she liked best to tell of births and funerals and such-like things; and how the daughter of this or that corpse no sooner looked on the dead than broke down—*and fair roared and grat when she saw him there.* So folk called her the Roarer and Greeter for short.

Well, then, it was her, to get on with the tale, as she blinked her way in that morning in May, saw a woman come down the hill from the Kaimes, and stopped dumb-foundered: Who could she be?

Ag was real shocked, for the Kaimes was the place where spinners and tinks of that kind would go, of a Sab-beth evening, and lie on the grass and giggle and smoke and do worse than that—Ay, things that would leave them smoking in hell, as the old minister said that they would. So no decent folk went up there at night, this creature of a woman was surely a tink. And Ag gave a sniff, but was curious forbye, and crept canny along in the lithe of the dyke that hemmed in the lassies' playground from the lads'. So she waited there till the woman went by, hurrying bare-headed, with a stride and a swing and a country-like gait. And then Ag Moultrie near fainted with joy, though she didn't tell you that when she told you the story, she saw that the woman was Mrs. Colquohoun, the wife of the new minister of Segget.

Well, afore the day was well started all Segget had heard that the wife of the new minister had been seen by Ag Moultrie up on the Kaimes, she'd been out all night with a spinner up there, Ag had seen them cuddling and sossing in the grass. Folk said, *By God, she's wasted no time; and who would the spinner have been, would you say?* Old Leslie heard the story in the smiddy and he said the thing was Infernal, just. Now, he minded when he was a loon up in Garvock—And the sweat dripped off him, pointing a coulter, and he habbered from nine until loosening-time, near, some story about some minister he'd known; but wherever that was and why it had been, and what the hell happened, if anything ever had, you couldn't make head nor tail if you listened; and you only did that if you couldn't get away.

Old Leslie was maybe a fair good smith: he was sure the biggest old claik in Segget. He'd blether from the moment you entered his smiddy, he'd ask how the wife and the bairns all were, and your brother Jock that was down in Dundon, and your sister Jean that was in a sore way, and your father that was down with the colic or the like, and your grandfather, dead this last fifty years.

And syne he'd start on your cousins, how they were, and your uncles and aunts and their stirks and their stots, their maids and all that were in their gates: till your hair would be grey and your head fair dizzy at the thought you'd so many relations at all. And his face would sweat like a dripping tap as he hammered at the iron and habbered at you and then he'd start some story of the things he'd done or seen or smelt when a loon up in Garvock, and the day would draw in, the night would come on, and the stars come out, he'd have shod all your horses and set all the coulters and you near were dead for lack of some meat; but *that* damned story wouldn't have finished, it would be going on still with no sign of an end, he'd start it the next time he saw you or heard you, though you were at the far side of a ten-acre field—as you took to your Rhls and run.

Well, about the only soul that couldn't do that was his son, Sim Leslie, the policeman of Segget. He had joined the police and had been sent back to Segget, and still bade with his father, he was used to the blether: and folk said if he listened with a lot of care, for a twenty years or so at a stretch, he at least might find out what really *had* happened that time when his father was a loon up on Garvock. Folk called him Feet, Sim Leslie the bobby, he'd feet so big he could hardly coup, there was once he was shoeing a horse in the smiddy, an ill-natured brute from the Meiklebogs; and the creature lashed out at him fair and square and caught him such a clout on the chest as would fair have flattened any ordinary man. But young Sim Leslie just rocked a wee bit, his feet had fair a sure grip on Scotland.

Well, Feet heard the story of Mrs. Colquohoun, from his father, as the two of them sat at dinner. And he kittled up rare, there was something in this, and maybe a chance of promotion at last. So he went and got hold of Ag Moultrie, the sumph, and pulled out his notebook with his meikle red fingers, and asked was she sure 'twas the minister's wife? And Ag said *Ay,* and Feet made a bit note; and then he seemed stuck, and he said, *You're sure?* And Ag said *Ay, I'm as sure as death.* Feet made another note, and scratched at his head, and swayed a bit in his meikle black boots. *It fair was her?* And Ag said *Ay;* and by then it seemed just about dawning on Feet it really was her and nobody else.

But Ag was real vexed, as she told to folk, she hadn't wanted to miscall a soul, *God knows I'm not a body to claik;* and she said when she'd finished with Feet and his questions she went home and sat down and just Roared and Grat, so sorry she was for the new minister. And she'd tell you some more how the woman had looked, her face red-flushed, with a springy walk; and if you were married you well could guess why all of that was—damn't man, 'twas fairly a tasty bit news!

That night Feet went up and prowled round the Manse, with his bull's-eye held in his hand and his feet like the clopping of a Clydesdale heard on the ground. He didn't know very well what he was there for, or what he would say if Mrs. Colquohoun saw him; but he was awful keen on promotion. And he said he was fine at detective-work, like, and if honest merit were given its reward they'd make him a real detective ere long. And Ake Ogilvie said in his tink-like way *A defective, you mean? God, ay, and certificated!*

Well, Feet had prowled round to the back of the Manse, and had stopped to give his head a bit scratch; when sudden the window above him opened and afore he could move there came a bit splash and a pailful of water was slung down his back. He spluttered and hoasted and his lamp went out, when he came to himself he was shaking and shivering, but the Manse was silent and still as the grave. He thought for a while of arresting the lot—aye, he would in the morning, by God; and turned and went home, running home stretches to change his bit sark, in case he might catch a cold from his wetting.

And, would you believe it, next day as he sat in his office writing up his reports, his mother said, *Here's a woman to see you.* And Feet looked up and he knew the quean,

Else Queen, the maid at the Manse it was; 'twas said she'd
been brought up as a lassie in Segget, though her father
had moved to Fordoun since then, now she was fair a great
brute of a woman, with red eyes and hair, and cheeks of
like tint. And she said, *Are you Feet?* and Feet reddened a
bit. *I'm Simon Leslie the policeman of Segget.—Well, I'm
the person that half-drowned you last night; and I've come
to tell you when you want the same, just prowl round the
Manse at such a like hour.*

And she didn't stop only at Feet then, either. She made
for Ag Moultrie and told her the same, she would have
her sacked from her job at the school; and Ag broke down
and just Roared and Grat, she said she'd never said an ill
word of any, but what was the minister's wife doing on the
Kaimes? *Looking at the hills and the sunrise, you fool.
Did you never hear yet of folk that did that?* And Ag said
she hadn't; and who ever had? Folk shook their heads when
they heard that tale, if the woman at the Manse wasn't fair
just a bitch, damn't! you could only suppose she was daft.

Dite Peat heard the story and fair mocked at Feet.
What, you that were once in the barracks? he said, *and
lived in Dundon, and can't manage a woman?* And he told
a story, 'twas down in the Arms, about how once when he
was living in London he'd come here, he said, on a leave
from the Front, he hired a bit lodging near Waterloo.—
And old Leslie that was standing by said *Eh? Would that be
the place the battle was at?* and Dite Peat said, *Oh, away
to hell,* a coarse way to speak to an old bit man.—Well,
Dite had put up in his London room, he saw the landlady
was a gey bit quean, fair young and fair sonsy, her man at
the Front. And he tried this way and that to get round her,
keen for a woman but not a damn fool like some that come
back on leave from the Front, they'd spend all their silver
on whores, but not Dite, he wanted a gratis cuddle and
squeeze.

Well, he waited and waited about for a bit, and half-
thought of getting the woman at night, she was only English and they're tinks by nature, it wasn't as though she
was decent and Scotch. But she locked up her door and
went early to bed till there came one night that he heard
her scraich, and he louped from his bed and he went to
the door, and there she was standing down in the hall, in
her night-gown, the tink, and white as a sheet. She'd a tele-

gram held in her hands as she stood, and was gowking and gobbling at the thing like a cow, choked on the shaws of a Mearns swede. And Dite called down *What's wrong with you, then?* and she laughed and laughed as she looked up at him, she was young, with a face like a bairn, a fool, white, with no guts; like the English queans. And she said *Oh, it's just that my husband's dead,* and laughed and laughed, and Dite licked his lips, it fair was a chance, he saw it and took it.

Well, she wasn't so bad, but far over-thin; and God! she was fair a scunner with her laughing, every now and then she would laugh like an idiot, he supposed that the English did that in their pleasure. So he took her a clout or so in the lug, to learn her manners, and that quietened her down. Oh ay, she was tasty enough in her way.

Some folk in the Arms asked what happened next, did he bide there long? Dite said *Damn the fears. I nipped out next morning, afore she awoke. She might have tried on to get me to marry her.* And he went on to tell what tinks were the English, they'd rob right and left if you gave them the chance. He gave them damn few, but once out in France——

That fair was a sickener, you put down your glass, or finished the dram and rose up and went out; and Will Melvin looked mad as he well could look, Dite sitting and telling a story like that, sickening customers away from their drinks. But you couldn't do much with a billy like Dite, a dangerous devil when he got in a rage. He looked a tink though he kept a shop, he and his brother, wee Peter the tailor hadn't spoken for years, though they lived next door. His father had lived with Dite till he died, Dite saw to that dying, some said helped it on.

The old man had been one of the roadmender childes, he worked with old Smithie and that fool John Muir, he'd come back with his wages at the end of the week and maybe he'd have spent a shilling on tobacco. And soon's he saw that Dite Peat would fly up and take him a belt in the face, most like, and send him to bed without any meat; and as he lay dying the old man cried to see his other son, wee Peter, the tailor. But Dite snapped *Be quiet, damn you and your wants. You'll see him in hell soon enough with yourself.*

That was hardly the way to speak to your father, him dying and all; and some folk stopped then going to his shop,

spinners and the like, they said Dite should be shot; and
collected below his windows one night and spoke of taking
him out for a belting. But Feet, the policeman, came up
and cried *Now, you'll need to be moving if you're standing
about here;* and the spinners forgot the thing they'd come
on, and took to tormenting the bobby instead, they carried
him down the Drumlithie road and took off his breeks and
filled him with whisky; and the left the poor childe lying
drunk in the ditch; and went back and fairly raised hell in
the Arms, the Blaster and Blasphemer near scraiched herself hoarse, the spinners had new got a rise in their pay.

Ah well, that was how Dite Peat had escaped, spinners
and their like wouldn't trade with him now, though most
other folk weren't foolish as that. You went on as before
and waited the time when he and Ake Ogilvie would yet
get to grips, Ake hated Dite Peat as a dog hates a rat.

Chris found it took nearly a fortnight to settle, the whole
of the Manse wanted scrubbing and cleaning, she and Else
Queen were at it all hours, Robert laughed and locked
himself in his room. But he came out to help rig the curtains on rods, both he and Else were handy and tall, they
spent the most of one long afternoon tacked up to the walls
like flies in glue; and Chris handed up rods and curtains
and pictures, and this and that, and hammers and nails; and
Else and Robert would cling to the walls, by their eyebrows
sometimes, or so it would seem, and push and tug and hammer and pant. Else was willing and strong and enjoyed it,
she'd poise on the edge of a mantel and cry *Will that do,
Mem?* and near twist her neck from her shoulders to catch
a look at some picture or other. Chris would cry *Mind!*
and Else: *Och, I'm fine!* and nearly capsize from her ledge,
and young Ewan, watching below, give a yell of delight.

But at last all things were trig and set neat. That evening,
with Ewan bathed and to bed, Chris found Else yawning
wide as a door, and sent her off to her bed as well. Chris
felt she was almost too tired to rest as she sat in a chair in
Robert's room; and Robert knew and came and made love;
and that was nice, and she felt a lot better. In the quiet and
hush of the evening below you could see the touns drift
blue with their smoke, as though it was they that moved,
not the smoke. Robert sat in his shirt-sleeves, smoking his
pipe, planning his campaign to conquer Segget, as Chris

supposed, but she closed her eyes. In a minute she'd get up and go to her bed.

But Robert jumped up sudden and picked up his coat. *I know! Let's go and see Segget at night.*

Chris thought *If it wasn't that I am in love—Goodness, how far I could tell him to go!* But she said not a word of that, but went down, and he groped in the dark and found her coat, and she his, and next they were out on the shingle, it crunch-crunched under the tread of their feet, the moon had come and was sailing a sky lilac, so bright that the Manse stood clear as they turned and looked back, the yews etched in ink, beyond them the kirk that hadn't a steeple, set round with its row upon row of quiet graves, the withered grass kindled afresh to green, in long, shadowy tufts that whispered like ghosts. An owlet hooted up on the hill and through the quiet of the night round about there came a thing like a murmur unended, unbegun, continuous, the hum of the touns—and that was queer, most folk were in bed! Chris thought a thought and put it from her mind—an awful woman to have wedded a minister!

Then she slipped her arm in Robert's, beside him, Segget stood splashed in the light of the moon like a hiddle of houses a bairn would build. Their feet were quiet on the unpaved street, they smelt the reek of the burning wood, and Robert said sudden, his voice not a whisper, *It's like walking a town of the dead, forgotten, a ruined place in the light of the moon. Can you think that folk'll do that sometime, far off some night in the times to be, maybe a lad and his lass, as we are, and wonder about Segget and the things they did and said and believed in those little houses? And the moon the same and the hills to watch.*

Chris thought it most likely they would find these enough, the hills and the moon, and not bother about Segget, that lad and that lass in the times to be. So they passed quiet down through the wind of East Wynd, over to the right the hiddling of lanes where the spinners bade, nearer the road and black in the moon the school and the schoolhouse set round with dykes. They passed a joiner's shop to the left, Chris peered at the name and saw ALEC OGILVIE, then came to a place with shops all around, a grocer's shop with D. PEAT on the sill, fat lettering over a shoemaker's— HOGG; and a narrow little front that barked PETER PEAT. Beyond, to the right, a lane wound down to the

post-office kept by Macdougall Brown, so Chris had been
told, she hadn't been there.

East Wynd to the left was now bare of houses, beyond
its dyke was the garden of Grant. And once they heard
through the night a crying, some bairn frightened or waked
in the dark, and a voice that called it back to its sleep, all
in a drowsy hush through the night. *There's honeysuckle
somewhere*, said Chris, and stopped to smell, as they came
to the Square, *over here by the saddler's shop.*

But Robert was giving no need to smells, he had stopped
and he said *My God, what a slummock!* And Chris saw the
thing that had now ta'en his eyes, the War Memorial of
Segget toun, an angel set on a block of stone, decent and
sonsy in its stone night-gown, goggling genteel away from
the Arms, as though it wouldn't, for any sum you named,
ever condescend to believe there were folk that took a nip
to keep out the chill. . . .

Chris thought it was fine, a pretty young lass. But then
as she looked at it there came doubts, it stood there in
memory of men who had died, folk of this Segget but much
the same still, she supposed, as the folk she had known in
Kinraddie, folk who had slept and waked and had sworn,
and had lain with women and had lain with pain, and
walked in the whistle of the storms from the Mounth and
been glad, been mad, and done dark, mad things, been
bitter for failure, and tender and kind, with the kindness
deep in the dour Scots blood. Folk of her own, those folk
who had died, out in the dark, strange places of earth and
they set up THIS to commemorate THEM—this, this
quean like a constipated calf!

Robert said *May God forgive them this horror! And look
at the star on its pantomime wand. But still it's a star; not
a bundle of grapes. Folk'll think it a joke when we've
altered things, this trumpery flummery they put up in stone!*

His dream again he could alter things here! *But what kind
of change, Robert, what can you do? Things go on the
same as ever they were, folk neither are better nor worse
for the War. They gossip and claik and are good and bad,
and both together, mixed up and down. This League of the
willing folk of Segget—who'll join it or know what you
want or you mean?*

He leaned by the Angel, looked down at her, smiled,
cool and sure of his vision tonight. *Chris, if ever we've a
child, you and I, and when it grows up, it finds that that's*

*true—what you've said—then I hope it'll come here with
Ewan, and a host of others of their own generation, and
smash this Memorial into smithereens for the way that
we failed them and left God out. Change? It's just that men
must change, or perish here in Segget, as all over the earth.
Necessity's the drive, the policeman that's coming to end
the squabbling stupidities of old——*

Then he laughed. *What, sleepy as that? Let's go back.*

He fair had plenty on his hands that summer, Feet, the
policeman, as the days wore to Autumn. First, 'twas the
trouble in the roadman's place, old Smithie and the hay he
nicked from coles and carted home at night to his kye.
His house stood side by side with John Muir's, both under
the lee of the kirk and the Manse, their back doors opened
out on the land that stretched east under the scowl of the
hills to the lands that were farmed by Meiklebogs. Muir
kept no stock and he bought his milk, but old Smith on the
chap of dawn would be out, up out of his bed and round
to the byre, where his cows, and his two young calves were
housed, none knew where he bought the fodder to feed
them; and that wasn't surprising, he stole the damned lot.

He'd look this way and that, he'd a face like a tyke, thin,
and ill-made, with a bushy moustache; and then, as swack
as you like he would loup, canny and careful in over a
fence, and made up a birn of somebody's hay; and be back
and breaking his stones as before when the next bit motor
appeared on the road. Syne at night he would load the lot
on his bike and pedal canny without any light, and nip up
through Segget as the Arms bar opened and folk had gone
in for a bit of a nip, none out to see; and syne he was
home, and the cows, as hungry as hawks, would low, old
Smithie would give a bit low as well, and stuff them with
hay and pat at their shoulders, daft-like, he near was
crack about kye, he liked the breath of the creatures, he
said.

Folk said that the cows couldn't be so particular, else
they'd fair get a scunner at *his* bit breath. For he liked a
dram and he took what he liked, he'd no more than peek
round the door of an evening (though the house was his
and all the gear in it) than his daughter would cry *Here's
the old devil home!* and her bairns, the bairns of Bruce the
porter, would laugh and call him ill names as they liked.
And he'd smile and stand there and mumble a while, though

he wasn't a fool in the ordinary way; and syne he'd go down
to the Arms in a rage and swear that before another night
came he'd have Bruce and his birn flung out of his doors,
he was damned if he'd stand their insultings longer.

Well, damned he was, for he kept them on, folk would
once kittle up with excitement when they heard old Smithie
get wild and say that, they'd 'gree with him solemn and say
'twas a shame for a man of Segget to stand what he did;
and they'd follow him home when the Arms closed down
and stand by the door to hear the din. But all that they'd
hear would be Ellen his daughter, fat as a cow at the calving
time, cry *Feuch, you old brute, and where have you been?*
And Smithie would just mumble and gang to his bed.

He'd another daughter as well as his Ellen, he'd slaved
to give her an education; and faith! so he'd done, and made
her a teacher. She lived in Dundon and never came south.
And the only thing Smithie said that he'd gotten, for all his
pains and his chaving for her, was one cigarette: and that
wouldn't light.

Well, that Saturday afternoon in July, old Smithie was
wearied with chapping at stones, and instead of steeling
some hay outbye and rowing it home strapped over his
bike, he got on the bike and pedalled near home, till he
came to the new-coled hay of Meiklebogs. And old Smithie
got off and lighted his pipe and made on he'd got off for
nothing but that. There wasn't a soul to be seen round
about, the park was hidden, and old Smithie was quick, he
nipped in over and pinched some hay, and was back with
the stuff strapped on to his bike—so quick that you'd fair
have thought it a wonder that his corduroy trousers didn't
take fire. But no sooner was he gone than Dalziel jumped
up, he'd been hiding all the while in the lee of a cole; and
he ran to the close and got his own bike, and followed old
Smithie and shadowed him home. Then he went down the
toun and collected Feet, and they came on old Smithie as
he entered the byre, the bundle of stolen hay in his hands.

And Feet cried out *Mr. Smith, I want you;* and old
Smithie looked round and near dropped the birn. *Ay, do
you so?* he quavered, and syne the old whiskered creature
fairly went daft, he threw the birn in Meiklebogs' face.
*Take your damned stuff. I wouldn't poison my kye with
such dirt!*

Feet said, *Well, I doubt this'll be a case,* but old Smithie
was dafter than ever by then. He said, *Make it two, and to*

hell with you both! and went striding into his house as he hadn't, striding that way, gone in for years.

His daughter, that sumph that was Mistress Bruce, fair jumped as she heard the bang of the door, she cried: *You nasty old wretch, what's the din?* Old Smithie was fairly boiling by then, he said, *Do you know who you're speaking to, Ellen?* and she said, *Ay, fine, you disgrace to Segget;* and at that old Smithie had her over his knee, afore she could blink, she was stunned with surprise. She gave a bit scraich and she tried to wriggle, but she'd grown over fat and old Smithie was strong. And damn't! if he didn't take down her bit things and scone her so sore she grat like a bairn, her own bairns made at old Smithie and kicked him, but he never let on, just leathered his quean till his hand was sore, not so sore as her dowp. *That's a lesson for you, you bap-faced bitch,* he said, and left her greeting on the floor, and went down to the Arms, and near the first man that he met there was Bruce, old Smithie by then like a fighting cock.

Bruce was a dark and a sour-like childe, but he looked near twice as sour in a minute when old Smithie took him a crack in the jaw. *What's that for?* Bruce cried, and Smithie said *Lip,* and came at him again, the daft-like old tyke. Well, you couldn't expect but that Bruce would be raised, he was knocking Smithie all over the bar when Mistress Melvin came tearing in. She cried in her thin Aberdeen, *What's this? Stop your Blasting and Blaspheming in here.* Bruce said, *I haven't sworn a damn word,* she said *That's enough, take your tink fights out, sossing up the place with blood and the like. If you've any quarrel to settle with your relations, go out and settle it where folk can't see.*

And Bruce said *Right;* and took old Smithie out, and gey near settled him entire you would say. It just showed you what happened to a billy that stole, there's a difference between nicking a thing here and there, and being found out and made look a fair fool.

And next Sabbath MacDougall Brown, the postmaster, came down to the Square and preached on stealing, right godly-like, and you'd never have thought that him and his wife stayed up of a night sanding the sugar and watering the paraffin—or so folk said, but they tell such lies. He was maybe a fifty years old, MacDougall, a singer as well

as a preacher, i'faith! though some said his voice was the
kind of a thing better suited to slicing a cheese. During the
War he had fair been a patriot, he hadn't fought, but losh!
how he'd sung! In the first bit concert held in the War he
sang Tipperary to the Segget folk, with his face all shining
like a ham on the fry, and he sang it right well till he got
to the bit where the song has to say that his heart's right
there. And faith, MacDougall got things a bit mixed, he
clapped down his hand the wrong side of his wame: and
Ake Ogilvie that sat in the front of the hall gave a coarse
snicker and syne everybody laughed; and MacDougall had
never forgiven Ake that.

But he got on well with his post-office place, Johnnie his
son was a bit of a fool and MacDougall sent him to take
round the letters, it cost him little with a son that was
daft and MacDougall kept the cash for himself. Forbye
young Jock he'd two daughters as well, the eldest, Cis, was
bonny and trig, with a grave, douce face, she went to the
College but she wasn't proud, a fine bit quean, and all Segget liked her.

Well, MacDougall had a special religion of his own, he
wasn't Old Kirk and he wasn't of the Frees, he wasn't even
an Episcopalian, but Salvation Army, or as near as damn
it. He went on a Sabbath morn to the Square and preached
there under the lee of the angel, that the road to heaven
was the way he said. He'd made two-three converts in his
years in Segget, they'd stand up and say what the Lord
had done, how before they'd met Him they were lost,
ruined souls; but now God had made them into new men.
And faith! you would think, if that was the case, the Lord's
handiwork was failing, like everything else.

Well, that Sunday after the row at Smithie's, he was there
at his stance where the angel stood, MacDougall himself
with his flat, bald head, and beside him his mistress, a
meikle great sumph, she came from the south and she
mouthed her words broad as an elephant's behind, said Ake
Ogilvie. She thought little of Cis, that was clever and
bonny, but a lot of her youngest, the quean called Mabel—
by all but her mother, she called her Maybull. Well, they
both were there, and the daftie Jock, gleying and slavering
up at the angel, and a two-three more, the gardener Grant
and Newlands the stationy, them and their wives; with the
angel above with her night-gown drawn back, right handy-
like, in case it might rap against the bald pow of Mac-

Dougall Brown. Mistress Brown opened up the harmonica
they'd brought, it groaned and spluttered and gave a bit
hoast, syne they started the singing of their unco hymns,
Newlands burring away in his boots and MacDougall slicing
the words like cheese.

Syne MacDougall started to preach about stealing, with
a verse from Leviticus for the text, though the case of old
Smithie had supplied the cause; and they started singing
another bit hymn, all about being washed in the Blood of
the Lamb, the Lamb being Jesus Christ, said MacDougall,
he was awful fond of hymns full of blood, though he'd
turned as white as a sheet the time Dite Peat had come
over to kill his pig and asked MacDougall to hold the
beast down.

Well, they were getting on fine and bloody, and having
fairly a splash in the gore, when MacDougall noticed there
was something wrong, the words all to hell, he couldn't
make it out. Syne his mistress noticed and screwed round
her head, and she said *What is't?* and saw MacDougall,
red as rhubarb, he'd stopped his singing. The rest of them
had to do the same, for a drove of the spinners had come
in about, with that tink Jock Cronin at their head, as usual,
they were singing up fast and fair drowning MacDougall,
a coarse-like mocking at MacDougall's hymn:

WHITER than—the whitewash on the wall!
WHITER than—the whitewash on the wall!
    Oh—WASH me in the water
    Where you washed your dirty daughter.
And I shall be whiter than the whitewash on the wall!

MacDougall waited until they had stopped, then he cried
to Cronin *Have you no respect?—you, John Cronin—for
the Lord's Day at all?* And the tink said, *Damn the bit; nor
have you.* And MacDougall nearly burst to hear that, he'd
lived by the Bible all his life. And John Cronin said *You
believe all that's in it?* and MacDougall Brown said, *Ay,
I have faith.* But Cronin had fairly got him trapped now,
he said *Well, it says in the Bible that if you've got faith you
can move a mountain. That'll be proof. Move back the
Mounth there in front of our eyes!*

The spinners with him, a lot of tink brutes, all brayed
up then, *Ay, come on, MacDougall! Move a mountain—
you're used to move sand!* MacDougall habbered redder

than ever, then he cried *We'll now sing Rock of Ages.* Jock
Cronin cried *Where's the rock of your faith?* and as soon
as MacDougall and his converts began the spinners sang
up their song as before, about being whiter than the whitewash on the wall, and about MacDougall's dirty daughter;
and such a noise was never heard before in the Sabbath
Square of Segget.

Old Leslie came by and he heard the noise, and he knew
MacDougall and was right sorry for him. But when he
came over and tried to interfere, Jock Cronin cried *God,
here's Ananias!* And old Leslie walked away, fair in a rage,
and went up to the Manse to complain about them.

He arrived there just after the morning service, the
minister new back, and dinner-time done. And old Leslie
said 'twas Infernal, just, the way that they treated a man
nowadays. In his young days if a loon like that Cronin
had miscalled a man he'd have been ta'en out and libbed.
Ay, he minded when he was a loon up in Garvock——

But the new minister rose up and said *Well, I'll hear
that again, I've no time to waste,* with a look as black as
though he could kill you. And afore old Leslie knew well
what had happened he was out on the doorstep and heard
the door bang.

Chris heard the door bang and she saw old Leslie, he was
turning slow to go down the walk, crunching the shingle
under his feet; and suddenly you saw the old man that he
was, his back crooked into that queer-like shape, cruel and
a shame to get rid of him so, suddenly you wanted to weep,
but you didn't, biting your lips as you watched him go.
Only a tiring old fool, as you knew, and he'd come on
Robert in that mad, black mood. And yet——

Things like that caught you again and again, with a
tightening heart, when you had no thought—Robert in
weariness half an hour back, his head in his hands, as he
said *What's the use?* Robert's head as he prayed to that
God of his that you couldn't believe in, though you hid
that away, what need to hurt Robert with something that
never he or you could alter though you lived forever?

So, in the strangest of moments it would come, in a flame
and a flash, a glimpse into depths that wrung your heart,
you'd see the body of Else as she bent, a curve of pleasure
that would curve yet in pain. You'd see—frightening the
things if you cared to think in the dark of the night in the

quiet of Segget, the hush of the yews out there on the lawn—the hopeless folly of all striving, all hope. Sudden, in a Segget shop, maybe, you'd glimpse a face like your father's, near, alive and keen with its bearded lips, and you'd think of your father, long ago dead, bones rotted from flesh in Kinraddie kirkyard—what had life availed him and all his long years when he hoped for this and he strove for that? He died a coarse farmer in a little coarse house, hid in the earth and forgot by men, as forgot as your pains and your tears by God, that God that you knew could never exist. . . .

Only with Ewan you'd never these glimpses into the shifting sands of life, bairn though he was there was something within him hard and shining and unbreakable as rock, something like a sliver of granite within him. Strange that his body had once come from yours in the days when you were a quean unthinking, so close to the earth and its smell and its feel that nearly he came from the earth itself!

From that we all came, you had heard Robert say, but wilder and stranger you knew it by far, from the earth's beginning *you yourself* had been here, a blowing of motes in the world's prime, earth, roots and the wings of an insect long syne in the days when the dragons still ranged the world—every atom here in your body now, that was here, that was you, that beat in your heart, that shaped your body to whiteness and strength, the speed of your legs and the love of your breasts when you turned to the kiss of your Robert at night—these had been there, there was nothing but a change, in a form, the stroke and the beat of a song.

And you thought how long, long ago with Will, your brother, that time he came home from France, before he went back and was killed in France you'd said that the Scots were never religious, had never BELIEVED as other folk did; and that was fell true, and not only for you, MacDougall that brayed by the angel in the square, the folk that came to the kirk on a Sunday, Robert himself— even Robert himself!

There was something lacking or something added, something that was bred in your bones in this land—oh, Something: maybe that Something was GOD—that made folk take with a smile and a gley the tales of the gods and the heavens and the hells, the afterlives and the lives before, heaven on earth and the chances of change, the hope and

belief in salvation for men—as a fairy-tale in a play that
they'd play, but they knew the whole time they were only
players, no Scots bodies died but they knew that fine,
deep and real in their hearts they knew that here they faced
up to the REAL at last, neither heaven nor hell but the
earth that was red, the cling of the clay where you'd alter
and turn, back to the earth and the times to be, to a
spraying of motes on a raging wind when the Howe was
happed in its winter storms, to a spray of dust as some
childe went by with his plough and his horse in a morning
in Spring, to the peck and tweet of the birds in the
trees, to trees themselves in a burgeoning Spring.

You knew, and you knew that they knew—even Robert,
holding to God in his blackest hour, this God he believed
was the father of men, pitiful. He was Pity and a Friend,
helpless even in a way as men, but Kind and Hero, and
He'd conquer yet with all the legions of hell to battle.

So Robert believed: but now, as you heard his feet
coming down the stairs in haste, out of his mood and
happy again, you knew that he knew he followed a dream,
with the black mood REAL, and his hopes but mists.

Chris remembered that dream of her own—she'd been
daft! she thought as she fled about next week's work. There
was jam to make and she thought it fun, and so did Else,
they'd boil pot on pot and fill all the jars, and forget about
dinner. And Robert would come sweating in from the
garden and cry *Losh, Christine, where have you been?
I thought you promised to come out and help. What's
wrong—nothing wrong with you, is there, my dear?* Chris
would say *Only hunger,* and he'd say *Not love?* and the
two would be fools for a moment till they heard the stamp
of Else bringing in the tray. Syne they'd each slip into a
chair and look solemn but once Else caught them and said
to the minister *Faith, I don't wonder!* and looked at Chris;
and Chris thought that the nicest thing ever *looked* about
her.

Ewan ran wild, Chris seldom saw him all the length of
the summer days, he was out in Segget, exploring the
streets, Chris at first had been feared for him—that he'd
fall in front of a horse, or a car, or one of the buses that
went by to Dundon. She tried to tell him to be careful,
then stopped, he'd take his chances with the rest of the
world.

On the Saturday she and Robert looked up from their
work in the garden, and stood and watched Ewan, hands
in his pockets, no cap on his head, go sauntering out
through the gates of the Manse, his black hair almost blue
in the sun, and turn by the Meiklebogs, going to the
Kaimes, Chris wondered what he could want up there?

Robert said *He's seeking the High Places already*, and
laughed, and went on with his digging, Chris the same,
sweet and forgotten the smell of the earth, you thrust with
your spade, the full throw of your body, so, and the drill
built up as you dug. Then the rooks came cawing and
wheeling in by, and they both looked up from Segget to
the Mounth, rain drumming upon it far in the heuchs,
cattle, tail-switching, dots on the heath. Chris asked what
the clouds were, up there by Trusta, they piled up dome
on dome in the sky, like the roofs of a city in the land
of cloud. Robert said *Cumulus; just summer rain;* and a
minute later—*Look, here it comes!*

Chris saw it come wheeling like a flying of rooks, dipping
and pelting down from the heights, she looked left and saw
it through a smother of smoke, the smoke stilled for a
minute as it waited the rain, all Segget turning to look at
the rain. Then Robert was running and Chris ran as well,
under the shelter of the pattering yews. There they stood
and panted and watched the water, whirling in and over
the drills, the potato-shaws a bend in the pelt, the patter
like hail and then like a shoom, like the sea on a morning
heard from Kinraddie, *the empty garden blind with rain.*
And then it was gone and the sun bright out, and Chris
heard, far, clear, as though it never had stopped; a snipe
that was sounding up in the hills.

By noon they saw a drooked figure approaching. Chris
heard Else cry *Are you soaked!* and Ewan answer *I was;
but I dried,* he'd some thing in his hand. Turning it over
he came up to Robert. *Look, I found this up on the
Kaimes.*

Chris stopped as well to look at the thing, the three of
them stood in the bright, wet weather, Robert turning the
implement over in his hands, it was rusted and broken,
the blade of a spear. *Did they use it for ploughing?* Ewan
wanted to know, and Robert said *No, they used it for
killing, it's a spear, Ewan man, from the daft old days.*

Then Else came crying them in for their dinner, and in
they all went, as hungry as hawks. Ewan wanted to know

a lot more about spears, 'twas a wonder he managed to ask all he did, him eating as well, but he managed both fine; he'd a question-mark for a brain, Robert said!

But the most of his questions he kept until night, when Chris bathed him and took him up to his room. Why did the stairs wind? Why weren't they straight? Would it be long till he was a man? Where was Christ now, and had Robert met Him? *That's an owl, why don't owls fly in the day? Why don't you go to sleep when I do? Does Else like Dalziel of the Meiklebogs much? I like the smiddy of old Mr. Leslie, he says that when he was a loon up on Garvock he was never let gang anywhere near a smiddy, his mammy would have smacked his dowp; didn't she like it? I saw Mr. Hogg, he said 'What's your name?' Why is there hair growing out of his nose? Mrs. Hogg is fat, is she going to have a calf? Does she take off her clothes to have it, mother? Mother, have you got a navel like mine? I'll show you mine, look, there it is, isn't it funny—I'm not sleepy, let's sing a while. Why——*

He was sleeping at last, in the evening quiet, the Saturday quiet, the sun not yet gone. Chris went down to the garden and took out a chair and leaned back in it with her arms behind her, drowsy, watching the gloaming come. Robert was up in his room with his sermon, he wrote the thing out when he'd thought of a theme—he would think of a theme of a sudden and swear because he hadn't a note-book at hand.

This afternoon it had come on him suddenly. *I know! That spear-blade that Ewan brought—where the devil has he hidden the thing?*

At half-past ten next morning, the Sunday, Chris heard John Muir and looked out and saw him, his shoulder a-skeugh in his Sunday suit, come stepping up the path from the kirk *There's a fair concourse of the folk the day; and how are you keeping then, mistress, yourself?*

Chris said she was fine, and he gleyed at her cheery. *Faith, so you look, you take well with Segget. Well, well, if the minister hasn't any orders I'll taik away back and tug at the bell.*

Chris heard that bell in a minute or so beat and clang through the quiet of the air. It was time that she herself had got ready, she sought out her hymn-book and hanky and Bible, and inspected Ewan, and straightened his collar. Then the two of them hurried through the blow of the

garden, and out of the little door let in the dyke, and into
the little room back of the kirk. There the sound of the
bell was a deafening clamour. Chris brushed Ewan down
and went into the kirk, and put Ewan into a pew and herself went ben to the pews where the kirk choir sat, Mrs.
Geddes, the schoolmaster's wife, there already, smiling and
oozing with eau-de-Cologne, whispered right low and right
holy-like, *Morning. A grand day, isn't it, and such a pity
so few have come up to hear the Lord's word.*

Chris said, *Oh, yes,* and sat down beside her, and looked
round as the folk came stepping in, slow. Hairy Hogg, the
Provost, and his mistress, Jean, they plumped in their seats
and Hairy looked round and closed his eyes like a grass-
filled cow. Then the wife and queans of John Muir came
in, Chris had heard a lot about them from Else. Else said
she could swear there were times when Muir wished he'd
stayed where he was when he fell in that grave.

His wife was one of the Milton lot that farmed down
under Glenbervie brae, she deaved John Muir from morning till night to get out of his job, a common bit roadman,
and get on in the world and show up her sister, Marget
Ann, that had married a farmer. But John Muir would say
*Damn't, we all come to the same—a hole and a stink and
worms at the end* and his mistress would snap, *Ay, maybe
we do, but there's ways of getting there decent and undecent. And as for stinking, speak of yourself.* And, real
vexed, she'd clout Tooje one in the ear. Tooje was her
eldest, fairly a gawk, and then clout little Ted when she
started to greet because she saw her sister Tooje greeting;
and John Muir would get up and say not a word but go
dig a grave as a bit of a change.

Then Chris saw Bruce, the porter, come in, with the
mark on his jaw where his godfather hit him, then Leslie,
the smith, paiching and sweating, he dropped his stick with
an awful clatter. Then she saw Geddes, the Segget headmaster, sitting grim in a pew midway, his rimless specs
set close on his nose, looking wearied to death, as he was.
Robert had thought to make him an ally, but he'd said to
Robert, *Don't be a fool, leave the swine to stew in their
juice*—by swine he meant his fellow-folk of Segget. He
would stand hymn-singing with his hand in his pocket, and
rattle his keys and yawn at the roof.

Then Moultrie came in, a slow tap-tap, with his stick
and his glare, and stopped half-way, his wife, Jess Moultrie,

waiting behind, her hand on his arm, gentle and quiet. But when he moved on he shook her away. Chris had heard the story of him and of her and how he had never forgiven her her daughter, Ag, whom they called the Roarer and Greeter.

Then others came in, all in a birn, Chris didn't know some and of some was uncertain, she thought that one was Ake Ogilvie the joiner; and a trickle of folk from the farms outbye, a spinner or so, but they were fell few, and Dalziel of the Meiklebogs, red-faced and shy, funny how one couldn't abide him at all.

Syne John Muir finished with the ringing of the bell and came with his feet splayed out as he walked and his shoulder agley, down the length of the kirk; and went into the little room at the back. Robert would be there and Muir help him to robe. Syne the door opened and John Muir came out, and swayed and gleyed cheerful up to the pulpit, and opened the door and stood back and waited. And Robert went up, with his hair fresh-brushed, and his eyes remote, and sat down and prayed, silent, and all the kirk silent as well, for a minute, while Chris looked down at her hands.

Then Robert stood up in the pulpit and said, in his clear, strong voice that hadn't a mumble, that called God GOD and never just GAWD. *We will begin the worship of God by the singing of hymn one hundred and forty. 'Our shield and defender, the Ancient of Days, pavilioned in splendour and girded with praise.' Hymn one hundred and forty.*

Folk rustled the leaves and here and there a man glowered helpless while his wife found the page; and the organ started with a moan and a grind and the kirk was a rustle with Sunday braws, folk standing and singing, all straight and decent, except young Ewan, a-lean in his pew and Geddes the Dominie, hand in his pouch.

Chris liked this hymn near as much as did Robert, most folk stuck fast when they came to pavilioned, Robert's bass came in, Chris's tenor to help, Mrs. Geddes' contralto a wail at their heels. Then down they all sat; Robert said *Let us pray.*

Chris wondered what Robert was to preach today, his text was no clue when he gave it out. Folk shuffled in their seats, and hoasted genteel, and put up their hankies to slip sweeties in their mouths; sometimes Chris wished she could do the same, but she couldn't very well, the minister's wife.

And all Segget lifted its eyes to Robert, he flung back the
shoulders of his robe and began, slow and careful, reading
from his notes; and then pushed them aside and began
a sermon on that bit of a spear young Ewan Tavendale had
found on the Kaimes. He'd brought the thing up in the
pulpit with him, folk stopped in their sucking of sweeties
and gaped.

And Robert told of the uses the thing had once had, in
the hands of the carles of the ruined Kaimes; and the siege
and the fighting and the man who had held it, desperate
at last in the burning lowe as King Kenneth's men came
into the castle: and the blood that ran on this ruined blade
for things that the men of that time believed would endure
and be true till the world died; they thought they were
fighting for things that would last, they'd be classed as
heroes and victors forever. And now they were gone, they
were not even names, their lives and their deaths we know
to be foolish, a clamour and babble on little things.

So might the men of the future look back, on this Segget here, not of antique times, and see the life of our
mean-like streets an ape-like chatter as the dark came down.
For change, imperative, awaited the world, as never before
men could make it anew, men of good will and a steadfast
faith. All history had been no more than the gabble of a
horde of apes that was trapped in a pit. *Let us see that we
clean our pit-corner in Segget, there is hatred here, and
fear, and malaise, the squabbling of drunken louts in the
streets, poor schools, worse houses—we can alter all these,
we can alter them NOW, not waiting the world.*

Robert had launched his campaign on Segget.

That sermon fair raised a speak in the toun, as soon's
they got out Peter Peat said Faith! they'd fair made a
mistake in getting this childe. You wanted a sermon with
some body in it, with the hell that awaited the folk that
were sinners, and lay on the Kaimes with their unwed
queans, and were slow in paying their bills to a man. And
what did he mean that Segget was foul? A clean little toun
as ever there was, no, no, folk wanted no changes here.

Old Leslie said 'Twas Infernal, just, he minded when he
was a loon up on Garvock——

Rob Moultrie said *Well, what d'you expect? He's gentry
and dirt with his flat-patted hair; and speaking to God as
though he were speaking to a man next door—and a poor-*

man at that. Ay, a Tory mucker, I may well warrant, that would interfere in our houses and streets.

Will Melvin said *Did you hear him preach against folk taking a dram now and then? And if he himself wasn't drunk then I'm daft, with his spears and his stars and his apes and his stite.*

That fairly got Hairy Hogg on the go. He cried *Ay, what was all yon about apes? And him glaring at me like a thrawn cat. If he comes from the monkeys himself let him say it, not sneer at folk of a better blood.*

Folk took a bit snicker at that as they went—damn't, the minister had got one in there! And afore night had come the story had spread, the minister had said—you'd as good as heard him—that Hairy Hogg was a monkey, just.

Well, it made you laugh, though an ill-getted thing to say that of old Hairy Hogg, the Provost. Faith, he fair had a face like a monkey, the sutor of Segget and its Provost forbye. He'd been Provost for years, not a soul knew why, or how he'd ever got on for the job; or what was the council, or what it might do, apart from listening to Hairy on Burns. For he claimed descent from the Burneses, Hairy, and you'd have thought by the way he spoke that Rabbie had rocked him to sleep in his youth. His wife had once been at Glenbervie House, a parlourmaid there and awful genteel; but a thirty years or so in old Hogg's bed had fair rubbed gentility off of the creature, she was common and rough as a whin bush now, and would hoast out loud in the kirk at prayers till the bairns all giggled and old Hogg would say, loud enough for the pulpit to hear, *Wheest, wheest, redd your thrapple afore you come here.*

She would make him regret that when they got home, she'd little time for any palavers, her daughter Jean that was nurse in London, or Alec her son that clerked down in Edinburgh. Old Hogg he would blow like a windy bellows about Jean and the things she'd done as a nurse. For when the bit King took ill with a cough she was one of the twenty-four nurses or so that went prancing round the bit royalty's bed, she carried a hanky, maybe, or such-like. But to hear old Hairy speak on the business you'd have thought she cured the King's illness herself, and been handed a two-three thousand for doing it. Yet damn the penny but her wages she got, said Mrs. Hogg; what could you expect? The gentry were aye as mean as is dirt and wasn't the King a German forbye?

Young Hogg was at home now, on holiday like, he meant to attend the Segget Show. You had seen the creature, wearing plus-fours, east-windy, west-endy as well as could be, forbye that he said he had joined the Fascists. Folk asked what they were, and he said *they* were fine, Conservatives, like, but a lot more than that; they meant to make Britain the same as was Italy. And old Hogg was real vexed, he cried *But goodsakes! You're not going to leave your fine job, now, are you, and take to the selling of ice-cream sliders?* And Alec said *Father, please don't be silly;* and old Hogg fair flamed: *Give's less of your lip. What could man think but that you were set, you and your breeks and your Fashers and all, with being a damned ice-creamer yourself?*

Alec said nothing, just looked at his quean, and she and him sniffed, she was real superior, a clerk like Alec himself down in Edinburgh. He'd brought her up on holiday to Segget, he called her his feeungsay, not just his lass; she wouldn't be able to stay for the Show, and if any soul thought that a cause for regret, he'd managed to keep a good grip on himself. The first time they sat down to tea in Hogg's house Alec finished his cup and looked round the table. *Where's the slop-basin, mother?* he asked, to show his quean he was real genteel. But his mother was wearied with him and his airs. *Slop it in your guts!* she snapped as she rose, *and less of your Edinburgh touches here!*

Segget Show was held in a park that was loaned to the toun by Dalziel of the Meiklebogs. He blushed and looked shy, *Oh ay, you can have it,* when Hairy Hogg went out there and asked him. 'Twas a great ley park with a fringe of trees, the hills up above, the Kaimes to the left; and early on the evening afore Segget Show there were folk down there marking out this and that, the lines of the tents and the marquees and such, the circle where the bairns would run their bit races and folk that thought they could throw the hammer could stand and show what their muscles were made of. Folk came to Segget Show far and about, from Fordoun and Laurencekirk, Skite and Arbuthnott, early on the Saturday Segget awoke to the rattle of farm carts up through East Wynd, down past the Manse, and so to the park, carts loaded with kail and cabbage and cakes, and hens and ducks in their clean straw rees, and birns of bannocks and scones for show, and the Lord knows what that folk wouldn't bring to try for a prize at the Segget Show.

It was wet in the morning, folk looked out and swore, but by noon the rain had cleared off and soon, as the lines of folk held out from Segget, there came a blistering waft of the heat, men loosed their waistcoats, some took off their collars and paid their shillings and went in at the gates, all except a crowd of the spinners. They suddenly appeared near the big marquee, and Sim Leslie, him that the folk called Feet, went over and looked at the bunch fell stern, he hadn't seen them pay at the gate. But he wasn't keen on starting a row, just looked at them stern: and the spinners all laughed.

There fair was a crush as the judges began, Hairy Hogg was one, the minister another, Dalziel of the Meiklebogs the third. They started in on the hens to begin with, a lot from MacDougall Brown's of the post-office. MacDougall stood by, looking proud as dirt, he'd won first prize for his Leghorns for years. So he fell near fainted when he got a green ticket, the second prize only and not the red first; and he said to whoever stood by to listen that it was that minister had done this to him, he was scared at the way that MacDougall drew folk away from the Auld Kirk's preaching and lies. But faith! his Leghorns looked none so well, he'd been mixing lime in their feed and the birds had a look as though they'd like to lie down and burst. But they daren't, with MacDougall's eye upon them, they stood and chirawked, as though kind of discouraged when they saw that they'd ta'en only second prize.

By then the judges were through with the hens, the ducks as well, a childe from a farm out near by Mondynes had ta'en every prize there was to be took. Syne the judges turned into the big marquee, to judge the baked stuff and the flowers and the like. The minister was speaking as they went inside; Hairy Hogg turned round to hear what he said; and prompt his elbow knocked over the dish that was set with cakes of Mistress Melvin. The landlady of the Arms looked at the Provost as though she'd like to bash in his head, with a bottle, and syne carve him up slow with its splinters; but she daren't say anything, seeing it was him, and he'd given the Melvins the catering to do.

So the Blaster and Blasphemer just smiled, genteel, and got down and picked up her cakes from the grass, the minister got down and helped her; and smiled; (what was the creature laughing about?). But Hairy Hogg said, for the marquee to hear, *I want stuff set out plain and decent, not pushed right under my nose when I judge.* He spoke as though he were the Lord God Almighty, and the bannocks sinners on the Judgement Day.

They couldn't make up their minds on the pancakes, there were two fine lots, one rounded and cut, neat-shaped and fine as ever you saw, the other lot not of much shape at all, but bonnily fired, and the judges stopped, and each ate a bit, of the well-cut at first, they weren't so bad, but looked better than they tasted. Syne the judges bit at the ill-cut cakes, they fairly melted in a body's mouth, the minister had eaten up one in a minute, and Meiklebogs nodded, and Hairy Hogg nodded, and the Reverend Mr. Colquohoun gave a nod.

So old Jess Moultrie had the first prize, faith! that was fairly a whack in the face for that Mistress Geddes with her fine-shaped cakes, and her blethering of lectures at the W.R.I. She was daft on the W.R.I., Mrs. Geddes, she said that folk in a village like Segget wanted taking out of themselves. So she and some others started the thing, they'd collect at all hours, the women of the place, and speak about baking and minding the bairns, and how to make pipes from the legs of old sofas; and hear lantern-lectures on Climbing the Alps. Well, damn't! she'd have to do a bit of climbing herself ere she learned to bake cakes like the Moultrie wife.

By three nearly everything there had been judged, most of the folk had scattered by then, to see the games in the ring that Ake Ogilvie had set up for nothing, the previous night. And well so he might, damn seldom he worked, you couldn't get near to his joiner's shop for the clutter of carts, half-made and half-broken, lying about, and the half of a churn, a hen-coop or so and Heaven knows what—all left outside in the rain and sun while Ogilvie sat on a bench inside and wrote his ill bits of poetry and stite—he thought himself maybe a second Robert Burns.

He was broad and big, a fell buirdly childe, and it seemed fell queer that a man like that couldn't settle down to the making of money, and him the last joiner left in the place. But he'd tell you instead some rhyme or another, coarse dirt that was vulgar, not couthy and fine. He was jealous as hell of the real folk that wrote, Annie S. Swan and that David Lyall: you could read and enjoy every bit that they

wrote, it was fine clean stuff, not sickening you, like, with
dirt about women having bairns and screaming or old men
dying in the hills at night or the fear of a sheep as the
butcher came. That was the stuff that Ake Ogilvie wrote,
and who wanted to know about stuff like that? You did a
bit reading to get away from life.

Well, Ake Ogilvie, him and his poetry and dirt, there he
was, on the edge of the ring. And inside the ring, round
about the hammer, were a pickle of those that would try
a bit throw. And Feet cried *Back, keep out of the way,*
and went shooing bairns at the ring's far side; and folk
clustered around fair thick to look on, old Leslie and Melvin the judges here.

The first to throw was a man from Catcraig, Charlie
Something-or-other his name, and he swung himself slow
and steady on his feet and syne took a great breath and
leaped in the air, and swung, and syne as his feet came
down his arms let go and the hammer flew out and flashed
in the air and spun and then fell—ay, a gey throw, folk
cheered him a bit. But one of his galluses had split with the
throw and he blushed to the eyes and put on his coat.

Syne another childe threw, a farmer he was, the hammer
went skittering out from his hand, he laughed in an off-
hand way as to say he was just taking part to encourage
the others. Syne folk saw that the third was that tink Jock
Cronin, one of the spinner breed, he picked up the hammer
and waited and swung, and louped, and the thing went a
good foot beyond any of the earlier throws that were made.
'Twould be a sore business if the Cronin should win. His
friends all shouted, *That's the stuff, Jock!* they were fair
delighted with their champion's throw, with their rattling
watch-chains and their dirty jokings, the average spinner
knew as much of politeness as a polecat knows of the ab-
sence of smell.

The worst of the lot, folk said, were the Cronins, they
bade in West Wynd, a fair tribe of the wretches, old
Cronin had once been a foreman spinner till he got his
bit hand mashed up in machinery. He'd fair gone bitter with
that, they told, and took to the reading of the daftest-like
books, about Labour, Socialism, and such-like stite. *Where
would you be if it wasn't for Capital?* you'd ask old Cronin,
and he'd say *On the street—where the capitalists themselves
would be, you poor fool. It's the capitalists that we are out
to abolish, and the capital that we intend to make ours.*

And he'd organized a union for spinners and if ever you heard of a row at the mills you might bet your boots a Cronin was in it, trying to make out that the spinners had rights, and ought to be treated like gentry, b'God!

The worst of the breed was that young Jock Cronin, him that had just now thrown the hammer. The only one that wasn't a spinner, he worked as a porter down at the station, folk said that the stationmaster, Newlands, would have sacked him right soon if only he'd dared, him and his socialism and the coarse way he had of making jokes on the Virgin Birth; and sneering at Jonah in the belly of the whale; and saying that the best way to deal with a Tory was to kick him in the dowp and you'd brain him there. But Jock Cronin worked as well as he blethered, the sly, coarse devil, and he couldn't be sacked; and there he stood with a look on his face as much as to say *That's a socialist's throw!*

It was Newlands, the stationmaster, himself that came next, you hoped he'd beat the throw of the porter. But faith, he didn't, he was getting fell slow, maybe it was that or he wasted his breath singing at the meetings of MacDougall Brown, the hammer just wobbled and fell with a plop, if they didn't do better at the second round and third it was Cronin the porter would grab the first prize.

But syne folk started to cheer, and all looked, 'twas the Reverend Mr. Colquohoun himself, being pushed inside the ring by his wife. Ay, that was well-intended of him, now, you gave a bit clap and syne waited and watched. And the minister took off his coat and his hat and smiled at the childe that held out the hammer, and took it and swung, and there rose a gasp, he'd flung it nearly as far as the Cronin's.

The second bout he landed well over Jock Cronin's, plain it was between the spinner and him, the spinners stopped laughing, crying, *Come on, then, Jock! You're not going to let a mucking preacher beat you?* The Reverend Colquohoun looked at them and laughed, and syne spoke to Cronin, and *he* laughed as well, not decent and low as a man would do that spoke to a minister, but loud out and vulgar, he wished folk to think that he was as good as any minister that ever was clecked. Then the childe with the galluses threw once again, but he'd never got over the blush or the galluses, he landed fell short and went off the field, and Else Queen, the maid at the Manse, was his lass, and she laughed out loud; and that was ill-done.

Syne Ake Ogilvie threw—ay, not a bad throw, but shorter than Cronin's, Ake did it with a sneer. Syne Cronin again, and the hammer was flung with the whole of his weight and his strength and it fell, crack! a bare foot short of his very first throw. And as the minister stood up, arms bared, you knew well enough that he couldn't beat that; and then everybody knew that he wasn't going to try, he maybe thought it not decent for a minister to win, he swung the hammer to give it a good throw, but safe and not as far as Jock Cronin's.

But the spinners had broken into the ring, a birn of them down at the farther end; and as the Reverend picked up the hammer and got ready to swing, one of them cried, you couldn't tell which, *Jesus is getting a bit weak in the guts.*

The minister gave a kind of a start, you thought for a minute that he wouldn't throw. But instead he suddenly whirled him about, and spun and swung and had flung the hammer, so quickly you hardly saw what he did. And the hammer swished and twirled through the air, like a catapult stone or a pheasant in flight, and landed a good three feet or more beyond the furthest throw of the Cronin: and struck on a great meikle stone that lay there, and stotted and swung, the handle swung first, into the middle of the spleiter of spinners.

They jumped and ran and the hammer lay still, and there rose such a yell from the folk that watched, your lugs near burst in the cheering and din. The minister's face had reddened with blood, the veins were like cords all over his face; and then he went white as ever again, and put on his coat and went out of the ring, folk cried, *That was a fine throw, minister,* but he didn't say a word, just went off with his wife.

Chris said, *What's wrong?* Then she saw his hanky as he took it away from his lips; it was red. He said *Oh, nothing. Gassed lungs, I suppose. Serves me right for trying to show off.*

Chris said, *You didn't; I thought you were fine.* Robert said, *I'm afraid not, only a fool. There, I'm all right, don't worry, Christine. Come on, we've to watch Ewan running his race.*

The bairns' races were the next things set. Ewan Chris watched line up with the others, Geddes the schoolmaster in charge of the lot, disgusted as ever he looked with the job. They'd marked out a track through the middle of the ring, John Muir stood down at the further end, the bairns had to run to him and then back. Chris watched Ewan, he was eating a sweetie, calm as you please, his black mop blue in the sun, his eyes on the Dominie, he didn't care a fig. But as soon as Geddes cried *Run!* he was off, he went like a deer, his short legs flying, the other bairns tailed off behind, and Ewan was first to reach Muir and go round him, swinging round gripping at John Muir's trousers; and as he went by the place where Chris stood, he looked at her and grinned calmly as ever, and shifted the sweetie to the other side of his mouth, and looked back, and slowed down, no need to race. He was up at the Dominie first, at a trot, folk round about asked who he was, as black as all that, he was surely foreign?

Then somebody knew and saw Chris stand near, and cried out *Wheest!* but Chris didn't care; she watched Ewan take the prize and say *Thanks,* calm still, and put the shilling in his pocket, and come walking back to look for her, and stand grave in front of her as she smoothed down his collar. Robert gave him a shake and he smiled at that (the smile that so sometimes caught your heart, the smile you had known on the lips of his father). Then Robert said, *Well, since we've won all the prizes, let's go and look for tea in the tent.*

And the three of them set out across the short grass, through the groupings and gatherings of folk here and there, the show was fairly a place for a claik, one gossip would now meet in with another she hadn't seen since the last Segget Show, and would cry *Well, now, it's Mistress Mac-Tavish!* And Mistress MacTavish would cry back *her* name, and they'd shake hands and waggle their heads and be at it, hammer and tongs, a twelve months' gossip, the Howe's reputation put in through a mangle and its face danced on when it came through the rollers.

There was a great crush in the tent they entered, but Melvin came running and found them a table, the gabble of the folk rose all round about, they nodded to the minister and minded their manners, and reddened when they thought that he looked at them, and took a sly keek at the clothes Chris wore—faith! awful short skirts for a minister's wife. Mrs. Hogg was sitting at a table with her son, him that she'd told to slop slop in his guts, his quean had gone back, and folk saw the damned creature trying to catch the minister's eye. But the Reverend Mr. Colquohoun didn't see you were torn two ways with scorn of the Manse for being so proud, and with sheer delight at seeing the Hoggs get a smack in the face.

Then it was time for the band to begin, folk trooped out to see in the best of spirits, well filled with biscuits and baps and tea; but weren't such fools as go over close to the board where John Muir and Smithie were standing, crying, *Come on folk, now, will you dance?* Behind them the Segget band played up. Ake Ogilvie there at the head of it, fair thinking himself of importance, like, with Jim that served in the bar of the Arms and folk called the Sourock because of his face, tooting on his flute like a duck half-choked, and Newlands the stationy cuddling his fiddle a damn sight closer than ever his mistress, or else she'd have had a bairn ere this—not that you blamed him, she'd a face like a greip, and an ill greip at that, though you don't cuddle faces. And Feet was there, he was playing the bassoon, he sat well back to have room for his boots and looked as red as a cock with convulsions. God ay! it was worth going up to the board if only to take a laugh at the band.

But not a childe or a quean would venture up on the thing till at last Jock Cronin, that tink of a porter that came of the spinners, was seen going up and pulling up a quean. She laughed, and turned her face round at last, and folk fair had a shock, it was Miss Jeannie Grant, she was one of the teachers, what was she doing with a porter, eh? —and a tink at that, that called himself a socialist, and said that folk should aye vote for labour, God knew you got plenty without voting for't.

Socialists with queans—well, you knew what they did, they didn't believe in homes or in bairns, they'd have had all the bairns locked up in poor houses; and the coarse brutes said that marriage was daft—that fair made a body right wild to read that, what was coarse about marriage you would like to know? . . . And you'd stop from your reading and say to the wife, *For Heaven's sake, woman, keep the bairns quiet. Do you think I want to live in a menagerie?* And she'd answer you back, *By your face I aye thought that was where you came from,* and start off again about *her* having no peace, she couldn't be sweir like a man, take a rest; and whenever were your wages going to be raised? And you'd get in a rage and stride out of the house, and finish the paper down at the Arms, reading about the dirt that so miscalled marriage—why shouldn't they have to get married as well?

Well, there were Jock Cronin and Miss Jeannie Grant, they stood and laughed and looked down at the folk. Syne some spinners went up, as brazen as you like, giggling, and then a ploughman or so, syne Alec Hogg that was son of the Provost, he had up Cis Brown that went to the College, thin and sweet, a fell bonny lass, she looked gey shy and a treat to cuddle. So there were enough at last for a dance, and Ake waved his arms, and they struck up a polka. There was fair a crowd when the second dance came, you felt your back buttons to see were they holding, and took a keek round for a lass for the dance: and the queans all giggled and looked at you haughty, till you asked one, bold, and then she'd say *Ay*.

Charlie, the childe from Catcraig, went to Else, the maid from the Manse, and said *Will you dance?* and she said *Can you?* and he blushed and said *Fine*. Else was keen for a dance and she left Meiklebogs, he looked after her shy, like a shy-like stot, as she swung on the board, a fair pretty woman. God, you hardly saw her like nowadays, queans grown all as thin as the handles of forks, and as hard forbye, no grip to the creatures; and how the devil they expected to get married and be ta'en with bairns you just couldn't guess, what man in his senses would want to bed with a rickle of bones and some powder, like?

Well, Else was up with the Catcraig childe, it was *Drops of Brandy* and the folk lined up, Else saw the minister, he smiled like a lad with the mistress herself further down the line. Ake waved his arms and you all were off, slow in the pace and the glide, then the whirl, till the brandy drops were spattering the sky the board kittled up and the band as well, and you all went like mad; and Else's time when she did the line she found the minister the daftest of the lot, he swung her an extra turn right round, and he cried out *Hooch!* and folk all laughed—ay, fairly a billy the new minister, though already he'd started interfering with folk, and he'd preached so unco, a Sunday back, that old Hairy Hogg was descended from monkeys. . . . Had he said that, then? Ay, so he had, old Hogg himself had told you the speak, it was hardly the thing to have said of the Provost, fair monkey-like though the creature was. . . .

And just at the head of the dance as Else flew round in

the arms of her Catcraig childe, he gave a kind of a gasp
and his hand flew up to his waistcoat and Else cried *What?*
And the childe let go and grabbed at his breeks, his other
bit gallus had fair given way, he lipped from the board
with his face all red, and went home fell early that evening
alone, not daring to stay and take Else Queen home.

The teas were all finished and Melvin had opened up
one of the tents for the selling of drams, folk took a bit
dander up to the counter, had a dram, and spoke of the
Show and looked out—at the board, the gloaming was
green on the hills, purple on the acre-wide blow of heather.
There was a little wind coming down, blowing in the hot,
red faces of the dancers, you finished up your dram and
felt fair kittled up; and went out and made for the board
like a hare, damn't! you might be old, but you still could
dance, you hoped the mistress had already gone home.

There was old Smithie, well whiskied by now. He cried
each dance till he got to the Schottische, he stuck fast on
that and shished so long you thought the old fool never
would stop, his whiskers sticking from his face in a fuzz,
like one of the birns of hay he would steal. And just as he
paused to take a bit breath his eyes lit down on his goodson, Bruce, and he stopped and said *What the devil's wrong
with you, you coarse tink, that lives in my house, on my
meal, and snickers like a cuddy when a man tries to speak?*

Bruce glunched up, dour, *Be quiet, you old fool,* and that
fair roused the dander of Smithie to hear. *Who's a fool? By
God, if I come down to you*—and he made a bit step, just
threatening-like, but he was over-near the edge of the board
to be threatening, even, next minute he was off, on top of
Ed Bruce, folk were fair scandalised and crowded about,
snickering with delight to see the daft fools, old Smithie
and Bruce, leathering round in the grass. But down came
the minister and pushed folk aside, angry as could be, and
folk stared at him. *Get up there, confound you, the two
of you!* he cried, and in a jiffy had old Smithie up in one
hand and Bruce in the other, and shook them both. *Haven't
you more sense than behave like a couple of bairns! Shake
hands and shut up!*

And so they did, but before the night was well done the
speak was all over the Howe of the Mearns that the new
minister of Segget had come down and bashed Ed Bruce
in the face and syne Smithie, and cursed at them both for
ten minutes without stopping. And a great lot of folk went

to kirk next Sunday that never went afore, and never went again, for no other purpose than to stare at the minister, and see if he'd be shamed of the coarse way he'd cursed.

Well, that was the Segget Show and Games, by eight and nine the older folk were crying ta-ta and taiking away home, the farmers in their gigs spanked down by Meiklebogs, the Segget folk dandered homes low in the light, it lay like the foam of the sea on the land, soft, in a kind of blue, trembling half-mist, a half-moon, quiet, came over the hills and looked down on the board where the young still danced. Else sought out the mistress—should she take Ewan home? But the mistress shook her head, *I'll do that. Dance while you're young, but don't be too late;* and she smiled at Else the fine way she had, she looked bonny with that dour, sweet, sulky face, the great plaits of her hair wound round her head, rusty and dark and changing to gold, Else thought *If I were a man myself I'd maybe be worse than the minister is—I'd want to cuddle her every damned minute!*

Young Ewan was beside her, he stood eating chocolate, he had eaten enough to make a dog sick, as Else knew well, but he looked cool as ever, the funny bit creature, and said *Ta-ta, Else. Will Mr. Meiklebogs squeeze you under my window?* Else felt herself flushing up like a fire, *Maybe, if I let him,* and Ewan said *Oh, do,* and would maybe have said more, for bairns are awful, but that the minister had hold of his arm—*Come on, or I'll squeeze YOU, Ta-ta, Else.*

So the three went home through the night-quiet park, Robert and Chris the last of the elders to leave. It came sudden on Chris, with her feet in the grass, her hand in Ewan's, that that's what they were—old, she who was not yet thirty years old! Old, and still how you'd like to dance, out under the brightening coming of the moon, drop away from you all the things that clung close, Robert and Ewan and the Manse—even Chris—be young and be young and be held in men's arms, and seem bonny to them and look at them sly, not know next hour who would take you home, and not know who would kiss you or what they would do ... Young as you never yet had been young, you'd been caught and ground in the wheels of the days, in this dour little Howe and its moil and toil, the things you had missed, the things you had missed! The things that the folk had aye in the books—being daft, with the winds of young

years in your hair, night for a dream and the world for a
song. Young; and you NEVER could be young now.

Like a sea you had never seen plain in your life, you
heard the thunder and foam of the breakers, once or twice,
far off, dark-green and salt, you had seen them play, spouting and high on a drift of the wind, crying in the sun with
their crested laughters, hurrying south on the questing tides.
Youth, to be young——

High up and over the Kaimes two birds were sailing into
the western night, lonely, together, into the night Chris
watched them fade to dots in the sky.

The whispers went round the minister had gone, the
ploughmen and spinners gave a bit laugh and took a bit
squeeze at the queans they held; and some of the folk that
were hot with their collars pulled the damned things off and
threw them in the hedge. In Will Melvin's bar was a roaring trade, old Hairy Hogg's son and Dite Peat were there,
the both of them telling the tale, you may guess, Alec Hogg
of the things he had seen in Edinburgh, Dite Peat of the
things he had done in London. God! 'twas a pity they'd
ever come back. Meiklebogs came taiking into the bar,
near nine that was, folk cried: *Will you drink?* and he answered back canny, *Oh, ay; maybe one;* and had two or
three, and looked shyer than ever. Dite Peat roared *With
that down under your waistcoat, you'll be able to soss up
the Manse quean fine.* Meiklebogs looked a wee bit shyer
than before, and gave a bit laugh, and said, *Fegs, ay.*

Else had danced every dance since the dancing began.
When Charlie from Catcraig, the fool, disappeared, Alec
Hogg had taken her up for a while, and half Else liked
him and half she didn't, he felt like a man though he spoke
like a toff. He asked in his clipped-like way, *You're Miss
Queen?* as though he thought it should be *mistake.* Else
answered careless, *Oh, ay, so I've heard. You're the son of
old Hairy Hogg, the Provost?* He grinned like a cat. *So
my mother says,* and Else was fair shocked, a man shouldn't
make jokes about his own mother. So after a while she got
rid of the creature, and the next dance she had was with
Ogilvie the joiner, he'd left the band for Feet to conduct,
he swung her round and round in a waltz, his own eyes
half-closed near all that time. If he thought your face such
a scunner to look at, why did he ask you up for a dance?

Then Feet cried *The last,* and there was John Muir he'd

grabbed Else afore any other could get near, and he danced
right well, Else warmed up beside him, he cried out, *Hooch!*
and she did the same, if he dug graves as well as he danced,
John Muir, he should have had a job in a public cemetery.
As Else whirled she saw the blue reek of Segget, and the
dusk creep in, it was warm and blue, and the smell of the
hay rose up in her face; there was the moon, who was taking
her home?

She was over big and scared off the shargars; but one or
two childes she knew keen enough for a slow-like stroll up
to Segget Manse. But they looked at Dalziel, that was
waiting by, and turned away and left Else alone. And the
old fool said, with his shy-like smile, *Ay then, will I see
you home, Else lass?*

Else said *You may, since you've feared all the rest!* but
he smiled as canny as ever and said *Ay,* he didn't seem to
mind that she was in a rage. The dances were ended and
the folk were going, streaming from the park as the night
came down, the band with their instruments packed in their
cases, and their queans beside them, them that had queans,
them that had wives had the creatures at home, waiting up
with a cup of tea to slocken the throats of the men that
had played so well for Segget that afternoon. Here and
there in the park a bit fight broke out, but folk paid little
heed, they just gave a smile, that was the way that the Show
aye ended, you'd think it queer in a way if you didn't see
a childe or so with his nose bashed in, dripping blood like a
pig new knived.

Jock Cronin and his spinners had started a quarrel with
the three fee'd men at the Meiklebogs. Jock Cronin said
ploughmen should be black ashamed, they that once had
a union like any other folk, but had been too soft in the
guts to stick by it, they'd been feared by the farmers into
leaving their union, the damned half-witted joskins they
were. George Sand was the foreman at the Meiklebogs, a
great meikle childe with a long moustache and a head on
him like a Clydesdale horse. He said *And what the hell
better are the spinners? They've done a damn lot with their
union and all? I sit down to good meat when the dirt are
starving,* and another Meiklebogs man cried the same. *Ay,
or a porter down at the station? What the hell has your
union done for you? I've more money in my pouch right
the now, let me tell you, than ever you had in your life,*

my birkie. I could show you right now a five and a ten and a twenty pound note.

Jock Cronin said sneering-like, *Could you so? Could you show me five shillings?* and the childe turned red, he hadn't even that on him at the time, it had been no more than an empty speak, and he felt real mad to be shown up so. So he took John Cronin a crack on the jaw, by God it sounded like the crack of doom. Jock Cronin went staggering back among the spinners, and then the spinners and ploughmen were at it, in a minute as bonny a fight on as ever you saw in your life at Segget Show. You'd be moving off the Show-ground quiet with your quean, till you saw it start and then you'd run forward, and ask what was up, and not stop to listen, for it fair looked tempting; so you'd take a kick at the nearest backside, hard as you liked, and next minute some brute would be bashing in your face, and you bashing his, and others coming running and joining; and somebody trotting to Melvin's tent and bringing out Feet to stop the fight.

He was well loaded up with drink by then, Feet, and he'd only a bit of his uniform on. But he ran to the fighters and he cried *Hold on! What's all this jookery-packery now? Stop your fighting and get away home.*

But the coarse brutes turned on poor Feet instead, it was late that night when he crawled from the ditch and blinked his eyes and felt his head, the moon high up in a cloudless sky, the field deserted and a curlew crying.

All the folk had gone long ere that, even the youngest and daftest of them gone, home from the Segget Show in their pairs, there were folk at that minute on the Laurence-kirk road, a lad and his lass on their whirring bikes, the peesies wheeping about in the moon, the childe with his arm around the quean's shoulder, the whir of the wheels below their feet, the quean with her cheek against the hand that rested shy on her shoulder, so, home, before them but still far off; and the dark came down and they went into it, into their years and tomorrows, they'd had that.

Some went further in business, if less in mileage. Near Skite a farmer went out to his barn, early next morning, and what did he see? Two childes and two lasses asleep in his hay. And he was sore shocked and went back for his wife, and she came and looked and was shocked as well, and if they'd had a camera they'd have taken photographs, they were so delighted and shocked to see two queans that they knew in such a like way, they'd be able to tell the story about them all the years that they lived on earth; and make it a tit-bit in hell forbye.

Cis Brown had asked her father MacDougall if she could stay on late at the dance; and he'd said that she might, his favourite was Cis; and so she had done and at the dance end she had looked round about and had blushed as she wondered would anyone ask her to walk home to Segget? She was over young, she supposed, for all that, a college quean with her lessons and career, and not to waste her time on a loon. And she wished that she wasn't, and then looked up and saw a spinner, a boy beside her, about the same age as herself, she thought. He was tall like a calf, and shy and thin, he looked at her and he didn't look—*Are you going up home?*

She said she was and she thought as she said it, *What an awful twang those spinners speak!* She was half-ashamed to walk home with one. But so they got clear of the stamash of the fighting, saying never a word as they went through the grass. Then the boy gave a cough, *Are you in a hurry?* and Cis said *No, not a very great hurry,* and he said *Let's go down by the Meiklebogs corn and home through the moor to the Segget road.*

So she went with him, quiet, by the side of the park, the path so narrow that he went on ahead, the moon was behind them up in the Mounth, below them stirred the smell of the stalks, bitter and strange to a quean from Segget, she bent and plucked up one in the dark, and nibbled at it and looked at the boy. Behind them the noise of the Show grew faint: only for sound the swish of the corn.

Then the path grew broader and they walked abreast, he said sudden, but quiet, *You're Cis Brown from Mac-Dougall's shop aren't you?* Cis said *Yes,* not asking his name, he could tell her if he liked, but she wasn't to ask. But he didn't tell, just loped by her side, long-legged, like a deer or a calf, she thought, leggy and quick and quiet. They heard as they passed in that cool, quiet hour the scratch of the partridges up in the moor, once a dim shape started away from a fence with a thunderous clop of hooves in the dark, a Meiklebogs horse that their footsteps had feared.

Syne they came to the edge of the moor, it was dark,

here the moon shone through the branched horns of the
broom, the whins tickled your legs and Cis for a while
couldn't find her way till the boy said *Wait. I know this
place, I often come here.* And his hand found hers and
she felt in his palm the callouses worn by the spindles
there, he'd some smell of the jute about him as well, as
had all the spinner folk of the mills.

Water gleamed under the moon in a pool. Cis stopped
to breathe and the boy did the same, she saw him half
turn round in the moonlight and felt suddenly frightened
of all kinds of things—only a minute, frightened and curious, quick-strung all at once, what would he do?

But he did not a thing but again take her hand, still
saying nothing, and they went through the moor, the low
smoulder of Segget was suddenly below them, and below
their feet sudden the ring of the road. She took her hand
out of his then. So they went past the Memorial up through
The Close to the door of the house of MacDougall Brown;
and Cis stopped and the boy did the same, and she knew
him, remembered him, his name was Dod Cronin. And
he looked at her, and looked away again; and again, as
on the moor, queer and sweet, something troubled her,
she had never felt it before for a soul—compassion and
an urgent shyness commingled, sixteen herself and he
about the same, daft and silly to feel anything like this!
He slipped his hand slow up her bare arm, shy himself,
he said something, she didn't know what. She saw him
flush as she didn't answer, he was feared, the leggy deer
of a loon!

And she knew at once the thing he had asked. She put up
her hand to the hand on her arm, and next minute she
found she was being kissed with lips as shy, unaccustomed
as hers. And a minute after she was inside the door of
MacDougall's shop, and had the door closed, and stood
quivering and quivering alone in the dark, wanting to laugh
and wanting to cry, and wanting this minute to last forever.

Else Queen of the Manse had held home with Dalziel.
As they gained the road he turned round and said, with
a canny glance back to where folk were fighting: *Would
you like to come ben the way for some tea?* Else was still
in a rage, she didn't know why, or with whom, or how
it began, so she snapped: *No, I wouldn't, then. Do you
know what the hour is?* Meiklebogs looked shy-like—she

knew that he did, she could guess the soft-like look on his face, she felt half inclined to take it a clout—and said: *Oh ay, but I thought that maybe you would like to slocken up after the dancing about.*

She might as well do as the old fool said, even though there'd be no one else at Meiklebogs. Oh ay, she had heard the gossip of Segget, about Dalziel and his various housekeepers, though he did his own cooking now, as folk knew: It was said that two hadn't bidden a night, two others had come to the Meiklebogs alone and left in their due time, each with a bairn, a little bit present from the shy Meiklebogs. Well, that didn't vex Else, the stories were lies, old Meiklebogs—he was over shy ever to find out what a woman was like, unless it was out of a picture book, maybe: and even then it was like he would blush the few remaining hairs from his head. And even were there something in the Segget gossip she'd like to see the creature alive that would take advantage of *her*—just let him.

So she nodded, *All right, I'll come for a cup.* Meiklebogs said *Grand,* and the two went on, the moon was behind them, in front was the smell from the coles out still in the hayfield, tall, they'd had a fine crop that year of the hay. As they came near the house there rose a great barking and, Meiklebogs' meikle collie came out, Meiklebogs cried *Heel!* and the beast drew in, wurring and sniffing as they passed through the close. In the kitchen 'twas dark and close as a cave, the window fast-snecked, the fire a low glow. Meiklebogs lit a candle, *Sit down, will you, Else? I'll blow up the fire and put on the kettle.*

So he did, and Else took off her hat, and sat down and looked at the dusty old kitchen, with its floor of cement and its eight-day clock, ticking with a hirpling tick by the wall; and the photo of Lord Kitchener that everyone had heard of, over the fireplace, a dour-looking childe. 'Twas back in the War-years that Meiklebogs had got it, he'd cycled a Sunday over to Banchory, to a cousin of his there, an old woman-body; and she'd had the photo new-bought at a shop. Well, Meiklebogs had fair admired the fine thing, he thought it right bonny and said that so often that the woman-body cousin said at last he could have it. But it was over-big to be carried in his pouch, and the evening had come down with a spleiter of rain. But that didn't bog Meiklebogs, faith, no! He took off his jacket and tied the

damn thing over his shoulder with a length of tow; and
syne he put on his jacket above it. And the cousin looked
on, and nodded her head: *Ay, the old devil's been in a
pickle queer places. But I'm thinking that's the queerest
he's ever been in.*

The dresser was as thick with dust as a desert, Else bent
in the light of the candle above it, and wrote her name
there, and Dalziel smiled shy. *Will you get down two cups
from the hooks up there?*

Else did, and brought saucers as well, he gleyed at them:
Faith, I don't use them. I'm not gentry, like. Else said:
Oh, aren't you? Well I am.

He poured the tea out and sat down to drink it. And
faith! he found a good use for his saucer, he poured the
tea in it and drank that way, every now and then casting a
sly look at Else as though he were a mouse and she was
the cheese. But she didn't care, leaning back in her chair,
she was tired and she wondered why she'd come here, with
this silly old mucker and his silly looks; and why Charlie
had made such a fool of himself. Meiklebogs took another
bit look at her then, she watched him, and then he looked
at the window, and then he put out a hand, canny, on to
her knee.

It was more than the hand, a minute after that, he louped
on her as a crawly beast loups, something all hair and
scales from the wall; or a black old monkey; she bashed
him hard, right in the eye, just once, then he had her. She
had thought she was strong, but she wasn't, in a minute
they had struggled half-way to the great box bed. She
saw once his face in the light of the candle, and that made
her near sick and she loosed her grip, he looked just as
ever, canny and shy, though his hands upon her were like
iron clamps. She cried *You're tearing my frock,* he half-
loosed her, he looked shy as ever, but he breathed like a
beast.

Ah well, we'll take the bit thing off, Else.

Robert had gone to moil at his sermon: Chris heard the
bang of the door upstairs. Ewan was in bed and already
asleep, hours yet she supposed ere Robert came down. The
kitchen gleamed in the light of the moon, bright clean and
polished, with the stove a glow, she looked at that and
looked at herself, and felt what she hoped wasn't plain

to be seen, sticky and warm with the Segget Show. She'd have a bath ere she went to bed.

The stove's red eye winked as she opened the flue, and raked in the embers and set in fresh sticks; and on these piled coals and closed up the flue. In a little she heard the crack of the sticks, and went up the stairs to her room and Robert's, and took off her dress and took off her shoes, not lighting a light; the moon was enough. The mahogany furniture rose-red around, coloured in the moonlight, the bed a white sea, she sat on the edge and looked out at Segget, a ghostly place, quiet, except now and again with a bray of laughter borne on the wind as the door of the Arms opened and closed. Far down in the west, pale in the moon, there kindled a star that she did not know.

She stood up and went over and looked in the glass, and suddenly shivered, cold after the dancing; and drew the curtains and lighted the lamp, and took off her clothes in front of that other who watched, and moved in the mirror's mere. She saw herself tall, taller than of old, lithe and slim still with the brown V-shape down to the place between her breasts, she could follow the lines of the V with her finger. And she saw her face, high cheek-boned and bronze, quiet and still with the mask of the years, her mouth too wide but she liked her teeth, she saw them now as she smiled at the thought her mouth was too wide! She loosed the pins in her hair and it fell, down to her knees, tickling her shoulders, faith! it was worse than a mane, a blanket, she'd cut it one day, if Robert would let her. She caught it aside and suddenly remembered a thing she'd forgot, forgotten for years, and looked for the dimple she once had had, and found it, there still, and saw her face flush faint as she minded, now that she thought of the thing at all, she'd been told that first night two years ago that the dimple was there——

Funny and queer that you were with a man! You did this and that and you lay in his bed, there wasn't a thing of you he might not know, or you of him, from the first to the last. And you could speak of these things with him, and be glad, glad to be alive and be his, and sleep with your head in his shoulder's nook, tickling his chin, you supposed, with your hair—you could do all that and blush at the memory of a daft thing said on your wedding night!

Then she remembered she'd wanted a bath. She seemed

to have stood there dreaming for hours, and found her
dressing-gown and her slippers, and went down the stairs
and turned on the taps. The water came gurgling out with
a steam, she saw her face in the shaving-glass, and stared
at it—something happening tonight?

She splashed for a little thinking of that, the water
about her stung quick at first; she saw herself fore-short-
ened and fragile, but fair enough still, so she supposed—
yes, she would think that if she were a man! She lifted an
arm and the water ran down it, little pellets, they nested
under her cheek; and 'twas then she thought of the thing
she would do. Yes, she would do it this very night! . . .
And because that wouldn't bear thinking about, here, she
splashed herself and got out, Robert's mirror blinded in
a cloud of steam. She opened the bathroom door and listened, there was no one to hear or see for this once, she
caught up her gear and ran quick up the stairs, in the
moving pattern of splashed moonlight high from the window set in the gable, and gave a gasp as she felt a hand
on her shoulder, the arm came tight, she was kissed. Robert
coming down had seen the light splash as she opened the
bathroom door.

She struggled away, *I've no clothes on!*

He said that he'd half suspected that, teasing her a
minute, then let her go. Then he said he'd go down and
get ready their supper, and went lightly down the stairs
as a lad, it was Chris who now stood still and looked down,
high in her breast her heart beating fast. She would, and
this very night she would, in spite of what he had told
her and taught her!

She dressed and went down through the quiet of the
Manse, Robert popped his fair pow round the edge of
the door, *Supper in the kitchen, or shall we be grand?* She
said she would like the kitchen as well and pushed him into
a chair as she spoke, and took off Else's apron he'd draped
on his trousers, and set to the making of supper herself.
He sighed and stretched out and lighted his pipe, and drew
at it, looking out of the window. *There's something in the
night—or is it in you?* He stood up and walked to the window and peered, and came back and looked at Chris for
a while; and put out a finger upon her forearm. *Funny to
think that was once monkey-hair!*

She said that it wasn't, whatever his ancestors had been,
hers were decent, like Hairy Hogg's, hers (they'd both

heard the story). Robert chuckled over that as he sat
down again, the only result of his sermon so far to drop
a blot on the Provost's escutcheon. Hopeless, the Provost,
and most of the others, Geddes, poor chap, had mislaid
his guts; but he'd form that Segget League even yet, wait
till this young Stephen Mowat came home!

Chris asked when that was but Robert didn't know, he
thought very soon, then grew puzzled again. *Funny, there
really Is something about,* and Chris said, *Maybe,* and
keeked at him sly, as he sat there and puzzled, and restrained herself from suddenly and daftly cuddling him
tight. When she opened the kitchen window wide there
came a faint scent on the tide of the wind, from the garden,
the jonquils and marigolds glowed faint and pale in the
light of the moon.

Then Chris set the table and they both sat down, it
was fine to work in her kitchen untrammelled, good though
Else was as a general rule, if it wasn't for the fact that
the Manse was so big they could have done well without
a maid here. She said that to Robert, he said *Yes, I know,
I feel that way myself—for tonight! As though I could turn
our Segget myself into Augustine's City of Gold. . . .
Something in the night that's making us like this,* and
stopped and stared, *Why, Chris, you look different!*

She said he was silly—or 'twas maybe the bath! Then
she felt herself colour with his eyes upon her. He shook
his head, *An unusual bath!——A mental one? They're uncommon in Segget.*

He said *That's the first time I've ever heard you bitter,*
and she said she didn't feel bitter, she was fine; and they
washed up and dried in the moonlight quiet, together and
content and yet more than that, once he brushed her
shoulder as he went to and fro, carrying the dishes over
to the dresser; and he stopped and scowled, sore-puzzled
upon her, *It must be that monkey-hair that's electric!*

And then they had finished and a mood came on Chris.
Let's go out in the garden. And they both went out in
the honey-dark shadows that the hedgerow threw, warm,
a little mist crept up from Segget, under the nets in the
strawberry patches the berries were bending their heads
full ripe, Chris knelt by a bed and found one that was
big, and ate half herself, Robert the other, seeing it waiting
there on her lips. And, as he laughed and kissed her for
that, something caught them both to a silence, foolish and

quiet by the strawberry beds. The rooks chirped drowsily
up in the yews as they passed beneath to the sheltered wall
where love-in-a-mist and forget-me-nots bloomed blue and
soft even now in the night, under the wall that led to the
kirkyard, just low enough for Chris to look over.

And so for a little she stopped and looked, that third
Chris holding her body a while, how strange it was she
stood here by Robert, so close that the warmth of his body
warmed hers—when in such a short time she would die
down there on a bit of land as deserted and left. They were
gone, they were quiet, and the tears that were shed and
the folk that came and the words that were said, were
scattered and gone and they left in peace, finished and
ended and all put by, the smell for them of forget-me-nots
and the taste of a strawberry eaten at night and the kiss
of lips that were hard and kind, and the thoughts of men
that had held them in love and wondered upon them and
believed in God.

All that had gone by, now under the gold of the moon
the grass rose from those bodies that mouldered in Segget,
the curlews were calling up in the Kaimes, the hay lay in
scented swathes in the parks, night wheeled to morning
in a thousand rooms where the blood that they'd passed
to other bodies circled in sleep, unknowing its debt. Nothing else they had left, they had come from the dark as
the dustmotes come, sailing and golden in a shaft of the
sun, they went by like the sailing motes to the dark; and
the thing had ended, and you knew it was so, that so it
would be with you in the end. And yet—and yet—you
couldn't believe it!

Robert teased. *Choosing a place for your coffin?* and
Chris said *Just that, but don't plant me deep,* and he said
with a queer sudden fear in his voice, he startled Chris
and she turned to look, *Lord God, how I'd hate to be
'planted' myself! If I die before you, Christine, see to that,
that I'm sent for burning to a crematorium. I'd hate to be
remembered once I am dead.* Chris thought in a flash how
Segget would take it, should he die and she get him a
funeral like that, *They'd say, most likely, that I'd poisoned
you, Robert, and were trying to get rid of the evidence,
you know.* He laughed, *So they would!* and then laughed
again, a second laugh that was dreary, Chris thought. *My
God, were there ever folk like the Scots! Not only THEM
—you and I are as bad. Murderous gossip passed on as*

sheer gospel, though liars and listeners both know it is a lie. Lairds, ladies, or plain Jock Muck at the Mains—they'd gossip the heart from Christ if He came, and impute a dodge for popularising timber when He was crucified again on His cross!

Chris said *That's true, and yet it is not. They would feed Christ hungry and attend to His hurts with no thought of reward their attendance might bring. Kind, they're so kind. . . . And the lies they would tell about how He came by those hurts of His——*

And yet you don't believe in a God. I've never asked you, but do you, Chris?

She bent her head as she answered, *No,* not looking at him; but his laugh was kind. *You will sometime, however you find Him.*

Then he looked at his watch, it was nearly midnight; and suddenly Chris forgot the sad things. She ran away from him and he came after, playing hide and seek, daft bairns both, in the play and wisp of the moonlight's flow, till Chris lost breath and he caught her up: and she suddenly yawned and he said, *Bedtime.* And Chris minded now the thing she had planned, and lingered a minute behind his step, shy as a bride to go with him.

The room was in shadow, for the moon had veered, Robert moved about quiet and lighted the lamp, his close-cropped hair lay smooth on his head till his clothes ruffled it up as he pulled them off. He looked over at Chris, *I'm not sleepy at all.* And said in that voice that he sometimes used *You look very sweet, Christine, tonight. Did you know?*

She reached up then and put out the light, and changed in the dark though he laughed and asked why. She answered nothing, slipping in beside him between the cool sheets; and lying so, still, she heard her heart hammer.

He lay quiet as well, then the curtain flapped and bellied in the breeze and you saw like a shadow the smile on his face, it was turned to you and you turned to him; and he said in a minute, *Why, Christine!* solemn, and his hands came firmly under your chin to hold you so and to kiss you, stern. And you knew that you stood on the brink of that sea that was neither charted nor plumbed by men, that sea-shore only women had known, dark with its sailing red lights of storms, where only the feet of women had trod, hearing the thunder of the sea in their ears as they gathered the fruit on that waste, wild shore . . .

So: and his lips were in yours, and they altered, and you were gladder than you'd been for years, your arm went round his bared shoulder quick . . . and suddenly you were lying as rigid as death. Robert said, *Tired out, after all, Christine?*

For months after that she remembered that moment, her voice hadn't come from her lips for a minute; then she said, *Just a bit,* and heard him draw breath, and she said again, soft *Not TOO tired, Robert,* and had set her teeth fast after that, for an age, the thunder of that sea cut off by a wall, as she herself was, by a wall of fire; but she said not a word of either of these, stroked his hair where it clung to his brow; and he put his head on her breast and slept, after a while: and the house grew still.

She'd sleep soon herself, she'd put that damn dream by, the dream of a bairn fathered by Robert—not now, maybe never, but she could not tonight, not with memory of that scar that was torn across the shoulder of this living body beside her, the scar that a fragment of shrapnel had torn —but a little lower it would have torn his body, grunting, into a mesh of blood, with broken bones and with spouting blood, an animal mouthing in mindless torment. And she'd set herself to conceive a child—for the next War that came, to be torn like that, made blood and pulp as they'd made of Ewan—*Oh, Ewan, Ewan, that was once my lad, that lay where this stranger's lying the night, I haven't forgotten, I haven't forgotten, you've a Chris that lies with you there in France, and she shan't bring to birth from her womb any bairn to die as you for a madman's gab. . . .*

Quiet, oh, quiet, greet soft lest he wake, who's so kind and dear, who's so far from you now. But you'll never have a bairn of his for torment, to be mocked by memorials, the gabblings of clowns, when they that remained at home go out to praise the dead on Armistice Day.

Faith, when it came there was more to remember in Segget that year than Armistice only. There was better kittle in the story of what happened to Jim the Sourock on Armistice Eve. He was aye sore troubled with his stomach, Jim, he'd twist his face as he'd hand you a dram, and a man would nearly lose nerve as he looked—had you given the creature a bad shilling, or what? But syne he would rub his hand slow on his wame, *It's the pains in my breast that I've gotten again;* and he said that they fairly were awful sometimes, like a meikle worm moving and wriggling in there. Folk said he fair did his best to drown it, and God! that was true, the foul brute would go home, near every night as drunk as a toff, and fall in the bed by the side of his wife, she'd say *You coarse brute, you've come drunken again;* but he'd only groan, with his hand at his stomach, the worm on the wriggle like a damned sea-serpent.

Well, the Sourock and his mistress kept a pig, and the night of November the tenth Dite Peat closed up his shop and came over to kill it. He fair was a hand at a killing, was Dite, and the pig looked over its ree as he came, and knew fine what the knife and axe were for. So it started to scraich, and Dite grinned at the brute, *Wait a minute, my mannie, I'll let that scraich out.* And the Sourock's wife, that was standing by, felt queer as she saw that look on his face, she thought him a tink, but he fair could kill, not useless entirely like that gawpus Jim.

So she asked Dite in for a dram ere he started, and down he sat with his dram and his cake, and he drank down the one like a calf with its milk and ate up the cake like a famished dog. Syne he said it was over late tonight to cut up the beast out there in the ree, he'd come over the morn and see to that, Armistice Day would be a fine time to do a bit cutting about among flesh—*Fegs, mistress, I've seen humans carved up like pigs, like bits of beef in a butcher's shop, and it fair looked fine, as I often thought, you couldn't wonder at those cannibal childes——*

The Sourock's wife asked if he'd like to see her sick, Dite said, *Be sick as you like, I won't mind; you've an uneasy stomach for a potman's wife.* And she broke down and grat then and said what a fool she had been to marry a creature like Jim, her that was a decent bit parlourmaid once, with her wages her own and her fine new clothes, Jim had sworn in those days he was fair tee-tee, now he drank like a drain and stank like one, too, he wouldn't care a fig though he came of a night and found her lying dead in her bed. Dite thought, *B'God, if he'd sense he'd dance!* but he didn't say that, he didn't care a damn for the Sourock's wife, or the Sourock's troubles, why should you care about any man's troubles, there were damn the few that had cared for yours—not that you'd asked them, you could manage them fine.

So he rose up and said, *Well then, I'll go out and have a bit play with that beast in the ree.*

She asked if he'd manage the thing by himself, she was off for the night to her sister in Fordoun, soon's she'd laid his supper for the Sourock, not that she supposed the sot would eat it, he'd come home and just stiter to his bed, as usual. Dite said he would manage fine on his own, and went out, and the Sourock's wife a bit later heard the grunt of the pig turn into a scream, nasty to hear, and then it came shrill, and she put on her hat and took her bit bag and went out and down by the ree as she went, not wanting to look and see Dite at his work of killing her pig for the winter dinners. But something drew her eyes in over the ree, there was Dite Peat, he was covered with sharn, he'd tripped in a rush he had made at the pig, now he'd cornered it up at the back of the ree. Its mouth was open and its bristles on end, and it whistled through its open jaws like the sound of the steam from an engine in Segget station.

So she didn't look longer, went hurrying on, it had been a fine beast, the pig, she remembered, would stand on its trough with a pleased-like grumph as she scratched the bristles on its back and lugs, fair a couthy beast, though scared at the rats, it had once near tripped her as she stood in its ree, she thought the creature was aiming at her: but instead it had caught a glimpse of a rat and was trying to get behind her for safety. So she turned the corner by Moultrie's shop and heard up in Segget the pig scream again, and she found herself hoast, like a fool of a bairn, with water in the nose—where was her hanky? And she suddenly thought of Dite Peat as a rat, a great rat with its underhung jaw and cruel eyes, creeping on the pig that was frightened at rats and had run once frightened to hide behind her—och, she was daft or soft or just both, and damn it! she couldn't get at her hanky.

But Dite had cornered Jim's pig at last, as it swithered its head he saw it set fine, and swung the bit axe, the blade of it up, the pig screamed again and fell at his feet with a trickle of blood from its snout and its trotters scraping and tearing at the sharn of the ree. So Dite turned the brute over, slow, with his axe, and took out his knife and cut its throat, slow, and held the throat open to let it bleed well. Syne he slung it on his shoulder and took it to the kitchen, and hung it on a hook and left it to drip.

It was fell dark then, as he slung the brute up, its flesh was still warm, and it minded him well of the bits of folk that a shell would fling Feuch! in your face with a smell of sharn, out in the War—He had liked it fine; there was something in blood and a howling of fear that kittled up a man as nothing else could. So he left the pig to drip in the dark, and it moved quick once, when the sinews relaxed, and Dite gave a laugh and gave it a slap.

'Twas near to ten when he took a bit dander back again to the Sourock's house, a blatter of rain was dinging on Segget, sweeping and seeping up over the Howe, lying at night on the winter's edge with its harvests in, potato-crops with dripping shaws in the rigs of red clay. Dite pulled down his cap and lifted the sneck and went into the house of Jim the Sourock. He cracked a match and looked at the pig, it was getting on fine, had near finished to drip, he would leave it now till the morn's night. And then—he was aye a coarse brute, was Dite Peat, though you couldn't but laugh when you heard the tale—a grand idea came into his head, and he sat down and thought it all out and syne laughed, and took down the pig he had killed from its hook and slung it over his shoulder and went ben to the bed the Sourocks slept in, a great box-bed that was half-covered in.

Dite threw back the blankets and put the pig down, the near the side of the bed where Sourock's wife slept—all the wives of Segget slept at the front, a woman aye sleeps at the front of the bed where she can get quicker out than a man, that's sense, for the lighting of the morning fire or getting up in the dark to be sick, as a woman will, when she's carrying a bairn, and not disturbing her man from his rest.

So Dite dumped down the pig in the bed, and covered it up, careful and canny. And he took a bit dander up through Segget, to freshen himself, as he said, for the night; and syne he went home, for he was fell tired.

'Twas an hour or so later ere the Sourock came home, he'd had to clear up the bar in the Arms, and lock the doors and hand over the silver, and stoke up a fire for a traveller childe that was spending the night in the Arms' best room. What with one thing and another that night, the drinks he had ta'en and the heat of the Arms, Jim came through Segget with a head fair spinning. As he crossed the Square he keeked at the angel, and damn't! there were

two of the things up there, he stared at them fairly stern
for a while; not decent for angels to cuddle like that. But
then he decided he was fell drunk, and shook his head,
two angels still there, and went slithering up through the
lurching East Wynd.

Well, he got home at last through the drift of the rain,
there was hardly a light to be seen in Segget, it cuddled up
close in its beds and slept, with its goodmen turned to
the wall and its wives wearied with a day of bairns and
of claik, the bairns lying three-four in a bed, though five
or six among the tink spinners, they bred like lice and
they slept like them, too, Ake Ogilvie said—an ill bit speak,
a man couldn't help the bairns that came, sometimes a
woman was just of the kind that would take if you gave
her no more than a squeeze, the next was cannier: you just
couldn't tell.

Well, Jim the Sourock had been lucky so far, a fell
good thing, one Sourock enough; but he wasn't thinking
that or aught else, for a while he couldn't lay hands on his
sneck. But he got it at last and let himself in, and sat down
on the chair that stood by the door, and gave a great
paich and rubbed at his middle.

Syne he loosened his boots, not bothering with a lamp,
he knew better than that, he might fire the damned house;
so he got his boots off and left them lie there, and made for
the bedroom, holding to the wall, he would know the way
in his sleep by now. Then the first thing happened that
jaggered his night, his knees went bang 'gainst the side of a
tub; he tumbled half-way into the tub, the bottom was full
of some sticky soss, the Sourock swore and lurched up to his
feet and wiped his hands on the seat of his breeks, he supposed that the wife had been washing fell late—the careless bitch to leave the tub there!

Well, he edged round about it and got to the door, and
stitered inside and grumbled out loud, *Do you know you've
near broken my neck, eh, woman?*

His wife said nothing, that wasn't surprising, considering that she was a five miles off. But the Sourock had forgotten all about that, he went shoggling and stitering about
the room, pulling off his breeks and his socks, nothing else,
he aye slept in his drawers and kept fine and warm. Syne
he made for the bed and went in by the foot, his left hand
on the hump he took for his wife. So he pushed back the
blankets and got in below, and felt about with his feet a

while to lay them on his wife and get himself warm. But
damn the warmth could he find the night, so he reached
out to give the creature a joggle—*Jean, are you wake?*

Well, the hump said nothing and the Sourock by then
had his head a bit cleared through the fall in the tub. And
he felt in a rage—*Here, answer me, can't you? What's
wrong with the like of you, eh, the night?* And he put his
hand under the blankets to feel her, so he did, and nearly
shot out of the bed. *Jean—God, Jean, but you're awful
cold!*

She said nothing at all and he sudden felt ill. He put out
his hand, she was cold as a stone—worse than that, the hair
frozen hard on her skin, the Sourock was dribbling and
yammering by then. *Jean, Jean, waken up; you're near
frozen stiff!* And at last he could bear the thing no longer,
and got from his bed and found a match and lighted it up
and pulled back the blanket. And he saw a great gaping
throat in the light, and the spunk went out, his yell maybe
blew it.

That was the story he'd tell to folk. For the rest, you
gathered he pulled himself together, and went out to get
some body go for the doctor: he was maybe a bit fuddled,
but he knew what he wanted and was keeping quite calm,
or so he would swear. That maybe was so and maybe it
wasn't, 'twas strange anyway if he felt like that, that when
Peter Peat heard a bellow and yammer and somebody beat
on the door of his house like the angel of God on the
Judgement Day—and Peter got from his bed and looked
out, there was no angel but Jim the Sourock, in his sark,
with no boots or breeks on either, his face and neck all
covered with blood. And he yammered in the light of Peter
Peat's candle—*Let's in, Peter Peat. Oh, God, let me in!*

But Peter wasn't near such a fool as do that. *Go home to
your bed,* he said, *and keep quiet. Is this a time to disturb
decent folk? Go home and sleep by your good-wife's side*—
And he couldn't say more, the creature of a Sourock was
fairly daft, he decided, for he yelped like a dog hard-
kicked, and vanished from the range of Peter Peat's eyes;
and Peter closed down the window and went back, canty,
to sleep by his meikle wife's side, like a calf cuddling up to
a haystack, folk said.

The Sourock was fair demented by then, he tried the
house of old Hairy Hogg, and the Provost came down and
keeked through the slit that was set in the door for letters,

fair gentry. And the Sourock cried *Let me in, oh, I'm
feared.* And old Hogg said *In? To your sty, you drunkard!
You're a fair disgrace to Scotland and Segget. Go home
like a decent man to your wife.* The Sourock vanished so
quickly at that that the Provost was fair convinced he'd
obeyed—ay, there still were folk had the power to rule,
them that came of the Burns' blood.

Well, where do you think that Jim ended up? Down in
the house of MacDougall Brown. MacDougall let him in
and heard his bit story. Cis got from her bed and came
down to hear. MacDougall cried on her to go back, but
she wouldn't, she said *All right, I won't look*—not decent
for a lassie to look on a man when he hadn't on breeks, or
not at least till she'd married one herself, syne she'd think,
said Ake Ogilvie, his breeks fair the best bit of the bargain,
and the Scythian childe that invented the things the greatest
benefactor of the human race.

Well, Cis boiled some water to wash the Sourock, and
MacDougall, it fair must have been a sore wrench, made
tea for the creature and he drank it up, and his stomach
for once didn't turn at the taste. And he felt a bit better
and washed his foul neck, telling how his wife lay with
her throat cut out. MacDougall said, *Ay, she has met the
Lord, as you yourself one day must do. Repent and come
to the arms of Jesus*—that's what he'd planned from the
first, you gathered. Well, the Sourock said that he would,
by God, he'd fair be tee-tee from that minute, he would;
and MacDougall was pleased as punch and near kissed
him, he was awful fond of bringing souls to God, was Mac-
Dougall, and threatening the souls with the pains of hell if
they traded at any other shop but his.

So he loaned a pair of his breeks to the Sourock, and
out the pair of them went together, and went canny up to
the Sourock's house and ben to the room where the red
corpse lay, MacDougall carrying the lantern he'd lit. And
he lifted the lantern and glowered at the thing that was
lying there in the Sourock's bed, and cried *Hoots, man, this
is no the mistress* and pulled back the blankets and showed
Jim the pig. And the Sourock glowered at it, *Well, then,
I'm damned. Man, but it fair looked her image to me.*

They were into Armistice Day by then, though neither
MacDougall nor the Sourock cared, they shifted the pig
and went to their beds, the rain held on through the night,

and morning came soaking laired across the clay parks, the parks that begirdle Segget in red, in a wheep of gulls driven in from the coast, if you drove into Segget that day you'd have seen enough glaur around to make you believe the tale that they never took a good wash in Segget till the harvest was over and the bills all paid. That was no more than a speak, you knew, but it made a fine hit at the Segget folk, them so damned proud of their Burgh and Kaimes, and their new bit kirk that hadn't a steeple, not so proud of their mills and the spinners that made up the most of their population. And faith, by the time Armistice was out, it was less proud than ever of its spinners, Segget.

The day had cleared by eleven o'clock, and folk came taiking in round the angel that stood so bonny in Segget Square. Ay, fairly a gey bit gathering, impressive—except for the smell, Ake Ogilvie said. But he aye was sneering something like that, the coarse brute, why couldn't he let folk a-be? And you saw him there in the midst of the lave, with his medals pinned on his waistcoat flap, and his hands in his pockets, looking at the angel as though he wouldn't sleep with the lass though she tried to come down and crawl into his bed.

Sim Leslie, the bobby, that folk called Feet, tried to form a half-circle here, the Provost to the right, all hair and horns, with his popping bit eyes and his ancestor Burns, he was telling how Burns was a patriot childe, aye ready to shed his blood for the land. Ake Ogilvie said *Ay. He slew a fell lot of the French—with his mouth. He was better at raping a servant quean than facing the enemy with a musket.* And Hairy Hogg said that was a foul slander, Ogilvie mad with jealousy, just because the dirt that he wrote himself was worse than dirt, compared with the Bard; and Ake said he'd rather be just plain dirt than slush on a dung-heap, disguised as a flower; and young Alec Hogg, that was home from Elinburgh, cried *Cannot you leave my father alone?*

Ake looked him up and down with a long, cold stare. *I never touch dung except with a fork, but give's none of your lip, or I'll break my rule.* Alec Hogg cried *Try it!* and maybe in a minute there would have been a fine bit fight on the go, right there by the angel in Segget Square, folk round about looking shocked as could be and edging nearer for a better look, when they saw the minister coming from

East Wynd, and the choir coming with him; and folk cried, *Wheest!*

'Twas him, the minister, that had started the thing and had you all out in the Square today, old Greig, that filled the pulpit afore him, hadn't bothered to hold any service at all, he'd over-much sense to catch cold in the Square. But the Reverend Mr. Colquohoun was fell keen, he'd bad-gered folk to close up their shops and gotten the mills to close down as well, he fair was a go-ahead billy, like, though some folk said he was more than that, he'd barely started interfering yet. 'Twas said he'd already the kirk session against him, with his preaching for this and that daft-like reform; and he'd badgered Hairy Hogg near from his wits—or what little wits were left the old Provost—about the town council and where it might meet, and what it could do, and who were the members, and why didn't they light Segget at night, did they know the drains in West Wynd were bad, when were the mills inspected and how? . . . Folk said the next thing you'd find him keen on would be shifting the Kaimes for a seat in his yard, ay, if the creature went on at this rate he'd soon have all Segget on his hands to fight.

A raw wind blew down the Howe through the Square and fluttered the minister's robes as he prayed, his thin white face down-bent as he prayed, his prayer just said in an ordinary voice. It made a man kind of uneasy to hear the way that he spoke to God like that—not as any other ministers would do, as though they'd only half-swallowed their dinners and had the remainder still in their throats.

No, no, the Reverend Colquohoun spoke plain, some liked it that way, you were damned if you did: and he asked the mercy of God on a world unawakened yet from a night that was past. And he said that God had made neither night nor day in human history, He'd left it in the hands of Man to make both, God was but Helper, was but Man himself, like men he also struggled against evil, God's wounds had bled, God also had died in the holocaust in the fields of France. But He rose anew, Man rose anew, he was as undying as God was undying—if he had the will and the way to live, on this planet given to him by God. *A pillar of cloud by day and a pillar of fire by night*—they had hung in the sky since the coming of men, set there by God for the standards of men, clouds and the shining stan-dards of rain, the hosts of heaven for our standard by night . . . A trumpet had cried and unsealed our ears; would it need the lightning to unseal our eyes?

And after a bit you stopped listening to that, you didn't know much about preaching and the like, but was that the way a minister should speak? You were damned if you thought so: fair heathen it sounded. And you took a canny bit keek round about, at the throng of the Segget folk that were there—hardly a spinner, where were the dirt? There was Mrs. Colquohoun, anyway, bonny in a way, with a sulky-life face, a common bit quean the minister had wifed, folk that had known her well in Kinraddie said she had once been as blithe as bonny; but now she was altered out of all manner, if they met her and spoke to her and cried, *Chris!* she would smile and speak and be friends enough, but different somehow—ay, she'd grown damned proud.

Well, there she was, and her son as well, the son of her first bit man you had heard, with a cool, dark face, but not a bad bairn. Nearby was the Provost and next him his son, the Fasher, rigged out in his baggy breeks. MacDougall Brown was well to the fore, not that he'd fought in the War, but he'd sung; and Peter Peat, the tailor, a terrible patriot; and Dite, the foul tink; and Dominie Geddes, and the three women teachers; and the porters and stationy, Smithie and Ake. Will Melvin you could see near the Station folk, John Muir and Bruce and a birn of the like. Syne the minister held up his hand for quiet, and you knew that it was eleven o'clock.

And faith! The quiet would have been fell solemn, but for a great car that came swishing up, from the south, and turned, and went up East Wynd. Folk had stood still like stooks of rags, but they moved then and stared at the thing go by—all but the minister, he stood like a stone. Then he said, low and clear, *We will now sing the hymn 'Our God, our help in ages past.'*

You cleared your throat and looked right and left, felt shy to be such a fool as stand there and sing without a bit organ to help; and the first few words were a kind of growl till you heard the minister himself sing up. And just as folk were getting in the swing, the dirt of spinners came down to the Square.

They came marching down through the Close from West Wynd, a twenty or thirty of the ill-getted creatures, with their mufflers on, not in decent collars, their washy faces

crinkled with grins, marching along there four by four. In
front of the lot was that tink John Cronin, and over his
shoulder he carried a red flag, and the spinners behind him
were laughing and joking, two-three of them women, the
shameful slummocks. Well, your mouth fell open, as it
damn well might, you had never yet seen such a sight in
Segget; and you stopped your singing, and so did some
more, and some after that, till the only folk left were the
Reverend Colquohoun, and his wife, and Cis Brown, and
that gawpus Else Queen. And then Ake Ogilvie that hadn't
yet sung took a look round about and started to sing, as
loud as could be, as though he'd new-wakened; he did it
to be different from others as usual.

But afore folk could pipe up again to the thing the spinners were close and Jock Cronin cried *Halt!* And they
swung round about him and stood in a circle, and next
minute they'd started singing themselves, loud as could be
and fair drowning the hymn, a song about shrouding their
dead in red, and about their bit limbs being stiff and cold;
and God alone knows what kind of stite.

Well, that fairly finished the Memorial Service. The minister had turned as white as a sheet, he finished his singing
and so did his wife, here and there a man in the crowd
cried out, *Have you no manners?*—speaking to the spinners.
And Feet, the policeman, went over to them, *Now then,
you're causing a disturbance,* he said, he was awful proud
of that word, was Feet, that he'd got in a book on how
bobbies should speak. But they took no notice, just stood
round and sang, till he pushed through the ring round that
tink John Cronin; then they stopped and Cronin said *Well,
Feet, what's up?*

Feet was fair roused, a patriot-like childe, he hadn't been
out to the War himself, they wouldn't let him go with
feet like that in case he might block up the trenches, folk
said. But he'd fair been a one for the War all the same,
and he wasn't to see its memory insulted by a pack of
tink brutes that didn't wear collars—them and their song
about flinching and sneering from a scarlet standard and
God knows what. Who ever heard of a scarlet standard?—
Just a tink way of calling their betters bloody. . . . So he
said to Jock Cronin, *Aren't you black ashamed to break
in on the War Memorial service?* And Jock Cronin said
*No, we're not, you see, Feet, we all had a taste of the War
ourselves. Take a keek at our chests now, Feet my lad, and*

*then have a look at your own and see if there's anything
on it the like of on ours!*

And then you saw plain what he meant, he himself, and
all of the spinners that had marched to the Square, had War-
medals pinned on their jackets or waistcoats, they were all
of them men who had been to the War: except the three
women, and they wore medals sent on to them after their
folk were dead. Well, that fair staggered Feet, and you
felt sorry for him, especially as you had no medal yourself,
you hadn't been able to get to the War, you'd been over-
busy with the shop those years, or keeping the trade going
brisk in the Arms, or serving at Segget as the new stationmaster. And well you might warrant if the King had known
the kind of dirt that those spinners were he wouldn't have
lashed out as he'd done with his medals.

But Jock Cronin pushed his way past Feet, and jumped
on the pedestal under the angel, and cried out *Comrades—
not only mill folk, but others as well that I see down there:
WE went to the war, we know what it was, we went to
lice and dirt and damnation: and what have we got at the
end of it all? Starvation wages, no homes for heroes, the
capitalists fast on our necks as before. They're sacking men
at the mills just now and leaving them on the bureau to
starve—that's our reward, and maybe it's yours, that's the
thing we must mind today. Not to come here and remember
the dead, they've a place that's theirs, and we'll share it
some time, they're maybe the better compared with some
that live here in Segget worse-fed than beasts. It's the living that's our concern, you chaps. Come over and join us,
the Labour Party. You first, Mr. Colquohoun, you were
out there, you've sense.*

And as the impudent brute ended up he waved his hand
to the Reverend Colquohoun, and for a minute after that
there was such a quiet you could near have cut it and eaten
it in chunks, it was that damned solid, while all the folk
stared. Syne the minister just turned his back and said,
cool, *I think we'll go home, Chris,* to his wife; and she
nodded and said nothing, they were both cool and calm. It
made a man boil to see them so meek, damn't! if you had
been a minister, would you let yourself be insulted like
that? No, you wouldn't; and neither would any minister in
the days before the coming of the War, the War had fair
been a ruination, letting tinks like the Cronins find out
that their betters ate and smelt just the same as themselves.

Well, next there was near a fight broke out. Ake Ogilvie
cried to Jock Cronin, *Oh ay, and where the hell did YOU
serve in the War?* And Jock Cronin said *Up in the front,
my lad, not scrounging behind with the Royal Engineers.*
——*No, you hadn't enough brain for them you poor fool,*
Ake Ogilvie said, and would maybe have said more, if
the minister hadn't turned round and cried, *Ogilvie!* And
Ake went off, and the spinners all laughed. Some folk
stayed near to hear what they'd say, most decent bodies
went over to the Arms and spoke of the things they'd
have done to the spinners if they'd stayed behind in Segget
Square.

Chris ran nearly all the way from the Square, Mr.
Geddes and his teachers were coming for lunch (as they
called it, but they ate it just as a dinner); and the meat
was cooking in the Manse's oven. Else you could see flying
on in front, as anxious as you, you'd left Robert behind,
he'd laughed and slowed down and lighted his pipe. But
you ran up under the drip of the yews, through the Manse
front door and through to the kitchen, and there was Else
with her face like a fire, leaning panting up by the kitchen
back door, and a burning smell from the open oven. Else
cried *Well, I was just in time!* and pointed to the chicken
out in its ashet, it had just begun to burn at the top. And
you said *That was fine, you're a blessing, Else. Sit and rest
a minute.* Else took a look at herself in the glass, *I've a
face like that flag the spinners were carrying. Did you
ever see such nasty brutes?*

Chris said they hadn't much manners, she thought. But
she'd never before seen men with that flag, or heard them
singing the song about it—hirpling and sad, but it caught
you somehow, there was something in it that you knew was
half-true, true with a truth that drew your mind back to
Chae Strachan far in your younger days, who had said
the mission of the common folk was to die and give life
with their deaths forever. . . . Like Robert's God, in a way,
you supposed.

And maybe that was Robert's own thought, Chris came
on him in the sitting-room, standing and staring queerly
at Segget, harsh-blue, rain-driven, in its clouded noon.
Chris put up a hand on his shoulder. *Not vexed? The service was fine, and I liked what you said.* Robert squeezed
her hand, *My vanity's vexed. That's all, I suppose, and
those spinner chaps—a perfect devil if they're right, Chris-*

tine. Chris said *How right?* and he said *Their beliefs—a war of the classes to bring fruit to the War. Remember the Samson I preached that day I tried for the kirk of Segget, Christine? I suppose we saw him in the Square today, with a muffler on and a thin, starved look. If his betters won't mend the world, HE may!*

Then his gaze drew in, *Lord, here they come. His betters —well, well. They're just at the door.*

Chris herself went and opened the door, Mrs. Geddes came gushing in over the mat, Miss M'Askill behind, sharp as a needle, the second teacher at Segget school. She eyed Chris up and down as a ferret might, *How d'you do, Mrs. Colquohoun? Disgraceful exhibition down in the Square!* Chris had heard of Miss M'Askill from Else, straight as a pole and nearly as bare, and she wore her hair in two great plaits, low down on her brow, and it gave her a look like a stirk with its head in a birn of hay; and whenever she saw a new man in the toun she'd stare at him till the man would blush, up and down in the line of her stare; and she'd give a bit sniff (or so said Else), as much as to say *What, marriage with you?*

But damn the soul had offered that yet, not even for a night at the furthest gait, Ake Ogilvie had said he would rather sleep with a Highland steer in the lee of a whin. Chris tried hard not to remember that, she would laugh if she did: and so she did not, but shook hands instead with Miss Ferguson next, her that they called The Blusher in Segget. And she started to blush as though someone had couped a jar of red ink on her head at that minute, the blush came thicker and thicker each second, till Chris felt so sorry she blushed as well. Then Miss Jeannie Grant, dapper and trig, with a fresh, fair face, *Hello, Mrs. Colquohoun! What did you think of the fun in the Square?* Last, Mr. Geddes, he looked at you bitter, as though he thought you poor stuff like the most of mankind, and shook your hand limp, and trailed after the others, his hands in his pockets, till he tripped on a toy of Ewan's in the hall, a wooden horse, and it fell with a clatter and Ewan came running out to see why.

Mr. Geddes had nearly fallen with the thing. Now he picked it up, a great splinter of wood torn out of its side. Ewan said *What a fool, man, why didn't you look?* and Chris cried *Ewan!* Mr. Geddes grinned. *He's right enough,*

I suppose I'm a fool. I'm sorry, young man. Ewan said *So am I.*

Chris wanted to giggle, but again did not, instead looked solemn as a funeral, near—or two funerals if you counted one of John Muir's; and separated the Dominie and Ewan ere worse came; and shooed Mr. Geddes in after his wife.

Robert was there, he'd greeted them all, and was standing by with the sherry decanter. Mr. Geddes had lost the smile plucked out for Ewan, like a last swede plucked from a frozen field, he said bitter as ever, *A drop, Colquohoun,* and sat down and looked round the room as though he thought damn little of any thing in it.

And then Ewan started to sing outside, in the moment when folk were sipping their sherry; and Miss M'Askill near dropped her glass. Chris got to her feet and felt herself blush, silly to do that, and she called out *Ewan!* and he cried back *Yes?* and opened the door. And Chris felt a fool, the whole room looking at her. *Why were you singing that song just now?*

Ewan said, polite, *I like it, mother. I think it's a bloody fine song, don't you?*

Else saved the situation, as usual. They heard her feet in the hall, Ewan vanished, and the door was snibbed with a sudden click. Miss M'Askill said it was dreadful, dreadful, those spinners corrupting even the children. Didn't Mrs. Colquohoun think the authorities ought to take steps to putting it down?

Miss Jeannie Grant was sitting by Robert, showing a fine length of leg, nice leg, she said *What's 'it'? Put a stop to singing the Red Flag, do you mean?* And Miss M'Askill said, *Yes, that for one thing, there are plenty of others— the ongoings in general of those paid agitators.* And Miss Jeannie Grant said, *Well, I'm an agitator, but I get no pay. Where do the others get theirs? I'd like to apply!* And Miss M'Askill looked at her so awful, 'twas a wonder she didn't shrivel up there and then. But instead she just winked blithe at Chris, and drank up her sherry and had some more.

Syne they were all speaking of the scene in the Square, Geddes said bitter that the spinners had behaved as you would expect such cattle to do, neither better nor worse than other Scotch folk. All Scots were the same, the beastliest race ever let loose on the earth. Oh no, he wasn't bitter, he'd got over that, he'd got over living amongst them, even: their gossip that was fouler than the seepings of a drain, there was hardly a soul in a village like Segget but was a murderer ten times over in word—they hadn't enough courage to be it in deed. Spinners were no worse than the rest, or not much. As for this business of a Segget League, well, he voted Tory himself every time, and no league could remain non-political long. His advice: Colquhoun leave the lot alone, if there's anything a hog hates it's cleaning its sty.

Robert asked Miss Ferguson what she might think, Miss Ferguson blushed till Chris feared for her vest, her underthings would sure be on fire in a minute, she stammered that she didn't know, for sure, some of the spinners' children were cruel, they'd get a girl in the playground and tease her, or worse than that—and Miss Ferguson blushed some more, a torrent, till Chris in pity looked away, and thought herself of her own schooldays and those things that were WORSE in the reek of the playground, hot and still on a summer day and a crowd of loons round about you, laughing, with bright, hot eyes and their short, fair hair, and cruel, eager fingers . . . but she hadn't much minded, she'd been able even then to look after herself, it needed a sudden twist of her mind to think, appalled, that Ewan might do that, might stand by some girl and pry beastly in things——

She switched to listening to the talk again, Mrs. Geddes was having all the say now, the three teachers had no other course, very plain, but listen to the Dominie's wife with attention. And Mrs. Geddes said what was really wrong, with the whole of Segget, not only the spinners, was Refusal to Co-operate in Fellowship. But the W.R.I. was to combat that, and she really didn't think that this League was needed. The W.R.I. was to organize socials, and teach the mothers all kinds of fresh things—basket work, now, that was very interesting. . . . And she shone and wobbled like a jelly from a mould, and Geddes' look of contempt grew deeper.

Miss Jeannie Grant put her sherry-glass down. *I don't see anything your League can do. But the Labour Party can here in Segget, if only we make the branch strong enough;* and she looked as sweet as an apple as she said it, and young and earnest, and Chris half liked her, as though she stood on a hill and looked down on her own youth only beginning to climb, half-liking its confidence, pitying its blindness. But she thought for that matter, again and

again (and more than ever since their coming to Segget)
that she was older than most she met, older even than
Robert himself—older than all but her own son Ewan!

Then they heard Else stamping out in the hall, and she
rang the bell and they went through to dinner, Mrs. Geddes
calling it lunch, of course, she was so genteel Chris thought
it a wonder she should ever open her mouth for food. But
she fair put away a good plateful and more, for the chicken
was golden and cooked to a turn, Robert sat and carved
when he'd said the grace, the grace that Chris thought so
childlike and kind:

> God bless our food,
> And make us good,
> And pardon all our sins,
> For Jesus Christ's sake.

Syne Miss M'Askill was asking Chris, sharp, *Are you
fond of social work, Mrs. Colquohoun?* and Chris said *Not
much, if you mean by that going round and visiting the kirk
congregation.* Miss M'Askill raised up her brows like a
chicken considering a something lying on the ground, not
sure if it was just a plain empty husk, or an interesting bit
of nastiness, like. Mrs. Geddes said she was very disappointed, she'd hoped they'd have Mrs. Colquohoun to help
—with the work of the W.R.I., she meant; and why didn't
Mrs. Colquohoun like visiting?

And suddenly Chris understood her and hated her—she
minded the type, oh, well, well enough! So she smiled sweet
at her and said *Oh, you see, I wasn't always a minister's
wife. I was brought up on a croft and married on one, and
I mind what a nuisance we thought some folk, visiting and
prying and blithering about socials, doing everything to
help us, or so they would think—except to get out and get
on with the work!*

Robert's face went queer, a half-laugh, a half-scowl, but
Miss Jeannie Grant was delighted, she said *And get off your
backs, you could surely have added! You're a socialist the
same as I am, you know.* Chris shook her head, she knew
nothing about it, sorry already she had spoken like that,
Mrs. Geddes had gone quite white for a minute, Chris knew
she had made an enemy in Segget. The Dominie stared at
his plate with a sneer; Miss M'Askill looked at Robert,
brows up; Miss Ferguson looked at her plate and blushed;

only Ewan ate on, as calm as ever, except when he said, *Can I go now, please?*

Chris caught Miss M'Askill's eye when he'd gone, it said, plain as plain, *A very spoilt child.* And you supposed it really was true, the truth as she'd see it, who'd never had a child, who didn't know the things that bound you to Ewan, as though his birth-cord still bound you together, he tugged at your body, your heart, at your womb, in some moments of pity it was sheer, sick pain that tore at you as you comforted him. But THAT you could never explain to a woman who'd never had a bairn, had never, you supposed, yet lain with a man, known all the shame and all the red splendour and all the dull ache and resentment of marriage that led to the agony and wonder of looking on the face, sweet and blind as the eyes of love, of a child new-born from your body's harbour. . . . And Chris roused herself, *Mr. Geddes—pudding?*

Robert was trying to keep the talk going, but some thing had spoiled the talk at the table—herself, Chris supposed, with telling the truth. And she thought *They're just servant-queans, after all, with a little more education and a little less sense*—these, the folk Robert had thought could save Segget! It was hardly likely he thought so now; what would he do with his League and his plans? Still wait for young Stephen Mowat to come home?

Suddenly in the midst and mid of them all—the words she now used, the thoughts she thought, the clothes she wore and the things she ate—Chris would see her father's face from long syne, the jutting beard and the curling lip— *Come out of that, quean, with your dirt of gentry!* And because she knew in a way it was true, the gentry that or but little more, sometimes she'd stop in the middle of a talk, in the middle of a walk, in the middle of a meal, and stare for so long that Robert would say, *We've lost her again! Ewan, bring back your mother!*

That feeling came over her later that day, when it brought Stephen Mowat to tea at the Manse. Though none of them guessed the fact at the time, it had been his car that passed the service at eleven o'clock in Segget Square; but ere well the car had reached Segget House the news had spread all around the toun, young Stephen Mowat had come home at last, from wandering about in foreign parts after leaving his English university. And his shover told as they passed the Square young Mowat had looked and seen

the angel, and had groaned aloud, *Oh God, even here—
another bitch in a flannel shift!* The shover said they'd seen
birns of the statues as they motored up from England that
week, lasses in bronze and marble and granite, dancing
about on pedestal tops, he'd thought them bonny, Mr.
Stephen hadn't, he said that Britain had gone harlot-mad,
and stuck up those effigies all over the place, in memory
no doubt of the Red Lamps of France.

And the shover said he should know about queans, young
Mowat, considering the number he'd had since he'd left
the college a six months back. No doubt he'd soon have
them at Segget House, he intended to bide there and fee a
big staff, and bring back the good old days to the toun.
He was going to look after the mills for himself, the estate
as well, and the Lord knows what.

Chris heard all this when the school-folk had gone,
from Else, when she went to the kitchen to help. But Else
needed no help, she'd a visitor there, Dalziel of Meiklebogs
it was. He smiled shy and rose when he saw Chris come
in, and she told him to sit, and Else poured out the news.
Chris didn't feel excited, but she thought Robert might.
*Well, that'll be fine, no doubt, for Segget. Oh, have we
made any cakes for tea?*

Else said they hadn't, but they damned soon would. *Out
of the way, there, Meiklebogs, now!* and pushed him into
a chair, he sat canny, his cap in his hands, and watched
while she baked. Chris went back to Robert and told him
the news.

He said *Mowat home? It's an answer to prayer. And just
as I heard the black dog come barking! Let's celebrate!*
And he caught Chris, daft, and twirled about the room in
a dance. So they didn't hear the knocking at the door, Else
did, and went and brought Stephen Mowat in. They came
to the door of the sitting-room and watched, till Chris saw
them and stopped, and Robert did the same. And Else
said, *Mr. Mowat, Mem,* and vanished.

He'd a face that minded her of a frog's, he was younger
than herself by a good few years, with horn-rimmed specta-
cles astride a broad nose, and eyes that twinkled, and a way
of speaking that in a few days was to stagger Segget. His
brow went back to a cluster of curls, he was charming, you
supposed, as a prince should be, and very likely damn
seldom is; and he said he was pleased to be back in Segget,
looking at Chris as though she were the reason, Chris had

never met in with his like before and stood and looked at him, cool in surprise, taller than he was, he was to say later he felt he was stared at by Scotland herself.

And once, when drunk, he was to say to the Provost that she couldn't get over her blood and breed, she was proud as all the damned clodhoppers were, still thought in her heart they were the earth's salt, and thought the descendant of a long line of lairds on the level with the descendants of a long line of lice. And he said by God, had it been a four hundred years back he'd have tamed that look quick enough in his bed, maybe she lost something of her sulkiness there. And Provost Hogg boasted and said *Not a doubt;* and started to tell of his ancestor, Burns. And Mowat said, *Who? Oh, Robbie Burns? A hell of a pity he couldn't write poetry,* and the Provost was vexed, but then, 'twas the laird, just joking-like; and he was the *laird*.

Chris heard of that later, she'd have needed second sight to know of the gossip that would be in the future: she said she was glad to see him, she wasn't, neither glad nor sad, a funny little thing, was this what Robert depended upon? Funny that the like of him for so long had lived on the rent of folk like hers. Syne she went to the kitchen to see how the cakes came, they were brown and steaming, set on the table, and Meiklebogs, shy, like a big, sly steer, was sitting and eating one by the sink. And because she just couldn't thole him at all, he made her want to go change her vest, Chris smiled at him and was extra polite, and hoped that he'd stay to tea with Else, and helped Else pile the things on a tray; and they carried it through and found Robert and the laird already deep in the talk that was planned by Robert himself when he first saw Segget.

Mr. Mowat's English bray sounded so funny that Else gave a giggle and near dropped the tray. *Is the creature foreign?* and Chris said *No;* and Else said no more, but went solemnly in, and took only a keek or so at the creature, a little bit thing in baggy plus-fours. And he said *Oh, thenks!* and *I say!* and *How Jahly!* Else nearly giggled again, but she didn't, till she got to the kitchen and there was Meiklebogs, and she gave him a poke, *I say, how Jahly! You old devil, I've a good mind to make up to the laird. What would you do then, eh, would you say?*

Meiklebogs smiled canny and said he would manage, and Else stared at him and wondered again why she'd ever allowed the old brute to come near her since she'd wept in his bed that night of the Show; she supposed she was still in a kind of a daze at finding the old brute as coarse as they'd said.

Chris sat in the sitting-room and listened to Mowat, and handed him tea, he said he'd come back to look after the mills and Segget in general, the curse of the age was its absentee landlords, not social conditions or unrest or such-like. He was Jahly well sure he could buck up the village— didn't Mrs. Colquohoun approve of that, now? he'd want her approval ever so much. And he flashed her a long, bright, toothy smile, he'd fine teeth and knew it; and Chris said, *I don't know. I'll wait and see what the bucking con- sists of. My father was a crofter and he used to say you should trust a laird just as far as you can throw him.*

Stephen Mowat said he thought Mrs. Colquohoun's father Jahly, and glinted charming, and Chris gave him up, and cleared off the tea things and came back and listened. By then, so it seemed, Robert had told of his plans, and was sitting now harkening to Mowat's reply. And the reply was: The thing that was needed everywhere was Discipline, hwaw? and order, and what not. The hand of the master— all the Jahly old things. He had been down in Italy the last few months and had seen things there, Rahly amazing, the country awakening, regaining its soul, its old leaders back— with a new one or so. Discipline, order, hierarchy—all that. And why only Italy; why not Scotland? He'd met other men, down from 'varsity of late, who were doing as he did, going back to their estates. Scotland a nation—that was the goal, with its old-time civilization and culture. Hwaw? Didn't Mr. Colquohoun agree?

But Chris had been listening, and now she must speak, she'd been trying to think as well as to listen, it was hard enough, but words suddenly came: they both turned round with a start as she spoke. *And what's going to happen when you and your kind rule us, again as of old, Mr. Mowat? Was there ever the kind of Scotland you preach?—Happy, at ease, the folk on the land well-fed, the folk in the pulpits well-feared, the gentry doing great deeds? It's just a gab and a tale, no more, I haven't read history since I was at school, but I mind well enough what that Scotland was. I've been to Dunnottar Castle and seen there the ways that the gentry once liked to keep order. If it came to the push be- tween you and the spinners I think I would give the spinners my vote.*

Mowat said *Rahly?* staring at Chris, Robert stared as well at her down-bent face—suddenly she'd seen so much she didn't say, all the pageant of history since history began up here in the windy Mearns Howe: the ancient rites of blood and atonement where the Standing Stones stood up as dead kings; the clownings and cruelties of leaders and chiefs; and the folk—her folk—who kept such alive—dying frozen at night in their eirdes, earth-houses, chaving from the blink of day for a meal, serfs and land-workers whom the Mowats rode down, whom the armies harried and the kings spat on, the folk who rose in the Covenant times and were tortured and broken by the gentry's men, the rule and the way of life that had left them the pitiful gossiping clowns that they were, an obscene humour engraffed on their fears, the kindly souls of them twisted awry and veiled from men with a dirty jest; and this snippet of a fop with an English voice would bring back worse, and ask her to help!

And then that went by, she was suddenly cool. It was only a speak, a daft blether of words, whatever else happened to Segget, to Scotland—and there were strange things waiting to happen—there would never come back that old darkness again to torment the simple folk of her blood. Robert was speaking, he knocked out his pipe.

I'm afraid my wife and I think the same—as all folk worth their salt in Scotland must think. There are changes coming—they are imminent on us—and I once thought the folk of some teaching would help. Well, it seems they won't—the middle class folk and the upper class folk, and all the poor devils that hang by their tails; they think we can last as we are—or go back—and they know all the while they are thinking a lie. But God doesn't wait, or His instruments; and if in Segget are the folk of the mills, then, whatever their creed, I'm on their side.

Chris started and moved, she nearly had frozen, leaning up here while the night went on, she thought to be down in her bed, she supposed. The rain had cleared and the stars had come out, frost was coming—there, bright down in Segget, was a mantling of grey where the hoar was set, sprinkled like salt on the cant of the roofs. Beyond them there rose a red, quiet lowe, from the furnaces stacked for the night in the mills.

She stamped her feet and drew up her collar, watching that coming of the frost below. This impulse to seek the dark by herself! She had left Robert up in his study at work, Ewan in bed, young Mowat gone, and herself gone out for a walk through the rain that was closing in the end of Remembrance Day, wet and dank, as she'd seen it come. And it might be an age ere she came here again, too busied with living to stand looking at life, with Ewan at school and the campaign of Robert to conquer Segget for God and his dream.

A pillar of cloud by day and a pillar of fire by night.

She raised her eyes and looked where the frost lay bright in the west, where the evening star wheeled down to midnight to lead her feet home.

III

STRATUS

IT was funny to think, this forenoon in June, how long it had been since she climbed the Kaimes, here rose the walls, in their mantle of heather, a blackbird was whistling up in the yews, as she turned around slow she saw the light flow up and down the hill as though it were liquid, Segget below lying buried in a sea, as once all the Howe had lain, Ewan said. Still weak, Chris halted and sat on the wall, her hands below her, and looked at Segget, and drew out her hands and looked at those so thin that almost she could see through them, so thin her face when she put up her hand that the cheekbones that once curved smooth under flesh now felt like twin jagged crags of rock—a long time ere she'd look comely again!

She leant her head in her hand a moment and waited for the hill below to cease reeling—maybe she'd come out too early from bed, this walk, Else had said she mustn't go far. But the Kaimes had called her after those weeks of the smell of medicines, close fires, and the pain that ran up and down her and played hide and seek with every sinew and bone that she had. So up she had come, the sun was up here, she was out of it for an hour or so, out of the winking flash of the days, to sit and look from the high places here, as Christ one had done with the devil for guide.

Idly she minded that and smiled—it came of being a

347

minister's wife. What had the devil said to Christ then? Maybe *Just rest. Rest and have peace. Don't let them tear you to
bits with their hates, their cares and their loves, your angers
for them. Leave them and rest!*

Yes, He'd said that, there wasn't a doubt, just as He
stood by her saying it now, telling her to rest for the first
time in years since that night when she last had climbed
up the Kaimes, telling her to rest and leave them a-be, her
cares for Robert, for that other who came and yet never
came—for that third, that stranger whom slow through the
years she had grown to half-know as a traveller half-
knows the face of another on a lone road at night, in the
summer light of a falling star. . . . How Segget would snigger
if they heard her say that that stranger desired was her own
son Ewan!

Being young Ewan Tavendale wasn't all fun, you'd to
get up as early as half-past six in the little room that looked
down on Segget. But it *was* a good room, the best in the
Manse, you could look of a night right into the trees when
the rooks came nesting, they had a great time, fighting and
mating and playing the devil. Once you nearly fell out when
two rooks were at it—mating, you'd wanted to know how
it was done. But that was a long time ago, when a kid, you
knew all about it now, humans or rooks, mother or Robert,
and there wasn't much in it, though the spinner kids of
West Wynd thought so. Charlie Cronin drew pictures in
the lavatories at school, the silly ass couldn't draw at all.
So you drew some yourself to show how things were, he
turned red-faced when you drew IT so well. *Ewan, that's
dirty!* What was dirty about it?

You would lie and mind these things of a morning and
stare at the ceiling and hark to the rooks—moving and chat-
tering and swearing in the cold—how they *did* swear as the
daylight grew! Sometimes you'd wanted to swear yourself,
and you'd tried once or twice when you were a kid, but it
sounded half-witted, so you gave it up. You couldn't see
sense in rubbish like swearing, any more than in speaking
Scotch, not English as mother did sometimes, and so did
Robert, and so did Else (but she couldn't help it). Scotch
was rubbish, all ee's and wee's, you didn't even speak it in
the school playground. And the other kids had mocked you
at first, but they didn't long, with a bashing or so.

Chris (and once Else) rigged you out of a morning,

now you did it yourself, nearly twelve years old. The clock went birr as you looked at its face and you got out of bed and out of your pyjamas, Charlie Cronin slept in his shirt, he said only gentry wore things like pyjamas. You were glad you were gentry, then, shirts got sticky. Then you'd hear the clock going off down below, where the new girl slept, she was shy and said *Eh?* A perfect fool, she near fainted one morning, in summer it was, when she first came here. You'd thought you'd go down and get a bath first before either Robert or Chris should be at it. So you'd nipped down the stairs without anything on, and as you came back she came from her room, and gave a screech like a frightened hen, as though she'd never seen folk without clothes. Charlie Cronin said that his father, old George, would take off his clothes slow bit by bit, the top bits first, and cover himself up, and then the lower, and he'd cover *that*—you'd supposed that Maidie herself was like that, a fool, maybe frightened to look at herself.

So after that you had promised Chris that you'd wear some clothes when outside your room, she'd said that she herself didn't care—and you said *Yes, mother, I know that you don't. I once saw you with nothing on coming up the stairs—a night long ago when I was a kid. I think it was the night of a Segget Show.*

She'd blushed, as though nearly as bad as the others, but she wasn't: you were glad that your mother was Chris. She didn't know that you called her that, to yourself, not aloud, aloud you said *Mother.* But Robert, just *Robert,* he wasn't your father. Robert was fun when he wasn't at work, with the kirk or the spinners or his Labour plans—summers he took you and Chris on your bikes out on far jaunts up and down the Howe, to Edzell, to Brechin, to Garvock Hill where they boiled the sheriff but not Leslie the smith—you asked Robert what he meant by that say, and he and Chris laughed like a couple of fools.

But out on picnics he changed and was young, and would teach you to throw and do the high jump, he could jump like anything, Robert, and box. Everybody knew that in Segget now, they hadn't at first, especially the spinners, and had mocked at Robert till he taught them manners. Charlie Cronin had been jealous of him and of you, that was at first when you first went to school, the first day he came swaggering up and said *Oh, you're the dirt from the Manse, are you?* And you said *I'm not dirt, I'm Ewan Tavendale,*

and he mocked at you till you hit him a bash, right on the
nose, and he bled and bled, though it was only a baby bash,
you were both of you just babies yourselves. But you won
that fight all the same, Mr. Geddes had watched it all from
a window; and he went to the Manse and told Chris about
it; and she asked that night *Did he hurt you, Ewan?* and you
said *Ay,* all the kids had said *Ay;* and Chris said *Oh, Ewan,
that was real like your father!* Father had been killed by the
Germans in France.

Time for breakfast: and there was Robert, busy with
letters, and Chris, looking sweet. But she always did that,
even when she was angry, she could do nearly anything,
answer you anything, she couldn't run maybe as fast as you
could and she was a perfect fool about flints, but she always
told the truth about things, most grown-up people told lies
half the time. You didn't yourself, it wasn't worth the
bother, explaining and trying to straighten things later.

And Chris would say *It's nearly schooltime,* and you'd
look at the clock, and see that it was, and Robert would
say, *He's dreaming about flints!* But you hadn't been dreaming, you'd been thinking of Chris, she'd looked different of
late in a puzzling way. Now, if it had been any other woman in Segget, you'd have known—but not Chris! It made a
cold water come in your mouth, as though you were going
to be sick, that thought. And Chris said *What's wrong?
That's a funny-loon stare.* And you said *Oh, nothing. I'll
need to be going.*

You kissed Chris every morning, one kiss a day; kisses
were sloppy except for that one—like the taste of honey up
on a hill, clear, with the wind in the summer south. Robert
cried *Ta-ta!* and you did the same, and were out in the
hall, where Maidie would be, tweetering about and worrying again, wondering if breakfast were over yet. You hardly
ever took notice of her, not since she'd screeched that time
on the stairs. She'd call *Master Ewan, is the breakfast done?*
and you'd say *I don't know* and leave her to twitter—who
wanted to be *mastered* like a kid in a book?

Out from the Manse and down through the shingle, giving it a kick and a plough as you went, under the ferny
tops of the yews, the rooks all wakened and screeching, or
off—all but the young ones, pecking, gaping. If it was
summer you passed under quick, they dropped dirt down
when you least expected, they dropped it once on the
Provost of Segget when he came to see Robert and he

walked back home with it white on his hat and everyone laughed, and he nearly had a fit when he found out about it.

He was frightened to be laughed at, most people were, you didn't care a button one way or another, they might laugh themselves blue in the face at you, you were yourself—and what did it matter?

And there was the land and there were the touns, Segget half-blue in its early smoke, you started early and with time to spare to go round the toun and back up to the school. So you'd stop and pull up your stockings to your knees, in shorts, and the shirt and tie that Chris tied, you couldn't get the knack of the thing, she would say *Oh, Ewan, you've forgotten to tie it at all!* and you'd say *I forgot,* and she'd ruffle your hair, *Thinking about flints again, I suppose?* She and Robert were always joking about flints, and calling them wrong names, and thinking that funny.

Down by Meiklebogs the curlews were calling, you heard them above the shoom of the Mills, Robert said something about that once—*Twin daughters of the Voice of God.* You hadn't bothered to find out what he meant, though you bothered about most things right to the end, sense to find out why this went like this, and that was so, and the wheels went round, and some stars twinkled and a lot did not, why people were ashamed to be seen without clothes and didn't like girls to go out late at night, and hated capitalists, if they were spinners, and hated spinners if they were New Toun.

The curlew called and you stopped and listened, Else would hear it at the Meiklebogs, you'd liked Else a lot, though not all the time. Once she'd come to your room late in the night, harvest, and was sloppy and kissed you about, you hated slop and threw a book at her, it hit her, she stared, you were sorry a bit.

There was a seagull up on that post, try a stone at it— nearly its tail!—and there was Ake Ogilvie's shop beyond. Most mornings you loitered about at Ake's, he'd lean from the door with his compass in hand and cry *Well, then, have you learned your Burns?* 'twas a joke between you, the poetry of Burns, silly Scotch muck about cottars and women, and love and dove and rot of that sort. Ake would recite you some of his own, his green eyes twinkling and his eyebrows twinkling, with a coating of sawdust sprayed on the hairs, and his long moustache going up and down, so, and

you'd stare at him and listen a while, it was good enough,
better than Burns's rot. Poetry was rot, why not say it
plain, when a man kissed a woman or a woman had a baby?

Down past the house of Jimmy the Sourock, the road
had a dip and a hollow for years, the rain would gather,
deep, in a pool, you used to march through it, your feet
close together, and watch the water soak in at the eyelets,
and feel it trickling betwixt your toes: that was when you
were only a kid. Then Mrs. Sourock would look out and
see, and cry she would tell the Mem at the Manse, that was
Chris she meant, and you didn't care. It was no business
of *hers* to get mad because you liked to wade in the water,
especially as she herself was so proud that her husband, the
Sourock, drank nothing but water, since he got that fright
with the pig in his bed. And every Sunday he went down
to the Square, to the service-meeting of MacDougall Brown,
and sang about blood, and you thought that funny, he'd
been so frightened at the blood of the pig. You'd once
played truant from the kirk to go down and watch Mac-
Dougall Brown as he prayed, he opened his mouth and
looked as though blind, with his eyes like glass and his
teeth all black, perhaps he was frightened to go to the
dentist.

A dentist came twice a week now to Segget, he hired
a room at the back of Dite Peat's: and the first time he
came Charlie Cronin was there, hiding and listening under
the window to hear the howls when the teeth came out.
And the first to come was old Mrs. Hogg, she had a wart
on her nose like Cromwell and hair growing out of the wart
as well, and she groaned like anything, Charlie told. Then
she said to the dentist *How much will that be?* and he said
Half a crown, and Mrs. Hogg said *What? Half a crown for
that, just pulling out a tooth? Why, old Leslie the smith
down there at the smiddy used to pull me all over the place
with his tongs, and never would ask a meck for it, either.*

But you liked Mrs. Hogg, she would cry as you passed,
Hello, Ewan lad, is there anything fresh? And you'd show
her the latest flints that you'd got, and she wouldn't just
laugh or blither about Druids, as everyone else in Segget
would do but would ask what the hunters had done with the
things, and she'd say that that was amazing, just, what a
thing it was to be learned and young. She'd sense, Mrs.
Hogg, more sense than her son, who sometimes came home
on a holiday; he spoke bad English and wore bad breeks,

and patted your head and said *Little man*, or tried to pat you, you just stepped aside.

Sometimes you'd look into Peter Peat's shop, where he sat on a table making a suit, he'd frown and motion you to get off, he came every Sunday and listened to Robert and hated his sermons and Robert as well. You'd heard him one Sunday say to the Provost the minister was nothing but a Bolshevik, just as bad as that tink John Cronin, the porter. Bolsheviks lived in Russia, you knew, they'd closed all the kirks and they all worked together and they hadn't a king; and it sounded sense.

By now you'd got to the end of East Wynd, to the Square where the War Memorial stood, the angel that looked like Miss M'Askill, Miss M'Askill had eyes that would lift up that way when she found something dirty drawn on a slate. In lower East Wynd of a winter morning half the lane was frozen to a slide, you took a long run from Peter Peat's shop and shot down the Wynd on the frozen slide that came from the leaking drains of Segget. By the Moultrie shop you'd to plan your turn, else you'd batter yourself on the wall of their house, as you'd done your second winter in Segget, the whole of Segget seemed fallen upon you, and your face had shifted, you sat on the ground and thought you had lost it and felt it all over, it still was there, grown bigger than ever, growing bigger and bigger every moment, it seemed.

It was while you were sitting there, licking the blood, it trickled from your lips and tasted salt, that old Mrs. Moultrie came out and found you, she'd heard the bang as you struck the wall, she said to Chris when she took you home she thought that it was a cart and horse. But you liked her in spite of clyping to Chris, her face, brown, old, and tired and quiet as she bathed you and *whished* as though you were a baby, till you sat up and said *I'm fine. Many thanks.* Old Moultrie was sitting in his corner, glaring, reading a Bible, and you said *Good day.*

He'd taken no notice at all before that, he glared some more, but you didn't mind, you saw he really was awfully shy underneath all the hair and the horns, so you said, while Mrs. Moultrie went out for a towel, *Do you like the Bible? There's a lot of rot in it.* He stood up, shaking all over, funny, and asked, *And you're the minister's bairn?* And you shook your head, *Oh no, I'm not. Robert's only my stepfather, didn't you know? My father was a crofter down in Kinraddie. Much better than being a minister, I think.*

Funny, he was friendly enough after that, and started telling you stories of Segget, when there weren't so many of the gentry dirt sossing about with their motor-cars. And you listened, polite, because he was old, a pity besides that he was so shy. But Mrs. Moultrie said to Chris that you were the only soul in Segget he'd treated to a civil word for years.

There was the Arms, not worth looking at, you threw a stone at a cat in the Square and watched the dog up against the angel, funny that dogs were so fond of that. They really couldn't *want to,* so often. Every day that dog of Newlands came down, as you turned in the Square to go up the Close, and did that against the Memorial stone, you'd once told Robert, and he'd laughed and laughed and said that the dog was a pacifist, maybe. But one morning you stood and watched for the dog and sure as anything along it came, and stopped, and relieved itself by the angel; and the door of the Arms opposite opened, and Mrs. Melvin came out and said that you were a dirty little brute to stand and look at a dog doing that—Weren't you black burning ashamed of yourself? She was soft in the head, why should you be ashamed? Maybe she was drunk, but you didn't say anything, just looked her all over, from top to toe, to see if she'd fallen while she was drunk, and then raised your cap and went on to school.

Round by here you could see the Mills, in the big glass windows across the field the whirr of the wheels as they caught the sun, the spinners at work in the dust and the smell; but you liked the Mills, you'd been down there twice, with Charlie, he said the folk in New Toun were daft to speak of the folk in the Mills as only spinners, there were foremen and weavers, and a lot more besides; but they all *looked* like spinners.

To the right, in the Spring and most of the year, as you passed up The Close you would see in the park the donkey that was kept by MacDougall Brown. If you whistled one note, high up in your throat, you'd found that the donkey would bray every time. So nearly every day as you passed you whistled that note and the donkey brayed, and you laughed, and he'd bray some more and come trotting and push his long nose through the fence and snuffle, but he never bit you as once Mabel Brown. Mrs. Brown spoke

funny, and she called her May-bull, and had a long story
how the donkey once *bat May-bull* when she went to play
in the park.

There was the smiddy and it once was great fun, when
you were a kid, to lean up by the door and look at old
Leslie blowing the bellows, he'd turn round and sweat, *Ay
man, is that you?* He called you *man*, but he blithered a lot,
you would hardly heed at all what he said—about Chris,
was she ill-like of late, would you say? and *The minister'll
be gey fond of her, eh?* and *D'ye mind your own father that
was killed out in France?* And you said you didn't know to
all of these questions, because you couldn't be bothered
with them, and he said, *Eh man, when my father died I just
roared and howled—ay, loon, I'd a heart.* And you said
Like the Roarer and Greeter, Miss Moultrie? And he
stopped and stared with his mouth fallen open, and muttered that you were an impudent get.

You'd take the West Wynd through the Old Toun then,
with its crumbling white houses and its washing to dry,
there was always washing to dry, never dried. You knew a
lot of the kids in West Wynd, they'd be finishing porridge
and pulling on boots, and they'd cry *Wait, Ewan!* but you'd
never wait, except for young Cronin, he'd come slouching
out and say *Ay, Ewan,* and you'd say *Hello, Charlie,* and go
on together not saying a thing till he'd ask, as always, *Have
you done your sums?* Then you'd know that he hadn't done
his and would bring out your book so that he might copy.

Funny that he couldn't do things like sums, you could
nearly do them with both eyes shut, and lean back and go
off on a think on flints while the other scholars were finishing theirs; and Miss M'Askill would cry out, *Ewan! Have
you finished already? Show me your sums.* And you'd show
them to her, she'd stand over close, with an arm around
your shoulder, like so; and you'd move away, though as
slow as you could; and she wrote in your report to the
Manse that you were brilliant, but you hadn't enthusiasm;
you supposed because you hadn't enthusiasm for cuddling.

It had been different in the first two years, the youngest
room with Miss Jeannie Grant, Miss Grant was pretty and
laughed at you, and at everyone else, and kept her cuddles
for Charlie's brother, or so you supposed. She was going to
be married some time to him, Jock Cronin, that was only a
railway porter, Chris said that job was as good as another.
But you didn't think much of John Cronin, yourself, he

didn't believe what he himself said, he just said things and then tried to believe them—you knew that well while you watched him sit, with Robert, up in a room at the Manse, and talk of Segget and socialism coming—it was all a fairy-tale, and he knew it, why didn't he say the things that he thought?

You said that to Chris and she took your two shoulders, and shook her head and looked at you, strange, *Oh Ewan, you're hard and cool as—grey granite! When you too grow up you'll find facts over much—you'll need something to follow that's far from the facts.* And she said something else, about a pillar of cloud, and was suddenly angry, *Don't stare at me so!* And you said *I'm sorry,* and she shook you again. *So am I, Ewan—but oh, you're so cool!*

Well, you saw nothing to make you excited, except now and then a broad-flake flint. It was worth reading history to get at these people, the makers of flints and their lives long ago. Though most of the histories were dull as ditch-water, with their kings and their battles and their dates and such muck, you wondered how the people had lived in those times. But especially before the history-book times you wanted to know how men had lived then and had read all the books you could find in the Manse, and got money from Chris to send and buy others, the lives of the people ere history began, before the Venricones came to the Mearns. And young Cronin would listen and say *What's the use? Father says that the only things we should learn are how to fight the caPITalists.* You didn't know about them, you asked who they were, and Charlie said *Folk like that mucker Mowat.*

Mr. Mowat lived sometimes in Segget House, but most of the time he was down in London, sleeping with whores, Charlie Cronin said. You asked what whores were and he told you about them, what they did, how they slept for money with men. You said that you didn't see why they shouldn't, and Charlie said you'd a dirty mind, and would soon be doing the same as Mowat. That was rot, you hadn't any use for girls, they could only giggle and drift along roads, with their arms twined, and screech about nothing. Or they played soft games in their own playground, once you'd run through there for a cricket-ball and the bigger girls were playing a game, *When will my true love come from the sea;* and the silly fools pulled you in the middle and kissed and slobbered you one after the other, you stood

it as long as you could, then pushed out, you didn't want
to hurt the fools and you didn't; but you had felt almost
sick in their hands.

You told Chris that when she heard about it, she laughed
and said *All lasses aren't fools, and they think you a good-
looking lad, I believe.* So you said that you didn't care about
that, could you have a piece now and go up to the Kaimes?

You went often up there to seek round for flints, when
they dug the Kaimes they must have dug deep, in a squat-
ting-place of the ancient men, and mixed the flints with the
building-earth. You had nearly thirty specimens already,
properly labelled in a press in your room, and each described on a ticket near. And you had a catalogue, fairly
complete, with diagrams of the ripples, hinge-fractures, the
ovates and such, and a drawing of the best, a tortoise-core
from the Leachie bends. Most of the stuff was late Bronze
Age, when the hunters in Scotland had still only flints.

Dinner-times you went home by the near way, quick,
stopping to throw up a stone at the rooks. Robert would
sometimes be there at the table, and sometimes was out
and about the Mearns, trying to raise his fund for the
miners, and raising little but temper, he said. Chris never
went with him at the dinner-hour, she would stay at home
and help Maidie at work, Maidie couldn't cook a dinner
for toffee.

Sometimes Chris would be out at night when you came
back from the school for tea. So Maidie would give you
your tea, like a mouse, and you'd have it and help her to
clear and she'd say, *Oh, Master Ewan, I'll do it myself,*
but you took no notice, just went on and helped, not heeding her blether you should do your lessons, any fool could
do the lessons in ten minutes. Then you'd climb to your
room and look in your press, and dust here and there that
tortoise-core, and a fabricator-cone you had gotten near
Brechin, and take them out and turn them with care, the
light waning and dying in from the window as the day
waned west from the slopes of the Howe. And sometimes
you'd raise your head and look up, when the sun grew still
on the peaks of the Mounth, by the glens and the haughs
you had searched for flints, and think of the men of ancient
times who had made those things and hunted those haughs,
running naked and swift by the sunlit slopes, fun to live
then and talk with those people. Robert said that they

hadn't been savage at all, but golden hunters of the Golden Age.

And once Chris came up as you stood and looked at a new ripple-flake you had newly found, a summer night ere you went to bed, you'd taken everything off, to be cool, and stood by the window and traced out the whorls on the red and yellow of the antique axe. Chris opened the door, you felt the air waft, and turned and looked at her, her standing so still. You asked was anything wrong, she said *No*, giving a laugh, as though wakening up. *Only you looked like a hunter yourself, strayed and lost from the Golden Age!*

And Else went by, and looked through the door, and suddenly flushed and ran up the stairs, that was just a week ere she went from the Manse.

Faith, that had fairly set folk agog, when that coarse quean Else was sacked from the Manse. It just showed you the way that the world was going, dirty spinners that gave you their lip, worked hard to get, so many sweir—and ministers that couldn't look after their queans. Folk said they'd been at it a year and a half, her and Dalziel of the Meikle-bogs, afore that Sabbath night in July when Mr. Colquohoun came in on the pair, right bang in the Manse's own kitchen it was, Meiklebogs in the way you'd expect a man in, Else Queen in a way that no quean should be in, with a two-three bits of her rig laid by. The minister had said *This won't do, Else*, fair mad with rage at old Meiklebogs, for he himself had slept with his maid, and was over-mean to share the lass out.

Some said that that was all a damned lie, the minister had nothing to do with the quean, she'd left the Manse of her own free will. The Reverend Mr. Robert Colquohoun wouldn't bed with an angel sent down from heaven, let alone a red-faced maid in his house, he was over decent and fond of his wife. But you shook your head when you heard that, faith! it clean took the guts from a fine bit tale. If he wasn't the kind to go to bed with any bit quean could you tell a man why he was chief with the Cronin dirt, social-ists that said you might lie where you liked and didn't believe in morals or marriage?

And if some childe said that THAT wasn't true, you knew right well that he was a liar, you'd seen it all in the *People's Journal*, what the coarse tinks did in Russia with

women—man, they fair had a time with the women, would
you say 'twould be easy to get a job there?

Well, whatever the thing that took place at the Manse,
and well you might wyte it wasn't just prayer—with that
scowling brute, the minister himself, and his wife with her
proud don't-touch-me face, and that meikle red-haired bitch
of an Else—whatever happened Else left the Manse and
took a fee at the Meiklebogs. And what the two of them
did when alone, with the night in about and the blinds
pulled down, you well might guess, though you didn't ask.
All but Dite Peat, and he said one night, when Dalziel came
taiking into the Arms, with that shy-like smile on his unshaved face, and the yellow boots that he wore for scud-
dling, *Ay, Meiklebogs, you'll sleep warm now. She's a
well-happed quean, Else Queen, I should think.* Dalziel said
nothing, just smiled like a gowk and drank at his dram and
syne had another, he hadn't a yea or a nay to say, it showed
you the coarse old brute that he was, and you nearly
bursting your bladder to know.

Some said they didn't believe it at all, Dalziel of the
Meiklebogs a decent-like childe, and an elder of Segget
kirk forbye. So he must be, but you knew a man's nature,
he needed a woman just now and again—no, no, you didn't
blame *him* overmuch, but she fairly must be an ill tink,
that Else Queen. And you'd look at her hard the next time
that you met, not a bit of shame she would show as she
passed, just cry *Ay, Fusty Face, so it's you?* and go swinging
by with her meikle hips on the sway like stacks of hay in a
gale, well-fleshed and rosy, disgusting, you thought, you'd
feel as mad as a mating tyke at Meiklebogs and his shameless sin.

But faith! 'twas the same wherever you looked. There
was Mr. Mowat up at the House, folk said he'd come back
from a London jaunt with *two* of the painted jades this time,
you'd hear their scraichs all over the House; and once the
servant went in of a morning and what do you think he saw
in the bed? Young Mr. Mowat with a quean on each side,
he'd slept with the two and he fairly looked hashed, the
bitches just laughed as the servant gaped, and one slapped
Mr. Mowat in a certain place and cried *Hi Solomon, here's
the head eunuch!*

But you couldn't believe all the lies that you heard. Young
Mr. Mowat was fairly a gent, and right fine if you met him
outbye, and speak civil; and say he Rahly was glad that

you'd met. He was maybe a bit daft about Scotland and such, and a lot of dirt about history and culture. But couldn't a gent please himself with his ploys, it kept him from wearying and did no harm? When the Mills closed down for a fortnight once, they had over-much stock already on hand, he said he was Jahly sorry for the spinners—and he couldn't say fairer than that, could he now? So you couldn't believe about the two queans, and even were it true 'twas a different thing—wasn't it?—a gent with his play, and a randy old brute like that Meiklebogs man sossing about with a quean half his age?

Them that said Dalziel was an innocent childe fair got a sore shock ere the year was out. Else at her new place worked outdoor and indoor, she'd to kilt her skirts (if they needed kilting—and that was damned little with those short-like frocks) and go out and help at the spreading of dung, and hoeing the turnips and anything else, she was worth her own fee and a joskin's as well.

Well, the harvest came and it came fell heavy, Else helped at the stooking and syne at the leading. That was a windy September day, the other childes were down in the fields, Else and Meiklebogs managed a cart, out in the park Meiklebogs forked sheaves, big and thick, into Else Queen's arms; and she built them round and about the shelvins till they rose four high and syne it was time for Meiklebogs to lead home the horse, Jim, the roan, a canny old beast. So home they would go and the stour would rise under the grind of the iron wheels, up above the Mounth in its mist of blue, Dalziel would look back now and again and see that the corn was biding in place, and see Else as well, lying flat on the top, with her eyes fast-closed, the meikle sweir wretch.

So he led the roan, Jim, up the Meiklebogs close, and round to the back of the Meiklebogs barn, high in the wall a window was cut, and he planned that this load be forked through the window for early threshing with his new oil mill. He stopped the horse and he backed it canny, the roan was old and he gave it a bit groan, and Dalziel gave the roan a belt in the mouth, the brute of a beast to groan out like that, folk would think that it was ill-treated. The roan looked surprised, as though he'd done nothing; and Dalziel cried to Else Queen, *Come on, you'll have to be up and doing some work.*

She cried, *I'll soon do that, you old mucker,* she called
him the terriblest names to his face, and all he would do
would be to smile shy, and stroke at his chin, neither shaved
nor unshaved. So he held, splay-footed, to the front of the
barn, and got himself in and climbed to the loft, and keeked
from the window, and there was Else Queen, standing atop
of the rows of sheaves, her fork in her hand, waiting to fork.
She cried *You're fair getting old in the bones!* and flung in
a sheaf that near hit his face, he smiled and said nothing,
they both set to work, her working as fast and as fleet as
you liked, Dalziel inside was bigging the sheaves, ready for
the first bit thresh at the place, the sun a blind fall on the
cart outside. And once when Dalziel took a keek out he saw
the sweat in a stream from Else, and her eyes looked glazed,
it would take down her creash.

Well, there happened near next the kind of a thing
that surely Else Queen had expected to happen, unless she
were innocent as the Virgin Queen, Ake Ogilvie said: and
he doubted that. And even she was hardly that now, with
Burns a hundred years in heaven.—Folk said *What's that?*
and Ake looked surprised—they had surely heard of their
own Great Poet? Well, the creature died and he went to
heaven and knocked like hell on the pearly gates. And St.
Peter poked his head from a wicket, and asked *Who're you
that's making a din?* And Burns said *I'm Robert Burns, my
man, the National Poet of Scotland, that's who.* St. Peter
took a look at the orders, pinned on the guard-room wall
for the day; and he said, *I've got a note about you. You
must wait outbye for a minute or so.*

So Robbie sat there cooling his heels, on the top of the
draughty stair to heaven, and waited and waited till he
nearly was froze; syne the gates at last opened and he was
let in. And Burns was fair in a rage by then, *Do you treat
distinguished arrivals like this?* And St. Peter said *No, I
wouldn't say that. But then I had special orders about you.
I've been hiding the Virgin Queen away*—That was a real
foul story to tell, it showed you the tink that Ake Ogilvie
was, interrupting the real fine newsy tale of the happenings
down at the Meiklebogs.

For when they had finished with the forking 'twas told,
Dalziel took a bit of a look round the barn and saw he
would need a hand to redd up. *Get up from the cart and
come round,* he cried down, *I'll need you to lend me a hand
in the loft.* Else cried back, *Havers! Do you think I can't*

jump? And she put the end of her fork on a stone that
stuck out a bit from the wall of the barn, and the prong-end
under her arm, *so,* and next minute sailed through the air
like a bird and landed near by Meiklebogs' side. And then
she went white and then red of a sudden and Meiklebogs
thought of the groan he'd heard, it hadn't been Jim the
roan after all, 'twas Else had been groaning afore, as just
now. And he stood looking sly as she sat on the sheaves,
her face beginning to twist and to sweat, she said *I'm not
well, send off for the doctor.* Then her time came on her
and they heard her cry, the fee'd men out in the Meiklebogs fields, and came tearing home to see what was up.
But by then the thing was nearly all done, the bairn born
out in the barn, and Meiklebogs looking shyer than ever
and getting on his bike to go for the doctor.

But faith! that was all he would do in the business. He
wouldn't register the bairn his; and when the young doctor,
McCormack, came up, and Else was moved to her room
in the house, and McCormack said *Is the bairn yours?*
Meiklebogs smiled shy, *No, I wouldn't say that.* And Mc-
Cormack said *Who's is it, then?* And Meiklebogs never let
on a word, just looked past the doctor and smiled shy and
sly; and the doctor said *Huh—immaculate conception.
Something in the air of the Meiklebogs. You've had other
housekeepers ta'en the same way.*

Well, the story was soon all about the place, as scandalous a thing as ever you heard, Ag Moultrie, the Roarer
and Greeter of Segget, knew every damned thing that had
happened in the barn, more than an unmarried woman
should know, she said the bairn was Meiklebogs' image,
with his eyes and his nose—and Ake Ogilvie said *Ay, faith!
and his whiskers as well I could warrant.* So Ag told him if
he couldn't be civil and listen she wouldn't bother to give
him the news; and Ake said *D'you think I'll suffer for
that?*—not a neighbourly way to speak to a woman that
was trying to cheer you up with some news.

Soon Else was up and about the place, and the bairn, a
loon, tried to get its own back on its father Dalziel, if
father he was. Its howl was near fit to lift off the roof,
Else let it howl and worked in the parks; as the season wore
on, were the weather fine, she'd take the creature out to
the parks, and when it came to its feeding-time suckle the
thing on a heap of shaws. When the fee'd men blushed and
looked bashful at that, she'd cry *What the devil are you*

reddening for? You sucked the same drink before you met beer, fair vulgar and coarse she'd turned to the bone, you'd never have thought she'd worked in a Manse. Dalziel would hark, with his shy, sleekèd smile, saying neither yea nor nay to her fleers, she would tongue him up hill and down dale when she liked, and call him the foulest names you could hear. But the foreman said she still went to his bed, or he to hers—ay, a queer carry-on!

Till the business of Jim the roan put an end.

That came with the second winter's close, when Meiklebogs carted his grain to the station, he'd sold the stuff for a stiff-like price, and put a young fee'd loon, Sinclair his name, on to the carting with the old roan, Jim. He fair was a willing old brute, the roan, he'd pant up a brae till an oncoming body might think from the other side, out of sight, that a steam-mill and thresher was coming that way. But he never would stop, would just shoggle on, with his great wide haunches shambling and swinging, he'd a free-like way of flinging his feet, but he wasn't cleekèd; and he fair could pull.

Ah well, it came white weather of frost, the ground as hard and as cold as iron, ribbed with a veining of frost each morning, folk that you met seemed most to be nose, and red nose at that when it wasn't blue-veined, Melvin at the Arms did a roaring trade, the water-pipes were frozen in the Manse, and the horses of all the farmers out about were brought to the smiddy to have their shoes cogged.

But Meiklebogs was over busy for that, on the Monday morning, the worst of the lot, he sent off Sinclair with the last load of corn; and afore he had gone very far the loon was all in a sweat and a bother with his job, old Jim the roan on the slide all the time, and the weighted cart going showding and banging. Sinclair tried to lead the old horse by the grass that grew stiff-withered by the side of the road; and that for a little while eased up the beast, till they turned into Segget at the top of East Wynd. There was devil a speck of grass grew there, and near Ake Ogilvie's the ground was like glass, and young Ewan Tavendale that came from the Manse had been sliding there a half hour that morning.

So when Jim the roan came on that with the cart he did the same as the Manse loon had done—took a run and a slide, and cart, horse, and all shot down past Ake's like a falling star—so Ake Ogilvie said, a daft-like speak. The lot fetched up near the Sourock's house, the roan fell shaken, but he didn't coup; and nothing of the harness by a miracle broke. Young Sinclair had fairly got a fell fright and he leathered old Jim round about the head with the reins and kicked him hard in the belly, to make the old brute more careful in future.

Peter Peat looked out and he nodded, *That's it, nothing like discipline for horses and men;* and he looked fierce enough to eat up old Jim, that was bending under the ding of the blows his patient old head—ay, a fierce man, Peter. And Sinclair, that was only a loon and a fool, said, *I'll teach the old mucker to go sliding about,* and gave the old roan another bit kick, to steady him up, and got on the cart, and sat him down on a bag of corn and cried to the roan *Come on, you old Bee!*

So old Jim went on and he fair went careful, flinging his great meikle feet down canny, the loaded cart swinging and showding behind, the road below like a sheet of glass. And he went fell well till the East Wynd sloped, down and round by the Moultrie shop, and there they found it—a slide once again! all the lasses and lads of Segget had been there, the night before, with their sleds and skates, and whooped and scraiched and dirled down the wynd, on their feet sometimes, on their backsides next, near braining themselves by the Moultrie wall, young Ewan Tavendale the worst of them all—he fair could slide, that nickum of a loon, with his black-blue hair and his calm, cool eyes, he'd led the lot and could wheel like a bird just in time to miss the bit wall that was waiting there to dash out his brains.

Well, young Tavendale might, but old Jim mightn't, no sooner did his great bare feet come down on the slide than the same thing happened as before. He started to slip and the cart went with him, it half wheeled round with the weight of its load, and reeled by the wall of the gardener Grant and stotted from that, and the roan was down, braking with its feet, that did little good. Sinclair jumped off and fell on all fours. As he picked himself up he heard the crash, and the scream that rose with the breaking shafts, and he scrambled erect and looked down the lane; and the sight was sickener, old Jim the roan had run full tilt in the Moultrie wall, and one of the shafts of the cart had snapped and swung back right in the horse's belly, as though the old brute were a rat on a stake. He lay crumpled up, the cart broken behind him, young Sinclair started to greet at the sight: and the noise of the crash brought folk on the run.

Afore you could speak a fell concourse was round, old Moultrie came hirpling out with his stick, and cried *What do you mean, malagarousing my house?* and Jess Moultrie peeped, and looked white and sick; and Ag came out and then nipped back quick, no doubt in order to Roar and Greet. Will Melvin took Sinclair over to the Arms and had a drink down him afore you could wink; and young Sinclair stopped sniftering and habbering about it, he was feared he'd be sacked by Dalziel for this. *And what can I do in the middle of the season if I lose my job? I'll just have to starve. You can't get a fee for love or money, right in the middle of the winter, you can't. And that old mucker Meiklebogs*—But Mrs. Melvin came into the bar and said *None of your Blasting and Blaspheming in here. You'll have to go out with your swearing, young man.*

So Sinclair went out and gaped like a fool at the folk that had come in around to see Jim. He lay with his eyes half closed and at last he'd stopped from trying to rise from the ground, the end of the shaft was deep in his belly, and there was a smell fit to frighten a spinner; folk took a good look and went canny away, you hadn't time to stand there and stare, you might be asked to help if you did, let Meiklebogs look to his old horse himself. Sim Leslie, the policeman that folk called Feet, came down and took his bit note-book out and asked young Sinclair how it all happened; and wrote it all down and looked at old Jim, and frowned at him stern; and then wrote some more—no doubt the old roan's criminal record. Syne he said he'd ride over and tell Meiklebogs, and he did, and when Meiklebogs heard of the news he smiled canny and shy, and got on his bike, and came riding to Segget to see the soss.

By the time he did it was nearly noon. Ake Ogilvie down with his gun at the place, a crowd had gathered to see the brute shot; but Dalziel wouldn't have it, *No, bide you a wee. If the beast be shot there would be no insurance.* Ake Ogilvie said *Can't you see it's in hell, with the shaft of the cart driving into its guts?* But Meiklebogs just smiled shy and said nothing, except to Feet—that the horse was his property, and he lippened to him it wasn't destroyed. And Feet said *Ay. D'you hear, Mr. Ogilvie? You'd better take home that gun of yours.* And Ake Ogilvie stood and cursed at them both, and folk were shocked at the words he used, calling Meiklebogs a dirty mucker when the man was only seeking his insurance.

Well, there the roan lay all that afternoon, sossing up the road, and it wouldn't die. Folk came from far and near for a look at old Jim the roan as he lay on his side, as the afternoon waned he turned a wee, and the blood began to freeze round the shaft that was stuck so deep in his riven belly. But what with the folk that came in such crowds, a birn of the spinners down from the Mills, and the bairns as they left the school at four, the roan was splashed an inch deep with glaur and hardly twitching or moving by then. Meiklebogs had sent off a wire to Stone-hive, to ask about the insurance, like: but no answer came, and he didn't expect one, he'd the corn loaded on another bit cart and went off home to the Meiklebogs, attending to his work with his shy, sleekèd smile, the insurance his if the horse died natural.

Once or twice Jess Moultrie came out to the beast and held a pail for it to drink out of, it slobbered at the warm water and treacle, syne would leave its head lying heavy in the pail, till Jess lifted the head and put it away; and all the while her face was like death, the fool was near greeting over the horse, if she couldn't stand the sight of the soss, why did she ever go near the beast?

It looked like a hillock of dirt by dark, and then Ake Ogilvie that half the day had been seeking the minister, that was off down the Howe, found him at last and told him the tale. And folk said that the Reverend Colquohoun swore awful—*The bloody swine, the BLOODY swine!*—a strange-like thing to say of a horse. But Ake Ogilvie said it wasn't the horse but the folk of Segget the minister meant. And that was just daft, if Ake spoke true—that Mr. Colquohoun could mean it of folk, real coarse of him to speak that way of decent people that had done him no harm. It just showed you the kind of a tink that he was, him and his Labour and socialism and all

And he said to Ake Ogilvie *Get out your gun,* and Ake got it again, and the two came down, the roan lay still in its puddle of glaur, the cart behind and the night now close. And the circle of folk drew off a wee bit, and the roan seemed to know the thing that Ake meant, for it lifted its head and gave a great groan. The minister looked white as a drift of snow, he cried *Stand back there—damn you, stand back! Ake, aim canny.* And Ake said nothing, but went up to the roan, and folk looked away as they heard the bang.

Soon as Meiklebogs himself had heard of what happened, and he did that in less than the space of an hour, he was over at the Manse to see the minister, with the shy, sly smile on his half-shaved face. And he said *They tell me, Mr. Colquohoun, that you've had my horse shot down in East Wynd.* The minister said *Do they? Then they tell you the truth.* So Meiklebogs said he would sue him for that, and the minister said he could sue and be damned—*And I'll tell you a thing that I am to do—report you for cruelty by the very first post. You're the kind of scoundrel over-common in Scotland.* And Meiklebogs for once lost his shy-like smile. *Say of me again what you said of me now! Mind, there's a witness to hear us, minister.* The Maidie was near in the hall, he meant her, but Mr. Colquohoun was blazing with rage. He said *Get out or I'll throw you out,* and made at Dalziel, and he shambled out, not such a fool as face up to a madman, a creature that fair went mad on a horse.

Nor was that the end of his troubles that day, for when he got home the news had reached Else, she was waiting in the kitchen when Meiklebogs came. He smiled at her shy, *Have you nothing to do but stand about there and be idle, then? Get my supper ready, or I'll need a new housekeeper.* The foreman had come in at the tail of Meiklebogs, and he heard every word that the two of them spoke. Else said *Is this true that I hear of the roan?* and Meiklebogs said *Ay; will you give me my supper?* and Else said *No, but I'll give you my notice. I've stuck queer things at your hands, Meiklebogs. I've been crazed or daft that I've stuck them so long. But I wouldn't bide another night in your house.* And Meiklebogs smiled sleekèd and shy. *Ah well, just gang—with your fatherless bairn.* And Else said she'd do that, but the bairn had a father, God pity the littl'un, the father it had.

She was greeting by then, she'd been fond of the roan. She hardly looked the Else that the foreman knew well, raging and red-haired and foul with her tongue, she stared at Meiklebogs as a body new waked out of the horror of an ill-dreamt dream; and she packed her things and wrapped up her bairn.

The foreman met her out in the close and asked her where she would spend the night, and he made a bit try

to give her a cuddle, maybe he hoped that she'd spend it
with him, her a tink-like quean, him buirdly and brave.
But instead she banged her case at his legs, near couped
him down in the sharn of the close, and held up through
Segget and down to the station, and took the late train to
her father's in Fordoun—the ill-gettèd bitch that she was,
folk said, to leave Meiklebogs without warning like that,
her and her blethering over a horse.

There wouldn't have been half the steer and stour if
Mr. Colquohoun had kept to himself. He'd need to leave
other folk a-be and heed to his own concerns, him, that
tink-cool stepson of his, for one—wasn't *he* the loon what
had led the others in making the slide that mischieved the
horse? He led most of the bairns in ill-gettèd ploys, folk
told after that, though you hadn't heard even a whisper
before. 'Twas said he would sneak in the lassies' playground,
and cuddle and kiss them when they were at games, the
ill-gettèd wretch, and at his age, too. Ay, Mr. Colquohoun
was more in need of trying to reform young Ewan Tavendale than interfering with a good, quiet childe like old
Dalziel of the Meiklebogs.

Old Leslie said *Ay*—it was down at the Arms—*or getting
that proud-looking wife with a bairn—damn't! is that an
example to show, none of a family and married five years?
Now, when I was a loon up in Garvock* . . . and folk began
to hem and talk loud, and look up at the room and hoast in
their throats, and you couldn't hear more, and that was a
blessing, the old fool could deave a dog into dysentery. But
still there was something in what he was saying, other folk
had bairns, they came with the seasons, there was no escape
were you wedded and bedded.

But Dite Peat said *Isn't there, now? Let me tell you*—
and he told about shops in *that lousy hole, London*, where
things were for sale that a man could use, right handy-like,
and what happened then? You never fathered a family, not
you, you could sin as much as you liked and pay nothing.
And Dite said forbye it was his belief that's what that
couple did up at the Manse, that was why Mrs. Colquohoun
went about like a quean, with a skin like cream and a figure
like that, hardly a chest on the creature at all; instead of
the broadening out and about, looking sappy and squash
like a woman of her age. Damn't, what was a woman in
the world for, eh?—but to make your porridge and lie in

your bed and bring as many bairns into the world as would help a man that was getting old? Not that the London things weren't fine for a childe when he went on a holiday, like. But if he himself were tied up, b'God, he'd take care he'd his wife in the family way—ay, every year, with a good bit scraich when it came to her time, that fair was a thing to jake a man up.

That was a dirty enough speak, if you liked. Folk looked here and there and Jim the Sourock, that had gotten religion, cast up his eyes, he had grown so holy with Mac-Dougall's crush that he called the watery the w.c., and wouldn't have it that women had bodies at all more than an inch below the neck-bone. But Hairy Hogg had come in and sat down, folk cried, *Ay, Provost, and what would you say?* And Hairy said he thought Scotland was fair in a way, and if Burns came back he would think the same; and the worst thing yet they had done in Segget was to vote the Reverend Colquohoun to the pulpit—him and his Labour and sneering at folk, damn't! he had said we were monkeys, not men.

Some folk in the bar took a snicker at that, the story was growing whiskers in Segget, but the Provost had never forgiven the minister. And Hairy said it was his opinion, from studying folk a good fifty year—and mind you, he was no fool at the job—the minister took up with some other woman. They said that the father of Else Queen's bairn was old Dalziel of the Meiklebogs, but he, Hairy Hogg, had his doubts of that. Had the minister ever cast out with the quean? No, when he'd meet her out and about he'd cry to her cheery, as though nothing had happened. If he couldn't give a bairn to his mistress, the minister, it was maybe because he was hashed other ways.

Damn't, that was a tasty bit story, now, queer you yourself hadn't thought of that. But long ere another day was done the news was spread through the Segget wynds that the Reverend Mr. Colquohoun, the minister, had fathered the bairn of that quean, Else Queen, the Provost had seen the two of them together, him making ardent love to the lass.

Ake Ogilvie heard the tale from the tailor, and Ake said: *Blethers, and even if it's true what has the business to do with old Hogg? He himself, it seems, has done a bit more than just lie down by the side of his wife—or that gawpus he has for a son's not his.*

That was just like Ake Ogilvie to speak coarse like that,
trying to blacken the character of a man that wasn't there
to defend himself. Peter Peat said *Well, I'm a friend to
my friends, but a man that's once got himself wrong with
me*—and he looked fierce enough to frighten a shark; but
Ake Ogilvie laughed, *And what's Colquohoun done?* And
Peter said *Him? A disgrace to Segget, that should be a
good Conservative. What is he instead?—why, a Labour
tink.* But Ake Ogilvie just said *To hell with their politics,
I don't care though he's trying to bring back the Pretender,
same as that snippet, Jahly young Mowat.*

But Peter wouldn't hear the gentry miscalled, and he said
that Jahly would come to himself, and take his rightful
place, you would see—at the head of the Segget Conservative branch. Ake said *He can take his place on a midden,
if he likes*—*and he'll find they've much the same smell.*
Peter asked what had much the same smell and Ake said
Tories and middens, of course, and Peter Peat looked at
him fierce, and left; that would learn the ill-gettéd joiner,
that would.

Well, the news reached Cronin, the old tink in West
Wynd, him that was aye preaching his socialist stite; and
he said that he thought the whole thing a damned lie, an
attempt to discredit the socialists in Segget. Jock Cronin
at the station heard it and said *He's all right, Colquohoun,*
in an off-hand way, to let you know he and the Manse were
fell thick and slobbered their brose from the very same
bowl.

Ag Moultrie, the Roarer and Greeter (for short), took
the news to the servants at Segget House; and it spread
about there, and when young Mr. Mowat came home from
a trip he had gone to Dundon, he laughed out aloud. *Some
have all the luck. But if Mrs. Colquohoun's in need of a
a bairn I'll give half a year's profits to provide her with one.*
And you couldn't but laugh at the joke of the gent.

Robert was away that New Year's Eve, into Aberdeen, he
wouldn't say why; but Chris could guess and had laughed
at him. *Mind, nothing expensive.* And he'd said *What, in
drinks? I'm going to squat in a pub and swizzle confusion
to all the dour sourocks in Segget!* Chris wished that it
wasn't a joke, and he would; he kissed her and went striding away down the shingle, turning about to wave from the

yews, his kiss still pressed on her lips as she stood, and tingling a bit, like a bee on a flower.

It was frosty weather as the day wore on, the sky and the earth sharp-rimed with steel, no sun came, only a smoulder of grey, Chris cooked the dinner with Maidie to help, and remembered Else, she'd have been more use. Maidie still *Memmed* like a frightened mouse, and once when up and above their heads there came a crash like a falling wall, she nearly jumped from her skin with fright. Chris said *It's just Ewan, he's moving his press,* and Maidie said, *Oh, I got such a fright!* and looked as though it had lifted her liver. Chris left her and went up to Ewan's room, and knocked at the door, he bade her come in, the place was a still, grey haze with dust. She saw Ewan through it by the window ledge, he'd stooped to look in the press he'd moved, it was filled with his precious array of flints.

Chris asked what he was moving today? He said *Everything* and set to on the bed, she sat down and didn't offer to help. His hair fell over his eyes as he tugged, funny to look at, funny to think he had been your baby, been yours, been you, been less than that even—now sturdy and slim, with his firm round shoulders and that dun gold skin he got from yourself, and his father's hair. He stopped in a minute and came where she sat: *I think that'll do, I'll dust after dinner.*

So the two of them went down and had dinner alone, Ewan said he'd have everything moved in his rooms ere the New Year came and Chris asked why. He said *Oh, I like a new angle on things,* and then he said *Mother, you wanted to laugh. What about?* and Chris said *You, I suppose! You sounded so grown-up like for a lad.*

He said nothing to that, but went on with his meat, they didn't say grace when Robert wasn't there, that was funny when you came to think of the thing, Robert knew and knew that you knew he knew. But he was too sure to vex about that, sure of himself and his God and belief, except when the angry black moments came—seldom enough in this last three years. Once he'd raved *Religion—A Scot know religion? Half of them think of God as a Scot with brosy morals and a penchant for Burns. And the other half are over damned mean to allow the Almighty even existence. You know which half you belong to, I think.* Hate and fury in his face as he said it, the day after the killing of Meiklebogs' horse. Chris had looked at him cool and remotely

then, as she'd learned with the years, and he'd banged from
the room, to return in an hour or so recovered. *What a
ranter and raver I am, Christine! I think you'll outlast me
a thousand years!*

And now, on a sudden impulse, she said, *Do you ever
think of religion, Ewan?*

He never said *What?* or said your last word the way
other boys of his age would do; he looked up and shook
his head, *Not now.* She asked when he had and he said,
long ago, when he was a kid and hadn't much sense, he
used to be worried when Robert was preaching. Chris said
But he never tried to fear you, and Ewan shook his head.
*Oh no, it wasn't that. But I hated the notion God was there,
prying into every minute of my life. I wanted to belong to
myself, and I do; it doesn't matter a bit to me now.* She
understood well enough what he meant, how like her he
sometimes was, how unlike! *So you think God doesn't matter, then, Ewan?* and he said, *I don't think He's worth
bothering about. He can't make any difference to the world
—or I should think He'd have made it by now.*

The evening came down before it was four, up in the
Mounth the snow came thick, sheeting hill on hill as it
passed on the wings of the howling wind from the haughs.
But the storm passed north of Segget, lying lithe, Chris in
the kitchen looked out at it pass, she was making cakes
and pies for the morn, Maidie tweetering about like a bird
Eh, Mem, but that's RICH, that'll be a fine one!

Chris said *Then be sure you eat a good share, you're still
thin enough since you came to the Manse. Are you sure you
are well?* And Maidie said *Fine.* She blushed and stood like
a thin little bird, Chris looked at her quiet, a thin little lass
—what did she think, what did she do in her moments
alone, had she a lad, had she ever been kissed—or more
than that, as they said in Segget? Not half the life in her
that poor Else had; what would Else Queen be doing today?

Dark. As they took their tea together, Ewan and Chris,
they left the blinds drawn and could see the night coming
stark outbye, growing strangely light as the daylight waned
and the frost, white-plumed, walked swift over Segget.
Ewan sat on the rug by the fire and read, his blue head
down-bent over his book, Chris stared in the fire and tired
of that and finished her tea, and wandered about and went
to the window and looked at the night. Then she looked at
the clock. She would go and meet Robert.

She turned to the door and Ewan jumped up, she said not to bother, she was going a walk. He said absent-mindedly, *See you keep warm,* and his eyes went back again to his book.

Outside, she went hatless, with her coat collar up, she found at the door of the Manse a wind, bright, keen, and edged like a razor-blade, the world sleeping on the winter's edge, about her, dim-pathed, wound the garden of summer, she passed up its aisles, the hoar crackled below her, all Segget seemed held in the hand-grip of frost. A queer thought and memory came to her then and she turned about from going to the gate, and went back instead by the side of the Manse, up through the garden where the strawberry beds lay covered deep in manure and straw, to the wall that girded the kirkyard of Segget.

Here the wind was still, in the Manse's lithe, she put out a hand on the hoar of the dyke, it felt soft as salt and as cold as steel; and idly, standing, she wrote her name, though she couldn't see it by then in the dark, CHRISTINE COLQUOHOUN in great capital letters. And she minded how once she had stood here before, four years or more, after Segget Show; and she and Robert were there together and she'd thought of the vanished folk in the yard, and planned to add to those that supplanted. And the war-time wound that was seared on Robert had seared that plan from her mind as with fire. . . .

It seemed this night remote from her life as the things she'd dreamt as a quean in Blawearie, when she was a maid and knew nothing of men, the kind of play that a bairn would play: for her who stood here with life in her again, unexpected, certain, Robert's baby and hers.

And she found it strange in that icy hush, leaning there warm, her hair bare to the cold, to think how remote was that life from her now, even bairn for the thing that lay under her heart was a word that she'd hardly used a long time, thinking of it as a baby, in English—that from her books and her life in a Manse. She seemed to stand here by the kirkyard's edge looking back on the stones that marked the years where so many Chrises had died and lay buried— back and back, as the graveyard grew dim, far over those smothered hopes and delights, to that other Chris that had been with child, a child herself or so little more, and had known such terror and delight in that, young and raw and queer and sweet, you thought her now, that Chris that had

been—the Chris far off in that vanished year who had lain
in terror as nights came down with knowledge of the thing
that moved in herself, the fruit of her love for the boy she
had wed, Ewan sleeping so quiet and so sound in her bed.
Remote and far to think she was YOU!

Quiet in the dark she wrote with her finger another name
across that of her own, on the kirkyard dyke, and heard
as she wrote far up in the Kaimes a peesie wheep—maybe
a lost memory from those years in Kinraddie, a peesie that
had known that other Chris! She heard a long scuffling
through the long grass, silver beyond the rim of the dyke,
some rabbit or hare, though it made her heart jump; and
slowly she felt her finger rub out the name she had written
in hoar on the dyke—ill-luck to have done that, she minded
folk said.

A month ago since she'd known for sure, had puzzled for
days with the second no-go. Robert would frown, *What on
earth's gone wrong? You're dreaming, Christine!* and smile,
and she'd smile, and puzzle again when he'd left her alone.
So it came on her in the strangest places, she stood in Mac-
Dougall Brown's to shop, and MacDougall asked thrice
what thing she might want—*Now, Mem*—and she said—
Did I want it at all? and then came to herself at his cod-
like stare. So she gave her order and went out and home,
she supposed MacDougall would manage to make out that
was another proof of her pride!—all Segget for some reason
thought her proud, maybe because she had taken to thinking, not stayed as still as a quean in a book or a quean in
a bothy from year unto year.

And when once Stephen Mowat came down to see
Robert, and she gave them supper and sat by to listen,
Mowat broke off the talk to say *Rahly, Mrs. Colquohoun,
do tell us the joke!* She said *What joke?* And he said *The
one that's making you smile in that charming way.* She said
Oh, I suppose I am full up of supper! And he'd said he
thought that a Jahly untruth, joking, polished as a mart-day
pig.

So at last she had known and woke one day sure; and
lay and dreamt; and Robert got up—*Feeling all right?*—
and she had said *Fine. Robert, we're going to have a baby.*
He stared—*We?*—the thing had staggered him, she lay and
watched, something moved in her heart, laughter for him,
a queer pity for him—oh, men were funny and just boys
to be pitied. *Well, I am,* she'd said, *but you had a share.*

He was standing half-dressed, with his fair hair on end, he sat on the bed and stared and then smiled, slowly, with that crinkling about the eyes she had loved near the very first time she met him. *Really and honest-to-God that we are?* And she'd said it was real enough, how did it happen? And he'd said he hadn't the least idea, and that struck them as funny, they giggled like children; and after 'twas Robert that went into long dreams. She'd say *What again?* and he'd say *But Christine! A baby—Good Lord, I hope it's a girl! What does it feel like being as you are—a nuisance, just, or tremendous and terrible?* And Chris had said that it made you feel sick, now and then, and Robert had laughed at that, he wasn't so easily cheated as Mowat. *Oh Chris Caledonia, I've married a nation!*

Now, standing beside the dyke in the dark, she minded that, it was true enough, somehow you did hide away the things, Scots folk had always done that, you supposed—in case they'd go blind in their naked shrine, like a soul in the presence of Robert's great God—God he followed unfaltering still, and was getting Him deeper in dislike than ever, with his preaching in Segget the cause of the Miners. These were the folk that were going on strike, in May, unless their wages were raised. Robert said their case was a testing case, the triumph of greed or the triumph of God.

Chris herself had hardly a thought in the matter because of that nameless doubt that was hers—doubt of the men and method that came to change the world that was waiting change—all the mixed, strange world of the Segget touns, with its failing trade and its Mills often idle. The folk of the Mills would hang round the room where their dole was paid by a little clerk, they'd laze there and snicker at the women that passed, and yawn, with weariness stamped on each face; and smoke, and whistle, and yawn some more. Once she'd passed and heard some of them quarrelling out loud, she had thought it must surely be over politics; but instead 'twas the chances of a football match! She'd told Robert that and he'd laughed and said *Demos!—didn't you know that the chap was like that? But we'll alter these things forever in May.*

May: and the baby wouldn't come till July, a good enough month for a baby to be born, though Robert said if they had planned it at all they would surely have planned it better than that. July might be far too hot for comfort. But he didn't fuss round her, stood back and aside, he knew it her work and that he'd little help—oh, different as could be from the Ewan long ago, the frightened boy who had so fussed about her—how they'd quarrelled, how wept, how laughed in that time of the coming of that baby that was now in the Manse—a boy, grown up, remote from it all, remote enough with his books and his flints, far enough off from being a baby, rather like a flint himself in some ways, but of a better shape and grain, grey granite down to the core, young Ewan, with its flinty shine and its cool grey skin and the lights and the flashing strands in it. Different from that, Robert's baby and hers——

She stamped her feet and woke from her dreaming as down through the dark she heard on the shingle the coming footsteps of Robert himself.

And next morning he said, *Let's go out a walk, up in the hills somewhere—are you keen?* Chris said she was and well before eight they were off, they met with Ewan in the hall as they went, he said nothing at all about going out with them, he always knew when he wasn't much wanted. Chris kissed him and said they'd be back for dinner; syne she and Robert went up by the Kaimes, and Ewan stood and looked after them—you could hardly believe that Chris was so old.

Underfoot the frost held hard and firm in the rising sun of the New Year's Day, that sun a red smoulder down in the Howe, the hoar was a blanching on post and hedge, riming the dykes, far up in the Mounth the veilings of mists were draping the hills, except that now and then they blew off and you saw the coarse country deep in the haughs, remote with a flicker of red on the roofs of some shepherd's sheiling high in the heath. Robert was walking so fast that Chris for a while could hardly keep up with his stride, then she fell into that and found it easy, the Kaimes was past and above it the path opened out through the ragged fringe of the moor that came peering and sniffling down at Segget as a draggled cat at a dish out of doors, all the countryside begirdled with hills and their companions the moors that crept and slept and yawned in the sun, watching the Howe at its work below.

They passed a tarn that was frozen and shone, Chris tried the edge with her stick and it broke, and she saw herself for a minute then, with the looped-up hair and the short-cut skirts and the leather jacket tight at her waist, high in the collar; and the blown bronze of her cheeks and hair and the stick in her hands and the fur-backed gloves, she smiled at herself for this Chris that she'd grown. Robert stopped and looked back and was puzzled and came and stood by her side and looked down at that Chris that smiled remote in the broken ice. *Yes, not at all bad. See the childe by her shoulder? Do you think the two can be decently married?*

Chris said that she thought not, they'd something in their eyes—and Robert kissed her then, iron, his hard, quick kiss, the kiss of a man with other passions than kissing: but wonderful and daft a moment to stand, on the frozen moor, her head back on his shoulder, and so be kissed, and at last released, Robert panting a little, and they both looked away; and then they went on, swinging hand in hand for a while till they tired and needed their sticks.

Robert went first, bare-headed, black-coated, he was whistling *Over the Sea to Skye*, clear and bright as they still went on, up through the wind of a sheep-track here where the Grampians pushed out their ramparts in fence against the coming of life from below.

By eleven they were high in the Culdyce moor, winding the twist of its slopes in the broom that hung thick-rimed with unshaken frost for the sun had died away in a smoulder, the Howe lay grey in a haze below, as they climbed that haze betook itself from the heights to the haughs, Leachie towered high, its crag-head swathed with a silk-web mutch. Trusta's ten hundred feet cowered west as if bending away from the blow of the wind, the moors a ragged shawl on her shoulders, crouching and seated since the haughs were born, watching the haze in the Howe below, the flicker of the little folk that came and builded and loved and hated and died, and were not, a crying and swarm of midges warmed by the sun to a glow and a dance. And the Trusta heights drew closer their cloaks, year by year, at the snip of the shears, as coulter and crofter moiled up the haughs.

Once Chris and Robert came to a place, out in the open, here the wind blew and the ground was thick with the droppings of sheep, where a line of the ancient stones stood ringed, as they stood in Kinraddie far west and below, left by the men of antique time, memorial these of a dream long lost, the hopes and fears of fantastic eld.

Robert said that they came from the East, those fears,

long ago, ere Pytheas came sailing the sounding coasts to
Thule. Before that the hunters had roamed these hills,
naked and bright, in a Golden Age, without fear or hope
or hate or love, living high in the race of the wind and the
race of life, mating as simple as beasts or birds, dying with
a like keen simpleness, the hunting weapons of those ancient folk Ewan would find in his search of the moors.
Chris sat on a fallen stone and heard him, about her the
gleams of the wintry day, the sailing cloud-shapes over the
Howe; and she asked how long ago that had been? And
Robert said *Less than four thousand years,* and it sounded
long enough to Chris—four thousand years of kings and
of Gods, all the dark, mad hopes that had haunted men
since they left the caves and the hunting of deer, and the
splendour of life like a song, like the wind.

And she thought then, looking on the shadowed Howe
with its stratus mists and its pillars of spume, driving west
by the Leachie bents, that men had followed these pillars
of cloud like lost men lost in the high, dreich hills, they
followed and fought and toiled in the wake of each whirling pillar that rose from the heights, clouds by day to darken
men's minds—loyalty and fealty, patriotism, love, the
mumbling chants of the dead old gods that once were worshipped in the circles of stones, christianity, socialism, nationalism—all—Clouds that swept through the Howe of the
world, with men that took them for gods: just clouds, they
passed and finished, dissolved and were done, nothing endured but the Seeker himself, him and the everlasting Hills.

Then she came from that thought, Robert shaking her
arm. *Chris, you'll be frozen. Let's climb to the camp.* He
had once been here with Ewan, she hadn't; the moor shelved
smoothly up to its top, as they climbed in view Chris saw
two lines of fencing climbing each slope of the hill, new-
driven and stapled, the fences, they met and joined and
ended up on the crest. But before that meeting and joining
they plunged through the circles of the ancient camp that
had been, the turf and the stones had been flung aside,
Robert told that the hill had been recently sold and the
lands on either side as well, and two different landowners
bought the hill and set up those fences to show their rights
—what were dirt like the old heathen forts to them? Symbols of our age and its rulers, these clowns, Robert said, and
the new culture struggling to birth—when it came it would
first have to scavenge the world!

Then he started talking of the Miners, of Labour, of the coming struggle in the month of May, he hoped and believed that that was the beginning of the era of Man made free at last, Man who was God, Man splendid again. Christ meant and intended no more when He said that He was the Son of Man, when He preached the Kingdom of Heaven— He meant it on earth. Christ was no godlet, but a leader and hero——

He forgot Chris, striding up and down the slope, excitement kindled in his harsh, kind eyes. And Chris watched him, standing, her stick behind her, her arms looped about it, saying nothing to him but hearing and seeing, him and the hills and the song that both made. And suddenly she felt quite feared, it was daft—as she looked at the scaling heights high up, the chasms below, and her Robert against them.

She put out her hand and caught him, he turned, something in her face stopped questions, all else, the pity and fear that had been in her eyes. He didn't kiss her now, his arms round about her, they were quiet a long moment as they looked in each other, they had never done that that Chris could remember, seeing herself globed earnest, half-smiling, and with trembling lips there in the deep grey pools that hid away Robert—never hers for long if ever at all, unceasing the Hunter of clouds by day. The men of the earth that had been, that she'd known, who kept to the earth and their eyes upon it—the hunters of clouds that were such as was Robert: how much was each wrong and how much each right, and was there maybe a third way to Life, unguessed, unhailed, never dreamed of yet?

Then he said *Now we surely know each other,* and she came from her mood to meet his with a laugh, *If we don't we've surely done shameful things!* And they sat in the lithe of the heath-grown dyke and ate chocolate Robert had brought in his pocket, and Chris fell fast asleep as she sat, and awoke with Robert sitting still lest he wake her, one hand around her and under her heart, but far away from her in his thoughts, his eyes on the sailing winter below and his thoughts with the new year that waited their coming down through the hills in the Segget wynds.

Chris watched the coming of that spring in Segget with her interests strange-twisted back on themselves, as though she re-lived that Chris of long syne, far from the one that had taken her place, that Chris of kirks and Robert of books—they sank from sight in the growing of the spring, quick on the hills, on the upland parks, you saw the fields of Meiklebogs change as you looked from the window of that room in the Manse that John Muir had set with Blawearie gear. It was there you intended the baby be born, the only sign of insanity yet, said Robert, laughing, and helping you change.

He seemed to have altered too with the Spring, the black mood came seldom or never now, nor that red, queer cough that companioned it. You'd hear him of a morning go whistling away under the yews, on some kirk concern, blithe as though the world had been born anew. It wasn't only the coming of the baby that had altered him so and kindled his eyes, all the air of the country was filled with its rumour, that thing awaited the country in May, when the Miners and others had threatened to strike. Robert said that more than a strike would come, the leaders had planned to seize power in May.

The red-ploughed lands steamed hot in the sun as Meiklebogs' men drove slow their great teams in the steam of the waiting world of Spring, the rooks behind them, Chris stood still and watched, and remembered, and put her hand up to her heart, and then lower, by belly and thigh: and slow, under her hand, that shape would turn, May close and July coming closer now, she felt fit and well, contented, at peace.

Ewan knew now, he had stared one morning; and then asked if she was going to have a baby. Chris had said *Yes, do you mind very much?* and he had said *No,* but hadn't kissed her that morning, she watched him go with a catch of breath. But by night he seemed to have got the thing over, he put cushions behind her when she sat at tea, grave, and with care, and Robert winked at her. Ewan saw the wink and flashed his cool smile; and they all sat silent in front of the fire, with its smouldering glow, they had no need to speak.

Then Maidie knew, as she watched Chris at work, and tweetered the news to some quean outbye, and the quean gasped *Never!* and told Ag Moultrie, the Roarer and Greeter, met in the street. And Ag had nearly a fit with delight, and before that night came down in Segget there was hardly a soul in both touns but knew the minister's wife had taken at last—ay, and must be fell on with it, too, by her look, so the lassie Moultrie had said. Had Ag seen her? you'd ask, and they'd tell you Ay, she'd fairly done that, and Mrs. Colquohoun had told the bit news to Ag Moultrie herself; and syne broke down and just Roared and Grat on Ag's shoulder.

Old Leslie said 'twas Infernal, just, you'd have thought a minister would have more sense. He never had thought it decent in a minister to show plain to his parish he did *that* kind of thing; and he minded when he was a loon up in Garvock—Those nearest the door of the smiddy nipped out, Ake Ogilvie near was killed in the rush, and he found Old Leslie habbering to himself, hammering at a horseshoe, and far off in Garvock. *What's up then, Leslie?* Ake Ogilvie asked, and Leslie said *What, have you not heard the news?* and told of the thing that was on at the Manse, and might well have begun to tell of Garvock, but that Ake, the coarse brute, said *Well, what of it? Didn't your own father lie with your mother—the poor, misguided devil of a childe?*

Syne out he went swaggering and met with John Muir, and asked if he'd heard what the scandal-skunks said? Muir gleyed and said Ay, and it made him half-sick, and Ake said the same, they were both of them fools, and cared nothing at all for a tasty bit news.

John Muir went home, never told his wife, she found out herself nearly three days late; and fair flew into a rage at that, to be so far behind with the news. *Did you know the news of Mrs. Colquohoun?* she speired of John and he gleyed and said *Ay.* And she asked could he never tell her a thing, her that had to bide at home and cook, and wash and sew and mend all the time, with himself and two meikle trollops of daughters, working her hands to the very bone? And John said *Well, it's nothing to me if Mrs. Colquohoun has been ta'en with a bairn—I'm not the father, as far as I know.*

Mrs. Muir reddened up. *Think shame of yourself speaking that way in front of the lassies.* Tooje was standing with her meikle mouth open, drinking it up, afore she could close it her mother took her a crack in the gape. Tooje started to greet and Ted in the garden heard the greeting, as aye she would do, and came tearing in, and started to greet to keep Tooje company; and John Muir got up with his pipe and his paper and went out to the graveyard and sat on a stone, and had a fine read: decent folk, the dead.

In the Arms Dite Peat said *Wait till it comes. She's the*

*kind that takes ill with having a bairn—over narrow she is,
she'll fair have a time. I warrant the doctor'll need his bit
knives.* Folk thought that an unco-like speak to make, he'd
a mind as foul as a midden, Dite Peat: but for all that you
went to the kirk the next Sabbath and took a gey keek at
Mrs. Colquohoun—ay, God! she fairly was narrow round
there, more like a quean than a grown-up woman, with her
sulky, proud face and her well-brushed hair, she'd look not
so bonny when it came to her time.

Then Hairy Hogg heard it and minded the story of what
Mr. Mowat had said he would give—to take the minister's
wife with a bairn. *You well may depend that was more than
a speak.* Folk had forgotten it but now they all minded,
it was said in Segget it was ten to one the bairn wasn't the
minister's at all, young Mr. Mowat had been heard to say
he'd given half of a whole year's profits for lying with that
proud-like Mrs. Colquohoun. MacDougall Brown said 'twas
a black, black sin, and he preached a sermon in the Square
next Sabbath, about scarlet priesthoods living in shame;
and everybody knew what he meant by that, his son Jock
wabbled his eyes all around, and Mrs. Brown shook like a
dollop of fat; only Cis looked away and turned red and
shy, and thought of Dod Cronin and his hands and lips.

The spinners didn't care when the news reached *them*,
though an unco birn came now to the kirk that had never
attended a kirk before, the older men mostly, disjaskèd, ill-
dressed, with their white, spinner faces and ill-shaved chins,
like raddled old loons, and they brought their wives with
them—the minister was fairly a favourite with them. So
might he be, aye siding with the dirt and the Labour stite
that the Cronins preached; and twice he had interfered at
the Mills and forced Mr. Mowat to clean out his sheds.
But the younger spinners went to no kirk, just hung about
of a Sabbath day, and snickered as a decent body went by,
or took their lasses up to the Kaimes as soon as the Spring
sun dried the grass.

Most of the gossip Chris heard of or knew, and cared
little or nothing, folk were like that, she thought if you'd
neither books nor God nor music nor love nor hate as stand-
bys, no pillar of cloud to lead your feet, you turned as the
folk of farm and toun—to telling scandal of your nearest
neighbours, making of them devils and heroes and saints,
to brighten your days and give you a thrill. And God knew
they were welcome to get one from her, she found herself

liking them as never before, kindled to new interest in every known face, seized again and again in the Segget wynds—looking at the rat-like little Peter Peat, at MacDougall's bald head, at the lizard-like Mowat—with the startling thought, *He was once a bairn!* It nearly put you off having one sometimes; and then again you'd be filled with such a queer pity, as you passed, that Hairy Hogg would go in and say to his wife—*That Mrs. Colquohoun she goes by me and SNICKERS!* and his wife would say *Well damn't, do you want her to go by you and greet?*

So April was here, with its steaming drills and the reek of dung in the Meiklebogs parks; and in Segget backyards a scraich and chirawk as the broods of the winter gobbled their corn, you could hear the ring of the smiddy hammer across the still air right to the Manse—above it, continuous, the drum of the Mills. Young Mr. Mowat had new orders on hand and most of the spinners were at work again. But early that week that he put them on Stephen Mowat came down to the Manse, with a paper in his hand and a list of names. He wanted Robert to join the list, the O.M.S., a volunteer army, that was being prepared all over the country to feed the country in the Miners' strike. And he said that they didn't always see eye to eye, him and Colquohoun, but that this was serious: you Jahly well couldn't let a push like the miners dictate to the country what it should do. And he said that Rahly Robert must join, and Mrs. Colquohoun as well, if she would; and he smiled at her charming, and showed all his teeth.

Robert said *Well, Christine, what do you say?* and Chris didn't much care for she didn't much hope. Then she looked at Mowat, elegant, neat, in his London clothes, with his tended hair and his charming look; and the saggy pouches under his eyes. And it seemed she was looking at more than Mowat, the class that had made of the folk of Segget the dirt-hungry folk that they had been and were—made them so in sheer greed and sheer brag. You had little hope what the Miners could do, them or the Labour leaders of Robert, but they couldn't though they tried make a much worse mess than Mowat and his kind had done, you knew. So you just said *No;* Robert smiled at Mowat. *That's Chris's answer, a trifle abrupt. And I can't help the O.M.S. myself—you see, I've another plan afoot.* Mowat said that was Jahly, what was the plan? And Robert said

*Why, do all that I can to hinder the O.M.S. or such skunks
as try to interfere with the Strike.*

Chris had never admired Stephen Mowat so much, he
kept his temper, charming, polite, she and Robert watched
him stride from the door, down under the yews, and they
later heard he had gone to the Provost and gotten his help,
and the same from Geddes, and the same from Melvin that
kept the Arms. Near everybody that counted would help,
except the spinners, the Manse, and Ake Ogilvie—Ake had
told Mr. Mowat they could hamstring each other, strikers and
Government, for all that he cared. And neither would Mac-
Dougall Brown give his name, he said his living depended
on spinners: and if all the world renounced its sin the cares
of the world would be ended tomorrow.

And all the time he was saying this he was mixing sawdust under the counter, canny-like, in a bag of meal.

Chris put the whole thing out of her mind, busied in
making the baby's clothes, busied in going long walks by
herself, the last day in April she took Ewan with her, across
by Mondynes, till they saw far off, crowning the hills, the
roofs of Kinraddie. *You were born over there twelve years
ago,* she thought aloud as they sat to rest, Ewan with his
head cupped up in his hands, his arms on his knees, his
blue-black hair rumpled, untidily tailed, in the glow of the
sun. He said, *Yes, I know,* and then looked at her sudden—
*but I say! I never really thought of that . . . Or anyway,
never as I thought just now.* She asked how was that, and
he looked down the Howe. *Well, that I once was a part of
you; though, of course, I know all about how babies come.*

And for almost the first time in years he seemed troubled,
her boy, the fruit of herself, so cool, so kind and sure and
so stony-clear, troubled to a sudden, queer brittled pity.
Mother! And he looked at her, then away, then came and
cuddled her tight for a moment, his arms round her throat
Chris nearly was stifled: but she didn't move, didn't say a
word at that strange embracing on the part of Ewan.

And May and tomorrow waited their feet as they turned
back quiet up the Segget road.

Ewan in his bed; in the May-time dark Chris wandered
the sitting-room of the Manse, looking again and again from
the window at the mist that had come and grew thicker each
minute. Beyond her vision the yews, the hedge: she could

see but a little space from the window, a space translit by a misty star, the lights far up in Segget House.

What had happened to Robert—had he been in time?

And at last she could bear it no longer, went out, into the hall and put on her coat, and opened the door and went down through the path, through the slimy, slow crunch of the shingle, mist-wet. A light gleamed faint in the house of John Muir and a dog barked loud from old Smithie's shed as he heard her footsteps pass in the mist, it came draping its cobwebs across her face, she put up her hand and wiped off the globes, from her lashes, and stopped and listened on the road. Nothing to be heard, the mist like a blanket, had Robert come up with the spinners in time?

They had gone to blow up the High Segget brig, a birn of the spinners and one of the porters, the news had been brought to the Manse by John Cronin, panting—*They've gone to blow up the brig and prevent the trains that the blacklegs are running reaching beyond this, or south from Dundon.* Robert had jumped up—*When did they go?* and Cronin had said *Ten minutes ago, I heard of it only now in Old Town, this'll mean the police and arrest for us all.* Robert had said *Oh, damn the fools and their half-witted ploys—blowing up brigs! Right, I'll be with you,* and hadn't waited his coat, had told Chris not to worry and kissed her, and ran, long-striding down through the shingle, Cronin at his heels and the mist coming down.

Where were they now, what had happened at the brig?

She pressed on again, that fear for an urge—a fool to be out, maybe Robert would miss her. The mist was so thick she could hardly see a thing on the other side of the Wynd, she kept the leftward wall and held down, past the locked-up shop of little Peter Peat, the shop of the Provost locked up as well, and Dite Peat's as well, all three of them specials enrolled by Mowat to help Simon Leslie. But the station folk and the spinners were out, so Robert had told her, and here in Segget, as all over the country, the Strike held firm.

Had he and Cronin reached the brig in time?

Now she was down in the Square, so she knew, the lights of the Arms seeped up through the mist, the Arms crowded with spinners as usual, few of them knew of the thing at the brig, John Cronin had said the folk who had gone to blow up the place were no more than boys, and daft at that, with their blasting-powder gotten or thieved from the quarry at Quarles.

As Chris crossed the Square she met in the mist two men who were holding up to East Wynd, Sim Leslie was one, and a man with a brassard, one of the specials, she thought it Dite Peat. They peered in her face and Sim Leslie coughed, and the man with the brassard laughed a foul laugh. Chris felt her blood go cold at that laugh, she heard them engage in a mutter of talk as she hurried down the road to the station.

There were lights down there, but still as the grave, she stood and looked down, her heart beating fast. And so, as she stood, slowly, quietly, under her heart her baby moved. She gasped a little, she must go more slow, she shouldn't be out in the mist at all. Robert and Cronin must have reached them in time.

But even yet she could not go back. She stood and listened in the mist and heard the fall of it on the grass, on the hedge, beyond the wall where she stood and leaned—soft, in a feathery falling of wet, blanketing sound away from her ears. She ought to go home, but how could she, unsure?

In that minute, far to the south the mist suddenly broke and flamed: she stared: the flame split up through the mirk from the ground. Then there came to her ears the crack and crinkle of such explosion as she'd heard before up in the Mounthside Quarles quarry. She knew what it meant; and started to run.

Beyond the railway lines was the path that wound by the lines till it reached Segget Brig. Here the hawthorns brushed her face and the grass whipped wetly about her legs as she ran, not thinking, trying hard not to think, to run fleetly, and gain the Brig, as she must—Robert was there—Oh, and those fools!

The second explosion laid hand on the night and shook the mist as a great hand might. Then it died, and Chris found the true dark had come, it had seeped through the mist like spilt ink through paper, and she couldn't run now, but walked and stumbled, and heard no more for it seemed an hour.

Till far behind her there rose a whistle, a long-drawn blast remote in the night.

She stopped at that and turned about, a whin-bush lashed her face as she turned and then stood listening and looking beside her. And far away north up the side of the Mounth a line of lights twinkled suddenly bright, and moved and slowed and came to a stop.

Clenched hand at her throat, for that seemed to help, she gasped and stared at the cluster at halt—some Dundon train that had halted at Carmont, in five minutes more it would be in Segget, and the brig was down, and it wouldn't know——

Running again she felt that change, slow and dreadful and sick in her body, her arms held out as she kept the path; and she cried to the thing unborn in her womb, *Not now, not now;* and it moved again. Then up the line she heard the skirl of the starting train, its windows flashed, it purred from sight as it climbed through the woods—she never could do it, try though she might!

Yet, so at last, running, she did; and gained the road with the station below. Down there was a flurry and scurry of lights, behind on the road a scurry of feet. She turned at that sound, saw a drift of men, she seemed to know one: and cried out *Robert!*

The night quietened away in a mist of faces and a kindled lantern and Robert's voice. So later Chris minded, and then the next hours closed suddenly up as a telescope closes. One minute she was standing, her teeth in her lip, harkening Robert tell how he'd gained the brig, just in time, they'd done no more than test off the powder, he and Cronin had stopped them at that; and the next she was up in the Manse with Robert, as she stood in the hall and he closed the door the hall rose up and spun twice round her head, she stared at the grandfather clock in the hall, for a minute she couldn't breathe, couldn't move. Something suddenly flooded her mouth, she sopped the stuff with her handkerchief—red, and saw as last thing Robert's startled scowl as he leapt to catch her; and then he quite vanished.

She opened her eyes in bed the next time, sick and weak with the May light high and pouring into the room in a flood, somebody she didn't know near the bed. Then the somebody turned and looked and Chris knew her, she whispered *It's Else!* and Else said *Shish! You mustn't move, Mem,* and crinkled her face as though she would cry. Chris would have laughed if she hadn't been weak, so she closed her eyes for another rest, maybe another day, maybe a minute, and woke, and the dark was close outbye, the first thing she heard as she came from the dark the rake and tweet of the rooks in the yews.

She looked round about and saw Robert and Ewan,

Robert was over by the window, hunched, with his shoulders
and head black-carved in the light, Ewan was sitting by the
side of her bed, a hand on his knee, his head down-bent,
looking at a little flint in his hand. She coughed: and both
of them turned at the sound, and she coughed again and
saw with surprise the stuff that spilt from her mouth on
the sheet, not red, it was brown, and she suddenly saw,
vividly clear and distinct, it was awful, horror and horror
in Robert's face.

.   .   .   .   .   .

Night, with a setting of stars, all alone, in the May-time
dark, she knew it still May. There was a hiss of rain on the
roof, light rain, and all the house set in silence but for that
whisper of the falling rain. She lay and suddenly knew the
Thing close, a finish to the hearing of rain on the roof, a
finish to knowing of that hearing at all, the world cut off,
she felt free and light, strung to a quivering point of impatience as she waited and waited and the night went by
—ready and ready she waited, near cried, because the
Thing didn't come after all. And grew tired and slept; and
the Thing drew back.

Lord, Chris, you've given us a devil of a time!
She lay and looked at him and suddenly she knew,
wakened wide, she said *And what happened to my baby?*
Robert said *You mustn't worry about that. Get well, my
dear*—he was thin as a rake, and near as ungroomed, his
hair up on end, she asked if Maidie had been doing the
cooking, for him and Ewan—and where was Ewan? He said
that Ewan was at school today, seeing the doctor had found
her much better. As for Maidie, she'd proved no use at all,
and he'd sent for Else, Else had done fine. . . .

So it hadn't been a dream Chris lay and knew as the
hours went by, and Robert went out and Else came in; and
later the doctor and all fussed about her; below the sheets
her body felt flat, ground down and flat, with an empty
ache; and her breasts hurt and hurt till they saw to them,
she hadn't cried at all when she knew what had happened,
till it came for them to see her breasts, for a minute she
nearly was desperate then. But that was just daft, she'd
given plenty of trouble, said the Chris that survived all
things that came to her. So she gave in quietly, and they

finished at last, and she slept till Ewan came back from the school, and came up after tea, and looked in and smiled.

Hello, mother, better?

He came to the bedside and suddenly cuddled her; for a minute she was hurt with the weight of his head on her breast, though she put up her arms about him. Then something hot trickled on her breast, and she knew what—Ewan to cry! that was dreadful. But he did it only a minute while she held him, then drew away and took out his handkerchief and wiped his eyes, and sat down, calm, but she didn't care, reaching out and touching his hand as he sat. Funny she should ever have feared she would lose him, that already she'd done so, him no longer a baby, remote from her thoughts or from thought of her. How nearer he was than any there were! She said *You must tell me Ewan, what happened. When was the baby born, was it dead?*

So he told her the baby was born that morning after the spinners were to blow up the brig. Robert had gone for the doctor and Ewan had stayed at home and tried to look after her, though he didn't know much of the things he should do: as for Maidie, the girl was a perfect fool. At last the doctor and Robert arrived, Robert sent off a wire to Else at Fordoun, and they put Ewan out of the room—he was glad, even though it was Chris, he'd a beast of a headache. The baby had been born then, it wasn't born dead, though it died soon after, or so Ewan heard. Else said that it was a boy, like Robert, but Ewan hadn't seen it: that was days ago, two or three days before the Strike ended.

Chris remembered: *What, is it ended, then? Who won?* and Ewan said the Government, Robert raved the leaders had betrayed the Strike, they'd been feared that they would be jailed, the leaders, they had sold the Strike to save their skins. Robert hadn't believed the news when it came, that was the morning that Chris was so bad and the two of them had sat in her room——

Chris lay still and said *Thank you, Ewan,* with a little ghost of a laugh inside to know that he called her Chris in his thoughts, as she'd thought he did; and soon, wearied still, she slept again, sleeping till supper-time, it brought Else up with a tray and hot bottle and all things needed, she cried, right pleased, *You're fine again, Mem?* and Chris said she was, she had to thank Else with others for that.

Else said *Devil a thanks—if you'll pardon a body men-*

*tioning Meiklebogs' cousin in a Manse. I liked fine to come
'stead of biding in Fordoun, with the old man glunching at
me and my bairn.* Chris asked how the baby was, and Else
kindled, *Fine, Mem, and fegs you should see how he grows.*
And then suddenly stopped and punched up the pillows,
and set Chris up rough, and began to chatter, like a gramo-
phone suddenly gone quite mad, with her ears very red and
her face turned away.

Chris knew why she did it, she'd thought of that baby
she'd carried out dead from this room a while back, she
was feared that Chris might take ill again were anything
said to mind her of babies. But Chris had never felt further
from weeping, appalled at the happening to Robert, not her.

Else told how the Strike had ended in Segget, folk said
that the spinners who went out that night and tried to blow
up the brig would be jailed. But there was no proof, only
rumours and scandal, and the burnt grass in the lee of the
brig. Sim Leslie, him that the folk called Feet, had come
up to the Manse like a sow seeking scrunch, but the minister had dealt with him short and sharp and he taiked away
home like an ill-kicked cur.

The spinners and station folk wouldn't believe it when
the news came through that the Strike was ended, they said
the news was just a damned lie, John Cronin said it, and
they wouldn't go back, he and the minister kept them from
that till they got more telegrams up from London. And Mr.
Colquohoun and Ake Ogilvie the joiner, John Muir and
some spinners had organised pickets to keep Mr. Mowat's
folk from getting to the Mills. Syne they heard how the
leaders had been feared of the jail, and the whole things
just fell to smithereens in Segget. Some spinners that night
went down the West Wynd and bashed in the windows of
the Cronin house, and set out in a birn to come to the
Manse, they said the minister had egged them on, him safe
and sound in his own damned job, and they'd do to the
Manse as they'd done to the Cronins.

But coming up the Wynd they met in with Ake Ogilvie,
folk said that he cursed them black and blue; and told them
how Chris was lying ill and wouldn't it have been a damned
sight easier for Mr. Colquohoun to have kept in with the
gentry, instead of risking his neck for the spinners? The
spinners all sneered and jeered at Ake, but he stood fast
there in the middle of the road, and wouldn't let them up,

and they turned and tailed off. A third were on to the
Bureau again, and Jock Cronin sacked from his job at the
station, and Miss Jeannie Grant hadn't gone to the school,
though all the nine days she'd been helping the spinners:
and when she went back Mr. Geddes said *No,* and folk told
that she would get the sack, too.

Chris said *So it ended like that? Else—was my baby born
dead, and was it a boy?* Else went white and wept a little
at that, Chris lay and watched and Else peeked at her,
scared, she looked strangely un-ill with that foam of bronze
hair, and the dour face thin, but still sweet and sure. Else
said that it wasn't, it lived half an hour, the minister came
up and baptized it Michael, a bonny bairn, tiny and quiet,
it yawned and blinked its eyes just a minute—*oh, Mem, I
shouldn't be telling you this!*

Chris said *But you should. Where is it buried?* and Else
said 'twas out in the old kirkyard, there were only the minister and Muir and herself, the minister carried the coffin
in there, and read the service, *bonny he did it, if it wasn't
for that fool John Muir that stood by, like a trumpet, near,
blowing his nose. And when the minister came to the bit
about Resurrection—I don't mind the words——*

Chris said *I do,* and heard her own voice tell them with
Else near weeping again: *I am the Resurrection and the
Life. He that believeth in me, though he were dead, yet shall
he live.*

Else gulped and nodded. *And after he said that—he
didn't know what he was saying, Mem, with his bairn new
dead and his Strike as well—he said AND WHO SHALL
BELIEVE? quiet and queer. . . . I shouldn't be telling you
this, but oh! you'll have to hurry and get well for him!*

Coming out of those memories given to the years, Chris
moved and looked at the waiting Segget, quiet in the lazy
spray of June sun, the same land and sun that Hew Monte
Alto had looked on that morning before Bara battle. You
were waiting yourself in a halt before battle: all haltings
were that, you thought, or would think if you weren't too
wearied to think now at all.

But that would pass soon, you'd to get better quick—
quick and quick for the sake of Robert. Better, and take
him out of himself, Ewan would help, maybe Segget even
yet——

She rose slow to her feet and smiled at herself, for that
weakness that followed her when she stood up, with the

drowse of the June day a moment a haze of little floating
specks in her eyes. Then that cleared, and a cold little wind
came by, she looked up and saw a thickening of clouds,
rain-nimbus driving down upon Segget.

IV

NIMBUS

Now, with the coming of the morning, the stars shone
bright and brittle on the Segget roofs, the rime of the frost
Chris saw rise up, an uneasy carpet that shook in the wind,
the icy wind from the sea and Kinneff. Under her feet the
dark ground cracked, as though she were treading on the
crackle of grass, and as she passed through the Kaimes'
last gate—far up, in the dimming light of the stars, there
fell a long flash from the arc of the sky, rending that brittle
white glow for a moment, its light for a second death-white
on the hills. Then she saw the sky darken, and the corpse-
light went: behind the darkness the morning was coming.

So, walking quick to keep her feet warm, and because
she'd but little time left for this ploy, she gained the Kaimes
and halted and looked—not at them, but up at the heights
of the hills, sleeping there on the verge of dawn. Nothing
cried or moved, too early as yet, but a peewit far in the
hidden hollow, she minded how it was here she had come—
almost at this very hour she had come—the very first night
she had lain in Segget. And here she climbed from those
ten full years, still the same Chris in her heart of hearts,
nothing altered but space and time and the things she had
once believed everlasting and sure—believed that they
made her life, they made her! But they hadn't, there was

393

something beyond that endured, some thing she had never yet garbed in a name.

She put up her hand to her dew-touched hair, she'd climbed bareheaded up to the Kaimes, she had seen a grey hair here and there last night. But it felt the same hair as she felt the same self, its essence unchanged whatever its look. Queer and terrible to think of that now—that all things passed as your life went on, but the little things you had given no heed.

The wind goeth towards the south, and turneth about unto the north; it whirleth aloud continually, and the wind returneth again according to his circuits.

That was Ecclesiastes, she thought; stilled; the dawn pallid on her coiled, bronze hair.

In Segget below a cock crew shrill, she turned and looked down at the shining of frost, remotely, and saw it gleam and transmute, change and transmute as though Time turned back, back through the green and grey of the years till that last time here when she'd climbed the Kaimes, her baby new dead and herself a live ache——

She had shown as little of the ache as she might, in spite of the waste, she had hated that. So she told to Robert and he laughed and said *You sound like a woman in an Aberdeen joke,* his eyes with the beast of the black mood in them. *Waste? Good God, do you think that is all?*

He flung away from her and walked to the window, beyond it the smell and blow of the hay in the sleeping parks of Dalziel of Meiklebogs. Then suddenly he turned—*Christine, I'm sorry. But I'm weary as well, let's not speak of it more.*

And she left it at that, he'd drawn into himself, lonely, he sat for hours in his room with impatience for either her pity or help. So she buried herself in the work of the house, and sought in her pride a salve for the sting of the knowledge she counted for little with Robert, compared with his cloudy hopings and God. She could be strange and remote as he could. . . .

And it came with hardly an effort at all, they were hurrying nods that met on the stairs and went to bed at uneven hours; yet sometimes a hand seemed to twist in her heart as she watched him sit at his meat in silence, or at night when she woke and he lay asleep, with it seemed the tug of lips on her breasts and the ghostly ache of her empty womb—silent the yews in the listening dark.

Segget crowded the kirk the first Sunday in May after the General Strike collapsed, to hear what that cocky billy Colquohoun would say of his tink-like socialists now. But he never mentioned the creatures at all, he preached a sermon that maddened you, just, he said there was nothing new under the sun: and that showed you the kind of twister he was. Hairy Hogg, the Provost, came out of the kirk, and said that the man was insulting them, sly, trying to make out that the work they had done to beat the coarse Labour tinks was a nothing. Instead, now the Strike was ended so fine, you'd mighty soon see a gey change for the good, no more unions to cripple folks' trade, and peace and prosperity returning again: and maybe a tariff on those foreign-made boots.

But damn the sign of either you saw as that year went on and the next come in, there was little prosperity down at the Mills, they were working whiles, and whiles they were not, young Mr. Mowat went off to London and syne from there he went off on a cruise, as a young gent should; but he fair was real kind. For he wrote that he'd soon be back home again, and would see about pushing the Segget trade, that would mean more men—*but no union men*.

It wasn't his wyte that he had no work, in spite of the spinners and their ill-ta'en grumblings. For they grumbled still, though their union was finished—faith! that was funny, for you'd got from the papers that the men would be fine if it wasn't the unions—the Tory childes nearly broke down and wept on the way the unions oppressed the workers. The Cronins had all been sacked from the Mills and no more of a Sunday you'd hear them preach about socialism coming, and coarse dirt like that. Jock Cronin, that had once been a railway porter, was down now in Glasgow, tinking about, it fairly was fine to be rid of the brute. Folk said that that Miss Jeannie Grant had gone with him, some childe had seen her, down there at a mart, all painted and powdered, she'd ta'en to the streets, and kept Jock Cronin, he lived off her earnings. Ay, just the kind of thing you'd expect from socialists and dirt that spoke ill of their betters, and yet powdered and fornicated like gentry.

But young Dod Cronin, that was a mere loon, he heard the news, he worked out at Fordoun, and he went to the

smiddy and tackled old Leslie, with the sweat dripping
down from his wrinkled old chops. And Dod said *What's
this you've been saying of my brother?* and old Leslie said
What? And who are you, lad? And Dod said *You know
damn well who I am. And if ever I hear you spreading
your claik about my brother or Miss Jeannie Grant, I'll
bash in your old face with one of your hammers.*

Old Leslie backed nippy behind the anvil and said *Take
care, take care what you say! I'm not a man you must rouse,
let me tell you.* And he told later on that never in his life
had he heard such impudence—'twas Infernal, just, he'd
a might sore job to keep himself back from taking that
Cronin loon a good clout. Now, when himself was a loon
up in Garvock—And you didn't hear more, for you looked
at your watch, and said you must go, and went at a lick;
and left him habbering and chapping and sweating.

Young Dod was as mad as could be on the thing, he
went up to the Manse and clyped the Colquohoun; and
Else Queen, that was back there again as the maid, told
that the minister said he was sorry, but what could he do?
Young Cronin shouldn't worry, you could only expect a
smell from a drain.

Else said the minister was referring to Leslie: and folk
when they heard that speak were real mad. Who was he, a
damned creature that sat in a Manse, to say that an honest
man was a drain? There was nothing wrong with old Leslie,
not him, he'd aye paid his way, a cheery old soul, though
he could sicken a cow into colic with his long, dreich tales
and his habberings of gossip.

He'd aye been good to his guts, the old smith, and faith,
he grew better the longer he lived. At New Year he took
a bit taik down the toun, into the shop of MacDougall
Brown; it was late at night and what could Brown do but
ask the old smith to come ben for a drink—not of whisky,
you wouldn't find that at MacDougall's, but of some orange
wine or such a like drink, awful genteel, though it had a
bit taste as though a stray pig had eased himself in it. Well,
Leslie went ben, and there sat the creash, MacDougall's
wife, and Cis, the fine lass, and the other bit quean that
folk teased and called Maybull. Mrs. Brown was right kind
and poured out the wine, syne she went and took out a
cake from the press, there was more than half of the cake
on the plate, and Mistress Brown cut off a thin slice, genteel,
and held out the plate to the smith.

And what did he do but take up the cake, not the slice, and sit with it there in his hand, habbering and sweating like a hungered old bull, and tearing into MacDougall's cake, MacDougall watching him boiling with rage—faith! speak about washing in the blood of the Lamb, he looked as though he'd like a real bath in the smith's.

Well, old Leslie finished his bit of repast, and got up, though he hadn't near finished his story, about Garvock, but he never yet had done that, though you'd known him fine this last fifty years. But it was getting fell late-like by then and he thought he'd better go take a taik home, Mrs. Brown had gone to her bed, and Maybull, and the fine lass Cis had gone as well. MacDougall showed him out to the door, and cried goodnight, and banged it behind him; and old Leslie was standing sucking at a crumb that was jooking about in an old hollow tooth, when what did he see round the end of the dyke that sloped to the back of MacDougall's shop, but a body slipping over in the dark.

Old Leslie wondered who it could be, and stepped soft in the dark down the lithe of the dyke. Near to the end he stooped and stopped, and heard the whisp-whisp of some folk close by. And he knew one voice, but not the other, 'twas the voice of Cis Brown and he heard her say *Not tonight—Mabel is sleeping with me.* The voice that the smith couldn't put a name to said *Damn her, why doesn't she sleep with the cuddy?* Cis laughed and sighed and syne Leslie heard the sound of a kiss, disgusting-like, he himself had never all his married life so much as pecked at his old wife's face: and once when she saw him without his sark, he'd been changing it, careless-like by the fire, she nearly had fainted, and so near had he, they'd never been so coarse as look at each other, shameless and bare, in their own bit skins. . . .

Well, where was he now with this story of Cis?—Ay, her slobbering her lad by the dyke. In a little bit while they were whispering again, and the smith tried hard to hear what they said, they spoke over low, the tinks that they were, to make an old man near strain off his neck from his hard-worked shoulders to hear what they said. Syne that finished and Leslie heard footsteps coming and dodged in the shadow of the post-office door. And who should loup over the wall and go by but that tink Dod Cronin, that had so miscalled him, him it had been that was kissing Cis Brown!

But folk said that that was just a damned lie, Cis Brown
was as douce and sweet a quean as you'd find in the whole
of Segget, they said—old Leslie telling the tale in the Arms
was nearly brained by Dite Peat himself. Dite said he liked
a bit lie fell well, just as he liked to soss with a woman,
especially a woman he'd no right to, but he wasn't to hear
that kind of a speak of Cis Brown, he was fairly damned if
he was. And others cried *Ay, that's right, that's right!* and
Feet, the policeman, said to his father *You'd better away
home.* Off the old smith went, the coarse old brute; still
habbering his lies and swearing he'd seen Dod Cronin and
that fine quean Cis together.

Chris heard the tale, but she paid it no heed, with long
months of resting her strength had come back, she was out
in the garden of the Manse each dawn, digging and hoeing
as the Spring came in. Funny to think 'twas nearly a year
since she'd walked this garden, her child in her body, and
stood over there and looked in the kirkyard, and thought
of the folk that had once been bairns, and died, and nothing of them endured. And now she herself walked free and
young, slim as of old, if her face was thinner, but warm
and kind, warm blood in her body, she could see it rise
blue if she looked at her hands loosen their grip from the
shaft of the graip, and her hair was alive, that had gone
a while dead, and crackled its fire as she combed it at
night, long hair that still came near to her knees. And the
baby she'd brought in the world last year——

But she'd not think of that, not here in the sun, the
rooks a long caw out over the yews, sailing, sun-winking,
dots in the sun, the clouds went wind-laden down through
the Howe, all the Howe wakening below them to hear the
trill and shrill of the springs of Spring. So busied Chris
was as the days grew warm, she'd found in a garden what
once in the fields, years before, on the windy rigs of Blawearie, ease and rest and the kindness of toil, that she saw
but little or nothing of Robert—no loss to him, with his
bittered face, and no loss to her now, they went their own
ways.

Ewan was shooting straight as a larch, narrow and dark,
with a cool, quiet gaze, and a sudden smile that came
seldom enough, but still, when it did—Else said she could
warm her hands at that smile. He was out all hours of the
day, was Ewan, still at his flints, he'd raked half the Howe,
he'd been down by Brechin and Forfar for flints. He was

known in places Chris never had seen, the dark-faced loon from the Manse of Segget, that would ask if he might take a look at your fields, and would show the arrows and such-like of old that the creatures of hunters had used in their hunts. And the farmers would say, *Faith, look if you like,* and Ewan would thank them. Charming and cool, a queer-like loon, not right in the head, folk that were wice weren't near so polite.

Sometimes, as the light of the Spring days waned he'd come back from school and find bread and milk, and bring them out to the garden to eat, and set them down by a bed or a drill and take the hoe or the fork from Chris, and start to work with quick, even strokes, the down of a soft fine hair on his cheeks, Chris would sit with her knees hand-clasped, and watch him, the ripple of his smooth dark skin, he'd long lashes as well, that were curled and dark, he worked with a cool and deliberate intent at digging the garden as he did at all else. Once Chris asked him, one of those evenings in April, what he would do when he had grown up.

He stopped at the turn of a drill and looked at her, he was leaving school and going to Dundon, up to the college in the summer term. He said *I'd like to be an archæologist, but I don't suppose that I'll ever be that.* Chris asked *Why not?* and he said that he thought it unlikely you could be that without lots of money. He would just have to face up to things as they were, jobs scarce, and all the world in a mess.

Chris wondered what were his thoughts on the mess, he had read nearly every book in the Manse, had he read the books on Socialism yet? She asked him that and he said that he had, indifferently saying it, one of the books—by a Ramsay MacDonald, all blither and blah. Charlie Cronin, who had now left the school was a socialist, the same as MacDonald, they were both very muddled, they had no proofs and they hadn't a plan, it was spite or else rage: OR BECAUSE THEY WERE FEARED.

Chris looked at the fairy featherings of clouds that went south on the hurrying wind of the Howe, the green of the hedges trilled low in its blow, you could feel in your body the stir of the blood as the sap stirred sweet in the hedge, you supposed. Spring and the time of young folk and dreams, following cloud-pillars as they sailed the Howe! . . .

And maybe Ewan was doing no more in that he refused all clouds and all dreams!

She said *What are YOU going to do with the mess?* and he put down his cup and said *Oh, nothing,* and started to weed in the strawberry patch: *Unless I just must,* and he whistled to himself, calm and cool, with his dark, cool face, he whistled and hoed in the evening light. And Chris felt for him a tenderness, queer, not as though she were only his mother but as though he were all young life in an evening of Spring—thinking the world would dare hardly intrude in their lives and years, but would stand back and bow, and slip to one side to let them go by. . . . She held out a hand—*Help me up, son, I'm stiff. Growing old, I suppose;* he stopped and looked at her, his gravity suddenly drowned in that smile. *I thought just now you looked like a girl. There are some at school who look older than you.*

But he gave her his hand and she jumped to her feet, light enough still, and they looked at each other; and Chris put up her hand to his throat, making on that the button there needed re-sewing, it didn't, but she wanted to touch that cool throat. He let her, standing there quiet and alert, like the deer she had seen come down from the haughs, with brindled pelts, in the winter-time—not feared and not shy, cool, quick and alive, under her fingers a little vein beat as she fastened his collar, and Ewan said *Thanks,* and went on with his weeding, Chris went to the house and looked at the clock and made tea for Robert.

He was off at Stonehaven, a meeting of ministers, called together to discuss the reason why every kirk in the Howe grew toom, a minister would sometimes rise of a Sunday and preach to a congregation of ten, in a bigging builded to hold two hundred. So Robert told Chris as he wheeled out his bike, that morning, under the peep of the sun; and Chris had said *Well, they surely know why? Do they need a meeting to find out that?*

Robert had looked at her withdrawn, remote, the brooding anger not far from his eyes. *Do YOU know the reason?* Chris had said *Yes, the reason's just that the times have changed.*

His unchancy temper quite went with him then, *By God,* he sneered, *isn't that profound?* Chris flushed, with an angry retort on her lips; but she bit it back, as so often she did, and turned indoors as he wheeled down the Wynd—

what a fool she had been to say what she'd said! Like telling an angry blind man he was blind. . . . She would keep to herself, she was nobody's serf.

But sometimes she ached for kind eyes and kind hands. One night she had turned to him, kissing him then, and he'd shrugged away from her—*Not now, Chris, not now.* She had said in her hurt, *And maybe not again—when YOU would again,* and had turned her back and pretended to sleep, but had wept a little instead, like a fool. Spring was here, she supposed it was that, daft to desire what no one could give except with a flame of desire in the giving.

So she waited this evening, with pancakes new baked, they might live poor friends, with love and lust by, but she still ate his meat and she owed him for that. Else had the day off to go down to Fordoun, her baby bade there in its grandmother's care. In the cool of the kitchen Chris stood for a while and watched Ewan kneel to a thrawn-like weed, and saw him twist it up ruthlessly, sure; she sighed with a smile at herself for that sigh. Were she sure of herself as Ewan of himself, she might go her own way and not heed to any, have men to lie with her when she desired them (and faith, that would sure be seldom enough!), do and say all the things that came crying her to do, go hide long days in the haughs of the Mounth—up in the silence and the hill-bird's cry, no soul to vex, and to watch the clouds sailing and passing out over the Howe, unending over the Howe of the World; that—or sing and be glad by a fire; or wash and toil and be tired with her toil as once she had been in her days on a croft—a million things, Chris-alone, Chris-herself, with Chris Guthrie, Chris Tavendale, Chris Colquohoun dead!

She lighted the lamp as she heard Robert come and carried it through to the hall for him to see to hang up his coat and his hat. He said *You look very sweet, Christine, there with the lamp,* and held her a moment, lamp and all, Chris felt her heart turn, with gladness—then, queerly, she felt half-sick. . . .

He loosed her and followed her into the room, soft happed in shadow in the loglight's glow, she put down the lamp and looked at him again. There was something about him that wasn't him at all—a *filthy* something, she thought, and shivered. He said *Not cold?* and smiled at her kind—ROBERT with eyes like a kind milch cow!

She went in a daze and brought in the tea, they sat and ate by the open window, the world all quiet out and about, except, sharp-soft in the fading light, the click and scrape of the tools of Ewan as he redded and bedded by the kirk-yard wall. And again, as she looked at Robert, Chris shivered—*What's ta'en you Robert—Robert what is it?*

He raised up his head and she saw his eyes smile. *Just something you'll think is quite mad when you hear. . . .*

And he told her then of the thing that had come as he rode from the minister's meeting at Stonehaven grinding his bike through Dunnottar's woods, he had looked once or twice from the road to the woods and saw them green in the April quiet, the sunset behind him—*very quiet, Chris.* He had ridden up there till the way grew steep, the old bike was near on its last wheels now: and just as he gained the neard edge of the woods he got from his bike and looked back at Stonehaven, in that corridor of trees the light fell dim, a hidden place, no sun came there. And, as he stood there and breathed in the quiet, he saw the Figure come slow down the road.

He came so quiet by the side of the road that Robert hadn't heard His coming or passing, till he raised his head and saw Him quite close, tired, with a white strange look on His face, no ghost, for the hair blew out from His head and He put up His hand to brush back the hair. And Robert saw the hand and the pierced palm, he stood frozen there as the Figure went on, down through the quiet of Dunnottar's woods, unresting, into the sunset's quiet, a wood-pigeon crooned in a far-off tree, Robert heard the sound of a train in Stonehaven, he stood and stared and then leant on his bike, trembling, suddenly weeping in his hands.

Outside, the next day broke quick with wind, a grey quick drive that was bending the trees, blowing its blow in the face of the sun, Chris went to her room and dressed in short skirts, the rig she'd once worn—it seemed years before—that day she and Robert climbed up the Mounth. She'd no fancy at all for that walk today, she found a stick and went down through the shingle, and looked back as she passed in the whisp of the yews. Ewan in his room, he stood near the window, some everlasting flint in his hands. She waved to him, but he didn't see, then at the turn of the dyke the wind caught at her breath and her skirts and her hair.

Ake Ogilvie looked from his shop as she passed, and gave her a wave and bent over his desk, his poetry maybe, Robert said it was awful, the angry sneering of a poet born blind. . . . But Chris hurried on from the thought of Robert, swinging her stick, the wind in her face, the Sourock's wife looked out as she passed, and stared after the creature, that Mrs. Colquohoun, like a slip of a quean she was, not decent, her that had had her two bairns, one dead, the other upgrowing and nearly a man. She said later on she was black-affronted as Mrs. Colquohoun reached the bend of the Wynd, the wind blew up the creature's short skirts, all about her, and instead of giving a bit scraich and blushing to the soles of her feet as she should, she just brushed them back and went hastening on—what was *her* hurry, no hat on her head, and her fine silk breeks and nought else below?

(And folk said *What, had she nothing else below?* and the Sourock's wife said *Not a damned stitch, fair tempting the childes, half-naked like that, not to mention tempting her death with cold.*)

Past the shop of Dite Peat and Hairy Hogg's front, Alec, the son of the Provost, stood there, he had lost his job in Edinburgh, Alec, Chris liked him better than when she first met him, she cried *How are you?* and he raised his cap; and Chris sped on, Alec said that night when he looked in on Else, that Mrs. Colquohoun looked more of a boy than a grown-up woman who had a fine son. Else said *She both looks them, and makes them, my lad,* whatever she meant by that, if she knew; but she kept him at sparring distance, did Else.

Down at the edge of the Moultrie shop, where Jim the roan had had such an ill end, Chris found herself in the lithe of the dyke that shielded the plots of the gardener Grant. It was here she nearly ran into Cis Brown, running, with sober face and blown hair, Chris held her and laughed and they steadied themselves, Chris asked *And how are things at the college?* Cis coloured up sweet, she said they were fine. She loitered a moment and Chris looked in her face and caught there the glimpse of a desperate trouble.

Something (what Chris of them all?) made her say *I'm

*off for a long walk down through the Howe, I'm restless
today, would you like to come?*

At noon that day they stopped at a place, a little farm
high in the Reisk, over-topped by the wave of its three
beech trees, standing up squat in the blow of the wind that
came in a shoom from the Bervie braes. They were given
milk there, and new-baked cakes, and rested a while, Chris
glad of the rest, Cis lying back in her chair with her face
flushed to colour from the walk they had come. They had
come down the Howe from the Segget haughs, past Catcraig, out on the Fordoun road, Fordoun a brown, dull
lour to the north, and so swung on down past Mondynes,
Kinraddie to the left, and then reached the brig, Chris
stopped and peered in the water below and minded how
once she'd done that, long before, in a summer, and seen
the school-bairns plash, naked and dripping, in the shadowed shallows. Now the water flowed under, free and unvexed, east, to twine to the Bervie mouths, Cis leaned beside Chris and stared down as well, and then said *There is
something I want to tell you.*

And Chris had said, gently, *I think I know what.* Cis
flushed up a moment and bit at her lip, she wasn't afraid,
only troubled, Chris saw. And she said *We'll go on, to the
right, I think;* and so they had done, and climbed up the
brae to the Geyrie's moor, and looked back from there and
saw all around the steaming teams a-plod in the parks,
shoring the long red drills of clay. Up in the hills the mists
had come down, as they watched they saw a rain-cloud
wheel out, down from the Mounth on the roofs of Drumlithie, white-shining there on the road to the South. Back
and still back, line on line, rose the hills, the guardian wall
of the Mearns Howe, it came on Chris as she stood and
looked she'd never been beyond that wall since a bairn.
The peewits were flying in the parks outbye, in the wind
that came racing up from the east was the smell, a tingle
that tickled your nose, of the jungle masses of whins that
rose, dark as a forest, on the Geyrie's moor.

Chris said that she thought they might take that way,
Cis said *Is it safe?* she had heard it was nearly impassable
with bog holes in the earth where a cart could lair, they
sat on a gate and looked into its stretch, dark brown and
green in the hand of Spring. And Cis's shyness and con-
straint had gone, she was calm and young, they smiled one

at the other, and Chris said suddenly, *Oh, we're such fools—women, don't you think that we are now, Cis? To worry so much about men and their ploys, the things that they do and the things that they think!*

Cis said *But what else is there to do? They count for so much*—and sat and thought, grave, shy and sweet as a wing-poised bird. *Or maybe they don't as much as they think, but there wouldn't be children without them, would there?* Chris laughed at that and jumped down from the gate. *I suppose there wouldn't, but still—we might try! Let's go through the moor:* and so they had done.

There they saw the cup of the Howe rise up to the Barras slopes that led to Kinneff, on their right, dark-mantled, lost in its trees, Arbuthnott slept on the Bervie banks, clusters of trees, with the sudden gleam in the wind and the sun of the polished gear, bridles and haimes, on the straining shoulders of the labouring teams. Like going back into your youth, Chris thought, and sighed at that thought and Cis asked why, and Chris said *Because I am getting so old,* and Cis said *That's silly, I sometimes think you're the youngest of all the folk in Segget.* And was shy, *Please don't ever cut your hair, though I've had mine cut: it's lovely, your hair.*

Chris said that she thought it wasn't so bad, and they came to a little bare patch in the moor, where the whins drew aside their skirts and stood quiet, and right in the middle a great stone lay, maybe a thing from the antique times, and Chris sat on it and clasped her knees, and Cis looked at her and then sat at her feet, Chris with her gold eyes closed in the sun, the run and wheep of the wind in her hair, the sun on her face: she could listen to it now, aloof and sure and untroubled by things. And she said to Cis *Is the boy Dod Cronin?*

So she'd heard it all as she sat knee-clasped, there, in the play of the wind and the sun, a tale so old—oh, old as the Howe, everlasting near as the granite hills, this thing that brought men and women together, to bring new life, to seek new birth, on and on since the world had begun. And it seemed to Chris it was not Cis alone, her tale—but all tales that she harkened to then, kisses and kindness and the pain of love, sharp and sweet, terrible, dark, and the wild, queer beauty of the hands of men, and their lips, and the sleeps of desire fulfilled, and the dark, strange movements of awareness alone, when it came on women what thing

they carried, darkling, coming to life within them, new life
to replenish the earth again, to come to being in the windy
Howe where the cloud-ships sailed to the unseen south.
She fell in a dream that went far from Cis, looking up and
across the slow-peopled parks at the scaurs of the Mounth
and its flying mists, beyond these the moving world of
men, and back again to those clouds that marched, terrible,
tenebrous, their pillars still south. *A pillar of cloud by day
and a pillar of fire by night.*

She said *I must think, I'll get Robert to help;* and Cis said
The minister? and looked still more troubled. *Oh, Mrs.
Colquohoun, what have men to do with it, it's not their
concern, they don't understand. Dod doesn't—he's frightened—for me or himself, but he doesn't know this, how
queer it all is, and sickening, and fine—maybe I'm sickening myself to say that?*

Chris said she thought she was sweet to say it, and put
her arm round the shoulders of Cis, and the girl looked up,
and her lips came to Chris's; and Chris thought at that
moment that no men could kiss—not as they should, they'd
no notion of kissing. . . . Oh men, they were clumsy from
the day they were breeked to the day they took off their
breeks the last time!

The wind was coming in great gusts now, driving the
riven boughs of the broom, in times it rose to a scraich
round about and the moor seemed to cower in its trumpet-
cry. Cloud Howe of the winds and the rains and the sun!
All the earth that, Chris thought at that moment, it made
little difference one way or the other where you slept or
ate or had made your bed, in all the howes of the little
earth, a vexing puzzle to the howes were men, passing and
passing as the clouds themselves passed: but the REAL
was below, unstirred and untouched, surely if that were not
also a dream.

Robert with his dream of the night before, that Face and
that Figure he had seen in the woods. Chris had listened to
him with her head bent low, knowing she listened to a
madman's dream. And Robert to dream it! Robert who
once followed a dream that at least had the wind in its
hair, not this creep into fear and the fancies of old. But
she'd seen then, clear and clear as he spoke, the Fear that
had haunted his life since the War, Fear he'd be left with
no cloud to follow, Fear he'd be left in the day alone, and
stand and look at his naked self. And with every hoping

and plan that failed, he turned to another, to hide from
that fear, draping his dreams on the face of life as now
this dream of the sorrowing Face . . . And she'd shivered
again at the filth of the thing, not looking as she heard
that crack in his voice, he was saying he could almost have
touched the Figure—*God, Chris, it was HIM, whom I've
never believed! I've thought Him only a Leader, a man,
but Chris—I've looked on the face of God. . . .*

She'd sat and said nothing till that was impossible, so to
sit silent, and raised up her eyes, misty with pity, yet
repulsion as well. Robert had said quiet, *And you don't
believe?* And she said *I don't know, I don't know—oh, I'll
try!* And gripped his hand tight that he mightn't ask
more——

She jumped up then from that seat in the moor—*Come
on, I'm so hungry!* and the two of them went on through
the whins with the scud of the clouds overhead, that parched
their faces in the sharp sun-fall, a snipe was sounding up
by the Wairds as they came to the shaven lands of the
Reisk, shaven and shorn in the greed of the War. So, as
they climbed they came on the farm, with the three beech
trees, and, beyond the horizon, poised and glistening, the
tumbling sea.

And when they had finished with drinking their milk
and eating their cakes Chris offered to pay. But the farmer's
wife shook her head, she'd not have it, she'd heard of Chris
from her son, she said, he lived in London and wrote horrible books: but he and Chris were at college together.
Chris couldn't mind much of the son at all, she supposed
they'd met some time or another, but she didn't say that,
she and Cis cried their thanks, and went on down the road,
it was afternoon then, the sun had wheeled round and was
on the west slant.

Down in Arbuthnott they found a bus and with that were
carried down the road to Bervie, where the old brig hung
by the lazy drifts of smoke from the Mills that lay in the
hollow—mills half-idle, as were those of Segget, Bervie
above them, a rickle and clutter. They got from the bus
and looked at the shops, then went down to the sea by
a straggling lane, the sea was pounding into the bay where
no boats came because of the rocks—it frothed and spumed
like a well-beaten egg, out east a fisher boat went by, into
the mist and the Gourdon smell. Chris sat on a rock and
looked at the sea, very wakeful, but Cis went to sleep in

the sun, till Chris waked her up and they went back again, and found a new bus to take them to Stonehaven, where they'd get yet another to take them back, up the long roads, to Spring-green Segget.

And so, by the fall of night, they came back; and Chris was tired, but her mind made up. Not even for Robert could she change and pretend, though she'd not say a thing that would hurt, could she help. She had found in the moors and the sun and the sea her surety unshaken, lost maybe herself, but she followed no cloud, be it named or unnamed.

Next Sabbath the minister stood up in the pulpit and preached from the Sermon on the Mount of Segget, he said that the Christ still walked the earth, bringing the only message that endured—though all else faded, that was undying, they must search out the Christ, each soul by himself, and find in himself what the world denied, the love of God and the fellowship of men.

Folk listened and thought the man a fair scunner, damn't! you wanted a minister with spunk, whatever had come over this childe Colquhoun, bleating there soft as a new-libbed sheep? Once he'd glowered as though he would like to gut you, and thundered his politics, and you'd felt kittled up, though you didn't believe a word that he'd said. But this Sunday he blethered away in the clouds, folk came out and went home and were real disappointed, minding the time when he'd said from the pulpit, right out, that Hairy Hogg was a monkey—damn't! he'd fair fallen away since then.

And some of the spinners that came to the kirk, they were few enough now, remembered the name they had called the minister a long time back, they said that Creeping Jesus was back, he'd got feared at the gentry, the same as some others. Old Cronin himself it was that said that, and by others he meant his own son Jock that had led the Strike but a two years back, and had aye been a right coarse brute, folk thought, though fair the apple of his father's eye. But Jock had gotten on well in Glasgow, where he'd lived in sin with Miss Jeannie Grant, he'd gotten a job on a union there and went lecturing here and went blethering there, in a fine new suit and a bowler hat, and spats, right trig, and brave yellow boots. And he'd married Miss Grant, a three weeks back, and they had a fine house on the

Glasgow hills; and wherever he went Jock Cronin would preach alliance between all employers and employed and say to the folk that came to hear him that they shouldn't strike, but depend on their leaders—like himself; and take a smug look at his spats.

When news of that came up to old Cronin, he cursed his son in a sickening way, and he said he'd never guessed he had fathered a Judas that could sell out the workers for that—not even for silver or a hungered guts, but spats, and a house on the Glasgow hills, and a craze for a white-legged quean in his bed.

Folk took a good laugh when they heard the news, Jock Cronin was showing some sense, they said, he fair had changed since the days when he'd go and break up the meetings of MacDougall Brown. Next MacDougall himself got a sore stammy-gaster, and so did the whole of Segget; it gasped. That tale of old Leslie's had had the truth in it, though you'd hardly believe it again when you heard it— it was all a damned lie and Cis a fine quean.

But then, when you met with her out in the street, and looked, and heard the news from the Manse, she and Dod Cronin to be wed in a week—your throat went dry, you went into the Arms and had a bit dram and swore at the bitch, all the folk said she was a foul creature, but they said it with something catching their throats, they'd been proud of Cis, all Segget had been, and here she was showing herself in that way, no better than that tink Else Queen at the Manse.

Ake Ogilvie said it was only nature, Cis or Else or the whole jing-bang, what ailed the folk of Segget, he said, was that they'd seen Cis as *they* might have been—clean—and they'd liked her for what they had lost. He spoke that speak to John Muir, the roadman, Muir gleyed and skeuched and chewed the thing over, it didn't make sense, Ake seldom did.

He went out to dig a bit grave after supper, the moon far up out over the Mounth, the sunset still far, though the lines lay long, in long slants across the hayfields of summer, and smoke drowsed low on the Segget roofs. In the kirkyard the grasses lay scythed as he'd left them, and he walked through that grass, there was some of it clover, bonnily scented with dead men's manure. So he came to the kirkyard corner and stopped, and lighted his pipe and spat on his hands, and started in to dig the bit grave, for one of the old spinner wives of West Wynd.

All the land here about was thick with old graves, he'd soon have to stop or start carting the bones to a pit and bury them out and apart, to leave room for the rest of Segget down there, eating and sleeping and having its play, all coming to stour and a stink at the end. And Muir gleyed down at the grave and dug, and minded of Cis and the speak there was, Dod Cronin had been found a job in Dundon and he and the lass were moving up there, the best they could do to get out of their shame. God knew there wasn't much shame in the thing, a lot over-rated, this bedding with a quean—you worked yourself up and you got damned little, and where did it end then, all said and all done? Down here with the clay and the grass up above, be you rich, be you poor, unwedded like Cis, or as bonny as Mrs. Colquohoun was bonny, or a shameless limmer like one of the queans that young Mr. Mowat would bring to the House.

He fair was a devil among women, young Mowat, gents were like that, Peter Peat said; but he'd time yet to settle down bravely in Segget and take his natural place at its head: and that was the Segget Conservative branch. Maybe he *had* had more queans than he should, but he'd settle down bravely yet, you would see. Ake Ogilvie said, *No doubt—in his sharns,* a tink-like speak, just what you expected, he was jealous as hell of the gentry, Ake, nearly as bad as that creature Moultrie that was now over stiff to crawl out at all.

One of the Mills had been idle for months, though young Mr. Mowat had come back from his sail. He was no sooner back than a birn of the spinners went up to the House in a deputation. But when the deputation got there, and the servant had shown them into the hall, and they stood there twisting their caps, fell shy, they heard the crackle of a falling bottle and a hooting and laughing as though lunatics were loose; and out of a side-door a quean came running, without a stitch on, nothing but a giggle, she looked back and laughed at young Mowat behind her, running and laughing with his wee frog face; and up the stairs the two of them went.

Well, the deputation blushed from head to heel; syne one of them, the oldest operative there, said *That's where the cash goes we make in the Mills*, and they looked from one to the other, old, hungry, and some of them were gey bitter, most on the dole, on starvation's edge; and they stood in the rich, warm hall and looked round, at the log-wood fire and the gleam of deers' heads, and the patterned walls and the thick, soft rugs. But the rest said nothing to the speak of the first, they knew it was useless trying to complain or to start that kind of socialist stuff that the Cronins of old had preached in the mills, you'd seen the end of that with the Strike, young Mowat was the only hope of the Mills.

He came down at last and was charming, polite, and said it was Jahly to see them again. And he stood with his back to the fire and said *Hwaw?* and read them a lecture on the awful times, he said that taxation was killing the country, all they could hope at the coming election was that the Conservative folk would get back, stronger than ever in position and power, and reduce taxation on men like himself. Then perhaps he would manage to open the Mill. And he smiled at them, charming, with his horn-rimmed eyes, but he offered no drink, instead rang a bell, and the servant childe came and ushered them out; and young Mr. Mowat said it had been Jahly; and that showed that he had a real good heart.

Now, that was the first Peter Peat had heard about young Mr. Mowat and the wishes he had that the Tory Party should get back again, they'd been holding office but a bare five years and hadn't yet had time to set things right, being busied with breaking strikes and the like, and freeing the working men from their unions, and seeing that we had a real strong navy, and trying to get the coarse foreign tinks to reduce their armies, a danger to Europe. . . . Peter Peat had these facts at his fingertips and went up to the House to see Mr. Mowat, and ask a subscription for the Segget branch. And Mr. Mowat said it was Jahly to see him, Rahly Jahly, and sipped at his wine, and the quean did the same, exploding a giggle, sitting bare-legged on the back of his chair.

Yes, he believed in Devolution for Scotland, but not this mad nationalism now rampant, only the Unionist Party would see that Scotland got her just dues in the end. And he told Peter more of the coarse new Nationalists, not the flower of the country's gentry, as once, Scotland had lost her chance once again, the new leaders a pack of socialists and catholics, long-haired poets, a fellow called Grieve, and Mackenzie and Gunn, hysterical Highlandmen. Well, he had Jahly soon finished with *them,* and would be glad to give a donation some time to the branch of the Unionist Party in Segget.

And Peter Peat was fell happy at that—ay, the old blood flowed in the gentry's veins.

The Autumn came, the Election's results, and Segget was fair stammy-gastered at them, the Labour tinks had gotten in power, led by that coarse brute Ramsay Mac-Donald. You minded him and the things he had said, long before, when the War was on?—that we shouldn't be fighting the Germans, no, no, but leave them a-be, they were much too strong. Ay, that's what he'd said and here he was now, at the head of the country, lording it about, and not even maybe saying Sir to the King. But others said the creature would fairly swank now, and get the King to make him a lord, or a duke or something: and Ake Ogilvie said he'd heard the title was Lord Loon of Lossie.

But that was just one of his ill-natured speaks, damn't! was he against this Government as well?—after going to all that stour to vote Liberal, instead of decent and Tory like others. Hardly any of the spinners had voted at all, they just hung about and smoked their bit fags, or dug in their gardens back of the wynds, or stared at the Mills with their hungry eyes. But Ake Ogilvie had said he was voting Liberal, and had canvassed Segget for the Liberal childe, doing him a sight more harm than good, he said there was good in none of the parties, Labour or Tory or Liberal or any: but the Tory name fair stank in your throat, it was built on the purses and pride of the kind of half-witted loon that mismanaged the Mills; the Liberals were damn little better, he knew, but they *had* a great name that was worthy a vote.

Hardly a soul paid heed to his blethers, just smiled at him canny and said *Well, we'll see;* and got ready for the polling day to come to ride to Laurencekirk in the Tory cars. Ake Ogilvie borrowed a Liberal car, and its driver, and waited in Segget Square; and the Tory cars piled black with folk, getting off to vote for the gentry childes that had promised them reischles and reischles of tariffs; but not a damn soul looked near Alec Ogilvie, sitting with a sneering look in his car. And then the door of the Moultrie shop was flung wide open and who should come out, hoasting and hirpling slow on his stick, but that thrawn old billy, Rob Moultrie himself, leaning on a stick and his old wife's shoulder, he hobbled and hirpled over to the car, near bent down double, Jess Moultrie beside him. Ake jumped from his seat and helped the two in, and stood back with a queer-like grin on his face—were these all who championed Liberty Mere?

But there was a fourth; Ake had grown tired and was crying to the shover that they might as well go, when he heard a hail and looked over his shoulder. And there was Mrs. Colquohoun of the Manse, crossing the Square, running like a lad, with a spray of blood on her dark, soft skin. *Sorry I'm late, Ake,* she said, and jumped in; and Ake got in himself and could nearly have cuddled her.

But the Liberal man got a mighty few votes, the Tory got in, as you knew he would do, if the rest of the country had done half as well, where would these tinks of social-ists have been? Selling spunks in the London streets, or that coarse brute Ramsay MacDonald tracts. And the Provost said in the Segget Arms 'twas an ill day this for our Scottish land. What was it the poet Robert Burns had written?—an ancestor, like, of the Hoggs, Rabbie Burns. *A man's a man for a' that,* he wrote, and by that he meant that poor folk of their kind should steer well clear of the gentry and such, not try to imitate them at all, and leave them to manage the country's affairs.

Deeper and deeper as that year slipped by, Robert slipped from the life of his parish, he hadn't bothered to vote at all, he locked himself up long hours in his room, dreaming or reading or just sitting still—alien to Chris as that Figure he dreamt he'd met in the dark at Dunnottar woods.

Nor was that meeting the only one, there were others haunting the paths of his feet, times when he'd know that Presence in his room, once in the midst of a sermon he stopped, not staring or wild, but all the kirk watched him, and he watched the door, and his eyes moved slow as though following a figure that came down the aisle; and folk turned round and stared where he stared, and saw nothing at all but the winter gleam of the cold kirk floor, and beyond that the glass of the far, stained window that looked on the tossing boughs of the trees. Chris half-rose from her seat in that silence, she saw the sweat bright on

Robert's still face. Then his eyes left the aisle and he wiped his forehead, and went on in an even voice with his sermon.

For outside these moments he was quiet and kind, with a kindness Chris hated—for it was not his. It was something borrowed from his unclean dream, not Robert at all, a mask and a pose, a kindness he followed with Fear for an urge. And a dreadful loneliness came upon Chris, and a shivering hate for that cloud he followed, that sad-faced Figure out of the past, who had led such legions of men to such ends up and down the haughs and hills of the earth. Christ? So maybe indeed He had lived, and died, a follower of clouds Himself.

That Figure she minded from school-time days, and even then it had not moved her, it seemed a sad story, in mad, sad years, it was over and done: and it left her untouched. And it left her so still, it was only a dream that could alter nothing the ways of the world. . . . Oh, why wasn't Robert like other ministers?—easy and pleased and hearty and glib, with no religious nonsense about them, they led hearty lives and ate well at table and took the days as they found them come, and didn't leave their wives to think daft thoughts, and cry here, quiet, in the dark, like a child, sometimes with the fear of a child for the dark.

But she just had to meet it: and her life was still hers. So she worked through that autumn tending the garden, till almost the earth rebelled from her touch, she thought with a smile, and welcomed the winter. New Year's Eve came in a bluster on Segget, in snow and a breaking of sleet for sharp hours, there were spinners starving down in Old Toun John Muir told Chris as he came in on Sunday. And he said that another twenty were sacked, it was likely the second Mill would close down.

Robert heard that story as well, and listened, and said not a word, who once would have flamed into curses and anger on the cruelty of men. But now he stood up in the pulpit and preached, his text the saying of Christ, *Feed my lambs*. And Chris sat and listened to the gentle voice, and shivered as though at a filthy thing. And she looked round quiet at the people he preached to—the Provost Hogg with his heavy face, John Muir, with his skeugh and his puzzled eyes, Peter Peat the tailor, red-eyed, like a rat, and the mean, close face of the publican, Melvin. What hope in appealing to them for help?—were there but a flicker he had sold his soul to that fancy and Figure for something at least. But they heeded as little the whine of his Christ as the angry threat of his Struggling God.

And that New Year's night as she lay by Robert, in the quiet and the dark, she knew fear again, fear for the new year come to birth, for the man who lay so quiet in his sleep, beside her, turned away from her touch, low in the grate the coals were drooping, in a little red glow, she watched them sink and fade and grow grey as the dawn came dim over a world that was wrapped in white; and out in the yews the frozen rooks stirred: and down in the kitchen Else Queen did the same.

That year brought plenty of changes to Else, before it began there were rumours about her, Ag Moultrie one morning was going by the Manse when she saw the door of the kitchen open, and out, as quiet as an ill-gettèd cat who should come stepping but that loon Alec Hogg? And he turned and gave a bit nod of his head, and Else Queen looked out and nearly saw Ag, but she dropped down smart in the lithe of a bush and watched the two part, and was fairly ashamed—to think that the son of a man like the Provost should have taken up with a harlot, just. And the more Ag thought of it, the more she was shamed, till she just broke down and fair Roared and Grat.

Well, she passed the news on in a neighbour-like way, and folk were fair shocked, and snickered at the Provost— ay, that was a nasty smack in the face for old Hairy Hogg: had he heard the news yet? And when it came out that he hadn't, just yet, there were half a dozen that took him the news, you yourself were nearly killed in the rush, there was never such a birn of boots needing mending, Dite Peat went in with a pair, and his brother, and Bruce the roadman, and syne Will Melvin. And old Hairy sat like a monkey and blew on how well he could sutor, and Dite Peat said *Ay, and we hear you'll be sutoring soon for a marriage. Or is it a christening?* And they all took a sly bit look at the Provost; and he habbered and said *What?* and so he was told.

Well, he couldn't believe that speak about Alec, the loon might be a bit of a fool and had lost his work in the Edinburgh office, the place had closed down, that wasn't his wyte: but he wasn't such a fool as take up with a quean that once warmed the bed for that wastrel Dalziel. And as soon as young Alec came home that day from some gardening work he had gotten outbye the Provost cried out, *Come into the shop,* and told him the coarse-like speak in Segget. Alec Hogg said, *Well, then, there's something in it. I like Else well and I mean to marry her.* When he heard him say that old Hairy near burst, and he asked Alec Hogg did he want to bring them, respectable folk, in shame to the grave? And Alec said No, he didn't think so, he only wanted to bring Else to tea. And the Provost said 'twould be over his dead body if he did.

When that got around folk fair took a laugh—faith, man! that would fair be a funny-like sight, Else Queen stepping over old Hairy Hogg's corpse, and the old ape, dead or alive, you could swear, taking an upward keek as she passed. Else and Alec were watched fell close after that, and once, when they took a walk up the Kaimes, that Spring, a windy Sunday in March, and sat in the lithe to have a bit crack, there was nearly a dozen that kept on their track, and Ag Moultrie, the Roarer and Greeter of Segget, was up in the Schoolhouse watching the pair with a spy-glass she'd borrowed at racing speed. And the childes that had crept up the Kaimes to watch near froze to death, for they didn't dare move, and Alec and Else did not a damn thing, they didn't even kiss all the time they were there; and you well could warrant if they didn't kiss then, it was only because they had come to a pass when neither kisses nor cuddles contented.

Well, Alec couldn't marry, he hadn't a meck, Else's wages went to the keep of her bairn, Dalziel of the Meikle-bogs wouldn't pay a penny. When Else had written and asked him for that he had just smiled sly, and torn up the letter. So things might well have stood as they were but for the tink row that broke out in the house of Smithie, the whiskered old roadman of Segget.

He hardly had seemed to alter at all, except that his whiskers looked more and more still like the birns of hay he would pinch from the parks. He still bade on with his daughter and goodson, Bruce, folk said he had hell for a life, though the house was his and all the gear in it, the kye in the byres and the kirns in the creamery. But he'd come home still of an evening from work and get no friendly greeting from any unless 'twas the kye, and only from them if he brought them their meat: otherwise, they would sulk. In his house his daughter would say, *Oh, it's you? Then clean your nasty big feet on the mat.* And old Smithie would glower at her sore, but say nothing, it was years since the old bit creature broke out.

But one Saturday afternoon in April, just as old Smithie had stopped from his chapping out on the road that led to Stonehive, and had wiped his long whiskers and took a keek round, a lorry came down the road and went skeugh, and nearly went into the west-side ditch. Well, the lorry-driver swore like a tink, which wasn't surprising, he probably was one, and cried on old Smithie to give him a shove. And he shoved, and old Smithie, they shoved and they heaved, and swore at the lorry, and chaved a good hour, 'twas a lorry-load of crates of whisky and beer going north to Dundon, the lorry-man told. And he said that he hoped that their guts would rot, them that would drink but a drop of the stuff.

Well, at last they got the wheel from the ditch, and the lorry-driver said he was bloody obliged. He looked at his watch and said he must go, but syne he reached back in a small bit crate. *Here, I pinched two bottles of this for my-self, but you try one, it's a fine-like drink.* And he said some more and syne he drove off, leaving the bottle in old Smithie's hands.

Old Smithie took a bit keek at the thing, a fattish bit bottle of an unco-like shape; and he took off the cork and gave it a lick. That tasted as unco as the bottle looked, sugary and sweet, and old Smithie thought, *Well, damn it, he surely thinks I'm a bairn, it's a lemonade drink this Benny Dick Tine.*

So he held the bottle to his mouth for a suck, and down the stuff gurgled, and old Smithie paiched, and wiped his long whiskers and curled up his nose—feuch! it was sickening; but he fairly was dry. So he drank down a half of the lemonade stuff, and corked the bottle and put it in his pouch, and got on his bike and rode home to Segget.

God knows what happened atween there and Segget, he rode through the Square at the awfullest lick, and nearly killed Melvin opposite the Arms. He was singing that his heart was in the Highlands, not here, Will Melvin sore vexed to see him like that, if the coarse old creature wanted to get drunk why couldn't he come down and get drunk at the Arms? Will Melvin cried *Hi!* and louped like a goat, and Smithie cried back *That'll teach you, I hope, to bide out of my way, you whiskied old wife!* Syne he wheeled round and up the East Wynd like the wind and narrowly missed running into the dyke, and swung the bike over to the other bit side, and nearly killed a lone chicken there; and vanished through Segget in a shower of stour, with Will Melvin and the angel gaping together.

Ake Ogilvie told that he saw him go by, like a Valkyr riding the wings of the storm—whatever that fool of a joiner meant. But the next thing that happened for sure was the Smithie got off at the door of his house and went in. His goodson Bruce sat canny by the fire and hardly looked up as he heard Smithie's step. Then Smithie said *Just a minute, you, the sweir swine there, and I'll deal with you!* and Bruce looked round and there was old Smithie, with a bottle upended, sucking like mad. And then he had finished and flung off his coat, the daft old tyke, and let drive at Bruce, and near knocked him head first into the dinner that was hottering slow on the swey by the fire. Well, Bruce got up, he would soon settle this, and his wife, old Smithie's daughter, cried out *Crack up his jaw—don't spare the old tink!*

But God! she nearly died at what followed. Old Smithie had fair gone mad of a sudden, he didn't heed the bashings of Bruce, not a bit, but took him a belt in the face that near floored him, syne kicked him right coarse, and Bruce gave a groan and caught at himself, and as he doubled up old Smithie took him a clout in the face with a tacketty boot, and for weeks after that it looked more like a mess in a butcher's shop, than a face, that thing that the childe Bruce wore. Bruce was blinded with blood, he cried *Stop— I can't see!* But old Smithie had gone clean skite, what with his wrongs and the Benny Dick Tine. *Oh, can't you? Well then, you can damn well feel!* And he took Bruce and swung him out through the door, and kicked him sore in the dowp as he went, and threw a chair at him, and Bruce had enough, he ran like a hare, half-blind though he was, and the Muirs all stood next door and gaped, Mrs. Muir and Tooje and Ted, all but John, he sat indoors and gleyed quiet up the lum.

The next thing the Muirs saw was Mrs. Bruce herself, kicked out like her man and running like him, and syne the bairns, and syne they heard sounds inside the house like a wild beast mad. Then old Smithie started to throw out the things that belonged to his daughter and his goodson Bruce, a sewing machine and their kists and clothes, a heap in the stour outside the door. Bruce had cleared his eyes by

then and come back, but old Smithie saw him and chased
him away, with a bread knife, and came back and danced
on the gear, he looked like the devil himself, said Ake,
who had come up to see what the row was about—if you
could imagine the devil in whiskers raising worse hell than
was usual in Segget.

Well, he closed the door next and after a while some
folk went over and chapped at the door, but they got not a
cheep, and waited for Bruce, he'd gone to the smiddy to
borrow an axe. He came back with a fair-like crowd at his
heels, Feet the bobby came with him as well, and just as
they started in on the door Ake Ogilvie cried *No, damn't!
that won't do.* And he said to Bruce *Is this your house, or
his?* Bruce told him to mind his own mucking business, and
was raising his axe to let fly at the door when Ake Ogilvie
said, *All right, then, all right. It's up to you, Feet. You're
supposed to defend the law here in Segget. Here's a man
that has locked himself up in his house, and you're standing
by and aiding and abetting a burglar trying to get into the
place.*

That hadn't struck folk afore, now it did, they cried, *Ay,
that's right,* and Bruce glared around; and Feet scratched
at his head and took out his note-book. And he said to
Bruce that he'd maybe best wait, he himself would call on
old Smithie for a change, to open the door in the name
of the Law. But all that they heard after Feet had cried
that were the snores of old Smithie asleep on his bed.

He wasn't seen in Segget till the Sunday noon, when he
crawled out to give some meat to his kye. But he never
left the house but he locked up the door, the Bruces got
tired of trying to dodge in, they said they couldn't bear the
old brute, anyhow, him and his stink, and they flitted to
Fordoun, and Bruce got a job on the railway there; and
old Smithie at last had his house to himself, thanks to the
lorry-man's Benny Dick Tine.

And what all this clishmaclaver led to was Alec Hogg getting the job on the road that had once been Bruce's, and
the seat by the fire in old Smithie's house that was Bruce's
as well. For young Alec Hogg was a skilly-like childe, right
ready and swack and no longer polite, he called a graip by
its given name. As for looking around for slop-basins these
days, he'd have eaten tea-leaves like a damn tame rabbit,
and munched them up with contentment, too.

And he said to old Smithie as they mended the roads
there was nothing like a damn good taste of starvation to
make you take ill with ideas you'd held, he had starved
down south when he lost his job, and near starved when he
managed to get back to Segget, his father, the old mucker,
would glunch and glare at every bit mouthful he saw his son
eat—*his* hands had never held idleceit's bread. He'd sneer
at the table, the monkey-like mucker. *And what have your
fine friends, the Fashers, done for you?* And it was but the
truth, they had done not a thing; as for Fascism's fancies
on Scotland and Youth—well, starvation's grip in your
belly taught better. Scotland and its young could both go
to hell and frizzle there in ink for all that he cared.

And old Smithie thought that a fell wice speak, and so
did John Muir, and they'd sit and crack, the three of them
by the side of the road, and watch the traffic go by to Dundon, the cars with gentry, the buses with folk. And John
Muir would gley *Ay, God, and that's sense. I was once
myself a bit troubled about thing—fair Labour I was, but
to hell with them all. Poor folk just live and die as they
did, we all come to black flesh and a stink at the end. . . .
And like fools we still go on with the soss, bringing grave-
fodder into the world. For I hear that you're courting Else
Queen, are you, Alec?*

Alec reddened up a bit and said maybe he was; and John
Muir said Well, and he might do worse, since women there
were you'd to bed them sometime. And he asked when Else
and Alec were to marry, and Alec said *Christ, I haven't an
idea—we've no place to bide though we married tomorrow.*

And 'twas then that old Smithie said *Have you no? You're
a decent-like childe and I like you well. Let you and your
wife come bide in with me.*

Else came to Chris and told her the news. Chris said she
was glad—*and I know you'll be happy.* Else tossed her
head, *God knows about that. There are worse folk than
Alec—at least, so I hear. And as for being happy—och,
nobody is!*

Chris laughed at that and said it wasn't true, but she
wondered about it in the fresh-coming Spring, maybe it was
Else had the sense of the thing—not looking for happiness,
madness, delight—she had left these behind in the bed of
Dalziel; only looking to work and to living her life, eating

and sleeping and rising each dawn, not thinking, tiring by night-time and dark—as Chris did herself in the yard of the Manse. And Chris raised her head as she thought that thought, and heard the trill of a blackbird, shrill, and saw the spirt of its wings as it flew, black sheen of beauty, across the long grass: and the ripple and stilly wave of the light, blue sunlight near on the Manse wall. And she thought that these were the only glad things—happiness, these, if you found the key. She had lost it herself, unlonely in that, most of the world had mislaid it as well.

She minded then as she worked at that tree, an apple tree, and set smooth the earth, and reached her hands in the cling of the mould, that saying of Robert's, long, long ago, the day he unveiled the new-hallowed Stones up by the loch on Blawearie brae—that we'd seen the sunset come on the land and this was the end of the peasants' age. But she thought, as often, we saw more than that—the end forever of creeds and of faiths, hopes and beliefs men followed and loved: religion and God, socialism, nationalism—Clouds that sailed darkling into the night. Others might arise but these went, by, folk saw them but clouds and knew them at last, and turned to the Howe from the splendid hills—folk were doing so all over the world, she thought, back to the sheltered places and ease, to sloth or toil or the lees of lust, from the shining splendour of the cloudy hills and those hopes that had followed and believed everlasting. She herself did neither, watching, unsure: was there nothing between the Clouds and the Howe?

This life she lived now could never endure, she knew that well as she looked about her, however it ended it could not go on; she was halted here, in these Segget years, waiting the sound of unhasting feet, waiting a Something unnamed, but it came. And then——

She stopped in her work and looked down at herself, at her breast, where the brown of her skin went white at the edge of the thin brown dress she wore, white rose the hollow between her breasts, except where it was blue-veined with blood; funny to think that twice in her life a baby had grown to life in her body and herself changed so to await that growth, and still she looked like a quean, she thought, breast, hips, and legs, and she liked her legs, even yet, as she looked at them with a smile, at the line of herself as she squatted to weed, nice still to cuddle spite her sulky face!

Had she lived in the time of the golden men who hunted the hills by the Trusta bents there would have been cuddles enough, she supposed, fun and pain and the sting of the wind, long nights of sleep in a heath-hid cave, morns shining over the slopes of the hills as you stirred by your man and peered in his face, lying naked beside you, naked yourself, with below the Howe just clearing its mists as the sun came up from an alien sea—the Howe unnamed and shaggy with heath, with stone-oak forests where the red deer belled as the morning grew and the Bervie shone; and far over the slopes of the Howe you could see the smoke rise straight from another cave, and know your nearest friends a day off; and you'd not have a care or a coin in the world, only *life,* swift, sharp, and sleepy and still and an arm about you, life like a song, and a death at the end that was swift as well—an hour of agony, or only a day, what woman feared death who had borne a child? And many enough you'd have borne in the haughs and been glad enough of their coming in that day, undreaming the dark tomorrows of the Howe that came with the sailing ships from the south. . . .

And, kneeling and cutting at a wallflower clump that had grown over-large for its portion of earth, Chris smiled as she thought of her talk with Else on this matter of human-kind itself growing over-large for *its* clump of earth. Else had stood and listened with red-tinted ears, and stammered and blushed, it was funny and sad, Chris knew how she felt, she had once felt the same. Else said *Oh, Mem, but I couldn't do that—it wouldn't be right to do anything like that!* Chris said *It's surely better to do that than have the bairns that you can't bring up?* Else shook her head, *They'll just come, and we'll manage. But I couldn't do things to myself like that.*

Robert had overheard Chris as she talked, he had heard the talk through the kitchen door, coming down the stairs in his silent way. And when he and Chris were alone to-gether, he said *You shouldn't have said that, Christine,* gentle and quiet and even of speech. Chris had shivered a little and drawn further away. *Why not?* she asked, and he said *Because we have no rights in these matters at all. We have meddled too much with our lives as it is; they are God's concern, the children who come.*

For a minute Chris hardly believed what she heard, she

had stared at him, at his masked face; they themselves had done this thing he denounced. . . .

All the next afternoon, as it seemed to Chris, she heard the rumour and hum of the wedding, down in the hall of the Segget Arms. It had turned to a day sunblown and clear, the earth was hard as she weeded the beds, clumps of begonias under the dykes, back of the Manse the chickens of Muir were deep in a drowsy scraiching, well-fed. Chris went and looked over the wall and watched, and laughed a little at the courting play of an over-small cock with a haughty, shamed look, as though it thought mating a nasty thing, but yet was right eager to make half a try. There were lots of folk who had minds like his!

Robert and Ewan were both at the wedding, Robert returned as soon as he might, Chris heard him climb up the stairs to his room. The noise went on far into the night, stirring in sleep towards the Sunday morning Chris heard the light step of Ewan go by. Next morning he wasn't stirring as usual, and she carried a cup of tea to his room, and knocked and went in and he still slept fast, lying straight, his dark hair thick as a mop, she stood and looked at him and tickled his arm, and he woke up lightly, as he always woke. *Oh, it's you, Chris!* and stared a moment: *I'm sorry, Mother!*

She said *Oh, I'm Chris as well, I suppose,* and sat on the side of the bed while he drank, the morning growing in the yews outside, promise of another day of summer yellow on the ivied walls of the Manse. She asked how the wedding had gone, and he yawned, so grown-up, and stretched while she caught the cup; and he said that the wedding had gone off fine, except that folk were afraid of Robert, he'd changed so much, with never a laugh. Ewan had heard Dite Peat say of Robert——

Chris said *Yes, what did he say of Robert?* and Ewan lay and looked at her, calm and cool. *He said that Robert had lain with Else, he knew bed-shame in a man when he saw it.*

Chris said *You didn't believe that, did you?* Ewan yawned again, *I don't know; he might. Though I shouldn't think it likely, he has you to sleep with; and you must be very nice, I should think.*

Chris felt the blood come swift in her cheeks, and a

moment the wildest feeling of fear; and then that went by, she'd be honest as him. She said *Oh, I think I am nice to sleep with. You've to be terribly in love with someone for that—it makes all the difference, as you'll know some time.*

He said, politely, *Yes, I suppose so,* he hadn't much interest in the matter at all; and told some more of the fun at the wedding, the Provost and MacDougall Brown had both sung, the Provost banking and braeing, bass, MacDougall strong on the Blood of the Lamb. There had been lots to eat and lots of dancing, Ewan had danced with most of the women, rather fun, though most were too fat round the hips, the hips were the things that counted, he'd found. He'd told Else that and she'd said she was shocked, but he didn't suppose that she was, very much.

And then Ake Ogilvie and Dite Peat had quarrelled, it seems they had hated each other for years, and kept away from each other for years, neither one nor the other sure that he'd win. It was round about seven o'clock that it happened; they went out to the back of the Arms to fight, Ewan didn't hear till the fight was near done and went out and saw Dite Peat on the grass, his eyes closed up and rather a mess, Ake Ogilvie being helped into his coat and wiping a trickle of blood from his nose. And Ewan had felt a bit sorry for Dite—goodness knew why, the *dirtiest* rat.

Chris asked what time he'd reached home and he said *Not till this morning some time, nearly two. I took a friend of Else's to Frellin, the servant-maid at the Manse up there.* Chris asked was she nice and Ewan gave a shrug. *I thought her rather a boring young beast, she wanted me to make love to her—up to a point, I suppose, I don't know.* Chris asked *And did you?* and Ewan said *No, but I thought I would try to teach her a lesson. You know I've got strong wrists?—I get them from you—so I held her with one hand and smacked her with the other, and patted her all neat and nice again, and put her in through the Frellin Manse gate, and came home to my bed: I felt a bit tired.*

Folk said he fair was a nickum, that loon, young Ewan Tavendale that came from the Manse, and went to the college at Dundon each day, cool and calm you'd see him swing by, no hat on his head be it sun, be it sleet, folk said he was proud as dirt: and for why? He was only the

son of a crofter, just, killed in the War, and only his luck
his mother had married into a Manse. He never went by
with a loon-like slouch, or reddened up, loon-like, over the
lugs, if he met with a covey of queans in the Square—
damn't, there was something unnatural about him, a sly
young brute, you could well believe. And what though
they said he did well at college? No doubt his stepfather,
the minister Colquohoun, did all his lessons and he got the
credit.

Then the speak got about from the Frellin Manse that
he'd taken a lass from the wedding of Else, the lass that
idle young thing Jeannie Ray, and she'd thought to have
a bit play with the loon—she often would play about with
the loons and get them sore in a way to have her, syne leave
them looking and habbering like fools. But she'd got a sore
stammy-gaster with Ewan, the coarse young brute assaulted
the quean, and left her greeting on the Manse door-mat.
And she told the news to a crony in Frellin, and the crony
giggled and passed it on, and it reached Ag Moultrie, the
Roarer and Greeter, and she nearly exploded with shame
and delight. And next time she met in with Ewan she cried,
*Ay, Ewan, what's this that I hear about you and that lass
Jeannie Ray down at Frellin Manse?* And the loon said
*I'm sorry I don't know what you've heard, Miss Moultrie,
but no doubt Segget soon will. Good morning.* And he
smiled, polite, and passed on, not a bit ashamed, and
left Ag to gape. And not only that, she felt a bit feared, it
was fair uncanny, a loon like that.

And a queerer thing followed, her father was dying,
Rob Moultrie that said he wasn't her father, the coarse old
brute still tormented his wife with the speak that Ag was
no daughter of his. Well, he was down and fast sinking at
last, about time that he was, the snarling old sinner. And
near to the last, when he'd got gey low, he said that he'd
like to see the young man, Ewan Something his name was,
up at the Manse, he'd like to see him and nobody else. Ag
sat by his bed and she heard the bit blither, and she said
to him, soothing, *You're wandering a bit. He doesn't know
you, the young man at the Manse.* And Rob Moultrie said
*Go get him at once, you goggle-eyed gowk, with your claik-
ing tongue. He's more kin of mine than you'll ever be, you
with your half-dozen fathers or more.*

So Jess Moultrie trudged away up through Segget, and

gave in the message, and young Ewan came down, and went
in and sat by the bed of old Moultrie, not feared as a loon
at the breath of death, but cool and calm, as though it
were nothing. Folk sat outbye and couldn't make out the
words that the two spoke one to the other, except that they
heard Ewan Tavendale say *Yes, I've noticed that,* and *Yes,
that's worth knowing.* And he shook hands with Rob when
at last he stood up, and didn't make on, as any other would,
that old Rob would soon be up and about, instead he
shook hands and wished him Goodbye, and went out as
calm as he had come in—ay, a heartless young mucker if
ever there was one, whatever could Moultrie have wanted
with *him?*

Rob wouldn't hear of the minister coming, and died
without a prayer in the house, and that was queer in a
childe like him, fell religious and fond of his Bible. Ag cried
that her father had died unblessed; and when he was dead
she just Roared and Grat.

They buried the old tyke on a hot, quiet day, Mr. Colquohoun thinner and quieter than ever; but he had a
fine voice as he read out the words, lower than once it had
been, more genteel, he fairly had quietened down, had
Colquohoun. Once on a time at a burial service folk said the
minister would speak out as though he fair meant that the
dead would rise up some day, and live once again, and it
made your hair crawl—it was all in the Bible, no doubt,
and right fine, but you knew the whole thing just a stutter-
ing of stite. But now the minister spoke earnest and low,
with a kind of a whine that you heard undisturbed as they
lowered old Moultrie down in the clay, with his ill-led life
and his ill-gettèd ways, his hatred of gentry, his ill-treating
of Jess. Well, that was his end, and you felt undisturbed, all
but John Muir, as he told to Ake later.

For it came on him when the folk had gone, and he
worked there alone in the stilled graveyard, and watched
the figure of Colquohoun move off, that something was
finished and ended in Segget, more than old Moultrie, older
than him. And a queer qualm came in the pit of his wame,
he stopped in the sun to gley in a dream, 'twas as though
they were shadows in the sunblaze he saw, nothing enduring and with substance at all, kirk and minister, and stones
all around graved with their promised hopes for the dead,
the ways and beliefs of all olden time—no more than the

whimsies a bairn would build from the changing patterns
that painted the hills.

And faith, there were more than enough of those changes,
folk woke to the fact of ill changes in Segget, you'd to
count your silver now ere you spent it, there wasn't a soul
but was hit some way, prices so high and the spinners, the
dirt, with hardly a meck to spend in shops. Whiles one of
the Mowat mills still joggled along, as it wore to Autumn
you'd see its smoke like a lazy snake uprise in the air. But
it joggled half-hearted, there was fell little traffic, the stationy, Newlands, said so little jute came in he wondered
the Mill kept going: and he tried to get spinners to do what
he did, bawl for the Blood of MacDougall's Lamb; and no
doubt he fair was a pious childe, though you thought yourself that praying for blood was hardly the way to start a
jute mill.

The Segget wynds were crowded with spinners, lolling
about in the sun, the dirt, you turned one moment from
cursing the brutes for their sweirty and living off the like of
yourself, and the next you had nearly moaned your head
off that there wasn't a thing they now bought in your shops.
Dite Peat was the first to feel the bit nip, he'd never done
well with the spinners, Dite, since that time long back he'd
mishandled his father. But up until late he'd managed to
live, with trade from the rest of Segget New Toun, though
most from the countryside out around. Well, he found that
the farms were failing him now, cottar folk got their meat
from the vans on the roads, and all the farmers had gotten
them cars and went into Stonehaven or even Dundon: in
the end Dite Peat was rouped from his door. It lent a bit
of excitement, that, Dite's stuff sold up while he stood and
looked on, still bearing the marks of the knocks he had got
in that tink-like fight with the joiner of Segget.

Folk wondered what would become of him now, it was
said he hadn't a meck of his own: and though when it
seemed he owned a bit shop folk bore with him and his
dirty jokes, they weren't such fools as to do that now and
cold-shouldered him everywhere that he went. And down
in the Segget Arms one night when he started in with his
dirty tales, Alec Hogg was there and he said *You shut up,
we're sick of you and the things you can do—though you
can't keep your shop-roof over your head*. Dite bared his
rotten brown teeth like a dog, but other folk was crying

That's right, and he didn't dare make a set at young Hogg.
That was near the end of the brute in Segget, he went to
Meiklebogs and asked for a fee, folk told that Dalziel had
ta'en him on cheap—Dalziel whose new housekeeper was
in the old way; faith! with Dite Peat at the Meiklebogs as
well, the question of fatherhoods in the future would be
more of a complication than ever.

For bairns came thick as ever they'd come, folk cut their
costs in all things but cradles, down in Old Toun they
squawked into life, the bairns, in rooms that were packed
out already. The less the work the more of the creatures,
they bred fair disgusting old Leslie would say, and it
showed you the kind of dirt that they were, living crowded
like that, four-five in a room, in houses that were not fit
for pig-rees. 'Twas Infernal, just: the men should be libbed:
now, when he himself was a loon up in Garvock——

But his trade at the smiddy was failing as well, though
he habbered and blethered as much as ever, you'd fell
often hear the anvil at rest and look in and see old Leslie
sit there, sitting and staring down at his pipe, it gave you
an unco-like feeling to see him. There were fell few jobs
came down from the Mills and a mighty few from the
farms outbye, with their new-like ploughs that needed no
coulters, if they broke a bit they looked in a book and sent
away to the makers for't. Not like the days of the crofter
childes, when in and about from Kinraddie, Arbuthnott,
and half the hill-land betwixt Segget and Fordoun, the folk
of the lost little farms would ride with plenty of trade in
a small-like way.

The only creature that seemed to flourish as the harvest
brought a dour end to the weather and the clouds rolled
slower over the Howe was Will Melvin that kept the Segget
Arms, him and that sharp-tongued besom his wife, the
spinners would go down to the Arms and get drunk, instead
of biding at home in their misery and cutting their throats,
as decent folk would.

Mr. Mowat came suddenly home to Segget and sacked
every servant he met in the House; he said that he Jahly
well must, he'd no choice, he was taxed to death by those
Labour chaps. Then he went to the kirk, the first time in
years, and sat and listened to a dreich-like discourse—
God! there was something queer with Colquohoun. But
he kept his eyes, Mr. Mowat, folk told, on Mrs. Colquohoun and not the minister, as she sat in the choir with her

sulky-proud face, and her swathings of hair, ay, she'd
fairly fine hair, herself looking up at the pulpit as though
she didn't know Mr. Mowat looked at her—and didn't
know as everybody else did in Segget, that he'd been the
father of that bairn of hers that died away a three-four
years back.

Mr. Mowat never went near the Manse now, he hadn't
done that since the days of the Strike, nor the Geddeses
either since Mrs. Colquohoun had raised a row at the
W.R.I. And what do you think that row was about? A
socialist creature had offered to come down from Dundon
and lecture on birth-control: and all the folk were against
it at once, except the tink bitch the minister had wed. . . .
And what might IT be? you asked, and folk told you: just
murdering your bairns afore they were born, most likely
that was what *she* herself did.

She did her own work in the Manse nowadays, they
had had to draw in their horns as well, no other maid
took the place of Else. And the Sourock's wife was fairly
delighted, she said getting down on the floors to scrub
would be an ill-like ploy, she would warrant, for the brave
silk knickers that Mrs. Colquohoun wore. For the Sourock's
wife had never forgiven the minister's wife her bit under-
things, and the way she voted at the General Election.

But syne news came that fair raised a stir, the Labour
Government thrown out at last, and that fine-like childe,
Ramsay MacDonald, was in with the Tories, and said they
were fine. And them that had wireless sets listened in, and
Ramsay came on with his holy-like voice and maaed like
a sheep, but a holy-like sheep, that the country could yet
be saved: and he'd do it. Ay, he'd grown a fine chap and
had got back his guts, you were pleased to hear as the maa
went on, now he had jumped to the gentry's side. And no
doubt you would see fine changes in Segget.

But Chris watched that and the life in Segget with a
queer apprehension holding her heart. One evening she
climbed up to Ewan's back room, where he sat at a little
desk he had there, reading a text-book, his head in his hands.
He jumped up when she came and found her a seat, polite
and kind, though remote with his book till she asked him
what the book was about. So he told her the stuff was geol-
ogy, he was studying the strata of the last Ice Age that
came in Scotland long years ago, when the bergs came
drifting down by Dundon and folk looked out from their

mountain eyries and saw the peaks and the glaciers come.
Chris sat and listened, hands clasped round her knees,
looking at Ewan's head in the light, smooth and dark and
yet shot with gold, the pallor of the lamplight upon his
hair—grey granite below as grey granite above.

Then her mind switched away to what he was saying, she
thought *And the thing is happening again*—all over the
world the Ice was coming, not the ice-time that ended the
Golden Age, but the Ice of want and fear and fright, its
glacier peaks on the sky by day, its frozen gleam on the
sky by night, and men looked out bewildered to see it,
cold and dank, and a dark wind blew, and there was neither direction, salvation, nothing but the storming black
lour of the Clouds as the frosts and the fog of this winter
came. . . .

Ewan had twisted around, he said *Mother!* sharp, and
jumped to his feet and shook her. Chris came to herself
with a start, and stared. *What's wrong?* she asked, and he
said *You looked—fey.*

She seldom heard a Scots word from Ewan, he brushed
them aside as old, blunted tools, but the word had come on
his lips as though sudden he'd sought in English and English
had failed. She laughed and said *Did I?* and ruffled his hair,
and he grinned at her, quiet, he'd been quick, but not
feared—he'd do strange things yet in the world, Ewan,
who hadn't a God and hadn't a faith and took not a thing
on the earth for granted. And she thought as she held him
(he endured that, polite) he was one of the few who might
save the times, watching the Ice and the winter come, un-
flustered, unfrightened, with quiet, cold eyes.

And she smiled at that and her prideful dreamings for
the child of her womb, an idle woman's pride: and bade
Ewan good-night and went down to the kitchen to leave it
neat for the morning's work. 'Twas then that there came a
knock at the door and Else Queen that was now Else Hogg
stamped in, with the washing she did each week for the
Manse, she cried *Well, Mem, have you heard the news?*

Chris asked *What news?* and Else sat down and gasped,
*I fair had to run to tell you. It's about Mr. Mowat—but
surely you've heard?*

The story, she said, was all over Segget, Mr. Mowat was
ruined and hadn't a penny, the whole of Segget mortgaged
to the hilt. The last time he came back from London he'd
tried to raise a bit loan at any damn price; and he'd gone

to his Dundon bankers and tried, and they'd said they must see the jute in his mills. So they sent a man down, Mr. Mowat met him and dined him and wined him up at the House, it minded old Sinclair, the last of the servants, of the good old days when young Jahly Mowat would come back with a half-dozen whores in his car. Ah, well, the banker childe was fell canny, he drank but little, and that with suspicion; but Mr. Mowat soaked like a drouthy fish, and then said *Right O, we'll go down to the mills*.

There were two main storage sheds at the Mill, one was near empty, said young Mr. Mowat, the other well filled with new bales of jute. And Mr. Mowat showed the first of the sheds, there was only a bale or so in the place, but when they came to the other bit shed, and the sliding doors slid back in their slots, there were the bales packed up to the roof, so tight they nearly bulged through the door. *You see, we've a Jahly good stock at the Mill*, said Mr. Mowat, and the bank man agreed.

So the bank childe went back to Dundon and reported, and they loaned Mr. Mowat a five hundred pounds. And the creature vanished, none knew where he'd gone; and this last week or so the bank grew suspicious. It sent a man down to Segget yestreen, and he went to the Mills and what did he find, down there at the shed that had seemed so packed? That there was no more than a curtain of bales, stacked up to the roof at the shed's near end, the rest of the shed was as toom as your hat, Mr. Mowat had swindled the bank to the end: and now the bank had ta'en over the Mills.

Chris asked what that meant and Else didn't know, except that all the folk left at the Mills had been sacked that evening and the Mills closed down. And folk were saying they never would open, it wouldn't be worth it, with trade so bad; and nobody knew what the spinners would do that had waited for years for their jobs to come back.

And the winter was coming. Down in Old Toun a weary indifference lay on the wynds, they paid no heed to the new Election, Chris herself didn't bother to vote—were the liars and cheats called Labour or Tory they'd feather their own nests and lie to the end.

Rain held the sky at November's end, she saw the streaming parks of Dalziel lift and move under the freezing haze that sailed and swam by the base of the Mounth, the curlews had ceased to cry on the Kaimes and of nights the

sounds the trains came blurred, those nights that the great
lighted buses would lighten, suddenly, firing the walls of
the room where she lay by the side of Robert unsleeping,
him sleeping so sound that he sometimes seemed dead. How
to sleep, how to sleep, when your mind took hold, in the
dark, of the plight of the Segget wynds?

They had brought in a thing they called the Means Test,
spinners who had had the dole over-long were told that
their relatives must keep them in future. Chris had stopped
by the door of Ake Ogilvie's shop, and he told her that
things were black in Old Toun, the Wilsons had been cut
off the dole altogether because their old grannie had the
Old Age Pension—the three of them to live on ten shillings
a week. How could they pay their rent on that?

Since the Mowat creditors took over the place they were
forcing the payments right through the nose, they'd already
had Feet up at the eviction of a two-three families out of
their houses, if houses you could call them—they smelt like
pig-rees. Old Cronin had been cut off the Bureau as well
because young Charlie was fee'd up at Frellin, and stayed
at home to look after his father: and how could they live
on the pay of a loon? And there were worse cases than
these, far worse, God damn't! you had never much liked
the spinners, but the things that were happening near turned
you sick, it was kicking in the faces of the poor for no
more than delight in hearing the scrunch of their bones.

Chris said *They won't stand it, there'll be revolution,* and
Ake sneered *Revolution? They'll starve and say nothing.
Or 'Come walk on my face and I'll give you a vote!'*

Then the news went round that old Cronin was dead,
found dead in his bed by his young son Chae, Chae blub-
bered the old man had no firewood for days, and nothing
but a pot of potatoes to eat. Folk wouldn't believe that
blither at all, it couldn't be true, for it made you shiver—
no, no, 'twas only another damned lie, that kind of thing
never happened in Segget. Would you find that news in the
Mearns Chief?—you wouldn't, so you knew that it couldn't
be true, the *Chief* said week by week we were fine, and
Scotland still the backbone of Britain, and the Gordon
Highlanders right gay childes, not caring a hoot though
their pay was down, and Progressives just the scum of the
earth that planned to take bairns out of the slums and rear
them up in Godless communes, and a woman Naomi
Mitchison coarse, for she said not a word about Christ in

her book. . . . Ay, the *Mearns Chief* was aye up-to-date, and showed you a photo of Mrs. MacTavish winning the haggis at a Hogmanay dance.

That son of old Cronin's, Jock was his name (you surely minded when *he* was in Segget?) had done right well for himself, folk said. He was now a National Labour supporter, one of Ramsay's new men down in Glasgow, and would likely get into the Parliament soon: and he was starting on a lecture tour—*The Country First, Parties Must Wait*. By that, of course, he meant the political parties, not the kind he would hold in his Glasgow house—he spoke and acted the gent to the life.

But Charlie said his old father had seemed to shrivel up when he heard of the tour; and the last time Charlie had been to his father he hardly had spoken a sensible word, just muttered over one of his socialist books, by Ramsay MacDonald, till the light grew dim, so faint that he couldn't have seen to read.

He told that to Ewan when he came to the Manse to arrange the burial in Segget kirkyard, he and Ewan hadn't met for a long time past, chief enough though they'd been at the school together. And Charlie was shy and he said to Ewan, *I hear, Mr. Ewan, you're clever at college,* and stood and shuffled his great glaured boots, and his hands were heavy and calloused and cold, holding the clumsy cap in his hand. Ewan said *I'm all right. Sit down. Like some tea?* and went ben to the kitchen where Chris made a cake. *It's young Charlie Cronin, and mother, he's hungry.* Chris said she'd bring some food on a tray, but Ewan said *No, you see he would guess I knew he was hungry and that would offend him. I'll take in some and we'll eat it together.*

So he did, though he'd only new-finished his dinner, Chris peeped at the two of them, sitting and talking, with a tinge of pride and wonder for Ewan, and a twist of pity in her heart for his friend, with his shy red face and his clumsy hands. Then she went back to her work, and they ate; and when Charlie Cronin at last went away she heard Ewan make a dive for the bathroom and be suddenly, exceedingly, very sick there. She took him a glass of water to drink, and he smiled and drank and said that was better: white-faced and black-haired, but still cool enough. Chris thought at the time 'twas because of the food he'd eaten to keep the Cronin lad company; but she wasn't sure later, for she found out that Charlie had told him black tales of the things in Old Toun.

And that night she went up to his room and found Ewan, staring out at the fall of sleet, a pelt and a hiss in the moving dark, his head in his hands, not reading as usual. She touched him, quiet, and he started a little.

Oh, nothing, he said, *I'm fine, don't worry, I was trying to remember old Cronin's face.*

He was turning to look in the face of Life.

That was the Sunday; on Monday folk woke to a blinding pelt of rain-sheets on Segget and down and across the steaming Howe where the churned earth lay with its quagmired pools, the hills corona'ed dark with their clouds. Robert went early up to his room and Chris was making the dinner in the kitchen when she found John Muir at the kitchen door. He looked stranger than ever she had seen him look, John Muir, and forgot to call her Mem. He said a gey thing had happened last night: and gleyed at her queer and gave a queer cough.

Chris said, *What's happened? Sit down, you look queer.* And he sat and told her the unco-like tale.

She had heard of the Kindnesses? Well, they were folk that bided down in Segget Old Toun. At least they had done till a three days back, Kindness himself was an ill-doing childe, and weeks behind with his rent, folk said. His wife was a lass from Kinraddie way, she'd a bairn only a three weeks old, and had near gone daft when the landlord's folk came down to the house to turn them out. Sim Leslie had gone to see it was done and thought nothing of it, he was used to that now.

Well, out they'd been turned, their bit gear in the streets, you minded that Saturday streamed with sleet, and the house they'd been in was at Segget's tail end, and few folk saw the thing that went on, or cared to be out in weather like that, and Kindness himself was a surly brute. He got sacks and happed up the most of his gear, and prowled Segget for hours to look for a place. But he wasn't well known and he wasn't well liked, so he came back at last somewhere about midnight, and broke in a window and put his wife in, she had stood in the lithe all those hours in the sleet with her bairn in her arms and must near have been dead. She sat in the kitchen the rest of the night, Kindness himself had brought in a chair, then he prowled some more, for he couldn't sleep.

But worse was to come with the Sunday morning; the policeman, Sim Leslie, that folk called Feet, came on them early and miscalled them for tinks, and took Kindness's name in his little note-book, as though the fool didn't know it by now, and said there would be a court-case about this. Syne he turned them out and boarded the window, and went off and left them, and a neighbour nearby took in the wife and bairn for a while. But she hadn't an inch of space to spare, and at last, as the night came, Kindness came back and said he'd gotten a place where they'd bide, he didn't say more, a surly bit brute.

Well, his wife went with him through the pelt of the sleet, and got to the end of Old Toun to the place, and that was an old deserted pig-ree, from the time when folk in Segget bred pigs, long ere the Mills or the spinners came. You could get inside if you got down and crawled, Kindness had taken a mattress in there and a stump of a candle and some of their things. Mrs. Kindness was feared at the dark and the sounds that the old ree made as the night wore on, but they put out the light at last, fell tired, and went to sleep in the sound of the rain.

It must have been somewhere near morning they woke, Mrs. Kindness woke up with her bairn screaming, not just the cry of a bairn in unease but a shrill, wild cry that near feared her to death. She tried all she could to comfort its wail, then the light began to peek in the pigsty and they saw the reason for the bairn's screams, the rats in the night had gnawed off its thumb.

John Muir cried *Mistress, don't take on like that!* and caught Chris's arm and put her in a chair. And then as he straightened up from that he saw the minister stand in the door, he'd come quietly down as he came these days, and he looked like Chris, he had heard it all. But he only said *John, where are they now?*

Muir skeughed and said that he didn't well know, he'd heard that folk had ta'en meat to the ree, and Kindness was off for a doctor, 'twas said, walking all the way to Stonehaven. Robert said *Walking?*—his face looked queer —*WALKING? Chris, I'll go for those folk. Will you get a room ready before I come back?*

She worked as quick as she could when he'd gone out

into the shining pelt of the rain. But it nearly was noon ere
Robert came back, the woman looked only a slip of a quean,
Robert carried the bairn, it had ceased to cry, whimpering
and weeking soft like a kitten. The woman stopped and
looked at Chris with the shamed, strange eyes of a frightened beast, Chris squeezed her hands for a moment, just,
and was rough, and told her where her room was, and was
rough that she mightn't break down and weep. And she
took the bairn and bathed the torn thumb, though it nearly
turned her sick as she worked; and the bairn weeked like
kitten hurt. Then she carried it up to its mother, waiting,
in the spare bedroom with the blazing fire.

She left them there and came down to find John Muir
come back with the Kindness gear. He told her the minister
was off to Stonehaven, on his bike, to try and overtake
Kindness, the minister himself would hold on for the
doctor.

Kindness reached back to the Manse about three, and an
hour or so later Robert and McCormack, Robert soaked
and shivering from his ride in the rain. The doctor went
up and bade a long time and then came down to the hall
and Chris. He shook his head and snibbed up his bag.

*I came over-late. Poison and shock. The woman didn't
know it though she had it beside her. The baby's been dead
this last hour or more.*

In the dead of the night three nights after that, Chris
woke, she was sharply and suddenly awake. Robert beside
her coughing and coughing. She got up and padded to his
side of the bed, and he had not known that her warmth
had gone, all his body was in such a heat; but he saw her
against the light from the windows. He said *I'm all right,
go back to your bed* and instantly fell to his coughing again.

Chris put on a dressing-gown and went down, and made
and brought up a hot lemon drink, he drank it and thanked
her, she put out the light, his body still burned as she lay
by his side. But presently the cough died away and she
slept, and didn't awake till the morning came, Robert's
cough awoke her, that and the sound of the wind as it
swept the snow down on Segget, piled up on the edge of
another New Year.

With the coming of the day the wind rose and rose and
rattled at the window-hasps of the house, the skirl of it in
the old roof-tops and wailing down the long, winding chim-

neys. Robert kept to his bed, Chris had made him do that, almost by force, he had suddenly smiled—smiled so that her bowels had seemed turned to water, with that flare of the hot old love that was gone. *If I was a man again, I'd hold YOU, you wretch of a woman to bully me like this!* Chris said *You'll be welcome to hold me as you like— when that cough's better, not until then.* He stroked her arm, the flame in his eyes: *Strong and comely still—I've neglected you, Chris!* Then he coughed for a while and when he came to, lay quiet, listening to the day go on.

The Kindnesses had gone to friends in Dundon, and left no relic but a snow-happed grave, and this cough that Robert had got in his throat, and that memory that woke you, sick in the night, of the rats that fed on a baby's flesh. And men had believed in a God and a Christ, men had believed in the kindness of men, men had believed that this order endured because of its truth and its justice to men. . . . Robert was sound beside you in sleep, but once he moved and muttered in dreams. He said *Oh, I can't, I can't—oh, my God!* Chris happed him close and again sought sleep, and the next day came, and he woke to that coughing, and Chris saw a spray of blood on the pillow.

She said *I must send for a doctor, Robert,* fear in her heart, though none in her voice. But he shook his head, his eyes grown remote. *I'll be all right, I'll look after myself.* And after he'd eaten a slice of toast and had drunk some tea, he didn't cough more, and asked for a pad of paper and pencil, he wished to write out his tomorrow's sermon.

Chris knew he wouldn't be able to speak it, a week at least ere he'd rise from his bed; but she took him the paper and pencil to quiet him, and stood by a while till at last he looked up—*Yes, Christine?* his eyes far from her again. So she turned to her work with a daft, dull pain, daft ever to think that THAT could come back.

Ewan helped her that morning, scrubbing the hall, bringing in coal, the wind still raged, a steely drive that was edged with sleet; as the day wore on it froze up again. When she went up that afternoon to Robert's room the door wouldn't open a while though she pushed, then it did, and the stinging air smote her face, the window wide open, the room ice-cold, Robert lying half-naked asleep in his bed. He woke as he heard the sound of her come, his face was flushed in spite of the cold, he said that he'd tried to sleep

and couldn't, he'd felt choked and opened the window and
slept. Where had the pad for his sermon gone?

Chris went down to Ewan to wire for the doctor. When
he came in the evening he sounded Robert's lungs, Robert
lying quiet, his eyes far away; and the doctor was puzzled,
though he chatted and joked. But later, downstairs, he said
to Chris, *There's something queer in Mr. Colquohoun's
lungs—oh no, this cold's not on to them yet. Was he ever
gassed in the War, do you know? There's the strangest con-
traction in both upper lungs. I'll be back fell early the
morn's morning, keep him in bed and keep him warm.*

Ewan went up about six and came back and said that
Robert was sleeping again, but there was blood on his pillow, fresh. Chris got up to change it, she ached in each limb,
but Ewan said that he'd done that already, and Robert
wasn't waked up from his sleep. *Sit down and rest,* and
he forced her to sit, and they sat a long time looking into
the fire, hearing the blast of the wind over Segget. But near
eight or nine when they went to their beds the wind seemed
to die in the cry of the yews, Ewan went to the window
and called Chris to look. So she did, and stood by his
side in the dark, and looked on a sky that was burnished
in steel, rimed with a pringling frost of stars, nothing moved
or lived, the yews stood black, the garden hedges rose up
in the silence as if to listen to the void star-glow. . . . Ewan
said *You'll catch cold,* and blinded the window, and above
their heads they heard Robert cough.

Next morning John Muir came early to the Manse, he
said that he'd tell the congregation there wouldn't be a service; and Chris agreed. But then, as they stood together in
the hall they heard the sound of an opening door, and
looked up, and Chris gave a gasp and cried, *Robert!* He
was coming down slowly, his hand on the rails, he said *I'm
all right; I MUST take the service.* He'd a handkerchief up
to his mouth, saying that, and stopped and coughed, and
Chris wrung her hands. *Robert, go back to your bed—you
must.*

He shook his head, he was fully dressed, even shaved,
*I'll take the service as usual. There's nothing in a cough to
stop me, is there? AND I HAVE SOMETHING TO SAY
TO THE FOLK.*

Chris had stood enough, now she knew at last if she
didn't win now she never would win. She said *Robert, for*

*me. I've never asked much—for me, and I'll never ask an-
other thing: Will you please go back?*

Ewan had come out of his room and looked down, and
he saw Robert's face for a moment twist, as if in pain,
then it altered again, back to the dark, dreaming look that
they knew. *It's you or the kirk, Chris, and I'm the kirk's
man.*

For a second it seemed to Chris she'd be sick, she gave
the funniest dry laugh at that thought, with that gripping
in her stomach and that pain in her throat. Then that went
by, she was suddenly cool, she heard herself say, *All right,
here's your coat;* and found a coat for him in the hall, and
a muffler, and wrapped it about him, as she finished with
that he stared at her queer, the ice broke round his eyes. He
said suddenly, *Chris—my dear, dear Chris!* and kissed her
with that look, not with his lips, not in front of John Muir,
and she smiled at him, white. Then he went out across the
chill blow of the wind, his feet rang sharp on the frozen
ground. Chris caught Ewan's arm and shook it—*Go with
him! I'll come as soon as ever I'm dressed.*

She fled and changed in a flurry and was down, and
across through the snow-wrapped garden before the kirk
bells had ceased from their sudden clamour. She raised her
eyes as she hurried through the kirkyard, and saw the
Mounth as though suddenly halted, watching, and staring
down at Segget, the far peaks under their canopy of cloud,
the nearer bare but for a snow-pillar she saw rise up from
the Leachie bents and whirl in the icy blow of the wind.

Folk said that the kirk at Segget nowadays was a fine bit
place to go for a sleep, the Reverend Colquohoun was as
quiet as a cow with his blethers of Jesus and Brotherhood
and Love and the Sacred Heart that still bled for men. You
could pop a sweetie or so in your mouth and take a bit
snore as the sermon went on; even Hairy Hogg confessed
it was quiet, they had fairly tamed that creature Colquohoun, with his coarse-like suggestings the Hoggs came from
monkeys, when instead they were all descended from Burns.
And Ake Ogilvie said *Well, monkeys for me!*

They were both of them there, both Ake and the Provost,
that Sunday, and Mistress Hogg came as well, she was failing a bit, but still as sharp-tongued, she had said to her son
when he married Else Queen—*Ay, you're keen on the bowl
in spite of the slop.* She sat by her man, Else and Alec sat
near, and it tickled you a bit to see Meiklebogs—behind,

ill-shaved, smiling shy to himself, he had come back to kirk since Colquohoun quietened down.

The kirk began to fill up a bit, old Leslie came in, he was getting fell done, and you thought as you watched him paich down the aisle he never would finish that story about Garvock. And damn't! you felt almost sorry about that, worse folk than old Leslie, his son Sim for one, promoted now, he was leaving Segget, if it wasn't he had such feet as he had you'd have said he'd grown overbig for his boots.

That fair was a hell of a clamour Muir raised, Will Melvin came in in the middle of the ring, like a pot-bellied cat, his thin mistress behind, they were making money like dirt, folk said. *Dirt unto dirt, 'twas the way of all flesh* was Ake Ogilvie's speak about that—aye the same, he'd miscall both the good and the bad in Segget, and didn't seem to see any difference at all 'tween an ill-doing brute like that tink, Dite Peat, and his brother, Peter, that owned his own shop.

There was wee Peter Peat up near the choir, looking round him right fierce to see folk were quiet, his mistress beside him, and the Sourock's wife, the Sourock himself would be down in the Square, singing about Blood in MacDougall's band—he'd never gotten over that mess in his bed when Dite Peat had left the pig he had killed.

God! the frost was fair driving the folk to the kirk; you moved over a bit to let a childe in: young Cronin, you saw, from the Manse at Frellin, the only one of the spinners that had come; the coarse creatures hadn't a care for religion. Charlie Cronin blushed and opened his Bible and sat like a duck on the edge of egg-laying, fell decent-like and shy; and you thought to yourself that Geddes, the headmaster, might well take a lesson, there he was, all asprawl in his pew, showing no respect or example at all; and that nasty bit sneer on his face as he sprawled.

Syne you saw the choir was beginning to fill, Miss Ferguson first; God! how she still blushed. Ake Ogilvie said she'd have a blush on her face if ever they exhumed her corpse from its coffin. Beside her Miss M'Askill sat down with a jerk that couldn't have been good for her spine, you'd have thought, especially as the bottom of that looked ill-padded. She hadn't got a man, and there seemed little chance that she ever *would* now, things as they were—damn't, Segget affairs were fair in a state, you could only hope, with the National Government, they'd alter some time afore Segget was dead. Ramsay MacDonald had said that they would, if we all went poorer, ate less, and spent more—ay, fair a fine childe, with a right clear mind. Ramsay MacDonald, as the English knew well, they couldn't breed the like of Ramsay in England: though Ake Ogilvie said they smothered them at birth. But that was just one of his tink-like says, the English aye needed the Scots at their head, right holy and smart at the same bit time.

John Muir had finished with his ringing at last, and went gleying down the aisle as of old, one shoulder first, and brought in the minister. Faith, he looked white, you'd heard he'd been ill, some cold or such like, a nothing at all. He climbed to the pulpit and coughed and sat down, and looked down the kirk—damn't a queer-like look, near the kind he would give in the days long syne when he was so keen on changing the world.

Syne you saw that you'd fair been mistaken in that, he was praying, with his head laid down in his hands; you felt a bit better to see him like that, decent and douce, as a minister should be—not trying to alter things as he'd done—who the hell wanted alterations in Segget? Folk were fine, if it wasn't that there wasn't any work, and meat a bit scarce, and you hadn't a notion what your bairns would find to do in the world, when they grew up and found it full up of the ill-gettèd bairns of spinners, and such. Ah well, they'd just have to gang their own gait, with the help of some guts and the rock of Christ's kirk.

Young Ewan Tavendale came in and sat down, and looked round the kirk and up at the pulpit as though he owned both and was frightened at neither—faith, folk were right, an impudent get, with no respect for God or man. Then, as the playing on the organ stopped, the far door opened to Mrs. Colquohoun, white-faced and proud, like a proud quean still, hurrying to take her seat in the choir. Half-way to that she stopped and looked up, at her man who sat so quiet in the pulpit—folk saw the look and kittled to interest, could the two of them have had a row in the Manse?

The minister gave out the psalm, but so low you hardly heard the words that he said; and you spent so long looking up the passage that the singing was over afore you had found it. Syne the minister was praying, you bent your head, a fell dreich prayer and only half-heard. But then as he finished and gave out his text folk fairly louped in their seats as he spoke, his voice had a ring like a sudden bell;

My text is from the twenty-third chapter of St. Luke, verse forty-two: AND HE SAID UNTO JESUS, LORD, REMEMBER ME WHEN THOU COMEST INTO THY KINGDOM.

It is nineteen hundred years since that cry was heard, it is sixteen hundred years since the holy Catholic Church was established in temporal power. In the early days after the death of Christ His return was hourly awaited—His followers, scanty, assured, looked to His coming within a few months or years at the most, they were certain He would come again and redeem the evil of the world that had murdered HIM. And the years went by: and He tarried still. But that Hope and that Promise it was that bore the Cross to triumph at last in Rome, all over Europe; that uplifts it still. And still the Christ tarries and the world remains.

LORD, REMEMBER ME WHEN THOU COMEST INTO THY KINGDOM.

In Segget a week ago tonight, in this Christian village, a man and a woman were driven from their home and had no place to lay their heads. In the night a rat came and fed on their child, eating its flesh in a sacrament of hunger——

LORD, REMEMBER ME WHEN THOU COMEST INTO THY KINGDOM.

In the years when the Great War ended the world seemed to turn in its sleep and awake, a new promise cried all about the earth, the promise of the Christ fulfilled in Man —fulfilled in the movements of pity and hope that men called by many names, meaning the same. Against ignoble oppressions and a bitter tyranny the common people banded themselves at last—in a Christ-like rage of pity to defend their brothers who sweated their blood in the mines, to give warmth and light and ease to us all. And the leaders of the great Nine Days, days filled with the anger and pity of the Christ who drove the money-changers from the Temple courts, looked in their hearts and found there fear,

heard the crunch of the nails that were driven in through
the shrinking hands of the Christ. And they sold Him again,
his promise in Man, each for their thirty pieces of silver.

LORD, REMEMBER ME WHEN THOU COMEST
INTO THY KINGDOM.

This year, when hunger and want filled the land, the
counsellors of the nation told for our guidance that more
hunger and poverty yet must come, an increasing of stripes
in the name of the Law, of Good Government, Order, in
this Christian land, in this nineteenth century since the
Christ died and came into that Kingdom of the Soul which
the Churches proclaim that He came into——

LORD, REMEMBER ME WHEN THOU COMEST
INTO THY KINGDOM.

AND IT WAS ABOUT THE SIXTH HOUR, AND
THERE WAS A DARKNESS OVER ALL THE EARTH
UNTIL THE NINTH HOUR.
AND THE SUN WAS DARKENED, AND THE VEIL
OF THE TEMPLE WAS RENT IN THE MIDST.

So we see, it seems, in the darkened sun, in the rending
veils of the temples and kirks, the end of Mankind himself
in the West, or the end of the strangest dream men have
dreamt—of both the God and the Man Who was Christ,
Who gave to the world a hope that passes, and goeth about
like the wind, and like it returns and follows, fulfilling noth-
ing. There is no hope for the world at all—as I, the least
of His followers see—except it forget the dream of the
Christ, forget the creeds that they forged in His shadow
when their primal faith in the God was loosed—and turn
and seek with unclouded eyes, not that sad vision that
leaves hunger unfed, the wail of children in unending dark,
the cry of human flesh eaten by beasts. . . . But a stark,
sure creed that will cut like a knife, a surgeon's knife
through the doubt and disease—men with unclouded eyes
may yet find it, and far off yet in the times to be, on an
earth at peace, living and joyous, the Christ come back——

His voice had sunk near to a whisper by then, so that
folk in the back of the kirk couldn't hear, all the kirk sit-

ting and staring in silence. Then he started again, he said,
very clear, and once again, slowly, terrible to hear, as a
man who cried from his soul on a friend who had passed
beyond either helping or help:

*LORD, REMEMBER ME WHEN THOU COMEST
INTO THY KINGDOM!*

Chris was never exactly sure of what followed. But she
got from the choir stalls and ran up the aisle, the frozenness gone that had hemmed her in—took scarcely a second
to move from that moment when Robert had stopped, the
queer look on his face. For he stared down the kirk as
though Someone stood there. And then a bright crimson
thing came on his lips, and down at the kirk's far end a
loon screamed.

John Muir reached the pulpit as quick as she did, she saw
Ewan, swift and dark, stand up. Ake Ogilvie as well, the
rest of the folk stared and stared in a frozen silence, from
them to the silent figure up there. Chris ran up the pulpit-
stair, opened the door, Robert's head had fallen forward
in his hands, and all the pages of the Bible below she saw
soaked in the stream of blood from his lips.

And somehow it did not matter, she had known, she put
out her hand and put back the hair, from his forehead,
gently; and looked at the faces of the congregation. She
wetted her lips and tried to speak, to be cool and tell them
the minister was dead, and the service was ended, would
they please go? And then at last she heard herself speak,
in strange words not her own, unbidden to her lips:

It is Finished.

Now, with the broadening of the day, she could see the
peaks of the Mounth wheel one by one into the line of the
flow of the light, dun and sun-riding they rode down the
Howe. Trusta towered first and north and north the peaks
came fast, sun on the Howe and day on the Howe, her last
day in Segget ere she went elsewhere, to new days and
ways, to changes she could not foresee or foreknow. Round
her the new year wakened to life, she saw the steam of a
ploughing team, a curlew was calling up in the broom.

She moved and stretched in weariness then, the morning
weariness before you right woke, so standing she minded

the way that Robert would bless the folk of Segget on Sabbath. And, queerly, her hands shaped into that gesture, with Segget rising in its driftings of smoke, and the hills behind, and all time before.

Then that had finished; she went slow down the brae, only once looked back at the frown of the hills, and caught her breath at that sight they held, seeing them bare of their clouds for once, the pillars of mist that aye crowned their heights, all but a faint wisp vanishing south, and the bare, still rocks upturned to the sky.

THE END

GREY GRANITE

CONTENTS

CAUTIONARY NOTE

THE 'Duncairn' of this novel was originally 'Dundon.' Unfortunately, several English journals in pre-publication notices of the book described my imaginary city as Dundee, two Scottish sheets identified it with Aberdeen, and at least one American newspaper went considerably astray and stated that it was Edinburgh—faintly disguised.

Instead, it is merely the city which the inhabitants of the Mearns (not foreseeing my requirements in completing my trilogy) have hitherto failed to build.

L. G. G.

I

EPIDOTE

ALL around her the street walls were dripping in fog as
Chris Colquohoun made her way up the Gallowgate, yellow fog that hung tiny veils on her eyelashes, curled wet,
and had in her throat the acrid taste of an ancient smoke.
Here the slipper-slide of the pavement took a turn that she
knew, leading up to the heights of Windmill Place, and
shortly, out of the yellow swath, she saw come shambling
the lines of the Steps with their iron hand-rail like a
famished snake. She put out her hand on that rail, warm,
slimy, and paused afore tackling the chave of the climb,
breathing deeply, she could hear her heart. The netbagful
of groceries on her arm ached—she looked down through
wet lashes at the shape of the thing—as though it was the
bag that ached, not her arm. . . .

Standing still so breathing that little while she was suddenly aware of the silence below—as though all the
shrouded town also stood still, deep-breathing a minute in
the curl of the fog—stilling the shamble and grind of the
trams, the purr of the buses in the Royal Mile, the clang
and swing of the trains in Grand Central, the swish and roll
and oily call of the trawlers taking the Forthie's flood—all
pausing, folk wiping the fog from their eyes and squinting
about them an un-eident minute——

Daft, she said to herself, and began climbing the stairs.

451

Midway their forty steps a lamp came in sight, at last, glistening, it flung a long dirty hand down to help her. Her face came into its touch, it blinked surprised, not expecting that face or head or the glistering bronze coils of hair that crowned them—hair drawn in spiralled pads over each ear, fog-veiled, but shining. Chris halted again here under the lamp, thirty-eight, so she couldn't run up these steps, stiff's an old horse on a Mounth hill-road.

Old at thirty-eight? You'll need a bath-chair at fifty. And at sixty—why, as they'd say in Segget, they'll have carted you off to the creamery!

Panting, she smiled wry under the lamp at the foul tale told of Duncairn crematorium—the foul story that had struck her as funny enough even hearing it after the burning of Robert. . . . Oh, mixed and queer soss that living was, dying, dying slowly a bit of yourself every year, dying long ago with that dim lad, Ewan, dying in the kirk of Segget the time your hand came red from Robert's dead lips—and yet midmost the agonies of those little deaths thinking a foul tale flouting them funny!

Daft as well as decrepit, she told herself, but with a cool kindness, and looked over the Steps at the mirror hung where the stairs swung west, to show small loons the downward perils as they pelted blue hell on a morning to school. She saw a woman who was thirty-eight, looked less, she thought, thirty-five maybe in spite of those little ropes of grey that marred the loops of the coiled bronze hair, the crinkles about the sulky mouth and the eyes that were older than the face. Face thinner and straighter and stranger than once, as though it were shedding mask on mask down to one last reality—the skull, she supposed, that final reality.

Funny she could stand here and face up to that, not feel sick, just faintly surprised! Once it had been dreadful and awful to think of—the horror of forgotten flesh taken from enduring bone, the masks and veils of life away, down to those grim essentials. Now it left her neither sick nor sorry, she found, watching a twinkle in sulky gold eyes above the smooth jut of the wide cheek-bones. Not sad at all, just a silly bit joke of a middle-aged woman with idle thoughts in a pause on the Steps of Windmill Brae.

Below the quiet broke with the scrunch of a tram wheeling down from the lights of Royal Mile to the Saturday quietude of Gallowgate. Chris turned, looked, saw the

shiver of sparks through the fog, syne the sailing brute
swing topaz in sight, swaying and swearing, with aching
feet as it ran for its depot in Alban Street. Its passage
seemed to set fire to the fog, a little wind came and blew
the mist-ash, and there was Grand Central smoking with
trains. And now, through the thinning bouts of the fog,
Chris could see the lighted clock of Thomson Tower shine
sudden a mile or so away over the tumbled rigs of grey
granite.

Nine o'clock.

She lowered the netbag and stretched her arms, saw herself wheel and stretch in the mirror, slim still, long curves,
half-nice she half-thought. Her hands came down on the
railing and held it, no need to hurry to-night for a change,
Ma Cleghorn would have seen to supper for them all—the
nine o'clock Gallop to the Guts as she called it. No need
to hurry, if only this once in the peace of the ill-tasting fog
off the Forthie, in the blessed desertion of the Windmill
Steps so few folk used in Duncairn toun. Rest for a minute
in the peace of the fog—or nearly a peace, but for its foul
smell.

Like the faint, ill odour of that silent place where they'd
ta'en Robert's body, six months before——

She'd thought hardly at all what she would do after
Robert's funeral that so shocked Segget, she'd carried out
all the instructions in the will and gone back with Ewan to
the empty Manse, Ewan made her tea and looked after her
—cool and efficient, only eighteen, though he acted more
like twenty-eight—at odd minutes he acted eighty-two she
told him as he brought her the tea in the afternoon stillness
of the sitting-room.

He grinned the quick grin that was boy-like enough, and
wandered the room a bit, tall and dark, unrestlessly, while
she drank the tea. He hated tea himself, with a bairn-like
liking for bairny things—milk and oat-cakes would have
contented Ewan from breakfast to dinner and some more
for his supper. Ayont the windows in the waning of the
afternoon Chris could see the frozen glister of night on the
Grampians, swift and near-moving, Ewan's shoulder and
sleekèd dark head against it. . . . Then he turned from the
window. *Mother, I've got a job.*

She'd been sunk in a little drowse of sheer ache, tiredness from the funeral and the day in Duncairn, she woke

stupid at his speak and only half-hearing: *A job?—who for?*

He said *Why, for little Ewan Tavendale all by his lone. But you'll have to sign the papers first.*

—But it's daft, Ewan, you haven't finished college yet, and then there's the university!

He shook the sleekèd head: *Not for me. I'm tired of college and I'm not going to live off you.* And thought for a minute and added with calm sense, *Especially as you haven't much to live off.*

So that was that and he fetched the papers, Chris sat and read the dreich things appalled, papers of apprenticeship for four years to the firm of Gowans and Gloag in Duncairn. Smelters and steel manufacturers—*But, Ewan, you'd go daft in a job like that.*

He said he'd try not to, awfully hard, especially as it was the best job he could come by—*and I can come out in week-ends and see you quite often. Duncairn's only a twenty miles off.*

—And where do you think I am going to bide?

He looked at her curiously with cool, remote eyes, black didn't suit him, hair and skin over dark. *Eh? Oh, here in Segget, aren't you? You used to like it before Robert died.*

Sense the way he would speak of Robert, not heartlessly, just with indifference, as much as to say what did it matter, would a godly snuffling help Robert now? But a queer curiosity moved Chris to ask *Does anything ever matter to you at all, Ewan?*

Oh, lots. Where you're going to stay, for one thing, when I've gone.

He'd slipped out of that well, Chris thought with a twinkle, sitting in the deep armchair on her heels, her head down bent, he ran his finger along the curve of her neck, coolly, with liking, as she looked up at last:

I'm coming to bide with you in Duncairn.

When they'd sold the furniture and paid off the debts there was barely a hundred and fifty pounds left, Segget took the matter through hand at the Arms, the news got about though both Chris and Ewan had been secret about it and never let on. But Segget would overhear what you said though you whispered the thing at the dead of night ten miles from a living soul in the hills. And it fair enjoyed itself at the news, God man! that was a right dight in the face for that sulky, stuck-up bitch at the Manse, her with her braw clothes and her proud-like ways, never greeting when her man died there in the pulpit, just as cool as though the childe were a load of swedes, not greeting even, or so 'twas said, when they burned the corp in there in Duncairn. And such a like funeral to give a minister, burning the man in a creamery!

And the Segget Provost, Hairy Hogg the sutor, said the thing was a judgment on the coarse brutes both, he never spoke ill of the dead, not him, but what had his forefather, the poet Burns, said?——

Ake Ogilvie the joiner was having a dram and he sneered real coarse: *You and your Burns! The gawpus blethered a lot of stite afore they shovelled him into the earth and sent all the worms for a mile around as drunk as tinks at Paddy Fair. But I'm damned if he'd ever a tongue like yours. What ill did Robert Colquohoun ever do you—or his mistress either, I'd like to know, except to treat you as a human being?—B'God, they showed themselves soft enough there!*

Alec the Provost's son was in having a nip, he wanted to fight Ake Ogilvie for that, the coarse Bulgar of a joiner to curse that way at a poor old devil like the Provost his father. But the wife of the hotel-keeper was back of the bar, folk called her the Blaster and Blasphemer for short, she was awful against a bit curse now and then: and she nipped Alec short as a new-libbed calf. *None of your cursings in here,* she cried, *I won't have the Lord's name taken in vain.* Alec habbered he'd nothing against the Lord, it wasn't Him he'd called a Bulgar, but the other one—and got in a soss, fairly upset at the Blaster's glower. Folk thought her an interfering old runt, ay God! she'd find her custom go.

So the most in the bar took a taik to the door with their drams in their hands and sat on the steps and looked at the sky, evening in Spring, bonny the hills, the seven o'clock dirling down Segget High Brig, peesies out on the long flat field that went mounting up to the bend of the hills. You minded Colquohoun, how he'd haunt those hills, the temples of God the creature would call them, him that died in the pulpit preaching a sermon—fair heathen it was, ay a judgment of God. And now this slip of a wife of his had less than a two hundred pounds to her name, living up there in one room, folk said, all by her lone now that her loon, Ewan (ay, a son by her first bit man) had gone to work in Duncairn toun. It just showed you what happened to proud-like dirt, she'd intended the loon for an education and a braw-like life in a pulpit, maybe, nothing to do but habber and haver and glower over a collar on back to front: and instead he'd be just a common working chap.

Ake Ogilvie had new come out and heard that last speak of wee Peter Peat's. *Well, God, YOU'RE common enough,* he said, *though it's damn little work you ever manage.* And then he went swaggering across the Square, past the statue of the War Memorial Angel, a trig-like lassie with a pair of fine hips, and spat at it, coarse-like, fair a tink Ake, aye sticking up for the working men, you were maybe a working man yourself, but were hardly such a fool as stick up for the brutes.

Syne Feet the policeman came dandering along, he was due to leave for a job in Duncairn, folk cried out *Ay, Mr. Leslie, fine night,* respectful-like, for he'd fair got on. And he stuck his thumbs in his belt and said *Ay,* majestic-like, like a steer with the staggers, and squashed out his great feet and looked up at the Angel as though to speir where she'd mislaid her stays.

Syne folk saw that he'd gotten his sergeant's stripes, he'd come out to give the bit things an air; and he said he was off to Duncairn in a week, he'd been kind of put in charge of the toun, you learned, him and some other skilly childes, or at least in a bit that they called Footforthie where the factories were and a lot of tink workers, low brutes, or they hadn't a meck to their name and lived off the Broo and Ramsay MacDonald, draining the country and Ramsay dry. But did that content them?—No, faith it didn't, they were aye on the riot about something or other, stirred up by those ill-ta'en Bulgars, the Socialists. . . . Feet said that he'd use a firm hand, by God you thought if he used his feet there wouldn't be a Socialist left in Duncairn that didn't look like an accident with a rhubarb tart. God, how the meikle-houghed devil could blow!

Folk ganted a bit and began to taik off, but halted at the hint of a tasty bit news, and cried *No, man?* and came tearing back. *What's that? God is here!* and Feet swelled out his chest and started to tell his tale over again.

And the gist of the thing when you got to the bree was that Sergeant Sim Leslie had been in Duncairn, on business,

like, that very forenoon—colloguing with the other heads
of the Police and learning the work that he'd have to take
on. Well, he'd finished the business and looked out for
lodgings, awful expensive up in Duncairn you needed a fine
salary, same as he had. The second bit place that he keeked
intil was a boarding-house on Windmill Brae, fell swell it
looked, a braw bit house on the high hill that rises over
Duncairn. But the terms were hardly as much as he'd
feared, and he clinched for a room with the mistress o't, a
meikle bit woman, Cleghorn the name.

Well, they had a bit crack when he'd ta'en the room and
she told to Feet, fair newsy-like, she'd had the place all
decorated of late at an awful expense she couldn't have
afforded but that she had advertised for a partner with a
bit of silver to lay down as deposit, and syne help as a
maid attending the lodgers. Feet had said *Ay?* and *Well,
that's right fine,* not caring a damn one way or the other
till she mentioned the new bit partner's name.

But when he heard THAT Feet fairly sat up, as every
soul did now in front of the Arms: *Mrs. Colquohoun?
Where might she come from?* And the Cleghorn body had
said *From Segget. Her man was a minister-creature there,
though I'm damned if she looks it, a fleet trig woman that
could muck a byre more ready any day than snuffle a psalm.*
At that poor Feet was took sore aback, he never could
stick the proud bitch at the Manse; but he'd made a deposit
for the lodgings already and couldn't well ask for the silver
back. So off he'd come home and got ready to pack—and
faith, did you ever hear the like of that?

Afore night was out all Segget had heard, and half of
the Mearns afore the next day, postmen ran for miles over
parks with the news, old Hogg hammered four soles on the
same pair of boots he was in such a fash to give the tale
out. And when Mrs. Colquohoun went down to the station,
straight and cool, with her trig-like back, her hair coiled
over each lug, fair daft, some thought it bonny, you were
damned if you did—the half of Segget was keeking from
its windows, and wondering about her, how she'd get on,
what was she thinking, what was she wearing, had she had
a bath on the previous night, did she ever think of a man
to sleep with, how much did she measure around the hips,
could she greet if she liked, what was her temper, how
much of the hundred and fifty was left, was that loon of

hers, Ewan, as dour as he looked, would he land in jail
or would he get on?

At half-past five the clock would go *birr!* in the narrow
long room you had ta'en for yourself, you'd wake with a
start and find yourself sprawled in weariness right across
the great bed, dark the guff of the early Spring, no cheep
of birds here on Windmill Brae, clatter of the clock as it
started again with a hoast and a rasp; and you'd reach for
the thing and switch it off and lie still a minute, hands
under your neck in the pad of your hair, fingers rough-
seamed and scraping your skin. And you'd stretch out under
the bedclothes, long, till your muscles all creaked, legs, hips
and ribs, blessedly, you'd still a passable figure.

Syne you'd throw off the blankets and get from the bed,
the floor-cloth cold as a Christian's heart under the naked
soles of your feet—off with your nightie and stretch again
and look from the window at the coming of dawn, lacing
its boots and grabbing its muffler and pelting across the
roofs of Duncairn. In a hurry the same you'd wriggle in
your vest, stockings and knickers, slip on your dress, getting warm already in spite of the floor and the frozen gleam
of grey granite outside. And you'd open the door and go
down the stairs, quick, and looping back your hair, to the
cold prison walls of the kitchen, smelly, fling open the window, in rushed the air and a smell of cats you could cut
with a knife. At first that smell had made you near sick,
even Jock the house-cat, a clean beast enough, but you'd
no time for such luxuries as sickness now-a-days, lighting
the gas, the kitchen range, your hands swift on kettles and
frying-pans, eyes on the clock and ears wide open for the
first stir of life in the morning's morgue.

At six you were up at Ma Cleghorn's room with a cup
of tea and a knock at her door and go in and draw back
the window-curtains, let up the blinds, bang! She'd wake
up and groan, *Is't you, Chris lass? Losh, you spoil me, just,*
she meant the tea, and you'd say *Oh, havers,* she spoke
Duncairn and you'd got the same gait. And Ma Cleghorn
would give another bit groan and drink up the tea and loup
from the bed, swack as you like, an old woman only a
minute afore but filled now with tea and a fury to work
The Bulgars'll soon be on the howl for their meat. What-
ever made me take to the keeping of lodgings?

You'd say *A BOARDING-HOUSE, please, Mrs. Cleg-*

horn, one of the jokes that the two of you shared, Ma'd give a great snifter through her meikle nose: *Boarding? B'God, it's leathering they want. And I haven't a pair of bloomers to my name that's no darned so a body can hardly sit down. I've a fair bit padding of my own to ease it, you haven't, get out of the damn trade, lass, afore you're like me and take to bloomers instead of them frilly things you wear—God be here, they'll kill you yet dead with cold. Aren't your legs frozen?*

You'd say *Not them; fine legs,* and Ma struggling into her blouse would say *You're no blate. Who told you they're fine?* And you'd say *Oh, men,* and she'd nod to that, great red face topped with greying hair like the face of a war-horse out of Isaiah (as you'd once thought, minding back through the months to Robert's reading from the Bible in Segget).—*Ay, no doubt, they had, and enjoyed them fine. And would again if you gave them the chance.*

Syne you'd to tear to the kitchen again, in time for the ring from Miss Murgatroyd's room, dying for her tea the poor old wretch, solemn you'd carry it up to her room, the best in the house, three guineas a week. She'd quaver out of a lace nightcap: *Is that you, Mrs. Colquohoun? And you have my tea? Oh, that's Such Fine,* she was awful genteel, poor spinster body with her pensions and potterings, not a soul in the world hers and respectable down to her shrivelled toes, wabbling hands and meek quiet eyes, Episcopalian, serving tea for the whist drives up at the Unionist Club. . . .

And Ma Cleghorn, watching her taik down the street, would ask who in God's name would be an old maid? She'd often used to think when her Jim was alive and would come back from the Fish Market stinking so bad that his shirts hung out on a washing day would bring the cats scraiching for miles around—she'd used often to think *I wish I were single, trig on my own, not handled, not kenned, with nobody's seed ever laid in me!* But losh, when he died she had minded him sore, night on night and would fain have had him again though he smelt like a kipper mislaid in a drain when he'd cuddle you, feuch! They were sosses, were men, but you'd only to look at the Murgatroyd creature to make you mad to go tearing out and grab the first soss that you met in breeks—*Half-past six, Chris; will you waken your Ewan?*

He slept in one of the two rooms of the upper floor, the

other empty, his window looked down on the glare of Footforthie at night that changed to a sick yellow furnace-glow,
unstill, staining the sky on the morning's edge. You'd
wanted him to change to another room, and he'd asked
you why and you'd told him he'd surely get sick of it—
working down there all day and seeing it all night. But he'd
shaken his shapely, sleekèd head, no fancies or flim-flams
with Ewan at all: *It'll neither wake me nor send me to
sleep. Only a light in the sky, you know, Chris.*—So you'd
turn the handle of his door and go in and meet the sting
of the sea-wind there, the window wide open, the curtains
flowing. Ewan dim in the light of the early dawn, lying so
still, so still he slept that near every morning you'd be
startled the same, feared that he lay there dead, so quiet,
you'd shake his shoulder and see as you bent the blankets
he'd thrust away from himself pyjamas open wide to the
waist, curling dark down on a boy's breast.

Strange to think that this was your Ewan, once yours,
and so close, so tiny, so small and weak, sexless, a baby
that had grown a body tall as your own, slimmer, stronger,
secret and strange, blossom and fruit from that seed of
yours. . . . In a queer pity you'd look and shake him awake:
Ewan, time you were up!

He'd start awake quietly, at once, like a cat, and look
at you with those deep, cool eyes, neither grey nor green,
grey granite eyes. *All right. Thanks. No, I don't want tea.
I'll get an apple for myself, mother. MOTHER! I said I'd
get it for myself!* And he'd be out of bed and have reached
the dish and caught an apple afore you got near. *You've
enough to do without waiting on me.*

—*But I like waiting on you. Wouldn't you wait on me?*

—*I suppose so, if you were sick or insane. What's the
time?* And lean out half-naked from the window ledge to
peer over Duncairn to Thomson Tower. *Splendid. I've time
for a dip in the Forthie.*

He'd be out of the house as you gained the kitchen, an
uproar by then of banging pans, Ma Cleghorn cooking porridge and bacon and sausages and coffee and cocoa and tea,
and swearing out loud at the younger maid, Meg, who slept
at her home away down in the Cowgate and was supposed
to come up each morning at seven. *Call that seven?—Then
you're blind as well's sweir. Stack up the range and be
nippy about it. Mrs. Colquohoun, will you lay the table?*

You were aye *Mrs. Colquohoun* when Meg was about,

Ma Cleghorn treating you distant, polite, for the sake of discipline, so she said. You'd gathered the way of setting the table in the big ben room so quick your eyes hardly followed your fingers, porridge plates for Sim Leslie (who'd come from Segget where they'd called him Feet) and Mr. George Piddle, the *Runner* reporter, thin and *he-he'ing*, minus his hair so that he could go bald-headed for news. Bacon for Miss Murgatroyd and Mr. Neil Quaritch: Mr. Quaritch worked on the *Runner* as well, a sub-editor creature, aye reading books and sloshing them to death in the *Runner* next day. But you rather liked the wee ferret man, red eyes and red hair and a red nose as well, and a straggle of beard on an unhappy chin, Ewan said he'd gone sozzled with reading rot rather than with knocking back gills of Glenlivet. . . .

Mixed grill for Miss Ena Lyon, the typist, powdered and lip-sticked, and awful up-to-date, baggy a bittie below the eyes and a voice like a harried peahen, poor lass. Porridge for young Mr. Clearmont, nice loon who went to the University and was awful keen on music and jokes, you could never make head nor tail of either as he always guffawed out, young and hearty, right at the point—if there was a point. Ma Cleghorn didn't think much of him, she said if ever he'd a thought in his head it'd be easy to tell it, you'd hear the damn thing rattling about like a stone in a tin. But she was jealous a bit, you thought, of the lad's university and books and book-learning. . . . Bacon for young John Cushnie, all red, the clerk in Raggie Robertson's Drapery Depot, half-sulky, half-shy and would spend half an hour roping up his neck in a speckled tie, he shared Archie Clearmont's room but nought else. . . . Eight o'clock and you hit the gong, breakfast all ready set on the table.

And down they'd all pour and sit in about, Miss Murgatroyd sitting neat as a pin, Such Fine, and eating her grapefruit up like a sparrow pecking at a bit of dung (you laughed: but you sometimes wished that Ma wouldn't say those things about folk so often: the picture stuck, true or untrue, and you never saw them in real likeness again); Sergeant Sim Leslie supping his porridge and goggling at you over his collar; Ewan eating quick, clean and indifferent, lost in his thoughts or else in a book, all squiggly lines and figures and drawings; Miss Ena Lyon, complete with complexion, eating her bacon and talking to Clearmont, he'd been to a concert the night before and Miss Lyon was saying she liked music as well—just loved a talkie with a Catchy Choon.

Poor Mr. Piddle with his long thin neck and his long thin head, as bald as a neep and something the shape, would snap up his meat in a haste to be gone in search of news for the *Daily Runner,* a fine big paper, the pride of Duncairn, and awful useful for lining your sleeves; Cushnie, red-eared and trying to speak English, would call out above the folds of his tie *Will ye pass the cruet? I'm in a gey hurry. Me and Mr. Robertson have the Spring Sale on;* and Mr. Neil Quaritch would push down his cup, *May I have another, Mrs. Colquohoun?* he'd left his breakfast untasted as usual.

And Ma Cleghorn would sit at the top of the table, her big red face set square on its neck, sonsy and sturdy, you'd liked her from the first, she you, you supposed you'd neither of you frills, you'd seen over much of this queer thing Life to try hide from its face by covering your own with a ready-made complexion out of a jar, or ready-made morals from the Unionist Club, or ready-made fear and excitement and thrill out of the pages of the *Daily Runner.* . . . And you'd sit and stare at your own porridge plate till Ma would call out: *Will you fill the cups?*

By ten the lot would have clattered away, on trams and buses, on foot and a-run, tripping along like a sparrow, Miss Murgatroyd, Mr. Piddle whirring away on his bike like a snake going pelting back to the Zoo, Miss Ena Lyon with her heels so high that her shoulders drooped and her bottom stuck out, quite up-to-date, Ewan in dungarees, no hat, books under his arm, black hair almost blue, shinning down the Steps of Windmill Brae two at a time, hands in his pouches. . . . And they left the real work of the house to begin.

You and Ma Cleghorn couldn't run to more help than Meg for the washing-up in the kitchen, Ma took the first floor with the dining-room and sitting-room and swept them and dusted them and tore up the rugs and went out to the back and hung them on the line and thrashed them to death in a shower of stour. You had the bedrooms, Ma'd asked if you'd mind—*Some of them stink like a polecat's den.* You'd said you didn't care, we all stank sometimes. And Ma had nodded, *Fegs, and that's true. But fancy you being willing to let on—you that was wed to a minister body!*

You'd mind that speak as you redded the rooms, gathered the mats and pulled wide the curtains, opened the windows and made the beds, swept out and polished each of the rooms, emptied the slops and carried down washing, and cleared the bathroom of razor blades and bits of paper stuck with shaving-soap hair, other things that Miss Murgatroyd would half-hide, so would Miss Lyon in a different way. . . . Wife to a minister—wife to Robert: it faded away in the stour of the days though only last Spring you had been in Segget, had slept beside him in those chill hours that come trailing down a blanket of dark to cut you off one from the other, Robert sleeping sound while you woke and heard the wail of sleet from the Grampian haughs.

All ended, put by, Robert himself no more than a name, you'd loved him so deep that the day he died something had broken in you, not in your heart, it didn't break there, something in your belly went numb, still, and stayed so . . . but the queerness of things! You could hardly mind now the shape of his face—his eyes, were they grey or blue? —Oh God! . . . And you'd sometimes stop and feel sick to think how quickly even your memories went, as though you stood naked in an endless storm shrilling about you, wisp by wisp your garments went till at last you'd stand to all uncovered—love, pity, desire, hope, hate put by under the sail of the endless clouds over Cloud Howe, the Howe of the World——

Then you'd shake yourself to sense, get down with pail of water and a scrubbing-brush, scrub and scrub till your fingernails, so smooth and round-shaped in your years at Segget, come jagged again, hacks in your fingers that caught the blankets as you turned in unease of a night and sent a shrill stream of pain up your hands. Queer to work again in such fashion, use all your body till you ached dead tired, by the time you'd finished the upper floor your hips were filled with a stinging and shooting, like a bees' byke with bees, bad as having a baby, sweat in runnels either side your nose—you felt like a greasy dish-clout, just, ready to be wrung and hung out to dry. And when you got down to the kitchen at last Ma Cleghorn would skeugh at you over her specs, *Fegs, lass, you take well with a slammock of work. Like a cup of tea?—Here, gi'me the basses, I'll take them out while you sit down a minute.* You'd say *I'll shake them myself, I'm fine,* and she'd look at you grim,

It's your funeral, then. But die where it's easy to spread out the corp.

A blessed minute that when you'd gotten back, though, sat down to drink the strong tea Ma made, hot, steaming and thick, Ma drinking another cup the other side of the table, Meg pleitering still at the kitchen sink. You felt all revived, throat, belly and—better not further. (Miss Murgatroyd you were sure never went further, Ma Cleghorn on the contrary seldom went higher.) You'd see yourself as you sat and drank, your head and hair and face and breast in the kitchen mirror over the range, flushed face, not pretty, it was never that, sulky eyes and the mouth men had liked well enough in your time—long ago, afore you grew old and took to scrubbing! . . . And you'd finish your tea and loup to your feet and be gone to finish the rest of the ploy, and be back in the kitchen to lend Ma a hand to plan out the dinner for those that came home—Mr. Clearmont from the University, Ewan seldom, Mr. Piddle sometimes, Mr. Quaritch and Miss Ena Lyon never, John Cushnie when Raggie's rag Sales would allow, Sergeant Sim Leslie sure as the clock.

Ma had a great cookery-book of her own, made up of recipes cut out of the papers, daft ones and good ones and plain damn silly ones, Ma'd say *What stomachs some folk must have to eat the dirt that the papers say!* But she cooked well enough, passable yourself, Jock the cat would sit and purr under the red-hot glow of the range, half-roasted the brute had been since his birth, and liked it; Ma said he'd enjoy hell. And she'd lift him aside with a meikle great foot, impatient-like, and he'd purr all the time, while the foot was under him, while he sailed through the air, while he landed with a thump out under the sink. And Meg would give a bit scraich of fear, and maybe drop a plate, inviting death.

In the first few days you'd been sorry for the lass, Ma Cleghorn treated her worse than dirt, bullying her, sneering at her, upbraiding God for making such a trauchle to pest decent folk. Syne you saw that Meg, thin, schlimpèd and pert, wasn't feared a wee bit, sleekèd and sly with a sideways glint in her eyes at Ma, taking her in and her measure unfeared. And Ma that could skin a body alive with her tongue and hang out the hide in the sun to dry wouldn't send Meg out on a message if it rained, heaped her plate with great helpings of dinner, and when she saw the bit maid over-trauchled with a job would swear at her and go tearing to help. . . .

So you didn't interfere but got on with your own work, plenty of that—how you'd ached at first afore dinner-time, hungry as you'd never been in the manse; genteel appetite going with all else, walking now with a quick and a hasting step not the long lope that had once been yours, face altering as well from the drowsy mask that had come on you under the yew-trees of Segget—waiting, half-asleep, sitting deep in a chair, for Maidie to bring tea out on the lawn, the peesies flying over Segget blue in smoke, smoke in sun smother, long ago; and Robert coming striding across the lawn, whistling—and you looked, and he hadn't a face——

And once Ma came on you as you stood and wept, tearless, sobbing dry-eyed, and stared and knew, shook you and hugged you tight, it hurt: *Don't greet, nothing's worth it, not a damn thing, no man that ever yet was, Chris!* You'd stopped from that daft carry-on at once, shamed of yourself, bothering Ma, weeping like a fool over something as common as kale, losh, weren't there thousands of widows in the world worse off than you and not snivelling like bairns? And you'd shaken Ma off, gentle as you could: *I know, I'm just giving myself a pet. My father would have said it was salts I needed.*

Dinner and the feeding of all the faces, funny to think a face was mainly for that; and then out shopping for the morn's meat. You went down Windmill Steps in the blue Spring air, the grey granite walls rising about you, if the day was clear you'd see below Duncairn spread as a map for show, far off, north-east, the sheen of the Beach beyond the rolling green of the Lings, Footforthie a smother of smoke ayont the Docks, the Fish Market and the trawlers' rig, the Forthie gleaming grey under its brigs. Cleaving the jumble of warrens and wynds went Royal Mile like a south-driven sword, to the left the new biggings of Ecclesgriegs, Town Hall and courts and Thomson Tower, the Tangleha' trees that hid the University, the gentry's quarters, genteel Craigneuks—to the right in jumbles around Grand Central the Cowgate and Gallowgate, Paldy Parish, and far off in the west beyond Footforthie the fishers' wee toun, called Kirrieben.

You waited a tram by the Windmill Steps, it came showding and banging up from the Station, green like a garden slug, in you got, and sat down and closed your eyes

and thought hard, the things you'd to order, where you'd
best get them. Fish, beef, eggs, butter, go swear at the
grocer, the laundry hadn't sent back those sheets, Ma Cleghorn wanted the chimney-sweep, you needed a new frock
and must bear with the need. . . . Out into Royal Mile you
stepped—there on his stance, unmoving, King Edward,
bald as a turkey and with much the same face, ready to
gobble from a ton of grey granite. In the seats round the
plinth the unemployed, aye plenty of them, yawning and
wearied, with their flat-soled boots and their half-shaved
faces, they'd cry their bit bars as they stared at the stir, or
chirp a bit filth to a passing quean, sometimes though
seldom they did it to you. You didn't much mind, were you
wearied yourself and half-fed, you thought, with nothing to
do, you'd do worse than chirp.

Only once had that worse ever happened to you, you'd
run down the steps from the Mile to the lane that led to
the Gallowgate's guff one evening, to a dairy there that
sold good eggs. Day above, but already half-dark in that
place, nobody about as you hurried along, or so you
thought till you sighted the man. He'd been leaning in the
doorway of an empty warehouse, heard you coming and
looked up and down: and as you came near he got in your
way. *I'm starving, wifie. Gi'me a tanner.*

His face was thin and dirty and brown, he'd no shirt,
his jacket pinned over his breast, smelt awful, great knuckled
hands, should you scream? And then you'd known that
that would be daft, you'd said *All right, though I haven't
one to spare.* And you'd opened your bag, heart thumping
as you did it, what if he grabbed and made off with the
lot? But he didn't, stood waiting, face red with shame.
You'd found him the sixpence, handed it over, he'd nodded,
no thanks, and looked away. And you'd hurried on down
the lane to the dairy, suddenly trembling and your lips
grown wet.

You'd get back to tea with the netbag full, have a first
cup ere the others came, Archie Clearmont first, banging
up stairs, he'd meet you and smile, *'Lo, Mrs. Colquohoun.
That's a nice frock.* You'd tease him and say *There's a
nice woman in it*, and he'd blush, boy-clear, *I know that as
well*. If only Ewan were as simple as he! . . . Mr. Piddle
tearing in from his office, all in a fash to be off to the
Station and catch the 6.30 bound for Dunedin. Not that
he'd catch the train himself, he'd send off the latest news

of Duncairn and make a bit extra salary, *he-he!* from the linage the *Tory Pictman* would print. . . . Miss Ena Lyon trailing in half-dead from the work in her office, half the rouge gone, the other half sprinkled about like a rash, she'd drawl on the Awful Rush in the firm, and the Boss no more than a Vulgar Keelie. . . . Ewan at last black-streaked, black-haired, as cool and composed from Gowans and Gloag's as he'd been when haunting the hills of the Howe seeking the flints of the ancient men.

More clearing away, more tidying-up, getting ready supper, eating it, clearing it—you might almost have hated the sight of food with the number of times you messed the stuff. But you didn't: instead, you were hungry all day, ate a large supper at nine o'clock, found work nearly done and yawned a bit, and sat listening to Ma's radio in the sitting-room, a deserted place most nights but for you. And you'd listen to talks on ethics and cocktails and how to go hiking on the Côte d'Azur, minding the baby, copulation in cat-kins, and the views of Jacob P. Hackenschmidt on Scotland and Her Ancient Nationhood; and you'd switch the thing off, lost, that was better, worth paying a licence to keep the thing quiet, drowse instead and think of the country-side, corn coming green in clay parks this night as often you'd seen it when you were a quean, wedded to Ewan in Kinraddie long syne—you that waited the feet of another Ewan now.

In Paldy Parish as the June came in there came a wave of heat with the month, it lifted the guffs from the half-choked drains and flung them in under the broken doors down through the courts to simmer and stew, a body could hardly bear the touch of his sark as he lay in bed by his wife of a night, the weans would whimper and move and scratch on the shakedown over under the window—stewing in the front of a half-open furnace. And a man would get up in a Paldy tenement and go along the passage to the W.C., blasted thing crowded, served a score of folk, not decent, by God what a country to live in. On the Broo since the War and five kids to keep, eating off your head— och, why did you live?—never a minute of quiet to yourself, nothing but the girnings of the wife for more silver, the kids half-barefoot, half-fed, oh hell.

And the wife would turn as she heard him come back, lie wakeful and think on the morn's morning—what to give

the weans, what to give the man, fed he must be ere he
took the streets to look for that weary job he'd not find—
he'd never find one you had come to ken. Hardly believe it
was him you had wed, that had been a gey bit spark in
his time, hearty and bonny, liked you well: and had hit you
last night, the bloody brute coming drunk from the pub—
a woman couldn't go and hide in booze, forget all the soss
and pleither, oh no, she'd to go on till she dropped, weans
scraiching, getting thin and like tinks, and the awful words
they picked up every place, the eldest loon a street-corner
keelie, the quean—oh God, it made a body sick.

And the quean would turn by the side of her sisters,
see the faint glow of the dawn, smell the reek of the Paldy
heat—would she never get out of it, get a job, get away,
have clothes, some fun? If they couldn't afford to bring
up their weans decent why did father and mother have
them? and syne nag and nag at you day on day, on this
and that, the way that you walked, the way you behaved
(take care that the loons don't touch your legs), the way that
you spoke—nothing pleased the old fools, and what you
brought home they thought should be theirs, every meck
that you made, nothing for yourself, stew in the reek of
the Cowgate's drains till you died and were buried and
stank to match. My God, if a lassie couldn't do anything
else she could take a bit walk out to Doughty Park, fine
there, though the place was littered with Reds, fair daft,
the Communionists the worst of the lot, aye holding their
meetings and scraiching and bawling that the workers all
join up with their unions and fight for their rights and
down with the gents.

But no decent lassies would listen to them, for they knew
the Communionists were awful tinks who wanted to break
up the home.

Every day as the Cowgate stirred Meg was up at the
cheep of dawn, seeing to young Jessie and Geordie for
school, getting ready breakfast, snapping back at Mother,
Father the old devil lying snoozing in bed, he didn't go
down to the Docks till ten. He swore he could hardly get
a wink of sleep because of the old trawl-skipper next door,
awful religious and fond of a nip, who thrashed his old wife
near every night, singing out hymn-tunes like hell the
while. If other folk could sleep through the old skipper's

roar of *Rock of Ages, cleft for me* as he cleft his old woman under a bed, why couldn't Father sleep as well?

Alick, Meg's brother, would get into his clothes, grumbling as usual when he'd only porridge. He was barely Meg's age, an apprentice-lad down at Gowans and Gloag's in Footforthie. That might have been fine, the beginnings of a job, but when his apprenticeship was up—well, everybody kenned what happened to apprentices. They were sacked right off when they needed men's wages, and Alick like others would be chucked on the Broo.

Alick said this morning when Meg sneered that, *Ay, maybe to me the same as the others, but not to the dirty college lads*. And he said that Gowans took college pups now, with a special apprenticeship, easy as winking, they served the first six months at the Furnace, same as the others, but what happened to them then? They squatted their dowps in office jobs, and put on clean collars and gave out their orders, bloody toffs, though no better than you or me. There'd been two of them in the last two years, training as managers, *they* weren't sacked, when the last machinery came into the Works that would do all the doings without working-chaps: you'd still need somebody to oil it about, and they'd keep the mammie's pets to do that. Another had come a two months back—a black-haired, stuck-up gypsy Bulgar, over-fine to speak to a chap like Alick, he'd get a sock in the kisser something.

Meg said *Don't blether, you haven't the guts; you're jealous he's brains and you haven't, that's all*. Alick snorted *Brains? Him? He's only got swank. And me and the chaps in the Furnaces are planning a little bit of a surprise for Mr. Bloody Ewan Tavendale.*

—WHO?

Alick said *Wash out your lugs. Ewan Tavendale's the name if you want to know. Here, get out of my way till I get on my boots, the hooter'll be howling in a minute or so.*

So that was where HER son worked, was it then? What had She to be stuck-up about? A lassie could bear with old Ma Cleghorn, an orra old bitch, but not a bad heart. But the way that that Mrs. Colquohoun took on, and looked at you cool, put a body off. And who was she to put on her airs that kept a lodging-house for a living and had her son only an apprentice like Alick?

Meg grabbed her hat and set out for Windmill, the Cowgate slowly unreathing its fug, up in Royal Mile the lorries

were lolloping over the calsays, Paldy Parish littering its
doors with weans, snuffy and ragged, kids off to school,
scrawling dirty things on the pavement, some throwing
filth and cheeking a lassie . . . She'd get out of this place,
get a lodging somewhere in Tangleha' or the Ecclesgriegs.

But who should she meet where the Cowgate lane
climbed up to the stour and whirr of the Mile than Big
Jim Trease the Communionist, red-cheeked and sappy,
everybody kenned him and called him *Jim* when bobbies
weren't looking. But Meg had no use for those coarse
brutes the Reds that would do away with the gents and
her job, and when Big Jim smiled all over his face twinkling his wee pig eyes at her she made to go by with her
nose in the air. He'd a creature with him she didn't know,
thin, brown, ragged, with an ill-shaved face; and Jim cried
*Meg, I've been looking for you. Has your Ma still got that
spare bed to let?*

Meg snapped *Supposing you gang and speir at her?* Big
Jim smiled at her sappy and kind, she felt half-shamed
though the beast was a Red: *Right, and we will. Many
thanks, Meg.*

Would you credit that?—trying to land a Red in the
house, maybe rape you and gut you in the middle of the
night, as the coarse tinks did with hardly a break, night on
night, in that awful Russia. If Ma wasn't soft she would
keep the door snibbed. . . . *Oh to hell, there's the Windmill
tram!*

She caught the thing by the skin of the teeth and got out
under the Windmill Brae, ran up the Steps and met face
to face young Ewan Tavendale coming down them—three
at a time, no hat, in overalls, hands in his pouches, two
books alow his oxter, his eyes went over her, why need
he be proud? The like of him made you think the Reds
right, he needed to be jammed by a wall and shot.

Morning, Meg, he said, *Didn't notice you,* and smiled
as sweet as a kid at you. Oh, losh, and the things you'd
been thinking about him!

And the things Alick said they were doing to-day——

Gowans and Gloag made metal containers, bolts and
girders and metal trestles, fine castings for sections of
engine casings, a thousand men working in great rattling
sheds built to hold the labour of three times the number in
a rattle and roar of prosperity. Ewan Tavendale would

think of that now and then, Gowans had flourished just after the War, high wages and bonuses dished out to all, pap for the proletariats. Wonder what they did with the high money then?—Spent it on the usual keelie things, dogs and horse-racing and sleeping with whores, poor devils—it had nothing to do with him.

Hardly anything to do with the others at all, stoking his shot in the Furnaces, stripped to the waist, he stripped brown, mother's skin, and tightened his belt over shovel and barrow, cleared out the clinkers and wheeled up a load and flung it deep in the whoom of the flame, the Works kittling up as the morning woke, bells snarling hell if the heat now and then went low in one fire or another. In an hour or so Ewan'd be dripping with sweat, and drink and drink from the tap in the rear, water that gushed out again from him, a sponge-like life and tremendous fun. The other apprentices, keelies the lot, didn't seem anxious to chum up at all, thank goodness, it gave him time to tackle the books of the trade, metallurgy twice as exciting as flints. He stacked the books with his coat in the sheds, till dinner, and went up and scrubbed himself, put on his coat and went down to the Docks with books and a sandwich and swotted up Castings. But the other apprentices stayed behind and laughed and joked in the lavatories, insanitary devils, no business of his.

But this forenoon was the worst he'd faced in the Furnaces, hours clogged with heat, lungs going like bellows, once the foreman Dallas came swearing down, about fires, not Ewan's, it was drawing fine. He looked at Ewan and gave him a nod *Take it a bit easier, Mr. Tavendale. Yours is fine. It's the fires of those other muckers.* He'd hardly gone up the steps to Machines when the pimply keelie Alick Watson, called out to another of them, Ewan didn't know his name: *D'you know any poetry this morning, Norman?*
—*Oh ay, a fine bit. You other lads heard it?*—

> There once was a gent Tavendale
> (Oh-Rahly-the-guff-makes me pale!)
>   A pimp and a sucker,
>   A dirty wee mucker—
> And his name, as I've said, Tavendale.

. . . Oh ay, the toff bastard heard it fine, but he didn't let on, just went on with his work, all the lads laughed,

you'd known he'd no guts. Syne Norman Cruickshank sang
out another bit, you laughed till you split, a funny devil
Norman, about the toff mucker's mucking mother. He
threw down the shovel as he said that, Norman, getting
ready for the toff when he louped to bash him, as any
body would do when he heard THAT about his mother.
And he heard it all right and gave Norman a look, fair
damn well maddening, as though Norman were dirt and
not very interesting dirt at that: and went on with raking
the clinkers, calm. But Alick you could see was warming
up to him, you all warmed up, led him hell's delight, serve
him right with his bloody show-off. Wee Geordie Bruce
couped his barrow when he wasn't looking, and Norman
nipped back for the urine pan and slung it right slap in the
toff Bulgar's fire, it sent up a guff that near killed you all
and the toff had to stoke it up afresh.

He'd only just finished when the hooter went, Alick
Watson had nipped up a minute afore bent on some devil-
try you could be bound. When the rest of you got up the
stairs he was just coming out of the washing-sheds where
all the lads left their jackets and pieces. He winked and
you knew he'd been up to something, and grinned and
waited for Tavendale.

Ewan went in and washed and took down his jacket,
and put it on, and put his hand in his pocket. . . . For a
minute, certain, he knew he'd be sick, damned sick, and
then swallowed his throat and didn't think as he washed
his hand and wrenched off his jacket. Nuisance—miss most
of that section on phosphor bronze now.

The five keelies were waiting for him to come out, they
held their noses and capered and laughed, Ewan thought
The pimply keelie, I suppose, and walked quietly over to
where the five stood. The keelie's eyes in his thin, dour
face didn't change, scornful of gentry, hands in his pouches,
Damn shame, he's no chance, said Ewan's mind as he hit
him and felt his arm go numb.

Alick shot like a stone from a catapult half across the
yard, crash in a bowie of lime, Ewan knew he'd be back
in less than a minute, the only other dangerous one in the
gang the one called Norman, an unscrubbed little swine—
about three inches higher than yourself—still, little. And
he swung up his left, keelie on the point, he whirled about
and went flump in the stour; and it seemed to Ewan suddenly all the day cleared, Duncairn clear, bright and sharp

to his finger-tips' touch, he'd never felt so well or so keen for life, he laughed: and Alick Watson came at him head down.

The foreman and another man heard the fighting back by the sheds and came round to see. The childe with the foreman grunted *That's him; another of those gentry apprentice swine,* but the foreman Dallas of course had his favourite, he called out *Steady a bit, Tavendale!* Ewan dripped blood like a half-killed pig, but he didn't know that, infighting, they were both thick-streaked with blood and snot, holding and fighting, Alick tried to kick, Ewan felt a stab of pain like a knife, and loosened his hold and Alick broke away—looked, swung, and struck, it caught Ewan's neck, he gave a queer grunt and twist, the fight finished, queer that silence to Alick and the way the sheds shook.

When Chris woke next morning the first thought that came in her mind was of Ewan. She didn't lie in bed and stretch as usual, got out and dressed and went down to the kitchen. Outside the early dawn of Duncairn lay pallid on the rigs and rinds of grey granite stretching away to the feet of the morning, east wan-tinted, no birds crying, the toun turning to yawn awake below. Jock came and purred and circled her legs, sniffed and sneezed, but she hardly noticed, taking up Ma's tea, syne Miss Murgatroyd's, and so at last gained Ewan's room.

He lay fast asleep, head bandaged, neck bandaged, she thought *He's so young!* as she saw his arm, dimpled and smooth of skin, lying by his side. And then as she went nearer she saw his face, the bruises upon it, the broken skin, the swollen lips; and went soft inside in a blaze of rage. How could they—to Ewan, he was only a bairn!

She picked up one of the apples he'd want and sat down on the bed and shook him awake. He woke with the usual quick lack of blink, but half unguarded for a minute, Chris thought, as though she'd peeped down in his eyes for once to that queer boy-self that so puzzled her. Son of herself but sometimes so un-sib she felt more kin to Meg Watson the maid!

She told him that, idly, as though it were a joke, and he put his hands under his head and considered, and said something about hormones and egg-cells, whatever they had to do with it—*I'm not so different; but I want to*

*KNOW THINGS. And I love you up to that phosphor-
bronze hair—more than Meg Whatname'll ever do.*

Chris said it was Watson, not Whatname, and Ewan
said that was a funny coincidence, wondered if she were
any relation of the keelie that had bashed him so yesterday.
—*Perfect hiding he was giving me, Chris! and I struck
it unlucky, head bang on a girder. Fought like a rat and so
did I.*

Chris said *What was it all about?*

He lay still a minute, still in that posture. *Oh, filth.
Nothing you need worry about. They don't much like me,
the keelies, Chris.*

She'd heard him use that word before but the queerest
thing happened to her now. She said sharply: *What's a
keelie, Ewan? Your father was a ploughman afore we were
wed, and I was a quean in a crofter's kitchen.*

Bandaged, undisturbed, he lay looking at her. *A ploughman's not a keelie. And anyhow, Chris——*

Her heart tightened in a funny way. There was something else. She said *Yes?*

—*Oh—just that though my father was a ploughman and
you came from a kitchen—that's nothing to do with me,
has it? I'm neither you nor my father: I'm myself.*

All that day and the next Meg didn't turn up, Ma
Cleghorn swore at the lazy limmer and did all the washing-up by herself and broke two plates in the first half hour
—*all through that lazy bitch of a quean!* Jock hardly
knew where he was after that, his feet more often in the
air than not, as Ma kicked him from the range to the
dresser and back, he purring like a red-hot engine the
while, Chris saw the last act as she brought down a tray—
Jock scart his claws in Ma's sonsy leg and give a loud
scraich and shoot out of the window. And the sight was
so funny Chris heard herself giggle, like a bairn, Ma rubbing her leg and swearing:

*Malagaroused by a cat and forsook by a jade. Will you
go to the Cowgate and see what's come of her?*

So down Chris went, not taking the tram, better acquainted with Duncairn by now, down Windmill Brae with
its shelving steps, across the Meal Market where they didn't
sell meal, sold nothing, old, a deserted patch, dogs and unemployed squatting in the sun, through Melvin Wynd into
Little Mart where the ploughmen gathered in feeing-times

in Paldy Fair in the days long syne. They didn't now, two or three shops littered here, shops everywhere that a body might look, how did they all live and manage a trade? The pavements were sweating a greasy slime as she made her way to the Cowgate's brink, steps leading down to Paldy Parish.

She'd never been so far into Paldy before, seeing the broken windows and the tattered doors and the weary faces of the women going by, basket-laden, all the place had a smell of hippens, unwashed, and old stale meat and God knew what, if even He knew, Chris thought He couldn't. And she passed a Free Kirk with a twist to her thought: if there was a God as Robert had believed couldn't He put it into the heads of those folk they'd be better served filling the wames of their weans than the stomach of some parson clown in a Manse? But then she'd never understood religion, thought it only a fairy-tale, not a good one, dark and evil rather, hurting life, hurting death, no concern of hers if others didn't force it on her, she herself had nothing to force in its stead.

Robert once had had with his Socialism. And looking around that evil place in the stew of the hottering rising June she minded that verse he'd once quoted in Segget, long ago in that other life:

> Stone hearts we cannot waken
> Smite into living men:
> Jehovah of the thunders
> Assert Thy power again!

And dimly she thought that maybe that was what the Covenanters had believed when they faced the gentry in the old-time wars. Only God never came and they died for Him and the old soss went on as it always would do, aye idiot folk to take dirty lives and squat in the dirt, not caring a lot were they letten a-be to rot as they liked. No concern of hers—she belonged to herself as Ewan had told her he belonged to himself, she'd have hated the Covenant giving her orders as much as she'd have hated its enemies, the gentry.

. . . And all far off from a middle-aged wife looking for a missing maidie, Meg. Where was it Ma said the creature bade?

She found it at last, a deep narrow court, used to the

smells she went in and up the stone stairs, chapped at the door and waited and listened. In a tenement near a row was on, furniture crashing, Chris heard a woman scraich and grew white to the lips. Syne she heard a loud voice raised in a hymn:

> Count your blessings, name them one by one,
>   Count your blessing, see what God has done,
> Count your blessings, name them one by one
>   And it will surprise you what the Lord has done.

There followed a final thump on that, somebody cried *I'll ha'e the bobbies on you,* and then a door banged: and then a loud silence.

Chris chapped again, heard a noise inside, the door opened, she said: *Is Meg Watson in?*

The man who opened the door was the same who'd once stopped her in The Upper Cowgate and asked her for sixpence.

They both stared like gowks a minute, speechless, he'd shaved and wore a second-hand suit, over-big for him, bulging at paunch and bottom, the thin brown face didn't look so starved, cocky and confident till he met her eyes. Now he flushed dark and licked his lips:

Meg Watson's gone off to look for a job.

Chris nodded. *I see. Will you tell her I want to know why she left me? My name Mrs. Colquohoun and if she comes back the morn you can tell her that I'll say nothing about it.*

. . . So that was who the sulky bitch was, boorjoy and stuck-up—he'd heard the tale, Alick had sloshed her son down at Gowans. A stuck-up toff, he'd said; like the mother, damn her and her glower and her ice-brick eyes.

Meg was feared to go back when she heard from her brother he'd bashed your son in a bit fight at the Works.

Chris said *I see. Well, she needn't be,* and turned and went down the stairs, stare on her back; turned again: *I think you owe me a sixpence.*

He dived in a pouch and brought one out, flushing again, but looking at her cocky: *There you are, mistress. Enjoy your money while you have it. There's a time coming when your class won't have it long.*

Chris's temper quite went with her a minute, silly fool, the heat she supposed, she didn't care:

My class? It was digging its living in sweat while yours lay down with a whine in the dirt. Good-bye.

Ewan was tired enough of the going next week, lying in bed, reading in books, feeling the throb under the bandages go. If only they'd leave him alone with the books. . . . And he thought *Most people—how they hate you to read!*

They were at him all hours: Chris in the morning, decent sort Chris, though you'd never got very close to each other since that winter in Segget, further off now since you'd made it plain her notions on begettings weren't necessarily yours. But once or twice when she put her arm under your head and unwound the bandage in the early morning, stuck on the lint, hands and arms so alive you felt queer —as though you were falling in love! You gathered the re-actions were something like that, and possible enough for all that you knew, those psychoanalyst Jewboy chaps had had cases enough, record on record, Œdipus the first of the Unhanged Unhygienics—*Rot! Let's dig in the phosphor bronze!*

She'd hardly have gone than a thunderous chapp, and in would come waddling Mrs. Cleghorn, very fat, very oozing, you rather liked her. Suppose it was her jollity, easily come by, it didn't mean much and couldn't mean much, but a bearable ingredient—so damn scarce. She'd plump on the bed and ask how you were, not stop for an answer, instead start in to tell of the time when her husband, Jim, was ill—with mumps, so he'd said, and looking like a tattie scone. And he'd been fair ashamed to have mumps at his age, the daft old tyke, Ma had wondered a bit, funny-like mumps for a body to have. So she'd hauled in the doctor will he nill he, and then could you guess what his illness was? You couldn't, you were over innocent and young, but the cause turned out to be one of those trollops down in Fish Market, Jim had chased her and gotten her and got tally-ho. And he'd got more than that when the doctor left.

Ewan had said *Oh?* not caring a rap, and Ma had nodded, *Mind out for the women. You're over bonny a lad to be taken that way.* Ewan'd said, grave, he'd be sure to mind, and Ma had said *Fine,* and gone, thank God. Back to that chapter on phosphor-bronze smelting, house cleared with the others all off to their work. All?—No luck, a knock on the door.

Miss Murgatroyd this time, thin and peeking, tittering

and shy like a wren gone erotic, *Eh me, in a Gentleman's Room, such a scandal! I thought you'd maybe like an orange or so,* she'd brought two of the things, great bulging brutes. You said you were sorry you never ate them, and she shrivelled in a way and you really felt sorry—why couldn't old people leave one alone?—always in need of pity, compassion, soft words to fend off the edge of things, cuddling in words, oh, damn them all!

So you'd put on a kind face and said you were sorry—*it was nice of you to think of me.* And at that she'd un-shrivelled like a weed in the rain, peeking and chittering in your bedroom chair all about herself and her life and her likes; and Ewan'd sat and listened, half-wishing she'd go, half-wondering about her in an idle way. Queer to think she'd been born for that, been young once like oneself and wanted real things: food, wind on the sea, phosphor-bronze smelting . . . maybe not, but books and sleeping with men. Surely at least she had wanted *THAT*—her gen-eration had seemed to want little else, blethered in their books about little else, Shaw and the little sham-scientist Wells running a fornication a folio before they could pitch an idea across: gluey devils, the Edwardians, chokers and chignons, worse than the padded Victorian rabbits. . . .

And now at the end she had none of it, went to tea-fights, the Unionist Ladies, she liked Mr. MacDonald and the National Government and read lots of faded verse in Scots, the new Scots letters the Edwardian survivals were trying to foist on the Scottish scene—*Have you read Dr. Pitten-drigh MacGillivray's pomes? Such lovely, I think, and Clean and Fine. And Miss Marion Angus, though they're awful Broad.* And Ewan said he hadn't, he didn't read poetry. Then she tweetered from the room and came back with a book of Mr. Lewis Spence's for him to read, all about the ancient Scots, they'd been Awful Powerful in magic. And Ewan said that was nice; and he was sure they had.

Tired after that and a spot of sleep. Chris would wake him up at noon, with a tray and dinner, gleam of bronze hair dolichocephalic heads scarce in Duncairn, his own one only a betwixt-and-between. And he'd eat, not much, and read some more, Duncairn outside in its afternoon haze, far off the foghorn on Crowie Point lowing like an aurochs with belly-ache—the cattle that Cæsar said couldn't

lie down, no knee joints, they kipped up against a tree. . . .
What the devil had that to do with a chapter on Castings?

Five o'clock, shoes on the stairs, a guffaw, a knock, young
Archie Clearmont. Decent chap Archie, if a bit of a bore,
baby face, a long story about a Prof: he'd turned round in
the lecture-room and said to Archie, and Archie had turned
and said to the Prof—, and Ewan nodded and wondered
they hadn't grown dizzy. Rectorial elections coming off
soon, Archie thought he'd support the Nationalist. Ewan
asked why, and Archie said for a bit of a rag, the Nationalist candidate was Hugo MacDownall, the chap who wrote
in Synthetic Scots. Ewan asked *Why synthetic? Can't he
write the real stuff?* and Archie said *I'm damned if I know.
Sounds more epileptic than synthetic to me—that's why
I'm interested, I'm going in for Medicals!*

John Cushnie next, sure as fate, poor devil with his
English and his earnestness, smart, in a new Raggie Robertson suit, he'd brought Ewan an Edgar Wallace to read—
you must feel weariet with lying there. And he said 'twas
a gey thing when decent chaps, just because they spoke
well with a bit of class, were bashed by keelies down in
Footforthie. They were never letten into Raggie Robertson's
Depot, time the bobbies took they kind of wasters in
hand. . . . Ewan said *What wasters?—Raggie or the keelies?*
and Cushnie gawked above his tight collar oh ay, *ha-ha,* but
Raggie was all right, he'd a good job there and a chance
to get on. A chap didn't need a union to help if he put
his back into a job of work—though Labour wasn't so bad,
look at Bailie Brown. But the Communists—along in
Doughty Park on Sunday he'd stopped and listened to that
dirty Red, Trease, paid from Moscow as every body knew,
splurging away about all workers uniting and yet pitching
glaur as fast's he was able at decent folk like Bailie
Brown. . . . And then, thank God, the tea bell went, and
Cushnie with it, tie, spots, and all.

Mr. Quaritch came up in the evening to see him, with a
pile of review books from the *Daily Runner,* and his pipe,
ferret-twinkle, and unhappy wee beard: *Want anything to
read? What's that you've got?* Ewan showed him the text-
book and he shook his head: *Dreich stuff. Would you care
to review a novel?*

Ewan shook his head, couldn't be bothered with novels.
Mr. Quaritch said he might count himself lucky, *he'd* to
bother enough with the lousy tripe, twenty or so of the

damned things a week. Ewan asked who wrote them—and
what on earth for? and Mr. Quaritch said mostly wee chaps
without chins—but what for God might know, He kept
quiet about it, unless it was to provide the deserving re-
viewer with half a crown a copy when he sold them at
Burnett's.—*Piddle makes a fortune flogging reviews. Have
you hear what happened to my colleague last night?*

Ewan said he hadn't and Quaritch told him the tale,
Mr. Piddle was racing for the six-thirty train with his copy,
Duncairn news for the *Tory Pictman,* gey late, in a hell of
a sweat that he'd miss it. You knew the way the daft Bulgar
would ride?—head down over the handle-bars, neck out
like a gander seeking the water, all in a flush and a paddy
for time. Well, he wheeled out from the *Runner* offices in
Wells Street, into Royal Mile, and pedalled like hell up the
Royal, tramcars and buses and lorries about, dodging the
lot and beating them all. Dark was coming down and the
street-lamps were lighting and Piddle's feet were flying like
the wind when, keeking his head a bit to one side he noticed
a lot of folk yelling at him. Well, he took no notice, half
Duncairn yells whenever it sights our reporter Piddle, just
thought that the proletariat,—*he-he!*—was living up to its
lowness, *yes?*

And then next minute his bike left the earth, his head
went over his heels and vanished, and when he'd finished
wondering with a sheer despair how he'd ever get copy
about the end of the world down to the *Tory Pictman*
office when there wouldn't be a *Pictman* left to print it he
looked up round the curve of his haunches and saw two or
three folk looking down at him, one cried *Are you killed?*
Piddle wasn't sure, but he managed to stand up, and was
dragged from the hole by the crowd that had come, the rest
of the survivors of the end of the world. And then he
found what had happened was he'd fallen head-first into
road-digging in the middle of the Mile, he'd passed the red
lights with never a glance, that's what the shouts had been
for as he passed. The bike looked like a bit of string chewed
by a cow, but Piddle had no time to attend to it: the next
things the gapers around the hole saw were Piddle's legs
scudding away up the Mile, bent on catching the *Pictman*
train. . . .

Ewan lay with his hands under his head, drowsing and
thinking of Quaritch and his tale when both had gone down
to their supper. Now the night was coming in by, lamps

lighted; through the window and up through the night the ghost-radiance of Footforthie flecked the blind.—People thought that kind of a story funny, everyone laughed, Quaritch had expected him to laugh, and he hadn't, he'd seen nothing funny about it. What was funny in a queer old wreck like Piddle falling into a dirty hole in the Mile? He'd hurt himself a bit, no doubt—that the fun? Enjoyment of seeing another look ridiculous?

And he thought of innumerable stories he'd heard, overheard when a boy, been told in Seggett with loud guffaws and glazed eyes of mirth—about women and their silly, unfortunate bodies, about babies and death and disease and dirt, and something he supposed was lacking in him, Robert had once told him he was born a prig, he'd no humour and couldn't be cheerful and lusty and scrabble in filth and call it fun. Fun?

Real fun enough in the world—fun in the roar of the furnaces, in a sweeping door and a dripping trough of blazing metal a-pour on the castings, fun in the following of formulæ through trick on trick in the twists of maths, fun in the stars wheeling at night with long lights over the whoom of Footforthie, the breath-taking glister of the Galaxy. Fun in the deadness of Duncairn after midnight, you could stand by the edge of Royal Mile where it wheeled to the moving blackness of Paldy and think the end of the world had come—the shining dead streets of this land long hence, waving in grass, beasts lairing in culverts, the sea creeping up and up on Footforthie and a clamour of seals on the rocky points where once they launched the fisherfleets, men long gone from the earth, not wiped out, not lost vanished an invading host to the skies, to alien planets and the furthest stars, storming at last the rooftops of heaven, earth remote from their vision as the womb and its dreams remote from the memory of an adult man——

He woke late that evening to hear a commotion in the next-door bedroom, empty till then. Low talk and quick steps, Mrs. Cleghorn, Chris, then a shivering bang, silence, a cough. Then Ma Cleghorn whispering *Will that have waked Ewan?*

His own door was opened a minute later and Chris came in, walking pussy-foot, she stood and listened till he called out soft, *'Lo, Chris. What's all the row next door?*

She said she was sorry they'd woken him up, a new lodger

was coming in a hurry, late, and they were making her up
a bit bed.

Ewan said he saw. What was she like?

Chris didn't know, a lass up from Dundee, the new
schoolteacher at the Ecclesgriegs Middle—English, she'd
heard, though she hadn't yet seen her——

Then she saw with a smile that Ewan was asleep, human
beings were never of much interest to him.

Taking up tea to Ma Cleghorn next morning Chris found
the meikle creature already out of bed, getting into her
stays like wool into a bottle. *God, Chris, just give a pull at
they points, I'm getting a wee bittie stout, I'm half-feared.*
Chris put down the tray and pulled at the tapes, the house
a drowse in the Saturday quiet, she asked why Ma'd got up
so early, and Ma asked if she'd forgotten the new lodger-
lassie, was Chris herself to do all the work? Chris said *Well,
unless she's so awful big, she'll make no difference to me.
I hope. What's she like?* and Ma gave a bit of a snort:
*A stuck-up looking bitch from a school in Dundee.
Schlimpèd and English and thin as a sparrow, I never could
abide the stuck-up kind.* Chris said *Some folk say that I'm
stuck-up,* Ma said *So you are, and so's your bit Ewan. I'll
maybe thole two of you about the house bit I'll be danged
to a cinder-ash afore I hear with another of the brew. . . .
Och, lassie, go away, I'm in bad tune this morning. Take
the teacher creature her cup of tea.*

So Chris did, and went up and knocked, a cool voice
said *Come in* in she went, the lassie lying in the double bed
Chris and Ma Cleghorn had put up yestreen, window wide
open, curtains flying, Chris lowered her eyes to the quean
herself and saw her trig, neat, in a flowered nightie, slim
like a boy, like Ewan almost, short black hair and blue deep
eyes, great pools going down into darkness. She sat up and
took the cup and nodded: *You Mrs. Cleghorn's partner?*

Chris knew for certain then what was wrong, the English
lass was shy as could be but carrying it off with a brassy
front, the kind of cool courage Chris always had liked. And
as Chris smiled the brassiness went, the quean flushed sweet
as they looked at each other, was suddenly neat and demure
and forlorn, no more; like a prize pussy-cat, Chris thought,
with that faint line of down on her upper lip that one liked
the look of, most folk didn't—*I'm Mrs. Colquohoun and
you're Miss Johns.*

—*I say, you're different from what I expected.*

—You're a wee bittie different yourself, Chris said, carried down the tray and went on with her work, nice to have had a nice quean like that for one's own sometime: as well as had Ewan. But that was just dreaming—she wouldn't have been one's own any more than was Ewan, the pussy-cat, wave of nice black hair by her smooth, soft cheek and that funny down and that youngness—oh, but they made one feel like an old trauchled wife, the young folk here in Duncairn!

And suddenly, washing the breakfast things, there came a waft of stray wind through the window, a lost wean of the wind that had tint itself in play in the heights of the summer Mounth, Chris nearly dropped the cup she was drying. Ma Cleghorn louped: *Steady on, lass! Mighty be here, have you seen a ghost?*

Chris said *Only smelt one,* and then, on an impulse, *Ma, I want the day off. Can you spare me?*

Ma said *If you like: you're hardly my slave,* Chris said she knew that, but would Ma manage herself? Ma said she'd managed a good fifty-five years, off an on, and as far as she kenned at the moment she was neither a cripple nor had brain-concussion. So Chris laughed and said *I'm off to the country.*

And she ran up and knocked at Ewan's door and went in and found him not in bed, up, naked, a long, nice naked leg and that narrow waist that you envied in men, lovely folk men, he was standing and stretching, stark, the bandage gone from his head. No shyness in Ewan, just a cool disinterest, he turned and grinned *I'm feeling my feet. Too hot to lie in bed. Chris: let's take a holiday out in the country!*

She said *I was off for one on my own,* his face fell a little, then he nodded *All right. Have a good time.—But aren't you coming?—Not if you want to be on your own.* And Chris said that was daft, she would be always want him, and he said that was nice, and meant it, with a sudden glint of a grey granite smile nipped across to where she stood and cuddled her, funny to be cuddled by a naked man, she made out she was shocked, for fun, and he didn't see that, said *Oh, sorry,* and went back to his clothes. A minute Chris stood with the queerest feeling of lostness, staring at him, fun was beyond Ewan.

Then, because she knew that couldn't be helped, daft to expect him other than he was, she said *Be ready in half an hour,* and went down to her room and changed, looked at her clothes and found a light frock, took off all she wore and looked at herself, as of old, with cool scrutiny, seeing mirrored her face with the broad cheek-bones, seeing the long white lines of thigh and waist and knee, not very much need to envy men. *The queer years that I've been with you!* she said to the earnest thing in the mirror, and the shadow-self smiled back with golden eyes, shadow and self no longer woe, light-hearted suddenly as she dressed in haste to be gone for a day from Duncairn and herself.

She went into the sitting-room for a book, the place half in darkness, half the blinds drawn against the sting of the sun without. And the place wasn't deserted as usually it was, Miss Johns was sitting in the biggest chair, on her heels, not reading, chin in hand looking out through the window, a little lost pussy-cat Chris thought, with her trim black hair and her lobeless ears. She smiled up at Chris with that fenceless smile that came when the brassy shy-ness went: and Chris was moved to an impulse again. *I'm going for a jaunt to the country to-day. Would you like to come—if you've nothing else to do?*

She hesitated a minute, flushed, demure: *I'd love to. Terribly. Only—I've no money.* And in a sudden rush of confidence was telling Chris she'd come dead broke from Dundee and wouldn't get an advance until Wednesday, she'd nothing till then and had settled herself to mope the week-end in Windmill Place. Chris said that didn't matter, she'd pay, and Miss Johns could pay her back some time; and the pussy-cat was shyer than ever, and Chris asked her name, and she said *Oh, Ellen. Helen really, you know, but when Dad came down from London to work in Dundee I went to High School and they mis-spelt me Ellen. . . .* And Chris had almost expected that, she couldn't have been anything else but an Ellen!

She was dressed and down in the sitting-room a short minute before Ewan came down. Chris said *Ellen Johns— Ewan Tavendale. He's my son—sometimes. Ellen's coming out with us on our jaunt.* And Ewan, un-boylike, wasn't shy a bit, he said that would be nice, grey granite eyes on Ellen Johns as though she were a chapter on phospher bronze, they were much of the same straight height and look, both dark and cool, Ellen cool as he was, no blush now, indiffer-ently polite to each other. And a queer unease came on Chris that minute as she looked from one to the other: as though she were sitting in a theatre-stall and watching the opening of a dark, queer play.

But that fancy was lost in the hours that followed. The three went down to Mercat Cross and found an Aberdeen bus waiting there, ready to leave in a minute or so, crossing the Slug into Banchory, down by Deeside and Dunecht to Aberdeen, turning about and so back again. And they got in the bus, the two pussy-cats polite, not wanting either to sit by the other, manœuvring each to sit by Chris. Chris said *I think I'll sit by myself, right at the front,* and went and sat there, the other two on the opposite seat, Ellen by the window, hatless, hair braided, curling long lashes and secret face, Ewan hatless as well, cool and composed, staring about him as the bus moved off. Once he leaned over and asked where they were going, Chris didn't know, they'd get out at some place they liked.

In a minute, themselves near the only passengers, the bus was climbing Duncairn Rise up to the heights where the men of Montrose had marshalled three hundred years before, suddenly, on a Sunday, over-awing Duncairn and pouring down to a Sabbath of blood. Chris turned in her seat and looked down and saw the white sword gleam of Royal Mile, the haze that lay on the lums of Footforthie, shining boats dipping out to sea in the pelt and shine of the morning tide. And then the road wheeled up and around and paused: there below the Howe of the Mearns, crowned, shod, be-belted in green and gold, silver chains where the Mearns burns wound and spun to the Forthie's flow, Stonehaven forward, Bervie behind, far off the shimmer where the Grampians rode, the farms gleaming below the bents, haugh on haugh, tumbling green long cornswaths under the wind.

And syne the bus stopped and took on a farmer, thin and mean-looking, he starved his men and ate sowans to his meat, never cuddled his wife except on Sundays and only then if he'd been to kirk. And like a great squat beetle the bus crept on, oh, they were cutting the hay in a park, the smell in the bus, drifting, tingling—Blawearie's night and days, hush of the beeches in a still July, pastures sleeping around Segget Manse with Robert beside you as you drowsed on the lawn—Robert that you looked at, and he hadn't a face——

And Chris shook that woe dreaming away from herself,

let nothing spoil the sun and the hay and the goodness of
being alone and alive, peering through lids at July unfold,
birring, up the blossoming Howe, deep-honeysuckled ran
the hedges, in parks outbye the gleg-vexed kye were tearing
about with tails a-switch, some eident body would have sour
milk the night. Ewan and Ellen at last were speaking to each
other. Ewan had turned his head and Chris saw the English
quean looking up at him, cool, like a virtuous panther-
kitten exchanging tail-switchings with a black-avised leop-
ard.

The next thing she knew they were through Stonehive,
windy, guarded by Dunnottar Woods, and were climbing
up the heath of the Slug, no hay-smell here but the guff of
the heather billowing up to the quivering heights. And there
came a sudden memory to Chris—a winter night twenty-
three years before when father and mother and Will and
herself and the loons long-lost and the twins that died had
flitted across these hills in a storm, with battered lanterns in
the on-ding of sleet . . . twenty-three years before. Back and
back through the years as the bus climbed the Slug, years
like the rustle of falling leaves, dreams by night and dim
turnings in sleep, and you were again that quean in the
sleet, all the world and living before you unkenned, kisses
and hate and toil and woe, kisses at night when the byre-
stalls drowsed, agony in long deserted noons, hush of terror
of those moon-bright nights when you carried within your
womb seed of men—for a minute they seemed no more than
dreams as you drowsed, a quean, in the smore of the
sleet. . . .

But now below, creeping out of the heat, the Howe left
behind, came Banchory shining in its woods and far away
the long flicker of the ribboned Dee that went down through
the fine lands to Aberdeen. On the sky-line the mountains
marched snow-covered, lifting white faces to the blink of
July, in great haughs the fir-woods bourouched green, red
crags climbed the northwards sky to peer, hands at their
eyes, at Aberdeen. Sometimes a body would get off the bus,
sometimes it would stop by a tottering gate and a slow,
canny childe climb grinning aboard, or a sharp-faced
woman, Aberdeen, thin-voiced, thin-faced, with quick ferret look around, from Chris to Ewan, Ewan to Ellen syne
to the driver syne up to the roof, syne out of the window,
syne folding her lips and her hands, the world well and
respectable and behaving itself. And Chris sat and watched

the comings and goings, happy and happy and sweir to the bone.

Then at last here was Ewan shaking her: *Chris. Where are we going?—to Aberdeen?* She said goodness no, she didn't hope so, though the tickets were for there and 'twas a pity to waste them. And then she looked out and saw flash by a word white-painted on a crossroads sign, a word and a place she had long forgotten. *We'll get out at Echt and wait the bus back.*

So they did, Echt snoozing white in its stour, bairns playing about the doors of the houses, Ewan went into a shop and bought pieces, Chris went to help: loaf, butter and milk, some cakes and a knife, they looked loaded down for a feast or a famine, or tinks on the road, fair shocking Echt. Ellen showed her bit English mettle at once, no pride, she caught up the loaf and the bottles, some of the bairns cried after them, she laughed and didn't mind, kitten not cat. Then Chris led them off on the ploy she'd planned.

The Hill of Fare towered high in the sun, scaured and red, the flow of heather like a sea of wine, leftwards, dark, the Barmekin haunted even in July's sun-haze. Chris cried *Oh, wheesht!* to the others and they stopped, looked at her, listened, and heard through the sun, lonely, unforgotten, never-stopping that plaint, the peesies flying over Barmekin. Twenty-three years and they never had stopped. . . . And Chris thought half-shamed, in a desperate flyting: *Losh, but their throats must surely be dry!*

And at last through the litter of the wild-growing broom choking the upward track, they came to the croft of Cairndhu where Chris had been born, rank thistles all about, the windows were shuttered, grass crept to the door, another and bigger farm long syne had eaten up the land and the implements. They poked their heads inside the out-biggings, the barn musty with a smell of old hay, rats scampered there in the sun-hazed gloom, Chris wandered from place to place like one seeking that which she wouldn't know—maybe something of that sureness mislaid in the past, long ago, when she was a quean. But here was nothing, nothing but change that had followed every pace of her feet, quiet-padding as a panther at night.

When she turned away from the biggings at last she found Ellen and Ewan sitting on the mill-course, speaking low and clear to each other, not to disturb her, cat-like the two of them, unheeding the sun, haunted by no such memories as hers. Daft not to have known from the first that this meant nothing to them, ruined biggings on a little farm: her old fiere the land was nothing to them, children of touns by love or by nature, Ewan born in a croft in Kinraddie knew little of the land, cared less, not his job—that was stoking a furnace in Gowans and Gloag's!

He asked where now, and said Chris was the guide, and she pointed up to the Barmekin shining high and flat in the air against the tops of the further hills: *I haven't been there since I was a bairn.* Ellen said *Well, you don't look as though that was long ago,* and Chris asked *Am I as bairn-like as all that?* and Ellen flushed and said she hadn't meant that—*it's just you don't possibly look as though Mr. Tavendale here were your son.* Chris smiled at him. *But he is, worse luck,* Ewan nodded, a kindly joke in his compass: *The luck's all mine. Come along then. Carry your parcel, Chris?*

Chris said shortly she'd manage it herself, she wasn't in her second childhood, either; and they laughed and went up and left the road and waded through the whins and the broom and over fences and up steep braes, steep so's you'd to clutch up step by step with handfuls of heather and grass for holds, Ellen flinched with stung legs and Ewan slipped on smooth shoes, Chris laughed back at both of them, shinning the slopes light and free and sure of her hold, she looked back from the uppermost ledge and waved at them, poor fusionless creatures her father would have called them—her father who all his years in Cairndhu had never (that she knew) climbed Barmekin, over-busy with chaving and slaving his flesh, body and soul and that dark, fierce heart, into the land to wring sustenance therefrom. So the whirlimagig went round and on: Father, now Ewan, the hill little to either, only to her who came in between and carried the little torch one from the other on that dreich, daft journey that led nowhither——

But, standing up there, with the wind in her hair, the thought came to her that THAT didn't much matter—daft the journey, but the journeying good. And she looked at the slopes gay in their gear, useless and meaningless but fine fun to climb. . . . The other two thought the same when they came, Ellen with smooth braids tangled a bit, a damp lock over Ewan's high forehead, they laughed and said things about Excelsior, young and sexless both, like the angels, dark angels, folk of an older stock than Chris's, intenter and sharper, not losing themselves in heather dreams or the smell of broom. Ewan said he was hungry, *aren't you, Miss Johns?* and Miss Johns said *Aren't I! Hungry as hell.*

So they made their way in the brush of the broom along the outer wall of the old Pict fort built by the men of antique time, a holy place before Christ was born, Chris said they'd find shade from the sun in its lithe. Syne they came on a thing they had little looked for, Ewan swore, his old passion for old times rekindled—men had been here, a great gang of them, had torn down the walls and flung them aside, deep ruts showed where the carts had been driven: and within the inner walls of the fort were the char and ash of a great foolish fire.

Some celebration, Chris thought, not caring, Ewan did, he said it was a filthy outrage and justified nothing that had happened in Aberdeen since they told the first of their filthy stories—that was probably before Christ's coming as well. Chris had never seen him so angered, she herself wasn't, they were only rickles of stone from long syne raised up by daft childes who worshipped the sun. Ewan said *That's rot. You know nothing about it,* and Chris gave a laugh and sat down on a stone, clasping her knees, not caring a fig one way or another. Miss Johns said *I agree with Mrs. Colquohoun. What does it matter what happens to this rubbish? There are things more in need of worrying about.* Ewan turned his grey granite glance upon her: *I didn't expect that YOU would think different.*

So they sulked a bit, sitting each side of Chris, and she didn't laugh, but looked fearsomely solemn. Then Ewan opened the milk-bottles and got out the bread and Ellen spread out the papers for a tablecloth, two sleek black heads under Chris's gaze; and they fed her solemn, though Ellen peeped at Ewan through those dangerous lashes—she'd trip on them some time. But he wasn't thinking of her at all, his mind far off with his ancient men, he began to tell them of that time that had been, how close in the generations these men were, how alike ourselves in the things they believed, unessentials different—blood, bone, thought the same. For if history had any lesson at all it was just that men hadn't changed a bit since the days of the folk in the Spanish caves who painted the charging aurochsen—except to take up civilization, that ancient calamity that fell on

the world with gods and kings and culture and classes—
Ellen cried *But then you're a Socialist!*

Ewan looked blank, smooth boy face, angel-devil eyes
suddenly dragged from his ancient Picts: *What's that to do
with it?* And Ellen said *Everything. If there was once a
time without gods and classes couldn't there be that time
again?*

Ewan said *I suppose so. I don't much care. It won't
come in our time. I've my own life to lead*—and at that
the slim quean seemed to forget all her hunger, curling
lashes and dimpled ways, she said Mr. Tavendale was talking rot, how could anyone live a free life in this age?—
capitalism falling to bits everywhere, or raising up classes
of slaves again, Fascism coming, the rule of the beast——

Ewan sat and munched bread *They won't rule me. I'm
myself.*——*You're not. You're a consequence and product
as all of us are. If we're all the children of those old-time
men that you've told us about do you think for a moment
we aren't more the children of our fathers and mothers and
the things we've read and depended upon? Just silly to say
that we're not.* And Ewan asked what had that to do with
it?; and they lost their tempers; and Chris fell asleep.

When she woke they were nowhere in sight; far off,
drowsy, a ringdove crooned in the little woods scampering
down to Echt, remoter still a peesie cried. The sun had
wheeled to afternoon, red on the nearer mountain cliffs,
blue far in the upper heights. Mountain on mountain:
there was Bennachie ahint which the tired folk went in song.
Sitting with her hands so propping her, Chris found herself
aching, sun-wearied and sad, in the bright day's glister curiously lost though she knew that Ewan and the English
quean couldn't be far off, they'd come if she cried. Call?—
behave like a frightened old wife?

She lay back again in the heather bells, and under her
ears heard whispers unceasing, sounds soft and urgent and
quieter than mice, the little world of the little beasts about
its existence of sowing and harvest, feeding and fighting and
a pridesome begetting, moral and urgent and dreadfully
unsweir, pelting through lives as brief as a blink as though
the blink lasted a hundred years. It felt like God so to lie
and listen—so long's the beasts didn't come climbing up a
stalk and mistake one's ear for heaven.

When she rose and went to look for the others she found
them close on the ruined dyke, not sitting and kissing as

they might have been (some sense in that, said her mind, still sleepy), Ewan perched on a stone, hands clasping his knees, looking down at Ellen sitting clasping hers, nice knees and long legs and the lot forgotten, talking, still talking—about history and Socialism and freedom for people in the modern world. And Ewan was saying, *Yes, that seems sense and I'll look it up. I've always thought Socialism just a measly whine, MacDonaldish stuff and politicians' patter. Different when you think of it as history making, the working classes to be captured and led: all right, I'll give the keelies a chance.* Ellen said *And don't be so horribly superior; you'll never lead if you can't be an equal. . . . Oh, there's your mother. Coo-ee, Mrs. Colquohoun!*

It seemed that their talk had run them clean dry, quiet enough in the afternoon quiet gathering up the papers and burning them, carrying the milk-bottles down the hill, the sun was dimming, and all about bees homing like drunken men from a pub, one came bumbling against Chris's face and tangled itself in her hair. She brushed it aside, quickly and quietly, and Ellen shivered *I couldn't do that!* Chris asked *What?* and Ellen said *That bee—I'd have jumped and hit it and it would have stung me. I'm a ghastly coward,* and shivered again. Ewan didn't notice, far off in thought, treading down from the breach in the Pictman's fort to seek the like in the crumbling castle that prisoned the men of his time.

Alick Watson said *Och, let the swine a-be. He gave me as good as I gave him;* and Norman Cruickshank said *He gave you a mucking sight more; who'd have thought a toff Bulgar had a punch like that?*

So they wouldn't have anything to do with the plan of Wee Geordie Bruce to send a bit note, insulting-like, to Tavendale's address when he bade at home nursing a broken head he'd gotten in that fight with Alick in the yard—God, the place was splottered in blood, wee Geordie went out and glowered all about it and nearly got down on his knees to lick it, with his wee shrivelled face and shifty eyes, awful keen on blood and snot. Alick said *You're not right in your head, you wee whoreson,* he seemed hardly right himself all that week, snapping a chap's head off if you spoke to him praising him a bit how he'd bashed the toff Bulgar.

Norman wasn't much better, they both worked like tinks

doing Tavendale's furnace as well as their own, trying to stick it with the foreman, were they? They got little thanks if that was their hope, Dallas came down and glowered *Good God, is that the way to work at Gowans and Gloag's?* Alick said to him *Ach, away to hell. We're doing the work of a dozen here—if that doesn't please you, gang off and clype.* The foreman looked a bit ta'en aback, *We've all to do more than our shift in Gowans, so give's none of your lip, you Cowgate brat.* And Alick said when the foreman had gone what he'd like to give the bastard was one in the guts, syne dance on his face with tacketty boots.

For Gowans and Gloag were fair in a way, they'd sacked a dozen from Machines that week and were trying to cheese-pare all over the shops, they'd been on to Dallas and gotten out his rag. The apprentice chaps in the dinner hour sat out in the yard and swore at them, and smoked, and watched through the haze from the Docks the swinging cranes that loaded the ships, or the bridges open and a laggard trawler creep in from an antrin night on the sea, lost in the fogs of the Dogger Bank. And Alick said by God if he had the guts he'd run off from it all and take to the sea, a fine bit life if it wasn't that on a ship a common chap was near starved to death. And Norman said that he'd like a farm: and he'd near as much chance of getting that as of wee King Geordie making him his vallay.

Well, you couldn't but wonder what Tavendale would do when he got back to Furnaces on the Monday morning, stuck-up as ever, and acting the toff he looked when he came down and took up his shovel, you keeked sideways and saw he'd no sign of a bandage, froze up and don't-touch-me-I'm-awful grand. Syne the work started, all at it hell for leather till the hooter went, no larking or jookery-packery, Alick and Norman not looking at the toff, they were maybe a bit feared he'd reported them.

And then as you climbed up to the yard the toff turned round to Alick *Hullo!* and Alick gave a kind of a start *Hullo!* and they laughed, and Norman went dandering over *Hullo!* as well and a fag to the toff Tavendale. You'd never seen him smoking before, but he took it: *I'm going down to the Docks to eat my dinner. Coming, you chaps?*

Now Alick and Norman never left the yard, they would bide there all the dinner hour and raise hell with pitching stones at old tins, telling bit tales of their Saturday nights, they were both of them awful Bulgars with the queans,

Norman had gotten a tart into trouble, and laughed when her Ma came after him chasing him with a bit of a broken bottle from the Gallowgate half through Paldy Parish; and they'd tease Geordie Bruce, the dirty wee devil, and get him to do the dirtiest capers, rouse hell's delight and have a fair time. But now they just looked a bit tint and surprised, and Alick said *Och, ay,* as though he couldn't help it, and Norman Cruickshank gave a bit nod, and away the three of them went together.

That was the beginning of a gey queer time, it wasn't only the apprentices noticed it, the toff didn't go out of his way to be friends but if he came on you, joking-like, he'd sit down and listen and smoke a fag-end and give a bit nod, and he wasn't so bad, not looking at you now so that a childe felt his face was all wrong and his sark gey clarted up at the neck and he hadn't ta'en the trouble to wash that morning. Some said that his bashing had done him good, he'd gotten scared of the working chaps; but Alick Watson said that that was damned stite, *Ewan Tavendale could tackle any Bulgar here.* And had he gone clyping to the management?

He was in and out of the shops all the time, and Norman's father, in the Grindery, took him down to a meeting of the Union Branch, Norman didn't go, he couldn't be bothered, he said to Tavendale *They just claik and claik and grab your subscription and never give anything, they're a twisting lot of swine in the Union. But the old man's aye been keen on them.* And looked a bit shamed, *He's Labour, you see.*

Tavendale said *There are lots of chaps that, my step-father was,* and you all cheered up, sitting on buckets in the furnace room, a slack hour, and having a bit of a jaw, you were none of you Labour and knew nothing about politics, but all of you had thought that the Bulgars of toffs were aye Tory or Liberal or this National dirt. And somehow when a chap knew another had a father who'd been Labour you could speak to him plainer, like, say what you thought, not that you thought much, you wanted a job when apprenticeship was over and a decent bit time and maybe now and then a spare bob or so to take your quean to the Talkies—och, you spoke a lot of stite like the others did, about the queans that you'd like to lie with, and the booze you'd drink, what a devil you were, but if you got half a chance what you wanted was marriage and a house and a wife and a lum of your own. . . . Wee Geordie Bruce said *The Tories have the money, they're the muckers for the working man;* and Norman said *Blethers, the Bulgars have money, but they take good care to keep it for themselves or spend it on their lily-fingered whores, what's the good of Tories to us, you neep?* Alick said that maybe the next Labour Government wouldn't be so bad as the last had been, they were working folk themselves, some of them, though they'd birns of the rotten toffs as well. . . . And you all said what you thought, except Ewan—funny, you'd started to call him Ewan—he just sat and listened and nodded now and then, as though he couldn't make up his own mind: well, that's what a chap with sense would do. And when one of the chaps in the Stores said to you: *I hear you're all sucking up to the young toff* you nearly took him a crack in the jaw, and daft ass, young Ewan was as good as he was and a damn sight cleaner in the neck and the tongue.

Well, Ewan went to the Union meeting that night, next morning chaps asked him what he'd thought o't, and he said there hadn't been much on at all, there'd been less than a dozen members there—*I suppose you can't blame a union if the chaps who belong to it won't attend its meetings.* Norman asked what the hell was the good of attending, the Union had sold the pass time and again, the heads of the bloody thing down in London were thick as thieves with the viscounts and earls. Ewan said that was rotten if it was true, why didn't the Union give them the chuck? And Norman said he'd be Bulgared if he knew.

Alick Watson said that his Ma's new lodger, a chap called Selden, and he was a Red, was aye saying the unions should chuck out the leaders. And everybody laughed, you knew well enough what Reds were like, daft about Russia and its Bolshevists—tink brutes, it made you boil to think the way they mis-used the ministers there, the *Daily Runner* had pages about it and the Pope had been in a hell of a rage at atheists behaving near as bad as Christians.

And you all sat by the Docks, you'd go down there now and look at the two or three ships in the harbour sleeping an hour in the still July, smoke a slow pencil plume from the derricks, a dead cat or so floating under your feet, far off through the brigs you could see the North Sea fling up its green hands again and again and grab and scrabble at the breakwater wall—and you blethered about everything you could think of, Ewan wouldn't talk much unless Alick made him, Alick'd slap him on the shoulder, *Come on, man, tell us.* But he'd say *I don't know any more than you chaps— less, it's only stuff out of books.*

Well, wasn't that a lot? And you'd ask him about it, did *he* hold with this ongoing of the Bolshevists in Russia, closing down kirks and chasing ministers all to hell for just preaching, like? He said he didn't know anything about Russia but he thought the time of kirks was past. *But you surely believe there's Something, man?* and Ewan said *Maybe, but I don't think it's God.*

And you couldn't make out what he meant by that, funny chap, fine chap, you liked to go home with him, he called you Bob as you called him Ewan, and was awfully interested in everything, where you'd been born, and gone to school, and the stuff they'd taught you in Ecclesgriegs. And you felt a bit shy to invite him, like, the old man's house was a hell of a soss, but you'd like him to tea some Saturday night. And he said *Right, thanks. I'd like to come;* and you went home and maybe boasted a bit till your sister, the silly bitch, said *Tavendale: isn't that the toff that you couldn't stick?*

And out of the fragments of days and nights Chris saw her life shape to a pattern again. Getting up and working and going to bed—it had never been anything else in a way she thought as she scrubbed the floors, tidied the rooms, and helped Ma Cleghorn cook the meals or young Meg Watson wash up at the sink. Meg had come back and was fair subdued, looking at Chris with a frightened eye, afraid, poor lass, she'd be somehow blamed over that fight at Gowans and Gloag's. But Chris wasn't so daft as pay heed to that, Ewan could heed to himself, she thought, he was growing up with his own life to lead. And she had hers, and sleep, and food, work, and meikle Ma Cleghorn to laugh at—and what else was there a body could want?

Ma said B'God she should marry some childe, fair going to waste, a lassie like her. And Chris asked who she should marry—Mr. Piddle? and Ma gave a snort, she'd said marry, not martyr, he'd never get up from the marriage bed.

Chris said she thought that was fair indecent, drinking tea and pulling a long face; and Ma shook her meikle red face at her. Life was damn indecent as both of them

knew. The first time she'd lain with a man, her Jim, she
couldn't make up her mind to be sick or to sing. But there
was more of the singing than sickness for all that, even
though it felt awful like going to bed and being cuddled
by a herring-creel, not a man. But mighty, a lassie when
she was a lass just bubbled for a childe to set her on fire.
But now they were all as hard and cold and unhandled as
a slab of grey granite in a cemetery. Look at that creature-
teacher, Miss Johns, whipping in and out the house like
a futret, with books and papers and meetings to attend,
never a lad to give her a squeeze. Chris said *You don't
know, she's maybe squeezed on the sly,* Ma said *Not her,
she'd freeze up a childe. Not but she isn't bonny in a kind
of a way, though I never could stick they black-like jades
with a bit of a mouser on the upper lip.*

Chris thought of the faint, dark down on the lip of a
down-bent face, and the long lashes, curled, soft and tender,
blue in the sun. And she said that she thought it rather
bonny, and Ma said *Bonny? You've an awful taste. Though
the Cushnie and Clearmont think the same, they near eat
her up at a breakfast time. I suppose that most of the
queans about are all such a pack of scrawny scarts that a
sleek pussy-cat like our Really-Miss-Johns just sets a childe
fair a-tingle to stroke her.*

Chris had noticed how Ellen woke up the breakfast,
though she herself didn't seem to know it, canty and trig,
with her braided hair and her cool, blue eyes, John Cushnie
would pass the marmalade, and blush, and habber a bit of
English, making an awful mess of it above his tight-tied
tie, Mr. Clearmont would give his cheerful guffaw and fix
his round baby eyes on this titbit—*Coming to the Saturday
Match, Miss Johns, Students and Profs, it'll be great fun?*
And Miss Johns would shake her head, *Too busy,* and
Archie's face would fall with a bang.

Even Mr. Quaritch forgot his books, the pussy-cat had
snared him as well, he'd waggle his thin little beard at her
and tell her stories of the *Daily Runner,* and start to explain
the Douglas Scheme, the only Plan to Save Civilization by
giving out lots and lots of money to every soul whether he
worked for't or not. *Who would be such a fool as work at
all then?* Miss Johns would ask, but she'd ta'en it up wrong,
Mr. Quaritch would marshal bits of bread to prove the
Scheme again up to the hilt, and Miss Johns would say it
sounded great fun, she knew there was Relativity in physics,

this was the first time she'd met it in maths. Mr. Piddle would say, *He-he! Fine morning. And how is Miss Johns to-day yes—yes?* And Feet the Policeman would curl his mouser, a Sergeant, and give her a bit of a stare like a cod that wanted its teeth in a cat, instead of the other way round, as was usual. Chris would smile at the coffee-pot and meet Ellen's eyes, demure blue eyes with an undemure twinkle.

She and Ewan were indifferent, polite, Chris thought them too much alike to take heed of each other. But Miss Lyon couldn't abide her at all, and would sniff as she watched her, Just a Vulgar Flirt, she didn't let me take Liberties with *her*. She told this to Chris after breakfast one day, didn't Mrs. Colquohoun think the Johns girl Common? And Chris smiled at her sweet, *I don't know, Miss Lyon. You see I'm awfully common myself.*

The first bit of scandal on the pussy-cat Chris heard was brought by Miss Murgatroyd, *she* had heard it up at the Unionist Ladies—it was awful, and Miss Johns looking Such Genteel. And what the Tory women had been saying was that the new teacher in the Ecclesgriegs Middle was being over-quick with the strap, strict as could be, maybe not a bad fault. But worse than that she was telling the bairns the queerest and dirtiest things, Mrs. Colquohoun, drawing pictures on the blackboard of people's insides and how their food was digested and oh—And Miss Murgatroyd coloured over with Shame, and dropped her voice and nearly her cup—*the way that the waste comes out, you know*.

Chris said she thought that was maybe good and the bairns would be less constipated. Miss Murgatroyd tweetered like a chicken in the rain, and then bridled a wee, *Well, of course I'm Single, and don't know much about things like that.* Chris wanted to ask, but didn't, if being Single meant that you never went to the bathroom; but a question like that wouldn't have been Such Fine.

But more was to come, as she heard soon enough, the Unionist Ladies in an awful stew, and hot to write the Education Authority. Miss Johns had been explaining the Bible away, the whole tale told to Miss Murgatroyd by Mrs. Gawpus, the wife of Bailie Gawpus, she said her little niece had come home and said there wasn't a God at all, the new teacher had said so or as good as said so, He was

just a silly old man the Jews worshipped and the world had
really begun in a fire. . . . Just Rank Materialism, wasn't it,
now?—And who would think it of a girl like Miss Johns?

She told the same story to Ma Cleghorn that night, but
got feint the much petting for her pains. *Well, damn't,
there's maybe some sense in her say, Miss Murgatroyd, the
Bible's no canny. Mind the bit about Lot and his daughters,
the foul slummocks, him worse, the randy old ram? It's
better to speak to beginnings in fire than let the weans think
it began in a midden. Ay, there's more in the lass than meets
the eye, I'll have to see how she's getting on*

Chris met Ellen Johns a week after that, coming up the
stairs, her dark face pale, she smiled at Chris, a tired-look-
ing lass and Chris said she looked tired. She said so she was,
though not with the teaching, and then told she'd been
summoned before the Authority and reprimanded for telling
the Duncairn kids a few elementary facts about themselves.—*So I've to leave off physiology and it's Nature
Study now—bees, flowers, and how catkins copulate. Won't
that be fun?* But she didn't wait an answer, just smiled in
the sleekèd way she had, dark and cool and wise, a mere
slip, a little quean playing about with fire, and went on up
the stair to the room next Ewan's.

Jim Trease had planned the march for the Friday, Broo
day, with all the unemployed of Paldy and contingents from
Ecclesgriegs and Footforthie and a gang of chaps on the
Kirrieben Broo. The main mob marshalled up in the Cowgate, the Communists crying for the folk to join up—
*we'll march to the Council and demand admittance, and
see the Provost about the P.A.C.* And a man'd look shame-
faced at another childe, and smoke his pipe and never let
on till Big Jim himself came habbering along, crying you
out by your Christian name, and you couldn't well do anything else but join—God blast it, you'd grievances enough
to complain of. The wife would see you line up with the
other Broo chaps, looking sheepish enough, and cry out
Will! or *Peter!* or *Tam! Come out of that—mighty, it'll do
you no good.* And a man just waved at her, off-hand-like,
seeing her feared face peeking at him. But a bit of a qualm
would come in your wame, thinking *Och well, she'll be all
right. We're just marching down to the Castlegate.*

Syne the drum struck up and off you all marched, some
gype had shoved the handle of a flag in your hand, it read

DOWN WITH THE MEANS TEST AND HUNGER
AND WAR, the rest of the billies made a joke about it,
they would rather, they said, down a bottle of beer. Right
in front was Big Jim Trease, big and sappy in his shiny blue
shirt, beside him the chap he'd been helping of late, Stephen
Selden that had been an immigrant to Canada and come
back from the starvation there to starve here. The two of
them were in the lead of the march, wee Jake Forbes waddling behind, banging the drum, *boomroomroom*, he could
play a one-man band on his own, a Red musician, and played
at the dances with his meikle white face that had never
a smile. And on and up you rumbled through Paldy, clatter
of boots on the calsay stones, the sun was shining through
drifts of rain, shining you saw it fall on the roofs in long,
wavering lines and floodings of rain, queer you'd never
seen it look bonny as that.

But now all the chaps were lifting their heads as they
marched, and looking as though they hadn't a care in the
world, not showing their qualms to the gentry swine. Bobbies had come out and now marched by the column, a birn
of the bastards, fat and well fed, coshes in hand, there was
the new Sergeant, him they called Feet—and what plates
of meat! *Boomr-oom* went the drum and you all were
singing:

> Up wi' the gentry, that's for me,
> > Up wi' the gentry fairly,
> Let's slobber on King and our dear Countree—
> > And I'm sure they'll like me sairly.

And a lot more like that, about Ramsay Mac, stite, but
it gave a swing to your feet and you all felt kittled up and
high by then and looked back by your shoulder and saw
behind the birn of the billies marching like you, you forgot
the wife, that you hadn't a meck, the hunger and dirt,
you'd alter that. They couldn't deny you, you and the rest
of the Broo folk here, the right to lay bare your grievances. Flutter, flutter, the banner over your head, your feet
beginning to stound a wee, long since the boots held out
the water, shining the drift of the rain going by. And now
you were all thudding into step, and beyond the drum saw
Royal Mile, flashing with trams, thick with bobbies: and
here out from the wynds came the Ecclesgriegs men and
the fisher-chaps from Kirrieben, they looked the worst of

the whole caboosh. And Big Jim Trease cried *Halt a minute*, you all paiched to a stop while the other chaps drew in and formed fours.

Watching that you minded your time in the army, the rain and stink and that first queer time your feet slipped in a soss of blood and guts, going up to the front at Ypres— God, long syne that, you'd not thought then to come to this, to come to the wife with the face she had now, and the weans—by God, you would see about things! Communion- ists like Big Jim might blether damned stite but they tried to win you your rights for you. And all the march spat on its hands again and gripped the banners and fell in line, and looked sideways and saw the pavements half blocked, half Duncairn had heard of the march on the Town House—and och, blast it if there wasn't the wife again, thin-faced, greeting, the silly bitch, making you shake like this, the great sumph, by the side of those oozing creashes of bobbies, shining their capes in the rain.

But now you'd wheeled into Royal Mile, a jam of traffic, the trams had slowed down, flutter, flutter the banners, here the wind drove, your mates shrinking under the sleety drive, Woolworth's to the right, where all the mecks went, and there the big Commercial Bank and the office of the *Daily Runner*, the rag, it had tried to put a stop to this march, the swine had said you never looked for work, you that tramped out your guts day on day on the search—to the Docks, to the granite works, the country around, as far to the north as Stonehive. *Boomr-oomr*, wee Jake'll brain that damn drum if he isn't careful, Lord, how folk stare! A new song ebbing down the damp column, you'd aye thought it daft to sing afore this, a lot of dirt, who was an outcast? But damn't, man, now—

> Arise, ye outcasts and ye hounded,
> Arise, ye slaves of want and fear—

And what the hell else were you, all of you? Singing, you'd never sung so before, all your mates about you, marching as one, you forgot all the chave and trauchle of things, the sting of your feet, nothing could stop you. Rain in your face—that was easy to face, if not the fretting of the wife back there (to hell with her to vex a man's mind, why couldn't she have bidden at home, the fool?).

She'd take no hurt, you were all of you peaceable, the singing even in a wee died off, they'd shooed the traffic to the side of the Mile, a gang of the Mounted riding in front, their fat-buttocked horses swaying away, well-fed like their riders, the rain sheeting down from their tippets, the Bulgars, easy for them to boss it on us——

What the devil was up down there?

The whole column had slowed, came bang to a stop, more Mounties with their wee thick sticks in their hands strung out there across the Mile, rain-pelted, the horses chafing at their bridles, impatient, hell rotten to face if a brute came at you. And a growl and a murmur went through the column, what was wrong up there, why had they stopped? Chaps cried *Get on with it, Jim, what's wrong?* Syne the news came down, childes passing it on, their faces twisted with rage or laughing, they hardly bothered to curse about it, the police were turning the procession back down into Paldy by way of the wynds. It wasn't to be let near the Town Hall at all, the Provost had refused to see them or Trease.

And then you heard something rising about you that hadn't words, the queerest-like sound, you stared at your mates, a thing like a growl, low and savage, the same in your throat. And then you were thrusting forward like others—*Never mind the Bulgars, they can't stop our march!* And in less than a minute the whole column was swaying and crowding forward, the banners pitching and scudding like leaves above the sodden clothes of the angry Broo men. Trease crying *Back! Take care! Keep the line!*

And your blood fair boiled when you heard him cry that, a Red—just the same as the Labour whoresons, no guts and scared for his bloody face. And above his head you saw one of the bobbies, an inspector, give his arm a wave, and next minute the horses were pelting upon you hell for leather, oh God, they couldn't——

Ewan was down in Lower Mile when the police tried to turn the unemployment procession down the wynds to the Gallowgate. He'd just come from a bookshop and was forced to stop, the pavements black with out-staring people. And then they began to clear right and left, the shopman behind cried *Come back, Sir. There'll be a hell of a row in a minute*, he was standing on a pavement almost deserted. Then he saw the mounted policeman wave and the others jerk at their horses' bridles, and suddenly, far up, the policeman of Segget, the clown that the Segget folk had called Feet, not mounted, he'd come by the side of the column—saw him grab a young keelie by the collar and lift his baton and hit him, crack!—crack like a causeystone hit by a hammer, Ewan's heart leapt, he bit back a cry, the boy screamed: and then there was hell.

As the bobbies charged the Broo men went mad though their leader tried to wave them back, Ewan saw him mishandled and knocked to the ground under the flying hooves of the horses. And then he saw the Broo folk in action, a man jumped forward with a pole in his hand with a ragged flag with letters on it, and thrust: the bobby took it in the face and went flying over his horse's rump, Ewan heard some body cheer—himself—well done, well done! Now under the charges and the pelt of the rain the column was broken, but it fought the police, with sticks, with naked hands, with the banners, broken and knocked down right and left, the police had gone mad as well, striking and striking, riding their horses up on the pavements, cursing and shouting, Ewan saw one go by, his teeth bare, bad teeth, the face of a beast, he hit out and an old, quiet-looking man went down, the hoof of the horse went plunk on his breast——

And then Ewan saw the brewery lorry jammed by the pavement, full of empty bottles; and something took hold of him, whirled him about, shot him into the struggling column. For a minute the Broo men didn't hear or understand, then they caught his gestures or shout or both, yelled, and poured across the Mile and swamped the lorry in a leaping wave. . . .

That evening the *Runner* ran a special edition and the news went humming into the south about the fight in the Royal Mile, pitched battle between unemployed and police, how the Reds had fought the bobbies with bottles, battering them from their saddles with volleys of bottles: would you credit that, now, the coarse brutes that they were? The poor police had just tried to keep order, to stop a riot, and that's what they'd got.

* * * * *

The Reverend Edward MacShilluck in his Manse said the thing was disgraceful, ahhhhhhhhhhhh, more than that, a portent of the atheist, loose-living times. Why hadn't the police called out the North Highlanders? . . . And he read up the *Runner* while he ate his bit supper, and called in his housekeeper and told her the news, and she said that she thought it disgraceful, just, she'd heard that a poor old man was in hospital, dying, with his breast all broken up: would he be a policeman then, would you say? The Reverend MacShilluck gave a bit of a cough and said Well, no, he understood not—*Ahhhhhhhhhhhh well, we mustn't worry over much on these things, the proper authorities will see to them.* And gave the housekeeper a slap in the bottom, well-fed, and said *Eh, Pootsie, to-night?* And the housekeeper simpered and said *Oh, sir*——

.   .   .   .   .

Bailie Brown, that respectable Labour man, was interviewed and was awful indignant, he said that he fought day in, day out, the cause of the unemployed on the Council, none knew the workers better than he or the grievances they had to redress. But what good did this senseless marching do?—the Council had to impose the P.A.C. rates the National Government laid down for it, you could alter nothing for a three or four years till Labour came into power again. The unemployed must trust the Labour Party, not allow itself to be led all astray—And he shot Mr. Piddle out on the street, in a hurry, like, he'd to dress for dinner.

.   .   .   .   .

Lord Provost Speight was found in his garden, stroking his long, dreich, wrinkled face; and he said that this Bolshevism should be suppressed, he put the whole riot down to Communist agents, paid agitators who were trained in Moscow, the working-class was sound as a bell. If they thought they could bring pressure to bear on the Council to alter the rates of the P.A.C., by rioting about in Royal Mile, they were sore mistaken, he'd guarantee that——

.   .   .   .   .

Duncairn's Chief Constable said it wasn't true the police had run, they'd just given back a wee till reinforcements came and by then the crowd had dispersed, that was all. No, they'd made only one arrest so far, the well-known agitator Trease. And the old man who had died in the hospital had been struck down by one of the rioters——

.   .   .   .   .

And the men came back to their homes in Footforthie and Paldy Parish and Kirrieben, some of them walking and laughing, some glum, some of them half-carried all the way, with their broken noses, bashed faces, it made a woman go sick to see Peter or Andrew or Charlie now, his face a dripping, bloody mask, his whispering through his broken lips: *I'm fine, lass, fine.* Oh God, you could greet if it wasn't that when you did that you would die. . . .

And all that night they re-fought the fight, in tenements, courts, this room and that, and the bairns lay listening how the bobbies had run, of the young toff who'd appeared when Trease was knocked down and shouted *Break down the lorry for bottles!* and led them all off when the bottles were finished, him and Steve Selden, and told them to scatter. By Heavens, he'd lots of guts had that loon, though, toff-like, he'd been sick as a dog of a sudden, down in the Cowgate when binding a wound. You wanted more of his kind for the next bit time. . . . And the wife would say *What's the use of more bashing?* and you said a man had to die only once and 'twould be worth while doing that if you kicked the bucket with your nails well twined in a bobby's liver——

· · · · · ·

A week later the *Daily Runner* came out and announced that after a special sitting the Council had raised the P.A.C. rates.

Ma Cleghorn heard the story from Chris: *Ah, well, if that's how your Ewan feels. I'd never much liking for bobbies myself, though maybe the meikle sumph, you know, was doing no more than his duty, like.* Chris said *His duty? To bash a young boy—before the boy had done anything to him?* And Ma said *Well, well, you're fair stirred up. I'll think up some sonsy lie as excuse, and tell him the morn to look out other lodgings.*

And next morning Ma tackled the sacking of Feet, he'd spluttered a bit and put on the heavy as she told Chris when she came back to the kitchen. But she'd soon settled up his hash for the billy, telling him his room was needed for another, a childe they'd promised it a long while back. He'd told her she'd better look out, she had, and not get in ill with the Force, they'd heard things in headquarters about that quean Johns and were keeping an eye on the house already——

Ma had fair lost her rag at that and told him she didn't care a twopenny damn though all the bobbies in Duncairn toun were to glue themselves on to her front door knocker, the meikle lice—who was he to insult a decent woman who paid her rent and rates on the nail? *If my man had been alive, he'd have kicked you out, sergeant's stripes and all, you great coarse bap-faced goloch that you are.* Feet had habbered *I wasn't trying to insult you,* and Ma had said *Give me more of your lip and I'll tackle the kicking of your dowp myself,* and left him fair in fluster, poor childe, hardly kenning whether he stood on his head or meikle feet, fair convinced he was in the wrong, and packing up his case to get out of the house.—*So there you are, lass, and we're short of a lodger.*

Chris said she was sorry, she'd try and get another, and Ma said Och, not to worry about that, some creature would soon come taiking around. Chris thought the same, not heeding a lot, though it was a shame to lose Feet's fee. But he couldn't have bidden in the house at all after that tale that Ewan had told her—Ewan with a pale, cool angry face, stirred as she'd never seen him stirred.

She was thinking of that when the postman chapped, Ma Cleghorn went paiching out to the hall and silence followed till Ma cried up *A letter for you, Mrs. Robert Colquohoun.*

When Chris got down to the hall there she stood, turning the thing this way and that, all but tearing it open and reading, Chris nearly laughed, she was used to Ma. *It's from Segget,* Ma said, and Chris said *Is't now?* and took the thing and opened it and read, Ma giving a whistle and turning away and dighting with a duster at the grandfather clock, making on she was awful ta'en up with her work. And Chris read the long straggle of sloping letters and was suddenly smelling, green and keen, sawdust, sawn wood—queerly and suddenly homesick for Segget:

We've a new lodger coming on the Monday, Ma. A man that I used to know in Segget, Ake Ogilvie the joiner, he's gotten a job as a foreman up at the Provost's sawmills.

Chris started awake. The fog had re-thickened, blanketing Duncairn away from her sight as she stood here dreaming like a gowkèd bairn. Her hair felt damp with the pressing mist veils and the weight of the bag on her arm was as lead—funny this habit she aye had had of finding some place wherever she bade to which she could climb by her lone for a while and think of the days new-finished and done, like a packman halting hill on hill and staring back at the valleys behind. She minded how above the ploughed lands of Blawearie this habit had grown, long syne, long syne, when she'd laid and dreamed as a quean by the loch in the shadow of the marled Druid Stones, and how above Segget in the ruined Kaimes she had done the same as the wife of Robert. Robert: and Ake Ogilvie was coming from Segget with his long brown face and his rangy stride. How would he take with a place like Duncairn? How had he gotten the job with the Provost?

Autumn coming down there in the fog, down in the days you no more could glimpse than the shrouded roofs of Duncairn at this hour. . . . And Ewan—what was happening to Ewan? Once so cool and cold boy-clear, boy-clever, a queer lad you'd thought would never be touched by any wing of the fancies of men, grey granite down to the core—and now?

In the mirror she saw her face, dim in mist, and smiled at it with a kind dispassion. And what to herself?—just the trauchle of time, the old woman she'd believed herself at first in Duncairn—as she still did sometimes at moments of weariness—or that other quean that refused to die, that moved and looked and stole off her thoughts, and dreamed the daftest of old, lost dreams, blithe as though twenty, unkissed and uncuddled?

Well, time she went into those mists of the future. There was ten o'clock chapping from Thomson Tower.

II

SPHENE

As the day awoke great clouds had come out of the North Sea over Duncairn, with them the wind rose and rose, snarling at the gates of the dark, waiting to break through with the first peep of light. And now as that peep came glimmering, far off, beyond the edge of the Mounth, the storm loosed itself over the toun, sheeting down a frozen torrent of water. Sometimes the sleet was a ding-dong fall, and again the wind would whirl and lift, pitching great handfuls into your face though a minute before you had been in the lithe. The Windmill Steps were sheeted in slush, twice Chris slipped and nearly fell as she ran for the shelter of the mirror ledge, low below a first shrouded tram wheeled, moaning, and took the road to the Mile, the lights were going out one by one as the winter morning broke on Duncairn.

In the lithe of the mirror Chris stopped and panted and beat her frozen hands together, hatless still but muffled in a scarf to the ears for that last silly journey down to the doctor's. She'd finished with him, done everything proper, and now there was surely nothing else. And she felt—oh, she could sleep for a month—like a polar bear, with the sleet for a sheet——

Her hair faint-sprayed by the sleet that went by, not touching the rest of her, she raised her eyes and saw it,

half in the dark, half in the light, strange, a strange blind
glister and drift high in the lift, a bannered attack going by
in silence though you heard the shoom of the spears far
down. Stamping her feet to bring them to warmth, she
rested a minute, closed her eyes, yawned over-poweringly
and achingly, and ceased from that to stare sombre-eyed
down at the breaking of the sleet-hunted light. Whatever
next? Whatever next?

How could she had known that day in July when she
rested here and wondered on things that *this* would come,
that she'd stand here appalled, that she wouldn't know
which way to think or to move? Her mind shrank in a passion of pity a minute, strangely linked with a desire to
laugh. . . . And she shook herself, no time to stand here,
with the house above wakening and waiting her——

Oh, let it wait, let it rest awhile while she caught her
breath and tried to make out where she'd mislaid that
security hers and her own only a short six months before:

Long-mousered, green-eyed, with his ploughman's swagger, it had seemed to Chris six months before that Ake
Ogilvie's coming had brought to Duncairn something clean
and crude as the smell of rain—crude and clean as she
herself had been once before a playing at gentry enslaved
her, like turning round in a lane at night and meeting one's
own lost self and face, lost a long fifteen years before, smiling with cool and sardonic lips. Not that Ake had anything
very young about him, or old-like either, he was one of the
kind that seemed to stick to one age all their lives, swagger and pipe and clumping feet, met on the stairs as he
carried up his kist that Monday morning from the taxi
below.

Ay, Mrs. Colquohoun, you look bonny as ever. And
Chris said that was fine, but why was he carrying the kist?
The cabman would surely have given him a hand. And Ake
said he'd just had an argy with the billy and sent him off
with a flea in his lug, by God he'd wanted a whole half-
crown for bringing them up from the Central Station.

Chris said that was awful, cabmen were like that, but
Ake wouldn't be able to carry up the kist on his shoulder
further, the stairs drew in. So he lowered it down and syne
shook hands and looked her all over with his swagger green
glower. *Ay, you're fairly ta'en with Duncairn. D'you miss
the Manse?* Chris said *Not much. Shall I give you a hand?*

Ake looked a bit doubtful, he thought of her still as the wife of Robert in Segget, she saw, genteel and neat and fine and frail—she said *Come on!* and took hold of an end and Ake did the same, up they went to his room, made ready, and put down the kist in the corner for't. Syne Ake looked round and out at the roofs: *A hell of a place for a man to bide, the toun, though the room looks canty enough. You'll be gey busy here, no doubt then, mistress?*

Chris nearly cuddled him, calling her that, so long since a soul had called her mistress: *I've a lot to do, same as other folk. But we'll have a crack on Segget some time.— Ay, faith we will.* He had turned away, no frills or unnecessary politeness with him: *I'll be in to my tea, but not to my dinner. I've to gang up and see the Provost man.*

Chris said that she hoped he'd get on fine, and he said *No fear of that. Ta-ta.*

He made himself at home from the first, sitting arguing in the sitting-room with Mr. Neil Quaritch, thin, with his little tuft of a beard and his Douglas Scheme (that Ewan called the Bourgeois Funk-Fantasy), Ake beside him looking like a shorthorn bull taking up its spare time on a gossip with a goat. He looked over-real sometimes to Chris to be real as she'd meet him coming in at the door, slow and yet quick, throwing down his feet with a fine and measured stride, the earth's his, yielding the wall to none in Duncairn. And he'd clump up the stairs and into his room without a sideways look or a thought, he'd paid his fee and the room was his, would he creep up quiet for any damned body?

Chris never saw him at ease in his room. Rousing the first morning after he came she'd thought to make him a cup of tea and take it to him the same as to others. But while she was moving about with the cups and the kettle was singing and Jock the cat purring away for dear life by the range and the caller air of the August dawn coming up the Steps and into the house, she heard a pad of feet on the stairs, and there was Ake at the kitchen door, his mouser fresh-curled, in his waistcoat and breeks, no slippers, his kind never did have slippers Chris minded back to her farmhouse days: *Ay, mistress, I thought it would maybe be you. This'll be your kitchen place, no doubt.* Chris said it was— *Come in and sit down.*

And in he came and sat by the fire and gave the cat Jock a bit of a stroke, and sat and drank the tea that she poured him, not offering to help her as Quaritch would have done, Lord be here it was a woman's work, wasn't it now, who'd ever heard of a man who sossed with the cups? And Ake drank the tea through his curling moustache, and wiped that, and nodded *Ay, that's good brew. I think I'll taik down every morning for one.* Chris said *There's no need to do that, Mr. Ogilvie, I take up cups for the folk that want them.* And Ake said Oh to hell with that, he wasn't a cripple and could come for his own. Besides, he was used to getting up with the light and hadn't a fancy for stinking in bed. Chris thought *And suppose I've no fancy for you sitting about in my way in the kitchen?* But she didn't say it, just went on with her work, watched by Ake sitting smoking his pipe—Ay, God, she looked a bonny lass still, a bit over-small for her height, you would say, but a fine leg and hip, a warm bit quean. She'd fair set a-lowe and burned up Colquohoun in her time, you wouldn't but wonder; and maybe had never yet had a man to handle her as she needed handling.

So he got in the way of coming to the kitchen and sitting drinking his tea every morning, Ma Cleghorn heard and said to Chris that she'd better look out, for they weren't to be trusted, childes with curling mousers like yon. And then sighed: *Though, Lord, there's no need to warn you, I keep forgetting you're gentry yourself, a minister's widow, not for common folk.* Chris asked what Ma wanted her to do with him—or thought he was likely to do with her? And Ma said that if Chris couldn't guess about that there were other folk than the Virgin Mary had had their immaculate conceptions, faith.

Chris laughed and paid her but little heed, Ake as far (she knew) from such thoughts as herself, funny in a way to have him about, it wiped out the years, all the gentry in her, she was back in a farm kitchen again and the man sitting douce and drinking his tea and she getting ready the meat for him. . . . And Ake would give his bit mouser a curl and tell the latest take of the Provost.

Chris asked how he'd gotten the job and Ake said by the skin of the teeth and the will of the Lord, he'd been at school with the laddie Speight a thirty-five years or so back, they were both of them of Laurencekirk stock. Well, he'd been a gey dreich and ill-favoured loon, and Ake had ta'en him a punch now and then to kittle him up and mind him his manners. The result was he'd fair ta'en a liking to Ake

and would follow him about like a cat a fish-cadger, right
through their schooldays and a wee whilie after, when they'd
gotten long trousers and cuddled their bit queans. Syne
they'd tint one another, Ake had gone drifting south as a
joiner, to the feuching stink of the Glasgow yards, to that
windy devils' burrow, the capital, Edinburgh, syne drifted
up to the Howe again, he'd never felt much at home, as
you'd say, outside the cloud-reek and claik of the Howe.
And that was how he had come to Segget, not near so dead
in those times as now, the joiner's business with still enough
fettle to brink a man a bit meal and drink.

So he'd settle down there, as Mrs. Colquohoun knew, till
the place was fairly all to hell, with unemployment and all
the lave; and after her good man died and so on Ake fair
got sick of sitting about in his shed and looking for custom
to come, scribbling a wee bit of poetry the while, and
glowering up at the Trusta heuchs and wishing to Heavens
that something would happen.—And Chris said *Oh yes, I
mind your poetry. You still write it, do you?* and Ake said
*Ay. Bits. It would hardly interest you. Well, as I was say-
ing*—and went on to say that one day he was having a bit
look through the paper and what did he see there but that
young Jimmy Speight, him that he'd gone to school with
long syne, had been made the Lord Provost of Duncairn
toun.

At first Ake could hardly believe his own eyes, he'd
thought that talent must be fairly damn scarce to make
Wabbling Jimmy a Lord Provost, like. He'd heard about
him afore that, of course, how he'd been ta'en into his
uncle's business and heired when the old uncle wore away
a fine sawmill and a schlorich of silver. But he'd never
much bothered about the creature till he read this notice
of him being Provost.

Well, damn't, that fairly moved Ake a bit, if Wabbling
Jimmy was all that well off he'd surely scrounge up a job
for a body. So Ake locked up his place and put on his best
suit and got on the morning train for Duncairn, and took a
tram to the Provost's house, out in Craigneuks, a gey brave-
looking place with fal-lal ornaments forward and back and
a couple of towers stuck on for luck like warts on the nose
of Oliver Cromwell.

A servant lass came tripping and held the door open,
What name shall I say to the Provost, please? And Ake said
My name's Ake Ogilvie tell him, and ask him if he minds

*the time in Lourenkirk when I gey near drowned him in a
stone horse-trough.* Well, the lass went red and gave a bit
giggle, as a young quean will, and went off with the message, and into the room in a minute came Jimmy, gey
grand, but dreeping at the nose as ever. And damn't, he'd
come in fair cocky-like, but syne a funny thing happened
to him, it just showed you what happened when you were
a bairn—if you got a rattle in the lantern then you might
build a battleship in later life and explore the North Pole
and sleep with a Duchess, but you'd never forget the lad
that had clouted you, you'd meet him and feel a bit sick
in the wame though it was a good half-century later.

Well, something like that came on Wabbling Jimmy, he
dropped his politeness and his he-haw airs, and Ake took
his hand and cried out loud: *Ay, Jimmy lad, you're fair
landed here, with all these queans to see to your needs, at
door and table and no doubt in your bed.* And the Lord
Provost went as yellow's a neep: *Wheesht, Ake, wheesht,
the wife's on the prowl.* And Ake said he didn't know that
he'd married—*d'you mind what happened to Kate Duthie
long syne?* . . .

Now, that had been just a kind of blackmail, as Ake knew
right well, but didn't much care, in a minute poor Wabbling Jimmy was ready to offer him half his worldly
possessions if only Ake would keep quiet on the subject of
Kate. Ake said that he was on the look for a job, what
about this sawmill that Jimmy owned? And Jimmy said he
seldom interfered, he'd a manager, and Ake said he hardly
wanted *his* job, though he'd tackle a foreman's he'd manage
that fine. So Jimmy in a stew howked out his car and in
they got and drove to the Kirrie, a fine sawmill, and they
weren't there long afore the manager came over to ask if
Jimmy had yet ta'en on a new foreman in place of a childe
that had gotten the sack. And at that what could poor
Jimmy do but go a bit blue about the neb and say, *Ay, I
have; and this is him.*

So that's how he'd collared the Duncairn job, not that
he was over-keen on the thing, *D'you ken now, mistress,
what I've aye wanted?—Losh, a job on a ship at sea, the
fine smell and the pelt of the water below you, there's fine
carpentering work to be done on ships.* And Chris, with
the teacups cold on the tray, said she thought it a shame
he'd never got it, maybe he'd get a job like that yet. Ake
nodded, fegs, and he might, not likely, better to bang on

the Provost's tail, old Wabbling Jimmy that was feared at his past. *Not that poor Jimmy's an exception in that: We're all on leading strings out of the past.*

For days you couldn't forget that scream, tingling, terrified, the lost keelie's scream as that swine Sim Leslie smashed him down. Again and again you'd start awake, sweating, remembering that from a dream, Duncairn sleeping down Windmill Steps, all the house in sleep, quiet next door, that kid Ellen Johns not dreaming at all. Luck for her and her blah about history and Socialism: she hadn't a glimpse of what either meant. . . .

Oh, sick of the whole damn idiot mess, drifting about nowadays like a fool, couldn't settle to anything, couldn't read a book, caught in the net of this idiot rubbish. Your head had softened like a swede in the rain ever to be taken in with the rot—rot about leading new life to the workers, moulding them into History's new tool, apprehending a force more sure and certain than the God poor Robert had preached in Segget. . . . In the workers?—Rats, what was there in them that wasn't in the people of any class? Some louts, some decent, the most of them brainless, what certain tool to be found in crude dirt? You'd dug deep enough to make sure of that, playing the game as a keelie yourself, fraternising with the fauna down at the Works—hell, how they stank, the unscrubbed lot, with their idiot ape-maunderings and idiot hopes, their idiot boasts, poor dirty devils. They took you for one of themselves nowadays, so you'd almost become as half-witted as they.

Finished with it all quite definitely now. What have the keelies to do with you—except to make you feel sick? They don't like the same things, haven't the same interests, don't care a hang for the books you read (mislaid those textbooks this last week somewhere). And you pretending an interest in horses—dog-racing—football—all the silly kid-games that excite the keelies—find History's beat in their drivelling blah!

. . . That ghastly house that Bob took you to—father unemployed for over five years, mother all running to a pale grey fat like a thing you found when you turned up a stone, one of the brothers a cretin, rickets—sat giggling and slavering in a half-dark corner, they couldn't afford to have the gas on, a dead smell of dirt left unstirred and unscrubbed, disharmonic heads and moron brains; and outside the house as you came away: streets on streets, the fug of the Cowgate, keelies on the lounge in the gutter, in the dirt, their ghastly voices and their ghastly faces——

They DON'T concern you. BREAK with it all.

So when Alick and Norman that Saturday asked if you were coming to the Beach Pavilion, Snellie Guff the Scotch Comedian was On, you said *No, sorry, I've reading to do,* and saw their faces fall, damn them, they'd just have to learn as you had to learn. But when you got home and had finished dinner and been caught by that ghastly old bore Ake Ogilvie who thought himself God's regent on earth because Christ had been of the same trade as himself, and heard his lout swagger on this and that, you felt too restless to rout out the books. Damn nuisance, August blazing outside, birds high up in the Howe to-day, a bus would take you to Segget in an hour. . . . If only it could take you back over a year!

And you thought of the times when you'd haunted the Howe, as a schoolboy, seeking the old-time flints, Neolithic stuff, passable collection: you'd forgotten it since you'd come to Duncairn. Where could it be?

And in the chase of that you went down to the kitchen and knocked and looked in, Chris and Ma Cleghorn and Meg the maid, they all looked up and said *I'm sorry. Chris, d'you mind where my flints went to?*

Chris said she thought you had finished with them, they were up in the box-room under the eaves. Ma called as you turned away *Ewan man, why aren't you out at a game this weather? Or out with a lass?—that'd be more your age than bothering about with a rickle of stones. Your mother showed me them and I thought 'What dirt!'*

You said *Oh, really?* funny old hag, another keelie trying to keep you in the gutter—games and street-crawling and their blasted girls. Her face fell a bit when you spoke like that, the old fool should heed to her own damned business. Chris looked at you with her nice, cool eyes, a long time since you'd kissed her, she had a nice kiss. Then you went up the stairs to your flints.

They were thick with dust, lying higgledy-piddledy in the press, tortoise-cores and a scraper or so, you took them out and turned them about, and saw the watery lines of the knapping done long ago in the hills of the Howe, some day three thousand years before. Some careful craftsman had squatted to knapp, with careful knee and finger and eye,

looking up now and then from his work on the flakes to
see the grey glister of the Howe below, the long lake that
covered the Low Mearns then, with sailing shapes of is-
lands upon it, smoke of fires rising slow in the air from the
squatting-places of the Simple Men, deer belling far on the
hills as the sun swung over to the hazes of the afternoon,
things plain and clear to anyone then—you supposed: was
that no more than supposing?

But at least they had made the things they desired, finely
and surely and lovely as these, long long ago. Still, things
no lovelier than the shining giants that whirred and spun
in Gowans and Gloag's, power-dreams fulfilled of the flint-
knapping men. . . . And at that the little warmth they had
brought you quite went, you were staring down at a dusty
stone, chipped by someone no shape at all, a dim shadow
on dust, meaning nothing, saying nothing: and down there
in the heat of this August day the festering wynds of Paldy
Parish——

You closed the press and went down the stairs, out of
the house, down Windmill Brae, idiot-angry to escape your
soft self. Turning up to Royal Mile you went slower, wondering what you could do at this hour. A thin little gallop
of Autumn rain came pelting down the street as you wondered, and you looked up and saw the Library near and
beside it the Museum Galleries.

Inside there, breathing from running from the rain you
debated a minute to stay or go out, the place as usual dingy
and desolate, old chap in uniform yawning at a table. Then
you went past him into the hall and stood and looked at
the statues around, poor stuff the most of it, you'd seen it
before.

Plaster-cast stuff of the Greek antiques, Discobolus, blow-
sily mammalian Venus, Pallas Athene—rather a dirty lot
they had been, the Greeks, though so many clean things
survived. Why did they never immortalize in stone a scene
from the Athenian justice-courts—a slave being ritually,
unnecessarily tortured before he could legally act as a
witness? Or a baby exposed to die in a jar?—hundreds every
year in the streets of Athens, it went on all day, the little
kids wailing and crying and crying as the hot sun rose and
they scorched in the jars; and then their mouths dried up,
they just weeked and whimpered, they generally died by
dark.

There was a cast of Trajan, good head; Cæsar—the

Cæsar they said wasn't Cæsar. Why not a head of Spartacus? Or a plaque of the dripping line of crosses that manned
the Appian Way with slaves—dripping and falling to bits
through long months, they took days to die, torn by wild
beasts. Or a statuary group of a Roman slave being fed to
fishes, alive in a pool. . . .

You turned and went up the deserted stairs to the picture
galleries, dusty and dim, drowsily undisturbed but for one
room you passed where a keelie was cuddling a girl on the
sly, sitting on a bench, they giggled a bit, dried up as you
looked and stared and stared. You looked away and about
the room, flat seascapes and landscapes, the deadest stuff,
why did people make a fuss of pictures. Or music? You'd
never seen anything in either. You went and sat down
in the Italian room, on the bench in the middle, and stared
at a picture, couldn't be bothered to find out the painter,
group of Renaissance people somewhere: soldiers, a car-
dinal, an angel or so, and a throng of keelies cheering like
hell about nothing at all—in the background, as usual. Why
not a more typical Italian scene!—a man being broken on
the wheel with a club, mashed and smashed till his chest
caved in, till his bones were a blood-clottered powdery
mess?——

Passed in a minute, that flaring savage sickness, and you
got to your feet and went on again: but the same everywhere, as though suddenly unblinded, picture on picture
limned in dried blood, never painted or hung in any gal-
lery—pictures of the poor folk since history began, be-
devilled and murdered, trodden underfoot, trodden down
in the bree, a human slime, hungered, unfed, with their
darkened brains, their silly revenges, their infantile hopes—
the men who built Münster's City of God and were hanged
and burned in scores by the Church, the Spartacists, the
blacks of Toussaint L'Ouverture, Parker's sailors who were
hanged at the Nore, the Broo men man-handled in Royal
Mile. Pictures unceasing of the men of your kin, peasants
and slaves and common folk and their ghastly lives through
six thousand years—oh, hell, what had it to do with you?

And you bit your lip to keep something back, something
that rose and slew coolness and judgment—steady, white-
edged, a rising flame, anger bright as a clear bright flame,
as though 'twas yourself that history had tortured, trodden
on, spat on, clubbed down in you, as though you were
every scream and each wound, flesh of your flesh, blood of

your blood. . . . And you gave a queer sob that startled
yourself: Something was happening to you: God—what?

Ma said, coming down to Chris in the kitchen after collecting the lodgers' fees, she went round each room of a
Sabbath morning before the breakfast time or the kirk:
*The Murgatroyd creature's fair in a stew, her dividends
are all going down she says and she hardly knows how
she'll Pay her Way. She's a bittie of a shareholder in
Gowans and Gloag's and there's not a cent from the firm
this year. Aren't they brutes to mistreat a respectable woman?*

Chris asked if that meant that she'd have to leave, and
Ma shook her head, Oh no, not her, she'd a bit of a pension as well as an income, a three hundred pounds a year
from a trust. Chris stared: *Then what's coming over her?*
and Ma sighed that Chris didn't understand and hadn't a
proper sympathy, like, with financial straits of wealthy
folk—like herself and their wee Miss Murgatroyd. What
the old bitch really wanted of course was her runkled old
bottom kicked a bit and turned out into the streets for a
night hawking herself at a tanner a time. . . .

And Ma sat down and paiched a bit, smoothing out the
pounds and the ten bob notes, and said that Mr. Piddle was
short again, him that banked every meck that he got. Ma'd
told him she'd need the balance on Monday—and not to
he-he! at her like a goat. *Four, five, two halves, a one and
ten silver, that's our little bit English pussy-cat. Sitting up
there and reading a book—can you guess what the book is
about now, lass?*

Chris looked in the range and over at the clock, and
shook her head, only half-heeding Ma's claik—*Well, then,
it's a Manual of Birth Control. What think you of that and
our Ellen Johns, with her little mouser and her neat long
legs?*

Chris was over-surprised a minute to say anything, then
asked if Miss Johns tried to hide the book? Ma said she
hadn't, neither showing off nor hiding: *Ay, a gey keep our
Ellen, with all her quiet ways. And it's all to the good of
the trade, anyhow.* Chris asked *How?* and Ma said *Why,
she'll be able to sin as she likes and go free, with no need
to marry the gallus childe. So we'll be able to keep her our
lodger. . . . Twelve, thirteen, ten, Ake Ogilvie—ay, faith
he's made of the old-time stuff. If I'd been a ten years*

younger or so I'd be chumming up to him, a bonny man,
well-shouldered and canty, it's a pity you're gentry.

Chris had heard this before and now hardly smiled, if
it was gentry to know her own mind, the things that she
liked and the things that she didn't, well then, she was gentry
down to the core. And Ma had been watching her and cried
out *Hoots, now don't go away and take offence. I'm just
a coarse old wife and must have my bit joke.* Chris laughed,
half-angry, *Well, don't have it on me,* and Ma said she'd
mind and went on with her counting, Miss Lyon's Boss had
fined her two shillings. Awful the way that they treat Us
Girls, the Clearmont laddie was all a-blither and a-clatter
over his Rectorial election, fegs, what was this Nationalist
stite that had got him?

Chris minded back to her days in Segget and said that
this Nationalism was just another plan of the Tories to do
down the common folk. Only this time 'twas to be done in
kilts and hose, with bagpipes playing and a blether about
Wallace, the English to be chased across the Border and the
Scots to live on brose and baps. Ma said *Fegs now, and are
we so, then? Then I'm for the English. Eighteen, nine and
six, the lot for this week, and we're doing fine. Did I ever
tell you when I wanted a partner my niece Izey Urquhart
wanted to come in?*

Chris said she didn't know Ma had a niece, Ma nodded,
worse luck, a thrawn wee skunk that lived away down in
Kirrieben. Ma couldn't stick the creature at all but she was
her only living relation and kenned that when Ma pushed
off at last she'd get what bittie of silver there was; That
might be so, but Ma had made up her mind she wasn't to
have the long-nosed sniftering wretch skeetering around
while she was alive; and maybe when Ma died holy Izey
would find a bit of a sore surprise to meet—*I'm fond of
you, lass, and I'm sending next week for my lawyer man
to alter the will. What's in the house and all things I have
would be better in your bit keeping, I think, than as miser's
savings in Kirrieben.*

Chris said sensibly that Ma shouldn't be silly, it was likely that she would outlive them all. And Ma said she hoped
to Heaven that she wouldn't, if there was anything that
cumbered the earth it was some old runkle of a woman
body living on with no man to tend and no bairns, a woman
stopped living when she stopped having bairns. And Chris
laughed at that and said *What about men?* and Ma said

*Och, damn't, they never live at all. They're just a squeeze
and a cuddle we need to keep our lives going, they're nothing themselves.*

And Chris went out in the Sunday quiet to the little
patch of garden behind and worked there tending the beds
of flowers she'd put in early in blinks of the Spring, sooty
and loamy and soft the ground, clouds were flying high in
the lift beyond the tilting roofs of Duncairn, the hedge by
the house next door was a-rustle, soft green, with its bud-
ding beech, far off through the hedges some eident body
was at work with a lawn-mower, *clinkle-clankle,* a bairn was
wailing in a bairn's unease as Chris dug and raked, watered
the flowers, pale things hers compared with Segget's.

And somehow Ma's daft words bade in her mind, those
about a woman having finished with things when she
finished having bairns, just an empty drum, an old fruit
squeezed and rotting away, useless, unkenned, unstirred by
the agonies of bearing a bairn, heeding it, feeding it, watching it grow—was she now no more than that herself?—a
woman on the verge of middle age content to trauchle the
hours in a kitchen and come out and potter with weeds and
flowers, all the passion of living put by long ago, wonder
and terror and the tang of long kisses, embracing knee to
knee, the blood in a stream of fire through the heart, the
beat and drum of that tide of life that once poured so swift
in those moments unheard—never to be heard again, grown
old.

And, kneeling, she stared in woe at the fork in her hand,
at the prickly roses that leaned their pale, quiet faces down
from the fence: well, was she to greet about that? She had
had her time, and now it was ended, she'd to follow the
road that others took, into long wrinkles and greying hair
and sourness and seats by the chimney-corner and a drowsy
mumble as she heard the rain going by on its business in a
closing dark. Finished: when her heart could still move to
that singing, when at night in her bed she would turn in
unease, wakeful, sweet as she knew herself, men had liked
her well long ago, still the same body and still the same
skin, that dimple still holding its secret place—Och, Ma
would say that she wanted a man, that was all about it,
as blunt and coarse as a farmer childe that watched his cattle in the heats of a Spring.

But there was more to it than that, some never knew it,
but real enough, an antrin magic that bound you in one

with the mind, not only the body of a man, with his dreams
and desires, his loves, even hates—hate of Ewan, a wild
boy's hate, passionless coldness of Robert in shadow, they'd
given you hate with their love often enough, tears, with
such white tenderness as even now you might not unfold in
memory,—here, at this moment, kneeling here, still, the
August sun on your hair, dreaming and dreaming because
Ma Cleghorn had blithered on the curse of a woman growing old, because you had heard a baby nearby wailing soft
in a baby's unease!

And, suddenly remorseful at her terrible sweirty, she bent
and dug and smoothed out the earth, raked it again to a
loamy smoothness around the wide feet of the Michaelmas
daisies, they looked a bit like Sim Leslie the bobby. Babies?
(said her mind, though she tried to still it)—hadn't she had
Ewan, perfect enough, grown up though he was, distant
and cool? And wasn't he fine enough to have made with
a little help from his father long syne? And she minded
that other baby who had died in the days of the General
Strike, he came oversoon that night she ran to warn the
strikers who were out by the railway to blow up Segget
High Brig. Oh, long since she'd minded that baby at all, the
baby Michael, she'd never seen him, he'd died within an
hour of his birth, killing something in Robert as he died,
killing the last of the quean in herself she had thought
through the long drowse of years in Segget, my bairn, the
lost baby who might have been mine——

She heard light footsteps hesitating on the path and shook
the mist from her eyes a minute before she looked up to
see who it was, Ellen Johns, slim, sweet in a summer frock,
a blue cloud her hair in the August day, soft dark down
on her lip, blue eyes like pansies, dark and wet, looking at
Chris queer, half-poised like a bird to turn about and fly
off.

I'm sorry, Mrs. Colquohoun, I didn't know——

Chris said *That I was weeping a bit? Old women often
have a weep, you know. Coming to help, or only to watch?*

Ellen said *I'll help* and squatted on long, pointed shoe-
heels and began to weed with long, pointed fingers—*I was
sick of sitting indoors and reading.*

Chris minded the book that Ma had seen and looked at
her with a little smile: *You were reading something about
Birth Control?*

And she didn't blush and didn't look up, just went on

with the weeding, quick and calm, intent, and nodded: *Yes, I suppose I'll need it some time. Can't find out much and it sounds a mess, but it's a thing that's got to be learnt. Don't you think so?* and Chris nearly laughed, but didn't, *Yes, I think it has. But you'll want a baby sometime?*

Ellen shook her head and said she didn't suppose so. There were thousands of unwanted babies already and most of *them* should never have been born. . . . *Can I have the fork to have a go at those weeds?*

Thank Creeping Jay for the change at last, the six of you turfed out of Furnaces, three to Stores and two to Machines, Alick and Norman the lucky devils, they would be, they gave more lip to old Dallas, they two, than any half a dozen in the whole of Gowans and Gloag's: and he seemed to like them the better for't!

Not that Stores was bad, a fine change from the Furnace, your own bench and lists and pigeon-holes, rows on rows of the tools and castings, burns of stuff to unload for the Shops, finished with being a damn kid in the Works, though the older ones that had been there awhile looked gey glum when you got your shift. And they'd something to look glum about, poor muckers, for afore the change had been a week over there were six of the older hands got the sack, on to the Broo, och, hell, you couldn't help it. It was just the way that things were run.

Ewan Tavendale had been moved to the manager's office, blue-printing, they liked his prints in the shops, a clever young Bulgar as you'd found out in Furnaces. You didn't see much of him the first week or so, but syne he came into the Stores one morning and started talking to the foreman chap, wee Eddie Grant, he listened awhile and said *Ach to hell, I'll have nothing to do with it. Look out yourself, you'll be getting in the dirt.* But Ewan, he looked fairly the toff again, clean hands and suit, hair trig and neat, just nodded, *All right, if you feel like that. But maybe it'll be your turn next for the sack.* Wee Eddie burbled *Me? What the hell! And who's to take MY place I'd like to know? Another of you whoreson apprentices?* and Ewan said nothing, just nodded to you, *Hello, Bob!* and walked out, what the hell was he up to now?

Well, it was soon all over the works what it was, he was trying to stir up the Union men to threaten a strike if Gowans and Gloag carried on with the plan they'd had year in, year out—taking on apprentices and sacking the old ones, they saved a fair sum on the weekly wage.

You knew it was Ewan had started the thing, everybody knew, and the story came down to the Stores that the manager had had him on the carpet for't, Ewan hadn't denied it and the manager had asked if he knew what would happen to him, stirring up trouble? And Ewan had said Oh, yes, he knew well, he'd be sacked when his apprenticeship was done. And the manager had roared *Well then, less of it. You've had your warning, you won't get another*. And Ewan had said *Yes, thanks, I've been warned*.

There was nothing else for a chap to say, the Union wouldn't move a foot in the business, it was crammed with Broo folk to the lid already; and the stour died down; and the gleyed Stores mucker who had sneered afore at Ewan as gentry said *What do you think of your toff now?* and you said *He'd the guts to try something, anyhow, more than a sheep like you ever would*.

Then Norman came round in the dinner hour with a funny like story you could hardly believe, he said that Ewan'd ta'en up with the Reds, Jim Trease and his crowd, and was going to their meetings. And you said *Away; he's not so daft*, and Norman said *Ay, hell, but he is. What's the use of the Reds to any body? They just get out the Broo men and march down the Mile and get their heads bashed in in the end*. Well, surely Ewan knew that as well; why was he taking up with them, then? Norman said he was damned if he knew, some rubbish about all working parties co-operating, Ewan had asked him to go to a meeting but he'd said he wouldn't, he wasn't so soft, he'd a quean to take out on a Sunday, him, not mess about with a lot of Reds who were just damned traitors to the Labour Movement. Not that *it* was worth a damn either. As for Alick, he'd gone skite, same as Ewan, anything Ewan said went down with *him*.

Well, hell, that was coarse enough to hear, but whatever made Ewan take up with the Reds? Him a gentleman, too, as you all knew he was though he tried to deny it and that time at your home when he came to tea had acted so fine, you'd all of you liked him, it had been nearly worth spending the day before scrubbing out the place, and hiding the twin, the daftie, and getting in cakes for the tea. So you went now and looked him up in the office, making on you wanted a chit for some tools, he was sitting at his desk among the office muckers, all with their patted hair and posh ties, young college boys no better than you though they tried on their airs if you didn't watch.

Ewan cried *Hello, Bob!* and you said *Hello,* and *Ewan, I'd like to speak to you sometime.* And he said *Right, let's get out a minute,* and out he came and you asked him point-blank. And he said *I didn't know you'd be interested,* and you said *Hell, I'm not,* and he said *Yes, you are. Look here, come along to the Saturday meeting, in the Gallowgate, 3 Picarles Wynd.* And afore you well kenned what it was you had done you'd promised to be there—oh, damn the whole business!

But there you were at the chapp of seven, a little bit room with maybe twenty in't, chaps and some queans all much of your age, chairs and a table and a chair for the chairman and a picture of a chap above the table that had cheated the barber from birth by his look, that awful coarse old billy Marx.

Then Ewan came along and made you sit down, and went back to the table to sit by a lassie, a stuck-up bitch with black hair, fine legs, she'd a pen and a lot of paper afore her. And there was a piano up in the corner with a lad sitting at it, and he started to play and you all got up and sang about England arising, the long, long night was over, though the damn thing had barely yet set in, God, what a perfect fool you felt not knowing the words, a quean next you pushed a book in your hands, smirked at you, trying to get off, would you say? So you made on to sing, glowering about, there was Alick Watson, bawling like a bellows, if England didn't awake she must be stone deaf, and another chap you'd seen down in Gowans, an older apprentice out of Machines. Syne the singing stopped and down you all sat, and Ewan looked at the stuck-up get and said *Miss Johns will now read the minutes.*

It was only as the quean was doing that that you knew she was English, Haw-Haw-Really-Quite, and found out what the blasted meeting was about, Ewan and some others were getting up a party for the young in Duncairn, neither Labour nor Communist nor yet in opposition, but to try and keep the two of them working in harness for the general good of the working class, get rid of the cowardice and sloth of Labour and cut out the nonsensical lying of the Communists, the older generation in the workers' parties had made an idiot mess of things, it was up to the young

to straighten things out, join this new workers' league in
Duncairn. You said to yourself you'd be damned if you
would, hell, they'd have you out with a banner next.

But then Ewan stood up and started to speak, quiet, not
bawling blue hell like the Reds or cracking soft jokes like
a Labour man, but just in an ordinary voice and way, telling what he thought this young league could do to waken
up all the young workers in Duncairn, get strong enough
till the time might come when it would take over Duncairn
itself. First, the membership: they'd twenty or less, what
they'd now to discuss was a big drive for members: *Six
minute speeches, not a minute more, and practical sugges-
tions, not oratory, please.*

A red-headed kid of a quean got up, near gave you a
fit with what she wanted done—the whole lot go out and
march down the Mile with flags and collecting boxes, just,
and hold a meeting in the Castlegate. That was the way to
win new members and serve the workers. . . . And you
thought she was daft, had she never seen a worker? The
Bulgars would laugh and tell her what she wanted was
some chap to serve her in another way. Then the lad from
Gowans and Gloag's got up and said what they should do
was smuggle a lot of leaflets inside the Shops, and pass
them round quiet, you'd get interest that way. And the
quean who had given you the glad eye like a Garbo got up
and said in a he-haw voice, hell, another of the bloody
toffs, *What's wanted is to advertise the meetings and then
hold readings from the great revolutionary poets, beginning
with the greatest of all, William Morris.* And after that
everybody was over-stunned to say more, except young
Ewan, who'd been staring at the roof.

He got up and said it wasn't much use marching down
the Mile, they'd only get their heads smashed in by the
bobbies. Leaflets in the factories wouldn't help much, no
body read leaflets, there were too many about. And the
comrade who had suggested reading William Morris had
surely meant the Dundee *Sunday Post.* . . . What was
needed was something light and attractive.

And at that the English quean beside him, ay, a nice leg,
got up and said what they wanted was a tanner hop—she
said just that, fair vulgar-like, though you'd heard by now
that she was a school-ma'am. She said that would bring in
members thick and the dances would pay for themselves
twice over.

Ewan asked if he'd put that as a resolution? And the school-teacher said *Yes,* and Ewan put it, and you heard yourself saying *I second that,* your ears near burning off your head with shame, Creeping Jay, you were in for it now. And only as you were coming away from the meeting did it dawn on you with a hell of a shock that now you were some kind of ruddy Red.

Ellen waited for Ewan to lock up the room, the air was a stagnant unstirred pool, out by the Crossgate the autumn night lay low in pale saffron over Footforthie. As they turned from the door they could see far down through the winding corridors of the Gallowgate the smoulder of the sun as it lost itself in the smoking lowe of Footforthie by night. Ewan said there was night-work again at the shipyards, even Gowans and Gloag's were looking up a bit, didn't look much, did it, like capitalism's collapse?

They were trudging together up through the streets, half-lighted, smell of urine and old food seeping out from dark doorways, sometimes a grunt as a man would turn in his sleep in the heat, sometimes a snuffle of wakeful children. Ellen said nothing for a little while and Ewan had half-forgotten her when she asked of a sudden: *Are you losing heart?*

He said *Eh?* and then *Oh, about capitalism? Losing heart would do a lot of good, wouldn't it?*

She said then something, queer kid, he was to remember: *Anyhow, your heart's not in it at all. Only your head and imagination.*

—And I'm not in much danger of losing either. You don't quarrel with History and its pace of change any more than you quarrel with the law of gravitation. History's instruments, the workers, 'll turn to us some time—even though it's only for a sixpenny hop. You or I to see to hiring the hall?

Ellen said she thought it had better be him, the only one suitable was the Lower School, and they didn't trust her too much there already. And Ewan looked at her, pale kid, tired kid, and felt an indifferent touch of compassion. Where else might she be if it wasn't for this belief she'd smitten on him?—at a dance, at the pictures, in a pretty dress. And he dropped the thought, with indifference again. Much better as she was, seeing she wasn't half-witted.

They were into the Lower Cowgate by then, ten o'clock

and the pubs were spewing out the plebs, raddled with drink, kids crying in the gutter, Ewan saw a man hit a woman in the jaw, she fell with a scream and a bobby came up and an eddy of the crowd came swirling around, and they couldn't see more, going up Sowans Lane. But half-way up they came on a woman pulling at the coat of a man who was lying half in a doorway, half in the gutter. *Och, come on home, you daft Bulgar,* she was saying, *or the bobbies'll damn soon land you in the nick.* But the childe wasn't keen to go home at all, he was saying what they wanted was a little song—*Come on, you bitch, and give's a bit tune.* And the woman said of all the whoreson's gets she'd ever met he was the worst: and what song did he want then, the neep-headed nout? And he said he wanted the songs his mucking mother sang, and Ewan and Ellen didn't hear more, they were out of the Sowans Lane by then, on to the Long Brig where it spanned the Forthie, and stopping to breathe from the Gallowgate fug.

And then, as Ewan stood there and whistled underbreath, indifferently, far away in his thoughts, he became aware of Ellen Johns by his side wiping her eyes in helpless mirth: *History's the funniest of jokes sometimes. If we'd had the courage of our convictions do you know what we would have done back there?*

He said *No,* and stared a cool surprise.

—*Why, STOPPED AND SANG HIM SOME WILLIAM MORRIS!*

Ma Cleghorn had taken Chris to the Talkies, to get out of the stew of the house for a while, she said she was turning to a cockroach, near, and Chris to an earthworm out in that yard. Meg would see to the tea for the folk, wouldn't she, eh? and Meg said she would, Meg had kittled up a lot of late, Chris thought as she went to her room to change. When she came down Ma was waiting for her, dressed all in her braws with a big black hat, with beadwork upon it, and a meikle brooch pinned in under one of her chins. *There you are, lass, though, God be here, you're wearing so little I can see your drawers.* And Chris said *Surely not,* and stooped to see. *Anyhow, I can't wear more than I'm wearing.* And Ma said maybe but it was a damned shame to go about with a figure like that, half-happed and stirring the men to temptation. And they'd better get on, near the time already, what in Auld Nick's name were they gossiping for?

So they got on the tram and soughed down Royal Mile, and up Little James Street to the Picturedrome; and paid for their seats and went in and sat down; and Chris felt sleepy almost as soon as she sat, and yawned, pictures wearied her nearly to death, the flickering shadows and the awful voices, the daft tales they told and the dafter news. She fell asleep through the cantrips a creature was playing, a mouse dressed up in breeks like a man, and only woke up as Ma shook her: *Hey, the meikle film's starting now, lassie, God damn't, d'you want to waste a whole ninepenny ticket?*

So Chris had to stay awake and see that, all about a lassie who worked in New York and was awful poor but awful respectable, though she seemed to live in a place like a palace with a bath ten feet in length and three deep, and wore underclothes that she couldn't have afforded, some childe had paid for them on the sly. But the picture said No, through its nose, not her, she was awful chaste but sore chased as well, a beast of a man in her office, the manager, galloping about the screen and aye wanting to seduce the lassie by night or by day. And instead of letting him and getting it over or taking him a crack in the jaw and leaving, she kept coming home in tears to the bath, and taking off her underthings one by one, but hiding her breasts and her bottom, fair chaste.

Syne she met with a man that managed a theatre, though he looked from his face as though he managed a piggery and had been born in one and promoted for merit, a flat cold slob of a ham of a face with little eyes twinkling in the slob like currants, he was the hero and awful brave, and he took the lass to the theatre and made her sing that the skies were black and she was blue, and something that rhymed with that, not spew, and all the theatre audiences went wild not with rage, but joy, they'd been dropped on their heads when young: and the lassie became a famous actress and the film did a sudden close-up of her face with a tear of gratitude two feet long trembling like a jelly from her lower eyelid.

And then she and the slob were getting on fine, all black and blue, my lovely Lu, when along came the leader of a birn of brutes, a gang, and kidnapped the lass, grinding his teeth in an awful stamash to begin at last, and Chris was just thinking it fairly was time, would they never get the job over and done?—when in rushed the hero and a fight began and chairs were smashed and vases and noses, and the lass crouched down with her cami-knicks showing but respectable still, she wouldn't yield an inch to anything short of a marriage licence. And that she got in the end, all fine, with showers of flowers and the man with the face like a mislaid ham cuddling her up with a kiss that looked as though he was eating his supper when the thing came banging to an end at last.

Ma said Lord be here, now wasn't that fine? It must be a right canty place, this New York, childes charging about like bulls in a park trying to grab any lass they saw—even though the creatures were all bone and no breast and would give a man as much joy in bed as a kipper out of an ice-box, you'd think. Ay, she'd fair made a mistake a twenty years back when she stopped her Jim emigrating, faith. He'd been keen as anything on going to America, a man had loaned him a bit of a book about Presidents being just plain working folk, born in cabins and the queerest places; and maybe Jim thought that he had a chance, he'd been born next door to a cabin, near, his mother was bairned on the trawler *Jess*. But Ma'd put him off, like a meikle fool, to think she might now have been out in New York with big Jews chasing her in motor-cars and offering to buy her her undies free. . . . And Lord, the bit show was over, it seemed.

But she wouldn't have it that they should go home, they'd have tea at Woolworth's in the Royal Mile. And in they went in the Saturday crush, full of soldiers and bairns and queans, folk from the country, red and respectable, an eident wife with a big shopping bag buying up sixpenny tins of plums and her goodman standing beside her ashamed, feared he'd be seen by a crony in Woolies, and she'd be telling him, *Look, Willy, such cheap! Mighty, I'll need a pound of that;* and buy and buy till he'd near be ruined.

And hungry Broo folk buying up biscuits, and queans with their jingling bags and paint, poor things, trying on the tin bits of rings, and mechanic loons at the wireless counter, and the Lord alone knew who wasn't in Woolies, a roaring trade and a stink to match, Ma fought her way through the crush like a trawler taking the tide from Foot-forthie and Chris followed behind and felt sorry for a man

who'd left his feet where Ma's came down, he cried *Hey,
you?* and Ma said *Ay? Anything to say?* and he said *Ay,
I have. Who do you think you are—Mussolini?* And Ma
cried over her shoulder *Faith, I could wear his breeks and
not feel ashamed. You never had a thing under yours, you
runt.*

So up at last, sitting down in the tea-room, Ma ordering
eggs and scones and pancakes and butter and honey in little
jars, Chris gasped. *But whatever's all the feast for?* Ma said
Och, she was sick of cooking herself, and the sight of those
feeds that they had in America fairly stirred up a body's
stomach. Losh, wasn't it fine to think of the lodgers sossing
on their own?—*though your Ewan and our Ellen, the sleek
wee cat, are out again together the day. Would you think
the two of them are getting off?*

Chris said not them, they had just gone Socialist as young
folk would, some plan they had to link up the Labour folk
with the Reds. Ma nearly choked on a mouthful of egg,
Lord be here, whatever did they want to do that for? Chris
said for good—or so the two thought, and Ma said they'd
think mighty different soon, the Reds were just awful, look
what they did in Russia to that poor Tsar creature back in
the War—shot him down in a cellar full of coal, and buried
the childe without as much as God bless you. Chris said
she didn't know anything about it though it sounded as
though it maybe messed up the coals, as far as she knew
neither Ellen nor Ewan had yet shot anybody, even in a
cellar. Ma said No, but she wouldn't trust Ewan, a fine loon,
but that daft-like glower in his eyes—*Och, this Communism
stuff's not canny, I tell you, it's just a religion though the
Reds say it's not and make out that they don't believe in
God. They're dafter about Him than the Salvationists are,
and once it gets under a body's skin he'll claw at the itch
till he's tirred himself.*

Chris said she supposed she thought the same, had always
thought so, but that didn't matter, if Ewan wanted God she
wouldn't try and stop him; there was plenty of mess to redd
up in the world on the road to where He was maybe to be
found. Ma said she didn't believe there was, this daft Red
religion was maybe needed in places where there was a lot
of corruption, coarse kings that ran away with folks' silver
and prime ministers just drunken sots. But where would you
find the like in Duncairn? . . . *Now, don't start on me, we'll
just away home. Eh me, to think of those New York childes*

*tearing after the women like you! Where would you see the
like in Duncairn?*

With one thing and another it was late that night afore
Chris went up the stairs to her bed, Ewan had looked
round the kitchen door and cried good night a good hour
before, Ma had gone off to dream of New York, the rest
of the lodgers were sound in their beds. And Chris was taking off her clothes, slow, tired to death with the evening's
outing—why did folk waste their time in touns, in filth and
stour and looking at shadows when they might have slipped
away up the Howe and smelt the smell of the harvest—oh!
bonny lying somewhere on a night like this! . . . And just
as she sat and thought of that, not sad but tired, she heard
a commotion above her head, the clatter of footsteps, and
syne a door bang, a woman's voice—for a minute she was
back in the Picturedrome, watching and hearing that shad-
ow-play that was never limned in a toun like Duncairn—
And then as a bigger stamash broke out she opened the
door and ran up the stairs.

Ake Ogilvie told the tale the next day to Ma Cleghorn,
Ma lying at rest in her bed, she'd gone to bed with a steek
in her side and was lying fair wearied till Ake looked in.
He said *Ay, woman, I hear you're not well?* and Ma said
his hearing was still in fair order—*sit down and gie's a bit
of your crack. How are you and your Provost creature getting on?*

So Ake filled up his pipe, sitting sonsy, green-eyed, with
his curling mouser and Auld Nick brows, a pretty childe
as Ma had thought often. And he said the Provost's bit influence had been fairly heard in this house last night, hadn't
the mistress been waked by the noise? And Ma asked *What
noise? Was the Provost here?* and Ake said No, God, the
lass escaped that, it was only one of his Bacchic chums.

Syne he started to tell of the Saturday outing of the
Duncairn Council to High Scaur Hill. Ma knew of the new
waterworks built there?—Ay, she'd known, faith, or at least
her rates had. Well, the official inspection had been billed
for the Saturday and the Provost had come to Ake at the
sawmill and said that he'd want him to join the bit outing,
he'd want his opinion on the timber-work. And Ake had
said Ay, he didn't much mind, though he'd little liking for
councillors and such. *Still, the poor Bulgars have to live*

somehow, haven't they, Jimmy? and the Provost grinned sick and said he was still the same old Ake.

Well, the whole lot set out on the official treat, Speight, Bailie Brown and the Dean of Guild, all the Bailie billies and a wheen hangers-on, two coach loads hired with the Duncairn rates to give a treat to the City Fathers. And who should the *Daily Runner* send but the wee Mr. Piddle, like a snake on the spree, he squeezed into the back of the Provost's coach, *he-he!* and sat down by the side of Ake with his little note-book fluttering, grinning like an ape, the City Fathers all brave in their braws. And off the jing-bang had rolled to the Scaur.

Well, they got out there at the dinner-time, the staff all drawn up ready for inspection, and Puller, of Puller and Grind's, the contractors, was there with the finest of feeds made ready for the Duncairn Council and afore you could wink the contractor had wheeled in Jimmy the Provost and all his tail and sat them down to a four-course gobble, specially made and sent up from the Mile, with wines in plenty—they needed them after the heat of the drive. Mr. Piddle nipped in and sat by Ake and wolfed into the fodder like a famished ferret, with his wee note-book held brisk at hand for words of wisdom from the City Fathers. But they'd hardly a word, Provost Jimmy or the lot, they'd gotten such an awful thirst to slock.

That was about noon; about three the Fathers made up the mischances they called their minds to go up at last and look at the works. Jimmy Speight stood up and started a speech about how these works were a fine piece of work (aye, a habbering gawpus with his words, poor Jimmy), and carried through in every particular a credit to Duncairn and Puller and Grind. He might have gone on for God knows how long but that Ake beside him pulled the old devil down and whispered *You haven't seen the thing yet.* And Jimmy said *Neither we have; that's suspicious,* and turned on Puller with a gey stern look, but got suddenly mixed in a yawn and a hiccup. When Ake had slapped his back out of that they all set out for the new waterworks.

It was nearly a quarter of a mile from the shed where Puller had spread them their brave bite of lunch hot as hell the sun; and the first man to fall by the wayside was Labour's respectable Bailie Brown, he sat down and said he would take it on trust, the workers knew that he was

their friend, he was awful tired and would need a bit of
sleep. So they shook him a bit and syne left him snoring
like a pig let loose over-long on a midden, and went on a
bit further till the Dean of Guild, he'd been swaying a bit
with his meikle solemn face, suddenly wheeled round on
wee Councillor Clarke and told him he'd never forgiven
him, never, for that time he had voted an increase in the
tramwaymen's wages the last year of the War—September,
it was.

And wee Clarke said the Dean was a havering skate, it
wasn't the last year, but the year afore; and they started
to argue the matter out till wee Clarke had enough, he
punched the Dean one, all the folk around you may well
be sure looking shocked as hell and enjoying themselves,
the Dean sat down of a sudden on the path and looked
solemner than ever and syne started to sing; and the Lord
Provost who'd been looking on at it all, very intent, but
with both eyes crossed, got fairly as mixed in his mind as
his eyes and thought he was down at the Beach Pavilion
adjudicating on the Boxing Finals, and started a speech
about the manhood of Duncairn, how pleased he was to see
the young men were taking up the manly art of defence,
and not rotting their minds with seditious doctrines.

And Ake, standing by and wondering quiet what the
hell they'd do if they ever met in with a real booze-up, he
himself was as drouthy as a lime-kiln, near, saw Mr. Piddle,
with a fuzzy bit look, taking it all down in his little note-
book with a carbon copy for the *Tory Pictman;* and they
left the Dean singing that his Nannie was awa', and resumed
the trek to the High Scaur works.

Well, believe it or not, they never got there, Puller had
the wind up by then just awful, he saw he'd drammed up
the Councillors over-much, if he took the boozed Bulgars
up to the works they'd more'n likely fall head-first in. So
he rounded them back to the lunch-shed again, Ake dandering behind with a bit of a laugh, Jimmy Speight stopping
every now and again for another bit speech, he was fair
wound up. Puller tried to sober them up with coffee, two
of the workmen carried the Dean, they found Bailie Brown
had started to crawl home and when they tried to get him
to stand he said he was only playing at bears, couldn't a
man play at bears if he liked?

Ake saw Mr. Piddle taking that down as well, he was
just a kind of stenographic machine by then. But the Coun-

cil wouldn't have much of the coffee, the Dean said if Puller and Grind expected them to pass the new waterworks,
the works in the disgraceful state they were in, they were
sore mistaken he could tell them that. And Jimmy Speight
started his seventeenth speech, this time about corruption
rearing its ugly head like the sword of Damocles in every
avenue. So Puller called to the waiter childes to bring in
the whisky bottles again, they might as well go home
soaked as go home soft.

So our City Fathers lay the afternoon there, soaking up
truly, but Ake drinking cannily—*and I guess if a pickle of
those Communist childes had been there they'd have got
enough propaganda to start a Soviet the morn's morning.*
It was seven o'clock before Mr. Puller could get the soaked
whoresons back in their coaches. Then he routed out Mr.
Piddle from a sleep in the grass and told him he expected
he'd say nothing of this, and Mr. Piddle took that down in
his note-book as well, but said *he-he* he knew discretion, he
was a man of the world as well. And old Puller muttered
something about Heaven help the world and then dosed
Mr. Piddle with a dram or so to put him into a right good
tune and bunged him in aside Bailie Brown; and off they
all drove back to Duncairn, the coach-drivers were told to
take it slow and see they didn't get back till dark.

Well, they halted up at the top Mile rank and pushed
the Councillors into taxis; but Ake and Mr. Piddle made
for a tram; and were soon at their lodgings in Windmill
Place; and syne the bittie of trouble began.

Ake took the creature along to his room, and took off
his boots and gave him a bit shake, and went off to his
own bed, thinking no more on't. But it seemed that the
outing to the High Scaur works had fair let loose the ill
passions of Piddle, he made up his mind to go up the stairs
and pay his respects to little Miss Johns.

So, forgetting he'd taken off most things but his breeks,
he padded up the stairs and knocked at the door, and went
in, *he-he!* Miss Johns was in bed, the lass sat up and asked
what he wanted and he closed the door and giggled at her,
soft, it doesn't seem she was frightened much. But she
nipped out of bed as Piddle came nearer, and called out
Ewan! and a minute later there was a hell of a crash.

Ake was taking off his boots when he heard that crash,
and he tore from his room just as Mistress Colquohoun tore
out of hers, she'd less of a wardrobe on than he had and

fair looked a canty bit dame for a man to handle, he
couldn't but think. Ake cried *What's up, up there, would
you say?* and she laughed in her cool-like, sulky way *Sounds
more as though the ceiling was down;* and up the two of
them ran together and there Ake set eyes on as bonny a
picture as he'd seen for long, Mr. Piddle lying over the
bed like a pock, the lassie Ellen Johns in a scrimp of a
nightie, all flushed and bonny, red spot on each cheek, and
young Ewan Tavendale looking at Piddle—the two young
creatures with their earnest bit faces and their blue-black
hair a sheen in the light looking down at Piddle like a couple
of bairns at a puzzling and nasty thing on a road.

Ake cried to the quean *Has he done you harm?* and she
answered back cool, *Not him. He's just drunk,* and looked
at Ewan that was standing beside her: *You shouldn't have
hit him; that was quite unnecessary.*

Syne they all looked at Ewan's knuckles and saw they
were skinned and dripping blood, it seemed he hadn't
known himself, he looked kind of dazed and now wakened
up. *Yes, sorry. Damn silly thing to do. Ake, will you help
me carry him down?*

So the two of them carried him off like a corp leaving
the women to redd up the soss, the Piddle childe slept
through it all like a bairn. Ake said to Ewan as they laid
Piddle in bed that he'd given the poor devil a gey mis-
handling, and Ewan said so it seemed, he knew little about
it. He'd heard Miss Johns call and then things had gone
cloudy—interesting, supposed it was much the same thing
happened to stags in rutting time.

Ma said B'God 'twas the best tale she'd heard since a
gelding of her father's at Monymusk had chased a brood
mare into a ditch—*why didn't you let on to me about it?*
This was to Chris after dinner that day, Chris shook her
head, it wasn't worth mention. Mr. Piddle had made a fool
of himself, there was no harm done, he was only a bairn.
Ma said *And what about your Ewan, then?* and Chris
said she thought that that had been straightened, Ewan had
told Mr. Piddle he was sorry and Mr. Piddle had asked him
He-he! What for? he'd had no memory of the happening
at all. Now Ma mustn't worry, she was just to lie still, the
house would be fine and all the things in't.

Ma shook her head: *And to think of me lying flat on my*

back when there's all these fine stravaigings about! Speak of New York—damn't, it's not in't!

October came in long swaths of rain pelting the glinting streets of Duncairn. Going up and down the Windmill Steps with her baskets of groceries Chris would see the toun far alow under the rain's onset move and shake and shiver a minute like an old grey collie shaking in sleep. The drive of wind and rain cleared the wynds of the fouler smells; down in the Mile, shining in mail, the great houses rose above the wet birl and drum of the trams, buses creeping about like beasts in a fog, snorting, and blowing the wet from their faces, Duncairn getting out its reefers and bonnets, in drifting umbrella'ed afternoon tides the half-gentry poured down the Mile every day. Up in the house it was canty and fine, the wind breenging unbreeked into room after room whenever you opened a shutter a bit, Miss Murgatroyd thought it was Such Rough, and John Cushnie came home from Raggie Robertson's store and said they were doing a roaring trade, him and Raggie, in selling a new line in raincoats. Jock the cat shivered so close to the range Chris wondered he didn't get in and look out.

Ma got up the second day of her illness, she said it was no more than sweirty, just, she must redd out the kitchen press to-day. But halfway through she gave a bit groan, Chris caught her as she tottered and turned white, Meg was at hand and lended a hand, they got her to sit in a chair in a minute. Then Chris said *It's back to your bed for you, my woman,* and back to it they took her, Ma puffing and panting, *Lord Almighty, lass, don't look feared about a small thing like this. There's more old folk than me in their time been ta'en with a bit of a paich, you know. Get out for a bit of fresh air yourself.*

Chris went for a walk to fetch the doctor, a thin young country childe with pop eyes, he came in his car and looked at Ma and gave her a prod and listened to her lungs and said what she wanted was quietness and rest and not to excite herself on a thing. But to Chris he said she'd a swollen heart, serious enough, she'd have to look out. Chris asked what she'd better do, then? and the doctor asked were Ma's relatives near, and Chris remembered about the niece, only she didn't know where she bade. The doctor said that it couldn't be helped—*try and find out without fearing the old wife.*

So Chris waited till Ma was sleeping again and then went and took a bit look through her desk, beside the great curtain, worm-eaten, old, bundles of papers tied in neat pilings, a fair soss of ribbons and cards and circulars, paid bills and bits of tow and old brooches and safety-pins and a ring or so, and some letters fading off at the edges, Chris didn't read them or heed to them except to peer at the writer's name. She found no trace of the niece's address in the pigeon-holes, Ma sleeping as the dead in the bed out under the shadow of the patterned wall. So she opened the lower drawers, old clothes, old papers, a bundle of photos, a little pack tied up in tape which came away in her hands as she looked, she stared at the thing a puzzled minute.

It was the photo of a little lad with Ma's nose and eyes and promise of her padding, keeking at something the photographer did, no mistaking Ma's face in his. And below was written "James at 2" and inside the package two other things, tawdry and faded, a hank of bairn's hair, brown soft, dead and old, it had lost its shine, and a crumpled scrap of ancient crape. Long, long ago it all had happened. Why had Ma never told she'd a son?

And Chris stood with the things in her hand in a dream looking at the faded, pictured face of the little lad who had died, she supposed, when he was no more than a little lad, he'd finished quick with a look round about and gone from Duncairn and gone from Ma, queer that such things should be—all the care and heed and tears of pain that had once been given this little childe far back there in the years where he twiddled his toes. And he'd ceased with it all, a mistake, a journey he would not make, no rain to hear or grow to knowledge of the dark, sad things of life at all, no growing to books and harkening to dreams, like Ewan— no growing to be a queer young man far from Ma and all she had hoped, only leaving her a searing memory awhile and then a quiet glow that lasted forever. Not leaving an unease that washed as a tide through one's heart, unending ... dreaming on Ewan.

How she hated the splatter of the driving rain!

As that rain held on and pelted Duncairn with the closing in of the storm-driven clouds, great cumulus shapes that came wheeling down from the heights of the far brown lour of the Mounth, the roof-tops glistered in the lights of the Mile and far and near the gutters gurgled, eddied and warm, piercing down to a thousand drains, down through the latest Council diggings, down to dark spaces and forgotten pools, in one place out through an antique tunnel that the first Pict settlers had made and lined with uncalsayed stones, set deep in earth, more than two thousand years before. And far and near as the evening came under the stour a thousand waters by gutters and wynd and the swollen Forthie dark, brimming, wheeled down through the darkling night to seek the splurge and plunge of the sea pelting beyond the dunes of the beach. Ellen heard its cry long ere they reached it, harsh, soft, the patter of the rain on the waves.

Then Ewan and she had climbed through the Links and up the railings to the desolate front, wet-shining, with hardly the glimmer of a light. Here the rain caught their faces in swaths, warm rain, like corn felled in a reaper's bout, some Reaper high in the scudding lift. Ewan said *There's a shelter further along. Let's run for it*, and caught her hand and they ran together, both hatless, both wet, and gained its lithe and sat on the bench, panting, staring out at the dark.

Ellen closed her eyes and leaned back her head and stretched out her nice legs, she knew they were nice, and lovely and tingly, and put her hands up behind her wet hair. That run was fun, hard to believe that this was Duncairn, here in the darkness with the forgotten sea.

She peeped at Ewan, sitting near, queer Scotch boy, solemn and not, wonder if he's ever kissed a girl? And she thought not likely and was angry with herself behaving just like an idiot shop-girl. She'd been tired and drowsy tonight with that long, stuffy meeting of the League, Semple had come and talked for the Reds, she'd thought him a catty and snelly bore. So when it finished and they came out into the rain flooding the Crossgate she'd said to Ewan *Let's go a walk before we go home*, half-expecting he'd snub her, he could do that easily. But instead he'd said *Yes, if you like, where'll we go?* and she'd said *The Beach* and he'd said *Right-o*, not thinking her silly as any other would, Duncairn had stopped going down to the Beach now that Snellie Guff and his Funny Scotch Band had finished their season assassinating music. So down through the squelching Links they'd come and here they were, and there, a creaming unquiet, the sea.

And Ewan said suddenly out of the darkness *This would be a splendid night for a bathe.*

Ellen turned to the glimmer of his face: *What, now?— Why not? The rain's warm enough and I'm sticky still with the Crossgate heat.* The glimmer grew blurred: *I'm going to. Shan't be out long.*

Ellen said *You can't. You haven't a bathing-dress—or towels—or anything.*

—That's the beauty of it. Nothing at all.

And supposing he caught cramp down there alone? Ellen swallowed: *It might be fun. I'm coming in as well.*

As she threw off her coat and unbuckled her shoes she saw him about to go out of the shelter. Funny the tingle that touched her then, cool enough though she was: *There's plenty of room for both of us, isn't there?*

He called *I suppose so,* and stripped in like haste with herself, it was cold in the shelter, a long pointer of wind stroked Ellen's back as she wrenched off her stockings, Ewan asked suddenly out of the dark if a girl always took off her stockings last?

Ellen raised her head and saw him a white glimmer, goodness, shouldn't look; but why shouldn't she? He was looking at her, she supposed, thank goodness couldn't see much. She said *Yes, I think so. I've never noticed. Oh hell, it's cold!*

Ewan said *It's not. Come on. Can you swim?* And Ellen said she could or was trying to say it when the rain-laden wind whipped the words from her mouth, on the promenade they were caught and twirled, she thought in a sudden panic, *This is mad we'll never get back,* and next minute found Ewan had caught her wrist: *Down together. I know the way.*

They ran. The way lay over the sand, soft and wet and slimily warm, the pelting on the water drew their feet, they forgot Duncairn and the lights behind, all the hates and imaginings that drowned those sad children lost from the winds and tides, rain at night, sting of flesh smitten under rain. Suddenly Ellen's legs seemed stroked with fire: they ran out into the play of the sea.

Beyond the shore-beat they met a great wave, Ewan tried to cry something, failed, dived, vanished, Ellen felt herself lost, laughed desperately, dived as well. Ewan suddenly beside her: *Let's get back. Over-rough,* and she turned about, she seemed sheathed in fire, saltily grainily slipping through water, she fought off cramp, struggled, and found her feet abruptly on the shore again. . . . Idiots! Goodness, what idiots!

Next minute, wading, she gained the wet sand, saw a glister beside her, Ewan Tavendale, head bent and wiping the water from his hair. Then he whispered *Sh—look at that!*

Ellen peered up at the promenade and her heart peered up in her throat. The shelter had squatted dark on the slope but now it was lighted with a moving light. Some man or other had gone in there and found their clothes, he's switched on a torch——

Ewan whispered there was nothing else for it but to tackle him, and they ran up, the wind in Ellen's hair, she thought *I don't care, it's fun,* she felt warm suddenly tingling from head to heel. Ewan glimmered in front: at the sound of the pelt of their feet on the sand the light switched about and Ellen for a moment saw Ewan, she thought *He's nice hips,* and at that the light vanished, Ewan had caught it and flung it down the Beach.

Now then, now then, what's this that you're up to? Do you know you're assaulting the police, my lad?

Ellen nipped past and caught up her clothes, struggled into her vest, into her knickers, the bulk of the bobby hiding Ewan from her. He was saying *You'll come along to the Station with me, the two of you, there'll be a bonny bit charge, public indecency down at the Beach.*

Ellen gave a gasp, Ewan said nothing, she could see him move quickly and dimly, getting in his clothes, he was dressing more quickly than she was, she knew, her shift stuck to her, it didn't matter, yet she felt cold now, her mind a tumult. Oh, they COULDN'T charge anybody with THAT, just for nothing——

Come along, you're all ready. Mind, none of your tricks. Here you—this to Ewan—*have you matches on you?*

Ewan made on that he hadn't heard, the bobby swore and made to come between them. It was then that Ewan acted, Ellen saw the play, an instant, dim as a bad-made film, the bobby vanished, there came a crash and a slither from below, Ewan had said *There's a match for you,* and flung him from the top of the high Beach steps.

He grabbed her hand *Run like hell!* and they ran like that till she gasped that she couldn't do more, else she'd burst.

He told her not to do that, it would be a mess, and released his hold, and halted beside her.

Out in the Links they stood listening: Nothing, nothing but the far cry of a seabird desolate about the turning tide, forward the glimmer of Duncairn in the rain warm and safe and all unaware. Ellen asked with a sudden catch of breath: *What if the bobby has been badly hurt?* and Ewan said *Let him hurt, it will do the swine good,* cool and unperturbed, she felt sick a moment. *It was only that half-wit Sergeant Sim Leslie who used to dig with my mother, you know.*

Things were fair kittling up at Gowans and Gloag, a lad had to keep nippy with the new tools that came, packing and storing and wondering about them, damned queer frames for new castings, too, nobody kenned what the bits were for. But there were orders enough to hand and the management was taking on folk again, it just showed you the papers were right what they said—that the Crisis was over and trade coming back.

And meeting Ewan Tavendale outside the office you cried to him, *Ay! Ewan, what about the collapse of capitalism now? Doesn't look very much like it, does it?* He said *No? D'you know what the new orders are for?* You said you didn't and you didn't much care as long as it gave a bit of work to folk, better any kind of a decent job than being pitched off on the bloody Broo.

Ewan said *And better getting ready stuff to blow out another man's guts in his face than starving yourself with an empty guts? Is that what you think? Then your head's gone soft.*

You'd never seen him look angry before, you felt angry yourself and damned hurt as well, you asked who the hell he was calling names and he said *Clean your ears and you'll hear quick enough. Bob, be up at the League room tonight. There's a meeting on of all the chaps I can bring.*

Who the hell did he think he was ordering about? But you went to the meeting all the same, a fair birn of the Gowans and Gloag chaps there, half the young lads from Machines and Castings and that thin-necked Bulgar who worked in the Stores, Norman and Alick and wee Geordie Bruce. No League folk and thank God no queans, Ewan sat behind the chairman's table alone and banged it and stood up and began to speak: and afore he'd said much there was such a hush you'd have heard the wind rumble in the belly of a flea.

He said they'd all noticed the new orders coming into Gowans and Gloag's. Did they know what the orders were for—the new machinery, the new parts they made? Especially had they noticed the new cylinders? He could tell them: he'd found out that morning. They were making new ammunition parts, bits of shells and gas-cylinders for Sidderley, the English armament people.

Somebody cried up *Well, hell, does it matter?* and Ewan said if a man were such a poor swine that it didn't matter to him he was making things to be used to blow Chinese workers to bits, people like himself, then it didn't matter. But if he had any guts at all he'd join the whole of Gowans and Gloag in a strike that would paralyse the Works. Gas-cylinder cases: he hadn't been at the War, none of them had, but they'd all read and heard about gas-attacks. Here was an account by a hospital attendant that he'd copied from a book:

I RECEIVED AN URGENT MESSAGE FROM THE HOSPITAL TO BE IN ATTENDANCE IMMEDIATELY. I HURRIED THERE AND ALMOST AT ONCE THE STREAM OF AMBULANCES WITH THE UNFORTUNATE PRISONERS BEGAN TO ARRIVE. AT FIRST SCORES, THEN LATER HUNDREDS, OF BROKEN MEN, GASPING, SCREAMING, CHOKING. THE HOSPITAL WAS PACKED WITH FRENCH SOLDIERS, BEATING AND FIGHTING THE AIR FOR BREATH. DOZENS OF MEN WERE DYING LIKE FLIES, THEIR CLOTHES RENT TO RIBBONS IN THEIR AGONY, THEIR FACES A HORRIBLE SICKLY GREEN AND CONTORTED OUT OF ALL HUMAN SHAPE——

There was plenty more, but that gave you a taste. Well, that's what he'd summoned this meeting for. What were they to do about it in Gowans?

God, you'd felt sick at that stuff he'd read, but then wee Geordie Bruce at the back of the hall sounded a raspberry and everybody laughed, high out and relieved, you laughed yourself, only Norman and Ewan didn't. Ewan said if the chap at the back had anything to say let him get up and say it, and at that wee Geordie Bruce stood up and said

Ah, to hell with you and your blethers. What do you think you're trying to do?—play the bloody toff on us again? It doesn't matter a damn to us what they're going to do with the wee round tins. If you're a Chink or a Black yourself, that's your worry. And other chaps called out the same, who the mucking hell did Tavendale think he was?—daft as all the bloody reds. And afore you could wink the place was in a roar, Ewan you could see sitting at the table, listening, looking from this side to that. Then he stood up and said that they'd take a vote—*those in favour of a strike hold up their hands.*

The noise quietened away a bit at that, you looked round about, nobody had a hand up, and och to hell suddenly you minded the stuff that Ewan had been reading about chaps caught in gas, and you felt fair daft, up your hand shot, and so did Norman's, and so Alick's, and Ewan was counting: *For—three. Those against?*—But there was never a real count, chaps started whistling and stamping, raspberrying and banging out of the room and knocking over the chairs as they went. You sat where you were feeling a fair fool, in a minute there was only the four of you left.

Syne Ewan called out: *Bob, close the door. We've to make ourselves into a Committee of Action.*

At half past five it happened again. Running down the stairs Chris met Ake Ogilvie who'd newly letten himself in at the door. *Ake, Ma Cleghorn's ta'en ill again. Will you run for the doctor?* and Ake said *Eh? Oh, ay, I'll do that,* and asked the address and nodded and went stamping out into the dark, Chris glanced from the window and saw it coming down, dark early now the winter was near. Syne she turned and ran up to Ma's room again to ease her out of her stays, poor thing, lying black-faced and gasping and swearing like a soldier.

The doctor came as he'd done before, had another look, gave another sniff, and said that Ma must be kept fell quiet. Chris told him she'd found out the relative's address, should she send for her? The doctor pulled at his lip and said *Oh no, just keep the address by handy-like. And don't worry too much, Mrs. Colquohoun, I'll send up medicine,* and off he went. Chris went down to the kitchen to get ready the tea, Ma ill or Ma well folk would need their meat.

She went to bed dead tired that night. But she couldn't sleep, getting up every hour or so to look in Ma's room, after midnight the breathing grew easier. It had grown cold and looking out of the window Chris saw that snow had come on, soft-sheeting, the early soft seep of November snow whitening the roofs in a spilling fall. And she stood and looked at it a little while in the still, quiet house above the stilled toun, in a cold no-thought till the clock struck three—suddenly dirling beside her head.

Far away through the snow beyond Footforthie the lighthouse winked on the verge of the morning, and a feeling of terrible loneliness came on her standing so at that hour, knowledge of how lonely she had always been, knowledge of how lonely every soul was, apart and alone as she had been surely even at the most crowded hours of her life. And she went up the stairs in a sudden fear and listened outside Ewan's room a minute and heard his breath, low and even. In the next room the door hung open unsnecked, she'd have to see to that lock to-morrow. Closing the door she saw Ellen Johns a dim shape curled like a baby in sleep, and stood, the snow-hush upon the panes, looking at her in a kind of desperation, half-minded to waken her up to talk.

Then that daft thought went from her, she went down the stairs and into the kitchen, cold even there, the fire in the range had drooped to ash, she stirred it a little and Jock the cat purred a drowsy greeting a minute, grew silent; she sat and stared in the fading ash, alone and desperate—what would she do?

It was plain enough Ma wouldn't last long. And then— Chris hadn't enough money to carry on the house herself and whoever heired Ma mightn't want to come in with her. So out again, looking for some other thing in this weary life of Duncairn, seeking out some little shop, she supposed, somewhere where she and Ewan could bide and trauchle and fight with the going of the years, he wouldn't earn money of account for years. And so on and on, streets all about, slippery with slime, the reeking gutters of Paldy Parish, the weary glint of shop-fronts in the Mile—till she grew old and old and haggard, thin—who would have dreamed this for her long syne that night she wedded Ewan in Blawearie, just a night like this she minded now, lights and Long Rob and Chae at the fiddle, dancing, warmth, the daftness of being young; they'd seemed eternal, to outlast

the hills, those moments when Ewan had first ta'en her
in his arms, naked, unshielded, unafraid, glad to be his
and give and take for the fun and glory of being in love
. . . all far away in the snowing years down the long Howe
on Kinraddie's heights.

And she thought of the croft in the north wind's blow,
of the snow driving about it this night lashing the joists
and window-panes, the fly and scurry of the driving flakes
about the Stones high up by the loch, the lost rigs sleeping
under their covering, the peesies wheeping lost in the dark.
Oh idiot, weeping to remember that, all things gone and
lost and herself afraid and afraid and a morning coming
she was feared to face, lost and alone.

And again she got to her feet and wandered through the
hush of the sleeping house, and stood in her own room,
with the sickly flare of the gaslight behind her and looked
at herself in the mirror, hands clenched, forgetting herself
in a sudden wild woe that wouldn't stop though her mind
clamoured it was daft, things would redd up in time, she
wasn't hungry or starved, she had friends, she had
Ewan. . . . SHE HAD NOTHING AT ALL, she had never
had anything, nothing in the world she'd believed in but
change, unceasing and unstaying as time, light after light
went down, hope and fear and hate, love that had lighted
hours with a fire, hate freezing through to the blood of
one's heart—Nothing endured, and this hour she stood as
alone as she'd been when a quean in those wild, lost moments she climbed the heights of Blawearie brae. And she
covered her face with her hands and sat down and so
stayed there awhile and then rose and put on her clothes,
coldly, mechanically, looking at the clock. . . . Trudging in
the track of those little feet as a tethered beast that went
round and round the tethering post in the midst of a
park——

The Young League dance was fair in full swing, chaps
had gone flocking to buy up tickets at Gowans and Gloag's
and all over Footforthie, a tanner hop was a good enough
chance to take your quean to on New Year's Eve. And
she'd said *But aren't those creatures Red?* and you said you
were Bulgared if you knew, did it matter? And she said
Reds were awful, they believed that woman—och, stuff that
you wouldn't speak about. And you said you wouldn't but

these Reds were different, the head of them was a toff kind
of swine, Ewan Tavendale——

And your quean said *Bob!* or *Will* or *Leslie*—*don't use
those kind of words to me,* and you nearly went off your
head at the runt, trying to make a lad speak genteel. But she
turned up ready to go to the dance down in Long Hall,
and there was that Tavendale, you'd never spoken to him,
standing at the door and taking the tickets and nodding to
folk; and up on the platform Jake Forbes's band that was
wee Jake Forbes all on his own, hard at it banging out the
Omaha Pinks, Jake tootling away with his big white face
like a bowl of lard on the melt by a fire, queans and chaps
all over the floor, your quean looked the bonniest and awful
posh, how the hell did queans manage to dress up like
that?

Then the Pinks struck up and you gave her a grab, she
hadn't on stays or much else below, and off you all went,
slither and slide, one foot in and another out, like a cock
with concussion, tweetle the flute. And Jake stood up and
hit the drum and banged the bell and clattered the cymbals
and looked as though with a bit of encouragement he'd
have kicked hell out of the nearest wall. God, what a row:
but it kittled you up.

It was cold outside but the chaps didn't heed, you took
out your quean for a squeeze between dances cold though
it was, she breathed *You mustn't, not here*—to hell, she
liked it. Then she'd fix up her dress and back you'd go,
New Year coming fast, some of the chaps nipped over to
the pub and brought back a gill of the real Mackay, kittling everybody up, you forgot you'd got sacked the day
before, and father was cursing like hell and said he'd have
to keep you on the P.A.C. . . . or that your job was a
bloody stalemate with no chance of earning a penny piece
more. Funny how fine your quean felt and smelt, other
queans as well as you changed with chaps.

And there was that toff Ewan Tavendale, only he didn't
look a toff a bit, just one of the lads, he was dancing like
hell when Jake put on a Schottische. Everybody cried
Hooch! and wakened up more, a daft old dance, not up to
date, but you could swank and give a big prance, in and
out, now on your own quean's sleeve, now on that of the
schoolteacher folk said was Red, only a kid, she was
dressed in red, with black hair and a flaming skirt, she
laughed and cried *Hook!* not *Hooch!*: she was English.

Jake quietened a minute to wipe his fat face and Ewan carried him something to drink; and Ewan called *The New Year dance is next. Just a word to you all before it comes on. You know who're the people who've got up this dance. They say we're some kind of Reds: let them say. We're workers the same as all of you are and as fond of taking a girl to a dance and giving her a cuddle on the sly as the next. In fact, that's why we believe what we do—that every one should have a decent life and time for dancing and enjoying oneself, and a decent house to go to at night, decent food, decent beds. And the only way to get those things is for the young workers of whatever party to join together and stop the old squabbles and grab life's share with their thousand hands.* And he stopped and looked down at the chaps and queans, all kittled up as they looked, with flushed faces, the lasses bonny in that hour though they came from the stews of Paldy and Kirrieben and Footforthie, their thin antrin faces soft in the light: *And isn't it worth grabbing? And that's all the speech.*

And as they cheered him and cried his name, the dirty, kind words of mates in the Shops, a great chap that Ewan, just one of themselves . . . it seemed to Ewan in a sudden minute that he would never be himself again, he'd never be ought but a bit of them, the flush on a thin white millgirl's face, the arm and hand and the down-bent face of a keelie from the reek of the Gallowgate, the blood and bones and flesh of them all, their thoughts and their doubts and their loves were his, all that they thought and lived in were his. And that Ewan Tavendale that once had been, the cool boy with the haughty soul and cool hands, apart and alone, self-reliant, self-centred, slipped away out of the room as he stared, slipped away and was lost from his life forever.

And then Ellen Johns was pulling at his arm: *Ewan, you look funny, is there anything wrong?* and he moved and came out of that dreaming trance, and smiled at her, and Ellen's heart moved, not the cold smile at all, it might have been that of any kind boy. *Hello, Ellen. You look lovely to-night. Can I have the next dance?* and she said, wide-eyed, *You can have them all if you want them, Ewan.*

And he took her hand and drew her close and waved to Jake and Jake started it up, *tooootle* the flute, *cla-boomr* the drum, off they all went in the wheel of a waltz, winkle the lights and Ellen's head close under Ewan's shoulder as they spun. And he looked down and suddenly smelled her hair, strange and sweet, and felt dizzy a minute, at the tickle of it up under his chin, at the touch of her up against him close, breast and belly and legs, soft, sweet, something ran with a torch and fired all his body. And Ellen looked up and saw his face, white, and suddenly knew what she'd always known, that she was his for as long as he liked, and *she* would like that till the day she died.

And she knew then that all the old stories were true, while they wheeled together, while they paused and rested, standing together so that they just touched, her hand touched his and his fingers closed on it, quick and glad—troubling fingers—Oh, all true that they'd sung in the olden times in this queer Scotland that had felt so alien, the dark, queer songs of lust and desire, of men and women and this daftness of love, dear daftness in soft Scotch speech, on Scotch lips—daftness like this that she felt for Ewan, and it didn't matter what he thought or did, whatever he might do or say or believe, the glory of it would last her forever. . . .

Jake cried *A last one ere Ne'ersday comes. What'll it be?* and they cried back *A reell,* and the chaps smiling by then to their queans, the queans that had lost their clipped, frightened looks, their distrusts of men and hands and lips, forgetting the dark and the cold outbye and those dreary dawns that haunted Duncairn, thinking only of touches kind and shy, weak faces they loved, a moment to snatch when all this was over, somewhere, anyhow—to hell with risk when you liked him so well! And they flushed at their thoughts and said flyting things; and all lined up for the last of the reels; and Jake crashed out the tune, walloping the drum till it boomed like a bittern, tankle the melodeon, tootle the flute, and off they all went. Round and faster and faster still, Ewan with Ellen and holding her so she was frightened and struggled a wild-bird moment, Ewan lost in a queer, cruel flame of wonder, desire, and—heartbreaking—a passion of pity. Play on, Jake, play on, never stop, Ellen and I, Ellen and I. . . .

And far away Thomson Tower clanged midnight across the toun and into Long Hall, the long dark hall where the League had its dance; and Jake stopped in the middle of his clatter of playing and they all stopped and laughed, the

queans pulled at their dresses, and Tavendale stood with
the schoolteacher close, close as though glued, jammed up
against Alick and Norman and their queans; and Jake cried
out *Join hands—here's New Year:*

> And here's a hand, my trusty fiere,
> And gies a hand o' thine—

And Ellen wished the mist would go from her eyes; and
then they'd all stopped and the music was done and queans
were being pushed into their coats, and coddled, and everybody crying good-night. *A happy New Year! Good night,
then, Ewan. Good night to your lass—what's her name?—
Ellen? Ta-ta, Ellen.* And she cried *Ta-ta*, standing by Ewan
the mist quite gone, alive and tingling not heeding at all that
some cried back *Hell, it's snowing like Bulgary!*

They left Jake to lock up the hall and went out, snow
sheeting down on the snow-rimed streets, all around the
lighted wynds of Ne-ersday, first foots and greetings and
drams poured in tumblers, the bairns crying *Is't time to get
up?* and their mothers, tired, happy, crying back to them:
*Mighty be here, get into your beds. You'll get all your
presents on New Year's Day——*

But the streets were nearly deserted as they hurried,
Ellen and Ewan, from the Cowgate's depth across the Mile
and the Corn Market, the cold air blowing on Ellen's face,
Ewan looked down and saw her face a winter flower and
wanted to sing, wanted to stop and say idiot things, to stop
and go mad and strip Ellen naked, the secret small cat, slow
piece on piece, and kiss every piece a million times over,
and hit her—hard, till it hurt, and kiss the hurts till cure
and kisses and pain were one—mad, oh, mad as hell to-
night!

And she tripped beside him, sweet, slim and demure in
act and look, dark cool kitten, and inside was frightened at
the wildness there. So up Windmill Steps through the sheet
of the snow, a corner with a mirror, here the snow failed,
Ewan halted panting while she made to run on.

But he caught her arm and drew her down, she wriggled
a little, the light on her face, startled, eyes like stars and
yet drowsy, he drew her close to him and they suddenly
gasped, with wonder and fear and as though their hearts

broke and were shattered in the kiss, sweet, terrible, as their lips met at last.

Thin and lank, with a holy mouth and shifty eyes, she sat in the kitchen and had tea with Chris: *Eh me, and you think she won't last the night?* And Chris said, *No, I don't think she will. Another cup of tea, Miss Urquhart?* and Ma's niece Izey sniffled through her nose, godly, and pecked at her eyes with a hanky: *Have you had the minister up to see her?*

Chris said No, she hadn't, Ma had told her in a wakeful moment that day she didn't want any of them sossing about, if St. Peter needed a prayer for a passport he'd be bilked of another boarder, fegs. And Niece Izey held up her hands in horror, *But YOU don't believe that, do you, now?* and Chris said more or less, she didn't care, and Miss Urquhart drew in her shoggly mouth, prim: *I'm afraid we wouldn't get on very well. I believe in God, I've no time for heathen.* And Chris said *No? That must be a comfort. Try a cake, Miss Urquhart,* and sat watching her eat, she herself couldn't, over tired with running up and down the stairs and seeing to the lodgers' meals as they came, they needed something special on New Year's Eve, and letting Meg go early though she'd offered to stay. . . . And suddenly the lank Izey said *I suppose you know that I heir it all?—the share in the house and the furniture?*

Chris said she'd heard that and knew it to be true, whatever intention Ma had once had of altering her will to surprise Niece Izey she'd never had the time to carry it out. And Miss Urquhart pursed up her holy-like mouth and said she would realize her share, she'd no fancy for the keeping of lodgers herself, not a decent work, she'd always thought. Maybe Mrs. Colquohoun would buy her out?

Chris said *I've no idea what I'll do. But I'm dead tired now. Will you watch by your aunt?* Niece Izey gave a kind of shiver: *Oh, but I don't know a thing about nursing. You won't leave me alone with her, will you?*

Chris looked at her in an idle pity, too tired to hate the poor, fusionless thing, a black hoodie-crow scared of a body not yet quite a corpse but ready to pick out its eyes when it died. *I'm going up to rest in my own room a while. If there's any change you can run up and tell me . . .*

Without taking off her clothes she lay on the bed and drew the coverlet over her, not intending to sleep, only rest

and lose her aches in the dark. But afore she knew it she
was gone, sound, the last whisper she heard the fall of the
snow pelting Duncairn in its New Year's Eve.

She woke from that with a hand on her shoulder, the
lanky niece had lighted the gas, she was all a-dither and
the long face grey. *I'm feared she's gey ill, and Oh, how you
were sleeping. I thought I would never waken you.*

Chris got off the bed and tidied her hair. And as she did
so she heard from Ma's room an antrin sound—a blatter of
words, then a groan of pain. She was down the stairs and
into the room, Izey trailing behind in a lank unease, and
saw that it couldn't be very long now, she had better send
for the doctor at once.

Ma Cleghorn was fighting her last fight with the world
she had jeered at and sworn at throughout her life, gallant
and vulgar, untamed to the end, her arm beating the air in
this battle. Chris wiped the spume from the swollen lips,
the smell of death already in the air, and did not move as
she sat by the bed, the niece went out of the room to be ill,
down in Duncairn a late tram tootled; and the dreich fight
drew to its close, begun a sixty years before, ending in
this—what for, what for?

And suddenly Ma's lips ceased to twist and slobber with
their blowings of brownish spume, her hand in Chris's
slackened with a little jerk; and she stepped from the bed
and out of the house and up long stairs that went wandering
to Heaven like the stairs on Windmill Brae. And she met at
the Gates St. Peter himself, in a lum hat and leggings, looking awful stern, the father of all the Wee Free ministers,
and he held up his hand and snuffled through his nose and
asked in GAWD'S name was she one of the Blessed? And
Ma Cleghorn said she was blest if she knew—*Let's have a
look at this Heaven of yours.* And she pushed him aside
and took a keek in, and there was God with a plague in one
hand and a war and a thunderbolt in the other and the
Christ in glory with the angels bowing, and a scraping and
banging of harps and drums, ministers thick as a swarm of
blue-bottles, no sight of Jim and no sight of Jesus, only the
Christ, and she wasn't impressed. And she said to St. Peter
This is no place for me, and turned and went striding into
the mists and across the fire-tipped clouds to her home.

The sleet had ended. Looking up in the lift Chris saw it
lighten and the cumuli clear, a stiff wind blowing the New

Year's Day into the eyes of Duncairn below, wakening down there and about her, wakening while she stood here frozen like—oh, like a corpse, like Ma up there in the blinded room, if Ma *was* there, no day for her, just the dark, no snow, sun never again or shadow or cold.

Long ago Robert would have been able to put in fine words the things that you felt—or could even Robert? Could he have put in words both your pity and desire to laugh—laughter because death was so funny and foolish?

... And whatever next—oh, whatever next?

And then, as always at breaking point, she felt cool and kind and unworried no longer, brisk and competent, unwearied, she whistled a little as the sleet went by.

No worry could last beyond the last point, there was nothing awaiting her but her life, New Year and Life that would gang as it would, greeting or laughing, unheeding her fears.

And she went up the steps to death and life.

III

APATITE

COMING down the steps of Windmill Brae in the blaze of the late May afternoon Chris paused at the mirror, dust-sprinkled in summer's beginning, and looked at her blithe self with a cool curiosity. If finery made fine birds, she thought, she'd peacocks beaten to the likeness of sparrows, new hat and dress, new shoes, new gloves, new-bathed—oh, new to her skin at least!

And so she supposed, behind this newness and those cool eyes in the mirror, the fugitive Chris was imprisoned at last, led in a way like the captives long syne whom men dragged up the heights to Blawearie Loch to streek out and kill by the great grey stones. Caught as they were: she, who had often laid down in the shadow of the Stones—oh, daft to blether in her thoughts like this, when all that was happening to her to-day was as common a happening throughout the world as getting up, getting down, sleeping and waking. . . .

Sleeping——

Even the cool amusement behind which she shielded could not restrain that shudder of disgust, goodness knew why, what was disgusting about the business? Going back to a life again full and complete from a half-life, unnatural, alone and part. But she pulled off her gloves and stared at her fingers in a sudden unreasoning spasm of panic. Oh,

however had she come to betray herself so? Better the sleet
and the grey despair of that five months ago when she
last climbed here, no road or vision before her at all——

When young Alick Watson taiked home one night to the
Cowgate in the middle of January and told the news that
a strike was on, there was no going back to Gowans and
Gloag's till they'd stopped the making of shell-cases and
cylinders, Meg Watson asked *And what does that mean?—
that a lot of tink brutes like yourself'll gang idle?*

Alick said that it meant she could give him less of her
lip, hell, wasn't there even a cup of tea? And him on picket
the morn's morning.

Meg was wearied from her work at Windmill Place, she
said he could get the tea for himself, he'd have plenty of
time for cookery classes now he was out on his half-witted
strike. And who did he expect would keep him, eh? Father
or herself or that Red swine Selden? She'd aye known that
Alick was a silly gawpus, she could bet they hadn't ALL
come out on strike.

Alick said she could bet herself blue in the face, they'd
all come out that had any guts excepting a few of the swine
in the office. Meg said she was glad Mr. Tavendale and his
like had more sense, Alick stared at her and then gave a
laugh: *Ewan Tavendale? Why, you silly bitch, it's him
that's organized the whole mucking strike—he's been going
it for weeks now, him and his League. They'd never have
brought off the strike at all if it hadn't been for the speed-
ing-up as well—chaps doing double work in the same
spread of time. And we're all out the morn and the whole
damn business led by your Mr. Tavendale, see?*

Then he said in a minute he was awful sorry—*I didn't
mean to vex you, Meg.* And she snuffled and dabbed at her
eyes, making out she'd a cold, she hadn't—what had he
said, what was wrong with her? And he glowered at his
sister in the littered, cold room, with the rags on the beds
and the rickety chairs, something about her looked queer
to a chap. . . .

Why should she greet when he spoke about Ewan?

Stephen Selden, the lodger, came in at that minute,
Alick told him the news, he was fair delighted. He said that
the Communist local would help, they'd take over the running from this daft young League. Alick asked what the
hell it had to do with the Communists—or Tavendale's

League, if it came to that? It was only the concern of the Gowans chaps. But Selden said it was every worker's affair that another was fighting for his livelihood and to put down the manufacture of armaments. He himself would be along at the picketing the morn.

And there sure enough he was at the gates with a birn of others when the morning broke, a crowd of Broo chaps from all over Duncairn standing about easy and looking at the gates and watching the half-dozen men on picket. Folk took a bit dander across the causeys and cried out to ask what the strike was about? The pickets said there was a statement to be issued soon, they'd nothing to say until that was done. And they stood and gowked at the gates, damned cold, or looked back up the streets to the fug of Footforthie, Alick and Norman and the new stores chap, Bob, two old men who worked in Machines, and a young chap who looked like a toff, folk thought, 'twas said he was a gent who worked in the Office. Whatever could he be doing on strike?

At nine o'clock, with the crowd gey thick, two bobbies came barging through the press and stood up on either side of the gate, one a young constable childe from the country, that everybody liked, a mere loon, with no harm and a cheery smile that he couldn't hide though he tried to look solemn as a sourock now, standing under the eye of his sergeant, the big ugly devil that had come to Footforthie, some called him Feet and some called him worse, Leslie his name, a heavy-looking brute with bulging eyes and a grind of a voice. *Stand back there!* he cried to the folk round about, and somebody sounded a raspberry, and everybody laughed.

The folk looked round and saw that a car was coming, the manager's car, slow, Sergeant Leslie opened the gates and gave it a wave in. But one of the pickets, the young toff, held up his hand, every body stared, hell, didn't he know the manager?

But the car slid to a stop and Ewan went forward and talked a minute to the manager, he said *You is it, Tavendale? Yes, I've heard all the story. This'll mean one thing certain enough, anyhow: YOU'LL not come back to Gowans and Gloag's.* Ewan said they would see about victimization when the strike was over: what about the manager himself coming out? And the manager reddened and said to his chauffeur *Drive on!* and Sim Leslie caught

Ewan's shoulder: *Stand away there, or I'll have you ta'en in!*

A fair growl went up from the folk at that, no body could stop strikers picketing their works. Who did the fat swine think he was—Hitler? And two loons at the back threw a handful of clinkers over a baulk, they splattered all about the big sergeant's helmet and his meikle red face, like a sow's backside, went a mottled grey: *Stand away there!* though not a soul stood within ten feet. Some chaps cried *Let's pitch him into the Dock,* Broo chaps that had nothing to lose anyway, and God knows the mischief that mightn't have happened but that some of the older folk with sense cried out to the young ones not to haver, where the hell did they want to land—in the nick? And the young toff nodded to the bobby, Feet: *We've a legal right to be here to argue with anybody who tries to get into the Works. . . . Lads here's the first of the blacklegs coming.*

Sure enough they were, a dozen of the muckers, the most of them foremen like old Johnny Edwards, dandering along in a bouroch, fair hang-dog, though laughing out loud and gey brassy, fair brave if it wasn't for the wamble of their eyes and hands. They pushed through the stir, syne the picket tackled them, there rose a surge and a stour so that folk couldn't see. Then the gates were opened and in they all went, the dirty blacklegging lousy scabs. Why the hell hadn't the Reds flung them into the Dock! What the hell were Reds for but to take up a row?

Alick Watson pushed through to relieve Ewan Tavendale, Ewan said he didn't think more would come, the lot for the day, but the morn—well, there'd be a stamash, for the union wasn't supporting the strike and there'd be no strike pay unless they could raise it. . . . Then he said *You look fearfully solemn, Alick,* and smiled at a body that way he had, dark and kind, like a bit of a quean. Alick went a bit red and said *Don't haver.* And then: *That silly bitch, my sister, seemed awful concerned about you last night.*

Ewan said *Meg? Oh yes, I know her. Works at our house—she's a nice leg. Meg. But you wouldn't know, being only her brother. Bye, bye, I'm off to the committee rooms. Trease is to raise a fund for the strikers.*

He came home soaked to the skin that night with tramping the rain and helping the Reds to raise an unofficial striker's fund. But Gowans had been killed stone-dead for the day, they hadn't even got the furnaces going. He sat and told this to Chris in the kitchen, drinking hot cocoa, and then stretched and yawned: *But you're never bothered about such things, Chris. Wise woman. Goodness, I'm tired.*

Chris told him he wanted a bath and his bed, and off he should get; but he turned at the door to ask what next was to happen to the house? Was Chris to carry on without Ma Cleghorn?

Chris said she supposed so as Ma was in heaven or at least in the kirkyard of Kirrieben. Ewan laughed and yawned in a breath, *Yes, I know. But I meant*—Chris said she didn't know, she'd see, if he didn't get tired and into a bath she'd be carrying on without HIM, anyhow.

He nodded and came back and kissed her, kind, much slower and kinder than once he'd been, though his mind was far off with his strike, she supposed. Queer loon that he was, lovely loon, on even him change working its measure as sunlight on granite bringing out the gleams of gold and red through the cold grey glister. For a little while after he'd gone she stood still, thinking about him tender, amused, in a puzzled fear: then sat by the table and thought of herself and the awful soss that Ma's death had left.

Izey Urquhart had had a valuator in and valued Ma's things and share of the house at a price that had made Chris gasp. And Izey had said that unless they were ta'en over, she'd sell the gear and the houseshare as well, *she* had no fancy for the keeping of lodgings. If the lodgings could have spoken they might have answered up canty that they had no fancy for being kept by her, Chris had thought, but hadn't said it, just nodded, and been given a week to decide.

A week. And when that was over—what?

She went on with washing the supper dishes, Meg she'd sent home that afternoon, the quean had looked queer and nearly fainted, she'd almost ta'en Ma's place after her death and worked like a Trojan, too much for a girl of her size, Chris thought—absently, noting Meg filling out a bit, pale still, but not that slat of a board with a dress tacked on it that once she'd been.

Ewan met in with Ellen the evening of the next day, going up to her room, and they stopped close and smiled on the dark stair's turn. And a queer, sharp pang shot through Ewan's heart looking down on the sailing thought-shapes in her eye far down deep in the sweet kitten face. And he'd kissed her only once in his life!

Trembling, he put his hands under her arms, the lights changed to a hurrying, twinkling flurry, they kissed and quivered a minute together, and stood breathing, listening, and kissed again.

He said, mimicking her English phrase *That was fun!* and she flashed back *I've known worse!* and slipped from him: looked down from the step above: *Coming out a walk?*

He said he'd just come in; and anyhow it was raining like— She nodded, *Like hell, but I like the rain. Don't you?*

He put up his hand on hers on the stair-rail and felt the quiver of blood in her fingers: *I like you at any rate,* and stared at the fingers so that Ellen whispered *Aren't they clean?* And pulled them away and riffled his hair: *There, I'll be ready in less than a minute.*

She was ready in ten and they went out together to the windy squall of the February night, a flicker and flow of wet lights and sounds. He asked where they'd go and she said Doughty Park, and they made that in a little under twelve minutes, wide open heath that lay furth of the toun, the great trees shoomed and pattered to the rain, they passed two bobbies with glistening capes and came under the shelter of a strumming beech. Here the lads of Duncairn would take their lasses on summer nights, fair scandalous, and behave to them in that scandalous way that first had launched humankind on the globe. But this night was a treey desolation, rain-pelted, Ewan remembered that night of the year before when they'd gone that walk to the Beach and stripped and splashed a mad dip in the sea. He asked Ellen if she minded as well, she was close beside him, snuggled in the lithe.

Yes, Goodness, how silly we were! Dirty little tykes. . . . Oh, Ewan, listen to the wind!

So he listened, but only with half an ear. The night on the Beach—what had been dirty about it? Ellen said *Didn't you want to see me naked? I did you; but I didn't say. That was why it was dirty, you know.* And thought: *No, I don't suppose you did, funny Ewan.*

She was silent for a long while after that, leaning up against him, hearing the rain, content and content she could stay there all night. She said so and Ewan said he could as well, only he mightn't be so funny this time. And at that she said, sobered, that she didn't suppose he would, it was damnable for him to have fallen in love, much better to have stayed out safe and sound so's he didn't much care what she looked, how she was. And now——

So they began making plans for the future, they'd get married some time when Ewan had a salary, Ellen would be forced to leave her school. She asked how much of a salary he'd get and he said indifferently *Perhaps four pounds,* and she said *But I get as much as that now——Goodness, we'd have to stay in the Cowgate!*

He said nothing to that, she thought she had hurt him and was kind to him a little while, playing a child's game with him under the patter of the night-blinded trees, kissing him with eyelids against his cheek, butterfly kisses, rather fun. Abruptly he pushed her away, cool and quick: *Don't fool, Ellen* in his old-time voice, hard, the voice of the student Ewan that she hadn't heard since New Year's Eve.

She knew he was being only sensible, pity rather, and she said she was sorry, and they didn't stand over-close after that, the weight of the rain was seeping through the branches and now a great low gust of wind swept up the park, driving the soft ground spray in their faces. Ewan began to talk of the strike, he said that Selden and Trease and himself had already a good strike fund in hand though the union had been trying to force the men back. Ellen said it was rather a pity to have to work so closely with the Communist leaders, they'd a horrible reputation, both of them liars and not to be trusted; and Ewan said perhaps, he didn't know, anyhow their tactic of rioting for rioting's sake was pure insanity, it got nowhere, if a revolution were properly organized it should be possible for a rising class to take power with little or no violence.

But Trease and Selden were handy in the strike, stiffening it up. And laughed: *Anyhow, whoever goes back, I shan't. The manager made that plain enough. Doesn't sound bright for our marriage, does it? You should have left me alone that day on the Barmekin and I might have been good and respectable now, not mixing up with this mess of a strike, but a gent in a bowler, smoking cigarettes in spats.*

She said if he was sorry he'd mixed up with Socialism he need never mix up with her, either, then. . . . And flushed dark in the darkness, but he hadn't rumbled, innocent as a babe, nice babe. He sat down against the bole of the tree and patted the dry ground there, and caught her ankle in a gentle hand: *Sit by me a minute before we go back. You never know what'll happen to a striker to-morrow!*

As the dozen bobbies cleared the way for the scabs coming out of the Works, the dark was falling, there came a hell and pelt of a rush, you were all of you in it, young chaps and old, one bobby struck at you with his truncheon, missed, you were past him, slosh in the kisser the scab; and all about you, milling in the dark, the chaps broke in and hell broke out, the bobbies hitting about like mad, tootling on their whistles, crunch their damned sticks.

And then the fight cleared from its stance by the gates and went shoggling and wabbling over to the Docks, the dozen scabs held firm enough, the bobbies bashing to try and get them and rescue them. Old man though you were, you wouldn't have that, you pushed a foot in front of one of the bastards, down he went with a bang on the causeys, somebody stepped on his mouth and his teeth went crunch. And there, in the heave and pitch of the struggle, were sudden the waters of the Dock, dirt-mantled, greasy in oil from the fisher-fleet, the lights twinkling low above it, folk cried *In with them! Dook the scab swine!*

And in they went with a hell of a spleiter, one of them, the foreman old Johnny Edwards, crying *Lads, lads, I can't swim!* Alick Watson beside you gave him a kick: *You can't, you old mucker? Now's the chance to learn,* over he went, your heart louped in your mouth. Then some body cried to look out and run, the bobbies were coming in a regiment, near.

And you looked round and there b'God they were, the causeys clattering under their feet, waving their sticks, God, never able to face up to them. Around to the left was the way to take nipping by the timber yard over the brig. All the chaps running helter-skelter you scattered, the bobbies wouldn't spare pickets now except to bash in their brain-caps, maybe, after seeing one of their lot on the ground. B'God, this would be a tale to tell when you got back safe to Kirrieben.

And then the lot of you saw you were trapped, in the flickering light and the scud of the water, a gang of the bobbies had raced across and cut you off, big and beefy, they were crying *We've got you, you swine!*

And you all half-halted a minute and swore and ebbed back a bit, you couldn't see the bobbies' faces or they yours, they wouldn't mind, bash down and bash till their arms grew tired, and then haul a dozen of you off to the nick.

Then two of the chaps cried *Come on, lads!* and ran straight for the line of running bobbies, all of you like sheep at their heels, gritting your teeth, nieves ready for the crash. Then you saw the foremost of the running chaps throw up his hand and wave it in front of him right in the bobbies' faces, swish, the other did the same and a yowl went up, bobbies dropping their truncheons and clutching their eyes, you got a whiff running and staggered, and near sneezed your head off. Hell, that was neat, whoever thought of it.

But there'd be a bonny palaver the morn!

And next day the *Daily Runner* came out and told of those coarse brutes the Gowans strikers, and the awful things they'd done to the working folk that were coming decent-like from their jobs. And all Craigneuks read the news with horror, every word of it, chasing it from the front page to the lower half of page five, where it was jammed in between an advertisement curing Women with Weakness and another curing superfluous hair; and whenever Craigneuks came on a bit of snot it breathed out *Uhhhhhhhhhhhh!* like a donkey smelling a dung-heap, delighted, fair genteel and so shocked and stirred up it could hardly push down its grapefruit and porridge and eggs and bacon and big salt baps, fine butter new from the creamery, fresh milk and tea that tasted like tea, not like the seep from an ill-kept sump. And it said weren't those Footforthie keelies awful? Something would have to be done about them.

*   *   *   *   *

And the Reverend Edward MacShilluck in his Manse shook his bald head and pursed his long mouth and said to his housekeeper *Ahhhhhhhhhhhh,* what they needed in Duncairn were folk like the Fascists, they knew how to keep tink brutes in trim. And this nonsense about the keelies being on strike because Gowans were making shells and gas-cases—well, wasn't a strong man sure in defence? Wasn't it the best way to avoid a war for a country to keep a strong army in the field?

The housekeeper simpered and said she was sure, that must have been why the last War had happened, those coarse brutes the Germans and Frenchies, like, had had

hardly an army to their name, would it be, and that was
why the war had broke out?

The Reverend MacShilluck gave a bit of a cough and
said *Not quite, you wouldn't understand. Ahhhhhhhhhhhh,
a fine thing the War in many a way. Did I ever tell you the
story of the nurse and the soldier who was wounded in a
certain place, my Pootsy?* And the housekeeper, who'd
heard it only a hundred times, standing and sitting and
lying down, upstairs and downstairs and ben in the kitchen
and once in the bathroom, shook her bit head and made
out she hadn't, she'd her living to look after and she'd
long grown used to that look that would come in Mac-
Shilluck's eyes, a look she'd once thought in a daft-like
minute that *stank* with the foulest of all foul smells. . . .

· · · · · ·

Bailie Brown said it was that damn fool the Chief Constable, why hadn't he kept enough bobbies on hand? The
workers were all right, though misled by the Reds, if they'd
trusted their natural leaders, like himself, they wouldn't be
in the pickle they were in, drowning a foreman that had
aye been a right good Labour man, and throwing pepper
in the bobbies' eyes. They should wait till the next Labour
Government came——

· · · · · ·

The Chief Constable said it was that bloody Inspector,
he'd told him to look out for trouble at Gowans. Pepper
flung in the eyes of the men—by God, you'd find it revolver-
shots next. He was to tell the Council that unless he
had powers——

· · · · · ·

The provost motored out to his sawmill to get away from
the stir and stew, and wandered around, with his long
dreich face like a yard of bad milk, till he lighted on Ake
level-testing a lathe. And he said *Seen the news in the* Runner *this morning?* And Ake asked what news, and the Provost said about the murder down at the Docks, the strikers
drowning the old foreman Edwards and then throwing
pepper in the police's eyes. Ake said he'd seen it and hadn't
wept, a scab was a scab wherever you found him though
'twas swollen water-dead in the Duncairn docks or bairning
a quean that screamed in a hedge. . . . And the Provost

gave a bit hurried hoast and Ake thought if ever he was
walking alone on a dark-like night and Jimmy came on him,
he with his bare nieves and Jimmy with a knife, he'd stand
as much chance of getting home safe as a celluloid cat that
had strayed into hell. . . .

. . . . . .

The sub-editors' room gave a yawn and a grunt, Piddle
had done a nippy bit work of stealing the photo of that
drowned Edwards bloke. Any chance of a few of the bobbies being coshed good and proper in the next few days?—
half a dozen of them drowned would make a good spread.
Damned neat stunt that pepper-throwing, the Chief would
blame it on the Reds for sure. Tell the boy to get out
Trease's photo, bet he was under arrest by now——

. . . . .

Chris read the news and thought, far away, *Awful.* . . .
Three more days to decide on this house.

. . . . .

The Cowgate read it and a queer sound started, in tenement and wynd and went wriggling on like the passage of
a flying train of powder, twisting and glistering and louping
to and fro, back to Footforthie, up to Kirrieben, a growl of
laughing and cursing, God, some Bulgar had dealt with the
bobbies fine. And hungry Broo men that had made up their
minds to sneak down to Gowans and into the gate and try
and steal one of the striker's jobs gave a bit rub at their
hunger-swollen bellies—ah well, they must try the P.A.C.
again——

. . . . .

Jim Trease the Red leader gave a roar of a laugh and
called to his wife to bring him his boots. *They'll be coming
for me in an hour or so. Get on with the breakfast, will
you lass, I'll be hungry enough before they finish their
questioning down at the Station.* His mistress said *What,
are they after you again?* placid as you please, he'd had
so much arresting off and on in his life that she thought no
more of him marched off to jail than when he marched off
to the W.C. *And what have your gowks been doing now?*
He told her and she said that sounded gey clever, that
pepper business, and Jim Trease puffed *Clever? Some idiot*

*loon has been reading a blood. What we need are the masses
with machine-guns, not pepper. . . . To hell, and I suppose
if they heard me say that they'd chuck me out of the Communist Party!*

* * * * *

Ewan said to Alick Watson he thought he'd more sense—
who'd bought the pepper, Alick himself or that dirty little
swine Geordie Bruce?

* * * * *

Ellen met in with Ewan after dinner that day, he'd come
up from watching the pickets at Gowans, the bobbies were
keeping them aye on the move, a great birn of folk had
been there all forenoon. He told Ellen this as they went out
together, she to her school and he back to Gowans, in the
clearing weather she looked up in his face, he down at
hers—queer what a thrill that faint line of down sent
through one, funny biological freak, thought the old-time
Ewan that wasn't quite dead——

You can kiss me inside this nook, she said, lightheartedly;
and when he'd finished kissed him in return in a sudden
terror: *Oh, Ewan, be careful down at the Docks. I'm—
I'm frightened for you!*

Making early tea in the kitchen next morning Chris
looked out and saw that the rain had cleared, Spring was
coming clad in pale saffron—the sun hardly seen all the
winter months except through the blanket of Duncairn
reek. She stood and looked out an un-eident minute till
she heard the sound of feet on the stairs, Ake Ogilvie, big,
with his swaying watch-chains and his slipperless feet,
swinging into the kitchen: *Ay then, mistress.*

She said absently, her thoughts far away, still looking out
at that blink of sun, *Morning, Mr. Ogilvie,* her worries forgotten for a lovely minute. Ake sat down and tamped out
his pipe on the range: *Well, what are you doing about the
bit house?*

She'd told him something of her plight before, and he'd
listened, douce, with his ploughman's face, his stare of
impudent, grey-green eyes. *Ay, a gey bit fix,* he'd said, and
no more, he wasn't much interested; why should he be?
Now, she thought with a twinge of resentment against him,
did he think it light gossip to be taken through hand in

the early morning to pass the time? Pouring him a cup of tea she said shortly *I've no idea. Sell it up, I suppose.*

—*And after that?*

—*Oh, something'll turn up.* She turned away with the brimming tray.

He said *Well, just gi'es a minute of your crack. Let the sweir folk wait for their tea a while.*

Chris put down the tray. *Well, a minute. What is't?*

He sat and looked up at her, drinking his tea, a man from the farms and the little touns, the eternal barbarian Robert had once called him. Now he laid down the cup and gave his mouser a dight: *Ah well, this is it: I've a bit of silver saved myself—about enough to buy the share of the place that Mistress Cleghorn left to her niece. And I'm willing to come in as your partner, like.*

—*Ake! Oh, Ake, you really mean that?*

He said *Oh ay,* he meant what he said—a habit of his, like. Mistress Colquohoun was willing to take him on, then? He'd look after this lad of hers, Ewan, all right.

Something queer about that: *Ewan—what'll he have to do with it?*

—*Well, damn't, as his stepfather I suppose I'll have more than a bittie to do with him.*

Chris stared: *One or other of us has gone daft. You were proposing to share my house, weren't you, Ake?*

He looked up and nodded, douce and green-eyed: *Ay, lass, and your bed.*

Chris went through that day betwixt anger and laughter, the last would come on her in the funniest way, pour over her in a sudden red, senseless wave. Marriage?—marry a lout like him, lose all that she'd ever gained in her life with Robert, the Manse, Ewan her son? The impudence of him—Oh, the beast, the beast! And she'd stand and suddenly picture him, the sneering, half-kindly, half-bull-like face, the face of the folk of the Howe throughout, canny and cruel and kind in one facet, face of the bothies and the little touns . . . and she'd shiver away from the thought of him, thought of impossible touches, caresses, those red, creased hands and that sun-wrinkled body . . . awful enough to make her feel ill.

At the dinner hour he came back with the others, she served him and them, sitting where Ma Cleghorn once had sat, no faces missing from about the board. And Neil Quaritch looked at her: *Neat piece of goods. Sulky and sweet in a breath as one of those damned unbreeked little novelists would put it. Queer the resemblance between her and Ogilvie—chips of the same bit of stone in a way——*

John Cushnie, sweating, looked over his tie and wondered, lapsing to keeliehood a moment, if she were as put-you-off as she looked. *Should start with a woman twice your own age, he'd heard. . . .* And he coloured richly over his pimples, not decent to think of a woman like that, especially now he'd ta'en up with that night girl from an office, real superior, that he'd met at a dance——

Archie Clearmont thought, switching off Stravinsky, *Lord, what a thrill to kiss her just once!*

Ena Lyon thought she was putting on side, as usual, and her just a Common Servant.

Ellen looked up from her plate at Chris and smiled at her, dark, and thought she looked nice and queer in a way, as though newly cuddled.

Ewan had come back from the picket at Gowans, he thought *Chris looks queer,* and then forgot her, trying to work out in his mind the balance likely to be left in the voluntary fund when they'd paid out the first week's pay to the strikers.

Miss Murgatroyd called *Eh me, Mrs. Colquohoun, You're fairly looking Right Well to-day. Has your lad been sending you a love-letter now?* and beamed round the table like a foolish old hen, all the others looking down at their plates, uncomfortable . . . *silly old bitch . . . blithering old skate . . . randy dame . . . silly thing . . . sex-repressed . . . half-witted old wombat. . . .* And a sudden impulse came on Chris, looking down the table and smiling at Miss Murgatroyd:

No, though it's something much the same. I had a proposal of marriage this morning.

There was a dead silence round the table a second. Ewan hadn't heard, Chris saw his indifferent face and her heart sank, on that impulse she'd thought he'd ask *Who proposed?* and she'd tell the whole table and watch Ake's face. But he hadn't heard; and the others began a babble: Who was the lucky man? Was she to accept? Chris laughed and shook her head and said nothing and the talk passed on to other things.

Ake sat and ate up his meat, calm and sonsy, but biding when the others had gone. Then he looked up and pushed back his chair, slow, certain; and looked over at Chris.

Ay, mistress, you cook a gey tasty meal. But a word in your lug: try no tricks on me. I'm not your fool nor anybody's fool.

Chris looked at him in a curious pity, *It was a silly caper, Ake.*

He said that that was fine, then; and when would she let him know about this partnership business?

Chris said she didn't know, but soon, anyhow; and was moved to a stark curiosity: *Ake, why do you want to marry me so bad? Just to sleep with a woman: that all? I've been married twice already, you know, and it doesn't seem it was lucky for the men.*

He said he was willing to take his risk; and he didn't suppose that Colquohoun or Tavendale had thought themselves cheated, however they ended.

She said she had little mind for any man again, that was the plain truth of it. If she married at all it would be with little liking, necessity only the drive.

Ake nodded: *We'd soon alter that, never fear.* And fear itself leapt in her heart at his look. *There's no woman yet that I couldn't content.*

Trease wouldn't squeal, an old hand him, and the Station Inspector wouldn't let the chaps go into his cell and give the bastard a taste of what he needed, he could raise hell in the courts over-easily, he knew the law inside out and bottom up. So he was letten out, laughed, and went home; and still there wasn't the ghost of a clue to point to the names of the striker swine who'd flung the pepper or drowned old Edwards.

The Gowans gates pickets had a fair dog's life, bobbies badgering them backward and forward, keen to have out their sticks and let fly. The manager had ta'en on a bouroch of blacklegs with a bit of the plant on the go again, but bobbies or no to march by their side the scabs were scared to their marrowbones to be seen going in or out of the Works.

Sergeant Sim Leslie went to the Inspector and said he wasn't sure, but he had an idea, that the striker at the bottom of most of the business was the young toff Tavendale from the Gowans office. He'd known him back in the toun of Segget, as coarse a loon as you'd meet anywhere.—— And the Chief said *Is this a moral homily or what have you got to say about him?* And Feet habbered a little and then got it out: That assault on him at the Beach last year when he was taking a couple in charge for naked bathing—ay, not a stitch—he was nearly sure 'twas the Tavendale loon; besides, his stepfather had been a Red, a minister that fair demoralized a parish. And the Chief said he wasn't interested in genealogy, had Feet any clue to this Tavendale having drowned Johnny Edwards or thrown the pepper?

Feet said he hadn't; and went back on his beat on the Docks patrol that centred now round the Gowans gates. The picket was dozing away in the lithe from a stiff bit blow of wind from the harbour as Feet came bapping along the calsays. He stopped and looked at the nearest picket, a surly-looking young swine he was, cowering down in the shelter of a barrel. And this picket instead of raspberrying him as most of the impudent muckers would do, looked round about him sly and said low: *Hey, Feet, a word with you, there.*

Feet asked if he knew who he was talking to, and the picket said *Ay, fine that, think I'm blind? Look here, if you want to know who started the pepper business look out for the next birn of pickets that relieves us and spot a long, dark-like chap of my age.*

Feet near louped in his meikle boots, but he showed not a sign, just gave a bit purr: *Tavendale, d'you mean?* and the picket said *Ay. The bastard hasn't been able to keep his hands to himself—or other things about his rotten self either. He's done me dirty and it's my turn now.*

Feet said *You'll come and give evidence?* but the picket said *Away to hell with you. Think I'm your pimp, you bap-faced peeler? Find out your evidence for yourself.*

Feet thought of taking him a whack on the head, with his truncheon, like, to teach him manners; but the rest of the picket was getting suspicious and rising to its feet and dandering near, it wouldn't do to rouse the coarse brutes, they might heave even a sergeant into the Docks, they'd no respect for the weight of the Law. So Feet swung away down to the Gowans gate to the constable body that was stationed there; and the picket came up and cried *Hey, Alick, what was that whoreson gabbing about?*

Alick Watson turned up the collar of his coat, and the chaps thought it funny he was shivering like that.

Chris stood in her room and looked out of the window at the quick-darkening February afternoon. It was this day only a year ago that Robert had died in the pulpit of Segget, the blood gushing suddenly up on his lips as he preached his last sermon with a broken heart, Robert, kind, a dreamer, a lover of men, lover of his Chris once with passion and humour, sweet and leal and compassionate. And the world had broken his heart and his mind, his dreams grey ash that had once been fire. In that last sermon he'd preached for salvation *'A stark, sure creed that will cut like a knife, a surgeon's knife through the doubt and disease—men with unblinded eyes may yet find it—'* not Christianity, or love, or his Socialism, some dreadful faith that he might not envisage. And then he had died; and she minded his lips, stained red, bubbly red, and the curl of the hair on his head, dear alive hair on a head that was dead. . . .

. . . Oh, less kind to you than I might have been. And I can't help it now, that's by and put past, nothing helps now, as little as you can I ever see a way out of all the ill soss. Not that I think I would look if I could, I've no patience with crowds or the things they want, only for myself I suppose I can plan. And I stand in the bareness, alone, tormented, and you . . . Oh, Robert man, had you stayed to help somehow we might have found the road together. . . .

Daft old wife to weep over something long by that couldn't be mended, her nature hers, his his, all chances gone in that dust of days they'd known together in Segget, in love, in estrangement, in fear and disgust—all ash with him and finished forever. And on this day of all she must try to decide . . . sell herself like a cow, a cow's purpose, in order to keep a roof over her head.

And abruptly she was minding Robert's study in Segget, the panelled walls black-lined with books, the glint of peat-light on the chairs, the desk, Robert sitting deep in a chair, head in hands, she herself looking down at him in pity and disgust because of that weak God he feared and followed. And with that memory something seemed to blow through the room, blowing out the picture like a candle-flame . . . she had finished with men forever, and could never again stir to a semblance of life that something which died when Robert died. Better a beggar in Duncairn's wynds than sell herself as she'd almost planned.

And so she would tell Ake Ogilvie to-night.

When Alick Watson reached home in the Cowgate after coming off picket at Gowans and Gloag's he met the old woman going trauchling out, away to her afternoon cleaning up for a widow body that bade in Craigneuks. She said *God be here, are you back again? Well, try and do something for once for your meat. Your sister's lying in her bed, no well. If she wants anything, see that you get it her.*

Alick said he could do that without being blackguarded, Meg was his sister, wasn't she? And the old woman said not to give her his lip, the useless skulking striking swine, wasn't he black ashamed to live off his folk's earnings? And Alick said *Away to hell. Did I ask to be born in your lousy bed in this lousy toun?* and brushed past her, swearing soft to himself because of that stricken look in her eye.

Inside he got ready a cup of tea, bread and corned beef, and sat and ate, Meg asleep in the other room, he heard her turn and toss once, and stopped and listened, better to busy himself with such sounds he needn't think then of what he had done . . . slipped the pepper poke into Ewan's pouch, God! if the other chaps ever found out——

And then Meg called *Alick, I heard you come in. Will you bring me a drink of water?*

He carried it to her and put his arm under her, lifting her, she was heavy already though he was the only one of the silly swine that had seen it yet. And because he aye had liked her so well, as she him, though they'd never let on, he found a sharp pain in his breast as he held her. Then she pushed him away in a minute, and was sick.

Alick said that he'd better go get the doctor, and she said not to talk like a meep-headed cuddy, couldn't a lassie be sick now and then?

—*Ay, but not that kind of sickness, Meg. When was it you were bairned?*

She said *Eh?* and then lay still for a minute, staring; he said it was no good to look at him like that, he'd known a long time and she might as well tell.

She turned her face to the pillow then, away from him, and whispered *Six months ago. Oh, Alick!* and began to cry, soft, in the littered bed, in a misery he couldn't help, could only stare at helpless. *Where did he do it, the bastard? Up in his toff's room in Windmill Place?*

She turned her head and stared again, and he saw the flyting quean in her eyes: Windmill Place? What was he havering about? The beast was never at the Place in his life.

Alick said *Listen, you bitch, and answer me straight;* and bent over the bed and caught her wrists, crushing them in sudden, frantic nieves. *Who's the father? Be quick and tell me!*

When he heard her say *Steve Selden,* he knew he'd been done, had played the fool. And Oh God, Ewan—if Ewan were caught——

He tore from the room and out of the house, banging the door behind, down the steps, the old whaler captain was out in the court, lurching home and singing a hymn, Alick saw his old wife peering down in fear. But he brushed past the old carle and ran for the entrance, two chaps that he knew were entering the court, they tried to stop him, for a joke, and he flung them aside, and paid no heed as they cried was it daftness or dysentery? And out in the Cowgate he started to run, dodging in and out the ash-cans on the pavement, a black cat ran across the street in front, that for luck, hell, there was a bobby.

So he slowed to a walk going by the bobby, if a childe were seen by a bobby running in the Cowgate he was sure to be chased and caught and questioned. Out of range Alick took to his heels again and gained Alban Street the same minute as a tram.

Only as he climbed the steps did he mind that he hadn't even a meck upon him, and turned to jump off as the tram with a showd swung grinding down to the Harbour: suddenly shining in a glint of sun, gulls above it, the guff of the Fish Market meeting the tram like a smack in the face, it grunted and sneezed and galloped on through it. But the conductor had seen Alick and caught his arm: *Look out, you whoreson, jumping off here. You'll bash out your brains—if you've any to bash.*

Alick said he'd found he'd no money on him, he was one of the strikers at Gowans and Gloag's in the hell and all of a hurry to get down with a bit of news for the rest of the lads. He'd jump off here——

But the trammie held fast, a squat, buirdly bird with a face like a badly-made barn door. And he said Not so fast, wasn't he Union as well? Here, he'd pay the ticket. Sit down and wait.

That shortened the run, in a minute the Docks, the trammie slowed down at a bend where he shouldn't the nearest to Gowans, and Alick jumped off and cried his thanks and took to his heels and ran like the wind.

When the four o'clock picket went on that day there hadn't been as big a birn as usual of idle folk to look on and claik. The cold was biting across Footforthie gnawing through the thin breeks and jackets of Broo men, sending them taiking off to the Library to read last Sunday's *Sunday Post,* the racing news and the story of a lassie raped, bairned, killed, and fried up in chips—Ay, fairly educative, the Scottish newspapers. . . . But a dozen or so still hung about, not expecting much of a shindy at all: but you never knew when a strike was on, there might be a bit of snot flying ere long.

There was only one of the bobbies there, the young country cuddy, he grinned at the picket and once cried him the old tale of the bobby whose beat was fair littered with whores: and a new sergeant came on the beat one night and set the bobby to jailing each whore, but at last the bobby put his splay feet down: *I've run in my sisters and my auntie to please you, my wife and my daughter and my cousin Jean, but I'm damned if I'll run in my mother as well——*

And they all guffawed, they'd no spite against him, he none against them, funny a chap like that should have joined up with the lousy police though you couldn't much blame him, fine uniform to keep out the cold, good pay and a pension and perks for the picking. And you blew your chilled hands and spat in the Docks and were just thinking about dandering away home again when you looked up and saw a half-dozen police coming swaggering down to the Gowans gates, the meikle sergeant, Feet, in the lead. You cleared your throat and spat on the ground to get the stink of their wind from your thrapple, but the birn went by with hardly a look, they were all speaking low and chief-like together: what dirty business were they planning now?

The only chap of the picket who stood in the road was the young toff childe folk said was half-Red. He drew back a bit to let the bobbies gang by, but they weren't looking and one of the stots gave a stumble and nearly tripped over the toff. Then, afore you could wink, a queer thing was on, the bobby had grabbed the young toff by the neck and Feet cried out: *What's that—assaulting the police? Right, my lad, you can come up to the Station.*

Young Tavendale said not to talk rot, the constable had been stumbling all over the street. Some others of the picket came out from the lithe, hanging round the bobbies, and called the same, the cuddy of a bobby had had the staggers, or water on the brain—if he had a brain. But Feet cried *Stand back, or we'll take you as well;* and he asked Tavendale if he'd come peaceable or not and Tavendale lifted his shoulders with a laugh and said he supposed so, he was cool and unfeared: and turned round sudden on the bobby that had bumped him: *I can see that this is a put-up show——*

Afore he could say another word, God, what a crack! the bobby had his stick out and smashed him to the ground. Then he looked at Feet and the meikle swine nodded: *In self-defence, Dickson. All right, pick him up.*

You saw the toff as they carried him past, he was only a kid, his hair dripping with blood, he hung like a sack among their fat hands. The picket tailed after crying that they'd see about this: but at that the rest of the bobbies faced round and in half a minute had cleared the street, Feet said the picket was trying to prevent an arrest.

And off they carted young Tavendale; and just as you were slipping off home yourself to spread the news in Kirrieben you ran bang into a white-faced young fool, panting and habbering, *What's on at Gowans?* You told him, and he cried Oh God, he'd never meant it, and you thought he was probably drunk, or daft, or both, and left him to it, he looked soft enough to pitch himself head first in the Docks——

Every movement he made sent a stream of pain down his legs and body, he thought, but wasn't sure, that his right arm was broken where they'd twisted it; and thought again *Not likely, that would show too much;* and fainted off in the fire of the pain.

When next he woke he thought it near morning, his throat burning, he tried to cry for a drink of water. And after a minute the cell door opened, a blaze from the passage on the blaze in the cell, he saw a dim face, big, it floated, and the face said he'd get a drink if he owned up now it was him that had drowned Johnny Edwards and organized the throwing of the pepper at the Docks? And Ewan moved his swollen lips, dull mumble, and heard himself say *You can go to hell!* Then his head went crack on the bobby's boot. . . .

When he'd come-to after that time at the Docks he'd found himself on a bench in the station, they'd started to ask his name and address and take it down in a big casebook. He'd asked what charge he was arrested on, and the big sergeant at the desk said he'd know soon enough, none of his la-de-da lip here, the bastard. *Right, boys, rape him.*

Two bobbies had taken on the job, in a minute they'd come on a bag of pepper, he'd stared, how the devil had that got there? The sergeant had cried *What say you to that?* and Ewan, half-blind with a headache, had said *Rats. Some groceries I was buying for my mother, that was all,* and the sergeant said by God, was that so? If his mother knew him when he finished with the Force she'd be a right discerning woman, she would: *Take him off to No. 3 cell, Sergeant Leslie. See he doesn't try to assault you again.*

He'd thought that a lout joke, suddenly it wasn't, three of them came into the cell behind him. And he'd minded in a flash of a story he'd read of the ghastly happenings in American jails. Rot: this was Scotland, not America, the police were clowns and idiot enough, but they couldn't——

Two of them held him while Sim Leslie bashed him, then they knocked him from fist to fist across the cell, bodyblows in the usual Duncairn way with Reds, one of them slipped in the blood and swore, *That's enough for the bastard, he'll bleed like a pig.* Lying on the floor, Ewan had heard a queer bubbling, himself blowing breath through bloody lips.

Then, the cell wavering, they'd picked him up and flung him down on the wooden trestle. *Now, answer up or you'll get the works*—And they'd asked him again and again to declare it was he had caused the drowning of Edwards; and he'd bitten his lips, saying nothing, till their fumblings at last brought a scream shrilling up in his throat, a bit of it ebbed out and the bobbies left off, standing and listening, feared it might have been heard even down this deserted corridor of cells. Then they said they'd leave him alone for a while, they'd be back in a wee to the mucking Red swine. . . .

And still he'd said nothing, setting his teeth, though the pain behind his teeth had clamoured to him to let go, to confess to anything, anything they wanted, Oh God for a rest from this. But the real self that transcended himself had sheathed its being in ice and watched with a kind of icy indifference as they did shameful things to his body, threatened even more shameful, twisted that body till his self cowered in behind the ice and fainted again. . . . And now, as he thought, the morning was near.

He moved a little the arm he'd thought broken, it wasn't, only clotted with bruises, the dryness had left his throat, he lay still with a strange mist boiling, blinding his eyes, not Ewan Tavendale at all any more but lost and be-bloodied in a hundred broken and tortured bodies all over the world, in Scotland, in England, in the torture-dens of the Nazis in Germany, in the torment-pits of the Polish Ukraine, a livid, twisted thing in the prisons where they tortured the Nanking Communists, a Negro boy in an Alabama cell while they thrust the razors into his flesh, castrating with a lingering cruelty and care. He was one with them all, a long wail of sobbing mouths and wrung flesh, tortured and tormented by the world's Masters while those Masters lied about Progress through Peace, Democracy, Justice, the Heritage of Culture—even as they'd lied in the days of Spartacus, lying now through their hacks in pulpit and press, in the slobberings of middle-class pacifists, the tawdry promisings of Labourites, Douglasites. . . .

And a kind of stinging bliss came upon him, knowledge that he was that army itself—that army of pain and blood and torment that was yet but the raggedest van of the hordes of the Last of the Classes, the Ancient Lowly, trampling the ways behind it unstayable: up and up, a dark sea of faces, banners red in the blood from the prisons, torn entrails of tortured workers their banners, the enslavement and oppression of six thousand years a cry and a singing that echoes to the stars. No retreat, no safety, no escape for them, no reward, thrust up by the black, blind tide to take the first brunt of impact, first glory, first death, first life as it never yet had been lived——

Trease said *Ay, well, we'll do what we can—and a wee thing more. But I wouldn't advise you to come to the court.*

Chris asked why, and the big man with the twinkling eyes

in the great pudding face got up from the sofa in the sitting-room and looked at her as though passing a mild comment on the weather: *I'm feared your Ewan'll have been bashed a bit—all in bandages, you know, and a bit broken up.*

Chris stared: *But he didn't try to resist! All the rest of the picket saw his arrest.*

Trease twinkled his little eyes a bit, a mild joke: *Oh ay, but he's a Communist, you see, or he'll be by now, for his fancy League was no more than the dream of an earnest lad. Anyway, the bobbies think him a Red and they aye get Reds to 'resist' at the station, they generally mash them in No. 3 cell. And this is your Ewan's first go, you know, they try to kill off the Red spirit right off.*

Chris said that was daft, they couldn't do things like that in this country, anybody knew the police were fair and any-body accused got a fair trial. Trease nodded, faith ay, if you were of the middle class and wore good clothes and weren't a Communist. Och, anything else—a sodomist, a pervert, a white slave trafficker, a raper of wee queans—any damn thing that you liked to think of. But if you were a revolu-tionary worker you got hell. Fair enough, for the Reds weren't out to cure the system, they were out to down it and cut its throat.

He waited while Chris got her coat and hat and left the house to look after itself. At Windmill Brae they found a tram and were down at the court by ten o'clock.

Outside were already a birn of men, down-at-heels, un-shaven, they cried *Hello, Jim,* and stared at Chris and came drifting around Trease, unwashed, their stink awful, their faces worm-white, Chris stared at them with a sinking heart. Were these the awful folk that Ewan had ta'en up with?

Bobbies all about the entrance door, one or two had come down in the street, big-footed, and were pushing about, beefy and confident, truncheons out and shoulders squared. Trease stroked his chin and twinkled at the Broo men and strikers: *We'll demonstrate later, lads. You'd better disperse and not raise a row.*

So the two got into the court at last, Chris had never been in one before, panelled in dark wood, with a witness box with a curling bit of wood above it that vexed her because the thing looked so daft. She whispered to Trease asking what it was, and he twinkled back 'twas the sounding-board, and then leaned back in his bench and yawned, they'd not have her Ewan on for a while, they'd wait till the Bailie got hot up a bit.

They finished at last with the street queans ta'en up, a soldier who'd stolen cigarettes from a stall, a man who'd knocked over a boy with a lorry. But there wasn't much in any of the cases, Bailie Brown, the leader of Duncairn Labour, rapped out his sentences snell and smart, fair a favourite with all the bobbies and giving double the sentences a Tory would have given—to show that he was impartial, like. Then Chris saw an inspector go whisper to him and the Bailie look at his watch and nod; and the far door opened and some body in a bandage came in unsteadily between two bobbies, Chris knew one, Sergeant Sim Leslie of Segget.

And then she knew Ewan, and some body cried *Order!* and Trease gripped her knee so hard that it hurt, left her breathless and she couldn't cry again, couldn't do anything but stare and stare at the bandaged figure pass in front of her and stand in the dock, the bobbies all a-glower. A little neat man got up with a paper, and hitched his gown and gave a quick gabble, talking down his shirt-front low and confidential. Then he asked for a remand . . . death of John Edwards . . . brutal assault on police at Docks . . . incriminating evidence. . . . Violently resisting arrest——

The Bailie nodded and looked up at the clock, *Remanded till Friday,* and then stood up, everybody stood, and a bobby grabbed the bandaged figure.

As the bobbies passed by below Trease leaned forward: *Okay, Ewan?*

—*I'm all right. They've got nothing out of me. Hello, Chris. Don't worry.*

Neil Quaritch said he was damnably sorry but he couldn't do anything with the papers about it, he was only sub-ed and book-hound on the *Runner.* Besides, the *Runner* daren't make a comment on a case sub judice. Not that it would make it if it could. Oh, the police were a pretty low set of brutes, but he couldn't believe this tripe about Ewan being tortured—this was Duncairn, not Chicago; just Red blah Mrs. Colquohoun could discount. Pity Ewan had been led away by the Reds, if he wanted social change there was Douglasism. Financial Credit operated at Social Credit would ensure that the products of Real Credit, though privately owned, were not malac-credited.

Mr. Piddle said *He-he!* he was dreadfully sorry. Yes, he'd been in the court and seen young Mr. Tavendale, and yes, he'd written the story for the *Daily Runner.* No, he hadn't intended to offend anyone, but the public must have its news, Mrs. Colquohoun. Could she give him a photo for the *Tory Pictman?* And wasn't it the case that her husband, the late minister of Segget, had also held—*He-he!*—rather extremist opinions?

Jim Trease said plain that of course the Communists would exploit the case to the full—for their own ends first, not for Ewan's. They'd do all they could for him, but Ewan was nothing to them, just as he, Jim Trease, was nothing.

Miss Murgatroyd said Eh me, it was Awful, and young Mr. Ewan Such Fine to get on with, right interested in the books on old Scottish magic that she'd loaned him—they were Awful Powerful in magic, the Picts. However had he got in such company?—It was said he'd assaulted the police Just Awful and them so kind and obliging, Too. Ask some of her friends at the Unionist Club to interfere?—oh, she couldn't do that she was feared, it wouldn't be right, now, would it? And they all terrible against the Reds, not that Mr. Tavendale was really one, she knew, but there you were, oh, she was terribly sorry——

Archie Clearmont said *Hell, was that Ewan? Didn't know he was Red. So was Wagner. Anything whatever I can do to help*——

John Cushnie said nothing but handed in his notice, he couldn't very well stay on any longer, and him an employé of Raggie Robertson's, you ken——

Ellen Johns said, white, *Anything you want. I'm a Socialist, too, and I started him on it—he's a Socialist, not a Red, it's all a ghastly mistake. Oh, Chris, how did he really look? . . . Oh, Chris, I'm sorry, I'm a fool to cry, he'd think me a fool*——

Ake Ogilvie said to Chris not to fret. He thought he could maybe fix up this business.

He went off to his work and bade off the whole day while Chris went about with a mind gone numb, dead brain in her head, scrubbing and cooking and serving the meals, helped by the new maid, a big widow woman who was kind as she could be and never spoke a word about Ewan or the case. The blink of March daylight closed into dark and still Chris worked in a numbing fear; then at

last, as it drew to tea-time, she heard the front door open
and Ake on the stairs, his slow, independent clump on the
stairs. A wee while later he came down again and opened
the door: *Ay, mistress, a word with you.*

He sat in the sitting-room, filling his pipe: *Well, you're
looking on an unemployed man.*

Chris said *What?* and Ake nodded and struck a match,
and took a bit puff, and said Right on the Broo, Jimmy'd
finished with him and he with Jimmy. But that was neither
here nor there at the moment. The main thing was that
Ewan would be safe—or else Jimmy's bit secret would be
all over Duncairn as fast as Ewan's Red friends and Ake
could spread it abroad. Ay, a great thing, scandal.

Chris gasped *Ake, Ake, it's true?* and he said *Oh ay.
There, mistress, don't take on so. He's safe, your loon, they
won't push the case—that's the quality of justice we've got
in Duncairn. Sit you still a wee bit and I'll tell the tale.*

She realized later he told it her so that she might hide
in herself again. But her mind at the time frothed over the
telling like a wild thing mad to be out of a cage, trying to
think, to think that Ewan——

And Ake said he'd not made the sawmill that morning,
but sought out Speight and put it to him that he could get
this bit case against the young Red quashed—Ake knew
the lad, there was no harm in him, a decent student, and
he'd been sore mishandled already by the bobbies. And
Jimmy had listened with his long dreich face looking
dreicher than ever, and shaken his head, he couldn't interfere, he'd no power to influence the courts or the bailies.
Ake had told him for God's sake not to talk wet, they were
both of them out of their hippens by now, the Lord Provost
kenned as well as he did that there was as much graft in
the average Scots toun as in any damn place across the
Atlantic.

Who invited contracts for agreed-on tenders? Who arranged the sale of public land and bought it afore the offer
was made public? Who took a squeeze off the water rates,
and who made a bit thing from the Libraries? And where
did the bobbies, inspectors and sergeants get their extra
wages for houses and motors except by acting as pimps
for the whores, living off the lasses and running them in
when they wouldn't pay up their weekly whack? And was
there a bookie's pitch in Duncairn that didn't pay tribute,
week in, week out? Not one.

Speight said that all that was just coarse rumour and scandal, he knew nothing about it, and Ake said *Maybe. And you'll see that this young Tavendale's let off with a caution, or whatever the flummery's necessary?*

The Lord Provost had nearly burst with rage then, he'd said he'd be damned if he'd be badgered and blackmailed in this way any longer, all because of a small mistake in his youth—was he the first young childe to rape a lass in a hedge, with a bit of darkness to hide his identity? . . . And Ake had seen he half-meant what he said, a rat that was fair being driven in a corner, he'd pressed him over-hard and his nerve would gang, the next thing might be Ake himself in the jail.

So he'd laid his proposition in front of Jimmy; if he'd bring this off in the Tavendale case Ake would never again breathe a single word about that lassie raped in a hedge, never a whisper in public or private, nor seek for any advantage on't. And the Provost had said *And you'll leave my sawmill?* and Ake had given a big shrug and said *Ay. All right, Jimmy, it's ta-ta, then.*

When Alick Watson had settled with Red Steve Selden he looked more like a mess in a butcher's shop than a leader that had once been out in Canada and come back to Scotland all in a fash to see to the emancipation of the working class. They fought it out in a Cowgate wynd, four of the chaps had come to see fair play, in the end they held Alick and said to Selden he'd best give best else he'd get bloody murdered.

Selden coughed and spluttered and stood up again and said he'd never given any man best, it wasn't his wyte he had bairned the lass and it wasn't his wyte she'd never let on. Alick said *What the hell! You knew all the time!* but Selden swore by God he never had, if he'd known he'd have done the decent thing. And all the chaps that were standing around cried out to Alick he might believe that, it was true enough, those daft Bulgars the Reds were as scared and respectable about bairning a quean as though they went to the kirk three times on a Sunday and said a grace afore every meal, there was hardly a one but was doucely married, they never looked near a lass if they were, a damn lot of killjoys a lot of folk said. . . . So Alick had had all his fighting for nothing: and what the hell was his fury for?

Alick said they could mind their own mucking business;

and put on his coat and went up to the Slainges Barracks
direct and hung about outside the gates a while, half-feared
and yet desperate, the sentry looked at him and said *Hello,
chum!* And Alick said *Hello. Is this where you 'list?*

The sentry, he was swinging to and fro in his kilt and
carrying a wee stick, not a rifle, took a keek at the guard-
room and syne round about, and said *For God's sake,
what's ta'en you?*—*have you lain with your sister or robbed
a bank?* Alick said he'd done neither; and the sentry said
not to be a soft fool, why join up in this lousy mob? The
grub was stinking potatoes, worse beef, seven shillings a
week pay and about half of that docked in sports and fines.
It was just plain hell when it wasn't hell decorated.

Alick said Ah well, he'd just take his chance; and went
in through the gates to the office place, a wheen of poor
muckers were wheeling round the square, shoggle and
thud, they looked half-dead, punishment drill of some kind
Alick knew. And he half made up his mind to turn back,
then swore at himself for a yellow-livered fool, they couldn't
do worse to him, could they, than the bobbies had done to
Ewan?—Oh God! And he burst open the door of the office
place and went in and they asked who the hell he thought
he was, the Colonel, maybe? and closed the door; and
that was Alick Watson's end for the Cowgate.

Folk heard the news and took it through hand, he must
fair have gone skite, the silly young mucker, wearied no
doubt with the darg of the strike. Most knew he'd a hand
in the drowning of old Johnny Edwards—well, what of
that? More than a dozen had had a bit hand, and a damn
good job, the lousy old scab. And *they* didn't run off in a
fear to 'list, they marched with the band that Jim Trease
got up to demonstrate outside the Central Court where
young Ewan Tavendale was coming up on Friday.

Banners and slogans, Jake Forbes wth his drum, a cold,
dreich, early April day. One or two as they slumped along
thought of Alick ticking to another drum now. And what
would young Tavendale get, would you say?

Then they heard a bit cheer break out up in front, and
the news came flying down the ranks like fire, it was true
enough, no it wasn't, yes it was, there he was coming down
the steps himself, his head all bandaged: he waved a hand.
He'd been letten off with a bit of a fine, his mother had paid
it for him at once, there she was behind—*God, that his*

*mother? I could sleep with her the morn and think her his
sister. . . . Sulky-looking bitch. . . . Get out, she's fine. . . .
There's Ewan. Now, lads, give him a cheer!*

Into the procession, Chris never knew how, marching by
the side of Ewan up the Mile, *boomr* the drum in the hands
of the fat man, big Mr. Trease stumping ahead with his
grin and his twinkle, Ewan's hand in hers. She wished
they'd left her alone with her son, Ake had stood aside as
they came from the court, *No, not me,* he had said to Jim
Trease. *I'm no body's servant, the Broo folk's or the bobbies',* Chris had liked him for that for she felt the same,
had always felt so and felt more than ever that she belonged
to herself alone. Except for Ewan: Ewan's hand in hers.
And he looked down and laughed, strained, cool from his
bandages: *Cheer up, Chris, it'll soon be over and we can
slip off and be respectable!*

> . . . Come dungeon dark or gallows grim
>   This song shall be our parting hymn!

The procession halted below Windmill Steps, Trease had
seen to that, he did it for her, Chris knew: a little thing
that wouldn't hurt his propaganda. And the Paldy folk
grabbed hold of Ewan and raised him up on the Steps:
Come on, gi'es a word, Ewan! and a sudden hush fell,
Chris stood back and waited and knew herself forgotten.

And he said in his clear and cool boy's voice that they
needn't bother to make a fuss, he'd got no more than any
might expect who was out to work for the revolution. One
thing he had learned: the Communists were right. Only by
force could we beat brute force, plans for peaceful reform
were about as sane as hunting a Bengal tiger with a Bible.
They must organize the masses, make them think, make
them see, let them know there was no way they could ever
win to power except through the fight of class against class,
till they dragged down the masters and ground them to
pulp——

Then he fainted away on the Windmill Steps.

April was in with a wild burst of the bonniest weather,
fleecing of clouds sailed over Duncairn with the honking
geese from Footforthie's marshes. Out in the little back-
garden Chris saw the buds unfolding on bush and twig,
and got out her hoe from its winter sleep, over the walls

other garden folk were chintering and tamping on the drying earth. And Chris thought in that hour of the bright April
day as she hoed round the blackberry bushes and roses—
suddenly, with a long-forgotten thrill—what a fine smell
was the smell of the earth, earth in long sweeping parks that
rolled dark-red in ploughing up the hills of the Howe, earth
churned in great acres by the splattering feet of the Clydesdale horses, their breath ablow on a morning like this, their
smell the unforgotten stable smell, the curling rigs running
to meet the sun. Earth . . . and she sossed about here in a
little yard of stuff that the men she'd once known wouldn't
have paused to wipe their nebs with!

If Ewan had been as that other Ewan . . . and she paused,
bent over the hoe, at the thought. Was he so unalike? There
was something about him since that awful time when he'd
fainted on the steps of Windmill Brae that had minded her
of his father back from the War—not the Ewan of the foul
mind and foul speech, but that darker being she'd not
kenned in those days, only later when the tale of his death
was brought her: that being who had been the real Ewan
imprisoned, desperate, a wild beast seeking a shelter she
hadn't provided, a torn and tormented thing seeking a ref-
uge——

Och, she was silly to think that in this case of her little
lad whom those beasts had mistreated—though he'd had
no great mistreating, he'd told her, he was fine and would
soon be about again.

She heard the sound of footsteps coming from the house
and looked up and saw, and looked down again. And she
thought with a whimsical, cool dismay it was funny she
couldn't be letten a-be even out in the yard—a sore-harried
body! And the whimsy went, she was cool and kind.

Ay, mistress, I want a bit crack with you.

—*Yes, Ake.*

He blew out a cloud of smoke, brushed it aside, he was
standing with his big, well-blacked boots unlaced, his waistcoat open, his mouser well-curled, undisturbed, unhurrying,
she felt his gaze on the side of her face. And he said they'd
held up this business of a decision while he'd loaned her
the money to carry on the house and ward off Miss Cleghorn's holy bitch of a niece: but now came an accounting
one way or the other: *Are you going to have me, then, as
your man?*

And Chris unbent from the hoe and turned to him and

that thing that had once been a poet in Ake's heart and was strangled with rage ere it ever reached vision, started sudden within him, oh bonny she was, sulky and gay with her bonny bronze hair. And she said, quiet and sweet, Yes, if he'd have her. She was nothing of a bargain for all that he'd done.

He thought through the dark of every night *Oh God, if only I could sleep!* And sleep came seldom, hour on hour, while he fought to lock back in his memory those pictures: pictures of himself in that prison cell, in the hands of the bobbies while they mauled him about, pictures . . . and he'd cover his face with his hands, bury his face in the pillow to forget the sick shame of it. He, Ewan Tavendale, held like a beast, his body uncovered and looked upon, jeered at, smeared with the foulness of those filthy eyes as battered by their filthy hands, held and tormented like a frog in the hands of a gang of schoolkids. His body that once he'd hardly known, so easy and cool and sweet-running it had been: now in the dark it was a loathsome thing that he lay within, a foul thing he didn't dare look upon.

In the grip of that fear he locked his room every night, went about the house swathed up to the chin, Chris was watching, she'd know, Chris or else Ellen. Ellen and he once—sickening to think of, filthy and dirty, lips like hers on his. . . . *Oh, God, please let me sleep!*

Jim Trease called in that day with the news that the strike at last had come to an end, he sat with Ewan in the sitting-room, big, heavy and red, his little eyes twinkling. They'd all gone back and were cheerily at work making their armament bits again—'twas even said that Gowans were to install a gas-loading plant soon. Oh, the strikers had got the speeding up slowed down and a bit of an increase on all the piece-rates, Bolivia and Japan were in a hell of a stamash to get arms: and Gowans were dancing in tune.

—And I went through what I did—just for that?

Jim Trease nodded, Ay, just for that. And for just the same kind of result he'd been going through the like things a good fifteen years—living on a pay a little better than a Broo man's, working out his guts for those thick-witted fools. . . . He twinkled his eyes and smoked his cigarette, looking like a Christmas pig, Ewan thought, with some foolish toy stuck in its mouth by a butcher. . . . And he'd do it another fifteen years till the bobbies got him down in some bit of a riot and managed to kick in his skull, he supposed—*For it's me and you are the working-class, not the poor Bulgars gone back to Gowans.* And suddenly was serious an untwinkling minute: *A hell of a thing to be History, Ewan!*

And for awhile his words and the image they painted abided with Ewan when Trease himself had gone shambling away across Windmill Place, turning, stout, shabby, to wave ta-ta. A hell of a thing to be History!—not a student, a historian, a tinkling reformer, but LIVING HISTORY ONESELF, being it, making it, eyes for the eyeless, hands for the maimed!——

And then he was shrinking back from the window at the sight of Ellen; but she'd seen him; waved. And across his memory there swept again, picture on picture, an obscene film, something they'd stick in him while he writhed, a bobby's hand——

Ewan!

He kept his face buried in his arms, feeling her arms around him tight, her hair against his cheek, shivering away from the touch of that. And he said to her *Go away!* and she wouldn't, kept close to him, holding him, shaking him: *Ewan, listen, you're to tell me what's wrong with you— what I've done that you avoid me like this. Ewan, do you hate me so much and so suddenly?*

He told her he didn't hate her at all, it was just that he was white-livered, he supposed. And sat up and pushed her away, not looking at her, looking a boy still, with the scar down his temple healed by now. Ewan scarred: last time it had been the keelies, this time the police: who next? and she shuddered as he himself had done. And then in the queerest fashion it came to her that she knew what was wrong, suddenly, she tingled with a blush that spread all over her body, neck, cheek and breast, goodness knew how far, a blush of unbearable shame and compassion: Oh Ewan, poor Ewan!

But she didn't say that, crouched beside him with her chin in her hands looking at him and loving him so that she almost wept; and was desperate while her mind sought round and round for a way to get at him, to help him.

And slowly, with a queer unemotion, she realized the only way—if she'd take it for him.

He'd sat staring out of the window the while, now she ran

to that window and pulled open the curtains and stared up at the sky. April was in, the weather would keep all day she thought: *Ewan, what are you doing this week-end?*

He said Nothing. Read a book. Hadn't an idea.

—*I want to go out a long ride on a bus. Somewhere. I get so sick of Duncairn. Will you come with me?*

—*Oh, if you like. I'll be poor enough company.*

She said she'd risk that, she'd go and find out about the buses. Would he be ready in an hour's time?

It felt the most crowded hour of her life, dragging on her hat and running from the house down to the bus-stance in Royal Mile, long lines of buses like dozing dragons, the drivers yawning and staring at the sky, staring at news-papers, buses innumerable, with all signs on them: where would she go? Then she saw a bus with GLEN DYE upon it, and she'd never been there, it was safe enough. So she found out the time when the bus was to start, the conductor said in a fifty minutes—*Don't* be late, are you bringing your lad? And Ellen said *Quite* and smiled at him, a bonny black pussy-cat of a creature, he straightened his tie and looked after her—'Od, keeks of that kind were unco scarce.

But Ellen had scrambled aboard a tram, it shoomed down the Mile as though knowing her haste, she stared in the gaudy windows of Woolies—would that do? for she hadn't much money to waste.

So she hurried in and looked in the trays, at the glitter, at the dull dog eyes of the girl at the counter, and foolishly felt sick, sentimental idiot. No, she wouldn't, she'd get it real, silly though that was!

Out of Woolies and off the Mile and found a passable place in George Street, and went in there, into a great clicking of clocks and watches, glimmer of silver, and bought what she wanted, and came out in the flying sun-scud of Spring. *What next?—This'll try your courage, my girl.*

It did, but she stuck it, looking cool as a cucumber, the shopkeeper an elderly, slow-moving man, he listened to her wants in the little shop with the ghastly books and the half-hid door, and said he thought another thing better. Had she ever tried it? And showed it to her, and Ellen said she hadn't, was it really good? And the shopman said Ay, un-emotional as a boiled turnip, he could recommend that. And

Ellen said *Thanks, I'll have it then. And I'm in a hurry.* And he said *Fine weather.*

Back to the Mile—And now—what else? Rucksacks? She'd one of her own, Ewan hadn't, Woolies again and get one for him. Running up through the crowds she looked at her watch and found she had still a half-hour to spare, saw her face as she whipped into Woolies, flushed and dark, that hair on her upper lip horrid in a way, Spanish and nice in another way. Rucksack and straps and she was digging out the sixpences, three of them, and had the thing tied up in paper. Now for Windmill Place again and see Chris after she'd bought some chocolates and fruit.

Running up the door-steps she peeped through the window and saw Ewan sitting where she had left him, staring out, that nerved her for the thing she'd to do. She ran up to his room and looked about and saw the old wardrobe hid in the corner and opened the packet she'd bought from Woolies and stuffed in things from the wardrobe, quick, stopping and listening for feet on the stairs. Then into her own room like a burglar, quiet, panting and working there like a fury, running to and fro and cramming her knapsack, anything forgotten?—Oh Lord, the things from the little shop! Here they were, save, cheers, that was all.

Chris was making scones in the kitchen when Ellen looked in, looked sweeter than ever, Ellen thought, lovely those tall Scotch cheekbones, nice sulky face.

Hello, Ellen lass, come for a scone?

Ellen said she hadn't, but she'd eat one, though; and sat on the table eating it, and they smiled one at the other, mistrust long past. And Ellen said *Mrs. Colquohoun, Ewan's not well.*

The lovely, sulky face went dark in a minute, like her son's then despite all the differences. *Where is he?—Oh, nothing new happened. But ever since that time in the jail. I want to take him out to the country—somewhere; and I want to know if you'll mind.*

Chris looked at her a minute and then laughed, saying they surely could go where they liked, they were neither of them bairns, Ellen nodded and jumped off the table. *I know. But I don't know if we'll be back to-night.*

And then she thought Ewan's mother understood, her eyes changed and grew darker and glassed over with gold in that way that Ellen had seen before. She said quietly and kindly: *I won't worry. But, Ellen——*

—*Yes?*

—*It's your life and his, but I think I ken Ewan. He's like this for the time, but he won't be long. And when he's once better . . . he's a funny lad. I don't think he'll ever be any lass's lad.*

For a second Ellen felt cold to her spine. True in a way —and she didn't care! Chris liked the gay smile on the scared pussy-face: *We're only going hiking. Bye-bye, Mrs. Colquohoun.*

Plodding teams blue steam in the parks as the fat bus grunted up the Hill of Barras, Ellen beside Ewan looked up a moment, he'd just asked, in his soft Scotch voice and as though wakening up, what were a couple of rucksacks for?

She said *For fun. I've brought some lunch.*

Below them all the eastwards Howe lay spread, grey saffron and thinly wooded, cold-gleaming under the quick Spring sun—a bare and wild and uncanny land, she'd never be at home here she thought with a shiver, though she trilled her r's and lived to be a hundred. Hideous country, ragged and cruel . . . but Ewan's shoulder against hers sweet.

And Ewan looked out and saw the Howe and far away high in the air beyond the cold parks and the dark little bourochs and nestling trees under the lithe of the shining hills, the line of the mountains, crested in snow, unmelting, Trusta Peak over High Segget, the round-breasted hills like great naked women waking and rising, tremendous, Titanic. Watching, Ellen saw his face suddenly darken, she said *Headache going?* and he answered her hardly (poor Ewan!) *Yes. I'm all right.*

Down by the Pitforthies and by Meikle Fiddes into the main road winding broad, chockablock with traffic tearing south, loaded lorries and glistening cars, swaying shapes of the great Dundee-Aberdeen buses squattering the ancient tracks of the Howe. Cattle were out from the winter byres, flanks laired in sharn and eating like mad on the thin, lush pastures that couched from the wind under the shelter of the olive-green firs. With a chink and a gleam and a slow, canny stamping the ploughmen faced up against far braes, the dirl of little stones pattered the windscreen as the bus ran through a great skellop of tar, roadmenders resting and giving them a wave, every soul in a fairly fine tune to-day.

And then, queerly and suddenly, Ewan's heart moved. He said to Ellen: *We're into Kinraddie.*

She'd never heard of it, he'd been born there, away up in a little farm in the hills, they'd see the place in a minute or so. And sure so they did, ringed round with its beech, Blawearie wheeling and unfolding, high, Ewan minded a day as a little lad standing by the side of his mother by the hackstock and watching a man in a soldier's gear going out of the close and not looking back: and his mother paying no heed to the man, the man's hands trembling as he fastened the gate. . . . So bright and near and close was the picture he shook his head to shake it way, he'd never remembered it before. That man—his father, he supposed, in the days of the War, going to the War, had he and Chris quarrelled? . . . Long ago, it had nothing to do with him.

His movement made Ellen ask if he was cold, and he turned and looked into her face, bright, flushed, little beads of sweat along her dark brows, she had opened the neck of her dress, skin warm and olive, he stared at that, looked like silk, maybe felt like it to touch. She asked, peeping a smile, if there was a smut on her nose? and saw the grey-gold eyes lose their dull film a moment. He said *Nice of you to take me out. No, I'm not cold—and there isn't a smut. Devil of a stour this bus is raising!*

The roads were dry and they ploughed a dust cloud in the wake of a wandering bouroch of sheep, maa'ing and scattering, the shepherd waved a canny hand to the driver and the driver wormed a canny way forward. Then the bus picked up and shoggled up through Drumlithie, the steeple still there: tell Ellen the joke.

They both craned out to look up at it, the steeple bell with no church behind; and Ellen's smooth braid of short-cut hair, blue-black, whipped Ewan's cheek like the touch of a bird, swift, with the smell of the spring.

And his mind at that touch remembered again the Horror: but it was in some way dimmer, queer, as though something were hiding it away. And he sat and puzzled on that while Ellen looked sideways at him and thought in a panic he looked more shut-away and lost than ever, what if she failed?—Oh, she couldn't do that. . . . And again that flush started near the tips of her ears and spread out and under, cheekily, and the bus wheeled on and up into Segget, shining half-dead with its whitewashed walls.

Ewan looked back as they left the place and saw the Manse high up from the toun and above it the ruined castle of the Kaimes where he'd gathered flints when he was a kid—a million and a half or so years ago. God, what a solemn young ass he had been!

And he minded the rolling drummle of names of those hill-hidden touns through the parks of which he'd searched out the flints—Muir of Germany, Jacksbank, Tannachie, Arnamuck, Bogjorgan, Droop Hill, Dillavaird, Goosecraves, Pittengardener, Cushnien, Monboddo—he could run the list for a hundred more, queer he'd never before seen those names for the real things they were, the lives and desirings of many men, memories of their hopes and possessions and prides though their own names and dates had vanished forever. And he thought of Trease saying that he and the rest of the Reds were nothing, they just worked the will of history and passed. . . . And suddenly Ewan's mind trembled on the verge of something, something that he couldn't name, maybe God, that made this strange play with lives and beliefs: and it seemed a moment that the shambling bus was the chariot of Time let loose on the world roaring down long fir-darkened haughs of history into the shining ways of to-morrow.

They came into Auchinblae, clatter and showd, the mountains near now, and Ewan looked out. Ellen had the tickets: where were they going?

Ellen said she'd taken tickets for Glen Dye but they needn't go there if he'd rather not. And Ewan looked at her shoes and then at his own and said *Let's get out and climb Drumtochty and then go over to Finella.*

Down in the Strath an hour or so later they came into the road through the Garrold Wood, dark the pines, here the sun was lost. Ewan had taken one of the rucksacks and asked again what she'd brought them for? And Ellen had smiled a secret smile at the road—*Oh, for fun!*—slim, like a boy, not feeling like one, and stared up through the woods at the heights of Drumtochty towering far in the April air, dark at this time of the year, the sky behind waiting and watching with a fleece of clouds like an old woman's cap. Ewan looked up when she pointed that out, he said that that was Finella's mutch, had she never heard of Finella?

And they sat and talked on a little bridge, the water below spun coolly and softly down to the hidden Luther water, and he told her the tale of the Lady Finella and the old-time wars in the Howe of the Mearns. And Ellen, sleek

head uncovered to the sun, listened and asked were those
the Covenanting Times? Ewan said Oh no, they had come
long after, funny chaps the Covenanters, he always had
liked them—the advance guard of the common folk of
those days, their God and their Covenant just formulæ
they hid the social rebellion in. They had fought up here in
the 1640's and away in Dunnottar Castle the gentry had
imprisoned and killed them in scores. . . . And his face
grew dark, no boy's face: *There's nothing new under the
sun—not even torture.*

She said gently *Ewan, what did they do to you?*

He didn't change colour or alter at all, just turned and
looked at her and began to speak, low and steady, she
whispered in a minute *Ewan, oh my dear!* and then felt
sick, knew she'd faint, gripped herself not to, and felt sick
again, she'd fail him completely if she were that. So he
went on and finished; in the silence that followed they heard
the whisper of the Luther hushaweesh in the reeds and far
away in the listening trees—long and contented—the croon
of a dove, terrible in its soft and sleepy content.

Ewan took out his handkerchief and wiped his face, and
then queerly and tenderly wiped Ellen's sweat on it as on
his own though the wind blew snell. And holding his hand
below her chin something lost ran a strange quiver up his
arm, he didn't heed it, smiling into the misery of her eyes,
speaking Scotch who so seldom spoke it, that blunted and
foolish and out-dated tool: *You needn't fash for me. I've
been the gypedest of gomerils to let on and vex you so, but
I'm better now, I'll forget, we forget everything.*

They left the road and went into the wood and were
presently tackling the chave of the slopes, sharp and tart
the whiff of the broom, crackling underheel the old year's
whins. All the hills and the world in their background stilled
except that far off above the ploughed lands that shored
red in clay to Drumelzie woods the peewits cried, in a
breathing-space they halted and listened, *laplaplap*. Then
they took to shinning the haughs again and saw the scrub
open in front and far up, ridge on saffron ridge, Finella
riding the southern lift.

When they gained the utmost ridge in early afternoon the
Howe below was mottled in fog, sun with them here in a
little hollow high on the crest where they sat and ate the
lunch they had brought. Then Ewan lay flat and looked at
the sky, hardly they'd talked in the last hour or so, and

talked little now, Ellen squatting beside him said *You need a pillow,* and meant the rucksacks. And then didn't; and was sensible.

His head in her lap he lay quiet, nice head, the weight sent through her a queer delight, foolish and tender, she bent over to speak to him. Then she saw his eyes closed: he was fast asleep.

When he woke he was looking at the westering sun low down in the Howe of Drumtochty. He ached all over, sun-sleepy, sun-tired, yet vaguely refreshed and his sins forgiven. Then he found where his head still rested, heavy, and started up, Ellen moved at last and cried out at a sudden sting of cramp.

—*Why didn't you wake me? You must feel half-dead.*

She said, with a pretence at Perky Scots, *More whole than half, but you slept so sound,* and stood up beside him, dark as him. With the drowse still in his eyes he smiled at her: *That was nice of you.*

She said absently *I thought you were going to kiss me, don't bother now, there are still some oranges! . . . But what wouldn't I give for a cup of tea!*

He thought it must surely be late by now, but she showed him her watch, only four o'clock, they'd have plenty of time to get back to Auchinblae and get a bus to Duncairn in time, the last passed through at six o'clock.

So they sat down, yawning, and ate the last orange, and Ellen began to speak about socialism and the world revolution that was coming soon when the workers were led in a sane way to power, no blood and mess, reorganizing things for the good of all, building great healthy cities, schools (what fun there would be in gutting Duncairn!) endowing the sciences, endowing motherhood, no more weeping and no more tears: *I couldn't go on living if I hadn't that belief.*

And the dark Scotch boy shook his head and said you could go on living though you might believe in nothing at all—like Chris; and that struck Ellen as queer and then as true, and then queerer still. Funny freaks the Scotch, rather dears sometimes. . . . And she stopped her mind bothering about them at all, only about Ewan, and peeped at her watch when he wasn't looking, then at the sun and as she did so a long, cold shaft of wind blew up the heath at their feet and they raised their eyes and saw the fringes of the darkness on the land, below them the Howe stirring as though someone had stirred a dark drink in the mixture. Ewan jumped to his feet: *Your watch must have stopped.* And took her wrist: *Let's see.*

The watch had stopped. They packed up the rucksacks and slung them on their backs, Ellen's mind in a flurry. Shouldn't she have done it up here?—she could easily, nothing to have stopped her. Only—a mess; and she wanted it proper. What now, what the devil the best thing to do?

Ewan called to her not to take that way, the other was the nearest to Auchinblae, she cried back that here was a clearer track and he came to her side and they ran hand in hand, plunging and slipping from tuft to tuft, the woods stared up and came gambolling to meet them, bound on bound, Luther gleaming beyond, up in the opposite heights rode a castle, all curlecue-battlements, a pork-pie in stone. Then it vanished from view as they still fell west.

Ewan said it didn't matter, over late now to reach Auchinblae, and looked worried a minute, and a clump of larch came and a shoulder of hill and, winding wide and deserted, the road. Ellen stumbled against him of a sudden dog-tired, the outing had won, not her, no need to go on with the thing to the end—oh, thank goodness, for she'd never have managed!

He said *Ellen!* in a strange, hushed boy's voice and put his arms under her arms, she saw his face suddenly blind, she gave a little sob, kissing he drew her tight and a wild fear came and struggled and escaped, she didn't want to escape him, hadn't done this to help him, she just wanted him for herself, for delight. And she held him away and told him that and he blushed, funny Ewan who could kiss like so! But his voice was cool and clear as glass: *I'm going to kiss you all over. Soon.*

She said that would be fun, trying not herself to go foolish again; and told him to sit down and asked what he knew of the countryside here, he didn't know much, two or three miles away was a little inn, he thought, he'd once seen it, picture-book place with honeysuckle in the summer. . . . She said *Oh Lord, NOT honeysuckle!* and he said he was sorry, but it wouldn't be out; and they smiled at each other, stared, laughed, kissed once—too damn dangerous more than once.

And then she remembered and sought out the wedding

ring she had bought that day: *Ewan, will you put this on for me?*

When she woke near morning in the little inn-room he was sleeping beside her, hallowed and clean and made whole again, light faint on the dark face turned to her shoulder; and in tenderness she lay and looked at him and thought, *Yes, that was fun, Oh, Ewan, funny boy!*

He woke at her movement—quickly, at once, and knew her, put his right arm under her head, and said sleepily did he tell her last night that Yes, she felt as well as looked like silk? Some funny grain in skin-texture, no doubt: he'd find out some time, unless he first ate her. . . . And he'd forgotten to kiss her as completely as he'd promised.

But when he'd done that and slept again Ellen didn't, holding him in a quiet compassion that he wouldn't have understood and would never know; and that didn't matter, she was his forever, in desire or hating, his till they ended or grew old and remembered, far off, the terror and wonder of those first moments that made you suddenly so frightened of God because there must be a God after all.

And Chris stood with gloved hands on the hot May railings and looked down at Duncairn where her marriage was waiting. What a reel of things in a short few months, what an antrin world that waited to-morrow!

Well, that had to be faced, and whatever else it would be (she thought and smiled to her sulky self trigged out in the glass of the Windmill Steps) it wouldn't be the to-morrow she expected now. No to-morrow ever was though you planned it with care, locked chance in the stable and buried the key.

To-morrow.

Ake.

Ewan.

Ellen.

Ewan and his Ellen. What had happened with them? Nothing but the thing that had happened so often as any fool of a woman might know. And now that it had happened—what came next? And she thought *Ah, well, it's no matter of mine,* though her thoughts strayed a little even as she thought that, half in tenderness, half in anxiety, wondering what they'd said, what they'd done, what their compact was, not caring greatly they'd done ill by old standards though she hoped to God they'd at least been careful. And she minded their faces at breakfast that day and that look they'd exchanged while she sat and watched, Ellen's open and lovely, unashamed, Ewan's open as well, but the kind of smile that no lad ever yet kept for his lass. Grey granite and thistledown—how would they mix?

Oh, that unguessable to-morrow would tell!

IV

ZIRCON

The hill slopes were rustling with silence in the glimmer of the late June gloaming as Chris Ogilvie made her way up the track, litheness put by for a steady gait. On the bending slopes that climbed ahead to the last of the daylight far in the lift the turning grass was dried and sere, a June of drought and swithering heat, the heather bells hung shrunken and small, bees were grumbling going to their homes, great bumbling brutes Chris brushed from her skirts. Half-way up she stopped a minute and rested and looked down with untroubled eyes at the world below, sharp-set and clear each item of it in that brightness before the dark came down, mile on mile of coarse land and park rolling away to the distant horizons that tumbled south to her forty years in the distant Howe.

She looked down at herself with a smile for her gear and then took to the climb of the brae again, following the windings of the half-hidden path, choked with whins and the creep of the heather since the last time men had trauchled up here. Then, greatly cupped and entrenched and stone-shielded, she saw the summit tower above her, so close and high here the play of the gloaming it seemed to her while she stood and breathed if she stretched up her hand she could touch the lift—the bending bowl of colours that hung like a meikle soap-bubble above her head.

Treading through the staying drag of the heather she
made her way under the shoggle of the walls to a high,
cleared space with stones about, to the mass of stone where
once the astronomers had come a hundred years before to
take an eclipse of the moon or sun—some fairely or other
that had bothered them and set them running and fashing
about and peering up at the lift and gowking, and yammering their little supposings grave: and all long gone and
dead and forgotten. But they'd left a great mass of crumbling cement that made a fine seat for a wearied body—a
silly old body out on a jaunt instead of staying at home
with her work, eident and trig, and seeing to things for the
morn—that the morn she might get up and see to more
things.

That the reality for all folk's days, however they clad its
grim shape in words, in symbols of cloud and rock, mountain that endured, or shifting sands or changing tint—like
those colours that were fading swift far in the east, one by
one darkening and robing themselves in their grave-
clouts grey, happing their heads and going to the dark. . . .
Change that went on as a hurpling clock, with only bene-
diction to ring at the end—knowledge that the clock would
stop some time, that even change might not endure.

She leaned her chin in her hand and rested, the crumbling
stone below her, below that the world, without hope or
temptation, without hate or love, at last, at long last. Though
attaining it she had come a way strewn with thorns and set
with pits, like the strayings of a barefoot bairn in the
dark——

She'd not failed in her bargain she told herself that night
in the house on Windmill Place, been glad for the man with
kindness and good heart, given that which he needed and
that which he sought, neither shrinking nor fearing. And
he'd given her a pat *Ay, lass, but you're fine,* and thrust
her from him, assuaged, content, and slept sound and
douce, alien, remote. Her husband, Ake Ogilvie.

She bit her lips till they bled in those hours that followed,
seeking not to think, not to know or heed or believe when
every cell of her body tingled and moved to a shivering
disgust that would not cease—Oh, she was a fool, what had
happened to her that wasn't what she'd known, expected
to happen? Idiot and gype to shiver so, she'd to sleep, to
get up in the morning and get on with her work, get her
man's meat ready, his boots fresh-polished, sit by his side

and eat in a kitchen, watch his slobberings of drink and his mouthings of food while he took no notice of her, read his paper, laced his boots and went showding out to look for a job, a contented childe. . . . She'd all that waiting for her the morn, all morns: sleep and be still, Oh, sleep and be still!

And at last she lay still with memories and ghosts, Ewan with dark hair and boy's face, Ewan beside her, Ewan from the dust, who'd thought her the wonder of God in the wild, dear daftness of early love, Ewan whom she'd loved so and hated so, Ewan—oh, little need to come now, she'd paid the debt back that he'd given for her when they murdered him that raining morning in France, paid it to the last ounce, body and flesh. And then in the darkness another came, a face above her, blue-eyed, strong-lined, only a moment as that moment's madness between them long syne. Not in longing or lust had they known each other, by chance, just a chance compassion and fear, foolish and aimless as living itself. Oh, Long Rob whose place was never with me, not now can you heed or help me at all. . . .

Quiet and quiet, because not that third, not look at him or remember him. And she buried her face in the pillow not to see, and then turned and waited rigid: Robert.

And she saw him for the first time since he'd died Robert completed, who'd had no face in her memory so long, Robert with eyes and face and chin and the steady light of madness in her eyes. Robert not the lover but the fanatic, Robert turning from her coughing red in sleep in that last winter in Segget, Robert with red lips as he sat in the pulpit —she stared at him dreadfully in the close-packed dark, far under her feet the clocks came chiming while she lay and looked and forgot to shiver.

Not Ake alone, but beyond them all, or they beyond her and tormenting her. And she knew in that minute that never again in memory, or reality might any man make in gladness unquiet a heart passed beyond lust and love alike— past as a child forgetting its toys, weeping over their poor, shattered shapes no longer, and turning dry-eyed to the lessons of Life.

Ewan tramped Duncairn in search of a job—he knew it would be too expensive a job to try and fight on the apprentice's rights which Gowans and Gloag had torn up with his agreement. No chance of winning against them, of course, they could twist any court against a Red. He told that to Chris, cheery and cool; but his coolness was something different now. Cold and controlled he had always been, some lirk in his nature and upbringing that Chris loved, who so hated folk in a fuss. But now that quality she'd likened to grey granite itself, that something she'd seen change in Duncairn from slaty grey to a glow of fire, was transmuting again before her eyes—into something darker and coarser, in essence the same, in tint antrin queer. More like his father he seemed every day, if one could imagine that other Ewan with his angers and hasty resentments mislaid. . . . She told him that and he laughed and teased her: *Only I'm a lot better looking!* and she said absently he would never be that, there was over-much bone in his face.—*And what job are you thinking of trying to get?*

He said he'd no idea, any old job, there'd likely not be much opening for a Red: *I'm sorry to have upset your plans, you know, mother.*

Chris asked what plans? and he asked with a grin hadn't she wanted him to be respectable, genteel, with no silly notions and a nice office suit? Chris didn't laugh, just said she hadn't known she'd mothered a gowk: if he knew as little of the beliefs that had made him a Red as he knew of her—faith, it would be long before he and Mr. Trease ruled in Duncairn.

He sat and listened to that with a smile: *Faith, it'll be long anyway, I'm afraid. And as for what you call my beliefs, they're just plain hell—but then—they ARE real. And you ought to like them, you're so much alike!*

She asked what he meant, and he said *Why, you're both real,* and stood up and cuddled her, laughing down at her, Ewan who'd once had no sense of humour, had he found that in torment in a prison cell? *Didn't you know you were real, Chris, realer than ever? And stepfather Ake's pretty real as well.*

Real? She watched through the days that followed, manner and act, gesture and gley, with a kind, quiet curiosity. Like Ewan he was tramping Duncairn for a job, she'd listen to his feet on the stairs as he went, and the stride never altered, an unhastening swing. And at evening they'd sit long hours in the kitchen, Chris sewing, him reading, hardly speaking a word, Chris because she had nothing to say, Ake

because he'd no mind for claik. Then he'd drink his cocoa
and look at the clock, and say *Lass, it's time we went off
to bed,* and off he'd go, in his socks, no slippers or shoes,
she'd follow and find him winding his watch, feet apart, independent, green-eyed, curled mousered, taking a bit glance
at the night-time sky. And even while they undressed he'd
say no word, getting cannily into the bed and lying down.
Then he'd swing over on his pillow and off to sleep without
a good night or a single remark: would a man be as daft as
say good night to his own wife?

And Chris as those nights went by, padding at the heels
of unchanging days, slept well enough now without fears
at all on that matter that had set her shivering at first, she
shivered no longer, he came to her rarely, eidently, coolly;
and with a kind honesty, unhurtable now, she awaited him,
paying her share of the price of things, another function for
the woman-body, who did the cooking and attended the
house while he still kept up his hunt for a job.

Kisses there were none, or caresses even, except a rare
pat as she leaned over to set a plate in front of him. They
said bare things one to the other: *Ay, it's clearing. . . . Rain
in the lift. . . . Eggs up in price. . . . That'll be Ewan. . . .*
She was finding ease who had known little.

The Reverend MacShilluck had never heard the like, he'd
advertised for a gardening body and the morning the advertisement appeared in the *Runner,* the first to come in
search of the job—now, who do you think the young thug
was?

The housekeeper simpered and said she didn't know:
could it be the young man was an ill-doer, like?

The Reverend MacShilluck said Not only that, far worse
than that, ahhhhhhhhhhhh, far worse. And the housekeeper
said *Well, God be here. Was the smokie to your taste?* for
she wanted away back to the kitchen to add up the grocer's
account for the week and see how much she could nick on
the sly and save up against the day that would come when
she'd be able to clear out completely and leave the clarty
cuddy forever. . . . But he was fairly in full swing by then
and went on to tell that the young man who'd come was
no other than that thug Ewan Tavendale who'd led the
strikers at Gowans and Gloag's and been sacked for it, he'd
been in the jail and yet he had the impertinence to come
looking for a job about a Manse. So the Reverend had re-

fused him, sharp and plain, he'd seen the young brute was
a typical Red, born lazy, living off doles and never seeking
an honest day's work——

The housekeeper said *God be here, like that? Then he
couldn't have been seeking the job at all?* And the Reverend
MacShilluck gave a bit cough and said he would never trust
a Red, not him; had he ever told her the tale of the way
at the General Assembly he'd once choked off a Socialist,
Colquohoun—shame on him, and him a minister, too! . . .

Miss Murgatroyd said Eh me, it was Awful, but had Mrs.
Colquohoun—oh, sorry, she meant Mrs. Ogilvie—heard of
the Dreadful Occurrence at Gawpus's shop? And Chris said
she hadn't and Miss Murgatroyd said she didn't know how
to speak, she was sure Mrs. Ogilvie would understand her
point of view and that she didn't really believe that young
Mr. Ewan had behaved like that. And Chris asked what
was this about Ewan? and Miss Murgatroyd told her the
dreadful story, just as she'd heard from that dear Mrs.
Gawpus that afternoon at the Unionist Ladies.

It seemed that Mr. Ewan had got employment in the
basement of Bailie Gawpus's shop, and oh me, it was awful
to tell the rest. He'd been there only a day or so when the
other workmen in the basement started raising a din because there wasn't a proper, you know, W.C. there, and
Bailie had thought it would be just pampering keelies, wasn't
there the yard outside! The Bailie had gone down to see
what was wrong, and then he'd set eyes on Mr. Ewan, so
unfortunate, for the Bailie remembered him—he had seen
him when he was arrested for taking part in that dreadful
strike. Bailie Gawpus hadn't known that Mr. Ewan was
one of his employees, a foreman had engaged him—such a
nice man, the Bailie, but awful strict, a little stout, she was
sure it was in his heart——

Well, he became Such Indignant at seeing Mr. Ewan, and
sure that was the cause of the bother, that he ordered him
out of the basement at once, he was so against the Communists and the dreadful things they had done to the Common People in Russia. He told Mr. Ewan he was dismissed
on the spot. Such a Pity, Bailie Gawpus perhaps not as nice
as he might have been—in fact, Mrs. Gawpus admitted that
her husband perhaps exceeded his powers, he laid hands
on Mr. Ewan to push him out.

And then—it was dreadful, dreadful, a man old enough

to be his father—Mr. Ewan seized Bailie Gawpus by the
collar of his coat and ran him out to the yard at the back,
the Bailie almost dying of rage and heart-failure, and
showed him—you know, the place that those awful basement people Used. And asked he how the Bailie would like
to use it? And before the Dear Bailie could say anything at
all he was down on his hands and knees and his face being
Rubbed in It—feuch, wasn't that awful? Worse still, the
rest of the dreadful keelies came out from the basement
and cheered and laughed and when Bailie Gawpus got up
to his feet and threatened to send for a policeman Mr.
Ewan said there was no need to do that, he was off to get
one himself and report the sanitary conditions of the place.
So dreadful for the Bailie. He'd to pay up a week's wages
to Mr. Ewan and promise to have a proper W.C. con-
structed; and the Bailie was just Boiling with Rage. . . .

Almost every night after that week-end in Drumtochty
Ellen would slip through her doorway, sly pussy-cat, and
trip along to Ewan's room, scratch on the door and be letten in, and taken and kissed and looked at and shaken, because they were mad and the day had seemed—Oh, so horribly long! And Ellen would forget the vexatious Scotch
brats whom she tried to drum up the steep cliffs of learning,
sour looks and old women and the stench from the drains
of the Ecclesgriegs Middle, the sourly hysterical glares of
Ena Lyon—everything every time in that blessed minute
when inside Ewan's door she was inside his arms, tight,
arms hard and yet soft with their dark down fringe, Ewan's
face bent down to hers to that breathless moment when she
thought she would die if he didn't, in one second—oh, kiss
her quick!

And he did, and her arms went up round his neck, fun,
thrilly: you'd often wondered what men's necks were for.
And the two of you would stand still, so cuddled, not kissing, not moving, just in blessed content to touch, to hear
the beating of each other's hearts, each other's breathing,
know each other's being, content and lovely, without shelter
or shyness one from the other, blessed minute that was
hardly equalled in all else, not even the minutes that followed it later.

But first she made tea on Ewan's gas-ring with the kettle
and teapot they'd bought together in a Saturday evening
scrimmage at Woolies, China tea, Ellen kneeling to make

it, having made Ewan sit and be quiet and not fuss, tired out with haunting the streets for a job. And he'd say *But I'm not,* and she'd say then he ought to be—*Sit still and read and don't argue.* Ewan would laugh and drag down a book, silence in the room but for the gas-hiss, Ellen drowsy as she watched the bubbling gas-flame and the kettle begin to simmer and stir. House-keeping comfy and fun, alone in a room with Ewan: though the house wasn't theirs, nor the room, nor the furniture, nothing but a sixpenny kettle and teapot and cups and saucers at a penny a piece!

She'd glance up at him, deep in his book, and not heed the book, but only him, nice arms bare and the curve of his head, strange and dear, nice funny nose, lips too thick, like her own, brown throat—she could catalogue them forever, over and over, and know a fresh thrill every word every time—oh, damnable and silly and lovely to be in love!

And they'd drink the tea in a drowse of content and talk of his books and the men of old time, the Simple Men who had roamed the earth before Civilization came. If even men attained that elementary simplicity again——

And Ellen would rouse: *But then, what's the use? If we don't believe in that we're just—oh daft, as you Scotch people say, wasting our lives instead of*—And Ewan would ask *Instead of what?—Saving up to get married?* and laugh and hold her face firm between his hands, young rough hands, the look in his eyes that made her responses falter even while at his laugh and the thing he laughed at something denying struggled up in her, almost shaped itself to words on her lips. Sometime, surely—Oh, sometime they'd get married when the Revolution came and all was put right.

And sometimes she'd feel just sick and desolate the way he would talk of that coming change, he didn't expect it would come in their time, capitalism had a hundred dodges yet to dodge its own end, Fascism, New Deals, Douglasism, War: Fascism would probably outlast the lot. Ellen said that she didn't believe that a minute else what was the good of all their struggles, what was the good of dissolving the League and both of them joining the Communist Party? And Ewan would smile at her: *No good at all. Child's play, Ellen, or so it'll seem for years. And we've just to go on with it, right to the end, History our master not the servant we supposed.* . . .

He'd fall to his books again, dryest stuff, economics she

never could stick, she would reach up and catch the book from him and his eyes meet hers, blank a while, cold, blank and grey, horrible eyes like a cuttle-fish's—like the glint on the houses in Royal Mile, the glint of grey granite she thought once, and shivered. And he asked her why and she said she was silly and he said he knew that, eyes warm again, and they fooled about, struggling a little in the fading June night: and then were quiet, her head on his knee, looking out of the window at summer-stilled Duncairn, little winds tapping the cord of the blind, far off in the fall of the darkness the winking eye of Crowie Point lighting up the green surge of the North Sea night. And Ellen would say *Oh, aren't we comfy? Fun, this,* he'd say nothing, just cuddle her, staring out at that light wan and lost that bestrode the sky.

In bed, beside him, breathing to sleep, the little sleep after those moments that she still thought fun, she would tickle his throat with her hair, feel sure and confident as never in the light, here in the dark he was hers unquestioned, hers and no other's, breathing so, sweat on his brow, hair curling about her fingers from the dark, sleek head. He would stroke her with a swift, soft hand, like a bird's light wing, into that little sleep till somewhere between two and three she would wake, he wakeful as well, and they'd kiss again, cool and neat, and slip out of bed, slim children both, and stand hand in hand and listen, all the house in Windmill Place silent. Then they'd pad to the door and lug it open and peer out, nothing, the lobby dark below, no glimmer about but faint on the landing the far ghost radiance of Footforthie. Ewan would open her door for her, sleepily they'd hug, and yawn at each other in the dark, giggle a bit because of that, and Ellen close the door and slip into her bed, asleep before she had reached it, almost.

But one morning she saw his hands cut and bruised and asked why, and he said oh that was from his new job, up at Stoddart's, the granite-mason's, he'd been taken on there as a labourer.

The table looked at him, the first any had heard: Chris asked if he liked it, were the other folk nice?

Miss Murgatroyd simpered she was awful glad he had found Respectable Employment, like. Such Pity not to be in the office though; they were awful respectable folk, the Stoddarts.

Mr. Piddle said *he-he!* and ate like a gull landed famished on the corpse of a whale.

Mr. Quaritch cocked his wee beard to the side: *You'll be able to study the proletariat at first hand now. Tell me when you get sick of them, lad. I might be able to find something better.*

Ena Lyon sniffed and said she Just Hated gravestones.

Ellen sat and stared in blank, dead silence, feeling sick and forgotten while they all talked. Oh goodness, hadn't they heard, had they all gone deaf? Ewan—EWAN A LABOURER!

July came in slow heat over Duncairn, and with it the summer-time visitors. John Cushnie took his feeungsay down to the Beach every night that his mecks would meet, in to hear Gappy Gowkheid braying his jokes in the Beach Pavilion, awfully funny, God, how you laughed when he spoke the daft Scotch and your quean beside you giggled superior and said Say he was sure the canary's camiknicks, she was awful clever and spoke a lot like that that she'd heard at the Talkies—though if you had mentioned *her* camiknicks she'd have flamed insulted right on the spot.

Or you'd take her down of a Wednesday afternoon, when Raggie's had closed, birring on the tramcars loaded for the Beach, wheeling out from Footforthie, there glimmering and pitching and reeling in the sun the Amusements Park with its scenic railway, Beach crowded with folk the same as the cars, you and your quean would sit and listen to the silly English that couldn't speak proper, with their 'eads and 'ands and 'alfs and such. Then off you'd get and trail into the Amusements Park, you'd only a half-dollar but you wouldn't let on, your feeungsay was so superior and you only the clerk in Raggie Robertson's. She was fairly gentry and said *how* she'd enjoyed her holiday away with her Girl Friend, they'd gone for a week out in the country, and the farmers were awful vulgar and funny. And you said, Yes, you knew, hicks were like that, and she said *You've spilt it—with their awful Scotch words: Tyesday for Tuesday, and Foersday for Friday, and no proper drainage at all, you know.* And you said again that you knew; she meant there weren't real W.C.s but rather would have died than say so right out.

So you asked if she'd like the scenic railway, and she said *It's okay be me,* on you got, she screamed and grabbed you and the hair got out under her hat, you were awful proud of her but wished to hell she wouldn't scream as though her throat were chokeful up of old razor blades, and clutched at her skirt, and skirl *Oh, stop!* God, hadn't she legs like other folk and need she aye be ashamed of them? So you gave her a bit grab about the legs and she screamed some more and hung on to you: but when the ride finished she was real offended and said she wasn't that kind of girl, *Don't try and come it fresh on me.*

You said you were sorry, so you were and were just trying to make it up with her when she saw her friend and cried *Cooee, Ena!* and the quean came over, all powder and poshness, and who should it be but Miss Ena Lyon that you'd known at the lodgings in Windmill Place. She said she was just having a stroll about, and no, she hadn't a boy with her. And your quean giggled, and Miss Lyon giggled and you felt a fool, queans were like that; and as you followed them into the tea-tent you wished a coarse minute they'd stop their damned showing-off and be decent to a chap that was treating them—wished a daft minute you'd a quean who didn't care about Talkies and genteelness or was scared at her legs being touched or her feelings offended—one that would cuddle you because she liked it, liked you, thought her legs and all of herself for you, and was douce and sweet and vulgar and kind—like a keelie out of the Cowgate. . . . God, it must be the sun had got at you!

Your quean and Miss Lyon were at it hell for leather talking about their holidays and where they had bade, and how much they paid for digs in Duncairn. And Miss Lyon said she thought she'd move hers, the landlady had once been a minister's widow but now she had married an Awful Common person, a joskin just, that lorded it about the place and wasn't a bit respectful at all. Worse than that, though, the landlady's son was a Red. . . . You said that you'd known that, that's why you'd left, Raggie Robertson was dead against the Reds. . . . And your quean said *Don't be silly. Go on, Ena.*

And Miss Lyon said that another of the lodgers was a schoolteacher, Red as well, and she was sure there were Awful Things between them. She'd heard—and she giggled and whispered to your quean and you felt yourself turn red

round the ears, what were the daft bitches gigg-giggling
about? And your quean made on she was awful shocked
and said she wouldn't stay there a minute, the place was
no better than a WICKED HOUSE, just.

Miss Lyon said that she'd got no proof, of course, and
your quean mustn't say anything, and your quean said she
wouldn't but that Ena could easily get proof and show up
the two Reds and then leave the place. And then you all
talked together about the Communists, coarse beasts, aye
stirring up the working class—that was the worst of the
working class that they could be led astray by agitators,
they'd no sense and needed to be strongly ruled.

You told the queans that but they didn't listen, they were
giggling horrified to each other again, your quean said
What, did you really hear the bed creak? and Miss Lyon
said *Yes, twice,* and their faces were all red and warmed
up and glinting, they minded you suddenly of the faces of
two bitches sniffling round a lamp-post, scared and eager
and hot on a scent. . . . But you mustn't think that, they
were real genteel.

For your quean was the daughter of a bank clerk in
Aberdeen and Miss Ena Lyon's father had been a postmaster, some class, you guessed, you didn't much like to
tell them yours had only been the hostler at the Grand
Hotel, what did it matter, you were middle-class yourself
now and didn't want ever to remember that you might have
been a keelie labourer—God, living in some awful room in
Paldy, working at the Docks or the granite yards, going
round with some quean not genteel like yours but speaking just awful, Scotch, no restraint or knowing how to take
care of herself, maybe coming into your bed at night,
smooth and fine and kissing you, cuddling you, holding
you without screaming, just in liking and kindness. . . .
Your quean asked *Whatever's come over you, red like that?*
and you said *Oh, nothing, it's stuffy in here.*

And home you all went on the evening tram, your quean
and Miss Lyon sitting together and your quean telling Miss
Lyon what fine digs she had, the landlady so respectful,
a perfect old scream: and Ena should wait about to-night
and catch the two Reds and show them up, and leave the
place and come bide with your quean.

And Miss Lyon said that she would, too, she was sick of
the place, anyhow—the dirty beasts to act like that, night
after night. . . . And they giggled and whispered some more

and for some funny reason you felt as though you'd a stone in your gall, sick and weary, what was the use?— what was the use of being middle-class and wearing a collar and going to the Talkies when this was all that you got out of it? And your quean, whispering some direction to Miss Lyon, turned round and said *Don't listen a minute*, and you nearly socked her one in the jaw—och, 'twas the summer night's heat that was getting you.

Chris's roses were full and red in bloom, scentless and lovely, glowing alive in the Sunday sun as she herself came out to the little back garden. Ewan and Ellen were out there already, their backs to the house, one kneeling one standing, their dark hair blue in the sunlight, young, with a murmur of talk and laughter between them. And she saw indeed they were children no longer, Ellen a woman, slim, a slip of a thing, but that pussy-cat dewiness lost and quite gone, Ewan with the stance and look and act of some strange species of Gallowgate keelie who had never hidden or starved in a slum and planned to cut all the gentry's throat, politely, for the good of humankind. . . . And Miss Ena Lyon was no doubt right in all she had said: Chris must tell them somehow.

But standing looking at them she knew that she couldn't, not because she was ashamed to speak of such things to either but because they were over-young and happy to have their minds vexed with the dirty sad angers of Miss Ena Lyon, poor lass. She'd never had a soul slip into *her* room of a night, maybe that was the reason for her awful stamash about Ellen and Ewan exchanging visits. . . . She'd bade up last night, she had told to Chris, and waited on the stairs to confirm her suspicions. And sure enough it had happened again, oh, Disgusting, at Eleven o'clock Miss Johns slipping into Mr. Tavendale's room. And she couldn't stay on any longer in a place like this, it was no better than a Brothel, just.

Chris had looked at her in a quiet compassion and said there was no need to stay even a week, she'd better pack and get out at once. Miss Lyon had stared and flushed up raddled red: *What, me that's done nothing? You've more need to shift those——*

She'd called them a dirty name, Chris had said without anger *You'll pack and be gone in an hour,* and left her to that and gone down to the kitchen and shortly afterwards

heard a tramping overhead as Miss Lyon got her bit things
together—thrown out of her lodgings for trying to keep
keelies respectable.

Working in the kitchen with Jock the cat stropping himself up against her legs, Chris had thought that funny for
a moment, then it wasn't, she'd have to ask the two what
they meant to do. And she thought how awful it was the
rate that things tore on from a body's vision, only a year
or so since she'd thought of Ewan as a little student lad,
her own, jealous when he talked to the pussy-cat: and
now she'd have to ask him when he meant to marry!

So she'd made the oat-cakes and scones all the lodgers
cried for, Ake had come swinging in from outbye, out to
buy his bit Sunday paper, no collar, his boots well-
blacked, his mouser well-curled, he'd sat down and eaten a
cake while he read. Chris had brought him some milk
though he'd said he'd get it for himself, he'd taken to saying that kind of thing, queer, though she'd paid it little
attention, looking at him quiet and friendly, just, this business of getting a job was a trauchle. She'd asked was there
any sign of work and he'd said not a bit in the whole of
Duncairn, and folded back his paper and looked up at her
with green-glinting eyes as he drank his milk. *A job? The
Devil the one. And I'm thinking I know the reason for that.*

Chris asked *What reason?* and he'd said *Jimmy Speight,*
no doubt he'd sent a message all round Duncairn to the
joiners and timber-merchants and such warning them
against employing Ake. Chris said that surely he'd be feared
to do that seeing that Ake knew the scandal about him,
Ake had shaken his head, Ah, but he'd promised never to
use that knowledge again and Jimmy knew that he'd keep
the promise, a body must keep a promise made even to a
daft old skate like the Provost.

And then he'd said something that halted Chris: *I'm
sorry, mistress, that I drove you to marrying me.*

Chris had said *Why, Ake!* in surprise, and he'd nodded:
*Ay, a damn mistake. Queer the daft desires that drive folk.
I might well have known you'd never mate with me, you'd
been spoiled in the beds of ministers and the like. I'd forgotten that like an unblooded loon.*

Chris had stood and listened in a kind surprise, beyond
fear of being startled or hurt any more by any man of the
sons of men who brought their desires their gifts to her.
She'd said she'd done all she could to make them happy,

and Ake had nodded, Ay, all that she could, but that wasn't enough, och, she wasn't to blame. Then he'd said not to fash, things would travel out in time, he was off for a dander round the Docks.

So he'd gone, leaving Chris to finish the cooking and set the dinner and watch the taxi drive up and take away Miss Lyon's luggage, a pile of it, and hear the cabman ask if she shouldn't have hired a lorry instead? And Miss Lyon had said she wanted none of his impudence, she'd had enough of that already, living in a brothel. Chris had started a little, overhearing that, but the cabman just said *Faith now, have you so? Trade failing that you're leaving?* and got in and drove off.

And now, the pastry browning fine and Jock the cat purring away, Chris had come out to the noon-time yard to ask Ellen and Ewan what they meant to do over this business of sleeping together without the kirk's licence and shocking Miss Lyon.

But the picture they made took the plan from her mind, she saw now what it was they were laughing about, they'd gotten in the baby from over next door, the bald-headed father had been left in charge and had wanted to mow his lawn awful bad and the bairn had wakened up in its pram and started a yowl, frustrating the man: till Ellen looked over and said *Shall I?* And he'd handed it over, all red and thankful, and now Ellen squatted by the rose-bush, the bairn in her lap and was wagging a bloom in front of its nose. And the bairn near as big and bald as his father, was kicking his legs, gurgling, and burying his nose and mouth in the rose, sniffing, and then kicking some more in delight. And Chris saw Ewan looking down at the two with a look on his face that made her stop.

Not the kind of look at all a young man should have given his quean with a stranger's bairn—a drowsy content and expectation commingled. Instead, Ewan looked at the two cool and frank, amused and a little bored, as he might at a friend who played with a kitten. . . .

And Chris thought, appalled, *Poor Ellen, poor Ellen!*

Gowans and Gloag's had quietened down after the strike, the chaps went back and said to themselves no more listening to those Communist Bulgars that got you in trouble because of their daftness, damn't, if the Chinks and the

Japs wanted to poison one the other, why shouldn't they?
—they were coarse little brutes, anyhow, like that Dr. Fu
Manchu on the films. And wee Geordie Bruce that worked
in Machines said there was nothing like a schlorich of blood
to give a chap a bit twist in the wame. But you, though
you weren't a Red any longer, said to Geordie that he'd
done damn little blood-letting against the bobbies; and
Norman Cruickshank took Wee Geordie's nose and gave it
a twist, it nearly came off, and said *Hey, sample a drop of
your own. God, and to think it's red, not yellow.*

You took a bit taik into Machines now and then for a
gabble with Norman on this thing and that, the new wing
they'd built, called Chemicals, where the business of load-
ing the cylinders with gas was to start in another week or
so. Already a birn of chaps had come from the south with
a special training for that kind of work, Glasgow devils
and an Irishman or so. You and Norman would sneak out
to the W.C. for a fag, and you'd ask if Norman had seen
anything of Ewan? And Norman would say he'd seen him
once or twice at meetings of the Reds down on the Beach,
he'd fairly joined up with the Communists now and spoke
at their meetings—*daft young Bulgar if ever there was one,
and him gey clever and educated, Bob.*

You said rough enough that you knew all that, and Norman looked at you queer and said Oh of course, you yourself had been a bit of a Red a while back and belonged to
that League that Tavendale had raised. Why had you scuttled? Got the wind up?

You took him a smack in the face for that, he was at
you in a minute, you couldn't stand up to him, the foreman
came running in and pulled you apart: *Hey, what the hell
do you think this is? Boxing gymnasium? Back to your
work, you whoreson gets.* And back you both went, b'God
you'd given the mucker something to think of, saying that
you had the wind up—you!

It was just that you'd seen the Reds were daft, a chap
that joined them never got a job, got bashed by bobbies
and was sent to the camps, never had a meck to spend of a
night or a shirt that didn't stick to his back. Och to hell!
You wanted a life of your own, you'd met a quean that
was braw and kind, she and you were saving up to get
married, maybe at New Year and maybe a bit sooner,
you'd your eyes on two rooms in Kirrieben, the quean was

a two months gone already but you'd be in time if your plans came off; and you weren't sorry a bit, you'd told her, kissing her, she'd blushed and pushed you away, awful shy Jess except in the dark. So who'd time at all for this Red stite and blether that never would help a chap anyway, what was the use of getting your head bashed in for something worse than religion?

But that evening you and some of the chaps had a bit of overtime in the works, clearing up the mess of some university loons allowed down to potter about in Castings. You finished gey late and as you came out there was some kind of meeting on at the gates, a young chap up on a kind of platform speaking low and clear, who could he be? And you and the rest took a dander along, a fair crowd around, Broo men and fishers, stinking like dung, and a dozen or so of the toff students that had messed about that evening in Castings. The toffs were laughing and crying out jokes, but the young chap wasn't heeding them a bit, he was dressed in old dungarees, all whitened, a chap from the granite-works, no doubt, with big thick boots and red rough hands. And only as you got fell close did you see that the speaker was young Ewan Tavendale himself.

He was saying if the workers would only unite—when one of the university toffs made a raspberry and called *Unite to give you a soft living, you mean?* Ewan said *Quite, and you a hard death, we'll abolish lice in the Communist state,* and then went on with his speech, quick and cool, the students started making a rumpus and some of the fishers gave a bit laugh and started to taik away home at that, quiet old chaps that didn't fancy a row. But Norman Cruickshank called out to Ewan to carry on with his say, would he? they'd see to the mammies' pets with the nice clean collars and the fat office dowps. And Norman called to the Gowans' chaps: *Who'll keep order?*

Most of the others cried up that they would, you didn't yourself but taiked away home, you'd your quean to meet and were going that night to look at a bit of second-hand furniture in a little shop in the Gallowgate. Only as you turned the bend of the street you looked back and saw a fair scrimmage on, the whey-faced bastards down from the colleges were taking on the Gowans chaps, you nearly turned and ran back to join—och, you couldn't, not now, mighty, what about Jess? And you started to run like a

fool, as though feared—feared at something that wasn't
yourself, that leapt in your heart when you looked at Ewan.

Jim Trease said that was one way of holding a meeting,
not the best, you should never let a free fight start at your
meetings unless it was well in the heart of a town, with
plenty of police about and folk in hundreds and a chance
of a snappy arrest or so, to serve the Party as good publicity.

Ewan said Yes, he knew, but he'd taken the opportunity
to stir up antagonism between the Gowans chaps and students. Deepening the dislike between the classes. Obvious
enough that the day of the revolutionary student was done,
he turned to Fascism or Nationalism now, the fight for the
future was the workers against all the world. Trease
nodded, a bit of heresy there, but true enough in the main.
Anyhow, there was no great harm done, Ewan had barked
his knuckles a bit, he'd better come up to the Trease house
in Paldy and get them iodined. And maybe he'd like a
cup of tea.

Ewan said he would and folded up his platform, the fight
was over and the students had gone, chased up the wynds
by the Gowans men. But Norman Cruickshank came panting back: *All right, Ewan?* and Ewan said *Fine. Thanks to
you, Norman. When'll I see you?*

*—I don't know, but to hell—sometime. Never heard any-
body speak about things as you used to do in the Furnaces.*
And he asked what Ewan was doing now and Ewan told
him he was a labourer at Stoddart's, and Norman said God,
what a job for a toff, and Ewan said he wasn't a toff, just
a worker, and Norman said tell that to his grandmother:
only, where would they meet again? So they fixed that up,
Trease standing by, big and sonsy, with a twinkle in his
little eyes and his shabby suit shining in the evening light.

Mrs. Trease held out a soft hand and said *Howdedo? . . .
Jim, I'm away out to the Pictures. See and not start the
Revolution without me, there's two kippers in the press if
you'd like some meat, the police have been here this afternoon and the landlord's going to give us the push. That's
all. Ta-ta.* Trease gave her a squeeze and said that was fine,
so long as nothing serious had happened; and told her
to see and enjoy the picture, who was the actress? Greena
Garbage? Well, that was fine; and gave Mrs. Trease a clap
on the bottom, out she went, Ewan standing and watching.

And Trease came back and smiled at Ewan, big, creased: *Ay. Think her a funny bitch?*

Ewan said No, she seemed all right, was she a Communist as well? Trease gave his head a scratch, he'd never asked her, he'd aye been over-busy, her as well, moving from this place and that, chivvied by the bobbies, her ostracized by the neighbours and the like, never complaining though, canty and cheery—they'd had no weans and that was a blessing.

Ewan nodded and said he saw that, there wasn't much time for the usual family business when you were a revolutionist. And Big Jim twinkled his eyes and said No, for that you'd to go in for Socialism and Reform, like Bailie Brown, and be awful indignant about the conditions of those gentlemanly coves, the suffering workers. And Ewan grinned at him, he at Ewan, neither had a single illusion about the workers: they weren't heroes or gods oppressed, or likely to be generous and reasonable when their great black wave came flooding at last, up and up, swamping the high places with mud and blood. Most likely such leaders of the workers as themselves would be flung aside or trampled under, it didn't matter, nothing to them, THEY THEMSELVES WERE THE WORKERS and they'd no more protest than a man's fingers complain of a foolish muscle.

And Trease made the tea and they cooked the kippers and had a long chat on this and that, not the revolution, strikes or agitprop, but about skies and stars and Ewan's archæology that he'd loved when he was a kid long ago, Trease knew little or ought about it though he'd heard of primitive communism. He said he misdoubted they'd ever see workers' revolution in their time, capitalism had taken crises before and would take them again, it was well enough organized in Great Britain to carry ten million unemployed let alone the two and a half of to-day, Fascism would stabilize and wars help, they were coming, the wars, but coming slow.

Ewan said he thought the same, for years it was likely the workers' movements would be driven underground, they'd to take advantage of legality as long as they could and then prepare for underground work—perhaps a generation of secret agitation and occasional terrorism. And Trease nodded, and they left all that to heed to itself and Trease sat twinkling, his collar off, and told Ewan of his life as a propagandist far and wide over Scotland and England, agitprop in Glasgow, Lanark, Dundee, the funny occurrences that now seemed funny, they'd seemed dead serious when he was young. He'd tramped to lone villages and stood to speak and been chased from such places by gangs of ploughmen—once taken and stripped and half-drowned in a trough; he'd been jailed again and again for this and that petty crime he'd never committed, and in time took the lot as just the day's work; he'd been out with Connoly at Easter in Dublin, an awfully mismanaged Rising that.

But the things he minded best were the silly, small things —nights in mining touns when he'd finished an address to a local branch and the branch secretary would hie him away home to his house: and Trease find the house a single room, with a canty dame, the miner's wife, cooking them a supper and bidding them welcome: and they'd sit and eat and Trease all the time have a bit of a worry on his mind— where the hell was he going to sleep?: and the miner would say *Well, look this way, comrade,* and Trease would hear a bit creak at the back of the room—the miner's wife getting into bed: and he and the miner would sit and claik the moon into morning and both give a yawn and the miner would say *Time for the bed. I'll lie in the middle and you in the front;* and in they'd get and soon be asleep, nothing queer and antrin in it at all, not even when the miner got up and out at the chap of six and left you lying there with his mate, you'd as soon have thought of touching your sister.

And Ewan laughed and then grew serious and spoke of his work in the Stoddart yard, he was raising up something of a cell in the yard, could Jim dig out a bundle of pamphlets for him? They'd all been Labour when he went to Stoddart's, but already he'd another four in the cell. Trease said he'd give him pamphlets enough, Stoddart's was a place worth bothering about, how long did Ewan think he would last before he was fired by the management? Ewan said he thought a couple of months, you never could tell, damned nuisance, he was getting interested in granite. And that led him on to metallurgy, on and on, and Trease sat and listened and poured himself a fresh cup of tea now and then . . . till Ewan pulled himself up with a laugh: *Must clear out now, I've been blithering for hours.*

But Mrs. Trease came back from the Talkies and

wouldn't hear of it, Jim would need a bit crack and a bit more supper, she thought there was some cheese. Greena Garbage had been right fine, cuddled to death and wedded and bedded. Would Ewan stir up the fire a little and Jim move his meikle shins out of the way? *Ta-ra-ra, 'way down in Omaha*——

Trease twinkled at Ewan: *That's what you get. Not revolutionary songs, but Ta-ra-ra, 'way down in Omaha.* Mrs. Trease said Fegs, revolutionary songs gave her a pain in the stomach, they were nearly as dreich as hymns—the only difference being that they promised you hell on earth instead of in hell.

And Ewan sat and looked on and spoke now and then, and liked them well enough, knowing that if it suited the Party purpose Trease would betray him to the police tomorrow, use anything and everything that might happen to him as propaganda and publicity, without caring a fig for liking or aught else. So he'd deal with Mrs. Trease, if it came to that. . . . And Ewan nodded to that, to Trease, to himself, commonsense, no other way to hack out the road ahead. Neither friends nor scruples nor honour nor hope for the folk who took the workers' road; just *life* that sent tiredness leaping from the brain; that sent death and wealth and ease and comfort shivering away with a dirty smell, a residuum of slag that time scraped out through the bars of the whooming furnace of History——

And then he went out and home through the streets swinging along and whistling soft, though he hardly knew that till he heard his own wheeber going along the pavement in front, the August night mellow and warm and kind, Duncairn asleep but for a great pelt of lorries going up from the Fishmarket, the cry of a wakeful baby somewhere. And he smiled a little as he heard that cry, remembering Ellen and her saying that Communism would bring a time when there would be no more weeping, neither any tears. . . . She was no more than a baby herself.

A bobby stopped in a doorway and watched him go by: there was something in that whistle that was bloody eerie, a daft young skate, but he fair could whistle.

It was plain to Chris something drastic must be done to reorganize the house in Windmill Place. With Cushnie first gone and syne Ena Lyon and Ake still seeking about for a job she'd have to get new lodgers one way or the other.

But the price Ma Cleghorn had set on the house had made it for folk of the middle-class, except such rare intruders as Ake—and he'd come in search of her, she supposed, much he'd got from the coming, poor wight.

She asked Neil Quaritch when he came to tea, he looked thinner and stringier and tougher than ever, a wee cocky man with a wee cocky beard, pity his nose was as violent as that. Lodgings?—he'd ask some of the men in the *Runner*. Especially as they might never see Mr. Piddle again.

Chris said Why? and Neil licked his lips and thought *Boadicea probably looked like that. She'd strip well—and damn it, she does—for Ogilvie*. Then he pushed his cup over for replenishing, they were sitting at tea alone, and told the tale about Mr. Piddle that had come up to the office as he left. Mrs. Ogilvie knew this side-line of Piddle's?—sending fishing news to the *Tory Pictman*? Well, he'd been gey late in gathering it to-day, doing another side-line down in Paldy, prevailing on a servant lassie there to steal him the photo of an old woman body who had hanged herself, being weary with age. Back at last he'd come to the office, *he-he!* photo in hand and all set fine, and looked at the clock and saw he'd a bare three minutes to tear down the Mile and reach the train at the Station in time. So he flittered down the stairs like a hen in hysterics and got on his bike and tore up the Mile, and vanished from sight, the *Runner* subs leaning out from their window and betting on the odds that he'd meet the inevitable lorry right now—it was an understood thing that he'd die under a lorry some day, and be carted home in a jampot.

Well, it seems that he reached the Station all right, the lorries scattering to right and left and Piddle cycling hell for leather, shooting through the taxi-ranks at the Station and tumbling into the arms of a porter. And the porter asked who he thought he was, Amy Mollison doing a forced landing? Piddle said *He-he!* and dropped his bike and ran like the wind for the *Pictman* train, he knew the platform for it fine, he'd to run half-way up to the middle guard's van.

Well, he rounded into No. 6 platform and gave a bit of a scraich at the sight, the *Pictman* train already in motion and pelting out of Duncairn town. It was loaded up with Edinburgh students, clowning and playing their usual tricks, a bit fed up with their visit to Duncairn, they'd been leaning out to shout things to the porters when Mr. Piddle came hashing in sight, head thrust out like a cobra homing like hell to the jungle with a mongoose close on its tail. And they gave a howl and started to cheer, Mr. Piddle running like the wind by now to reach the middle brake.

The guard looked out and yelled to him to stop, he'd never make it and do himself a mischief. But the van was chockablock with students, they pushed the guard aside, a half-dozen of them, and thrust out their hands, Piddle thought that fine, if only he could get near enough to hand up the *Pictman* packet to them. And at last, bursting his braces and a half-dozen blood vessels, or thereabouts, he got close in touch—down came the hands, the students all yelled, and next minute Piddle was plucked from the earth and shot, packet and all, into the guard's van. And then the train vanished with a howl of triumph, an express that didn't stop till it got to Perth.

Chris sat and laughed, sorry for Mr. Piddle though she was, poor little weasel howked off like that. Then Ewan came in and heard the tale and laughed as well, ringing and hearty, no boy's laugh any longer, Neil thought—far from that lad who'd once thought those silly happenings to folk had little or nothing of humour in them. Damned if one liked the change for all that, a difficult young swine to patronize, growing broader and buirdlier, outjutting chin and radiating lines around the eyes—Quaritch knew the face on a score of heads, he'd seen them on platforms, processions, police courts, face of the typical Communist condottiere, cruel and pig-headed and unreasonable brutes with their planning of a bloody revolution to-morrow when Douglasism were it only applied and the maze of its arguments straightened out would cure all the ills that there were of our time: the only problem was distribution, manufacture and function couldn't be bettered.

It was as though a great hand had battered, broadnieved, against the houses that packed Footforthie. Windows shook and cracked, the houses quivered, out in the streets folk startled looked up and saw the lift go suddenly grey. Then, belly-twisting, the roar of the explosion.

Folk tore from their houses and into streets, pointed, and there down by Gowans and Gloag's in the afternoon air was a pillar of fire sprouting a blossoming to the sky, it changed as you looked and grew black and then green, blue

smoke fringe—God, what had happened? Next minute the
crowd was on the run to the Docks, some crying the fire
had broke out in a ship, but you knew that that was a lie.
And John—Peter—Thomas—Neil—Oh God, he was there,
in Furnaces, Machines—it was and it couldn't be Gowans
and Gloag's.

Then, rounding into the Dockside way you found the
place grown black with folk, bobbies were already crying
to keep back, forward the left of the Works like a great
bulging blister, a corral of flame, men were running out
from Gowans clapping their hands to blackened faces,
some screaming and stitering over to the Docks to pitch
themselves in agony into the water. And as they did that
the blister burst in another explosion that pitched folk head-
first down on the ground, right and left—Forward, against
the green pallor of the Docks, a rain of stone and iron
stanchions fell.

And out of the sunset, and suddenly, the lift covered
over with driving clouds.

.   .   .   .   .   .

The *Tory Pictman* got the news from Duncairn over the
telephone, clear-the-line, from Mr. Piddle *he-heing!* like
fun: all about the charred bodies, the explosion, the women
weeping, the riot that broke out against the Gowans house
up in Craigneuks when the windows were bashed in by
Reds. And the *Pictman* printed a leader about it, full of
dog Latin and constipated English, but of course not Scotch,
it was over-genteel: and it said the affair was very regret-
table, like science and religion experiment had its martyrs
for the noble cause of defending the State. The treacherous
conduct of extremists in exploiting the natural grief of the
Duncairn workers was utterly to be deplored. No doubt the
strictest of inquiries would be held——

.   .   .   .   .   .

The Reverend Edward MacShilluck preached from his
pulpit next Sunday and said the catastrophe was the Hand
of Gawd, mysteriously at work, *ahhhhhhhhhhhh, my
brethren, what if it was a direct chastisement of the proud
and terrible spirit of the times, the young turning from the
kirk and its sacred message, from purity and chastity and
clean-living?* And Craigneuks thought it a bonny sermon,
and nearly clapped, it was so excited; and the Reverend

MacShilluck went home to his lunch and fell asleep when he'd eaten it and woke with a nasty taste in his mouth and went a little bit stroll up to Pootsy's room, and opened the door and peeped in at her and shoggled his mouth like a teething tiger——

* * * * * *

Jim Trease said to Ewan they hadn't done so bad, twenty new members had joined the local, damn neat idea that of Ewan's to have the Gowans windows bashed in. Ewan was to take Kirrieben for the weekend meetings, he himself Paldy and Selden Footforthie. And be sure and rub in the blood and snot well and for God's sake manage a decent collection, he'd be getting in a row with the E.C. in London, they were so far behind with the Press contribution.

Eh? Of course the Works had been well-protected, that kind of accident would happen anywhere. But Ewan had been right, that was hardly the point, he could rub in if he liked that there had been culpable negligence. . . . Eh, what was that? Suggest it had all been deliberately planned to see the effect of poison-gas on a crowd? Hell! Anyhow, Ewan could try it. But for God's sake mind about the collection——

* * * * * *

Alick Watson said in his barrack-room: *See what's waiting us in the next war, chaps? Skinned to death or else toasted alive like a winkle in front of a fire, see?* And the rookies said *God, they all saw that,* what was there to be done about it? And Alick said to organize and stick up for their rights, would they back him to-day down in the mess if he made a complaint about the muckingmeat? They could force the swine to feed them proper, no fear of that if they'd stick together, no need to knuckle-down to the bloody N.C.O.'s. And if a war came and the chaps in the companies were well-organized: what the hell could the officers do to them then?

* * * * * *

Norman Cruickshank lay in the hospital and didn't say a word, quiet and unmoving, half of his face had been eaten away by the flame.

* * * * * *

Jess would never see Bob again. She thought at his grave-side, decent in her black, *Young Erchie's been awful kind to me. Maybe the furniture me and Bob's bought will do if he's really serious, like. . . .* But she mustn't think of that, even with her Trouble, poor Bob that had been so kind and sensible even though he'd once mixed with those dirt, the Reds——

　　　·　　·　　·　　·　　·

Ellen Johns said, sick, it was horrible, horrible, but, *Ewan, you know that THAT was a lie. It was sickening of you to suggest that they let loose the gas deliberately. . . . Ewan, it's just cheating, it's not Communism!*

Chris had said *But, Ake, why are you leaving me?*

He'd tapped out his pipe by the side of the fire, *Just for what I've said, Mistress: I want a change. So I've ta'en on the job of ship's carpenter, on the Vulture, bound for New-foundland. That's all about it.*

She'd said But it wasn't all; what was this stuff about not coming back? And at that the Ake Ogilvie of Segget had awakened, a minute, as he told her why: that he'd never had a minute since his marriage day, when he was a free and happy man, aye knowing how she looked on him, thought of him—oh aye, she'd done her best, he knew, it was just that the two of them never should have wed, *You were made for somebody different from me, God knows who, neither me nor Colquohoun. But it's been like hell, we just can't mix. Lass, do you think I haven't seen you shiver over things another woman would laugh at or like?*

She'd said that that was just foolishness, she'd liked him well and had aye done so. And he'd said she looked bonny standing there, trying to be kind. It was more than kindness he'd once hoped to get; and now they'd speak of the soss no more.

And he told her his plans, he was off in three days, and he'd maybe write her, had he anything to write about, when he got to Newfoundland or Canada. He thought of crossing over Canada and taking a look at Saskatchewan, plenty of work there for a joiner, he'd heard. Of what money he made he'd let her have half.

Chris had said quiet she wouldn't have that, if they parted she'd no need to live off him, they parted for good and all—if at all.

And Ake had nodded, *Ay, that would be best.*

So, watching from the doorway as he went this last morning, she minded in pity and smiled at him, kind. He hoisted the case on his shoulder and nodded, *Well, I'll away. Ta-ta, mistress.*

Her heart was beating high in her breast and her throat felt tight so that hardly she could speak: and all that meant little enough, as she knew. If she tried even now she could keep him by her—who would soon have so few to fall back upon. But he wasn't for her, she for any man, they'd each to gang their own gait.

She'd finished with men or the need for them, no more that gate might open in her heart, in her body and her soul, in welcome and gladness to any man. Quick and quick in the flying months she passed with hasting feet over ways that once had seemed ever-lasting: the need not only for a lover's caresses, but the need for anyone's liking, for care, kind words and safe eyes. . . . That dreadful storm she'd once visioned stripping her bare was all about her, and she feared it no longer, eager to be naked, alone and unfriended, facing the last realities with a cool, clear wonder, an unhating desire. Barriers still, but they fell one by one——

She stared from the doorway, standing still, motionless, almost the last sight Ake saw, it twisted his heart and then left it numb. *Ay, a strange quean, yon. And not for him.* He'd thought that glimmer in her eyes a fire that he himself could blow to a flame; and instead 'twas no more than the shine of a stone.

Ewan at last had been fired from Stoddart's he told to Ellen as they drove from Duncairn in the little car they'd hired for the week-end. Ellen had hired it and sat aside now while Ewan took the wheel and a reckless road through the lorry traffic of Kirrieben in the whistling spatter of December snow. She'd been deep in thought: on the road, on herself, on the week-end that waited them in that inn in Drumtochty. Now she started: *Oh Lord, what'll you do now?*

He said he hadn't the ghost of a notion, something or other, and whistled to himself, dark and intent, growing tall, still slim, with the mouth that was losing its lovely curves, growing hard and narrow she suddenly thought: dismissed that thought—he was just Ewan still.

And some time she'd tell him. But not to-night.

For a while Ewan drove without saying more. Topping
the Rise the storm had cleared, the snow no more than an
inch or so thick scarred with the passing of buses and lorries, a lorry came clanging to meet them, chains on, and
once the little car caught on a slide and skidded and
galumphed a wiggling moment till Ewan's hands switched it
into line again. Up here the full blow of the winds was
upon them; behind, down in its hollow, Duncairn was a
pelting scurry of flakes, browny white as smoke rose to
snow and commingled and presently drew down a veil,
capped with darkness in the early sunset, over the whitening
miles of grey granite. Forward the country wavered and
shook, no solid lines as they held the road, a warm, birring
dot, tap-tap the hardened flakes on the shield. Ellen snuggled up closer to Ewan and he reached out a hand and gave
her a pat and nodded thanks as she put a cigarette between
his lips. She lit it and then said *Goodness, we're comfy.*
Wish we'd a car like this of our own.

He said he'd have to get Selden's job for that: and he
doubted if it would be as easy next time! She asked what
on earth he was talking about and he steered through a
drifting drove of cattle, head down to the storm, drover
behind, and didn't answer her for a moment. Then he
asked her hadn't she heard the news—oh no, she hadn't
been down to the Communist local for nearly a couple of
weeks, lazy thing. *The point is that Selden's bunked with*
the funds.

—*Selden? With the funds of the Party?*

—*Every cent, and there was a decent amount. I thought*
it risky to have him treasurer, and so did Trease, but he'd
got in well with the E.C. in London. Cleared us out to the
very last copper.

She said the man was a beast, it was filthy; but Ewan had
started his whistling again, hardly heeding her, only the
road and the car, he said Selden had shown a lot of sense
in waiting till the local had a spot of coin. Been sick of
unemployment and his wife wasn't well—her that used to
be Chris's maid—remember?

—*You speak as though you might do the same.*

He laughed at that, cheerfully, *I'm a Communist.* And
fell to his whistling again, but soberly. And when he next
spoke there was steel in his voice, the steel of a cold
unimpassioned hate: *I could tell long ago that Selden would*
rat; you can tell a rat easily among revolutionists—yeasty

*sentiment and blah about Justice. They think they're in
politics or a parlour game.*

And what did he himself think it was? But she didn't
ask, didn't want to hear more, wanted to forget Duncairn
and all in it and that dreadful paper they had made her
sign. And Ewan drove as though he owned the road and
all the Howe and half of December and had specially
arranged the storm effects, the storm coming rolling down
from the Mounth and pelting across the grey fields in wan
tides, now snow, now sleet, once, curling and foaming,
combers of hail. The shrouded farms cowered in by their
woods, here and there a ploughman wrapped to the ears
went whistling up to the end of a rig, the lapwings flying,
Lost; lost! their plaint above the wheel and fall of the
snow.

Ellen drowsed against Ewan's sleeve, and woke and
looked out, they were past Auchinblae going down into the
Glen of Drumtochty, here no snow fell, far in the lift
Drumtochty rose with its firs going climbing to the racing
clouds. She said *Remember that day there, Ewan?* and
told him to be careful, he'd nearly turned the car in a ditch
kissing her, he laughed, he'd remembered as well, something
like a shadow went over his face, not from it, and a moment
she saw again the shamed hurt boy whom she'd loved, still
loved deeper and madder and worse than ever.

The landlady said God be here, they'd expected no
visitors on New Year's Eve, but they both were welcome.
If they'd wait a while she'd stir up those sweir meikle
bitches the maids and see that a room was set in order.
Och, she minded the two of them fine back in May and
she'd know another thing though she'd never letten on—
that the two of them had been on their honeymoon. Wasn't
that true?

Ellen said it was, but the landlady was looking at Ewan,
hardly heard, she said he'd take a bit dram with her?—
and his good lady too, maybe?

So they sat and had their dram, all three, and the landlady and Ewan were at it in a minute, gossip that somehow
left Ellen out, though she didn't know how, she was just as
interested in floods and storms and hens and chickens and
farm boys as Ewan was (and once a lot more). But as
always with the working people everywhere, however she
dreamed of justice for them, flamed in anger against their
wrongs, something like a wall of glass came down cutting

her off from their real beliefs, the meanings in tones and
intonation, the secret that made them bearable as indi-
viduals. But Ewan had now the soap-box trick of pretending
to be all things to all kinds of keelies—That was damn
mean and wasn't true, there was no pretence, he WAS all
things—sometimes, frighteningly, it seemed to her that he
was the keelies, all of them, himself.

But they were served a warm supper ben in the parlour
and sat there thawing in front of a fire, resin-spitting,
curling bright amber flames up the wide lum, it whoomed
in the blasts of the storm driving night, hunted, down
through Drumtochty. Sometimes the whoom in the lum
would still, then roust and ring as though the storm going
by beat a great bell in the lowe of the lift. And Ellen felt
happy and content again, sleepy as a cat, a little bit like
one: and something a moment touched through to Ewan,
a hand from other days, other nights, queerly. He said
*You're thinner, you were always slim, but plump in a way
as well that time we climbed the Barmekin.* She shook her
head, she was just the same, only horribly sleepy, was he
coming now?

He went to the window and looked out at the storm,
solid in front of the inn it went by, speckled in the lights,
a great ghost army hastening east, marching in endless line
on line, silent and sure; and he thought a minute *Our
army's like that, the great lost legion, nothing to stop it in
heaven or hell;* and that thought lit him up a little moment
till he closed it away in impatient contempt. Bunk sym-
bolism was a blunted tool.

So he said he'd look in at the bar a minute, and sent
Ellen to bed: looked a tired kid. When he got up the stairs
in a half-hour or so the house was shaking in every gust,
the candle-flame leaped as he opened the door, Ellen lying
in bed in silk nightie, pretty thing, drowsy, she said *Hurry,
it's cold.*

But soon it wasn't, the candle out, the lights from the
fire lay soft in the room, he said *Warm now?* and she said
That was fun; remember the first time I said that? And she
laid her head in the hollow of his arm sleeping the New
Year in.

The storm was over when they woke next day, breakfast
ready and a tramp in the snow to follow, they climbed to
the top of Cairn o' Mount, bare ragged and desolate under

the snow, no exaltation of the storm left; around them, mist-draped, the jumble of hills. It seemed to Ellen the most desolate place that God ever made, and she hated it.

But Ewan said one could think up here and sat on a stone and filled his pipe, and dusted the stone clear of snow: *Sit down. I've something to ask you.*

She sat down and cuddled up close to his shoulder and said if the question was if she still loved him, the answer was in the affirmative, worse luck. And did he know he was, oh damnably thrilling?

He said *Listen, Ellen. About the Party. Why haven't you been to the meetings of late?*

She watched a puff of wind come over the snow, ruffling it like an invisible snake, nearer and nearer, and caught her breath, if it didn't reach them—for a luck, a sign. . . . It blew a white dust over her hands.

She said quietly as him *Just because I can't, or I'd lose my job.*

He said *Oh,* and knocked out the pipe and filled it again with the cheap tobacco, his suit was frayed and the coat collar shiny, she saw, sitting away from him: funny she had never noticed these things before. . . . *What's happened, then?*

She laughed and caught his shoulder *Ewan! Don't use that tone to me! EWAN!*

His face was a stone, a stone-mason's face, carved in a sliver of cold grey granite. *You might as well tell me.*

Suddenly frightened she stared at him, and told him she couldn't do anything else. The Education Authority had got to hear and had put the choice plainly enough. She'd to sign a paper saying she'd take no more part in extremist activities and stop teaching the children—what she'd been teaching them. *Oh, Ewan, I couldn't help it!*

—Does that mean you've left the Party as well as left off attending its meetings?

And then anger came on her: *Yes, I've left the Party! And it wasn't only that. I've left because I'm sick of it, full of cheats and liars, thieves even, look at Selden, there's not one a clean or a decent person except you and perhaps Jim Trease. And I've left because I'm sick of being without decent clothes, without the money I earn myself, pretty things that are mine, that I've worked for. . . . Oh, Ewan, you know they're hopeless, these people—the keelies remember you used to call them?—hopeless and filthy; if ever*

*there's anything done for them it'll be done from above,
not by losing oneself in them. . . . Oh, CAN'T you see?*

He nodded, not looking at her. And colour came back
into Ellen's cheeks—oh, he was going to understand! She
leaned forward and told him all that she planned: he
would get away from ridiculous jobs, Mr. Quaritch had
promised to find him another. They could save up like
anything and get married in a year or so, have a dinky little
flat somewhere in Craigneuks. Even that car down there at
the inn—it had been hired with her money, hadn't it? Well,
they'd soon get one of their own, you couldn't have any fun
without money. And it needn't mean they must give up
social work completely, there was the Labour Party——

He stood up then, dark and slim, still a boy, and brushed
her off carefully, and the snow from his knees: *Go to them
then in your comfortable car—your Labour Party and your
comfortable flat. But what are you doing out here with me?
I can get a prostitute anywhere.*

She sat still, bloodless, could only whisper: *Ewan!*

He stood looking at her coolly, not angered, called her
a filthy name, consideringly, the name a keelie gives to a
leering whore; and turned and walked down the hill from
her sight.

The extremists were getting out of hand again said the
Daily Runner in a column and a half; and Duncairn was
the centre of their sinister activities. There had been
several strange and unexplained phenomena in the blowing
up of the new wing of Gowans and Gloag's: and though
no definite charge might be laid at any door hadn't there
been similar occurrences abroad inspired by the Asiatic
party of terrorism? And what had followed within a few
months of the explosion?—a soldier of the North Highlanders arrested and court-martialled for circulating seditious literature in the barrack-rooms—an ex-employee of
Gowans and Gloag's. He had been dealt with with the
severity appropriate to his case, but behind the muddled
notions of Private Watson what forces were aiming at the
forcible overthrow of Society and suborning the loyalty of
our troops? It was true the soldiers had no sooner become
aware of the contents of the leaflets than, with admirable
promptitude, they had seized the culprit and marched him
off to the guard-room. The tales of the barrack-room riots
in his defence might be discounted as malicious gossip. . . .

And here the sub-editor who wrote the leaders stopped and scratched his head in some doubt and stared at the Spring rain pelting Duncairn and streaming from the gutters of the grey granite roofs. He wondered a moment what had really happened when the furniture was smashed in two barrack-rooms and five rounds issued to the N.C.O.'s? Better cut out that bit and keep bloody vague. Something about the absolute and unswerving loyalty of our Army and Navy throughout the hundreds of years of their history? What about Parker and the Mutiny at the Nore? Or, closer in memory, the Navy at Invergordon? Or the Highlanders in France? . . . Better miss it all out. Some blah about the bloody hunger march now——

. . . In civil affairs the same state of things, culminating in the organizing of this hunger march down through Scotland and England to London. Hunger—there was none anywhere in Duncairn. For their own ends extremists were deluding the unemployed into the privations of a march that would profit them nothing, a march already disowned by official Labour——

* * * * *

Bailie Brown said Ay, B'God that was right, the Labour Party would have nothing to do with it: if the unemployed would wait another three years and put the Labour Party back in power, their troubles would all be solved for them. But, of course, it was no class party, Labour: wasn't it Labour had instituted the Means Test? It stood for a sound and strong government, justice for all, peace and progress, sound economy and defence of our rights. . . . And hurrying to the police court at ten o'clock he sentenced two keelies to two months a-piece, for obstructing the police near the Labour Exchange, and to show the low brutes what Reform would be like——

* * * * *

The Reverend MacShilluck said straight from the pulpit we could see the mind of Moscow again, deluding our unemployed brothers, ahhhhhhhhhhhh, why didn't the Government take a stern stand and put down these activities of the anti-Christ? The unemployed were fully provided for and the Kirk was here to guide and to counsel. Straitened means and times were the test-gauge of God. . . .

And he wondered what Pootsy would have for lunch; and finished the service and got into the car and drove home, the streets shining white in the rain. And he let himself into the Manse, rubbing his hands, and called for the woman to come take his coat. But he heard no reply, the place sounded empty; and he couldn't find her ben in the kitchen or yet upstairs or yet in the sitting-room. In the dining-room he came on his desk smashed open and gaping, the Kirk fund gone, and where had the silver gone from the sideboard? But there in the middle of the desk was a note: *I've cleared off at last and taken my wages—with a little bit extra as a kind of a tip for sticking your dirty habits so long. Just try and prosecute and I'll show you up so you can't show your face anywhere in Duncairn——*

.   .   .   .   .   .

In Paldy Parish and the Gallowgate, the Kirrieben, Ecclesgriegs and Lower Footforthie, folk stood and debated with a bit of a laugh this hunger march that the Reds were planning. And those that had jobs said *God, look out, they're just leading you off to get broken heads, they don't care a damn for themselves or any other, the Communists, the devils aren't canny.* And those that hadn't jobs said *Maybe ay, maybe no. Who got the P.A.C. rates raised if it wasn't the Reds, tell us that?*

Not that you were a Red, hell no, you had more sense, and you wouldn't be found in this daft-like March, you hadn't the boots for it for one thing. And the wife said *Mind, Jim . . . or Sam . . . or Rob . . . you're not being taken in by this coarse March of the Reds, are you now?* And you said to her *Away to hell. Think I've gone gyte?* and took a stroll out, all the Gallowgate dripping and drooked, most folk indoors but chaps here and their nipping in and out of the wynds and courts, what mucking palaver was on with them now?

Then, afore you could do a sneak back and miss him, there was Big Jim Trease bearing down upon you, crying your name, he'd been looking for you as one of the most active and sure of the chaps. The March wouldn't be a march unless you were in it to stiffen the backbone of the younger lads. And you said To hell, you hadn't any boots; and he said that they'd be provided all right and wrote your name down in a little book, and you saw Will's there and Geordie's and Ian's and even old Malcolm's—God you could go if they were going; and it was true what Big Jim said, you wanted a pickle of the older men to put some guts in the younger ones——

. . . . . .

And in and out through the courts and wynds and about the pubs all through that last week were Trease and that mad young devil Ewan Tavendale, prigging with folk and taking down names and raising the wind to buy chaps boots. The bobbies kept trailing after them, the sergeant called Feet and a couple of constables, who the hell were they to interfere? They'd never let up on young Tavendale since he'd shown up the explosion at Gowans and Gloag's as the work of the Government testing out gas to see its effect in a crowded shed. So you guarded him and Trease in a bit of a bouroch, a bodyguard, like, wherever they went, young Tavendale whistling and joking about it, a clever young Bee—and God, how he could fight! They said he was a devil with the queans as well, though you hadn't heard that he'd bairned one yet.

. . . . . .

Trease said the last afternoon to Ewan that he'd better get home and put in a bit of sleep, he'd want it afore setting out the morn to tackle the chave of the march down south, the windy five hundred miles to London. Lucky young devil that he was to be going, Trease wished it was him that was leading the March, but the E.C. had given its instructions for Ewan and intended keeping him down there in London as a new organizer—right in the thick. . . . *And for God's sake take care on the line of march to keep the swine from straying or stealing or raising up trouble through lying with queans,* they'd find the Labour locals en route were forced to give them shelter and help, never heed that, never heed that, rub it well in through all the speeches that the workers had no hope but the Communist Party.

Ewan said with a laugh that Jim needn't worry, rape Labour's pouches, but not its wenches, he'd got that all fixed; *well, so long, comrade. You'll lead us out with the band to-morrow?* And Trease said he would, and then *So long, Ewan,* and they shook hands, liking each other

well, nothing to each other, soldiers who met a moment
at night under the walls of a town yet unstormed.

The workmen from Murray's Mart had come up and
bade in the house all the afternoon tirring the rooms of
their furniture. Chris had made the two men each a cup
of tea, they'd sat in the kitchen and drank it, fell grateful:
You'll be moving to a smaller house then, mistress? Chris
said Yes, and leaving Duncairn, and the older man gave his
bit head a shake when he heard the place she was moving
to. He doubted she'd be gey lonely, like. He was all for
the toun himself he was.

Now, in the early fall of the evening, Chris went from
room to room of the house locking the doors and seeing
the windows were snibbed up against the beat of the wind.
The floors sent up a hollow echo to her tread, in Miss Murgatroyd's room a hanky lay in a corner, mislaid, she'd be
missing it the morn and maybe sending for it. She'd said
Eh me, she was Such Sorry that the place was breaking up,
but maybe for the best, maybe for the best, she'd be Awful
Comfortable in her new place she was sure. And would
Mrs. Ogilvie take this as a Small Bit Present? And this for
young Mr. Ewan, if he'd have it—two Awful Nice books
about the ancient Scots, such powerful they were in magic,
Mr. Ewan had once read the books and So Liked them.

Chris closed that door and went ben the corridor, to
Archie Clearmont's, and peeped in a minute; he'd flushed,
standing in that doorway, trunk behind him: *I say, I'm
damnably sorry to leave. Given you a lot of trouble, often.
I say*—and flushes again, looking at her. And Chris had
known and smiled, known what he wanted, and kissed him,
and watched him go striding away, and thought, kind, *Nice
boy;* and forgotten him.

Nothing in here, nor in Mr. Quaritch's, except the pale
patches along the walls where his books had rested, still the
fug of his pipe. He'd said *You were never meant for this,
anyhow. Mind if I ask: Is your husband coming back?*
Chris had shaken her head and said No, they had separated,
Ake was settling in Saskatchewan. And Neil had fidgeted
and then proposed, she could get a divorce, he had some
money saved, get a decent house and he wouldn't much
bother her. When she shook her head he gave a sigh: *Well,
luck go with you if you're not for me.*

Mr. Piddle hadn't bidden good-bye at all, he'd brought a

cab and loaded in his goods, and gone cycling off in the
rear of it, head down, neck out, without a *He-he!* And,
queer, that had hurt Chris a bit she found—that the funny
thing couldn't have said good-bye. The cracked pane in
his window was winking in the light from lamps new-lit outside as she looked round his room: then closed it and locked
it. That was the lot. Oh no, there was one.

So she climbed up the stairs and stood in that, the room
above her own, next to Ewan's, half-dark and quite empty
but for its shadows. It had had no lodger a three months
now, Ellen Johns herself had never come back from that
week-end she'd gone away with Ewan: Ewan himself had
come back mud-splashed as though he'd been walking the
roads like a tink. And then next day a messenger had come
with a little note, asking Mrs. Ogilvie if she'd pack Ellen's
things, Ellen was too busy to come herself and here was a
week's pay in place of notice. And she hoped Mrs. Ogilvie
would be awfully happy. . . .

Chris had ceased wondering on that long ago; but now,
going down to the kitchen where Ewan sat and the fire was
whooming and the supper near ready, she minded it as in
an ancient dream. As she closed the door Ewan looked up,
he'd been deep for hours in papers and lists, marking off
items of marching equipment, addresses, routes, notes for
speeches: Chris had looked over his shoulder earlier and
seen the stuff and left him a-be. But now with that distant
stare upon her, she asked if he'd ever seen Ellen since
then?

He said *Seen whom?* and looked blank, and then shook
his head. *Not a glimpse. Why?*

Chris said Oh nothing, she'd just wondered about her;
and Ewan nodded, forgetting them both, finishing his lists
while she laid the supper, the house unquiet without fur-
nishing, filled with rustlings and little draughts. Then she
called Ewan to supper and they ate in silence, night without close down on Duncairn.

He said suddenly and queerly *The Last Supper, Chris.*
Will you manage all right where you're going?

She said that he need have no fear of that, she was going
to what she wanted, the same as he was going. And they
smiled at each other, both resolute and cool, and Chris
cleared the table and re-stoked the fire and they sat either
side and watched the fire-lowe and heard the spleiter of
the wet on the panes. And Ewan sat with his jaw in his

hand, the briskness dropped from him, the hard young
keelie with the iron jaw softening a moment to a moment's
memory: *Do you mind Segget Manse and the lawn in
Spring?*

Chris said that she minded, and smiled upon him, in
pity, seeing a moment how it shook him, she herself beyond
such quavers ever again. But his thoughts had gone back
to other things in Segget: that day that Robert had died in
the kirk—did Chris mind the creed he'd bade men seek out,
a creed as clear and sharp as a knife? He'd never thought
till this minute that that was what he himself had found—
in a way, he supposed, Robert wouldn't have acknowledged,
a sentimentalist and a softie, though a decent sort, Robert.

Chris stirred the fire, looking into it, hearing the Spring
wind rising over Duncairn, unending Spring, unending
Spring! . . . Rain to-morrow, Ewan said from the window,
rotten for the march, but they'd got those boots. Then he
came and sat down and looked at her, and asked her,
teasing, of what she was dreaming. She said *Of Robert and
this faith of yours. The world's sought faith for thousands
of years and found only death or unease in them. Yours is
just another dark cloud to me—or a great rock you're
trying to push up a hill.*

He said it was the rock was pushing him; and sat dreaming again, who had called Robert dreamer: only for a
moment, on the edge of to-morrow, all those to-morrows
that awaited his feet by years and tracks Chris would never
see, dropping the jargons and shields of his creed, thinking
again as once when a boy, openly and honestly, kindly and
wise:

*There will always be you and I, I think, Mother. It's the
old fight that maybe will never have a finish, whatever the
names we give to it—the fight in the end between FREE-
DOM and GOD.*

The night was coming in fast Chris saw from her seat on
the summit of the Barmekin. Far over, right of Bennachie's
ridges, a gathering of gold cloud gleamed a moment then
dulled to dun red. The last of the light would be going
soon.

Alow her feet, under the hills, she could see the hiddle
of Cairndhu, all settled for the night as she'd left it, the two
kye milked and the chickens meated, her corn coming fine
in the little park that ran up the hill, its green a jade blue

in the soft summer light. To-morrow she'd be out to tackle the turnips, they were coming up fairly choked with weed.

At first they'd been doubtful about letting her the place, doubtful of a woman-body at all. But they'd long forgotten her father, John Guthrie, and the ill ta'en in which he had flitted from Echt twenty-three years before. To them she was just a widow-body, Ogilvie, wanting to take on the coarse little place that hadn't had a tenant this many a year. She'd moved in early in the April, setting the house to rights, working till she near bared her hands to the bone, scrubbing it out both but and ben, the room where she herself had been born, the kitchen where she'd sat and heard her mother, long syne, that night the twins were born. . . . And sometimes in the middle of that work in the house or tinkling a hoe out in the parks she'd close her eyes a daft minute and think nothing indeed of it all had happened—Kinraddie, Segget, the years in Duncairn—that beside her Will her brother was bending to weed, her father coming striding peak-faced from the house, she might turn and see her mother's face. . . . And she'd open her eyes and see only the land, enduring, encompassing, the summer hills gurling in summer heat, unceasing the wail of the peesies far off.

And the folk around helped, were kind in their way, careless of her, she would meet them and see them by this road and gate, they knew little of her, she less of them, she had found the last road she wanted and taken it, concerning none and concerned with none. . . .

Crowned with mists, Bennachie was walking into the night: and Chris moved and sat with her knees hand-clasped, looking far on that world across the plain and the day that did not die there but went east, on and on, over all the world till the morning came, the unending morning somewhere on the world. No twilight land anywhere for shade, sun or night the portion of all, her little shelter in Cairndhu a dream of no-life that could not endure. And that was the best deliverance of all, as she saw it now, sitting here quiet—that that Change who ruled the earth and the sky and the waters underneath the earth, Change whose face she'd once feared to see, whose right hand was Death and whose left hand Life, might be stayed by none of the dreams of men, love, hate, compassion, anger or pity, gods or devils or wild crying to the sky. He passed and repassed in the ways of the wind, Deliverer, Destroyer and Friend in one.

Over in the Hill of Fare, new-timbered, a little belt of rain was falling, a thin screen that blinded the going of the light; behind, as she turned, she saw Skene Loch glimmer and glow a burnished minute; then the rain caught it and swept it from sight and a little wind soughed up the Barmekin. And now behind wind and rain came the darkness.

Lights had sprung up far in the hills, in little touns for a sunset minute while the folk tirred and went off to their beds, miles away, thin peeks in the summer dark.

Time she went home herself.

But she still sat on as one by one the lights went out and the rain came beating the stones about her, and falling all that night while she still sat there, presently feeling no longer the touch of the rain or hearing the sound of the lapwings going by.

GLOSSARY

GLOSSARY

As implied in the note at the beginning of this book, most of the Scots words are untranslatable except in their context setting. Otherwise there would have been little point in using them: English would have served, as elsewhere. So the following "translations" are very faulty—the English a mere approximation to the Scots.

When various constructions compete for translation, the verb-form only is given and translated.

L. G. G.

Awful. Extremely.

Billy. Young man.
Birn. Load, burden.
Bit. A mildly deprecatory adjectival handle.
Bothy. Bachelor farm servants' dwelling.
Bout. Swath.
Bree. Water, gravy, liquid.
Brose. A sketchy oatmeal dish.
Brute. One mildly antipathetic to the speaker.
Byre. Cow-house.

Chakie. Diminutive of Charles. The order is: Charles, Charlie, Chae, Chakie.

Chave.	To toil back-breakingly.
Chief-like.	Over-friendly, intimate.
Childe.	A full-grown, responsible male.
Claik.	Gossip.
Clart.	A byre implement.
Cleck.	To give birth to.
Clour. } *Clout.* }	Hard knock.
Coarse.	Wicked.
Coup.	Overset.
Couthy.	Known and kindly.
Creash.	Fat (adipose tissue).
Cuddy.	Donkey.
Dawtie.	Darling.
Deave.	To annoy.
Douce.	Wholesome.
Dowp.	Posterior.
Drookèd.	Deep-drenched.
Dyke.	Stone wall.
Fair.	Quite, certainly.
Feint.	Hardly.
Fell.	Exceedingly.
Fleer.	To scoff, to flare.
Futret.	Weasel.
Gey.	(Sardonically) rather, very.
Girn.	To whine hardily.
Gley.	To squint.
Glour.	Black, viscid mud.
Glunch.	To mutter half-threateningly, half-fearfully.
Gomeril.	Half-wit.
Gowkèd.	Stupid.
Greeve.	Good.
Greip.	A kind of cow-shed drain.
Happed.	Well covered.
Heuch.	Sickle; hollow.
Hippens.	Babies' napkins.
Hoast.	"A hacking cough."
Hubbley-jock.	A turkey-cock.
Jobe.	Probe.

Keek.	To look slyly. An impudent, innocent girl.
Kittle.	To tickle. The itch.
Ley.	Fallow land.
Libbed.	Castrated.
Limmer.	Sharp-tongued woman.
Lithe.	Shelter, lee.
Lowe.	Glow.
Lug.	Ear.
Meikle.	Great, much, large.
Mucker.	A euphuism for "bugger"; i.e., a Bulgarian heretic; i.e., suspected of nauseous practices.
Orra.	Odd, untidy, wicked.
Pernickety.	Fussy.
Pleiter.	To wade aimlessly.
Pretty.	Handsome.
Prig.	Urge.
Quean.	Girl.
Rangy.	Lanky.
Redd.	To clear away.
Schlorich.	A shapeless, unchartable sticky chaos.
Scraich.	To screech.
Scunner.	To disgust.
Sharn.	Dung in a semi-liquid state.
Shelvin.	Section of a farm cart.
Sholtie.	Pony, young horse.
Skite.	Daft (used flippantly).
Slummock.	A lumpish slattern.
Smit.	To infect.
Smore.	To smother.
Sneck.	Latch.
Sniftering.	Snuffling.
Sonsy.	Handsome; flattishly burly.
Soss.	A static mess.
Sotter.	To bubble stagnantly.
Sourock.	A little sour plant.

Spleiter.	A wettish mess.
Spunk.	Essence, courage, grit. A lucifer match.
Spurtle.	A stick for stirring porridge.
Stamash.	Blind fury.
Stammy-gaster.	To puzzle.
Stirk.	Bullock or heifer.
Stite.	Gibberish.
Stock.	Person.
Stour.	Dust, commotion.
Strainer.	The main upright of a wire fence.
Sumph.	Lout.
Swack.	Agile.
Swick.	Sly cheat.
Swither.	To swish draggingly.
Thrapple.	Throat.
Tocher.	Inheritance.
Trig.	Neat.
Wame.	Stomach.
Wean.	Child.
Well-kenspeckled.	Trim.
Wheeber.	To whistle birringly.
Wight.	Blame, fault.
Yavil.	Land in harvest the previous year.

Important Works of Modern Fiction

Donald Barthelme

———82304 CITY LIFE $2.25

———82305 THE DEAD FATHER $2.25

———82306 UNSPEAKABLE PRACTICES, UNNATURAL ACTS $2.25

John Casey

———81870 AN AMERICAN ROMANCE $2.25

Don DeLillo

———81935 AMERICANA $1.95

———82012 END ZONE $1.95

Lawrence Durrell

———82428 BALTHAZAR $2.25

———82427 CLEA $2.50

———78958 JUSTINE $1.95

———80304 MONSIEUR $1.95

———82460 MOUNTOLIVE $2.50

———78012 TUNC $1.25

Bernard Malamud

———82568 THE FIXER $2.50

———78810 IDIOTS FIRST $1.75

———80481 THE NATURAL $1.95

———80509 A NEW LIFE $2.25

———80147 PICTURES OF FIDELMAN $1.75

———78735 REMBRANDT'S HAT $1.50

———80635 THE TENANTS $1.95

1F3-78